TALES OF THE PHOENIX TITAN
VOLUME ONE
HERITAGE

S.M. WARLOW

COPYRIGHT

"When something bad happens you have three choices. You can either let it define you, let it destroy you, or you can let it strengthen you"

—Theodore Suess Geisel

PROLOGUE

For countless generations, the people of Earth would look to the skies and ask; *What is it that lies beyond those millions of twinkling stars?*

It was a question that permeated every generation that graced the pale blue planet. History told us that everyone from the Ancient Greeks to the Vikings pondered the subject at least once in their fleeting moment of existence.

For thousands of years, many would claim to have the answers to all the great questions. The dreamers would argue that other species were living out their own fleeting existence on some distant planet, far off in the cosmos. The believers would claim that an all-seeing, all-knowing deity was watching humanity stumble through its flawed continuation. The realists —as they preferred to be called— proposed the most terrifying theory of all: that humanity was alone; that there was no other form of intelligent life in the universe and that there was no omnipotent creator or caretaker.

The tragedy is that the people of Earth would never see past the things that divided them. Wars were waged, and blood was spilled: all because the race of man couldn't see beyond their differences. After all the bloodshed, arguing and fighting, none of it mattered.

The sixth of June was the day that the Revenant came. The Earthers didn't have a chance to open their arms in acceptance. The Revenant attacked without restraint, laying waste to the pale blue dot without mercy. As mankind stared out at the end of its inconsequential existence, it didn't matter if you were a realist, a dreamer or a theorist: nobody was safe from the Revenant.

In Earth's final hours, there wasn't one *realist* that didn't turn to the skies and plead for intervention. Those who'd denied the existence of anything beyond themselves were proven very wrong.

In the thirteenth hour of the assault, the Commonwealth arrived, and Earth found its saviour. The 'wealthers saved as many as they could, but the damage was already done: Earth was but a shell of its former self. The sixth of June was a day that went down in Earther history; a day now referred to as the Fall.

With the pale blue dot reduced to a ball of toxic ash, Earth's people were taken in by the Commonwealth. When the survivors of Earth laid eyes upon their saviours, they were astonished to see that the Commonwealth were both alien and human. Somehow humanity had developed outside the boundaries of Earth. As it turns out, we weren't as unique as we'd thought.

I didn't survive the Fall, but the good news is that this is most certainly not my story.

This is the story of Nathan Carter and the Phoenix Titan.

Twenty-five years have passed since the Fall, and the war between the Commonwealth and the Revenant continues...

CHAPTER ONE

"It'll be an easy job, Nate," Guttasnype said. "Sneak aboard, grab the goods then make a break for it. Five thousand is more than generous".

Nathan Carter shook his head as he peered across the table at the brown-furred Icktus. Guttasnype did what he always would when trying to negotiate restitution for a risky job: he opened his desk-side drawer and produced two dirty glasses and a bottle of something cheap.

"Nathan, my boy, we've known each other a very long time," Guttasnype poured a glass for each of them as he spoke. "Work ain't easy for folks like you to come by..."

Nathan watched as the lanky weasel opposite climbed from his chair and circled the desk toward him. Guttasnype handed him the foul-smelling liquor and continued to negotiate;

"After everything that Jack did for me, I suppose I could stretch to seven thousand," Guttasnype said, straightening his cheap pin-stripe suit.

Nathan didn't answer immediately and instead sipped his drink, which tasted more like engine fuel than liquor. He knew what Guttasnype was doing by referring to Jack: a cheap attempt to appeal to the part of Nathan that missed his long-dead uncle. Fortunately, Nathan knew better than to fall into such obvious traps.

There is no room in our line of work for weakness, Jack had once said.

So Nathan followed his uncle's lesson and remained silent. Several awkward seconds passed before Guttasnype cracked;

"Okay fine, eight thousand, but that's the best I can do".

Nathan grabbed the datapad in the middle of Guttasnype's desk to examine the exact details of the job. The suited Icktus was asking him to sneak aboard a docked Commonwealth warship and steal a piece of *precious cargo*. It was certainly something that could be done, but it was also incredibly risky. The 'wealthers didn't take too kindly to outsiders; especially those engaged in criminal activities.

Nathan pulled up the stolen schematic of the mile-long Commonwealth warship. He spent several seconds checking the location where the cargo was believed to be in storage. The strange thing was that the item was not in the cargo bay, but on the fifth floor of the ship near the escape pods.

This was not a typical grab-and-go job. Guttasnype was asking him to venture onboard a densely-crewed ship, sneak into one of the busier decks and grab something that wasn't a conventional payload. It wasn't impossible for someone with Nathan's experience, but he wasn't risking his neck for a measly eight thousand credits.

"Thirty-five thousand," Nathan said. "Cash".

Guttasnype almost choked on his cheap drink.

"Nate? You're killing me here," Guttasnype said, circling back around his desk. "We're like family. How do you expect me to afford that kinda money".

Nathan rolled his eyes at the comment and repeated;

"Thirty-five thousand. Cash".

Guttasnype's yellow eyes seemed to dart around the dingy little office rather than look at Nathan. The Icktus was clearly attempting to backtrack the conversation in his mind to find some way to get the best possible price.

"Nate, c'mon?" Guttasnype said, setting his eyes back on Nathan. "I'm offering you work. Not many folks in your predicament get opportunities like this".

"What kinda two-bit-gun-for-hire do you take me for?" Nathan tossed the datapad across the desk. "Commonwealth military doesn't keep weapons, medical supplies, food or anything you usually steal on the fifth floor next to the pods. Rule one in the Commonwealth: follow the rules".

Guttasnype's cheeks fell a millimetre and his thin brows knotted. He knew that Nathan could see straight through him. Nathan swallowed the rest of his drink and then leaned forward to look Guttasnype in the eye.

"The 'wealthers are hauling something important in that room. Something worth a whole bunch more than nine thousand," Nathan placed his glass down on the desk as he spoke in a low voice. "If you want me for the job, my price is thirty-five-thousand. In cash".

Guttasnype sighed in defeat;

"Alright, Nate, you win," the Icktus paused as he finished off his drink. "Twenty thousand".

"Thirty-four," Nathan said.

"Twenty-five. Half now, half when the job's done".

"Thirty-two," Nathan leaned back in his chair with an arrogant smirk on his face. "A third now and the rest when I'm back".

Guttasnype narrowed his yellow eyes, then nodded in agreement. He pulled a credit-chit from under his desk and tossed it to Nathan.

"You're an arrogant little bastard, Carter," Guttasnype grunted. "Just like that uncle of yours".

"And just like him, I'll get the job done," Nathan replied.

He checked that the funds on the chit were in line with their agreement and then tucked it into his breast pocket. He felt a smug sense of satisfaction knowing that he'd outsmarted the two-bit gangster just as Jack would have.

Nathan wasted little time in bidding Guttasnype farewell, refusing to spend any more time around the Icktus than he needed. He left the office and went down a flight of stairs into the busy club which served as a front for Guttasnype's amateur crime empire.

Maybe he's right, Nathan thought. *Perhaps I am turning into Jack.*

At thirty years old, Nathan was only five or six years

short of the age that Jack had been the day of the Fall: the day he'd saved Nathan from the Revenant. The sixth of June had become a day known to Earthers and 'wealthers alike as the Fall. Nathan could recall almost everything that had happened but tried to push it into the deepest recesses of his mind. The memories were just too painful.

Never let them see you bleed, Jack had said.

▲

Nathan exited Guttasnype's club and stepped out onto the rain-soaked slums of the mining planet Gararre. The sun was about to set on the tiny little rock, which meant he had little over ten hours to complete his job for Guttasnype. Nathan made for the tavern where he'd been bunking the last couple of weeks to gather his things.

Nathan couldn't wait to pay for an off-world transport and get somewhere with a friendlier climate. It had been a very long three weeks on the miserable planet of Gararre, but he'd needed to go where there was work and cheap places to stay.

Gararre was not a Commonwealth world, it was an independent planet controlled by The Lorde Industrial Group. The mineral-sucking corporation was just one of many businesses that operated outside of Commonwealth jurisdiction. It was easier for giant corporations to conduct their businesses on planets like Gararre because they could avoid the heavy taxation that the Commonwealth imposed. They could also employ who they wanted, not who the Commonwealth told them to.

Jack had once described the 'wealthers as communists: a giant superpower that manipulated its populous into never questioning anything it did. That was the very reason why Jack had kept Nathan and his cousin James as far away from them as possible.

'wealthers will never accept people like us, Jack had said.

When Nathan was older, he'd done his research into the Commonwealth and what he'd found had contradicted what Jack told him. He read that the Commonwealth's main intention was to bring other species into their alliance so that they may stand a chance against the Revenant. All creatures were equal in the Commonwealth. There was no rich or poor. Every man, woman and child had a role to play in creating a better galaxy.

On paper that didn't sound like such a bad thing, but when Nathan delved deeper into his studies, he'd found that the state controlled absolutely every facet of its people's culture. Nobody was allowed to question a thing that the Commonwealth or its leadership did. Everything was censored and controlled and the citizens had to obey.

As Nathan walked down a quiet side-street toward the tavern, he thought about the job he'd agreed to take. As a rule of thumb, Nathan would usually avoid situations that involved the Commonwealth. Getting on the wrong side of a galactic communist superpower was not wise.

Nathan only accepted the job because he was so desperate to get off of Gararre. Nathan knew that with the money he'd get from Guttasnype he'd have enough for an off-world transport and be able to set himself up for a couple of months.

Just gotta sneak onboard and grab whatever the 'wealthers are hauling, Nathan told himself.

▲

Once Nathan reached the tavern, he gathered his things and then settled up with the owner. Everything that he had ever owned was contained in a single ruck-sack. It was just as Jack used to say:

Travel light; no more than a couple of bags. Carry a decent gun, some clothes for your back, and whatever it is you need to function.

Nathan found it almost maddening to think of that most other people would have homes or ships to store their belongings; whereas his entire life fit into a single bag. As per Jack's lesson, Nathan kept a few treasured family photographs, his gun, a datapad, and clothes. Anything else would just weigh him down.

Nathan's dream was to one day own a ship: somewhere he could call home. It had been that way once before, with Jack and his cousin James. A few years after the Fall, Jack had got them aboard a separatist vessel called the Loyalty. They'd had cabins with their own beds, hot water, a meal three times a day. Though the Loyalty's work was not exactly legitimate, it had given Nathan a semi-stable environment to live in. The ship was by no means perfect, but Nathan had considered the ship his home and its twenty-man crew his family.

For around fifteen years, Nathan, Jack and James had lived aboard the Loyalty right up until the day that everything went wrong.

All good things come to an end, Nathan reminded himself. *Just the way of the world.*

An hour later, Nathan boarded an inner-planet transport that dropped him at a village on the southern hemisphere. He then walked two miles in the pouring rain to the transportation docks.

Doesn't matter where you are on this fuckin' planet you're always gonna get rained on, Nathan thought.

When he finally got to the docks, Nathan used a forged identity pass to get through a security checkpoint. Today he was assuming the character of Engineer Calz Frombire; a freelance gear head from Maru Four.

The officer at the booth was of a spider-like species known as the Urdak: a Commonwealth race known for their short tempers. Like most of his kind, the Urdak officer had over a dozen black eyes that stared at Nathan as he handed over his forged pass.

"Why are you so wet?" The uniformed spider said as he placed Nathan's ID into a computer.

"My inner-planet transport broke down," Nathan shrugged. "Had to walk the whole way".

"Uh-huh," The officer replied.

The Urdak kept at least seven of his dozen eyeballs on Nathan while the others examined the screen before him. Nathan knew he simply had to remain calm to maintain his cover. This security officer was simply doing his job and didn't want any trouble. There came a musical ping from the Urdak's computer, and he returned the pass. Just as Nathan had predicted his forged ID was perfect.

"Make sure you go dry off before working," the officer remarked. "You'll probably be working on the Commonwealth ship we've got up there. The powers that be won't like you dripping all over the customer's floors".

Nathan tucked his ID into his pocket; "I'll keep that in mind".

He made his way into the dock and immediately saw the Commonwealth warship several miles above. It was a massive vessel, spanning almost a mile in length, with the name Vertex emblazed across its angular metal hull. Nathan knew that this tub would have a crew of around three-hundred; all of which would have had the necessary combat training to graduate from the Commonwealth's military academy. Nathan moved toward a service elevator which would take him up into the magnificent warship. There were a few 'wealther officers around, but none of them batted an eyelid to him. He passed through another security checkpoint, and his fake ID got him inside. The elevator took Nathan up several miles into the Vertex. When the doors hissed open Nathan laid eyes on the impressive interior. Everything was just as Nathan expected — functional, immaculate and efficient.

A pair of crewmates wandered past Nathan, discussing productivity improvements for the ships sensor array. Another sat at a bench talking on a comms device, and a pair of marines guarded a doorway. Just by looking at the room confirmed what Nathan thought of the Commonwealth: every 'wealther knew the role they had to play, and that's what made them the well-oiled machine they were known to be.

Nathan didn't waste any more time in looking around, he had a job to do. He casually walked past the marines, flashing his forged ID at the men when they asked. Neither of them challenged as he passed by. Nathan made his way toward a staircase and climbed to the fifth floor where he knew the cargo was being kept.

The entire time he remained nonchalant and calm; as though he was supposed to be there. It was the most obvious way not to get caught, but it was a tried and tested method that Nathan had used on many occasions. He followed his datapad toward the location that Guttasnype's intel suggested. Eventually, he arrived at a corridor leading to a number of crew quarters.

What the fuck has that oversized weasel got me into? Nathan thought.

He continued to follow the datapad until he turned a corner. At the other end, he spotted an entire squad of heavily armed marines, guarding one of the doorways.

That's gotta be it, Nathan thought. *Why leave six jugheads guarding a nondescript room?*

Nathan knew it wasn't wise to fight a group of marines, he'd faced worse, but this job relied on subtlety. Instinctively, he darted into the environmental control station a few feet away.

If you can't shoot them, punch them or stab them; outsmart them, Jack's words had never been more apt.

The forged ID gave Nathan access to the room no smaller than a broom cupboard. After a few seconds of searching, Nathan found an entrance to the ventilation. He pulled a tool from his jacket and jimmied open the hatch, then crawled on his belly through the tight shaft and reached a junction. He rechecked his datapad and headed left toward the room that the marines were guarding. It was a relatively short crawl before he was directly above his destination. Nathan peered through the grate beside him and into the guests quarters that contained the precious cargo. There was no sign of life, so Nathan quietly opened the grate and sleuthed inside.

He instinctively pulled a pistol from under his jacket as he examined the quarters. The room was much like the rest of the warship, furnished and decorated in the utilitarian style that 'wealthers preferred.

So what am I looking for? Nathan thought. *Is this the right room?*

He lowered his gun and referred to his datapad to check he was in the right place. According to the data that Guttasnype had provided him, this was the spot. Nathan wondered if perhaps his datapad was malfunctioning. He took a few steps forward to ensure that the location settings on his device were picking up his movements correctly. It was only when he heard a woman's voice that he realised that something wasn't right;

"Excuse me? What do you think you are doing in here?"

Nathan spun around in reaction to the voice, lifting his gun at the same time. The sights of his weapon landed on a pale woman with dark hair and green eyes. Nathan stared at her for a second, deciding whether or not she was a threat. Before he could make up his mind, the woman raised both of her palms up, but not in surrender.

What followed was a blast of energy that was so powerful it sent Nathan hurtling through the wall and into the next room. He crashed into a piece of functional furniture and suddenly felt overcome from the attack.

That bitch was an Evoker, Nathan thought.

The last thing he heard before blacking out was the brunette calling out to the marines.

CHAPTER TWO

Astrilla didn't need to call out to the marines for protection. The commotion from her elemental summon alerted them before she'd even said a word. The attack sent the curly-haired assailant smashing through the wall and into the next cabin.

In a heartbeat, the marines had knocked down the door to her quarters and to the room next door. Astrilla looked on as the marines dragged the attacker from her cabin. The scruffy reprobate was unconscious —not dead— which was precisely what Astrilla had hoped. All the others had either died or committed suicide before they could be captured.

"Are you okay? A marine asked.

She nodded in response, though his question was null and void.

In truth, Astrilla hadn't been *okay* for a considerable amount of time. This had been the sixth attempt to abduct her in the last four months, and she knew that the Revenant weren't going to stop any time soon.

It would seem that the target on my back is growing with every passing day, Astrilla thought.

Over the last few months, she'd spent her days in hiding, always moving between Evoker compounds and Commonwealth warships. Her life had been disrupted beyond all recognition, and it was all thanks to someone with a very loose tongue —or worse a traitor. Someone had sold her secret to the Revenant, and now she was at the top of King Seig's list. It was a soul-crushing feeling to know that the Revenant king would stop at nothing to capture her.

This attacker had been different from the others: he'd acted alone, and he'd hesitated to shoot her. Not that a simple gun would be enough to put down an Evoker, but still, it was significant.

Surely Seig wouldn't be so foolish to send such a mismatched foe after me, Astrilla thought.

Something didn't make sense.

Astrilla climbed to her feet then shuffled to the exterior of her room. Outside, a senior officer was getting an update from the marines. For the second time in thirty seconds, she was again forced to answer;

"Are you okay?"

Astrilla was so sick of the question that she didn't acknowledge it. Instead, she folded her arms to show her displeasure.

"I want to speak to Commander Rooke," Astrilla demanded.

The Uvan officer shuffled nervously.

"Commander Rooke is currently in a meeting with The Admiralty," he answered. "Lieutenant Oxarri will be on his way shortly".

Astrilla frowned at the officer's answer. The Vertex's Commander, Harlmam Rooke, was a good man and an excellent military leader, but his greatest flaw was his unwavering focus on the war and not the task at hand. To send his first mate, Lieutenant Harrt Oxarri was standard practice, but he wasn't inside Astrilla's circle of trust. If the ships CO wouldn't give her the time of day, then Astrilla was going to take charge of the situation.

"Tell Lieutenant Oxarri to meet me at the brig," Astrilla said. "Tell him that I'll be questioning my attacker".

Astrilla pushed past the officer and headed toward the brig, refusing to hear out his objections. For once, one of her attackers had survived, and Astrilla would get answers.

▲

After almost a month onboard the Vertex, Astrilla had grown tired of the humdrum, sterile environment. Commonwealth citizens were by definition, utilitarian, and that carried over into every facet of their lifestyle. Their clothes, food, even the way they decorated their homes lacked imagination. The whole experience served as a reminder to Astrilla of just how different the Commonwealth and Evokers were. Despite their alliance existing over five-hundred years, the Evokers had retained their individuality and beliefs. They'd set themselves apart from the Commonwealth, which was incredibly rare.

When the Commonwealth inducted new worlds into their regime, the planet's population would —over the course of a generation or two— lose everything that made up its cultural identity. New member worlds would shed their religions, traditions and political ideologies, all in the name of sovereignty. The Commonwealth didn't publicly force its member worlds to cast off the aspects that made them unique; instead the loss of societal individualism was not through force, but through the collective desire to survive.

The war with the Revenant had lasted over a millennia, and countless lives had been lost: something Astrilla had borne witness to first-hand. The Revenant had dominated a myriad of planets in the name of their cause, and they'd shown no sign of slowing down. The Commonwealth was formed to stand against them as a galactic superpower.

Strength in numbers.

The brig was much like the rest of the Vertex: functional. When Astrilla stepped inside, she saw her dark-haired attacker slumped on the floor of his cell, still in an unconscious state. The marines had searched him and placed his belongings on a table at the back of the room.

A security officer was rooting through a tattered old back-pack that the assailant had been carrying. The marine peered at Astrilla as she entered the room.

"Ma'am, I don't think you should be down here," he said.

Astrilla didn't acknowledge the suggestion, and

instead, walked to the energy shield that separated her from the attacker. She peered down at the unconscious human sprawled out on the ground. He was human, maybe in his early thirties: pale skin, unkempt beard, long curly hair that reached his shoulders. Whoever he was, he certainly wasn't Revenant —probably an off-world freelancer or a desperate junkie.

"Ma'am" The marine repeated.

Astrilla's response was short;

"Get out," she said. "I want to speak with him when he comes around".

The marines didn't usually take her orders; after all, she was just a guest aboard the ship. But Astrilla wasn't just any guest. She was an Evoker, and her title carried with it a reputation. Either out of fear or submission, the marine scuttled out of the room, leaving behind the attacker's belongings.

"I'll be outside if you need me," he said.

Astrilla pulled up a chair and sat down, waiting for her would-be attacker to wake up. Several minutes passed, and she grew impatient, so Astrilla decided to root through the prisoner's belongings. The gun that he'd pointed at her earlier was undeniably unique; certainly not Revenant or Commonwealth. She picked it up and immediately, noticed the weight of the weapon. Astrilla ascertained from the archaic shell that it had originated on a primitive world and its owner had likely modified it into an energy weapon.

A professional bounty hunter would have carried a better gun, she thought.

Astrilla placed the weapon down and moved to his fraying backpack. Inside she found a locked datapad, some old clothes, a leather-bound book and a very valuable Arcane chest.

He must have paid a small fortune for this, Astrilla thought as she examined the box.

Arcane was a highly sought after metal from the outer-worlds, often used by smugglers to carry plunderage through security checkpoints. There was something unique to the chemical properties of the metal that made it undetectable to scanners: that was the reason why it fetched such a hefty price-tag in the right circles.

This must be how he got through security with a gun, Astrilla thought.

Along with its use in the criminal underworld, the rare metal had once served as the primary building material for the galaxies forerunners: the Enkaye. The long-extinct species had used the metal to build their ships and temples. Historians had theorised that the technologically advanced race chose Arcane for the same reasons as a modern-day smuggler.

Astrilla carefully examined the box, noticing a latch on one side. She flipped it open, expecting to find another gun inside. Instead, she found something that surprised her: a collection of two dozen printed photographs.

That's what the people of Earth had called the capture of images: photographs.

Out of curiosity, Astrilla examined the picture on the top of the pile. The image depicted an old man wearing a white lab coat and smiling at the camera. The next one depicted a man and a woman holding a small child, no older than five years old. As she was about to look at the third picture, a voice called out from the cell;

"Get your fuckin' hands off my stuff".

She turned around with the pile of photographs to hand and peered at her curly-haired attacker. He'd sat up on the floor and was shooting her a furious glare.

"Are you deaf? I said get your fucking hands off of my stuff!" He said, this time raising his voice.

His use of the rarely heard profanity confirmed Astrilla's suspicions: he was an Earther. She took a few steps toward the energy shield that divided them, keeping the photographs in her hands. The scruffy-looking assailant climbed to his feet as though he were preparing for a fight.

"Tell me…" Astrilla said, stopping at the edge of the forcefield. "What exactly is an Earther doing working for the Revenant?"

The dark-haired prisoner on the other side of the shield took a step back in disgust. Astrilla noticed his jaw tense and his eyes dart from side to side.

"You think I'm working for the Revenant?" He said, both outraged and humoured by her accusation.

"You snuck aboard a Commonwealth warship and broke into my quarters," Astrilla replied. "What did the Revenant pay you to do exactly? Kill me or kidnap me? Which one was it?"

The Earther arrogantly smirked through the shield, almost as though he was antagonising her. Astrilla could practically feel the hubris oozing off of him.

"I don't care who the fuck you are," he shook his head. "I don't work for the Revenant, and you are certainly not what I was hired to steal".

He took a step closer, leaving only a couple of inches between them. Astrilla stood her ground, knowing that the forcefield would bounce him across his cell if he touched it. As the troublemaker looked her up and down, Astrilla felt for a second as though he was mentally undressing her. She quickly realised this wasn't the case; his eyes were locked on the photographs in her hand.

"Tell you what," he said. "Put 'em back in the box, and I'll give up the guy who hired me. Doubt he's linked to the Revenant, but if he knew I was coming face to face with an Evoker, then he screwed me over. I don't like being screwed over".

Astrilla recognised that the old photos were clearly of some importance to the reprobate, so out of politeness she did as he asked.

"I was right, wasn't I?" Astrilla said. "You're an Earther. Aren't you?"

She noticed that her inquiry had made the pale scoundrel uncomfortable. He scratched the back of his head as if searching for a good lie, but Astrilla could see straight through him.

"It's rare for your kind to venture this far from Paradisium," Astrilla remarked.

The expression that filled the miscreant's face was both of offence and annoyance. He scowled through the shield but didn't say anything.

It would appear that I've touched a nerve, Astrilla thought.

Before she could demand the name of the man who'd hired him, Astrilla heard the doors behind her hiss open. She turned around and came face to face with Commander Harlmam Rooke.

The Commander of the Vertex was a mixed-race Human-Uvan in the winter years of his military service. It was evident that the human genes had been dominant in the case of Harlmam Rooke. Everything to his visage was human: the dense facial bones, the dark skin, even the close-knit grey hair on his head. The only thing that was Uvan was his striking purple eyes.

"My office, now!" Rooke said.

CHAPTER THREE

Lieutenant Harrt Oxarri had served as first mate aboard the Vertex for over three years. It wasn't the most glamourous of postings, but the Vertex felt like home. The life of an XO aboard a Commonwealth warship was never dull. Harrt was high enough in the ranks that he commanded the respect of the crew, but it was only through loyalty; not out of fear. He had to earn the admiration of the crew, and that was the way it was meant to be: the Commander would bust the chops, and the first-mate would gauge the crew's reaction.

Since the Evoker had come on board, the crew had been on edge, which was to be expected. Even the most hardened Commonwealth soldier would find the presence of an Evoker to be unsettling at best, but this was different. When Evokers travelled on Commonwealth warships, it would be for their strategic acumen or as an emissary. Astrilla was neither of those. She had come on board and stayed within the confines of her quarters for the entire four-week journey. The *official* reason for her extended stay was for transportation to the Capital Worlds. Of course, Harrt was too experienced to take anything on face value. The executive order to divert the Vertex and pick up the Evoker came from High Command, and for Harrt that meant one thing: Astrilla was involved with something classified.

Harrt's day had been like any other. He'd climbed out of bed, said the Commonwealth Pledge and then gone to work. The Vertex had to stop at a dock on Gararre to refuel and collect some food supplies. Harrt hated the days when they'd dock at the non-Commonwealth planets or stations as it meant security would have to pull double shifts. Pirates and scavengers were rife on non-member planets like Gararre. It was the result of rejecting the law and order that the Commonwealth valued so much. As the ship's first-mate, Harrt would do the same eighteen-hour shift as the security personnel as a way to show unity. At the end of his long day, there were only a few things on Harrt's mind: a stiff drink, an hour of the newscast and then a decent sleep. That, of course, hadn't gone to plan. As he'd sat down with a glass of Maruviun Kor, his communicator had sounded the emergency alarm.

Before Harrt had thrown on his uniform, the threat level was lowered to neutral, and an update was issued to the ship's leadership team. An unknown assailant had been caught inside the Evokers quarters.

He's either got a deathwish, or he's the unluckiest criminal alive, Harrt thought after he'd read the report.

Despite the reduced threat level, Harrt made his way down to Astrilla's quarters. One of the senior security officers reported that she was agitated and demanding an audience with Commander Rooke. When Harrt arrived on the scene, there was no sign of Astrilla, so he questioned the marines.

"Where is the Evoker?"

"She went to the brig to question the intruder herself."

"You said she was agitated?"

"She was pretty angry, sir," the jarhead nodded. The marine then took a step closer to Harrt and said in a lowered voice; "Not as pissed off as the Commander though. Guys on the first deck are saying he's been yelling at her for the last ten minutes".

Harrt had spent enough time serving under Rooke to know that the old man had a temper. It was common knowledge that Evokers would —if provoked to do so— reduce anyone they deemed hostile to a pile of ash. Harrt's day had been long enough, and he had no desire to sweep up the charred remains of his CO. It was for that reason alone that Harrt rushed to Rooke's office.

It didn't take long and as Harrt approached he could hear the Commander's raised voice from down the hall. He quickly knocked on the door, and the yelling stopped.

"Come in," Rooke's order was abrupt.

Harrt entered and found the Commander standing at his desk; his face flushed with anger. Harrt had only seen the enraged expression on the Human-Uvan's face once before, at Maru Seven. At the other side of the standard military office was the Evoker. Astrilla stood at the foot of a giant window that spanned one side of the room, looking out onto the dockyard. Harrt was unable to see her face, but judging from her body language, she was none too impressed.

"Thank the Founders!" Rooke said as Harrt wandered in. "Someone who actually knows how to follow the chain of command!"

Harrt sensed that Rooke said it as a means to taunt the Evoker rather than providing him a compliment. Still, mocking an Evoker was not a wise thing to do, and Harrt felt as though he needed to calm the situation before it escalated. Before he could say a word, Astrilla made her stance on Rooke's insult clear;

"You do not give me orders," she said, pointing her finger at the ship's CO "I am an Evoker, not one of your soldiers".

Rooke sat down and gestured to Harrt to take one of the two chairs tucked under the other side of his wooden desk. Lieutenant Oxarri took a seat and watched Rooke produce a bottle of alcohol from his drawer.

"While you are under the protection of my ship and my crew, you will do as you're damn well told," Rooke glared across the room at her. "Questioning prisoners does not fall into the remit of guests. Do I make myself clear?"

It seemed strange that Rooke was so riled up by the Evoker's minor actions. The prisoner would have been sealed in a cell behind a high-grade JIME forcefield. For Astrilla to question this prisoner was at worst a mild imposition. It was this simple thought that confirmed Harrt's hunch —Astrilla was tied to a classified operation.

Astrilla didn't acknowledge Rooke's demand. Instead, she moved over to the desk and took the seat beside Harrt. She folded one leg over the other and sat up straight in her chair, regarding the Commander with an expression of indifference.

"For the record, I think you're mistaken about our prisoner," Astrilla said. "He's a freelancer; not Revenant".

"What makes you so sure about that?" Rooke asked as he poured himself a drink.

"Revenant don't carry keepsakes," Astrilla said. "He had old pictures in his bag. I think he's an Earther".

Rooke pushed a shallow glass of blue alcohol across the table to Harrt.

"My marines ran his facial scan through the database," Rooke said, peering at Astrilla.

The Commander tapped his datapad and a hologram formed at the base of his desk. The holographic representation of a shaggy-haired human male assembled in front of Harrt. Astrilla was right. Her attacker was anything but Revenant.

"Who is he?" Harrt asked.

"That's the golden question," Rooke replied. "Seems our fugitive doesn't show up on any Commonwealth database. If he is an Earther, then how do we not have any record of his existence?".

Harrt couldn't help but agree with his CO's very valid argument. Earthers had been one of many victims in the Revenant's campaign. Twenty-five years prior, the Revenant had struck the primitive world without mercy. By the time that the Commonwealth had arrived over ninety-percent of planets population were gone. The survivors were taken in by the Commonwealth and rehomed on a new world called Paradisium. Each citizen had every facet of their identity recorded by the Commonwealth; from DNA to facial scan.

"So what are we gonna do about him?" Harrt said.

"When we reach the Capital Worlds, I want Dines to interrogate him," Rooke said. "He'll get the answers we need".

"Before we go down that route, I'd like to speak with

him again," Astrilla insisted.

"Out of the question," Rooke snapped. "You are too valuable to—"

Harrt noticed that The Commander stopped himself from saying any more. Rooke waved off his mistake and instead started on a new tangent:

"I've received new orders from the Admiralty. It seems our current route to the Capital Worlds is not as direct as they'd hoped".

Rooke changed the holographic projection on his desk to a star map, displaying the planned journey of the Vertex. Rooke tapped on his datapad and a new trail appeared on the map.

"We are to travel through the Yandi System to shave three days off of the journey".

That is less than ideal, Harrt thought.

Harrt knew his star maps well enough to know that the Yandi System was not safe. A group of corporations controlled the long stretch of space, and they didn't take too kindly to Commonwealth presence. On the other hand, the Revenant was just as loathed, if not more so.

"Isn't that a little reckless?" Astrilla remarked. "If the corporations find out we're there—"

"Better than going toe to toe with the Revenant," the Commander interrupted. "We need to keep you as far away from them as possible. Agreed?"

For the first time since the Evoker woman had come on board, Harrt noticed that she looked almost vulnerable. Astrilla lowered her brow and sighed at Rooke's question.

"Very well," Astrilla conceded. "Have your navigator avoid any busy patches of space. We shouldn't take any risks".

Once she'd said her piece, Astrilla climbed from her chair, regarding both of the military men with the same indifferent expression that she'd worn for the entire conversation. Harrt felt a sense of relief as she made for the door. Rooke hadn't been reduced to a pile of ash, and their uneasy alliance remained intact.

As the Evoker took her leave, Harrt wondered;

What's so important about this woman?

Commander Rooke exhaled into his glass before knocking back the rest of his drink.

"Admiral Wexell tells me that you put in a request for extended leave?" Rooke said, topping up Harrt's glass as he spoke.

Harrt's gut sunk at the question. It wasn't something he'd wanted to discuss with the Commander. It was personal business, and besides, Rooke would try to talk him out of it.

"Please tell me you're planning a relaxing trip to Tonna Five or that station that overlooks the Praxxian Nebula?" Rooke said with a knowing look on his face. "Not *the other thing*".

Harrt sighed. He couldn't lie to his Commander: honesty was one of the many values that the Commonwealth demanded of its people.

"I wish it was Tonna Five, sir," Harrt said.

Commander Rooke swirled the booze inside his shallow glass and placed it back down on his desk. Harrt watched as his superior officer leaned on the desk between them.

"His time will come, Harrt," Rooke said. "Don't go throwing away your life in pursuit of retribution".

Harrt shook his head in frustration, knowing that Rooke was going to decline his request for extended leave.

"This is about justice; not retribution," Harrt lifted his head. "It's been eight years since Maru Seven. I still have nightmares".

"As do I," Rooke nodded. "Maru Seven will haunt the people on the ground, like you and I, until the end of our days".

"With respect sir, you didn't lose what I did," Harrt said. "That's why I need to do this. That's why I need to make things right".

Rooke pursed his lips together; either out of frustration or sadness, Harrt couldn't tell. The Human-Uvan reclined in his seat and sipped his drink in quiet contemplation, studying Harrt from the other side of the desk.

"Prep the crew for take-off and get us on our new

course," Rooke said.

Harrt masked his frustration as best as he could. Rooke had neither declined or signed off on the personal leave, and the ambiguity was irritating. Of course, questioning authority was not an option.

"Aye, Sir," Harrt replied.

As Harrt made for the door, he stopped and peered back at Rooke. For all of his life, Harrt Oxarri had been a good citizen. He'd never questioned orders and always upheld the values of the Founders. For some reason, he found himself asking his commander a question out of impulse rather than duty;

"What's so special about Astrilla?" Harrt asked.

Rooke's expression didn't change, and he allowed the silence between them to answer. Harrt knew that Rooke was a man loyal to the Commonwealth: he would obey his orders to the letter, but he'd also survived Maru Seven; thanks to Harrt.

"The fate of every single life in the universe rests on Astrilla's shoulders," Rooke said, saying it as a sobering statement of fact. "We cannot let her fall into Revenant hands".

Harrt could tell that Rooke wouldn't say anything more on the matter, but from the gravity in the Commander's voice, he didn't need to do so. Harrt had served with Rooke long enough to know that he'd meant every word of his statement.

CHAPTER FOUR

There had been three moments in the life of Nathan Carter that had truly defined him. The first had come on the day of the Fall, where he'd bore witness to the bloody slaughter of his parents and Grandmother. For years, Nathan had tried to block out the memories, but it never worked. They would always find a way to resurface. Months after the Fall, Nathan experienced vivid dreams where his mind would replay the entire experience to him. Every time it played out, he was helpless to save his family; almost as though he were paralysed.

He would see the Revenant soldiers ferociously cut down his Grandmother in a hail of weapons fire. Her blood would splash against the ivory white kitchen and alarm Nathan's parents in the next room. In the dream, like his memories, Nathan's father, Dylan, would rush toward the attackers armed only with a fire iron. Nathan had never seen the moment his father died, as his mother had grabbed him and made a break toward the rear of the house.

The final harrowing memory Nathan had of his father was of sheer terror. He'd see Dylan Carter stand his ground against a savage creature known as a Revenant hunter. If Revenant Footsoldiers were considered to be cold, calculating monsters then a hunter would be a wild, untamed beast. Nathan would hear the sound of the hunter, cutting through his father's flesh with its dagger-like claws. The agonised screams of Dylan Carter would be forever etched into the back of his mind.

The dreams would always end at the same point: the moment when a Revenant officer shot his mother as she begged for their lives. The callous man would then turn his gun on Nathan. The dream would abruptly end there, and Nathan would wake up in a cold sweat, screaming for the whole thing to stop. Of course, in reality, the Revenant officer had never been able to kill Nathan; thanks to Jack. By some miracle, Jack and his son James had arrived and saved Nathan from the Revenant.

One night aboard the Loyalty, Nathan had the same dream again, and woken up half the ship with his screaming. The crew's medical expert, Cobie, had helped Nathan to calm his breathing, recognising that he was suffering the symptoms of a severe panic attack. Once Nathan had regained his composure, Jack had taken him off of the ship for a man-to-man talk. They'd sat in the quiet docks of the space station where the Loyalty had been harboured for several days. That night in the humid confines of Pasargadae Station, Jack had said;

What happened to you shouldn't have happened to anyone, but it did, and you've gotta learn to live with it.

At eight or nine years of age, the advice his uncle had offered was harsh but necessary. Nathan hadn't been sure how to deal with his trauma up until that point, but Jack was right: he *had* to deal with it. They didn't live on Paradisium with the other Earthers, so they didn't receive the counselling and cushy lifestyle that came with living on the idyllic world.

Grief can destroy a man from the inside, Jack told him. *Your mother and father wouldn't want you to end up like that, and neither do I.*

Jack had always been tough and stoic, and it had got him through the Fall and everything else before. So that night, Nathan decided that he would be like Jack. He would be brave in the face of his demons. He wouldn't let the dreams in, and even if they did, he wouldn't let them frighten him. From that moment on, Nathan was not going to be the helpless little boy he'd been back at the family home. He would not let anything hurt him again. Facing his demons head-on had made Nathan stronger. Ever since that night at Pasargadae Station, Nathan had never allowed his weaknesses to show.

Even at the age of thirty, those same dreams would sometimes crawl their way through the recesses of his mind. Rather than be the screaming child, Nathan would do the same as Jack and allow it to replay in his mind. Sometimes he was able to fight off the Revenant soldiers and other times he wasn't, but Jack had given a piece of advice which had stuck by him ever since;

Never let them see you bleed.

Nathan had lived by those words for over two decades, and it had hardened him to the harsh realities of life after the Fall. Ever since that night at Pasargadae Station, Nathan never allowed his weaknesses to show.

For Nathan, the defining point of this experience was simple; he had to be tough, just like Jack. That was one of many lessons that Jack had bestowed upon him, and Nathan had lived by them since.

Ever since the Evoker had left, Nathan had seen little of anyone else and by his best guess, the other cells were empty. He'd felt sorry for himself for several minutes, having not been captured in over fifteen years. He slumped against the wall at the back of the cell with his forearm resting atop his knee.

It suddenly dawned on him that the Evoker woman had seemed sympathetic. Nathan wondered if perhaps he could talk his way out of the situation, risky as though it may be.

There was another thought which ran through his mind as he debated how to escape;

I am gonna kill Guttasnype for this one.

It hadn't been the first time that the Icktus had screwed him over with a bad job, but this occasion was different: this had resulted in Nathan's capture rather than a laser bolt to the shoulder. *Had Guttasnype's intel been way off, or had he known that Nathan would stumble on the Evoker?*

Before Nathan could even think about how he'd return the favour, the doors to the brig opened. The Evoker woman from earlier stepped inside with a dark hood pulled over the top of her head. She walked passed Nathan to his belongings at the other side of the room.

"Hey, what the hell do you think you're doing?" Nathan scrambled to his feet in protest.

The Evoker seemed to ignore his objections and took ahold of his Arcane storage box. Though she had her back to Nathan, he could tell that she was examining it closely. After several seconds, she walked to the shield at the front of his cell, clutching the Arcane box in her hands.

"I know that there are some Earthers who've left the confines of Paradisium, but most of them are business-people trying to create an empire. You certainly don't look like one of them," she said. "So, I'm going to ask you this once: who are you?"

"I'm the guy who is gonna be really pissed off if you don't leave his stuff alone," Nathan narrowed his eyes.

He refused to give up his name to an ally of the 'wealthers. Nathan knew that the moment he gave up his identity, everything about him would be loaded into the Commonwealth database. He'd lose anonymity and his freedom.

The Evoker held the Arcane box up almost as if she were toying with him. To Nathan's surprise, she returned to the table and gently placed it down.

"Have it your way. The Commonwealth will process you when we reach the Capital Worlds. You will be questioned by one of their agents. Chances are he'll treat you as a terrorist". She stopped at the shield and focussed her gaze on him. "I assume that's what you are then? A Revenant Terrorist, sent here to kidnap me".

Nathan remained silent, refusing to answer the question. She knew that he wasn't Revenant, Nathan could feel it. It was all an attempt to manipulate him.

"Tell me something.." the Evoker said. "How does a freelancer, like yourself, get his hands on a box made from solid Arcane?"

The Evoker began to pace back and forth, waiting for his response.

"That's none of your business," Nathan answered.

He watched as the pretty woman in front of him pulled back the dark hood over her head. She regarded him with an almost warm expression which seemed unusual, given the circumstances.

"It's a long journey to the Capital Worlds. Maybe you should take some time to think long and hard about your stubborn nature," she said. "I don't believe you are Revenant anymore than you ever intended me harm. So when you choose to put your pride to one side and are willing to have a civil conversation, have the guards send for me".

Nathan watched the Evoker woman leave the brig. He refused to give up any information regarding his identity. Jack's advice on the 'wealthers had always been very clear;

Stay the fuck away from them.

Guess I failed to uphold that lesson, Nathan thought.

When the brunette had left, a thought ran through Nathan's mind;

She isn't a 'wealther. She's an Evoker.

▲

The Vertex eventually lifted off and left Gararre behind. From his tiny cell window, Nathan watched the green and brown rock disappear from view. He'd wanted to get off of the planet since arriving, but certainly not under the circumstances he now found himself in. The Vertex had swiftly jumped into a faster-than-light slipstream and Nathan had felt the full force of a Commonwealth engine for the first time.

After the Fall, the people of Earth learnt that they'd barely scratched the surface of space travel. The Commonwealth, much like the Revenant and every other space-faring faction that existed, had harnessed the power of faster-than-light-travel. The rich and expansive history of the Commonwealth told of a blueprint left behind by the galaxies forerunners; the Enkaye. Thousands of years prior, the race of small grey men had discovered the means to travel from planet to planet in a matter of hours. It had likely been that stepping stone that had elevated the Enkaye to an almost god-like status.

Before the Commonwealth began to repress the idea of religion, many of the inner-world faiths had cited the little grey men as the creators of all life in the galaxy. There was one issue with that theory though; the Enkaye had died out, and nobody could say how or why. Besides the blueprints to FTL travel, the Enkaye had left little else behind. All the temples and buildings that had once been theirs now laid dormant. Relics and technology were utterly unresponsive, and nobody knew why. The Enkaye had been the foremost dominant species in the universe, and yet, they'd succumbed to the cruelties of the universe. Despite their extinction, they had left their mark on modern culture. Even though two different worlds could have been separated by billions, if not trillions of miles, there would be many cultural similarities. Languages would often be very alike, if not identical. Old traditions and rituals could be shared across thousands of worlds. Ancient religions bore similarities that simply couldn't be ignored. The assumption by many historians and scientists was that the Enkaye had passed down their cultural teachings, long before their demise.

Even in the case of Earth, the similarities were striking. The biggest was that the human race had spread across the galaxy, far beyond the confines of Earth. For some unknown reason, life, God or maybe even the Enkaye themselves had enabled human beings to develop across the cosmos. Of course, humanity wasn't the only race in the universe; there were thousands. The likes of the Uvan empire had risen, fallen and then become a part of the homunculus unit known as the Commonwealth. The Sphinax had evolved from simple felines into a complex culture of clans and tribes. The Horrus had gone from primitive canines and were now one of many leading races in the 'wealth. Thousands upon thousands of species had progressed from nothing, and many believed it was thanks to the Enkaye.

As the FTL engine bubbled to life beneath him, Nathan felt his stomach churn under the abrupt gravitational shift.

The feeling of having one's insides suddenly slammed from one side of the body to the other wasn't pleasant, but it was completely harmless. Once the Vertex had careened into the slipstream, Nathan felt the ship's simulated gravity take back control, and his body felt normal once again.

Knowing that it was going to be a long journey to the Capital Worlds, Nathan settled in. He climbed into the ergonomic bed in his cell and closed his eyes, but it was impossible to sleep.

I've gotta find a way off of this tub before the 'wealthers set their Agent on me, Nathan thought.

CHAPTER FIVE

Harrt Oxarri had always found something oddly relaxing about the FTL slipstream. He'd somehow blocked out the primitive part of his brain that told him being hurtled through space wasn't natural. He simply accepted it. Huge blue streams created by the extreme forward motion passed over the command centre windows like a flowing river, and Harrt took comfort in it.

By the end of his shift, Harrt checked the star map to ensure that their course was on track. The route provided by High Command was risky, but the Vertex wouldn't encounter too much attention provided it stayed on course and didn't stop during the FTL transit.

Satisfied that his job was done for the day, Harrt walked to Rooke in order to provide his CO with a handover. The Commander was on the other side of the bridge, reading something from his datapad. He regarded whatever it was on his screen with the level of scrutiny that was to be expected for an officer of his rank.

"The route looks good," Harrt said. "We should be through Yandi in twelve hours".

Rooke continued to read the datapad, as though he'd not even acknowledged Harrt's sentence.

"Sir?"

Rooke shook his head as if to clear his daze and placed the datapad down. He looked at Harrt with a distant expression and struggled to form a proper response. Harrt could tell that whatever Rooke had just read was not good.

"We need to turn around," Rooke finally said.

"What do you mean?" Harrt replied, seeing the sudden anxiety on his Commanders face.

Rooke glanced around at the crew who were busy going about their routines. He then stood from his seat and spoke in a lowered voice;

"The situation with our Evoker guest is far more severe than High Command initially anticipated." Commander Rooke then paused for breath as though he were regaining his composure. "Get every marine and security officer down to Astrilla's quarters and see that she has around the clock protection. I need to have eyes on her the entire time".

"Aye sir," Harrt nodded.

As he pulled his datapad to relay Rooke's orders, Harrt heard the CO address the bridge crew.

"I need your attention people," Rooke said, standing beside his Commanders console. "We've just had new orders from High Command. We need to turn this ship around and reroute to the Heslem System where Admiral Wexell and the fifth fleet will rendezvous with us".

As Harrt keyed the new orders into his datapad, an alarm began to sound from the tactical station opposite.

Must be a malfunction, Harrt thought.

He finished relaying the message to all security personnel and then walked to the tact-terminal. The Ensign who had been stationed there was frantically checking the readings that were suddenly flooding the screen.

"What is it?" Harrt said.

Before the Ensign could reply, an alert flashed up in bold red letters. Harrt's eyes took in the new information before his mouth could say it aloud;

ALERT—MISSILE—LOCK

What followed was a crash that sent the Vertex spiralling out of the FTL slipstream. For a moment, everything slowed down. The artificial gravity tried its best to guess which way the ship was supposed to orientate. The overhead lights smashed under the enormous pressure of a failed FTL drop.

The Vertex's onboard computer must have kicked in seconds later, as the engine ceased and the blue waves of the slipstream faded into non-existence. Gravity returned to normal, and the emergency lighting kicked in, soaking the bridge in a scarlet hue.

By the time Harrt climbed to his feet, chaos had erupted on the bridge. Rooke was yelling orders to anyone that was able to listen over the emergency siren. Something had attacked the Vertex in mid-FTL, which was a near-impossible thing to do.

"Battlestations!" Rooke yelled.

Harrt caught his breath, then made his way over to the Commander, who'd sustained a bloody cut across his forehead. When Harrt stumbled across the gangway, Rooke helped him to regain his balance.

"Oxarri, are you okay?" Rooke said. The CO then turned to the helmsman; "Get the FTL drive back online".

Harrt lurched forward again as another missile struck the Vertex. He managed to secure his footing and then looked back to the window, seeing what had attacked them.

"Revenant!"

Harrt counted nine warships, equal in size and combat ability to the Vertex. Harrt had been in enough battles to know when the enemy had the advantage: this was one of those occasions.

"Helmsman!" Rooke was yelling again. "Get us the hell outta here".

The male Horrus at the helm was so overwhelmed that it took him several seconds to fathom a reply;

"Sir, the engines…" the helmsman stuttered. "The engines are gone!".

"What do you mean *gone*?" Rooke snapped.

Another missile struck the ship, causing it to shake under the impact.

"I mean, we don't have engines," the helmsman stuttered. "The Revenant blew them straight off the ship. The entire engineering deck is gone".

For the first time in all the years that Harrt had known Harlmaan Rooke, he looked vanquished by the situation. Once Harrt finished calling into his communicator to the marines, Rooke grabbed him by the collar and marched him toward the rear of the bridge.

"Get down to the armoury and prep every man, woman and child for a Revenant incursion," Rooke said. "Tell the marines to take the pods and get that Evoker off this ship".

"Sir, we're in the middle of hostile space," Harrt replied. "Where are they supposed to take her?"

Rooke pulled out his datapad and gestured to a planet that was dangerously close to the Vertex. He then shoved the datapad into Harrt's chest.

"The planet is called Yenex," Rooke said. "Tell them to hide her down there and do not let her fall into Revenant hands. Follow her down there!".

Rooke then shoved Harrt into an elevator;

"You make sure that she gets off this ship," Rooke said, tossing him a sidearm. "Once she's away, evac the crew and rendezvous with her".

"Yes sir!"

"And Harrt…" Rooke said. "The Evoker is important. You must keep her safe. I wouldn't be asking you to do this if I didn't trust you".

As the elevator doors sealed between them, Harrt relayed Rooke's order to the marines. He knew that their backs were up against the wall and that Rooke would go down with the ship. The Evoker was involved with something significant and whatever it was, had warranted the presence of nine Revenant warships.

Suddenly another missile collided with the Vertex and an alarm sounded. Harrt grimaced as the automated voice filled the elevator cab;

"Mag-lock failed; brace for impact".

That was the moment that Harrt Oxarri realised that he was going to miss the fifth floor by several decks. With the mag-locks gone, the elevator would free-fall in whichever direction the artificial gravity was pointing.

He plummeted downward for what felt like a lifetime.

Seconds after passing the fifth deck, the elevator cab crashed into the bottom of the lift shaft. The full force of the impact sent Harrt smashing into the ceiling, and then gravity dragged him back to the ground. As Harrt sat up, he heard the emergency announcement that was being broadcast across the Vertex;

ATTENTION: A HOSTILE FORCE HAS BOARDED THIS VESSEL. PLEASE ATTEND YOUR DESIGNATED SECURITY CHECKPOINT. THIS IS NOT A DRILL.

Harrt took up the sidearm that Rooke had given him, knowing that there would be an arduous battle ahead.

▲

Everything around Nathan shook like he'd been caught in the middle of an earthquake. A piercing siren started wailing from a speaker in the corner of the brig.

Before Nathan could climb from his bed, he was flung from it by the sudden shift in gravity. After he'd crashed into the floor with a bone-jarring thud, the overhead lights failed, and for several seconds he lay in darkness.

What the hell just happened? Nathan thought.

Emergency lighting kicked in and bathed Nathan and his surroundings in crimson. As he climbed to his feet, an automated ship-wide broadcast announced that a hostile force had boarded the Vertex.

Without warning, something crashed on the next deck, causing the ceiling over Nathan's head to buckle. The translucent forcefield that had contained him for the last few days disappeared. Nathan wasted no time in dashing from his cell before any backup system could kick in and seal him inside. He gathered his belongs from the table where the marines had left them, noticing that his pistol was gone.

Another rumble caused him to lurch forward. He used both of his outreached palms to steady himself against the table and turned to face a window at the other end of the brig. It was at that moment that Nathan saw what was attacking the Vertex.

Against the harsh darkness of space, Nathan saw at least nine Revenant warships and several dozen fighters; all of which were firing on the very ship he was standing aboard. He could only assume that the Vertex was flying solo and was, therefore, heavily outnumbered. In addition to the Revenant Armada, Nathan saw that the Vertex was in orbit around a grey planet.

I ain't dying aboard a Commonwealth ship, Nathan thought.

He quickly concluded that the planet below was his best method of escape. There was no point in trying to steal a fighter from the dock as the 'wealthers would have locked down the area.

DRILLERS INCOMING.

The ship-wide announcement sent a chill down Nathan's spine. He'd never encountered a Driller before, but he'd heard enough accounts over the years to know what was about to happen. He spotted one of the arrow-shaped transports from the window. Seconds later it smashed into the Vertex several decks below.

That means that the Revenant must've knocked out the shields, Nathan thought.

He knew that at that moment, the Driller was magnetising itself to the hull and creating a vacuum seal. In a matter of seconds, it would cut through the metal skin of the Vertex and offload a boarding party. Nathan heard the sound of more Drillers colliding with the Vertex as he threw his backpack over his shoulder and made for the door. He stepped out onto a barren corridor which was covered in the same red emergency lighting. The sound of gunfire was coming from the direction that Nathan had to go.

First objective, get a gun, Nathan thought.

He began to make his way toward the weapons fire, hoping that he'd be able to sneak past whoever was causing the ruckus. As he turned a corner, Nathan noticed the remains of two dead 'wealther marines. One had been stabbed through the chest with a sharp object, while the other had suffered a decapitation. Nathan immediately recognised the distinct scratch marks on the first victim's armour.

Hunters, Nathan thought.

Instinctively, Nathan readied himself to sprint in the opposite direction, but as he did so, he came face to face with the murderer.

The hunter towered over Nathan, standing around seven-foot in height. At first glance, it's bulbous head looked something akin to a primate with two deformed eyes and a mouth filled with jagged teeth. It's once human body was covered in ceremonial Revenant armour, which appeared to be a dull grey colour under the emergency lights. Nathan noted that the monster was not only armed with it's dagger-like claws but it also carried a jagged sword which was sheathed at the hip.

The hunter took two steps toward Nathan.

"Human…" It spoke with a deep and broken voice.

Nathan grabbed a gun from one of the dead marines and proceeded to fire wildly at the mutated beast. With every laser-bolt that tore through its torso, the hunter howled. Its mutated grey blood sprayed against the wall as each shot collided, but it showed little sign of backing down.

It's gonna take a hell of a lot more than a few bolts to put this thing down, Nathan thought.

He fired until the gun overheated, by which point the hunter started to cackle. Before Nathan could react, it grabbed him by the leg and swung him into the opposite wall. He crashed into the hard metal bulkhead with a thud and felt the full force of the attack in his ribcage.

For a moment, the hunter stopped to moan in pain. Nathan peered up to see the monster checking the gunshot wounds that he'd inflicted.

"You are one ugly mother—"

Nathan was cut off as the hunter grabbed him by the

throat and lifted him off the ground. It slammed him against the metal bulkhead and then proceeded to squeeze on his neck. As Nathan began to choke under the hunter's grip, it studied him with its freakish black eyes and uttered in a low growl;

"Human….."

It began to cackle as it pulled Nathan closer.

Once Nathan was within an inch of the hunter's face, he seized the opportunity to strike. He grabbed at the sword at the hunter's waist and yanked it from its sheath. Survival instinct kicked in. Nathan plunged the jagged blade deep into the beast's thigh, and the hunter recoiled in utter torment, releasing its vice-like grip on Nathan's neck.

As Nathan gasped for air, he watched the hunter yank the sword from its flesh. The monster shrieked for several seconds before tossing the weapon aside in a fit of animalistic rage. Instinctively, Nathan crawled toward the body of one of the dead marines in the hope of securing a new firearm.

The hunter focussed its soulless eyes on him and pounced. Nathan was able to grab a gun from one of the bodies and fired. The laser bolt pierced through the creature's neck and sent it hurtling past Nathan and into the wall opposite.

When it comes to hunters, always go for the head. Another of Jack's life lessons played back in Nathan's mind.

Nathan scurried away from the wounded beast and took up the discarded sword from the floor. He drew close to the hunter, armed with a pistol in one hand and the creature's blade in the other. Nathan fired a bounty of gunshots into the monster's body as it climbed to its feet. When Nathan was within metres, he tossed the gun aside and took up the sword in both hands.

The swing was powerful enough to ensure that jagged steel connected with mutated flesh. For a moment, Nathan wondered if perhaps his strike had been sufficient enough to defeat the beast. The fact was that the blade had sliced through the leathery meat of the creature's neck and severed its head from its torso. Nathan straightened up as the headless carcass fell to the ground and its armoured head rolled down the corridor. He tossed the blood-soaked sword to one side and stopped to catch his breath.

I really hope there's no more of those guys, Nathan thought.

He checked that his newly acquired pistol was loaded and continued to make his way toward the escape pods on the fifth floor. Nathan passed through the intricate corridors of the warship, avoiding a Revenant patrol in the process. It felt like a different ship from the one he'd snuck aboard two days prior. The bloodied bodies of 'wealthers were littered everywhere, and the walls were covered with scorch marks and blood.

When Nathan turned a corner, something startled him, and he impulsively pitched his gun up in defence. The man opposite Nathan did the same, but he didn't pull the trigger.

Both of them stopped. Nathan's eyes settled on a human male in his mid-forties, wearing a Commonwealth officers uniform. Six-foot-two, with green eyes and short dark hair with the odd grey at the sides. Even before the man opened his mouth, Nathan could tell from the look in his eyes that he wanted to live.

Lt. Harrt Oxarri, Nathan read the name tag on the man's uniform.

"I won't shoot if you don't," the 'wealther said.

CHAPTER SIX

For several seconds, Harrt kept his weapon trained on the scruffy-looking Earther. He immediately recognised the intruder who'd been captured a few days earlier. Unlike his holo-profile, the man was covered in grey Revenant blood.

The good citizen in Harrt wanted nothing more than to recapture the criminal, but the survivalist in him objected. One of the most key values of the Commonwealth was *unity in the face of adversity*. It was that teaching which had served as the cornerstone for the Commonwealth's foundation.

There's something to be said about strength in numbers, Harrt thought.

He knew that the Earther wanted to survive; he could see it in the younger man's dark eyes.

"I won't shoot if you don't," Harrt said.

The curly-haired man, at least fifteen years Harrt's junior, didn't react to his statement. There was something nervous about the Earther's demeanour, as though he were debating something internally.

Another crash struck the Vertex, and both men stumbled under the impact.

"Listen to me," Harrt straightened up. "We can either shoot each other, or we shoot at the Revenant and survive this".

Harrt's datapad began to alarm, but he didn't reach for it. Instead, he kept the barrel of his gun trained on the unkempt younger man.

"Aren't you gonna get that?" The Earther finally spoke up and pointed with his chin to the ringing device. "I passed a dozen Revenant soldiers back that way: that noise is gonna bring them our way".

"That depends," Harrt replied. "Are *you* gonna shoot *me*?"

The Earther tilted his head to one side;

"Are you planning on putting me back in a cell?"

Harrt had seen the full military capability of the Revenant on many occasions. His gut told him that if this had been a one-on-one battle, the Vertex would have held her own, but this was very different. They were outnumbered and outgunned. The Revenant had already boarded and would rip the Vertex apart piece by piece.

Time was of the essence. Harrt decided to lower his gun, and to his surprise, the curly-haired stranger did the same.

"Good," the Earther said. "Now answer that fuckin' message before the Revenant sends a squad up here to investigate".

Harrt frowned at the younger man's use of Earther profanity but didn't acknowledge it. Instead, he grabbed his datapad from his belt and tapped the screen.

"Harrt…"

The worried voice of Commander Rooke came through the tiny speaker. Harrt tried to adjust the settings on his datapad as there was only audio being transmitted on their channel.

"Sir?" Harrt said into the device. "I couldn't get to the fifth deck to evac the Evoker".

There was the sound of an explosion on the other side of the transmission which made Harrt pause. A silence dragged for a few seconds before Rooke's voice continued;

"She made it off the ship five minutes ago in an escape pod," Rooke coughed. "The marines went with her as well".

Harrt breathed a sigh of relief.

"Harrt, the Vertex is lost. The Revenant are trying to breach the doors to the bridge". Rooke's voice disappeared behind the sound of laser-fire for a few seconds. "I'm activating the ship's self destruct function. Abandon the ship and find the girl; she must be kept safe."

Before Harrt could reply, a ship-wide announcement blared over the speakers;

SELF-DESTRUCT SEQUENCE INITIATED. TEN MINUTES UNTIL DETONATION.

"I will," Harrt said into his communicator. He waited for a reply from Rooke, but there was nothing. All that came through the other side of the transmission was the sound of gunfire and screaming. When the comms link finally cut out, all that came from Harrt's datapad was the sour crackle of static.

The grim reality of the situation hit Harrt in the gut. He knew that if Rooke had activated the self-destruct sequence, then the Vertex was a goner. The CO's final order was simple; *find the girl and keep her safe.* Harrt intended to follow those orders to the letter.

He buckled his datapad to his belt and peered at the apprehensive Earther opposite. The younger man was busy checking around the corner for any pursuers, but Harrt noticed that he'd kept one eye on him the entire time.

"We should move," the Earther said, shoving his way past Harrt. "I don't wanna become one of those brainless husks".

Harrt watched the dark-haired man head down the corridor.

"You're going the wrong way," Harrt said. He then pointed in the correct direction and added; "Escape pods are this way".

It was apparent that the scruffy-looking rogue didn't appreciate being corrected. He scowled as he waltzed back toward Harrt.

"How about you lead the way," he grunted.

▲

Nathan didn't trust anyone. He'd been burned enough times to know that the only person he could rely on was himself. Maybe that was why he couldn't keep his eyes off of his newly acquired ally. Something was itching at the back of his mind as they dashed toward the escape pods:

Is this guy just gonna shoot me the moment my back's turned?

Nathan followed his gut and kept his gaze glued on the Lieutenant's back. There was something robotic about the way the officer navigated through the ship. He'd creep down a corridor with his weapon raised, then stop at a junction to check for Revenant soldiers. Then the whole process would start all over again.

The ship's announcement system had continued to loop the self destruct message for several minutes. Nathan was very wary that time was slipping away and they didn't have long to escape.

"We need to get a move on," Nathan insisted. "The Revenant will be on the main deck, gathering as much of the dead as possible".

The 'wealther glanced over his shoulder as they reached a stairwell.

"Trust me; I know what the Revenant do in situations like this," the officer said. "You're right. Under normal circumstances, they'd be gathering the dead for mutation, but this is very different".

Nathan looked around the gloomy blood-stained walls of the Vertex and then whipped his head back to the Lieutenant.

"Different how?" He gestured to the destruction as he spoke.

"This whole thing is about the Evoker," the 'wealther answered. "They'll have soldiers searching for her".

"Didn't your pal say she'd gotten off the ship?"

"He did, but *they* don't know that!"

"And they'll be near her quarters. Right next to the escape pods," Nathan said.

They moved up the stairs to the fifth floor and stepped into the middle of another long corridor, even darker than the previous one. Nathan could hear the percussive chorale of gunfire echo in the opposite direction. Evidently, the Revenant were finishing off the last survivors, and he had no intention of joining them.

Nathan took the lead, replacing his mistrust for the 'wealther, with a burning desire not to become a Revenant drone. The Lieutenant followed close behind, and together they moved deeper into the corridor.

We're not alone, Nathan thought.

Just as he made the assessment, a Revenant soldier appeared at one of the junctions with his rifle raised. Nathan was the first to react, cutting down the soldier with a single laser bolt to the chest. Nathan's heart sank as the sound of his gun echoed throughout the hall.

That's gonna draw a whole bunch of trouble, he thought.

Almost a heartbeat after he'd killed the first soldier, another two darted into the corridor ahead. They aimed their weapons at Nathan and his 'wealther companion. Nathan shoved the Lieutenant into a doorway and watched the array of laser bolts fly down the corridor.

THREE MINUTES TO DETONATION

Only the Revenant's soldiers would carry on fighting aboard a ship about to explode, Nathan thought.

He fired blindly around the corner, causing the enemy soldiers to dive into cover. The 'wealther beside him looked ready to fight and tapped Nathan on the shoulder:

"We *need* to move!" the Lieutenant yelled over the gunfire.

Nathan moved from cover and spotted another three soldiers running toward them from the other end of the corridor. It was an attempt to surround them, but the second group didn't anticipate that Nathan had an ally.

Nathan fired at the three approaching guards, while his 'wealther companion darted from cover and began picking off the first group. Within seconds, all five of the hostiles were down. Nathan stood over one of the dying soldiers who helplessly tried to pull his sidearm. The killing shot that Nathan delivered was precise and merciless; just as the Revenant had been on Earth. The laser bolt demolished what had once been the skull of a human into a grey cloud of mutated blood.

"C'mon, pods are up ahead" the Lieutenant said.

Nathan allowed the 'wealther to take the lead. They turned a corner onto a shorter hallway that Nathan immediately recognised. The escape pod bay was halfway down on the right side, and there was no sign of any Revenant soldiers.

We're nearly out of the woods, Nathan thought.

The Commonwealth Lieutenant began sprinting toward the pods, and Nathan followed close behind. As he picked up the pace, Nathan sensed something but didn't have ample time to react.

He felt the excruciating burn of a laser bolt sear into his shoulder blade. Nathan stumbled forward in shock as the round seared into his flesh. It wasn't a severe wound, but it was still agonising to feel the heat of the blast boiling his skin. The 'wealther must have noticed, as suddenly he turned and opened fire on the attacker. The two Revenant soldiers behind fell as quickly as they'd appeared. The Lieutenant darted over and offered him a hand, but Nathan had already started climbing to his feet.

"You okay?" the 'wealther asked.

"Ain't the first time I've been shot," Nathan barked. "C'mon let's get outta here".

They got to the pods a few seconds later. Only one of the fifteen capsules had been ejected, which meant that the Evoker and her bodyguards were the only ones who'd made it off the Vertex.

They jumped into the closest pod as the overhead announcement began to countdown from sixty seconds. The 'wealther paused as they worked to seal the door behind them.

"What is it?" Nathan said hurriedly. "You hear that countdown, right? We have to move now!"

The 'wealther pulled his datapad again and tapped a

few buttons on the screen. Despite his injury, Nathan continued to close the hatch on his own. He noticed that the Lieutenant was running a ship-wide scan; undoubtedly checking if any of his crewmates had survived the incursion.

"What the fuck are you doing?" Nathan demanded.

The 'wealther didn't reply, and a split second later his datapad beeped. The expression on the Lieutenant's face as he examined the readings was one that Nathan had seen many times before. It was the look of a defeated man.

"They killed all of them," the 'wealther said bitterly. "Every last one of them".

The Lieutenant suddenly sprung into action as soon as he'd said it. He double-checked the hatch which Nathan had closed and then moved to a control panel at the front of the escape pod. After the officer had punched a few commands into the console, Nathan felt the floor shake. The escape pod whirred to life and a split second after it fired into space.

Nathan slumped down in a chair near the officer. Together they looked out on the damage to the Vertex. The once-proud symbol of the Commonwealth's military prowess had been reduced to a floating piece of wreckage.

The warship's hull had suffered a plethora of fiery wounds where the Revenant ships had battered the vessel into submission. Nathan counted over a dozen Drillers that had attached themselves to the ship. The Revenant Armada had begun to move to a safe distance, undoubtedly anticipating the imminent blast from the Vertex's self destruct.

There's no way they'll detect a pod this size with what's about to happen, Nathan thought.

When the countdown reached zero, the Vertex erupted into a massive ball of green fire. The blast sent debris out in every direction, and for at least thirty seconds all that could be seen from the escape pod was an emerald inferno against the cold darkness of space. When the fire cleared, all that remained was a field of debris.

Nathan peered at his new ally. The Lieutenant was pulling several harnesses over his lap and shoulders as though he knew something else was about to follow.

Shockwave, Nathan thought.

He did the same as the 'wealther and strapped himself into his chair. Seconds later, the fallout of the explosion struck the pod and sent it hurtling toward the planet of Yenex at an alarming speed.

"Was your ship carrying warheads?" Nathan yelled over the loud rumbling.

The 'wealther didn't reply, and instead tapped something on the armrest beside him.

As the escape pod entered the atmosphere of the planet, it began to slow down. Nathan felt the artificial gravity deactivate, allowing the new world's downward pull to take over. From the window, all that could be seen was the pod's exterior beginning to burn up on entry. Automated air-brakes activated and further slowed the pod's descent. Nathan allowed himself to sigh in relief as the air-pressure and gravity returned to normal.

All of a sudden, there was a loud crash which startled both men. It quickly became evident that something had struck the rear of the pod and destroyed the engines along with the air-brakes.

Nathan looked back to the window as they cleared the thick clouds of Yenex. He saw the skyscrapers and sprawling city below them, just as the pod glanced a moving ship. The impact caused their straight fall to transform into a violent downward spiral.

Nathan and his new 'wealther companion had just enough time to exchange concerned expressions before they felt the full force of Yenex's gravity.

CHAPTER SEVEN

The second of Nathan's life-defining moments came at the age of twenty. After the Fall, Jack made it his mission to impart every ounce of his knowledge to Nathan and James. He taught them to survive; how to fight; how to hold, aim and fire a gun. Then there were the subjects that Jack didn't understand; space flight and engineering: all the things that were alien to an Earther. Rather than bumble his way through a lesson he couldn't teach, Jack had the other members of the Loyalty's crew share their wisdom with the boys.

For Nathan, this had mostly worked. He'd been young enough to climatise to the new world around him and take in the information that Jack and the crew passed on. By fifteen years of age, Nathan was a functioning member of the Loyalty's crew and would often play a part in their missions.

For Nathan's cousin James, it wasn't the case. At the tender age of sixteen, James survived the Fall. While Nathan was growing up, his cousin never spoke about what had happened on that fateful day. Instead, James opted to always put on a brave face, just like his father.

Nathan always looked at James as a big brother growing up. His cousin had always been *the cool guy,* practically oozing charisma and charm from every blonde hair on his head. Nathan could recall James saying that the girls back on Earth would fall over themselves for a chance to date him. For many years Nathan saw him as a role-model, but as he grew, so too did the cracks in James' facade.

By the time Nathan was a teenager, he could see straight through the shroud with which his cousin had hidden behind. The charisma and charm were replaced by hubris and vanity, and Nathan saw his cousin in a different light.

It was only when a mission went sideways, and all hell broke loose that Nathan called his cousin on his bullshit. The pair had almost come to blows aboard the Loyalty after a narrow escape and Jack was forced to separate them. After things cooled down, it transpired that James had been high on an outer-planets' narcotic known as Ice during the mission. The harsh truth was simple; James had a drug habit, and it had been going on for a very long time.

The crew weren't happy about James, his habits or his actions, but Jack defended his son, vowing to help him get clean. James' girlfriend, Merri, backed up Jack, and they made it their mission to help James kick the habit and get clean.

Months down the line, the Loyalty and her crew were gone, including Jack. The Loyalty's final moments were spent being piloted by James into a gang's hideout as an act of revenge.

Justice, he'd called it. *For what they did to my father.*

The reality was that James had no proof of the gang's involvement. After days of searching for his father, James shot-up with a double dose of Ice and chose to disregard everything he'd been taught.

Nathan had watched helplessly as James crashed the Loyalty directly into the floating structure which served as the gang's hideout. The fallout from the explosion was significant. Not only did fifty gang members perish in the blast, but so too did a further eighty-three civilians when the complex crashed into the town below. James had destroyed the ship which had served as their home for over twelve years.

When Nathan found his drug-fuelled cousin a few

hours later, he was sat at the bar of a grimy nightclub, nursing a drink as though nothing had happened. Nathan immediately confronted his cousin about the civilian casualties and what James said, changed Nathan's life forever.

Their lives mean nothing.

Nathan snapped, and they'd gotten into another fight, but this time Jack wasn't there to stop it. In the middle of the packed nightclub, Nathan had beaten his cousin to a bloody pulp. When James had pulled a gun, Nathan was forced to act. They wrestled for the gun, and Nathan broke his cousins arm. He still remembered the crunch of James' bones, followed by screaming.

Nathan wanted to shoot his cousin then and there, but something inside told him not to do it. Instead, he left James —the only member of his family— in the middle of the nightclub and never looked back. Within an hour, Nathan spent the last of his money to chart a ship for the Purian system.

From that day on, Nathan was alone, left with only Jack's life lessons and the bag on his back. Unlike the first life-defining moment in his life, Nathan associated this one to his own advice rather than Jack's;

If I can't trust my own flesh and blood, how can I trust anyone else?

He'd asked himself that question countless times and never found the answer. All the people Nathan had ever trusted were gone. They were either dead, missing or like James. So he learned from the experience never to misplace his trust again.

"How could you do that to us? How could you do that to our home?"

When Nathan opened his eyes, he saw the Commonwealth Lieutenant looming over him. The first reaction Nathan had was of pure instinct. He tried to shove the 'wealther aside in a desperate bid to get to safety. A second later, everything came crashing into the forefront of his mind. He recalled escaping his cell aboard the Vertex and allying himself with the officer.

Everything became clear again, and Nathan released his grip on the 'wealther's collar. The Lieutenant must've recognised the clarity that filled Nathan's eyes and took a step back.

"You were shouting in your sleep," he said. "First thing you've said that actually made any sense in six hours".

"Six hours?" Nathan said.

It took Nathan a moment longer to process the statement as the length of time didn't sound correct. He felt groggy and sluggish, as though someone had struck him in the head with a blunt object: far worse than any hangover he'd ever experienced.

Nathan sat up and quickly realised he was no longer inside an escape pod. Nathan stared around at what he could only assume was an alleyway.

"What do you remember?" the Lieutenant asked as he handed Nathan a flask of water.

Nathan gulped down the contents of the bottle before answering.

"Those Revenant fuckers got the jump on your ship," Nathan said. "How the hell did they shoot you out of an FTL slipstream".

The 'wealther's jaw tightened at the question.

"That doesn't matter right now," he shook his head. "We've got bigger things to worry about right now".

We? Nathan thought.

He didn't acknowledge the 'wealther's use of the word, but it didn't make him feel any less uncomfortable. Nathan climbed from to his feet, noticing his shirt had been removed and that a medical dressing was applied to his shoulder.

"I treated your wound," the 'wealther said, handing Nathan a fresh shirt from his bag.

"Thanks," Nathan muttered, pulling the dark top over his head. "So, where the hell are we?"

"The planet is called Yenex," the 'wealther said. "It's a corporation controlled world in the Yandi System".

Nathan knew of the star system but had never travelled to it. From what he'd gathered the corporations ruled the planets with an iron fist. Unlike the Commonwealth, there was no such thing as equality: every man, woman and child had to plunder to survive. Simply put, if you had money, the corporations would allow you to thrive, but if you didn't, they would either work you to the bone or leave you to rot.

"What about the escape pod?" Nathan asked.

"We hit a ship and a building before we reached the ground. It was not my finest landing, but we're still in one piece," the 'wealther answered. "I think you hit your head on the back of your chair as we were coming down. By the time we... *landed*... you were out cold".

"That explains my headache," Nathan remarked. "So, how'd we end up here?"

"I carried you to a public transport and got us the hell out of there before the local authorities turned up". the Lieutenant said.

Experience taught Nathan that when people went out of their way to help others it was for one of two reasons: the first being that they wanted something out of the person they were saving. The second was that they were simply a fool: the 'wealther didn't look like the latter.

"You could've just left me for dead," Nathan said. "Why save me?"

The 'wealther's lips pressed together until they were almost white.

"Why would I leave you behind?" he said uncomfortably. "The Founders taught our people that an ally is a friend. You don't leave your friends behind".

Nathan cynically rolled his eyes at the Commonwealth doctrine, which had evidently been drilled into his new-found ally.

"Is that what we are?" Nathan said. "*Friends?*"

The 'wealther shrugged.

"The Revenant put a blockade in place over the planet. They aren't letting anyone off-world. It's causing huge civil unrest, and the corporations haven't exactly been accommodating for them," the officer said. "The way I see it we need one another to survive".

"This is about the Evoker".

"It is," the 'wealther nodded. "She crashed here as well with a squad of my marines. If we can get to them then maybe—"

"*We?*" Nathan interrupted. "Up until a few hours ago, I was being kept prisoner aboard you're fuckin' warship."

"You snuck aboard and tried to kidnap a high profile guest," the 'wealther folded his arms. "We thought you were a Revenant spy: everyone except the girl you were trying to kidnap".

"Clearly, I'm not a Revenant spy," Nathan said, raising both of his arms in protest. "For the record, I didn't take a job to kidnap anyone. It was a simple cargo grab. As it stands, I'm starting to think the guy who hired me was trying to fuck me over".

The Lieutenant's dark eyebrows rose.

"I think you should take a good look at the people you are working for," the 'wealther said.

Nathan scowled at the remark, but he couldn't deny that the military man was right. Perhaps Guttasnype knew the Evoker would be there. Maybe the Icktus had planned that Nathan would get caught or killed in the process. The question was, *why?*

Maybe it was some kind of act of revenge against me, Nathan wondered. *Or Jack...*

"Listen, I don't care what you did or who you were working for," the 'wealther said. "You're clearly not a Revenant spy, and you handled yourself well back on the Vertex. I'd like to propose that we work together to find Astrilla and then get the hell off of this planet".

Nathan smirked at the ham-fisted attempt to appeal to the optimist inside him. Nathan's very thought of being an idealist had died on the day that James destroyed the Loyalty, as had his trust of other people. Jack's lessons had always been clear;

Do not trust the Commonwealth.

Something itched at the back of Nathan's mind. This 'wealther had saved him both on and off of the Vertex. He'd also treated the gunshot wound on Nathan's shoulder despite owing him nothing. He didn't like to admit it but getting off a Revenant controlled planet would be nigh on impossible alone.

This guy needs my help as much as I need his, Nathan thought. *Maybe this could be an opportunity to get a clean slate, especially if the Evoker is important to them.*

After considering the Lieutenant's offer, Nathan said;

"I'll help you on two conditions." He began to count out his demands on his fingers. "One; I want a full pardon for the *supposed kidnap attempt on* the girl. Kidnapping is not my style."

"I'll vouch for you," the 'wealther said. "And the second?"

"I want a ship," Nathan said. "Doesn't have to be anything fancy just something to get me from A to B".

The 'wealther nodded reluctantly. He climbed to his feet and then offered his hand to shake with Nathan.

"My name is Harrt Oxarri," he said.

Nathan shook his hand, debating whether or not to give a fake name. In the end, something about this particular 'wealther made Nathan ignore the voice of Jack and instead, trust the feeling in his gut.

"Nathan Carter".

CHAPTER EIGHT

By the time Harrt and Nathan departed the alleyway, night had settled in. Despite the absence of the sun, the planet of Yenex was alight. Thousands of windows across a plethora of skyscrapers could be seen for miles in every direction. Like most Corporate controlled worlds, Yenex boasted an incredible array of architecture. Each high-rise superstructure was carefully designed and constructed by the finest materials money could buy.

There was a distinct hustle and bustle on the streets that Harrt found almost overwhelming. Like most of the Corporate controlled worlds, Yenex was crowded and overpopulated. Billions, if not trillions, would flood from the Outer Worlds to planets like Yenex in search of paying work. Non-'wealthers had a burning desire to accumulate riches, and the Corporate lifestyle was advertised to the desperate as a means to climb the social ladder. The reality was that these so-called careers were menial and poorly paid. More often than not, most workers would end up spending all of their gains to keep a roof over their head. Inequality was rife on worlds like Yenex. The rich would live in high-rise penthouses, miles above the city, while the poorest would live in slums on the lower levels.

Such injustice didn't exist in the Commonwealth. Each and every citizen was equal regardless of the role they played in society. Seeing the way the corporations treated their employees made Harrt grateful to have been born and raised as a proud member of the Commonwealth.

The same could certainly not be said for Harrt's new ally. It was evident that the unkempt vagrant who'd introduced himself as *Nathan Carter* had lived a tough life. Even though Harrt had saved Nathan's life, the curly-haired Earther hadn't taken his eye off of him.

What would the Founders do in my situation? Harrt wondered. *How do I win this guy's trust?*

Commonwealth history had told of twelve ordinary people who'd come together in the face of great adversity. They all came from different species, shared opposing creeds and political beliefs and yet, despite all of the differences between them, they'd formed the Commonwealth. Perhaps Harrt could do the same with this Earther and forge his very own alliance; just like the Founders.

"You're an Earther, aren't you?" Harrt asked.

The scruffy man appeared to pause, as though he were contemplating his response.

"You already know the answer to that question," Nathan replied coldly. "Your Evoker friend figured that out when she rooted through my stuff. I'm guessing what you really wanna ask is *why ain't I living with the others on Paradisium?*"

"I mean, sure," Harrt mumbled. "It is very rare to see your people anywhere else".

Like most Commonwealth citizens, Harrt was surprised to see an Earther outside of the comforts of the idyllic world of Paradisium. Harrt had never been, but he'd heard that the planet was a beautiful paradise complete with all the amenities that Earth's people would need to live a carefree lifestyle.

To many 'wealthers, the gift of Paradisium was seen by some as a gesture of apology to the Earthers, while others saw it as a frivolous gift. The truth was that the Commonwealth should have prevented the Fall, but news of the attack had reached the Council too late. As a result, most of Earth's population were wiped out, and the Revenant had a few billion footsoldiers added to their ranks.

That wasn't to say that all Earthers stayed on Paradisium. There was the rare few that ventured off-world like business tycoons and the odd politician. Corporations like Jareth Corps, Roth Industries and Belfort Transport were all Earther-run companies that had gained notoriety over the last two decades.

"I'm nothing like the people on Paradisium," Nathan scowled. "I'd sooner spend my time earning a living and travelling the galaxy. Not spending my life sitting on a fuckin' sun-lounger".

Harrt lifted his eyebrows at the contempt Nathan clearly had for the Earther refugees. *Care for your fellow citizen,* was one of the Commonwealth's core values. Therefore, Harrt couldn't help but wonder what had spurred Nathan's distaste for his own people. Before he could enquire any further, Nathan turned to him:

"If we wanna find this Evoker friend of yours we need to get some local knowledge," he said. "Looking for one person on a planet will be like finding a needle in a haystack".

Harrt didn't quite understand the colloquialism, but he got the gist. They needed to find out where Astrilla and the marines had landed. As this world and its ways were utterly unfamiliar to Harrt, he'd have to rely on Nathan's intuition.

"Where do you propose we gather this local knowledge?" Harrt asked.

There was a slight upturn at the corners of Nathan's mouth; almost forming a smile.

"I dunno about you, but I could use a drink," Nathan replied.

▲

It was only a couple of minutes before the pair stumbled upon a dingy back-alley bar. The first thing that Harrt noticed was the musky aroma of alcohol and exotic herbs. Green clouds emanated from the back of the room where a group were taking turns to smoke from a large glass pipe.

The patrons mingled about in the smoke riddled air,

sipping their drinks and engaging in conversation. It was noticeably crowded: far more so than outside. Loud music blared from speakers at every corner of the room. The thump of the bass moved through the air with a punch that rattled Harrt's gut with every beat.

"I don't think Astrilla will be hiding in here," Harrt said, turning to look at Nathan.

The Earther seemed to ignore him and continued into the crowd. When they reached the bar, Nathan leaned against it with a tight jawed expression on his face. Harrt noticed something in the Earthers stony visage: it had the same quiet arrogance of all the CO's he'd ever known. It told Harrt that Nathan Carter was in his element.

"Places like this are a cesspit of local intel," Nathan said. "Your Evoker won't be here, but I'll bet we can find out some info on her location".

While Nathan ordered them each a drink, Harrt stared around the busy watering hole, wondering how many of the customers could be a threat. There would have been bigger dives on the main street, with better music and cheaper booze, but Nathan clearly hadn't picked this place for either of those reasons. It made Harrt realise that his new ally was far more shrewd than he'd realised.

When Harrt turned back to Nathan, he discovered that the Earther was no longer standing behind him. Instead, Harrt spotted his new ally at the end of the bar flirting with a purple-haired woman.

I hope that's not his idea of gathering intel, Harrt thought.

With his companion otherwise indisposed, Harrt moved to an empty table in the corner. He watched Nathan work his charm on the woman, suspecting that his new ally wasn't sticking to the mission. Harrt's doubts were proven wrong when the woman produced a datapad from her bag and began to show Nathan a map on the screen.

Something drew Harrt's attention away from Nathan: the sound of a low and threatening voice from the table behind.

"Mr Venin says you're behind on your payments".

As Harrt listened to the exchange, he made a conscious effort not to turn around. He'd vaguely recalled passing the three men earlier: one Sillix and the others were human.

"I swear I'll get the money. I just need more time".

The next thing that Harrt heard was the native tongue of the Sillix. Though many of them were multi-lingual, some still used the pre-Commonwealth dialect. Though he couldn't speak the language, Harrt knew enough to understand what the Sillix said;

"Your time has run out".

Harrt heard the unmistakable click of a loaded handgun. At worst, the two-bit gangsters were planning on killing the man over Harrt's shoulder right then and there: at best they were planning on executing him in the alley out back.

Logic told Harrt not to do anything. Taking action would simply create a scene, draw attention, and ultimately attract Revenant soldiers or Corporate enforcers. Harrt's face would be plastered on every datapad, newsfeed and city-screen. A non-Commonwealth citizen in Harrt's situation would've done nothing: that was the smart thing to do, but it wasn't right.

Every life is precious, Harrt recited the Commonwealth teaching in his head before slowly climbing to his feet.

"Mr Venin wants us to make an example of you," the Sillix threatened, this time in broken English. "Now we can do this the hard way or the—"

The thug didn't have the chance to finish his sentence. Harrt violently slammed the Sillix's head into the table then pointed his pistol at the mobster's human accomplice.

"Consider the debts repaid," Harrt threatened. "Now walk out of here and forget your qualms with this man".

The victim of the mobster's threats looked almost as stunned as his would-be killers. Harrt kept his pistol trained on the first man while mashing the Sillix's skull against the table. Several patrons around the area noticed the altercation and were watching the scene play out before them.

Despite having a gun pointed at his face, the human mobster didn't look the slightest bit nervous.

"Do you have any idea who I work for?" the thug said.

"I don't care," Harrt replied, refusing to back down. "Walk away".

"Believe me, you *will* care". The mobster jerked his head in the direction of two men at Harrt's shoulder.

Harrt craned his neck to peer back at the pair of thugs who were coming to the aide of their compatriots. The first was a burly Uvan, and the second was human with a cheap ocular enhancer grafted onto his face.

Before Harrt could take action, he was knocked back by the first mobster into the middle of the dance floor, dropping his gun in the process. By the time Harrt climbed to his feet, the four men had surrounded him.

The big Uvan was the first to take a swing. He was quicker than Harrt expected but evidently lacked any formal training. Ducking the hook, Harrt charged forward, knowing that the amateurish gangster and his friends would not expect such an aggressive move at such an early stage in the fight.

Harrt slammed into his attacker, tackling the chunky thug across the bar and onto a table. For several seconds the other goons couldn't get in a clean swing at the Commonwealth officer. Harrt landed two precise jabs into the Uvan's skull, the first into his forehead and the second into his exposed windpipe. Harrt knew the offensive attack would both disorientate and incapacitate the Uvan for several minutes.

That leaves three more, Harrt thought.

Two of the other mobsters wrenched him away from their wheezing companion. As they held Harrt back, the third gangster drew back his fist. He slammed two right hooks into Harrt's ribcage and then threw a third into the 'wealther's skull. Rocked by the blow, Harrt's head snapped back, then forward.

Sucking on his lower lip, Harrt spat blood and then eyed something over the thug's shoulder that made him smirk.

"You aren't the only one with backup," Harrt taunted.

Before the augmented mafioso could raise his fist,

Nathan slammed his foot into the man's knee. A loud crunch could be heard across the bar as the impact of Nathan's boot broke the attacker's leg. The sound of shocked gasps and winces came from the crowd gathered around the fight. The two men pinioning Harrt's arms were equally as shocked; so much so that Harrt was able to take advantage.

He slammed an elbow into the thug on his right while wrestling with the man on his left. The grappling didn't last long though, as Nathan slammed a glass bottle into the gangsters head. Poleaxed, the Uvan's eyes rolled back into his head, and he went down like a sack of root vegetables.

Harrt and Nathan turned back to face the one hostile that was still standing. To Harrt's dismay, the human mobster pulled a gun and aimed it toward them. It was the same human who'd been threatening the old man in the booth less than a minute earlier. The mafioso shot an arrogant, toothy grin as two of his companions scrambled to their feet.

"You see our boss doesn't take too kindly to folk interfering in his business," the thug drawled. "You two clowns just put yourselves in a very bad situation".

What had begun as a straightforward bar fight now threatened to get ugly. Harrt was unarmed, but Nathan still had a gun, but it wouldn't matter: each of the thugs had produced a weapon and their chances of surviving a gunfight at such close quarters were slim at best.

Suddenly, the distinct sound of razor-sharp gunshots erupted inside the bar. Harrt darted to the floor but quickly realised that the laser bolts had not been directed at him or Nathan. As the mobsters keeled over and hit the ground, Harrt realised that someone else had interfered in the situation.

A large male Sphinax emerged from the crowd, still holding a smoking handgun. A heavy coat of dark black fur hung from his stocky, two-metre feline frame.

"Show's over folks," the chunky creature said to the crowd.

As the small audience dispersed, Harrt straightened up, and his gaze met the Sphinax's wild cat-like eyes. His initial fear was that the Sphinax was hostile, but Harrt's concerns were quickly laid to rest. The cat-like creature holstered his weapon and pushed passed Harrt toward Nathan.

"Well, well," he said with a distinct drawl. "Nathan Carter".

Like Harrt, Nathan had hit the floor a few seconds earlier to avoid the gunfire. When the Earther's eyes met with the Sphinax, Harrt saw a mix of familiarity and confusion painted across Nathan's face.

"Koble?" The pitch of Nathan's voice was heightened in surprise. "I thought you were dead?"

CHAPTER NINE

The last thing that Koble had expected to see in Caltose Bar was Nathan Carter. Like most of his days on Yenex, Koble had gone down to the filthy watering hole for a drink, hoping he could gather some intel. It was only when the fight had stared that he'd recognised his long-lost crewmate.

Koble didn't know how to react at the sight of Nathan Carter. To see him alive and well was almost overwhelming. On the one hand, Koble could've hugged the Earther. It had been over a decade since the Loyalty, and ever since Koble had believed he was the only surviving member of the crew. On the other hand, Koble could have slapped the curly-haired Earther and his well-groomed accomplice. Picking a fight with Viktor Venin's goons would be considered suicidal by anyone with the slightest hint of local knowledge. Of course, when the mobsters pulled their guns, Koble knew he had to act. Putting down Venin's men would paint a target on his back, just like Nathan, but it didn't matter: he owed it to an old friend to keep Nathan safe.

Three of Venin's thugs had gone down with Koble's precise gunfire, while the forth was still sprawled out on a table gasping for air. Whoever Nathan's accomplice was, he'd been trained in hand-to-hand combat and had quickly dispatched the thug with a single strike.

Once the crowd dissolved, Koble helped Nathan up.

"I thought you were dead," Nathan said as Koble pulled him to his feet. "How did you—"

As much as Koble wanted to both answer and ask Nathan the same question, he knew they needed to move. Three of Venin's men were dead, and there were at least fifty witnesses. It was highly likely that Venin would have more men in the area; given the civil unrest that the Revenant presence had caused.

"We'll have time for that later, but right now we gotta get outta here," Koble said, interrupting the Earther mid-sentence. "You guys just messed with the wrong thugs".

▲

Koble led Nathan and his friend through the back of the bar to an alleyway. Walking through the main doors would have been unwise, especially if Venin's men had back-up on the way. From the back alley, they rushed through a complex set of winding streets that were off of the main promenade. After passing through the busy spice market, the group came to a public elevator, which was surprisingly empty. Koble tapped the control panel, sending them down to the lower levels of the city. He knew Yenex well enough to know that if Venin's men were following, they'd stop there.

The view from the elevator window became obscured by thick clouds of pollution as they travelled down to the slums. It was only around half a minute until the smog cleared and Koble could look down on the dense industrial metropolis that made up Yenex's lower levels.

Nathan's dapper counterpart tapped him on the shoulder as he looked out onto the slums.

"What happened here?"

"First time on a Corporate world, huh?" Koble asked, turning to regard the clean-cut man with a narrowed-eye expression. "This is what they do. The richest live on the top, and the poor live down here".

There was something about the tidy-looking human that didn't sit right with Koble. He didn't look like the kind of running mate that Nathan would have picked back in the day, but then again he'd started the fight with Venin's thugs. Still, there was something too *clean* about him.

"Have you two got any idea whose gang you picked a fight with back there?" Koble said, craning his neck to look at Nathan.

Nathan raised a brow in response, while his tidy accomplice folded his arms.

"You guys just picked a fight with Viktor Venin's mob," Koble said. "He's one of this planet's more influential businessman".

"Never heard of him," Nathan remarked.

"You haven't?" Koble took a step back in surprise. "I figured you were here to take back the Phoenix".

Nathan looked taken aback by his statement.

"What do you mean to *take back the Phoenix?*"

As the doors to the elevator parted, Koble turned to Nathan;

"I'll explain when we get back to my place," Koble said. "We should keep moving: Venin has eyes everywhere".

Nathan nodded in agreement, but the confused expression on his face told Koble something bothersome: Nathan didn't know a thing about the Phoenix Titan.

How? Koble wondered.

They stepped out of the elevator onto a dark downtrodden thoroughfare. The street was awash with civilians, going about their day to day lives; many of them dressed in old dirty clothing. Several run-down shops made up the left and right side of the street, most had closed down and were boarded up. Neon signs floated overhead, lighting up the area; all advertising the kind of vices the downtrodden would turn toward —alcohol, gambling joints, and one-day-loans.

Koble couldn't help but notice that Nathan's acquaintance was shaking his head in disgust. Whoever the tight jawed human was, Koble knew that he was naive when it came to the brutalities of the galaxy. To Koble, that meant one thing:

'wealther,' he thought. *What the hell is Nate doing running with a 'wealther?*

▲

Koble's hideout was a basement apartment under a mechanics workshop. It was tucked in a quiet corner of the slums, just a half-mile from the service elevator. The adjacent road was a melting pot of strip-joints and casinos: the kind of place where crime was currency.

It's the kinda spot Jack would have picked, Nathan thought. *Hidden in plain sight.*

When Jack had brought Koble onboard the Loyalty, he'd been around twenty cycles of age, which was considerably immature by a typical Sphinax lifespan: somewhere between a teenager and an adult. After that, Jack had taken Koble under his wing and the rest was history. There was just one piece of the puzzle that was missing:

Where had Koble been the day that Jack went missing?

In order to access Koble's apartment, they ventured through the closed garage, down a flight of stairs and through a set of reinforced metal doors. The apartment was exactly what Nathan had predicted; chaotic but practical. There were a few personal storage crates crammed into the corner of the tiny living space masked only by a hamstrung couch that was likely a decade older than Nathan. Two doors led to the bathroom and kitchen, both of which looked as though they hadn't seen a clean in years. The thing that caught Nathan's eye was the old Pluvium flag, which Koble had crudely nailed to the wall.

"I see some things never change," Nathan said, pointing at the flag.

"Never forget where you come from," Koble's lips turned up slightly, almost forming a smile.

He's still living by Jack's words, Nathan thought.

Harrt, who had been uncharacteristically quiet since the bar, offered his hand to shake with Koble.

"I ought to thank you for saving us back there," Harrt said. "You handle your weapon well".

Nathan could tell from the way Koble sceptically glanced at Harrt's hand that he was suspicious of the 'wealther. Regardless of any misgivings that Koble may have had toward the Lieutenant, he shook Harrt's hand.

"Picking a fight with Viktor Venin's crew... guess

you've got some real stones on you 'wealther," Koble replied. "Either that or you've got a death wish".

Harrt didn't say anything, but the bewildered expression on his face confirmed what Koble had said: Harrt Oxarri was a Commonwealth officer.

"Don't look so surprised, you might not be wearing the uniform, but you've got 'wealther written all over you," Koble remarked. "The way you fight is straight out of the Commonwealth Military handbook. Plus your haircut lacks imagination".

"You got something against the Commonwealth?" Harrt said, his voice lowering.

"No more than the average Sphinax," Koble shrugged. He turned to Nathan with a raised eyebrow; "But I gotta say, Nathan Carter working for the Commonwealth… I didn't see that one coming."

"I'm not working for them," Nathan shook his head.

"That's not what it looked like back at the bar when you came to the aid of 'wealthy here," Koble pointed a claw in Harrt's direction. "What was it Jack used to say? *Never trust the Commonwealth?"*

Nathan raised his brow at what Koble said. Jack, along with most of the crew, had disappeared during a mission that went awry. Nathan and James had been the only ones to survive. The others never made it back to the ship, and Nathan and what was left of the crew could only assume that the worst had happened. Several days later, James had taken the Loyalty in a drug-fueled rage.

For over a decade Nathan believed that Jack, Koble and the rest had perished. To see the dark-haired Sphinax in the flesh challenged everything he'd come to believe in the last ten years. Since leaving the bar, every single scenario he could possibly come up with had run through his mind. Now that they were safe inside Koble's apartment he could finally ask the question;

"What the hell happened?" Nathan said. "How did you —"

"Mirotose Station was a setup; at least I think it was," Koble interrupted. "After we all split up, all hell broke loose".

Nathan took a seat on Koble's old couch as he listened intently.

"Myles was the first one to go down, then Cobie, then Lish. I dunno about the others," Koble continued. "I got hit, but Jack bundled Sasha and me into a shuttle and told us to get the hell outta there".

Nathan swallowed a lump in his throat.

"What about Jack?" He asked. "What happened to my uncle?"

Koble's eyes took on a pained expression, and he made a motion as close to a shrug as he could manage.

"I don't know," Koble finally answered with a shake of the head. "Jack said he was going back for Merri, but they never came back. None of them did."

The answer wasn't what Nathan had hoped for. Jack's fate was still ambiguous. Even if there had been fifty well-armed mercs gunning for Jack Stephens, there was a chance that he could have survived just like Koble.

"What about Sasha?" Nathan asked, thinking of the portly Russian who'd lived amongst the Loyalty's crew.

"Dead," Koble answered. "When we got sabotaged, Sasha took a bunch of gunfire to the chest. I'm amazed he lasted as long as he did".

"Fuck," Nathan shook his head regretfully.

"By the time, I got back to the rendezvous point maybe a day later, I saw what happened to the Loyalty," Koble said. "Locals told me that it killed a hundred people when it destroyed the Xung-Sin hideout; mostly civilians. What happened?"

Nathan noticed that Harrt's ears had pricked up; either at the mention of the notorious gang or the number of casualties. Nathan ignored Harrt and answered Koble's question. It was far more painful than Nathan expected. In the last ten years, he'd never told anyone about the Loyalty: after all, no member of the crew had been around to ask. Nathan explained everything to Koble, and the Sphinax listened intently. He told him of how they'd escaped to the Loyalty and what James had done in the aftermath. When Nathan finished talking, Koble remained silent for at least thirty seconds. Harrt didn't say anything, likely out of sheer bewilderment.

"So, let me get this straight," Koble finally said. "You've been alone this entire time?"

Nathan nodded.

"That explains why you've got no idea about the Phoenix Titan," Koble said, snapping his fingers.

Something akin to a smile came across the Sphinax's face. He turned and excitedly rummaged through his storage crate. After a few seconds, he handed Nathan an old holo-projector, which Nathan recognised from the Loyalty.

"Say hello to the Phoenix Titan," Koble said, tapping a button on the side of the device.

A schematic of a ship appeared a few inches above Nathan's open palm. He imagined that the vessel was quite imposing in size; somewhere around one-hundred-fifty foot in length. It was clear that the spacecraft had been modified with additional weaponry, and reinforced hull and a significantly larger engine than the original Titan-class design.

"Why are you showing me this?" Nathan asked.

"This ship belongs to you," Koble answered.

CHAPTER TEN

I am the saviour that will bring order, where there is only chaos. I am the end, the start and everything in between. I am cleanser of this universe. I am death: I am birth: I am Seig; I am Revenant.

The Commonwealth described the conflict between themselves and the Revenant as a war, but Seig saw it as his cause. His people were created in the darkest parts of space: intended by their creator as the perfect organism.

The first king of the Revenant was born and bestowed the means to create an army: the vast waters of the river Prynn. He'd laid the groundwork for every single king that came afterwards by enslaving his enemies and converting them to the Revenant way.

After many generations, Seig was born in the Void, just like all the other monarchs before him. At the moment of his birth, Seig looked into space and knew that every world and all of its citizens belonged to him.

Seig was the first of his name —referred to by many as *the destroyer of worlds*. He was the ruling monarch of the Revenant and one of the few pure-blooded Revenant that remained. On the day of his birth, the Paladins and Priests prophesied that Seig would bring order to an otherwise sinful universe.

Seig had ruled for the last three hundred years, succeeding his father Mezug the Conquerer, who had sat on the throne for over a millennia. Mezug was a cunning warrior but had started to lack the required ambition that the river Prynn demanded. Seig had murdered his father and claimed the crown as his own. Ever since his coronation, Seig had been every bit as merciless as he was devout.

Darkness surrounded him as he perched in a meditative state atop a pool of water, filled from the river Prynn. In his naked state, the waters would both restore his wounds from battle while clearing his mind of the universe's chaos. Seig exhaled, allowing the silence of his chamber and the purity of the water to bring him comfort.

The grey liquid boiled from his touch and filled his chamber with a thick layer of steam. Just by touching the water, Seig could commune with the Void, and it would answer with the screams of those who'd been converted.

He began to recite one of the Revenants many mantras as he filled his lungs;

"I am wrath, I am fury, I am Revenant" he whispered.

He allowed himself to fall forward into the dark liquid. There, he found the solace he needed to commune with the Great Void.

"Allow me to capture the Evoker, and I will bring you many more souls to devour: to bend to our will. I swear it".

As always, the waters answered with the screams of its victims.

It reminded Seig that regret and remorse was a characteristic of the weak —of those who stood in his way. When the screaming subsided, Seig's mind became clear, and he reaffirmed his belief in the Revenant Cause.

The silence that Seig had craved for so very long was broken by the sound of the comms panel chiming. Begrudgingly he swam to the surface of the pool. Climbing from the water naked, he moved across the room and allowed the automatic lighting to kick in. A servant emerged from the corner and handed him a towel. Seig wiped away the water from his grey tattooed torso before his servants dressed him in his traditional royal robes.

Like most pure-blood Revenant, Seig was incredibly muscular, just as the creator had designed. Though his physical strength and cunning were a crucial attribute in combat, Seig didn't need to rely on them as he could summon dark energy. Unlike his father, Seig liked to fight on the frontlines of war. In his view, a monarch needed to look into the eyes of their enemy before destroying them.

As a result of his time in battle, Seig's body was ravaged with scars. Thankfully his ceremonial tattoos covered most of the severe tears in his skin. Each marking on Seig's body represented a world he had claimed for the cause.

Once he was dressed in his black robes, Seig moved to the communications panel at the side of the chamber. The holographic display activated and a projection of High Admiral Xax, one of Seig's chief advisors, appeared before him. Xax was a human convert, one that had surrendered himself to the will of the Revenant many years ago. Despite Xax's loyalty, Seig didn't trust him. Instead, he saw the human for what he really was: a useful resource and nothing more.

"Why have you disturbed me, Admiral?" Seig said.

Admiral Xax looked visibily nervous at the other end of the hologram, shuffling about before mustering up the courage to speak.

"Your majesty, we've had a communication from the planet's surface: a Mr Venin," Xax said. "He says that he has something of interest for you".

Seig circled the hologram and sighed in frustration. *Why was Xax wasting his time with such nonsense?* Seig wished that he could reach out to the bridge and set fire to Xax at that moment, but before he could even begin to conjure up any further thoughts, the human cut in:

"He claims to have found the Evoker, my lord,"

Seig's head snapped at the statement.

Impossible, Seig thought.

Over the last couple of months, Seig had sent soldiers, hunters and even a Paladin to capture the Evoker: none of them had returned. To think that a local thug could have overpowered a fully trained Evoker seemed absurd. Regardless, Seig had to know if it was true. Astrilla was the key to ensuring the Revenant's victory.

Seig glowered at Xax as he spoke;

"Patch him through".

Admiral Xax nodded to his king's command, and the hologram shifted to the projection of a human male.

Venin was an overweight middle-aged human with a well-kept beard and sharp brown eyes. Seig only had to look at the man for a split second to know he was a living embodiment of hubris. The greed was written all over his snake-like features.

"Ah, your majesty, it's an honour to make your acquaintance," Venin said.

Seig took note that the human didn't bow to him.

"Viktor Venin of Venin and associates," Venin continued.

Seig had heard of Venin Associates before: they were a smaller corporate entity controlled by the Earther-led Jareth Corporation. The only reason that Seig knew this was because Jareth Corps and its CEO had been more than just a thorn in his side since the Fall. The fact that Viktor Venin was standing before Seig with what he could only assume was going to be a business proposition made the King apprehensive. Either Venin was attempting to lure Seig into a trap, or he was rebelling against his corporate masters.

Seig waited a few seconds to reply; he wanted to make Venin nervous.

Only in the void of silence is the truth exposed, Seig thought.

Seig circled the hologram, and Venin began to shift his weight from one foot to the other; evidently feeling slightly intimidated. Seig waited until the human opened his mouth to break the silence before he addressed Venin.

"You had something of interest for me?" Seig asked.

Venin —for the most part— masked his nerves with a calm and collected facade.

"I certainly do your majesty," Venin nodded. "My men were able to capture an Evoker on the surface a few hours ago. She's sedated and for the most part unharmed."

Seig didn't sense dishonesty in the man's voice, but

that didn't mean a thing: corporate-types were very good at lying and he wasn't planning on falling into any traps.

"What of David Jareth?" Seig replied. "Does your associate know that you are contacting me?"

A thin, sinister smirk came across Venin's face before he answered the question.

"David Jareth is no associate of mine, your grace," Venin said. "The corporate world is highly competitive, and I don't like losing".

There was a commitment to Venin's voice that told Seig everything he needed to know. Venin was an atypical corporate-man motivated by one thing and one thing only: greed. There was some truth to what Venin was saying, but the only way Seig could be sure would be to initiate a trade for the Evoker.

"You will receive three hundred million in exchange for the girl," Seig said.

He keenly observed Venin's reaction. Based on the way his eyes softened, Seig could tell that he was delighted with the offer.

"I will send my men to the surface in due course, and when you deliver us the girl, you will receive your payment," Seig said.

"A pleasure doing business with you, your majesty," Venin bowed his head.

"Mr Venin, I must warn you that if you are trying to deceive me, I will burn you alive".

Seig deactivated the hologram before Venin could utter a reply. He knew that if this course of action resulted in Astrilla's capture, then the war would be over. The Commonwealth and the Evokers and even Jareth Corps would be finished. Experience, however, had taught Seig never to trust anyone, and that included the likes of Viktor Venin.

▲

Nathan had stared at the palm-sized projection of the Titan-class ship for several seconds; trying his best to comprehend what Koble had said. He'd never seen or heard of the Phoenix Titan. Jack had only ever owned the Loyalty, so to learn that he'd secretly been hiding away a top of the range, Titan-class frigate seemed bizarre at best.

After what felt like an awkward amount of time, Nathan turned to Koble; "What do you mean this ship belongs to me?"

Koble's answer had initially come in the form of a stiff drink. The chunky Sphinax had passed a bottle of Yandian rum to Nathan before answering the question:

"After everything went down with Jack and the Loyalty, I fell on hard times and ended up working a few jobs here and there," Koble waited for Nathan to swallow his rum before continuing. "So about two years ago, this Private Investigator comes to me, asking a bunch of questions about You, Jack and James. Naturally, I dodged every question and try to get the hell outta there".

"Why?" Harrt asked, screwing up his face in confusion.

It was evident that the 'wealther didn't understand what life outside the Commonwealth really meant. Nathan and Koble knew the lifestyle from the first-hand experiences they'd had aboard the Loyalty.

"When someone starts asking you about Jack Stephens, it's usually to do with a vendetta," Koble answered. He turned his head back to Nathan and continued; "Turns out this guy was working for a legal counsel from Paradisium, and he was tasked with settling Jack's will".

Nathan leaned back in his chair in surprise, and a cascade of thoughts burrowed into his brain;

Did Jack have anything to leave us besides the Loyalty? Nathan thought. *Why the fuck would he get an attorney on Paradisium? He hated the place.*

Before Nathan could express his thoughts out loud, Koble had already started talking again;

"So this lawyer tells me that the Phoenix Titan belonged to Jack. For some reason the old fool had kept it in a lockup on Paradisium," Koble said. The Sphinax then pointed at the hologram still at Nathan's palm; "Strange considering what a bucket of bolts the Loyalty had been. We could've lived like kings on a ship like the Phoenix".

Nathan couldn't help but agree. Just from looking at the holographic schematic of the Titan-class ship, he could tell that the Phoenix was far roomier than the Loyalty, with several cabins, a kitchen and even a living area.

There was a sudden crushing feeling that struck Nathan like a moving freighter: James was Jack's son and therefore the first in line to inherit anything. That is *if James were still alive.*

"What about James?" Nathan said, peering up at Koble. "Surely the Phoenix would belong to him before me?"

To Nathan's surprise, Koble shook his head:

"That's exactly what I thought," Koble replied. "Jack's wording in the will was pretty clear: he didn't want James to have that ship."

What Koble said raised more questions than answers, but Nathan accepted it. A Titan-class ship would be capable of fast aerial manoeuvres that they'd need to outrun a Revenant blockade.

It might just be our ticket outta here, Nathan thought.

"If he didn't want James to have it, then who did he leave it to?" Nathan said.

"You," Koble replied. "Seeing as you and the rest of the crew have been, well, *dead,* for the last ten years, I figured I would scoop it up".

There was an awkward silence. Nathan took another sip from the rum, wondering what was going through Koble's mind.

Have I just stolen your thunder? Nathan wondered.

Koble gestured to the bottle and Nathan passed it to him. After he'd knocked back a large gulp of the sweet liquor, Koble leaned forward in his chair and looked Nathan in the eye.

"The way I see it, that ship belongs to you," Koble said. "Not James, not me; yours. I owe you a lot, and I certainly owe Jack a whole bunch more".

Nathan found it reassuring to know that Koble's allegiance to Jack hadn't waivered. He was still the loyal friend that Nathan had known all those years ago. As comforting as it was, something wasn't right. Koble didn't have the ship and was instead living under a chop shop on Yenex.

"Why are you on Yenex if the Phoenix is in a lockup on Paradisium?" Nathan asked.

Koble frowned, and his large feline-ears twitched at the question;

"It's not on Paradisium anymore, it's here; owned by Viktor Venin," Koble answered. "The guy who's thugs I shot at the bar".

Koble leaned back in his seat; looked at Nathan and Harrt and added;

"Now you know why I'm here," Koble raised an eyebrow. "So, Nate, what the hell are you doing here with a 'wealther?"

CHAPTER ELEVEN

Harrt remained silent as Nathan recounted the events of the last few days to Koble. He'd chosen to stay quiet on purpose, seeing it as an opportunity to understand the Earthers perspective. To Harrt's amazement, Nathan's account of the last few days was mostly in line with his own: though the Earther had subtly left out the part explaining why he was aboard the Vertex in the first place.

When Nathan finished talking, Koble slumped back in his chair. Harrt couldn't help but wonder how the Sphinax was going to react. It was evident from his actions at the bar that Koble was a creature of action, but in contrast, he also had an easy-going demeanour; at least around Nathan, he did. It was that disparity in behaviour that put Harrt on edge. After a few seconds of quiet contemplation, Koble looked at Harrt, clearly aware that he'd been silent for too long.

"Anything to add, 'wealther?" Koble said.

Harrt leaned forward and laced his fingers thoughtfully. He knew that if he was to make allies of Nathan and Koble that he'd have to be direct with them.

"Astrilla is vital to the war effort," Harrt said. "I don't know why; the whole thing was way above my rank, but I trusted my CO with my life. He said that she must not fall into Revenant hands".

Koble chewed at the inside of his cheek before finally taking his cat-like eyes off of Harrt.

"You do realise that an Evoker is the last person that needs protection, right? Koble said. "I've heard they reduce men to ash just by looking at them. I met a guy on Darrum Five who told me that killing one is almost impossible".

Typical misconception, Harrt thought.

Koble was somewhat right about the ability to reduce men to ash, though Harrt had never seen it first hand. It was common knowledge that Evokers were incredibly dangerous in combat, thanks to their ability to summon elemental energy. Though this power gave them an edge in battle, Evokers could most certainly die: that was something that Harrt had seen first hand.

"Astrilla had been under the protection of my crew for weeks," Harrt said. "Before that, she'd been in hiding for months. All I know is that if they catch her, it'll be bad news for the entire universe; not just the Commonwealth".

Koble climbed to his feet and stared out of his apartment window.

"That certainly explains why the Revenant is here in such force," Koble remarked. "Civil unrest will eventually boil over with that blockade in orbit. Guess its only a matter of time before things get ugly".

Once again, the Sphinax was right. If it wasn't the civilians or the Revenant to fire the first shot, then the corporations certainly would. Chaos would ultimately ensue, and then the Revenant would likely level the entire planet from space.

"So, will you help us?" Harrt said.

He noticed Nathan raise a brow at his use of the word *us.* Koble moved away from the window and over to Nathan.

"Nate, do you trust this 'wealther?" Koble asked, pointing with his chin at Harrt.

For a split second, Harrt wondered how the Earther would respond to the question. Despite Nathan's apparent scepticism of 'wealthers, Harrt hoped that he'd at least earnt a part of his trust.

"He saved my life," Nathan shrugged. "So, yeah, I trust him".

As soon as Nathan uttered the words, Koble's eyes softened, and his jaw loosened.

"Good," Koble said, his voice returning to a more jovial tone. The Sphinax looked at Harrt, and with a shrug of the shoulders said; "I'll help you find the girl on one condition".

"Go ahead," Harrt said.

"Once we've found the Evoker, we take back the Phoenix Titan and get the hell off of Yenex," Koble said.

Harrt nodded, though he wasn't entirely comfortable with stealing: even if it was from a local crime lord. Viktor Venin was dangerous: at least that's what Koble said. Taking the Phoenix Titan from him could put them all at risk, but so would staying on Yenex.

"Why does it have to be the Phoenix Titan?" Harrt asked. "There will be thousands of off-world transports we could steal; why must it be that ship?"

Koble gazed at Nathan for a few seconds before turning back to Harrt.

"Those are my terms," Koble said.

Harrt looked to Nathan, and the Earther raised his eyebrows. To Harrt's surprise, Nathan's gesture appeared to be more of sympathy toward Harrt rather than agreement with Koble. It was evident that the Sphinax was headstrong, and Nathan trusted him.

"Provided that we find Astrilla first," Harrt said. "Those are *my terms*".

The corners of Koble's mouth turned upward, and he started laughing. The Sphinax pointed a meaty finger at Harrt as he chuckled sarcastically.

"You're alright, 'wealther". Koble patted Harrt on the shoulder before adding; "Don't worry, pal, you've got yourself a deal".

Harrt wasn't entirely sure how to perceive the Sphinax's laughter. *Was it a gesture of goodwill and camaraderie, or was there something more sinister to it?* Rather than waste any more time humouring Koble, Harrt asked the one question that had been on his lips for the last half-hour:

"So, where do we start looking for Astrilla?"

Koble grabbed something from behind his door and stuffed it into a backpack before answering;

"Word on the lower levels is that an escape pod crashed about three miles south of here". Koble slung the pack over his chunky shoulder, "Seems to me like the best place to start".

▲

After leaving Koble's apartment, the Sphinax led them through a maze of alleys. The level of poverty was just like every other corporate world that Nathan had visited, so it didn't come as a surprise to him when they passed a group of homeless, warming themselves around a fire. Eventually they came upon what Nathan could only assume had once been a town square. The street was bordered by rubble from where the buildings had begun to fall apart. At the centre of the square was a statue that had been defaced by the locals. Nathan noticed an area to the west that had been cordoned off to the public. It was entirely fenced off and the only way in was through a security checkpoint.

Koble pulled an ocular enhancer from his bag and took a long moment to examine the scene ahead.

"That's the crash site," Koble said, passing the enhancer to Nathan. "Looks like we've got company".

Koble was right. Three armoured humanoids guarded the entrance to the crash site, while another group patrolled the perimeter. Nathan could almost anticipate a further dozen-or-so inside. He turned his attention back to the guards, noticing that their armour was utterly unfamiliar to him.

"Is that local law enforcement down there?" Nathan said. "I've never seen armour like that".

"You wish," Koble snorted. He handed Nathan and Harrt a comms device each, and then added; "Those are Viktor Venin's guys".

"Is that Jareth Corps armour that they are wearing?" Harrt added. "Why the hell is a corporate crime lord using Jareth Corps materials?"

Nathan sensed Koble's apprehension at the mere mention of the Earther-run business. The Sphinax lowered his furry brow and stared at the crash site for several seconds.

"Viktor Venin is, or at least was, in-cahoots with David Jareth," Koble said. "The pair had a falling out a while back".

Before Nathan could say anything else, Harrt cut in;

"There must be a few dozen guys down there?"

"Way ahead of you 'wealther," Koble replied, pointing at a nearby rooftop. "I'll have you boys covered from up there".

"Covered with what exactly?" Harrt said.

"He'll be covering us with the high-powered sniper rifle that he stuffed in his bag," Nathan said. He turned to Koble and added; "I'm guessing you're still working the old Daxiniun MX's?"

Before Koble started to climb up to the roof, he patted the side of his bag in confirmation.

I *guess some things never change,* Nathan thought.

Once Koble disappeared onto the roof, Nathan and Harrt began to stroll to the checkpoint. It was clear that the Commonwealth Lieutenant didn't feel at ease knowing that Koble was covering from a distance, but Nathan knew better. He'd seen Koble's combat abilities first-hand and to say that the Sphinax was a good shot would be an understatement. Koble was already an impressive combatant before he came aboard the Loyalty, and when Jack started to train him with a rifle, Koble had come into his own.

"Don't worry," Nathan said, craning his neck to look at Harrt. "Koble's a very good shot".

"I hope you're right about that,' Harrt replied with a hint of scepticism to his voice. The 'wealther then spoke into his communicator; "So what's the plan here? Are we just supposed to walk straight through that checkpoint?"

Koble could be heard clearing his throat at the end of the transmission. Nathan knew that by now, the Sphinax would be set up on the roof, watching them through his scope.

"That's pretty much the plan," Koble replied sarcastically. "You see the guys guarding the entrance?"

Nathan and Harrt turned their attention to the security checkpoint where the three goons were casually leaning against their workstations, in a discussion.

"Sure," Harrt replied. "We see them".

Not for much longer, Nathan thought.

From his vantage point on the rooftop, Koble fired two silenced rounds in quick succession. The first bolt collided with one of the guards, sending him straight to the floor—the second took out the remaining two. Koble had lined up the shot precisely, just as Nathan knew he would. The silenced Daxiniun MX that Koble was using was almost completely silent and didn't draw the attention of the other guards in the area.

Nathan turned to Harrt and saw that the 'wealthers eyebrows were raised in surprise;

"Impressive," Harrt said.

"I told you he's a good shot," Nathan replied.

With the security checkpoint unguarded, Nathan and Harrt were able to sneak into the crash-site undetected. Once they were inside, Nathan surveyed the ravaged area. It was evident from the small crater at the centre of the site that the pod had not landed smoothly. Nathan looked to the upper levels, noting that there was some damage to the top of one of the skyscrapers.

"Must've hit that tower on the way down," Nathan nudged Harrt.

He didn't reply, and Nathan noticed that his attention was focussed on the crater. Nathan took a closer look and saw several scorch marks on the pod.

"Looks like a firefight broke out," Harrt remarked. "We need to get a closer look and find out what the hell happened here".

They snuck past another group of Venin's men who were going about their patrols. Nathan led Harrt behind a wrecked building to get a better view of the escape pod, but something else caught their attention.

The bodies of over a dozen Commonwealth marines had been piled up beside the wrecked escape pod. Nathan noticed that some of them had been riddled with gunfire, while others had succumbed to stab wounds and burns.

"This was the unit that my Commander sent to protect

Astrilla," Harrt said. "These guys were some of the finest marines that the Commonwealth had to offer: what the hell happened to them?"

"Guess someone got to them first," Nathan said. "I don't see the Evoker".

"Let's get to the pod," Harrt replied. "Hopefully the onboard computer will have some answers".

Once Koble confirmed that they had a clear path to the escape pod, Nathan and Harrt dashed past the bodies and made toward the wreckage. Nathan was the first to slither inside and take a good look at the damage on the interior. The right bulkhead was almost entirely ashen: burnt by something from the inside. Nathan moved toward the rear of the wreck, while Harrt made his way inside. The 'wealther keenly examined the charred remains of the bulkhead before saying to Nathan in a low voice;

"Looks like Astrilla fought someone off from the inside".

Nathan turned back to Harrt and noticed that the 'wealther was pointing at the scorch-riddled wall.

"Are you saying that she did all of this damage?" Nathan said.

Harrt's jaw tightened, and he nodded in response.

"Let's just grab the computer and get the hell outta here," Nathan said.

He tried his best to shut out the part of his brain that was questioning why the hell he was helping in this crazy endeavour. It was evident that Astrilla could take care of herself: Nathan had learnt that first hand a few days prior. He couldn't escape the feeling in his gut that told him something violent had happened prior to the crash. Of course, he couldn't say that out loud to Harrt; 'wealthers were always loyal to their own.

While Harrt took the pod's control console apart, Nathan studied the back of the wreck. Something on the floor caught Nathan's eye, and he leaned down for closer examination.

Looks like some kind of medal or brooch, Nathan thought.

He scooped it up from the floor, confirming his

suspicion. The silver brooch had a sigil delicately carved into its surface that Nathan didn't recognise. The unfamiliar marking appeared to depict a flying creature with an enraged expression on its face.

All of a sudden, Koble's voice came through the communicator; "Guys, we've got a big problem".

Nathan turned to Harrt, who was still disassembling the pod's control console.

"What is it?" Nathan said into his communicator.

"We've got company...Revenant company".

CHAPTER TWELVE

As soon as Koble's transmission reached Harrt's ears, he immediately yanked the computer's black-box from its cradle.

"What do you mean Revenant?" Nathan said into his communicator.

"I'm lookin' at a Revenant dropship landing just outside the crash site". Koble's tone was somehow both sarcastic and concerned.

Harrt knew from experience that a dropship would likely be carrying Revenant marines, not the usual rabble of mutated soldiers and hunters. This told Harrt that the Revenant were there either to take the bodies of his fallen comrades, to find Astrilla, or both.

We don't have the numbers to fight off a dropship's worth of soldiers, even if Koble is a good shot, Harrt thought.

Harrt called Nathan over to him and handed him the drive. While the Earther stuffed the device into his backpack, Harrt knelt down and opened a metal grate beneath the pod's control console.

"What are you doing?" Nathan asked. "We've gotta get outta here".

"Listen to me very carefully," Harrt said. "That dropship is carrying two, maybe three dozen Revenant marines: not husks or hunters, marines; fully conscious psychopaths who've willingly signed up to the Revenant".

"You mean non-mutated," Nathan shrugged, saying it as

though he wasn't surprised. "What's your point?"

Harrt reached under the grate and started to unscrew an electrical housing unit that was hooked up to the pod's engine.

"My point is that we can't shoot our way out of this one," Harrt replied. "We're gonna have to create a diversion and get the hell outta here, while Koble provides sniper fire".

Harrt allowed the Earther to digest what he'd said, and continued to undo the screws to the electrical housing unit. It was only when Harrt had opened it that Nathan spoke up;

"Okay, I'm with you," Nathan nodded. "Just one question: what are you doing?"

Harrt smiled, and he gestured to the device that he'd just accessed. Like the good soldier that he was, Harrt knew every function of every control panel aboard his ship, and that knowledge extended to the escape pods.

"Creating a distraction," Harrt replied, tearing a cable from under the metal grate. He turned a dial on the control panel to maximum and climbed to his feet.

"What kind of distraction?" Nathan asked.

"I just rigged this pods engine to overload," Harrt replied.

The expression on Nathan's face was a mix of both confusion and —for some reason— delight. The Earther clenched his jaw, evidently forcing himself to stay under control.

"So it's the explosive kind of distraction…"

▲

Koble knew his way around sniper rifles. In fact, he knew his way around almost every kind of firearm. When he first come aboard the Loyalty, Koble was already a skilled archer, but with Jack's help, he'd made the leap to firearms seamlessly. To say that Koble was a perfect shot was an overstatement, but he was very confident in his aim; both in long-range and short-range combat.

Koble watched the crash site through the scope of his rifle; trying to anticipate the movements of the Revenant marines that had swarmed the area. They were coming in formation, with seven out front in a ragged line heading toward the pod, while another dozen-or-so argued with Venin's mercenaries. Koble focussed his aim on the one that he assumed was in command of the squad.

Unlike the mindless soldiers that the Revenant were known to use, their marines were the true believers of the Revenant cause. It always sent a shiver up Koble's spine, knowing that people would actively choose to be a part of the Revenant: after all, they were responsible for the slaughter, and mutation of countless innocent lives.

As he stared down the scope, Koble thought; *How can somebody choose that life?*

Koble's attention was drawn to Nathan's voice in his communicator.

"We're gonna need covering fire, right now!"

It sounded as though the Earther was running away from something and Koble's suspicion was confirmed as he looked back down his scope. He watched Nathan and Harrt make a beeline toward the exit; drawing the attention of both the Revenant marines and Venin's men.

Koble wasted no time, in lining up his first shot and squeezing the trigger. The silenced laser bolt tore through the marine's metal armour as if it was paper-thin. Koble watched as the humanoid crashed to the floor in a haze of blood. He then promptly switched to his second target, picking the hostiles that he deemed the biggest threat to Nathan and Harrt. This time Koble's aim met one of Venin's men, but before he could open fire, the thug was dispatched by gunfire from Harrt.

"Not bad 'wealther," Koble muttered to himself.

Koble continued to lay down sniper fire until Nathan and Harrt made it past the security checkpoint. Before Koble could target any of the pursuing hostiles, a huge explosion erupted inside the crash-site.

There was a flash of blinding red light; so bright that Koble was forced to shield his eyes. What followed was an eruption of fire and debris accompanied by a roar that gradually resolved into people shouting and screaming.

When the dust settled, Koble peered down at what had previously been the crash-site. The escape pod was gone, along with the perimeter fences and security checkpoint. The Revenant marines had been consumed by the blast, along with most of Venin's thugs and the dropship.

"Nate? Harrt?" Koble spoke into his communicator. "You guys hear me?"

There was a long pause as Koble surveyed the devastation.

"Loud and clear," Nathan coughed over their comms feed.

It took Koble a few seconds to spot Nathan and Harrt taking cover behind a pile of rubble.

"That was one hell of an explosion," Koble remarked. "If we make it off this world alive, you're gonna have to show me how you timed that so well".

▲

Yenex is a powder keg just waiting for a match, Nathan thought.

On the way back to Koble's apartment, he couldn't help but notice that the civil unrest was growing. Large crowds had swarmed the streets and were clashing with the local law enforcement. Koble led them through an alternative route to avoid getting caught in the middle of the riots.

"Angry people tend to do stupid things," Koble remarked.

As they walked through a tight alley toward Koble's apartment, Nathan spotted a gang of thick-necked men in combat armour beating the crap out of two security officers. Harrt had wanted to intervene, but Nathan and Koble dissuaded him from taking such action. It didn't feel right, but Nathan knew that getting caught up in heroics would only result in drawing attention to themselves.

If Astrilla is as essential as Harrt says then he'll thank me later, Nathan thought.

By the time they reached Koble's apartment, dense rain had begun falling from the sky. Koble wasted no time in getting inside and ushered Nathan and Harrt in as quickly as possible.

After the chunky Sphinax closed and bolted the door, he turned to them:

"I swear, the rain on this world is so damn nasty," Koble remarked. "All the pollution and lack of plant life has really done a number on the ecosystem".

"That's exactly why the Commonwealth ensures any developed planet retains a percentage of its green spaces," Harrt replied. "Even the most densely populated Capital World has oceans and forests."

Nathan wasn't too sure if the 'wealther was simply stating a fact or if he was trying to promote his political ideologies. Harrt was right about the Commonwealth's retention of natural spaces: it was one of the few positives that Nathan could cite about the communist regime. Where the Revenant would destroy life, the corporations would exploit it for profit. In contrast, the Commonwealth sought prosperity; though Jack had always maintained that it was all a part of their *screwed-up agenda.*

Nathan pulled the pod's computer drive from his backpack and set it down on Koble's flimsy coffee table.

"We took a big risk getting this thing," Nathan remarked. "Let's hope it was worth it".

Harrt pushed his way past Koble and picked up the drive.

"It'll be worth it," Harrt nodded. "I'll need a minute to access the data".

He pulled a multi-tool from his pocket and began taking the drive apart. While the 'wealther was preoccupied, Nathan followed Koble to the next room. The Sphinax was in the process of unpacking his precision rifle and swapping out the ammunition.

"I see you haven't lost your aim," Nathan remarked. "Jack would be proud".

Koble tossed the empty ammo capacitor into the corner of the room.

"I sure hope so," he sighed.

Sensing something in the Sphinax's tone, Nathan moved into the room and asked;

"What is it?"

For a moment, Koble was silent as he placed his rifle back into its case. Finally, he folded his chunky arms and took a deep breath.

"You gonna tell me why the hell you were aboard a Commonwealth warship?" Koble said, his tone bordering on accusatory. "What's the deal? Are you one of them now?"

Nathan laughed.

"Fuck-no. I was running a grab-and-dash job while they were docked at Gararre. I snuck aboard, got to the pick-up-point and came face-to-face with the Evoker".

Koble's expression shifted to that of amusement.

"So... she handed you your ass in other words".

"Something like that," Nathan nodded. "Think my employer gave me shitty info".

Koble held up his finger.

"Wait a minute, Gararre?" Koble raised his brow. In a moment of realisation, he leaned forward; "You were working for Guttasnype?"

"It's been a bumpy couple of years, okay?" Nathan said defensively.

"Bumpy? More like turbulent to work for that sack of shit," Koble exclaimed. "I heard a rumour back in the day that he was running jobs for Prince Baylum".

Nathan shrugged.

"It was just a rumour".

"Has it crossed your mind that your *cargo* might've been that Evoker*?*"

"I don't do kidnappings," Nathan shook his head. "I've still got fuckin' morals".

Koble wrinkled his brow.

"Wasn't implying that you didn't," Koble drawled. "Sounds to me like Guttasnype set you up. Maybe he was hoping you'd complete the job and deliver him a high-value Commonwealth asset, or you'd fail and get killed in the process. Either way, it's a win-win situation for him".

Nathan lowered his head and thought about it. Koble had said what he'd been thinking for days, and to think he could've been a part of a Revenant plan was utterly sickening.

Before Nathan or Koble could say anything to the other, Harrt called to them.

"Guys, I've got it," he said. "I've found the recordings".

Harrt's timing couldn't have been better; Nathan was glad to stop their discussion about Guttasnype. Nathan made his way back toward Harrt, with Koble following close behind.

In the kitchen, Harrt was leaning against the kitchen counter, waiting for them patiently. Nathan noticed that the 'wealther had hooked up the pod's computer drive to a datapad using a web of cables.

"You are full of surprises," Koble remarked, as he patted Harrt on the shoulder. "Manually bypassing a drive like that is the sorta stuff I'd expect from an engineer".

"Basic engineering is covered in every Commonwealth academy and..." Harrt paused. "I have experience with this kinda thing".

There was something about the way Harrt answered the question that Nathan recognised in himself. On the surface, Harrt had played it as nonchalance, but something in Nathan's gut told him it was a mask: a way to detract from something painful. It made Nathan wonder what it was that the 'wealther was trying to cover for, but this was neither the time nor the place to ask.

"We gonna get this show on the road?" Nathan pointed at the computer drive.

Harrt took up his datapad and activated a holographic projection.

The hologram depicted Astrilla entering the escape pod along with her marine escort. There was a sadness in the woman's eyes that Nathan hadn't noticed back on the Vertex: as though she carried a heavy burden. Once Astrilla and the marines were strapped into their chairs, the pod disembarked the Vertex and started heading toward Yenex.

"Looks pretty routine," Koble remarked.

The footage skipped, and for a few seconds, there was only static. When the image cleared, it showed that most of the Commonwealth marines were out of their seats, and aiming their weapons at Astrilla.

"What the hell?" Harrt straightened up in surprise. "What are they doing?"

The next thing that played out in the footage showed a single marine placing himself between his companions and Astrilla. There was a couple of seconds while the marines argued amongst themselves before all hell broke loose. Astrilla launched in to a full-scale assault while the marine who'd been defending her was cut-down by his squadmates.

The speed with which Astrilla moved was unbelievable: Nathan had never seen anything quite like it. Despite being unarmed, the Evoker made light work of the dozen-or-so hostiles; using a mix of otherworldly hand-to-hand combat and lethal elemental magic.

The recording skipped to a point after the pod crash-landed. Astrilla had somehow managed to both climb to her feet and dispatch all of the marines, though it was evident she had sustained an injury or two. As Astrilla attempted to escape the pod, she was struck by something from the outside.

"Yandian stun-dart," Koble whistled. "That's gotta hurt".

Astrilla crumbled to the floor in a heap. For several seconds the Evoker didn't move, but then, she attempted to drag herself off of the ground. She clawed at the pod's bulkhead for leverage but was struck over the head by a hostiles, who rushed into the pod with a group of thugs.

Nathan, Harrt and Koble watched as the gang, wearing the same armour as Venin's men earlier, dragged Astrilla out of the pod and out of frame.

"Shit," Koble snarled. He pointed out a square-jawed male Uvan from the footage. "That is Grecko. He's Viktor Venin's right-hand man".

Nathan could tell from Koble's tone that the situation had changed drastically. Saving the Evoker would not be as simple as they'd first hoped.

"How do we find this *Grecko*?" Harrt said while

examining the footage.

The corners of Koble's mouth lifted and his brow raised as he answered;

"I think we're gonna need some help with this…" he answered. "I think it's time I introduce you guys to my landlady".

CHAPTER THIRTEEN

Nothing great lasts forever, Vol thought.

She drank the last of her Mironium kor and placed the glass down. Like every night since her husband's death, Vol lived out the same day to day ritual. She would spend the day working in her garage, then in the evening, she gathered intel around the local bars. Mostly this included interrogating the drunks, perverts and immoral regarding Vikor Venin's criminal operation.

Most nights, she would come up dry, and on those occasions, Vol would open a bottle of something sweet. Then there were the other nights, where there would be a breakthrough. No matter how insignificant Vol would open the good stuff: the Yandian kor.

You gotta celebrate the little things, she'd tell herself.

After losing her mother at a young age, Vol's father uprooted her from the Commonwealth world of Iuam Four and relocated them to Yenex. There had been no such thing as formal education for Vol, as the high fees for schooling on corporate worlds were way outside of her father's budget. Instead, Vol's father taught her his trade; the art of ship engineering. Everything else Vol picked up along the way. By the time she was a young teenager, they'd opened the shop and business had been steady for several decades.

At thirty-three Vol met the man who would eventually become her husband. Muhne was special; Vol recognised it the moment she'd laid eyes on him. Unlike the majority of the power-hungry Corporate vermin that flocked to Yenex: Muhne simply wanted to lay the foundation for a simple life. Vol's father must have seen it too as he instantly took a shine to Muhne, treating him like the son he'd never had. In the years that followed, Vol, Muhne and her father ran the shop and life was good, but Vol quickly came to learn that nothing good could last forever.

Vol had been off-world when it had happened: when her father and husband were murdered. At the time, it wasn't clear who had committed the act or why. Local law enforcement didn't care and simply concluded that it had been the work of a desperate junkie, but Vol knew they were covering up for someone in Yenex's elite.

Initially, Vol fell into a deep depression: paralysed by the sheer grief that weighed down on her. For days she would contemplate how life could have been different; what she could have done to prevent it from happening. In those dark times, Vol grieved; blamed herself, and lost sight of who she was, but then something changed.

There was a fleeting moment in the pit of her despair where Vol had debated taking her own life. She'd toyed with the idea for some time, but something had prompted her not to do it. When the moment to commit arose, Vol had an epiphany that changed her mind.

I'm gonna bring those bastards to justice, she'd thought. *If no one is going to help me, I'll do it myself. What have I got to lose?*

From that point, the daily cycle of work, investigation and planning began. It wasn't long before Vol had the name of the murderer; a Uvan hitman by the name, Grecko, who was under the employ of Viktor Venin. Despite having the killer's name, there was no motive for the murder. For days Vol debated, *why Venin would place a hit on two engineers from the lower levels?* She knew that her investigation had to change if she ever hoped to find out the answer to the question. Rather than look into Grecko, she focussed all efforts on understanding Viktor Venin and his criminal empire.

It took time, but eventually Vol discovered that Venin

had hired her father and Muhne to complete works on a prestige Titan-class ship. Around the same time, the name Koble kept cropping up around the local area. He was described to Vol as a Sphinax on a mission to bring down Venin.

The enemy of my enemy is my friend, Vol thought.

She arranged to meet with him, and Koble spilt his guts on the situation. For most people, going in to a meeting of that nature would be deemed foolish. Had Vol been a human, she would have treated Koble's intentions with a level of scepticism. He could have been insane, or perhaps working for the enemy, but Vol knew from the moment she met him that Koble was telling the truth.

As a Uvan female, Vol carried a particular chromosome which allowed some women of her species to read the thoughts of others; albeit sparingly. It wasn't something she could switch on and off, and neither was it something she could do on command. The thoughts of others were tricky to read, but most of the time, Vol could get a measure of a person within minutes: that's how she knew that she could trust the chunky Sphinax.

"The ship is called the Phoenix Titan," Koble said. "Venin doesn't want it getting out that he owns the ship. That's why I think he killed your father and husband".

Vol's question after that had been simple;

"What's so special about this ship?"

The reply that Koble gave raised more questions than answers;

"It's not the ship that's important: it's the man who it once belonged to".

After that night, Vol and Koble had agreed to take down Venin and steal the Phoenix Titan. She'd rented Koble the basement under the chop-shop, and together they'd started to put a plan in place.

Vol climbed from her armchair and moved to a digital display that spanned an entire wall in her living room. On the screen was the plan, the research and the faces of the men who were in Venin's close circle. She snarled at the surveillance photograph of Grecko, longing to cave in his skull with a blunt instrument.

There came a sudden knock at the front door, which made her jump.

"Yo, it's me". Koble's voice followed. "We need to talk".

"Give me a minute," she said, grabbing some clothes that she'd slung over the back of a chair. "Where the hell have you been? My spikes picked up a transmission from Venin that you are gonna want to—"

Vol paused as she pulled a top over her head, she felt another presence accompanying Koble: someone filled with deep regret and bitterness. She then sensed a third person outside her door, but they were harder to read.

"Who's with you?" Vol said.

"Revenant wizard men," Koble replied, his voice oozing with sarcasm.

Vol could almost imagine the chunky Sphinax rolling his eyes at her as he spoke. Despite his candour, Vol didn't feel any more at ease. She grabbed her handgun but holstered it, just to be safe.

When she opened the door, Vol saw Koble clutching a large duffle bag. The other two were human; both male, but that's where the similarities stopped.

The first was a handsome older man; clean-cut; possibly former military. She imagined he was the type that knew his way around a gun. By human standards, he was probably around the same age as Vol, but it was always hard to tell with the way humans aged.

The second was at least a decade younger than the first, with long curly hair tied back into a bun and a scruffy dark beard. He looked like the typical vagabonds that frequented the bars that Vol would visit for intel.

"Who are these two?" Vol said, turning to Koble.

"These two?" Koble shrugged with a sly grin on his face. "They are gonna help us steal the Phoenix and get the hell outta here".

The Sphinax then paused and tilted his head to one side. "Whats all this about a transmission?"

▲

The deal that Koble had made with the two humans was quite unusual, but it sounded worthwhile. Koble and the 'wealther, who called himself Harrt, had explained everything, while the scruffy one, Nathan, was mostly quiet.

Vol listened intently and tried to pick apart every word that was said: she needed to be sure that she could trust the pair of humans. There was an honesty to Harrt Oxarri; she could feel it. As for Nathan, she could only get a partial read on him.

When Harrt was finished speaking, Vol asked the one obvious question;

"What's so special about the Evoker?"

"I don't know," Harrt shook his head. "My CO told me she is critical to the war effort, and I trusted him with my life".

Vol could read the 'wealther like a book, and he most certainly was not lying.

"What about the part where your marines were pointing guns at her?" Nathan said from the corner. "I thought you guys were trying to protect her".

"That, I can't explain," Harrt's jaw stiffened. He turned back to Vol and Koble and asked; "Why would a crime lord like Venin want her?"

"That I *can* explain," Vol said, grabbing her datapad. "I've been investigating Viktor Venin for quite some time".

"Why?" Nathan asked.

Vol felt something odd as Nathan spoke; almost as though he was blocking something out of his mind. She could tell at that moment, that whoever Nathan Carter was, he was anything but a 'wealther. Rather than answer his question, and discuss her motivations relating to Venin, Vol simply continued;

"A few months ago I had a tip-off that Venin ran some very... *personal* communications off-world using a private satellite," Vol paused for a moment as she activated a hologram from her datapad. "A few weeks ago, I was able to plant a bug on his satellite, and since then, I've been keeping tabs on all the comms that Venin doesn't want his wife to see; including this one".

She tapped her datapad and a two-way hologram formed in the centre of the apartment. The first image was of Viktor Venin. The second made Harrt stand from his chair in shock.

"That is King Seig..." Harrt said in horror.

He watched as the life-sized hologram of the Revenant king spoke to Venin.

"You had something of interest for me?" Seig's deep voice filled the apartment.

Venin's eyes were wide with excitement.

"I certainly do your majesty. My men were able to capture an Evoker".

Vol peered at Nathan, Harrt and Koble as they watched the exchange between King Seig and Viktor Venin. All of them were silent throughout, except for Koble, who huffed at the mention of *David Jareth*.

When the recording ended, Harrt sat back down and looked at Vol:

"Where is Venin likely to do this exchange?"

"It'll be the top of Venin Towers," Vol answered without hesitation. "The place is built like a fortress. It's the perfect spot for a trade. Fortunately for your Evoker friend, I have a relatively safe way to get inside".

"*Relatively safe?*" Harrt frowned.

"Nothing is ever guaranteed," Vol blinked. "But something tells me that you are... adaptable".

Harrt straightened up awkwardly, as though Vol's mild flirtation had caught him off guard.

"So, I think the plan is simple," Nathan said. "Sneak in, grab the Evoker, grab the Phoenix and get the hell outta here".

"Wait you wanna do this in one hit?" Vol exclaimed. "Are you crazy?"

"Two fish one hook," Koble replied. "Besides, you've been talking about getting off Yenex since we first met. I don't think we're gonna get a second chance."

Vol weighed up the options and quickly came to the conclusion that Koble was right. Striking Venin Towers on one occasion would be tricky; striking it again would be damn near suicide.

"A Titan-class frigate has the manoeuvrability of a small fighter," Vol surmised. "It might just outmanoeuvre a blockade with the right pilot at the helm".

"Good thing that I'm a pilot," Harrt said.

"Well, that makes two of us," Vol rolled her eyes at the 'wealther's confidence. "Unlike you, I learnt to fly everything from junkers to racers. What's the standard training vessel in the Commonwealth? Six months behind the stick of an out-the-box fighter?"

Vol expected him to rise to the challenge, but instead, Harrt smirked;

"Closer to eight months," he answered. "I then spent another five years flying as a pilot in the Maru battles".

There was a moment of silence between them. Vol sensed something in Harrt's mind as soon as he mentioned the Maru System. There was only pain and agony, which felt very familiar to Vol.

"So it's a yes?" Koble asked with a slightly raised voice. He stared at Vol expectantly, impatiently waiting for an answer.

"It's dangerous," Vol nodded. "But if the rumours are true about what an Evoker can do in a combat situation; we might just pull this off".

Koble clapped his paws together and excitedly climbed to his feet. The Sphinax patted her on the shoulder, but Vol knew she had to make her terms clear:

"I want Grecko and Venin," Vol said, standing to meet Koble's gaze. "We get to them, and I'm the one who pulls the trigger".

"You know it doesn't have to be like that," Koble said gently.

"What would you do if you were in my situation?" Vol replied knowingly. "What if instead of Venin and Grecko, it was Kornell and Jareth? You wouldn't wanna be the one to pull the trigger?"

Koble tensed in response and nodded. Vol noticed Nathan sit up in his chair at the mention of the two men Koble most hated. Evidently, the Earther knew the Sphinax well.

With Koble agreeing to her first demand, Vol voiced her second to Harrt and Nathan:

"I want safe transport off of Yenex to a planet of my choice".

"You have my word," Harrt nodded, and Vol noted the sincerity in his voice. "So what is this way inside Venin Towers?"

Vol grabbed another bottle of kor from her bookshelf. She took a swig and answered, with a saying that her father used when they first set up the business:

"Everything great starts in the dirt".

CHAPTER FOURTEEN

Travel light; no more than a couple of bags. Nathan thought that Jack's words had never been more appropriate as he watched Vol and Koble gather their belongings. For Koble, it had been an easy process. The Sphinax's apartment was barren before he'd even filled his backpack. It was evident that he'd not let go of the wanderer's lifestyle. For Vol, the process of selecting a few prized possessions to take was far more complicated; though she'd done an excellent job in concealing her reluctance to leave. Nathan hadn't acknowledged it, but he'd noticed the Uvan staring mournfully at a tool rack in her chop-shop. Rather than pressuring Vol into hurrying, Koble suggested to Nathan and Harrt to grab some fresh air.

Outside, the rainfall had finally subsided, leaving several greyish-green puddles in the street: no doubt a result of Yenex's screwed-up ecosystem. In addition to the odour of dirty rainwater, there was a distinct aroma coming from a nearby vendor. Koble opted to go and purchase himself a snack, and when he returned to Nathan's side, the pungent stench of cheap tank-bred eels became apparent.

"Want some?" Koble offered.

In unison, Nathan and Harrt winced at the contents of Koble's snack-in-a-cup. Fortunately, they didn't have to give an answer as Vol finally emerged from her chop-shop.

"I'll be back in ten," she said, wrinkling her nose at the scent of steamed eel.

"Where are you going?" Harrt asked.

The tone with which the 'wealther spoke was borderline interrogative, but Vol didn't seem even slightly affected by it. Nathan noted her nonchalance, suspecting that Vol Volloh was far more than she appeared.

"I'm gonna go sell my place to the guy who runs the strip-joint opposite," she shrugged. "He's always liked the building: hopefully, I'll get a decent price for it".

She slung a backpack over her shoulder and crossed the street. Nathan turned to Harrt, noticing that he was watching her like a hawk.

"A woman shouldn't be going into a club like that unaccompanied," Harrt shook his head. "She's practically painting a target on herself by going in there".

To the 'wealther's surprise, Koble laughed so hard that he almost choked on his snack.

"You're kidding me, right? You'd have to be blind, deaf and dumb to mess with Vol," The Sphinax slapped Harrt on the shoulder as he continued to howl in laughter. "Guess the women must be softer inside the 'wealth".

It was clear from the scowl on Harrt's face that he didn't appreciate Koble's ridicule; regardless of its candour.

"We haven't got time for this," Harrt muttered. "I'll go keep an eye on her".

Koble continued to snicker into his food as Harrt rushed to catch up to Vol. Once Harrt was out of earshot, Koble leaned into Nathan;

"Do you think the lack of humour is how the 'wealthers come when they get off the assembly line?" Koble nudged at Nathan as he chuckled with his mouth full. "What in the hell would Jack say about all of this?"

Nathan shrugged;

"Probably something about the Commonwealth's lack of freedoms?" He took a few steps away in an attempt to avoid smelling the steamed eels. "Vol seems like she can handle herself," Nathan said, hoping to change the subject.

"That she can," Koble nodded while shoving a piece of fish into his mouth,

"So what's her story?"

Koble raised his brow.

"She's a good engineer; decent pilot; tougher than a good bottle of Sphinax Grog," he answered. "She can read minds too. So you best watch what that filthy Earther brain of yours conjures up, or she'll slap you upside the head".

Koble tapped the end of his wooden spoon into Nathan's forehead in jest.

"I kinda suspected," Nathan replied. "So, why was it so easy to talk her into doing this?"

Koble munched on the last bite of his snack before tossing the empty cardboard cup over his shoulder.

"Venin murdered her father and husband". Koble paused as he wiped his mouth. "She's got a vendetta; no doubt about it, but I've got to know her really well, and I say she's trustworthy."

"That's pretty clear already," Nathan said. He turned to look the Sphinax in the eye; "You told her about Jareth and Kornell?"

Koble stared back in silence, his jaw clenched hard enough to crack his teeth.

"Does she know the whole story?" Nathan questioned.

With a shrug, Koble answered; "She knows enough".

▲

After selling the chop-shop, Vol led the group through the undercity; taking them directly through the slums. The poverty in the area had been just as Nathan expected; abhorrent. The people were malnourished, the settlements were falling apart, and there was an atmosphere of utter desperation.

No different from any of the other corporate worlds, Nathan thought.

Harrt had been completely taken aback by what he saw: so much so that Vol reminded him not to stare. Nathan had always believed that the 'wealthers lived a slightly sheltered lifestyle, and the look in Harrt's eyes confirmed it. Fortunately, they didn't spend too long in the slums, and nobody gave them any trouble. Beyond the village, there was an abandoned mine from a bygone era.

"Why are we stopping here?" Harrt asked.

"You'll see," Vol pulled a flashlight from her belt. "Stick close".

She led them deep into the complex network of mineshafts. For over ten minutes, Nathan relied solely on the light from Vol's torch to find his footing. Eventually, she stopped and pointed the light toward a large metal pipe set into the wall.

"Seems whoever built the mine did a poor job," Harrt remarked.

The Uvan offered only a sarcastic chuckle as she handed him the flashlight.

"This pipe leads us into the sewers directly beneath Venin Towers," Vol said. "I need you to hold that light still while I cut this thing open".

Nathan watched as Vol produced a handheld port-torch from her backpack and proceeded to cut into the pipe. Less than a minute later, they were climbing inside.

The sewers of Yenex were anything but a tourist attraction. The foul stench that filled Nathan's nostrils was far worse than that of Koble's steamed eels from earlier —in fact, the eels seemed far more pleasant by comparison.

"It's a short walk," Vol said, noticing that he was struggling with the stench. "You humans really don't handle strong scents well".

"Guess so," Nathan growled.

He craned his neck to look at Koble and Harrt, who were a few metres behind. The pair appeared to be discussing Koble's modified rifle at some length.

"So," Vol said, grabbing Nathan's attention again. "I understand that you and Koble go way back?"

"Twenty years, give or take," Nathan exhaled. "My uncle brought Koble aboard our ship after the unpleasantness with Kornell."

Vol seemed to ponder his response, then nodded slowly.

"So, your uncle is the famous, Jack," she remarked.

"You've heard about him?"

"Koble speaks very fondly of him," Vol nodded.

"Sounds like a hell of a guy".

There was a pause that lasted longer than it should have. Nathan didn't feel at ease, knowing that Vol could read his mind at any moment.

"It would appear that this phantom ship of your uncle's cost the lives of two people that were very dear to me," she said.

"I heard," Nathan replied. "I'm sorry about what happened".

Vol turned her eyes away from Nathan and focussed on the path ahead.

"Not as sorry as Venin is going to be".

▲

There was something unusual about Nathan Carter that Vol couldn't quite pinpoint. Usually, her mind-reading abilities would allow some insight into a person's psyche; no matter how clear or clouded that reading was. In the case of Nathan, there was an indecipherable haze. It was something Vol had only ever experienced twice in her lifetime. The first was a pure-blood Revenant Duke who'd been on the run from his own people, and the second was a former Evoker. It was the ambiguity surrounding Nathan's mind that put Vol on edge; regardless of how trustworthy he appeared on the outside.

After walking for fifteen minutes through the rancid stench of Yenex's sewers, Vol halted the group at a junction point. She examined the readings from a datapad and then pointed at the wall on her right.

"We're here," she said. "Just need to cut through this wall, and we'll be inside Venin Towers".

"Oh boy, I've been waiting to test these babies out!" Koble excitedly grabbed an explosive charge from his belt, but Vol stepped in his way.

"Save it for later," she said. "If you detonate that thing you'll bring every crook on Venin's payroll to our position".

Harrt nodded, "We should try to do this as quietly as possible".

"Fine," Koble huffed. He tucked the explosive back into his belt and stepped back a few paces. "So what's the plan?"

"Just a bit of basic chemistry," Vol answered.

She knew that the sewers and lower levels of Venin Towers were constructed from a standard mix of Yandian Ores and Outer-world Ropelime, like most of the skyscrapers on Yenex. It would simply be a case of breaking down those components, using a chemical reaction.

Best way to avoid attracting attention, Vol thought.

Breaking into Venin Towers was always part of the plan; so Vol came prepared. She pulled two containers from her backpack and handed one to Harrt.

"I need you to spray a two-metre square on that wall," she ordered. "Oh, and try not to get that stuff on your skin".

The 'wealther examined the canister with a level scepticism, but he did as he was told. Once he'd drawn out a perfect square, Vol pulled open the second container, which immediately began to steam the moment it met oxygen.

"What the fuck is that?" Nathan backed up when he saw the chemicals bubbling.

Vol didn't answer straight away and instead ushered the three men to take a few steps back. She carefully placed the open container down where Harrt had applied the atomised X7 Barolinium.

"This is a mix of Carbonised-Brekon, Black Starseed and Diso-methylate," Vol said, taking a few steps back from the steaming container. "In tiny doses, you can use this stuff to clean comet dust off a ship's hull".

She watched the red steam meet with the Barolinium.

"Thing is, once Starseed mixes with oxygen, it becomes kinda... unstable. Throw a bit of Barolinium in there as well, and it can pretty much eat through anything".

The chemical mixture began to bubble violently as it devoured the square that Harrt drew earlier. A moment later there was a perfect two-metre opening that led directly into Venin Towers.

"See," Vol smiled. "Basic chemistry".

CHAPTER FIFTEEN

Sneaking through the basement of Venin Towers was too easy. A mix of past experience and the teacherly advice of Jack Stephens told Koble that he should remain alert. The basement was used for storage, with large floor to ceiling racks holding crates and shipping containers. Only one guard was patrolling the area which suggested that nothing in the stockpile was of significant value to Viktor Venin. After taking down the lone thug with a simple-but-effective forearm to the skull, Vol checked her datapad. She brought up a schematic of the building and highlighted the nearest service elevator.

"Looks like they were too arrogant to assume anybody would come in through the sewers," Harrt remarked.

"*Arrogance* may as well be Venin's middle-name," Vol said. The Uvan paused, noticing something on her datapad; "Shit!"

"What is it?" Koble leaned over Vol's shoulder to get a better look at the screen. It took Koble a matter of seconds to spot that Venin was mobilising most of his men on the roof.

"Perfect place for a trade," Vol turned to Koble and raised her brow. "Wouldn't you say?"

▲

The group rushed to the elevator, with Koble lagging several paces behind —though it didn't take long for the Sphinax to catch up. Vol was right: there was no other reason why Venin would gather most of his men at a single location. Making a trade with the Revenant was a high-risk move, even by Venin's standards.

The Revenant were not known for making deals or agreements: they took everything they wanted by force. To Koble, this meant one of two things —either the Revenant would kill Venin and his men the moment they had the Evoker, or they were so desperate to capture her that the Revenant would put aside their take-by-force nature in favour of a trade.

Doesn't make sense, Koble thought.

Once the group assembled inside the service elevator, Vol tapped on a mounted control panel, and within seconds they were heading up to the roof. Koble pulled his backpack over one shoulder and assembled his rifle. Once he was satisfied that the modified weapon was ready for combat, Koble checked his handguns, then the knife tucked behind the thick tuft of fur on his neck.

Always be prepared, Koble recited one of Jack's lessons in his head.

After passing several floors, it became apparent that the back wall of the elevator was, in fact, a window that looked out onto the city. For several seconds the horizon was dominated by the view of Yenex's skyscrapers.

"I ain't gonna miss this rock," Nathan remarked.

"That makes two of us," Koble replied.

Eventually, they ascended to a position where the sky was visible. Koble peeked at the rolling metropolis below, imagining what it had been like before terraforming and civilisation had ravaged the planet. Yenex was nothing like his homeworld, Pluvium. Koble recalled his birthworld as a beautiful, mostly forested paradise. Of course, it had been two decades since he'd left. For all he knew, Pluvium could have been stripped of its natural beauty by this point —just like Yenex.

Koble's attention was drawn to the matter at hand, as he overheard Harrt talking to Vol;

"Do you think he's keeping the Phoenix Titan on the roof?" Harrt asked.

Koble turned to listen in on their conversation:

"Unfortunately for us, no," Vol answered. "Viktor Venin may be arrogant, but he certainly isn't stupid".

"So where is it?" Harrt demanded.

Koble didn't appreciate that the 'wealther was talking to his friend like she was a soldier in his regiment. Before Vol could answer, Koble decided to butt into the conversation.

"We're doing as we all agreed," Koble folded his arms. "We get the girl out *then* steal the ship".

Harrt straightened, evidently sensing some hostility in Koble's voice. The Sphinax remained silent and didn't take his eyes off of the Commonwealth Lieutenant. It was just like Jack Stephens had said all those years ago;

The 'wealthers believe that they are better than everyone else.

Vol must have sensed a potential conflict between them, and rushed to answer Harrt's question.

"Venin keeps the Phoenix on the one-hundred-and-eleventh floor." The Uvan tucked her pistol into its holster and added; "Easiest floor to access in case of a security breach".

Before anyone could respond, a ship flew directly past the elevator window. Koble recognised the design of the angular ship from newscasts and books. It was a hideous, angular thing that looked otherworldly compared to the other ships in the Yenex skyline.

"That's a Revenant Royale," Koble swallowed. "I've only ever heard about these things, I've never seen one in the flesh".

Harrt stepped closer to the window to get a better look as the Revenant transport flew by them.

"Don't they use those things to transport their high ranking officials?" Nathan asked.

Harrt nodded, "A Royale could be carrying a Priest or an Admiral: it could even be carrying the King of Darkness himself!"

"The King of Darkness?" Koble laughed sarcastically. "He's just an entitled prick wearing a crown".

Koble immediately regretted his oversimplification, as Harrt took a half-step toward him. The 'wealther's lips were pressed thin, and his brow had lowered.

"How I wish that was true," Harrt frowned.

Koble didn't respond.

There was no denying that the Revenant were evil: Koble had witnessed the effects of their campaigns first-hand. He'd seen the burnt-out planets and mutated husks that the Revenant left in their wake. Before his disappearance, Jack had shared his own harrowing account of the Revenant attack on Earth; something so horrid that Koble would never forget it. After living with half a dozen Earthers aboard the Loyalty, Koble had a deep insight into the Fall that not many others could claim to have.

Every single Earther aboard the Loyalty had suffered some form of trauma or another. Nathan's cousin James had turned to hard-drugs to numb his pain. Jack bottled it all up; drank when nobody was looking and lived with a pang of guilt so heavy that he'd attempted to take his own life. Nathan was the most well-adjusted of the bunch, but even after all this time, it was clear that he was still struggling.

The problem was that the Commonwealth could never appear weak to its citizens. They couldn't be seen to lose in a *fair fight* —not that there was such a thing in Koble's eyes. The simple truth was that it sounded far more impactful to tell your citizens that they were fighting a war against *The Eternal King of Darkness.* That was how you kept your people loyal —by shrouding your enemy in myth.

I guess it sounds better than fighting an asshole with a god-complex, Koble thought.

▲

When the elevator reached the top floor of Venin Towers, Harrt was the first to step out with his weapon raised. Koble followed while Nathan and Vol covered the rear. Considering that the group had been working as a team for only a few short hours, it was stunning how efficiently they surveyed the new area. The room that they entered had large windows overlooking a landing pad on the level below. A lone sniper was covering the window, but he was quietly dispatched by Harrt. With the only threat in the room taken care of, Koble shuffled to the window to get a better view of the deck beneath them. He could see the Revenant Royale in the process of landing on a pad which extended over the edge of Venin Towers. Koble knew that was a tactical move by Venin to ensure that whoever the Revenant had sent would behave themselves or risk seeing their shuttle destroyed.

He took his eyes off of the Revenant and turned his attention to the small army that Viktor Venin had at his disposal. There must have been at least two-dozen armed men ready to fight in case the trade turned sour.

"There's Grecko and Venin..." Vol said, her voice growing hostile.

Koble didn't need to look back at her to know that her eyes would be hardened and full of vengeance. Instead, Koble craned his neck to where Vol was pointing. Viktor Venin was just as Koble had pictured; a tubby human with the same garish facial hair that you'd only see in the most elite of Yenex's social circles.

Grecko was taller than Koble imagined. Even from a distance, he could spot the telltale signs of a mercenary. Grecko's face was scarred from battle, and there he had the same laser-focused gaze that Koble had seen a hundred times before. There was an arrogance to the green-skinned Uvan that was eerily familiar as well. He watched Grecko puff on a cigar and toss it the ground.

Just like James, Koble thought, thinking about to his old shipmate, and Nathan's estranged cousin. *Well that's kinda creepy.*

Grecko and Venin were stood behind their wall of armed thugs, with a large containment chamber beside them. It was fair to assume that the coffin-shaped device was where Venin was keeping the Evoker.

Bold move, Venin, Koble thought.

Containment chambers were commonly used to transport dangerous criminals, keeping their occupants in a sedated state until they arrived at their destination. Still, the Evokers were said to be legendarily powerful. Koble wondered if the drugs held in a containment chamber would be strong enough to keep an Evoker out cold.

"That would be where they are holding your friend, " Koble nudged Harrt.

"We've gotta get down there now," Harrt said. The 'wealther looked at Koble's rifle and asked; "Are you good to give us sniper cover from up here?"

"Damn straight," Koble nodded. He grabbed some grenades from his belt and distributed them evenly between Nathan, Harrt and Vol. "You guys should take these. They'll cause a bit of havoc down there".

As the group dispersed, Koble set up his sniper position and watched as the Revenant Royale touch down below. He adjusted the scope on his rifle and watched intently;

"Here we go again," Koble muttered to himself.

▲

Nathan and Harrt followed Vol down to the next deck where they positioned themselves out of sight behind a set of storage containers. Nathan had counted at least twenty men under Venin's command, so going in guns blazing didn't feel right. There was a loud mechanical hiss as the Royale's landing gear connected with the platform and seconds later a boarding ramp emerged from the ship's hull.

Nathan watched as a small group of Revenant marines disembarked the ship in a tight military formation. These marine's were different from the ones Nathan encountered earlier at the crash site; wearing bronze armour and carrying heavy weapons.

"Kingsguard," Harrt whispered.

A pair of Revenant hunters were led out by a man in a dark cloak. He kept each of the savage creatures at a distance using shackles at the neck to keep the beasts under control.

"What the hell is this?" Vol shook her head. "Is this a game of who's got the bigger balls?"

"It's a show of force," Nathan replied.

"Shh," Harrt pressed a finger to his lips and gestured to the Royale.

From the interior of the dark angular spacecraft, a tall man in ceremonial robes stepped out. Just as Harrt predicted, this man was someone of great importance to the Revenant. For a moment, Nathan wondered if perhaps this hooded figure was the so-called *King of Darkness*. Nathan allowed the memories of the Fall to flood to the surface. He recalled all the nights where he'd lay awake swearing revenge against the Revenant: against King Seig.

"That's a Revenant Paladin," Harrt said, his mouth gaping in a mixture of shock and panic. "Things just got real complicated".

"What do you mean?" Nathan said. "What is he?"

"Paladins..." Harrt paused, apparently thinking about the question. "Think Evokers, but these ones are on the Revenants side. Very dangerous".

Nathan knew that Harrt's answer was a simplification, but it didn't matter: his response would have been the same, regardless of the level of detail.

"Fuck..." Nathan cursed, feeling the hairs on the back of his neck stand-up.

The Paladin stood at the foot of the Royale for several seconds; staring at Venin for what felt like an uncomfortably long time. He waited for Venin's men to bring the containment chamber forward.

"So what do we do now?" Nathan turned back to Harrt.

Harrt pressed a knuckle between his teeth, unable to look away from the Paladin.

"Plan doesn't change," Harrt answered. "We grab Astrilla; get on the Phoenix and get the hell outta here".

If Harrt's comparison of the Paladin to an Evoker was to be believed, then sticking to the plan was insane. Astrilla had bested Nathan without even trying, and she'd been merciful. Going up against a self-aware Revenant with the ability to control elemental energy was practically suicidal.

Nathan watched as Viktor Venin greeted the Paladin. Despite not being able to hear a word of the exchange, Nathan could tell it was intense. Venin had one of his men open the containment chamber, and Nathan saw the Paladin nod in approval.

Suddenly, he felt Harrt's hand on his shoulder.

"Where is Vol?" the 'wealther said.

Nathan looked over his shoulder to where Vol had been just seconds earlier. She was gone, and Nathan had no idea where.

"Shit," Nathan turned back to Harrt. "She was right there! Where the hell is —"

The sound of yelling caused Nathan to pause mid-sentence. A gut-wrenching sensation of utter dread filled his stomach, and for a moment, he couldn't breathe. In unison, Nathan and Harrt peaked out from cover to see Vol in the open, with her weapon pointed at Viktor Venin.

"Venin!" Vol yelled.

Nathan felt the element of surprise slip through his fingers, upon realising that every single eye on the rooftop was locked on Vol.

"Shit..."

CHAPTER SIXTEEN

The third of Nathan Carter's life-defining lessons had come at the age of five; mere weeks before the Fall. When Nathan's parents were working, he would spend his days with his maternal grandparents. They owned a big house with several floors and many rooms, which to a small child was an opportunity for exploration.

There was an occasion, however, when Nathan felt an urge to venture beyond the confines of the house. He wasn't too sure why, but he'd been drawn to his grandfather's shed at the rear of the property. The small wooden outbuilding wasn't anything significant to look at. It had been painted green, probably at the behest of his grandmother to match the plants.

The door was locked, but Nathan hadn't allowed that to stop him. He'd gained access to the interior by crawling through a small gap in the corner that James had pointed out to him a week earlier. Inside, he'd found tools and gardening supplies: nothing particularly exciting.

By chance, something had caught his eye at the back of his grandfather's workbench. It was a very old black and white photograph of a handsome man in a paisley jacket. Nathan had grabbed the picture and taken it back to the house, wondering who the man in the picture was. He'd eventually found his grandfather, Bill, in his study packing a bag for his next research trip.

Despite being beyond the age of retirement, Bill had

continued working, citing his love of science as his fuel to keep going. Many years later, Jack had described his father as a man committed to answering the big questions, which in hindsight, Nathan could most certainly agree with.

"What have you got there?" Bill pointed to the photograph.

Nathan handed it to his grandfather and asked;

"Who's that man?"

Nathan always remembered that the expression on his grandfather's face had been a mix of sadness and loss. He'd stared at the picture for several seconds before answering;

"That man was my father; your great-grandfather".

"Where is he now?" Nathan had asked with a level of childlike curiosity.

"I don't know," Bill shook his head. "He left before I was grown-up. This is the only picture I have of him".

"Why did he leave?" Nathan asked, blissfully unaware of how complicated his question was.

After some careful consideration, Bill replied;

"My father wasn't a good man".

"Why?"

Bill frowned, but it didn't stop him answering the question.

"I guess things got tough and he couldn't handle it".

In hindsight, Nathan wondered if perhaps his grandfather could ever understand the impact of what he said next;

"When you're older things will get tough, it's a part of growing up," Bill said. "Just remember this: no matter how bad it gets, there is always a way to keep moving forward. Never give up, no matter how hard it gets".

That was the last day Nathan saw his grandfather. Bill had flown to Russia as part of a special research project. Nathan could still remember Bill jumping into a car with a young man in thick-framed glasses and driving off into the distance.

Never give up, no matter how hard it gets, Nathan thought grimly. *Wonder if that applies to my current situation.*

Vol was the first to open fire. Sensing that Venin and the Revenant were taking up their weapons, Nathan tossed a grenade into the crowd. As Venin's men began to fire at Vol, Harrt tackled her into cover. Nathan craned his neck to make sure they avoided the onslaught of laser-fire.

Everything moved very quickly.

Koble began laying down sniper-fire, while Harrt and Vol scuttled to the next container for cover. Nathan took up his handgun and instinctively picked off one of Venin's thugs who'd made a beeline toward his position. Nathan's grenade detonated and the explosion was so great that his ears popped. He heard Vol and Harrt several metres to his right returning fire. There was another detonation which Nathan assumed had been from a grenade tossed by Vol or Harrt. The Revenant Royale and the landing pad holding it, fell from Venin Towers and into the city below.

There was a horrible feeling in the pit of Nathan's gut as he reloaded his weapon: they were outgunned, and if what Harrt had said about the Paladin was right, they were very outmatched.

"I've got no intention of dying here," Nathan said to himself. He reaffirmed that point by quoting his grandfather; "Never give up..."

Nathan searched the rooftop for the Paladin and spotted him just a few metres away. The crimson robed man was heading straight toward Nathan's position.

Fuck, Nathan thought. *I can't fight this guy.*

Then something dawned on him; *I can't, but maybe she can.*

Nathan turned his eyes to the containment chamber at the centre of the landing pad. Astrilla was their golden ticket out of the situation. If Evokers were as powerful and as mighty as the rumours said, then she'd make a perfect ally.

Without a second thought, Nathan darted from cover and fired his gun in the direction of the Paladin. He turned a corner and hastily dispatched another of Venin's thugs. Finally, when he reached the containment chamber, Nathan came face to face with a man clutching what he could only assume was a flamethrower. Throughout a single heartbeat,

Nathan prepared himself for one of two things to happen: One, he'd have to fight his way out, or two, he'd be burnt to a crisp. Neither of those things happened. The man carrying the flamethrower dissolved in a spray of blood as Koble cut him down from the other side of the building.

Nathan could almost picture the Sphinax saying in a boastful tone; *I've still got it.*

Nathan hurriedly tapped the containment chamber's controls. He waited until the panel turned green and then pulled the heavy door ajar. Before Nathan could fully open the coffin-shaped device, he was flung to the floor by a pulse of energy. As he rolled along the ground, Nathan felt the same bone-jarring sensation he'd felt back on the Vertex; when Astrilla had struck him with an Evoker attack.

The Paladin lowered his outreached palm. The elemental summon that struck Nathan was non-lethal, and he suspected that the Paladin had done so intentionally. Nathan raised his gun, but before he could open fire, the robed man sent another summon into him. The blast of untamed power ripped into Nathan, carrying him through the air and straight into the floor. The impact of the attack took the breath out Nathan's lungs as he smashed on the hard concrete with a gut-churning thud.

The Paladin, pulled back his hood, revealing the ravaged features of a man who'd once been human. His eyes had been blackened, and his face carried the scars of battle and the mutation process.

The fact that Nathan wasn't dead yet simply suggested that his attacker was toying with him: a point that was proven when the Paladin drew his sword;

"You shall be reborn in his image, my child. Do not fear death: it is the first step closer to him".

Nathan didn't listen to the rhetoric and instead, climbed to his feet, clutching his handgun. Knowing that he was about to go toe to toe with an enemy as powerful as an Evoker filled him with dread. There was a very good chance that he would die in the fight, but as Jack would say;

It's better to go down fighting.

▲

For Harrt Oxarri, the feeling of being in a gunfight was always the same. It didn't matter when, where or even the number of hostiles he was up against. Every time it happened, Harrt Oxarri's mind would switch to a kind of instinct fueled auto-pilot. Unconsciously, he was aware that the odds were stacked against them, but for some reason, his mind kept saying;

It's still not as bad as Maru Seven.

Chaos was everywhere. Most of Venin's men were disorganised and ill-experienced, meaning that they were the easy ones to kill. The Revenant Kingsguard were far more tactical. They took up cover behind whatever could be found and attempted to lay down suppressing fire on Harrt and Vol. It was a tried and tested tactic that felt all too familiar to Harrt: he'd seen it enough times to know. Revenant soldiers would often try to keep their target pinned down at a single location; thus enabling them to send in the hunters.

It didn't work.

The first hunter dashed toward Harrt, unaware that it was running into Koble's line of fire. The foul creature got to within three metres of Harrt's position before its head exploded in a shower of blood and brains.

Harrt darted from cover and laid down a barrage of weapons fire, cutting down two more Revenant guards in the process. At the same time, Vol launched one of her grenades toward the second hunter. The explosion that followed consumed the vicious creature and a handful of Venin's men.

Harrt turned his attention to Nathan at the centre of the rooftop. The Earther appeared to be in combat with the Paladin.

What the hell is he doing? Harrt wondered.

Something primitive in Harrt's mind compelled him to protect the Earther. He pressed forward and began firing in the direction of the Paladin, but was suddenly tackled to the ground.

The attacker was a muscular Uvan male. He laid a hard right hook into Harrt's ribcage but left an opening when he reached for his gun. As the Uvan turned to grab the pistol, Harrt delivered a strike to his attacker's throat and attempted to wrestle the weapon away. The pair tussled for the gun for several seconds, and for a moment it looked as though the Uvan would win. To Harrt's relief, Vol interrupted the fight by booting the hostile in the head. The kick was so hard that it sent Harrt's would-be killer crashing to the floor in a heap.

"Hello Grecko," Vol said, pointing her pistol at the bloodied Uvan. "You know who I am, don't you?"

"I know who you are," Grecko managed a nod, and then followed it up with a callous smirk.

Harrt looked on as Vol's face turned to rage. Without flinching, she pulled the trigger. A single round seared into Grecko's skull, sending his blood across the ground. Harrt warily climbed to his feet, and Vol handed him a new gun.

"Fight's not over," she said.

▲

Nathan turned his battle with the Paladin into a game of cat and mouse. He didn't like to admit it, but he was up against an enemy that outmatched his own combat abilities several times over. Nathan kept moving to draw the robed man into Koble's line of fire. He avoided several bursts of Evoker-like energy as he leapt over a group of shipping crates. Sure enough, the Paladin entered Koble's kill-zone, and as Nathan hoped, the sound of sniper fire rang out.

Nathan peaked out from behind the crates, hoping to see a dead Paladin. What he saw sent a cold shiver down his spine. The Paladin stood before him unharmed with the smoking bullet from Koble's rifle pressed between his fingers.

How the hell did he do that? Nathan wondered.

Before Nathan could finish his thought, the Paladin hurled a ball of fire toward Koble's position. Nathan spotted the Sphinax leap through the windows by his sniper's nest, narrowly avoiding the blast.

The Paladin turned back to Nathan and lifted his sword.

"Time to die," the robed man said.

The Paladin took a wide swing with his sword, which Nathan was able to avoid. He emptied the entirety of his gun's chamber into the Paladin's torso. Before Nathan could reload his weapon, the Paladin grabbed him by the throat and lifted him like a rag-doll.

"There is no shame in death," The Paladin looked at Nathan as he crushed the Earther's windpipe. "Rebirth brings strength".

Nathan tried to break free, but it was to no avail. His vision became maddeningly blurred under the weight of the chokehold. In what Nathan assumed was to be his final moments, there was one thought that sprung to mind:

Was it worth it? He thought. *Was anything I did ever worth it?"*

Nathan suddenly felt oxygen fill his lungs as the Paladin loosened his grip. The bald man was staring down at his chest, where a sword had been stabbed through his back. The Paladin released Nathan, and for several seconds, the Earther coughed and gasped for breath. He lifted his head to see the Paladin turn and face his attacker.

Astrilla wrenched the sword from the Paladin's back and tossed it to one side. Nathan looked on as the dark-haired woman summoned the elemental energy that her kind was known for. Something visceral in Nathan awoke at that very moment: an urge to run to safety. He could tell that what was to follow was not going to be pretty, but something innate implored him to look on.

Astrilla raised her palms, and a glow of blinding light formed at her fingertips. The beam of energy she cast hit the Paladin, and for a second, there was only the sound of a guttural scream. When the light cleared, all that remained of the Revenant man was a pile of ash.

Nathan didn't notice that the fighting had stopped; instead, he stared at the charred remains of his former opponent. There had been many odd things that Nathan had borne witness to over the years, but this was something else entirely. After several seconds, Nathan turned his attention to Astrilla, and she was looking at him. Her expression was one of both outrage and astonishment.

"You?" She said.

CHAPTER SEVENTEEN

After being pumped full of sedatives for the last however many hours, Astrilla felt sick to her stomach. She was aware that the drugs were still coursing through her veins —it explained why everything appeared to be playing out at triple speed. Despite the effect of the narcotics on her body, Astrilla's combat abilities were uninhibited. The Paladin had learnt that first hand.

Like all Evokers, Astrilla had been taught that bloodshed was a last resort. Evokers were trained to defend, disarm and disable: except for those occasions when your adversary was Revenant. Killing someone that was sworn to the Revenant cause was a necessary evil; regardless of whether or not they'd undergone the mutation process.

The Paladin disappeared behind her summon of raw energy, and the untamed blast consumed him. When Astrilla lowered her palms, all that remained was a cloud of grey ash. Astrilla was quick to examine her new surroundings, in case there were any other threats in the area. What she found was the last thing she expected to see.

"You," Astrilla said.

The Earther who'd broken into her quarters a few days prior stared back. The scruffy vagabond was clutching at his throat where the Paladin was choking him seconds earlier.

Somewhere at the back of her mind, something itched. It was an odd feeling; primitive and yet somehow deeply evolved. The Earther had faced a Revenant Paladin and survived. That feat was almost unheard of, for a non Evoker. Of course, he'd lived thanks to Astrilla's intervention. But still, Astrilla couldn't deny the fact that he'd engaged a Paladin in combat and not died in seconds. In the past, she'd seen fully trained Evokers fall to Paladins, which suggested the Earther was of some significance to the universe.

"You?" She said again, this time phrasing it more like a question than a statement. "What are you doing here?"

Before the Earther could answer, Astrilla sensed someone approaching at speed. Expecting another hostile encounter, she whipped around and raised her hands ready to fight. Rather than confronting another Revenant, Astrilla came face to face with a burly Sphinax. She still prepared to strike, but the hairy creature raised his paws skyward and said in a shrill, panicked voice;

"Whoa, whoa, I'm friendly!"

Astrilla took a moment to consider before lowering her palms and allowing him to pass. The Sphinax moved around her with caution, then patted his Earther counterpart on the back.

"Shave my fur and call me an Ickus," the Sphinax said with an unusually jovial tone. "Nathan, I've said it before, and I'll say it again, you are one crazy SOB".

The Earther's name was, Nathan. Astrilla recalled that he'd refused to answer that question back on the Vertex.

As The Sphinax helped Nathan to his feet, she asked,

"What are you doing here?"

The scruffy Earther dusted himself off and regarded her with a mixed expression.

"Saving you," Nathan answered. "At least that *was* the plan until that guy showed up," he pointed at the small pile of ash on the floor that had once been a Paladin. "Guess I owe you one" he added.

Before Astrilla had the time to process everything that had been said, she heard another pair of footsteps heading toward them. The first was a Uvan woman; pink skin, purple and blue hair with the most striking set of magenta eyes that Astrilla had ever seen. The second prompted Astrilla to raise her hands in rage:

"Lieutenant Oxarri," she snapped.

At that point, Astrilla was aware that the Uvan reacted by pointing a pistol toward her. She was pretty sure that the Sphinax had done the same but not as quickly as his Uvan ally. Astrilla knew she could kill them all if came to it. She took a step closer to Harrt, recalling the sabotage aboard the escape pod.

"Your men tried to kill me," Astrilla said through gritted teeth.

Harrt raised his hands in surrender and said in a very calm tone;

"I know, I saw the footage".

"Who gave the order? Was it Rooke?"

"He's dead, along with the rest of my crew," Harrt replied. "Rooke's final order was to protect you. He said that you can't fall into Revenant hands and I intend on sticking to those orders".

"That doesn't explain why your marines tried to kill me," Astrilla argued.

"It wasn't Rooke, and it damn sure wasn't me," Harrt objected. "My entire crew died keeping the Revenant away from you!"

Astrilla wanted to interrogate the 'wealther more, but to her surprise, Nathan spoke up:

"He's telling the truth!" The Earther holstered his gun and took a step closer toward her. "I heard what the Vertex's commander said to Harrt before we abandoned ship: find the girl and keep her safe."

Nathan turned to the Uvan and the Sphinax and prompted them to lower their weapons:

"Koble, Vol, put the fuckin' guns down," he said. "We're all on the same side here".

Astrilla noted the names.

It stood to reason that the Earther could be lying about Rooke, *but why? What could he possibly have to gain?* On the other hand, the rag-tag group had gone to all the effort to break her out: all while fighting off the Revenant. Astrilla lowered her hands, and everyone breathed a sigh of relief. She could only hope it was the right decision.

"When we get back to Commonwealth Space, I'll have Dines launch a full investigation into what happened with the marines," Harrt said, trying to reassure her.

Astrilla's response was cold; "See that you do, Lieutenant".

She immediately regretted her tone, but couldn't admit wrongdoing. Harrt had gone to some length to *rescue* her, and Astrilla had responded by almost reducing him to dust. Unfortunately, there wasn't ample time to apologise for her blunt response. The Sphinax, Koble, called out to them and gestured to something on his datapad:

"I hate to break up this little team-bonding exercise, but we've got a very big problem!"

"What is it?" Nathan and Harrt said at the same time.

Koble pointed toward the sky;

"We've got incoming".

▲

Astrilla felt a slight rush of vertigo as the elevator descended. She was aware that her lightheadedness was likely an after-effect of the containment chamber. Knowing that it would take some time for the drugs to wear off, Astrilla decided that her only option was to persevere —at least until they were off of Yenex.

Koble gave her what he'd described as a whistle-stop-tour of the plan. After he'd blurted out a rough explanation, Astrilla couldn't decide if the scheme was incredibly foolish or just plain impulsive. She'd expected a meticulously planned operation from the likes of Harrt Oxarri.

The next part of the plan was to steal a Phoenix-class ship, which for some reason or another belonged to Nathan. Once they had the ship they would use it to escape Yenex and, hopefully, outrun the Revenant blockade.

At least it's a plan, Astrilla thought.

The elevator doors slid open onto what Astrilla could only assume was a re-purposed warehouse. The ceiling was covered in large white panels, forming a grid, while the ground was made from concrete. While most of the room was bright and clear, there was an uncomfortable darkness that clung to the back of the room. Astrilla was so focussed on what was hiding in the shadows that she completely missed the trail of blood across the floor.

"Venin," Vol said, gesturing to the blood. "He's here. I knew I clipped him back there".

There was a certain indignation in the Uvan woman's voice that hinted at history with Viktor Venin. Astrilla didn't acknowledge it, they didn't have time.

The group followed the blood until they reached Viktor Venin. The rotund human was dragging himself across the floor, leaving a red trail behind him. Realising that the group were hot on his tail, Venin attempted to wrestle a gun from his blood-soaked jacket. As he grabbed the weapon, Vol shot him again, this time in the hand. Venin spent several seconds writhing in agony on the floor, before finally uttering;

"Shit…".

In the space of a heartbeat, Vol rushed over to him and pressed her gun to his head.

"Viktor Venin; you murdered my husband and my father," Vol declared. "Tell me why, and I'll make your death a quick one".

Venin seemed to laugh in response, and Vol responded by pressing her boot into his injured shoulder. Astrilla felt compelled to stop what she was seeing, but something primitive told her not to do anything: almost as though the universe had a purpose for this kind of barbarity.

After several seconds of screaming, Viktor Venin called out;

"Stop! Stop!"

Vol took her boot out of his gunshot wound and waited for his reply. Venin looked at her; smirked ambiguously and then gazed past her, to look at Nathan.

"The Phoenix Titan is an incredible ship," Venin snarled. "I think that's why he kept it a secret".

"What are you talking about?" Nathan stepped toward Venin, but Harrt halted him.

"We haven't got time for this," Harrt insisted. "Either

get him aboard the Phoenix and question him later or shoot him in the head now".

"He's right," Koble agreed. "Revenant fighters are less than two minutes out".

Astrilla breathed a sigh of relief when Vol stepped aside. Given their current circumstances, there was no time for bloodshed. Whatever had happened between Venin and Vol, it could wait.

▲

The Phoenix Titan was far more imposing in size than Nathan had anticipated. He guessed that the ship measured somewhere around sixty metres in length, but it was impossible to tell. The Phoenix Titan's mass filled out the stern to the midpoint of the ship, leaving a small prong on the starboard side. The stern housed the Phoenix's large cylindrical FTL engines, which had been installed for both agility and manoeuvrability.

As Vol and Koble predicted, the Titan-class frigate was modified in several places: additional gunnery chambers had been added to the underside of the ship, and the engine had undergone some alterations that Nathan didn't recognise. On both the port and starboard sides, there were two fixed missile turrets.

This thing can pack one hell of a punch, Nathan thought.

As he climbed aboard, banks of overhead LEDs flickered to life. Though he didn't have much time to examine the interior of the Phoenix, something felt oddly familiar. He passed through the corridor and entered the central-most point of the vessel, which was an unfinished living space. There was a mix of dark wooden flooring and new carpet spanning the length of the room. There was a mock-fireplace against one of the walls, which seemed unusual, but Nathan recalled that Jack always had a fondness for such things. Still, it didn't feel like Jack's ship at all, rather the property of an architect or designer. Nathan didn't have time to examine his surroundings any further, as

Harrt and Vol directed him toward the cockpit.

"C'mon, there will be time to check out your new digs later," Vol said.

She was right. Revenant fighters were inbound to their position, and there was a very good chance that they would reduce Venin Towers to rubble. Nathan turned back to Koble, who was dragging Viktor Venin by the collar of his diamante shirt.

"What do you want me to do with this piece of shit?" Koble asked.

"I assume this ship's got a brig?" Nathan replied.

Koble shrugged with his paw; "There's a cargo hold with a locking door: better than getting his blood all over the carpet, right?"

"That'll do".

Koble proceeded to drag the half-conscious, Venin to the rear of the ship, but Nathan halted him.

"Give him something for those gunshot wounds. I wanna have a conversation with him later".

Koble nodded in agreement with a frown on his face. It was very likely that the Sphinax was thinking the same thing as Nathan; that perhaps Viktor Venin had some intel on Jack.

Astrilla entered the living space, sidestepping Koble as he yanked their prisoner to the rear of the ship. She looked at Nathan for several seconds. It was interesting to see her pretend not to be anxious. Back on the Vertex, Astrilla had been in control of the situation: interrogating him with a high-energy brig-shield between them. Now the Evoker was in the middle of a chaotic situation and wasn't holding all the cards. It was clear that behind her calm facade Astrilla had been rattled.

Nathan grabbed Astrilla by the upper arm, and she seemed to snap back into the moment. The Evoker's eyes went wide, and her hands came up in defence. She blinked at him in confusion but then lowered her hands after a few seconds.

"Are you okay?" Nathan asked.

"This ship has a history..." She said.

CHAPTER EIGHTEEN

The Phoenix Titan was a good ship —state of the art. Harrt hadn't anticipated just how advanced the onboard systems would be. The navigation terminal was worth more than an entire Commonwealth fighter. From what he could tell, the FTL drive and thrust control was a hybrid, meaning that the ship would have the manoeuvrability of a small fighter while also reaching the kind of high speeds that Harrt expected from a racing shuttle.

Makes the average Commonwealth hauler look like a damn tugboat, Harrt thought.

He sat at the pilot's station and prepped the ship for take-off. There was a low rumbling, and then a roar as the engines came to life. A small green screen on the control console flickered to life, catching Harrt's attention. He tapped at the screen once, and a message popped up;

PRESENCE DETECTED...
INITIATE VALIDATION...
DNA SCAN: CONFIRM.
FACIAL RECOGNITION: CONFIRM.
VOICE RECOGNITION: CONFIRM.
IDENTITY CONFIRMED: NATHAN WILLIAM CARTER.
SYSTEMS CONTROL RELEASED.

Harrt raised his brow but didn't have the chance to question the onscreen readout. The message faded into obscurity almost as quickly as it appeared, and was replaced by a flashing red warning. A threat alert began to alarm throughout the entire ship. Harrt glanced at the proximity readings which loaded three times faster than the average Commonwealth warship. He didn't need to look at the screen for very long, as it became blindingly apparent why an alert had been triggered.

"That's an entire squadron," Vol said as she climbed into the co-pilot's seat. "That's a whole lot of firepower".

"What are you doing?" Harrt said, noticing that the Uvan was strapping herself into the chair beside him.

Vol shot him a cocky smirk;

"The way I see it, you need a co-pilot, and I'm it".

"You sure about that?"

"Between the Earther; the magic-chick and Koble, I'm your best bet!" Vol answered.

She made an excellent point.

Before long, the Phoenix Titan lifted from the ground and blew a hole in Venin Towers; creating the perfect escape path. Harrt was stunned by the sheer precision of the fixed cannons.

"This is gonna get really bumpy!" Harrt said, before punching the acceleration control.

The Phoenix's engines ignited, sending the ship hurtling out of Venin Towers. When they reached the city, fire rained from above. By Harrt's estimate, the weapons fire wasn't exclusively coming from the Revenant Fighters: some of it was coming from orbit. Harrt pushed on the throttle, forcing the Phoenix to accelerate even faster. Nathan loomed over Harrt's shoulder, clinging onto the back of his chair.

"Did they just shoot down a fucking skyscraper to try and kill us?" the Earther said.

"We aren't sticking around long enough to find out," Harrt replied. "I'm taking us up! Get yourselves strapped into a seat; things are gonna get bumpy!"

Harrt shared a companionable nod with Vol, and within seconds, the Phoenix was twisting skyward. It was at that moment that the Phoenix's agility became apparent. The vessel barely buckled as it began a steep ascent into the clouds. Harrt oriented the ship at a near ninety-degree angle, feeling only the slightest pull of gravity. After experiencing less than ten seconds of turbulence, the Phoenix cleared Yenex's atmosphere. The cold, dark embrace of space filled Harrt with a fleeting moment of pure serenity. It felt good to see the stars and to know that he was one step closer to Commonwealth space. Then the Revenant blockade came into view, and Harrt's moment of tranquillity was gone: replaced with the same sense of dread he'd felt back on Maru Seven. Dozens upon dozens of hostile warships and fighters blocked the Phoenix's path to FTL

One of the Phoenix's various control panels chimed aggressively, and when Vol examined the screen she yelled;

"They're targetting us!"

The Uvan pointed to the Revenant's flagship through the window. The colossal grey mass that loomed ahead must have measured at least five miles in length. Harrt's first impulse was to engage the Phoenix's manual flight controls: his second was to push the ship to its maximum zero-g speed. The rate of acceleration was alarming; far more so than the ascent. It suddenly dawned on Harrt that the vehicle he was flying could execute the same kind of aerial trickery that he'd been taught during dogfight training. He sent the vessel into an evasive spin, dodging several bolts of laser fire from the blockade. Despite his initial admiration of the Phoenix's manoeuvrability, Harrt knew that it wouldn't be a straight shot to clear space. They were going to have to fight to survive. Harrt recalled that he'd seen two modified gunnery stations when he'd come on board.

Along with the heavy artillery from the fixed cannons, we might just stand a chance, Harrt thought.

He craned his neck to look at Nathan, who was still clinging onto the back of his chair for dear life.

"I need two of you in those gunnery chambers," Harrt said. "We need to get them off our tail".

"Got it," Nathan snapped. The Earther turned and called out to Koble; "C'mon, we gotta get on those guns".

Harrt returned his gaze to the dense barrier of Revenant fighters and warships that stood in their path. He took a deep breath and pushed the Phoenix toward the blockade.

Vol turned to him; "So, is this the worst you've been up against?"

Harrt tried not to think of Maru Seven, but it was there regardless. Just as Rooke said, *Maru Seven would be there until the day he died.* Harrt turned to Vol,

"Believe it or not, I've survived worse".

"Sounds like an interesting story," Vol said, looking at the Revenant ships. "You'll have to tell me about that when this is all over".

Harrt started to answer but then heard Astrilla clear her throat behind them. He wondered if perhaps she knew about his service at Maru Seven: maybe that was why she'd interrupted. When Harrt turned to look over his shoulder, he found that Astrilla was strapped into a seat at the rear of the cockpit in a meditative state.

"Is she sleeping?" Vol's voice lifted an octave. "What the hell is she doing?"

"Oh, boy..." Harrt sighed knowingly; "Whatever you do, don't touch her".

▲

There was a mad dash to the gunnery chambers. Nathan wrestled against the mix of simulated gravity and the sheer velocity of the Phoenix. Somehow he made it through the lounge without falling over the bolted-down wooden furniture. He sprinted to the aft of the ship, with Koble not far behind.

When the pair reached the gunnery chambers, they stopped at a set of ladders: one going up, the other down.

"See you on the other side!" Koble punched Nathan on the arm.

The Sphinax scaled the downward ladder, and Nathan the upward. The small semi-spherical pod looked out onto the top of space, giving Nathan a full 360-degree view of the chaos looming around them. It was the kind of modification that had been designed for just such an occasion.

Nathan climbed into a leather seat at the centre of the

chamber and took ahold of the cannon's controls. Not only did the console enable Nathan to rotate the gun, but it also highlighted predicted enemy flight paths: it wasn't going to be perfect, but it would certainly give the Phoenix an edge in combat.

Several Revenant fighters soared toward the ship, and Nathan wasted no time in spinning up the guns. He looked on as the hostile crafts danced in the sky, rotating to avoid the oncoming cannon fire.

"I'm gonna get us close to the flagship," Harrt yelled over the communicator. "Koble, when we get in close enough, you need to fire on that warship's missile array. It's the only way we'll survive once we're in open space".

"Gotcha!" Koble replied.

Nathan listened in but didn't reply. Instead, he tracked the incoming fighters as they soared toward the Phoenix Titan. Once he was confident with his aim, Nathan opened fire.

▲

On the underside of the Phoenix, Koble twisted the gunnery chamber. He targetted the Revenant Flagship but had to manually adjust to pinpoint the missile array. Once he'd lined up his sights, Koble unleashed the full force of the Phoenix's weaponry. Small explosions erupted around the array, and after a few seconds, it collapsed into the hull.

Koble allowed himself a celebratory yell, which he shared over the communicator.

"That's some damn fine piloting 'wealther," he said into the communicator.

"Celebrate later! We aren't out of this yet," Harrt replied.

Koble continued to push down on the trigger, firing multiple shots into the Revenant warship as they passed over it. They'd have minimal effect, but it still felt good knowing that the Revenant would be scrubbing scorch marks off the hull for weeks.

▲

Despite losing over a dozen fighters in the chase, the Revenant continued their pursuit. It was the kind of unquestioning persistence that Nathan expected. He knew that they would not stop until their mission was complete — even if it meant throwing themselves in front of the Phoenix's cannons. Nathan's attention was drawn to what he assumed was the squadron leader. Not only was the fighter made from a different kind of metal, but it also moved more erratically —unlike its counterparts who stuck to a standard flight path. The squad leader pushed ahead until it was within firing range. It fired several times, but the Phoenix's shields managed to deflect most of its weapons fire.

"Nathan, take him out!" Harrt roared over the communicator.

Nathan tried to shut out the 'wealthers yells; choosing to concentrate on targetting the hostile. The fighter closed in, continuing to shoot. Nathan adjusted his aim, accounting for the ship's speed and trajectory and fired. The two blue bolts flew through space and connected with their target. Gunfire jumped from the Phoenix in steady succession until the Revenant fighter blew to pieces. Leaf-like shards of glittering metal flew in every direction as the vessel exploded.

Nathan began to breathe a sigh of relief, but was interrupted;

"We've got more incoming!" Vol yelled over comms.

He turned the gunnery chamber to the starboard quarter, and his heart sank. In addition to countless Revenant warships, Nathan was able to spot another wave of incoming fighters.

"Persistent bastards," Nathan punched the cannon controls.

▲

Vol wiped the sweat from her brow as she plotted a risky flight path. After the Phoenix completed its run over the Revenant Flagship, Harrt pulled the joystick. He followed the flight path and sent the ship spiralling toward the underbelly of another warship. It was a manoeuvre Vol had used a dozen times before but in far smaller ships. The plan was to throw the pursuing fighters off of their trail and force them to reroute to catch-up. It was a smart move, but it wasn't enough to throw the Revenant off course for long. When Vol checked the nav terminal, she found that an additional four squadrons had been deployed.

"They're hitting us from all sides," Vol turned to Harrt. "We need to punch a hole in that wall of fighters."

Vol expected Harrt to call out to Koble and Nathan in the gunnery chambers, but he didn't. Instead, the Lieutenant turned to Astrilla, who up until this point had remained in a meditative state.

"Astrilla, if you're gonna do something, now's the time!"

Astrilla didn't respond to his call.

"Damn," Harrt shook his head.

The Revenant fighters closed in from all sides. Just as Vol predicted, they were trying to box-in the Phoenix. The nav-control flashed and alarmed, but Vol ignored it. She didn't need the ship's systems to tell her that they were in an impossible situation.

Suddenly, Vol felt the Evoker looming behind her chair. Astrilla leaned over and placed a hand against the window. When Vol looked at Astrilla, she was shocked to see that the Evoker's eyes were glowing white. Astrilla pressed her palm flat against the window, and suddenly, Vol felt a surge of energy radiate from the Evoker. Astrilla screamed in agony over Vol's shoulder. The sound was incredibly unsettling: like an injured animal in the wild moments before death.

A dozen Revenant fighters erupted into white explosions as Astrilla screamed.

"What the hell is she doing?" Vol tried to yell over Astrilla's cries, but it was pointless.

Harrt seemed less unsettled by the Evoker's howls. He pushed the Phoenix through the new path that the Evoker had carved out for them. After several seconds Astrilla's screaming subsided and she collapsed to the floor. When the Phoenix cleared the wall of white fire, Vol turned to Harrt;

"What in the hell did she just do?"

The 'wealther didn't respond right away. Instead he flipped a couple of switches and tapped something into one of the screens.

"She just made us an escape route," Harrt said.

The 'wealther was right: the path for FTL was clear, so Vol punched in a jump route. Once the Phoenix was prepped, the engines rumbled, and the pressure behind them grew.

"Hold onto something!." Harrt yelled over the communicator. "This is gonna get bumpy".

He pulled a lever beside him and engaged the FTL drive.

Vol leaned back in her chair as the heightened gravity pressed against her chest. She watched as the stars around them disappeared into the blue flashes of the FTL slipstream. With the knowledge that the Revenant couldn't follow, Vol allowed herself to breathe. There was a moment of absolute calm as Vol and Harrt stared out at the slipstream.

"You're one hell of a pilot," Vol said.

Harrt turned to her and smiled: his expression a mix of relief and euphoria.

"A pilot is nothing without a decent co-pilot".

CHAPTER NINETEEN

Take comfort in the knowledge that through death, the sinful shall be reawakened as Revenant: reborn to serve a higher purpose. I am death; I am wrath; I am Seig; I am Revenant.

The bridge crew of the Revenant warship, Acan, was silent. Seig could almost taste the shame of defeat in the room as he watched the Titan-class frigate jump to FTL

Astrilla had been aboard that ship. Seig knew it.

Somehow it had outrun the full force of the Revenant's eighth fleet; destroyed an inordinate amount of fighters and crippled the flagship's missile array. There was no word to describe the sense of defeat that loomed over the Revenant king.

Such failure was unacceptable.

Seig looked out on the stars for several seconds, using it as a moment to absorb the fear among the crew. He could hear Admiral Xax grinding his teeth from across the room. One of the free-thinking-converts began to cry.

Finally, Seig moved from the window, passed the terrified crew and stopped at the Admiral.

"My lord..." Xax stuttered.

Seig could hear the human's heart rate increase.

"Your highness," Xax shuffled back. "I'm sorry my lord, I—"

In a single motion, Seig pulled his sword from its sheath and forced it through the Admiral's heart. The expression of horror on Xax's face was primordial; like the human brain was still fighting to survive even though it was aware that it was dying. It was an expression Seig had seen thousands of times. Blood poured through Xax's uniform and started to pool on the floor between them.

"Our lack of failure is what separates us from them," Seig hissed. "Do not fear death, my old friend. Embrace the dark and be reborn".

Seig pulled his sword from the Admiral's chest and stepped aside, avoiding a spray of blood from Xax's torso. The Admiral crumbled to the floor, dying in a pool of his own blood.

"Die now with the knowledge that soon you shall be cleansed of this failure," Seig declared.

He watched as Admiral Ujun Xax, a man who'd served him for fifty years, died in a bloodied heap on the floor. There was no such thing as honour in death —Seig didn't believe in such sentiments. Xax had failed him, and the price was death, followed by mutation.

Such defeat should have been met with a considerably slower and far more painful demise, but Seig recognised the Admiral's service to the cause. So, he granted Xax a far quicker death than he deserved.

Seig looked to Xax's first officer;

"Order the fleet to lay waste to that planet," Seig pointed at Yenex. "Ensure that the dead are converted. When it is done set a course for the Messorem and the rest of the fleet".

The first officer's reply was swift;

"Yes, your grace".

King Seig waited on the bridge for a few more minutes, watching as the fleet orbiting Yenex fired at the planet. Something was comforting about the chaos. Seig found it almost peaceful, knowing that soon he would welcome the converts from Yenex.

Of course, his peace of mind was fleeting. Astrilla was the key to unlocking the Messorem, and without her, the cycle of war would continue as it had since the dawn of time. Seig knew the moment he'd laid eyes on the Titan-class ship that she was aboard —he knew it. Seig swore that nothing would stop him from capturing her. He walked back to his royal hall in defeat, recalling the words that the Great Void had bestowed upon him as a boy;

The universe shall deliver you the hand of the catalyst, and with it, you shall turn the tides of war. You will forge a new order—one free of sin and chaos.

▲

Astrilla stood in a sandy desert, with nothing around her for as far as the eye could see. On some conscious level, she was aware that it was a dream, but she didn't force herself to wake. Instead, she embraced what was going on around her.

Most of the time, her dreams were pleasant, but there would be the occasions where her mind would conjure up disturbing images. The Evoker Elders called it a precognitive ability: that somehow the universe was showing her the path that lay ahead.

Astrilla was not sure if she believed it or not.

Unlike her usual dreams, this was different. Somehow it felt more real. The coarse sand between her toes was warm underfoot. A cool breeze from the east caressed her neck and created goosebumps on her skin.

How is this happening? The conscious part of her brain asked.

Like the sand, the sun and the breeze, Astrilla sensed something else around her: a presence. Whatever it was, it didn't care to show itself. Instead, the spectre remained in the background, watching her from a distance.

"You know what you are," it said.

The voice was neither hostile nor friendly, it simply was.

"I do," Astrilla replied. "What does it mean?"

"That you are both predator and prey to the Revenant," It reached out to her as it spoke. "You have the power of a million generations within you. That power can be leveraged to wipe out everything".

It felt hopeless, and the dream started to collapse around her. The sky turned a dark grey, and the sand around her began to spin in a whirlwind.

"So what do I do?" She asked.

The spectre was silent, and the dream ended.

When she awoke, Astrilla found that she was laying on a long couch in the Phoenix's living area. Someone had covered her in a patchwork blanket and left her a bottle of water. As she sat up, Astrilla felt a faint drag against the ships simulated-gravity. It was likely caused by an unconfigured system which should have been compensating for the FTL drive.

It took Astrilla a few seconds to climb off of the couch, and take a good look at the Phoenix's living area. It was a very unusual interior, at least, compared to the Commonwealth Ships she'd travelled on in the past. The decor was a combination of industrial and natural materials. Somehow, despite the mix of dark woods and metals, the Phoenix felt oddly comfortable. The seating area was a mix of soft armchairs and couches surrounding a mock-fireplace, set against the forward wall. Astrilla craned her neck to the back of the room, where its previous owner had begun constructing a bar.

"Rise and shine," a voice said from across the room.

Astrilla's eyes were drawn to Nathan on the other side of the bar. The curly-haired Earther was rooting through a cabinet when she spotted him.

"How are you feeling?" he asked. "Heard you passed out?"

Astrilla stood up and stretched her arms.

"I'll be fine," she answered. "My kind aren't supposed to summon that much power at once. It can be quite dangerous".

The Earther walked over to her with a bottle of liquor in his hand and unscrewed the cap. He offered her a drink, but she declined.

"No, thank you. Evokers don't partake. It numbs the senses".

Nathan shrugged and drank straight from the bottle;

"Isn't that the reason to drink?"

The Earther began a slow walk toward the cockpit, but he stopped and turned back. He sighed and started talking slowly as if the words were somehow heavy in his mouth;

"Back on the Vertex, I didn't know you were the target". Nathan stepped a few inches toward her. "I don't do kidnapping or murders. The guy I was working for told me that it... *you* were cargo".

Was that an attempt to apologise? Astrilla wondered.

Nathan took another swig from the bottle then reached into his breast pocket. He handed Astrilla the silver brooch that had been in her family for generations. Astrilla couldn't deny that it felt strange to be reunited with the family heirloom. She'd been all but certain that it had been lost in the chaos escaping the Vertex. And yet the small silver trinket had returned to her: Astrilla wanted to believe that it meant something. *Maybe it did?*

"I found this where your pod crashed," Nathan said. "Something tells me it belongs to you".

"I didn't think I'd see this again," she said tentatively. "Thank you".

Nathan's dark eyes softened for all but a second.

"I don't work for the Revenant," he said with a hard voice. "Never have, never will".

For a moment, she could see his regret. It was in the angle of his jaw and the way his dark eyes cut to the right, avoiding hers.

"Who was your employer?" Astrilla asked.

Nathan seemed to consider his answer for several seconds.

"His name is Guttasnype. He's just a low-level wannabe mobster on Jarrare". Nathan drank from the bottle again. "I doubt he even knew you were the cargo. Probably took a contract through a third party".

There was a moment of awkward silence between them. Astrilla wanted to push him for more answers, but she didn't. Suddenly a lot about the Earther became clear to her. The scruffy vagabond was alone, or at least had been for some time. Perhaps he'd been desperate for money and took the job because he didn't have any other option. Regardless, none of it mattered now. Despite what happened on the Vertex, Astrilla knew that Nathan meant her no harm. After all, he, along with the others, had risked life and limb to prevent the Revenant from taking her. More importantly, they'd undertaken that risk without knowing why she was so important.

Aside from the Evoker Elders and the small crew aboard the Phoenix, Astrilla couldn't trust anyone. The Revenant needed her alive, and wouldn't stop until they had her. In addition, someone inside the Commonwealth wanted her dead: the marines on the escape pod had proven that.

When she peered back at Nathan, she didn't see the criminal who'd tried to capture her. Instead, she saw one of the very few allies she had left, and he didn't even know why he'd saved her. As Nathan went to take another sip of alcohol from the bottle, Astrilla snatched it off of him:

"Gather the crew. I think it's time we all had a talk," she said.

Before Nathan could answer, there was the sound of angry yelling, coming from the aft quarter.

"Was that Venin?" Nathan said.

▲

Vol slammed a closed fist into Viktor Venin's head. The rotund human fell from his chair and choked on the blood now oozing from his broken nose.

After escaping the blockade, there was only one thing on Vol's mind, and that was Venin. She left the ship in the capable hands of Harrt and made her way to the rear of the Phoenix —being sure that she wasn't followed. When she entered Venin's makeshift cell, all of the hatred and rage that she had held onto boiled over.

Normally, the act of striking a bound and wounded captive would have been wrong in Vol's eyes, but striking Venin had been too easy. Vol had hit him more times then she could count until finally, he'd fallen from his chair in a heap.

Vol watched as the man who'd taken everything from her, tried to lift himself off the floor. It was like watching an infant take its first steps, but Venin wasn't a child, he was a killer.

"You know who I am, don't you?" Vol yelled, before booting him in the gut.

Venin writhed on the floor in agony for a few seconds, and Vol kicked him again; this time with enough force to send Venin onto his back.

"Why did you kill my husband and my father?" Vol demanded. She pulled her pistol and placed it against Venin's head. "Tell me! Tell me why! Why did you do it?"

Vol saw the primal sense of panic set in on Venin's face. His eyes became wide, and he began to whimper.

"They were a liability," Venin blurted out. "They knew too much!"

"About what?"

Vol raised her pistol in the air, ready to strike Venin with it, but something stopped her. She became aware that a gun was being pointed at her from the other side of the room. When she looked up, she found that Nathan had his weapon trained on her. The Evoker, Astrilla, was with him but didn't appear to react.

"What the hell do you think you're doing?" Vol said. "This was part of the deal. *I'm the one who gets to kill him*".

"Put it down," Nathan ordered. "I need that sack of shit alive so that he can answer my questions".

"You have no idea what he did to me. What he took from me!" Vol replied, pressing her gun back against Venin's head.

Nathan seemed to line up his shot in reaction but didn't open fire. Vol wondered if the Earther had the balls to shoot her. She didn't want a fight, but Venin was the only loose end left to deal with, and Nathan was trying to stop her.

Vol was surprised when Astrilla, placed her hand on the barrel of Nathan's gun, prompting him to lower the weapon. The Earther seemed to obey, but Vol knew his kind: the type to shoot first and ask questions later. Nathan would be quick to react if things went sideways. Astrilla stepped forward, placing herself between Nathan and Vol's line of fire. It was a strange move —almost crazy.

"Vol, isn't it?" Astrilla said calmly. "I understand that *this man* has wronged you, but if you kill him now, we lose our chance to know what he discussed with the Revenant".

"So what?" Vol said, pressing the barrel of her gun against Venin's skull. "He probably doesn't know anything".

"Maybe, maybe not," Astrilla said. "But we all have questions for him. If you kill him, those secrets die with him".

Maybe it was Astrilla's soft and soothing voice, that made Vol consider what she was doing. The Evoker had a point, but Vol had waited for this moment for a very long time. She wanted to pull the trigger, more than anything in the universe, but something inside her told her not to do it.

"Let us question him," Astrilla said. "Please".

"Yeah," Nathan added. "Then if you want him dead, be my guest. I'll even hand you the gun myself".

For a moment, Astrilla frowned at Nathan's comment, but her facial expression changed when she looked back at Vol.

"Or we can throw him in a Commonwealth cell," Astrilla said. "Just put the gun down, and we can talk".

Vol reluctantly holstered her gun. There was no point in turning this into a bloodbath —not yet at least. Letting Venin go to the grave with so many secrets seemed counterproductive. If Venin was going to die, he would only do so after he'd spilled his guts.

"Fine," Vol shrugged. "Let's go *talk*".

She stepped over Venin and booted him one more time for good measure. It felt good.

CHAPTER TWENTY

Nathan waited in the living area of the Phoenix, still nursing the bottle of Carumian rum from earlier. While Astrilla gathered the crew, Nathan glanced at Vol, who was sitting directly opposite. The Uvan had spent most of the time scowling at him. It was clear that she was pissed with him, but Nathan didn't feel bad in the slightest. Venin still had a lot of questions to answer, and Nathan wasn't going to allow Vol to kill him yet.

He took another swig of the rum, savouring the slightly sweet drink as he peered back at the Uvan.

"What?" Nathan finally said, choosing to adopt a slightly aggressive tone of voice.

Vol chewed the inside of her cheek and her brow lowered.

"You pointed a gun at me," she answered.

"I've pointed guns at lots of people," Nathan shrugged. "I couldn't let you kill him".

"You think I care about your family issues?" Vol snapped. "That man murdered the only people I cared about, and for what? A Titan-class ship?"

Nathan snapped back in his seat, outraged that the Uvan had read his mind.

"You read my fucking mind?"

Vol narrowed her eyes:

"It's not something I can just turn on, dumbass!" She replied. "It doesn't matter anyway! You pointed a gun at me, even though you didn't have the balls to shoot me".

Nathan placed his bottle on the coffee table between them and took a breath. There was no point in arguing with her. If Vol could read his mind, she was already one step ahead in the verbal sparring.

"I need to find out what Venin knows," Nathan said. "For over a decade, I was alone with nobody to look out for me —just like you."

Vol's scowl softened slightly.

"Venin might know what happened to my uncle," Nathan continued. "Killing him without airing all of his secrets is granting him an easy death. Is that really what you what?"

Vol crossed one leg over the other and sighed heavily.

"Fine, get your answers," she nodded. "I'll kill him after".

▲

Five minutes later, Astrilla, Harrt and Koble joined them in the living area. Nathan noticed that Astrilla seemed oddly tense. It was the anxiousness, he'd seen in her, back on the Vertex. Once they were all seated, Astrilla clasped her hands together tightly and laid them on her knees. After a moment of silence, Astrilla cleared her throat.

"I wanted to thank you all," she started. "You may not believe me when I say this, but you saved a lot of people by doing what you did".

Nathan and Koble exchanged a look, as Astrilla paused. It was a rather odd thing to say, but Nathan knew the Evokers were superstitious. Perhaps sweeping, grandiose statements were the norm in her culture.

"I owe you all a debt of gratitude I can never repay," Astrilla continued.

"Why do I sense the word, *but*, is about to come outta your mouth," Koble mused with a smirk. The Sphinax snatched Nathan's bottle of rum and took a large mouthful.

"*But*," Astrilla exhaled. "You four and the Evoker Elders are the only people I can trust in the whole galaxy. Someone in the Commonwealth tried to kill me. The Revenant will never stop hunting me. I have nobody else to turn to but you".

Nathan took his rum from Koble and wiped the bottle's rim with his shirt.

"So, what is it that makes you so important?" he asked.

Nathan sensed that Harrt was about to say something about *classified information*, so he interrupted the 'wealther before he spoke up.

"I know… it's a military secret," Nathan said, looking at Harrt. "Astrilla just told us that we are the only people she can trust. I think it's her choice to tell us".

Harrt pressed his lips together tightly in quiet consideration. Finally, after a few seconds, the 'wealther nodded in agreement. Everyone turned their attention back to Astrilla, who shuffled in her seat nervously.

"What do you know about the Enkaye?" she said, looking at the crew.

The group exchanged a few questioning looks with one another before Harrt answered:

"Commonwealth history is pretty clear," the 'wealther said. "The Enkaye were the galaxies' foremost dominant species before they went extinct. They laid the path for all of us, but nobody knows what happened to them. The Evokers have a slightly different view on the subject through".

"Back in the day, my old crew stumbled upon Enkaye ruins," Koble said. "Rumours say the 'lil grey bastards left behind a lot of dormant tech".

"Was that on the Loyalty?" Nathan's voice jumped up a pitch in surprise.

"Yeah, you were probably too young to remember," Koble nodded. "Jack nearly blew the damn thing up in an accident. Its a really funny story actually—"

Astrilla cleared her throat, interrupting the Sphinax mid-sentence.

"The Evokers believe that our power comes from exposure to Enkaye technology as a foetus," Astrilla said. "The teachings say that the Enkaye intended for people like me to become Evokers: defenders of the balance and warriors against evil".

"No offence, but that sounds like bullshit," Vol said. "For three-thousand years, my people worshipped the Enkaye as gods. They prayed to their monuments and pyramids for countless generations. They waged wars believing that some little grey man was going to deliver them to salvation."

Astrilla nodded, and she looked at Vol sympathetically.

"It was only until the Commonwealth came along, that my people became enlightened," Vol continued. "Sure, the Enkaye were technologically advanced, but they weren't gods".

From what Nathan understood of Uvan history, most of what Vol had said was historically accurate.

"Everyone is entitled to their opinion," Astrilla said. "But we can all agree that the Enkaye helped to develop modern civilisations".

There was a short silence, but nobody disagreed. Nathan didn't really know what to say. He was the odd one out in the conversation. All the others were born and raised on planets —or into cultures— where the Enkaye were a historical cornerstone. The same couldn't be said of Earth. Sure, there were theories that the Enkaye had visited Earth several millennia ago, but there was no proof. Some of the survivors on Paradisium compared the pyramids of Egypt to the Enkaye temples, stating that they were of similar design. The problem was that it was all based on assumption, and with Earth gone, nobody could verify the theories.

"A few months ago, I learnt that I am not like the other Evokers," Astrilla said, the words sounding heavy as she spoke. "My powers are not the result of exposure to Enkaye technology".

Nathan turned to Harrt. The 'wealther shared an equally confused expression.

"So, what are you saying?" Harrt asked.

Astrilla's jaw tensed hard enough to break a tooth, and she took a deep breath.

"I am Enkaye," she answered. "At least, I am part Enkaye".

There was a stark silence in the Phoenix's living area which lasted far longer then it should have. Nathan struggled for a moment to get his head around her statement. The Enkaye were extinct. They hadn't existed for over a few thousand years. If Astrilla was what she said she was the implications were ginormous.

Finally, the silence was broken by Vol.

"Bullshit," the Uvan said. "How is that even possible?"

"I don't know," Astrilla shook her head. "When I'm around their technology, it works".

"So, you've got a parent that was an Enkaye?" Nathan said.

Astrilla didn't answered the question.

Koble had been oddly quiet. The Sphinax had sat in his chair, tugging at one of his whiskers for the last few moments. Finally, he climbed to his feet and asked the question that nobody else had;

"Why do the Revenant want you?"

Astrilla slumped back in her chair and placed a hand on her forehead. Nathan sensed the same anxiety coming from her as before.

The Evoker took a deep breath.

"Six months ago, King Seig's son, Prince Baylum, unearthed an Enkaye weapon in the unknown regions". Astrilla curled her lips.

"What kind of weapon?" Harrt sat up straight. "Where did this intel come from?"

Astrilla didn't answer immediately, but the look on her face told Nathan everything he needed to know —it was the bad kind of weapon.

"Dines was the one who gathered the intel," Astrilla said, looking at Harrt. "He had an informant".

The 'wealther nodded at her statement, suggesting to Nathan that whoever *Dines* was, he or she was a reputable source of information.

"The device is called the Messorem," Astrilla continued. "It is an Enkaye warship, capable of destroying entire planets in the blink of an eye".

"And the Revenant need you to be some kind of battery to power this thing?" Vol said. The Uvan leaned forward in her chair in anticipation of Astrilla's answer. The scepticism was gone from Vol's voice.

When Astrilla nodded, Nathan felt the hairs on his arms stand upright. He'd seen first hand what the Revenant were capable of doing with their own warships. He could only imagine what they could do with working Enkaye technology. The thought of King Seig controlling a device made by a species that many believed to be gods, made Nathan's mouth dry.

"Commonwealth High Command knew about this?" Harrt asked. "Rooke knew about this?"

When Astrilla answered with a nod, Harrt leaned back in his chair. It was as though the gravity of the situation had finally hit him.

For several minutes there was silence. Nathan continued to drink from the bottle of rum and watched the rest of the group. Astrilla remained seated, while Harrt paced back and forth. As for Vol and Koble, the pair moved to the half-constructed bar and poured themselves a drink. Eventually, Nathan felt as though the lack of conversation had dragged for too long. Impatiently, he climbed to his feet;

"So," he said, drawing the word out to two syllables. "We need to decide what to do now".

Nathan looked at each of them, and Harrt was the only one to offer up a swift response:

"My orders were clear," Harrt said, nodding in Astrilla's direction. "Get her to the Capital Worlds".

Astrilla frowned at the suggestion and shook her head.

"The Capital Worlds is the last place I want to go," she argued. "Your people tried to kill me. It isn't safe for me there".

Astrilla was right. Going to the Capital Worlds would be signing her death warrant.

"Okay," Harrt sighed. "Then where do we go?"

Koble and Vol didn't offer up an answer. Neither did Nathan. Everywhere he'd been over the last few years was in the Outer Worlds. With the number of bandits, freelancers and general scumbags, he may as well hand Astrilla straight to the Revenant. He hadn't had a safe haven since the Loyalty, and even then it had been questionable at best.

"The Evoker Enclave on Pelos Three," Astrilla finally said. "We should be safe there".

▲

After some time, the group dispersed from the living area. Harrt and Vol headed to the cockpit to divert the ship to Pelos Three, while Koble sat at the bar in quiet contemplation. Nathan wanted to check on Astrilla, but she rushed to one of the cabins to meditate.

He decided instead that it was time to get his answers from Venin, so he returned to the cell. As he was about to open the door to the make-shift brig, Nathan's communicator chimed. He pulled the device from his pocket, seeing that Vol was requesting a channel. For a moment he considered ignoring the call but decided it wasn't worth offending the Uvan anymore than he already had.

Nathan answered the call; "What's up?"

"You need to come to the cockpit," Vol replied.

"Now?"

"Now," she insisted. "You *need* to see this".

Nathan huffed and deactivated the communicator. Getting answers from Venin would have to wait a little longer. He made his way toward the cockpit, noticing that Koble was no longer at the bar as he passed through the living area.

In the cockpit, the entire crew —including Astrilla— was gathered around the holotable, where a projection floated a few inches above. Nathan couldn't quite make it out at first, but when he got closer, he wondered if his eyes were deceiving him.

They were not.

The face of his uncle Jack stared back at him for several seconds. The way the holographic visage gazed at him was unsettling —almost life-like. It looked at him for several seconds before speaking;

"Identity confirmed: Nathan William Carter". The projection stopped, and its hardened facial expression became relaxed. "This is a message for Nathan Carter".

CHAPTER TWENTY-ONE

The old footage of Jack Stephens sent a shiver down Nathan's spine. It felt unsettling to see his uncle after such a long time, even if it was just a recording. Jack was leaning against a wall with a pistol drawn. He'd been shot in the shoulder and appeared bewildered.

Nathan, if you are watching this message, then you are standing aboard the Phoenix Titan, and I guess…I guess I'm dead. What I am about to tell you is going to be difficult to hear…

Nathan peered at Koble, and the Sphinax offered an equally puzzled expression. It was strange watching footage of someone who'd been gone for so long. Just hearing Jack's voice, made Nathan's arm hair stand up.

I'm recording this message on Mirotose Station, two hours after the Loyalty was ambushed. The people who attacked us were… let's just say it was the sins of my past catching up with me.

The list of people that Jack Stephens had pissed off was almost as long as the Phoenix herself. Nathan didn't understand why his uncle hadn't been more specific about his attackers.

I managed to get Koble and Sasha aboard a shuttle —I can only hope they are with you now. If either of you is watching this, I thank you for your service to the Loyalty.

Nathan felt Koble place a paw on his shoulder for comfort. He was grateful that at least half of Jack's statement was right.

I went back for Merri, I found her and I managed to get her aboard a shuttle. Problem is... this station is swarming with assholes who will stop at nothing.

Jack checked his gun for ammo and proceeded to grab a rifle from behind his recorder.

Nathan, the Phoenix Titan, is yours. Long story short, a man on Paradisium owed me a favour. Take care of her.

Nathan couldn't help but wonder who owed Jack a favour on Paradisium. His uncle had actively avoided the refugee world, so to think that he had a friend on the planet seemed like an alien concept.

The sound of banging and crashing came through the recording, and Jack disappeared from view. A couple of gunshots rang out, and then Jack's face came back into view.

Listen up... the path ahead is gonna be fuckin' hard, but I know you can do this.

Jack bore the same expression he always had going into a mission. It was severe and hardened, like a soldier about to go to war. Jack disappeared again and opened fire on someone off-camera. Gunfire soared past the recording device, but Jack continued to speak into it;

My Father used to close his lectures with a quote: greatness lies not in being strong, but in the right use of strength. Nate, remember those words. Don't end up like me. I spent so long pretending to be a far better man than I really am. Be somebody that our family would be proud of: be someone you can be proud of.

The gunfire in the recording continued, and the hologram twisted in and out of static. Jack returned fire from behind his cover. The footage became shaky, and the sound muffled. Then there was nothing. The hologram deactivated, leaving the Phoenix's cockpit in silence.

Nathan took a deep breath.

For the first time in ten years, Nathan finally knew what had happened to Jack at Mirotose Station. Regardless of the message's ambiguity, Nathan knew that Jack was gone. It was the closest thing to closure he'd ever experienced, and it felt strange. Part of him was angry and vengeful —desperate to know who Jack's killers were. Unfortunately, his uncle had been deliberately vague: likely knowing that back then, Nathan and the crew would rush to avenge him.

It was clear that Jack didn't want him to know who had sabotaged them all those years ago. To Nathan, that meant that whoever his uncle's killers were, they were incredibly dangerous.

There was another part of Nathan which felt a tremendous sense of relief. Up until this point, he'd never had any form of closure. The idea that Jack might still be out there had haunted him for over a decade. To know that his uncle was gone made Nathan feel mournful, but at the same time, there was a sense of acceptance which he allowed to wash over him. Nathan chose to take comfort in the fact that even moments before death, Jack had passed one final lesson to him.

Be someone that our family would be proud of: the words burnt into Nathan's skull.

The timing of Jack's message and the reveal of Astrilla's heritage minutes earlier was unsettling. Maybe it was fate or just dumb luck. Either way, Nathan chose to take it as a sign.

He suddenly became aware that the rest of the group were staring at him. It made Nathan feel awkward and vulnerable, which wasn't something he was used to. Rather than acknowledge the feelings, he gestured to the star map that had loaded in place of Jack's hologram.

"How many hours to Pelos Three?" Nathan asked.

He could almost feel the group clumsily exchange conversation through awkward stares. Everyone wanted to say something, but nobody knew what. Finally, Vol spoke up and answered the question.

"About ten hours". Her voice was noticeably softer than it had been earlier.

"Good," Nathan attempted his best stoic tone.

He left the cockpit.

Nathan didn't want anyone to ask how he was feeling,

or if there was anything they could do for him. He simply wanted to be out of the situation. Being visibly vulnerable around others was not something Nathan was accustomed to. For years he'd told himself that he had to be brave; *that he couldn't let anyone see him bleed.* That had been one of Jack's many lessons, and Nathan had lived by it for over twenty years. Part of him wanted nothing more than to break down in a corner, but that wasn't who he was. Instead, Nathan headed to the brig. It was time for Viktor Venin to answer his questions.

▲

Viktor Venin was still bound to the table. He wore the expression of a man who was not nervous under his current circumstances. It was as though Nathan was more of an inconvenience than his interrogator.

Nathan set down an empty glass and poured Venin a shot of rum. It was his hope that treating the man with some dignity may loosen his tongue, but Nathan suspected that the discussion would end in blood.

"You and I need to have a conversation," Nathan said, pushing the drink across the table.

Venin stared at him for an uncomfortable amount of time.

"Do you have any idea who I am, boy?" Venin snarled. "When my people hear about this, they'll—"

"We're not on Yenex anymore," Nathan talked over Venin. "Your people will already be carving up what's left of your empire. So the best thing for you is to talk".

Venin remained unmoved.

"A man called Jack Stephens once owned this ship," Nathan said. "Why is it of interest to you?"

Venin's eyes narrowed.

"I don't know anyone by that name," he said. "I stole this ship from Jareth Corps".

"Why?"

"Because two decades ago, I invested billions into David Jareth's little empire. I made Jareth Corps what it is today," Venin answered. "Then that Earther scum refused to pay me what I was owed. So I took this ship and my money. I also had my men destroy his space station as interest."

"So, why did Jareth Corps have this ship?" Nathan took a sip of rum from the bottle.

Venin leaned forward on the table;

"That sounds like a question for David Jareth".

"So that's it? You stole this thing to settle a debt?"

"It's called *business*," Venin nodded unapologetically. "Sometimes it gets dirty".

Nathan didn't allow his resentment to show. Venin's cold-blooded answer reminded Nathan of a few former employers —particularly Guttasnype.

"*Business*?" Nathan said. "Is that what you called it when you killed Vol's husband and father?"

Venin smirked;

"Ah, yes, the engineers. No, that wasn't *business*," Venin shook his head. "More like....*insurance*".

Nathan watched as Viktor Venin's lips went thin and curled upward. It was a callous expression, free of remorse. It was at that moment that Nathan realised that he knew Venin's type all too well. He was the kind of man that placed business and pleasure over everything else, and Nathan had worked for men just like him.

"Why'd you kill them?" Nathan asked.

The look of indifference on Venin's face sent a chill down Nathan's spine.

"My people hired that pair of Uvan idiots to fix a broken intake," Venin replied. "Sadly they wandered too far and saw something they shouldn't have".

"Let me guess," Nathan raised a brow. "They saw some *business*?"

"You could say that," Venin nodded. "I can't have a pair of peasants from the lower levels, spilling my secrets. They wouldn't take the money I offered them. The younger one, well, he didn't respond well when my boys started roughing up the old one".

Nathan climbed to his feet, but Venin didn't appear the slightest bit intimidated. Instead, the mobster continued;

"Funny, isn't it? The moral-codes of lesser men," Venin mused with a smirk. "You don't seem like those two. Correct me if I'm wrong, but, you seem more of the industrious type. You know I can make you a very wealthy man if you make this situation disappear".

Nathan placed his hand on his holstered gun, and the grin on Venin's face disappeared. He wanted nothing more than to shoot the rotund man between the eyes and be done with it, but something stopped him. Maybe it was the part of him that wanted Vol to get her closure, or perhaps he'd just had enough of being around men like Venin.

"We're done here," Nathan growled. "I'm gonna tell Vol what you told me, and if she doesn't kill you, then you'll rot in a Commonwealth cell till the end of time".

Nathan made sure to grab his rum and the glass from the table; refusing to allow Venin another drink or the means to slit his own wrists. He regarded the two-bit mobster with the same indifferent look that Venin had given him earlier. Nathan walked out of the brig, feeling as though he was leaving a part of himself in that cell. It felt good to walk away. Jack was right, it was time to *be someone that the family would be proud of*: it was time to start giving a damn.

▲

Nathan recounted to Vol everything that Venin told him. He could see the sadness on her face change to anger as she processed Venin's reasoning for murdering her loved ones. Nathan had even handed her his bottle of rum as a means to take the edge off. When he'd finished talking, the Uvan was silent for a long time. Finally, after her third mouthful of liquor, Vol said;

"My father and husband, were *insurance* to that man?"

Nathan nodded.

"I know it's not any consolation, but Venin told me that they refused a bribe. That's gotta say something about the kind of men they were".

Vol chugged back another mouthful of rum, spilling some down her chin in the process. She swallowed the booze and wiped away the excess with her forearm.

"They were far better men than him," she coughed. Then after shaking her head, "What a bastard".

"I don't disagree," Nathan replied.

He moved over to the Uvan and drew his gun from his holster. Nathan handed her the weapon and took a step back.

"A deal's a deal," Nathan said. "Kill Venin if it's what you need to do".

Vol nodded and quickly wiped a tear from her eye. She took a few steps towards the brig but stopped mid-stride.

"If you were me, what would you do?" Vol looked over her shoulder.

"If you'd have asked me that a few days ago, I'd have told you to put one between his eyes," Nathan admitted. "Personally, I think Venin should rot in a cell for the rest of his miserable fuckin' life. Rather than make him a martyr, make him an example".

It took Vol a while to process what he'd said. After a while, she moved back and handed Nathan his gun. She smiled through her mournful tears;

"Didn't have you pegged as the life-sparing-kind," she said.

Nathan appreciated that her candour was to cover for her vulnerability: he'd seen Koble do the same thing in the past. Nathan knew that something had changed, but he couldn't admit it; not yet anyway. For years, he'd believed that the only way to survive was *to be just like Jack.* In reality, his uncle Jack had wanted the exact opposite.

Be somebody that our family would be proud of; The final lesson of Jack Stephens was one that Nathan was going to live by.

CHAPTER TWENTY-TWO

Koble couldn't sleep. He'd been lying in his newly claimed bed for several hours staring at the grey ceiling, obsessing over Jack's final message. There was something unsettling about seeing the final moments of his mentor and friend that left Koble's gut in a knot.

It was the same feeling he'd experienced after Mirotose Station — the day Jack and most of the crew were murdered. Unlike Nathan, Koble had been at the centre of the chaos and seen many of his shipmates killed in the struggle. He still remembered holding Sasha in his arms as the husky Russian-Earther had succumbed to his wounds.

There was something that Jack had said in his final recording that stuck in the back of Koble's mind. Jack had helped Merri escape on the shuttle, but she'd never reached the rendezvous point, but then again neither had Nathan or James.

Merri Tautana had been pretty, even by human standards. Koble had never been one for cross-breeding, but he could recognise her kind-hearted nature. Maybe it was the reason why she'd gravitated towards the Loyalty's token junkie: James Stephens.

Koble had never been jealous of James, but he was concerned for Merri. She gave, and James took, it was as simple as that. Koble suspected that James had hit her in one of his drug-fuelled rampages, but he'd never witnessed it first-hand. If Koble had, James would likely be missing an arm or two.

Regardless of the past, it was fair to assume that Merri was either dead or simply didn't want to be found. Koble imagined his old friend living on a tropical planet with a couple of kids and a nice, non-junkie husband. Of course, it was the former that was probably true.

Mirotose Station had been what Nathan or Jack would describe as *a complete cluster-fuck*. Most of the crew died in the attack, and nobody could say who'd carried out the assault. Jack had deliberately left that detail out of his final message, which only served to frustrate Koble.

Rather than obsess over the second-worst day in his life, Koble decided to get up and try and take his mind off of things. He plundered the bar and managed to find a three-hundred year old bottle of Arumiun Kor.

"Shit..." Koble gasped out loud. "Don't mind if I do".

A single swallow of the drink was likely worth more than the Phoenix Titan itself. Carefully, he dusted off the bottle and carried it through to the cockpit. He found Harrt in the pilot's seat of the ship, watching the FTL slipstream pass by.

It was strange thinking that he'd found an ally in a 'wealther. Back in the day, Koble would actively avoid his kind, but Harrt had proven he was different. Koble sat down in the co-pilot's chair and presented the bottle of kor to the 'wealther. Harrt's brows lifted as he read the label.

"Isn't that kinda decadent?" he said.

Koble unscrewed the cap and sniffed the liquor.

"We just survived an escape through a Revenant blockade; learned that we are travelling with the descendant of a bunch of god-like grey dudes and I just saw my old friend die on hologram," Koble waved the bottle. "I think we've earnt ourselves a drink".

Harrt smiled and grabbed an empty mug from his cup-holder. Koble poured them each a cup-full; worth the equivalent of at least three Phoenix Titans. He thanked Koble and took the glass.

"Doesn't it seem kind of messed up that a thimble of this stuff is worth more than my old house?" Harrt said, examining the floral-smelling alcohol.

"The injustices of the galaxy," Koble drawled, taking a swig from his glass. He savoured the taste for several seconds, allowing the mild nodes of Theros Thistle and something smokey burn into his taste buds.

The flavour was underwhelming.

Koble and Harrt sat in companionable silence for several minutes. Harrt checked the ship's consoles between conservative sips of his drink, while Koble watched the slipstream.

"So where are you from?" Koble asked.

Small talk had never been his strong suit, but it was a long journey to Pelos Three, and Koble sensed that Harrt's presence aboard the ship wouldn't end there. He turned to look at the 'wealther, but the Lieutenant didn't meet his gaze. Instead, Harrt looked straight ahead and pressed his lips together in discomfort.

"I came from Maru Seven," Harrt answered.

Koble paused mid-sip and lowered his glass.

The tragedy of Maru Seven was not something that the Commonwealth broadcast to the rest of the galaxy. Koble only knew about it because he'd been running a job in 'wealther space at the time. Maru Seven was one of the Commonwealth's bloodiest losses. Many, including the Earthers on Paradisium, compared the attack to the Fall. Billions died in the slaughter, and most of the population were converted into Revenant soldiers, but that was where the similarities to Earth ended. Maru Seven was deep in 'wealther space and had a military presence in orbit, whereas, at the time of the Fall, Earth was both unprotected and primitive by the rest of the galaxy's standards.

The rumour was that a high ranking Commonwealth official betrayed his own people and provided the Revenant with a tactical edge. Of course, the Commonwealth would never publically admit that one of their own would do such a thing.

Aware that he'd been silent for an uncomfortable amount of time, Koble managed to stutter out the words;

"I'm sorry".

Harrt tilted his head in thanks and took another sip of

his *decadent* drink.

"Were you there?" Koble asked.

Harrt bit back something at the back of his throat and nodded.

"I was on the ground. I've never seen anything quite like it".

"I can only imagine," Koble said. "If you don't mind me asking, how'd you make it off the planet?"

Harrt's jaw tightened.

"That is a story for another day".

For a moment, Koble forgot that he was talking to Harrt. It felt like he was talking to Jack. The 'wealther had the same distant expression in his eyes that Jack would get when he talked about the Fall. It meant that Harrt Oxarri had lost so much at Maru Seven that he'd lost a piece of his soul.

▲

The cabin that Astrilla claimed was unfurnished, but at least it had a shower. In her thirty years of life, she couldn't recall a time where she'd been more desperate for a wash. Even though it had been days since she'd escaped the Vertex, Astrilla still had the blood of a dead 'wealther marine on her forearms.

She stripped off, placing her dirty clothes in a compact-washer and stood under the showerhead. Astrilla closed her eyes, allowing the water to wash over her. She felt everything that had happened to her over the last few days drain away, but something continued to itch in her mind.

Evokers were taught that the universe had carved a destiny for every living being. She wondered *if that were the case, why did she have to be the one to carry such a burden?*

Despite being made up of entirely human flesh and bone, she was somehow part-Enkaye. It was hard to believe that a species so advanced that many referred to them as gods would breed with humans. At the height of the Enkaye Dynasty, mankind would have been barely able to start a fire, let alone understand the complexities of cross-species breeding. Of course, if the Enkaye had started breeding with lesser species back then, there would be millions or even billions just like Astrilla.

None of it made sense.

When she finished showering, Astrilla dried off and threw on an oversized jumpsuit from one of the storage lockers. It was incredibly bulky around the upper torso, and the sleeves went way beyond her wrists, but it was better than her dirty clothes from days earlier.

As she tied her dark hair back, Astrilla felt her stomach growl. It had been days since she'd had a good meal and her body was reminding her of that fact. She stepped out of her cabin and headed to the galley, hoping to find something in one of the cupboards.

She found Nathan sitting at the dining table reading from his datapad. The first thing Astrilla noticed was that the Earther had brewed a pot of tea. The second thing she spotted was that Nathan tied back his dark curly hair. It allowed Astrilla to see his face in a different way. She'd failed to notice the dark shade of brown in his eyes up until that point.

"I see you scrub up well." he said, gesturing with his cup to her bulky flight suit.

It was an idiom that she didn't understand, but Astrilla assumed it was a compliment. Earther slang wasn't widely used in the Commonwealth, despite how eerily similar the 'wealther dialect was to the Earth language, English. It was another stark reminder of just how much the Enkaye had influenced modern cultures across the galaxy.

Nathan offered her a cup of tea, and she accepted. Astrilla sat opposite him and adjusted the collar of her flight suit while Nathan poured her a cup of the purple coloured tea.

"I see you've traded hard liquor for something a bit more light," Astrilla remarked.

"You can only take so much booze," Nathan shrugged.

They sat in silence for what felt like minutes. It was awkward, but at the same time, it wasn't uncomfortable.

Astrilla accepted that she'd somewhat misjudged his character back on the Vertex, but she didn't feel the need to apologise. Nathan had, after all, been an intruder in her quarters, and Astrilla was a high-value target for the Revenant. In reality, the Earther was lucky that she'd only flung him through a wall.

The silence continued, and it started to become very awkward. Astrilla debated asking Nathan about the message his uncle had left but quickly decided against it, as it was evident he wasn't one for sharing feelings. Before she could fathom another subject for small-talk, the Earther broke the silence between them.

"So, I've been thinking," Nathan said. "Assuming that the 'wealthers don't confiscate this ship when we land, I wanna help you".

Astrilla leaned forward in her chair, surprised by his response. It was the first time in months that someone had said something like that to her and actually meant it.

"Why?" she asked. "You don't owe me a thing."

"Ten years ago, I lost what was left of my family. I lost my crew, my friends, everyone I ever cared about," Nathan placed his cup down. "I spent the better part of a decade running jobs for people just like Viktor Venin. I'm done being someone I don't wanna be".

"Was it the recording of your uncle?" Astrilla said.

"No," Nathan shook his head. "I took a job to steal from the Commonwealth, and I bump into you. The ship we are on goes down over Yenex; there I randomly bump into an old friend that I believed died ten years ago. One thing leads to another, and I end up aboard a ship that somehow belonged to my dead uncle".

"Sounds like destiny to me," Astrilla smiled.

"Call it whatever you want," Nathan said, knocking on the table. "All of it has to mean something, right?"

"Perhaps," Astrilla nodded and took a long sip of her tea. As she stared across the table at the Earther, Astrilla couldn't help but wonder what he'd say to her next statement; "When we get to Pelos Three, I'd like for you to meet with the Evoker Elders".

Nathan leaned back in his chair with an expression of curiosity on his face.

"Why?" he asked.

"You faced a Paladin in combat and survived," Astrilla answered. "I just can't escape the feeling that our meeting is more than just happenstance".

CHAPTER TWENTY-THREE

When the Phoenix Titan dropped out of the FTL slipstream, Harrt breathed a sigh of relief. It had been four years since he'd been on Pelos Three, but just seeing the green and blue world filled him with a sense of hope. There were three Commonwealth warships in orbit around the planet ready to shoot anything that disobeyed the rules of access.

While Harrt waited in a small queue of ships to gain planetary-clearance, he rubbed his tired eyes. It had been a tough couple of days, and it was only just starting to hit him.

After a couple of minutes, Vol joined him in the cockpit. The Uvan sat in the co-pilot's seat beside him. Harrt felt as though her mood had lifted somewhat, and he was proven right when she turned to him and said playfully;

"You had a drink!"

For a split second, Harrt wondered if the Uvan had poked around inside his brain, and his suspicions were confirmed seconds later;

"A three-hundred year old bottle of Arumiun kor?" Vol exclaimed. "Isn't that kinda—"

"Decadent?" Harrt interrupted.

Vol pursed her lips together in amusement.

"No," she replied, drawing the word out. "I was gonna say, *celebratory*".

Harrt smiled back at the Uvan then tapped on a control panel to transmit his clearance codes to the warship. It was hard to ignore that Vol appeared far more upbeat than she'd been before.

"You seem to be in a better mood," Harrt said.

"I guess… I got some closure," Vol shrugged, her voice becoming noticeably soft. "It feels like a weight has been lifted off of my shoulders".

I'd love to know how that feels, Harrt thought.

When she smiled at him, Harrt noticed something in her eyes that he'd missed about himself for a long time. It was eight long years since Maru Seven, and he'd never found the closure he desperately craved. For years, he'd dedicated his life to serving the Commonwealth and doing his part in the war. He'd requested leave to go and seek out the justice his life was lacking. Harrt's chance to take extended leave had arisen, but Commander Rooke tried to talk him out of it.

Harrt recalled one of the last conversations he'd had with Harlmaam Rooke aboard the Vertex; *His time will come, Harrt. Don't go throwing away your life in pursuit of retribution.*

Rooke's voice reverberated in his skull. Harrt knew the old man would refuse his leave, believing that he was protecting him. The problem was Rooke would have denied Harrt the chance to finally get his closure.

I will have my justice, Harrt promised himself.

He became aware that Vol could hear his thoughts. He looked through the corner of his eye at the Uvan, and she was staring back at him.

"Don't worry," she placed a hand on top of his. "We've all got our demons; even you 'wealther".

Harrt withdrew his hand;

"Your demon is in a cell. Mine is the Grand-Admiral of the Revenant Fleet".

▲

Pelos Three was a vast green world, with several continents divided by a deep blue ocean. Even from orbit, it was clear that the world was mostly forested. There was the odd scattering of man-made structures in amongst the green patches of land, but compared to Yenex, Pelos Three was a natural paradise.

Having spent years in the outer worlds and some of the corporate systems, Nathan found it to be a welcome sight. It felt almost like a lifetime since he'd seen a world quite like it. As Nathan looked out of the port side window, Astrilla pushed into him to get a look at the landscape.

"It has been far too long," Astrilla said, barely able to stop herself from smiling.

The Evoker Enclave was made from a mix of grey stonework and metal built into the side of the mountain. For someone with little interest in architecture, even Nathan had to stop and stare.

Astrilla told him that the construction of the Enclave had taken place over a three-hundred year period, and it was certainly believable. The building was a feat of both technical and artistic mastery. Nathan saw no sign of the sterile and functional characteristics seen in the Commonwealth. Instead, the Evoker Enclave boasted the appearance of something built so that history would remember its builders.

A more modern dome-shaped structure had been added to the top of the mountain. Nathan assumed it had likely been added a few hundred years ago as a tactical combat station. It almost ruined the appeal of the original building, but with the Revenant threat everywhere you could never be too careful.

Noting a distinct lack of anti-aircraft cannons, Nathan turned to Astrilla and said;

"Are you sure we're gonna be alright here?"

"There is significant power here. Just because you can't see it doesn't mean it's not there". Astrilla answered.

"If it's so safe, why the hell didn't you just stay here?" Nathan asked.

Astrilla's smile disappeared and was replaced by a frown.

"For a time, I did," she said. "The Commonwealth insisted on moving me every couple of weeks. They thought that by constantly changing my location would throw the

Revenant off of my tail".

"Well, that tactic clearly worked well," Nathan remarked.

There was a slight bump as the Phoenix touched down on the landing pad. Although Astrilla didn't acknowledge Nathan's blunt assessment, he could tell she agreed with him. The fact was something had gone horribly wrong aboard the Vertex. Not only had the Commonwealth marines tried to assassinate her, but the Vertex itself was shot out of the slipstream.

Nathan wasn't an engineer, so he didn't understand the physics or dynamics of an FTL drive, but he knew that shooting a ship out of the slipstream was nigh-on-impossible. In theory, the only way you could force a vessel out of FTL was to know the exact timing, trajectory and coordinates of the jump. The only way the Revenant could have that kind of intel, was if a mole in the Commonwealth passed it to them.

Nathan walked down the boarding ramp toward the landing pad. He took a deep breath, allowing the fresh air to fill his lungs. The view from the Evoker Enclave was stunning. Asides from a small town at the foot of the mountain, there was nothing but nature for miles around.

Nathan shifted his focus from the view to the bottom of the landing pad, where an old woman was waiting for him to disembark. She stared at Nathan with a hardened expression for several seconds, but her features softened once she laid eyes on Astrilla. The old woman was human, around seventy years of age, with a head of thick silver hair.

Astrilla pushed past Nathan and rushed down to greet the woman with a tight embrace. Nathan was surprised to see the Evoker let down her guard so quickly. He assumed that the woman was Astrilla's mother or a close relative at least; *why else would she show such affection?*

"When news came in about the Vertex we thought all hope was lost," the old woman said, still clinging to Astrilla. "How did you survive?"

After a few seconds, Astrilla released the woman from the hug:

"I had help".

The Evoker nodded at Nathan and the others who were now making their way down the ramp. Astrilla beckoned Nathan to join her.

"This is Yuta, she is one of the Evoker Elders," Astrilla said. "Yuta, this is Nathan, he's one of the people who saved me on Yenex".

Nathan offered out his hand, but Yuta hesitated to shake it. The Evoker Elder studied him for a few seconds before taking his hand. At first, Nathan assumed that handshakes were simply a custom that the Elder wasn't used to, but he quickly realised that she was trying to assess him.

"You are an Earther," Yuta remarked. "We don't get many of your kind out this far".

Lucky guess, Nathan thought.

Regardless of whether or not Yuta was reading him, it was a comment that Nathan was too used to hearing. So he did what he always did and shrugged it off like it was no big deal. He didn't want his defining characteristic to be the planet of his origin. Earth and most of its population was gone. There was a lucky few that survived the Fall, and most simply lived out a pampered lifestyle on Paradisium —all at the expense of the Commonwealth taxpayer.

Some 'wealthers will view our kind as a drain on the precious resources, Jack had said. *That is why we have to keep our distance.*

After the last few days, Nathan couldn't help but question his uncle's advice from all those years ago. Harrt had shown no hostility to him, and neither had Astrilla. Yuta was no different, and it made Nathan wonder if Jack had been wrong about the 'wealthers.

▲

Introductions with Elder Yuta were brief. The old woman shook hands with Koble and Vol before she got to Harrt. There had been a strange awkwardness to the exchange, which Nathan had noticed immediately.

"Lieutenant Oxarri," Yuta paused for several seconds

before adding "It's an honour to finally meet you".

Harrt replied with a stiff nod of the head and said nothing else. Nathan recognised the 'wealther's gesture as a way to cover for his unease.

After Elder Yuta finished greeting the group, she ventured back into the Evoker compound with Astrilla at her side. Nathan watched as the pair disappeared into the building. He couldn't help but wonder if Astrilla was telling Yuta about what had happened with the Paladin. It was clear that Astrilla believed that their meeting was more than just dumb luck and Nathan worried that he was starting to think it too. There was no doubt in his mind that everything he'd lived through had been a series of random events, but it was hard to doubt Astrilla's theory.

Nathan decided to take a seat at the edge of the landing pad with his feet dangling off the side. He took a moment to reflect as he stared at the tops of the trees.

So much had changed over the last few days. There was a time where Nathan would have found the idea of being at an Evoker Enclave laughable. Even the idea of being so deep in Commonwealth space would have made him turn and run the other way.

Change is the only constant in this life, the voice of his grandfather, Bill, played out.

It was hard to believe that less than a week ago, Nathan had been negotiating terms with Guttasnype on Gararre. Upon reflection, it seemed as though a different man had made a deal with the mobster.

Nathan was still who he'd always been, but something had changed, and it was more than just his commitment to *start giving a shit.* For the first time, Nathan had a purpose, and it was to help Astrilla. He didn't know why he felt so compelled to help the Evoker, but it had to be done.

Nathan suddenly became aware of Vol sitting down beside him on the edge of the landing pad. The Uvan passed him a bottle of kor and gestured to the Phoenix;

"Hell of a ship," she said. "Of course, she's not finished yet, but when all the work is done she'll be incredible".

"Guess I'll need a decent engineer," Nathan took a sip from the bottle. "Are you game? You wanna stay aboard?"

"Why not," Vol shrugged. "Assuming the 'wealthers don't confiscate it for being too decadent".

Nathan offered out his bottle and the pair toasted.

"So as your chief engineer I guess its kinda my duty to provide you with meaningful advice," Vol said.

"What is it?"

"You need to be careful with Astrilla," Vol said.

"Why?"

"I can't read Evokers. They train their minds to be resistant to stuff like that," Vol answered. There was a short pause, and Vol added; "Plus you should *really* be careful with Astrilla".

Nathan sighed and rubbed his face with both hands;

"What's that supposed to mean?"

"*You know* what I mean," Vol lowered her brow.

"You read my mind again?"

"It's more like I overheard a few things," Vol said, nonchalantly. "I hear a lot of thoughts: some good, some bad; but in my experience, the people that you can't read are the ones to worry about".

"So because you can't read her, you're worried?"

"I don't think Astrilla wants to do harm to us or anything, but I think you should exercise a level of caution with her," Vol said. "It's evident that she's been through a lot, and Evokers tend to have a habit of reducing people to ash when they get pissed off".

"I'll keep that in mind," Nathan replied, drinking from the bottle. "So is this the kind of brutal truths I should expect from my engineer going forward?"

Vol turned to him and smiled;

"I prefer the sound, *Chief* Engineer?" she said. "It rolls off the tongue rather nicely."

CHAPTER TWENTY-FOUR

In Harrt's experience, prisoner transfers were often tedious and time-consuming, but it was entirely different in the case of Venin. Three marines and an administrator arrived on schedule and were quick to do away with any formalities. The fact that the whole thing took less than fifteen minutes made Harrt wonder if perhaps Venin was already wanted for crimes against the Commonwealth, but he knew not to ask questions.

Once Venin was escorted away, Harrt made it his priority to finish his report for High Command. Rather than go back to the Phoenix, Harrt found a quiet corner in the grounds of the Enclave. He settled at a bench under a large tree and began writing. He spent a couple of hours typing up a full account of the last few days; making sure to keep his writing straight to the point. He submitted the report using a comms terminal inside the Enclave. After he logged off, the screen returned to its default setting and played a loop of the top headlines from the daily newscast. One of them immediately caught Harrt's eye;

YENEX DESTROYED IN REVENANT ASSAULT.

Harrt had to read the headline three times before it finally sunk in. He tapped the screen and read the article in disbelief. Billions were slaughtered in the attack, and the planet had been reduced to ash. It made Harrt feel sick to his stomach, knowing that he had been stood on Yenex hours, if not minutes, before its downfall.

Harrt rushed back to the Phoenix to tell the others, but by the time he'd made it aboard they'd already heard the news.

"How can they just kill all those people?" Koble shook his head. "It ain't right".

In Harrt's view, the answer to Koble's hypothetical question was simple: the Revenant, at least the non-mutated ones, believed that all life in the universe belonged to them. The Revenant Creed was clear to all its disciples; convert all who stand in our way.

The Commonwealth taught its citizens that the Revenant were evil warmongers, but Harrt learnt after Maru Seven that it was so much more than that. The Revenant didn't see the act of killing and mutating as murder. Instead, they saw it as an act of nobility. That, of course, wasn't to say that the Commonwealth's teachings were wrong: far from it.

The Revenant were evil, and Harrt truly hated them, just like the rest of the 'wealthers, but there was someone else that Harrt despised far more. Admiral Densius Olbori was the man who'd aided the Revenant and betrayed his own at Maru Seven. He had cost Harrt far more than he'd ever care to admit.

Within an hour of sending his report, Harrt received a request from Admiral Wexell for an urgent meeting over hologram, which he accepted without question. Before the meeting, he showered, shaved and combed his hair and put on a clean shirt.

When Wexell's face formed upon the hologram, Harrt wasn't quite sure what to say. The dark-skinned Uvan stared at him for a few seconds, then cleared his throat.

"Lieutenant Oxarri," Wexell said. "You must be one of the luckiest men in the Commonwealth."

Harrt found he was tapping his fingers on the holo-table and forced himself to stop. Wexell's eyes darted to Harrt's hand and back up. The Admiral's hard facial expression softened as he said;

"You've done the Commonwealth proud".

"Thank you, sir, but I can't take responsibility for getting off of Yenex," Harrt replied. "It was a team effort".

"I've read the report," Wexell replied with a wave of the hand. "As has Grand Master Inon Waife".

It wasn't the first time that the most senior politician in the Commonwealth had read one of Harrt's mission reports, but it still sent a shiver down his spine. Inon Waife was a great and powerful leader, committed to winning the war. He'd faced re-election on five separate occasions and won by a landslide every single time.

"The Grand Master is very impressed," Wexell continued. "There will be a medal waiting for you when you get back to the Capital Worlds".

"Thank you, sir," Harrt nodded.

He wondered why Wexell hadn't acknowledged Commander Rooke's death or the destruction of the Vertex. It seemed odd that Wexell hadn't questioned him on the subject at all.

"We're sending Agent Dines to debrief you at Pelos Three," Wexell said. "After that take a few days to rest up".

"Understood," Harrt nodded. Sensing that Wexell was about to end the call, Harrt spoke up; "Sir, about the recommendation I submitted?"

Wexell paused, and he rooted through Harrt's report.

"You wish for the Earther to keep the ship?" Wexell replied. The Admiral seemed to skim the exaggerated report that Harrt had submitted and then asked; "According to your report, the Phoenix Titan is practically a piece of scrap metal".

"That's correct sir," Harrt lied. "It'll take a lot a hell of a lot of resources to fix the damn thing up".

He wondered for a moment if Wexell could see straight through the lie. The dark-skinned Uvan stared at him for an uncomfortable amount of time, and after a few seconds Harrt felt the need to say;

"I couldn't have done this without the Earther, sir. If it wasn't for him, Astrilla would be in the hands of the Revenant".

Wexell shrugged his shoulders;

"Be sure to thank the Earther for his services to the Commonwealth".

"Thank you, sir," Harrt nodded.

▲

Nathan couldn't deny that the sunset hours on Pelos Three were beautiful. He couldn't recall a time he'd felt more at peace as he looked out at the rolling landscape of forests, mountains and lakes. He'd spent the majority of the day cataloguing all the components that were missing from the Phoenix Titan. The list was far more significant than he'd anticipated, but Astrilla had assured him that the Evoker Elders would take care of it.

After a long day, he returned to the landing pad with Koble, and they'd watched the sunset, while sharing a bottle of Maruvian kor.

"So," Koble said, drawing the word out to two syllables. "You wanna talk about the message that Jack left us?"

"Not especially," Nathan replied. "I'm guessing you do?"

Koble nodded and stared up at the sky.

"I can't believe he's gone. I mean I kinda thought he was, but I guess that hologram was a confirmation".

Nathan pushed the bottle toward Koble, but the chunky Sphinax declined with a wave of the paw.

"You know there are two things I just can't wrap my head around," Koble continued. "Who do you think sabotaged us at Mirotose Station?"

Nathan took a long sip from the bottle and shook his head;

"Jack deliberately left that out of his message. He didn't want us going after them for a reason". Nathan said; "It doesn't matter anymore. He's gone, and we're not."

Koble didn't argue. Nathan knew the Sphinax well enough to tell that he agreed with what he'd said. Koble had always been loyal to Jack, and he would respect the old man's final wishes.

"So, what do we do now?" Koble asked.

"I can't help escape the feeling that I'm supposed to help Astrilla," Nathan replied. He handed the half-empty bottle to Koble and gestured to the Phoenix; "You know this ship is gonna need a crew?"

Koble raised his brows and grinned;

"I wouldn't have it any other way, brother".

They continued to watch the sunset and following twilight. After thirty minutes, Harrt joined them on the landing pad. The 'wealther sat between them and unbuttoned the collar on his formal shirt.

"Drink?" Koble offered out the bottle.

"No, thanks," Harrt shook his head. "I just finished speaking with the Admiralty, and I've got some good news".

"Go on?" Nathan said.

"I pulled some strings. As far as my superiors are concerned, the Phoenix is a hunk of junk," Harrt answered. "The ship is yours. They won't take it from you".

"Good to know," Nathan said, tipping the bottle as a mock-toast. He'd had no intention of letting the 'wealthers claim his newly acquired ship anyway, but he appreciated the gesture nonetheless. "So, what happens now?" Nathan asked.

"High-Command is sending someone to debrief me," Harrt replied. "They'll probably reassign me to another ship after that".

Nathan couldn't help but feel an odd sense of melancholy. He'd only known the 'wealther for a week, but the idea of parting ways didn't feel right. As Nathan reflected on Harrt's potential departure, he had to stop and think;

I guess a lot really can change in a week.

▲

The memories of the Earth's destruction forced their way into Nathan's sleeping mind like an unstoppable flood. Like always, the blue skies of Earth were replaced by fiery scarlet. He saw his grandmother cut down in a hail of Revenant gunfire. His father rushed toward the enemy, armed with a fire iron. The sound of Dylan Carter's tortured final moments played out like they always did.

Like every time Nathan experienced the dream, he attempted to fight back, but it was futile. His mother was gunned down as she begged for their lives, and there was nothing he could do to stop it.

That was usually where the dream ended, but this time it didn't.

Everything stopped, and the Revenant soldiers vanished. The gardens of Bill Stephens' home warped and twisted into darkness. On some sub-conscious level, Nathan became aware that he wasn't alone —like some part of him was aware that he was asleep in his bed. He allowed the thought to calm his mind, and after a few seconds, the darkness was replaced by a birds-eye view of the Phoenix Titan. The ship was still docked on the landing pad on Pelos Three. From the skies, he could see the Evoker Enclave in all its architectural glory, but he wasn't supposed to go there.

Nathan was dragged through the forest for several miles until he stopped at a white structure. The ornate building was nestled amongst the trees, appearing as though it didn't belong. Nathan wasn't sure why, but he felt compelled to venture inside. His fingertips brushed the stone door to the temple. There was a flash, and Nathan saw Astrilla. Instinctively, he drew his hand away from the stonework.

"I have foreseen our meeting," A deep voice surrounded Nathan. "I have foreseen your annihilation at my hands."

The defiant part of Nathan's mind told him to resist, and he pushed the door open. The interior was replaced by his grandparents' garden and at the centre stood Jack, covered from head to toe in blood.

Jack stared at Nathan with a look of sheer horror on his face.

"You must find it!" Jack screamed.

Before he could say anything, Nathan was dragged through the temple; across the forest and back to the Phoenix.

"And so, my friend, it begins".

▲

Astrilla awoke with a scream. For a moment, she didn't know where she was. All that she knew was that the dream —or nightmare— that her mind conjured up wasn't entirely of her own design. At the start of the dream she saw the deaths of three unfamiliar people. Then there was the blonde man. Astrilla had seen him before. He was the one who'd left the holographic message for Nathan.

Instinctively, Astrilla reached out for someone beside her, unaware of who it was she was searching for. Instead, her hand found unfamiliar coils of sweat-damp sheets around her. The rational part of her mind took over and reminded her that the dream was over and she was safe on Pelos Three.

Astrilla disentangled herself from the sheets and sat on the edge of the bed. She placed her feet against the cold stone floor, inviting the pull of gravity to settle her mind. It took less than a minute for Astrilla to centre herself, but there was still an unfamiliar feeling: an almost magnetic pull toward Nathan and the Phoenix Titan.

He was there, Astrilla thought. *Nathan was there in my dream.*

Astrilla climbed to her feet and walked over to a window that overlooked the Phoenix. She noticed that Nathan was sitting on the landing pad, looking directly up at her. The expression on his face confirmed what she already suspected.

Nathan had experienced the dream as well.

CHAPTER TWENTY-FIVE

Astrilla threw a robe over her body and rushed to the landing pad. By the time she got to Nathan, a light rain had started to fall from the sky. The words out of his mouth almost mimicked her own;

"What was that?"

They stopped and stared at one another for several awkward seconds.

"You saw it too?" she asked.

"Yeah," Nathan nodded. "The temple; then Jack telling me I had to find something. Ever since I woke up, I can't get this fuckin' itch outta my head. It's like—"

"It's like you can feel my presence," Astrilla finished his sentence. "I feel the same pull towards you".

They spent a couple of minutes comparing accounts of their dream, not noticing that the rainfall had become more intense. Even though Astrilla knew they had experienced the same nightmare, it didn't stop a chill running down her spine.

It has to mean something, Astrilla thought.

The whole thing was impossible, and yet they'd experienced it together. The Evoker Legendarium mentioned visions during deep meditation, but never in the form of a shared dream.

"We must seek advice from the Elders," Astrilla said. "They will know what to do".

To her surprise, Nathan shook his head.

"I say we go find that temple".

"Now?"

"Now". He pointed to the west. "It's pulling me toward it. Can you feel it too?"

"Of course," Astrilla nodded. "But we don't know what's in there. We should seek counsel before venturing out there".

Nathan shook his head and slung a backpack over his soaking wet shirt. Astrilla noticed that he'd already holstered a gun at his hip.

"You can go seek counsel as long as you want, but I'm going," Nathan said. "There's something in there, and I gotta know what it is".

"Why?" Astrilla asked impatiently.

"Because Jack was in that dream," Nathan replied. "What if he's there? What if all of this is something to do with him? I've gotta know".

"So your plan is to venture out into the forest in the middle of a storm?"

Nathan stared at the dark clouds, regarding them with an expression that said, *who cares?*

"That'd be about right," Nathan concluded and he started walking past her.

Astrilla grabbed him by the bicep in frustration. She wanted to knock him unconscious and seek advice from the Elders, but something stopped her.

This means something. I should go with him—the voice in the back of Astrilla's brain didn't feel like her own. It was impulsive and unruly; unbound by the order and logic that the Evokers had trained into her.

She felt the damp cloth of his shirt as she pulled him to stop. When Nathan looked back at her, there was a moment of uncomfortable tension between them.

"I'm going," Nathan growled.

"As am I, but can I at least get changed before we leave?" she said, gesturing at her rain-drenched robe.

▲

After Astrilla had changed into a hiking-appropriate outfit, she and Nathan ventured through the Enclave and into the forest. They trekked for several miles through the dense woodland, each barely saying a word to the other. Astrilla could feel something pulling at both of them —as though some force of nature was drawing them toward the temple.

Astrilla didn't like the way it felt.

She tried her best to process the concept of experiencing a shared dream, and tried to focus on the meaning, rather than its disturbing content, but it wasn't that simple. In the nightmare, Astrilla witnessed the murder of three people at the hands of Revenant soldiers. One of the victims had howled in complete torment as he was cut to pieces by a hunter—Astrilla could still hear his screams ringing in her ears. The whole thing felt like a memory, but it wasn't. Astrilla had never seen those people before, and the surroundings were completely alien. And yet she felt the fear of that moment in her heart as if it were her own.

As the sun began to rise, the rain ceased. Astrilla convinced Nathan to stop for water at a fallen tree. She passed him a bottle from her bag and watched as he gulped back a third of its contents.

"We're not too far now," he said, wiping excess water from his beard. "I can feel it".

Astrilla nodded as she took the bottle from him. For a moment, she felt as though Nathan was stating the obvious. Astrilla felt the same pull toward the temple as he did, but she forced herself to remember that this sensation was new to both of them.

"What do you think we're gonna find?" Nathan asked.

"I honestly don't know".

Nathan rubbed a hand through his hair, deep in thought.

"You lived on this planet as a kid, right?" he said. "I take it you know these forests like the back of your hand?"

Astrilla took a deep breath;

"When I was young I didn't spend much time away from the Enclave".

Nathan eyed her with a degree of scepticism and asked, "Why?"

"Because I had plenty of studies to complete," she

answered.

Nathan's frown deepened for all but a moment. Astrilla could feel him trying to bury an impulsive response to her answer. On the surface, it appeared to be a lot like envy, but Astrilla saw grief in the Earther's eyes.

"You and I had very different childhoods," Nathan said bitterly.

As soon as he'd spoken the words aloud, everything became clear. Astrilla fixed her eyes on him and summoned to courage to broach a difficult topic.

"In our dream, I saw a family slaughtered by Revenant soldiers," Astrilla said. She noticed Nathan's attention dart in an almost defensive manner, "That was one of your memories, wasn't it?" Astrilla questioned.

Nathan's breath trembled, and he replied, "Yeah…"

Nathan's lips pressed, bloodless and thin. Astrilla could feel his discomfort as though it were her own. She took a seat beside him on the fallen tree and placed a hand on top of his.

"I'm sorry," she fumbled. "I didn't mean to—"

"It doesn't matter," Nathan withdrew his hand. "What's done is done".

▲

They reached the temple thirty minutes later, and it wasn't as either of them expected. Nathan could hardly believe it was the same building. The once white stonework had become a muddy grey —faded by the ravages of time. The intricate carvings from the dream were replaced by a layer of thick green moss.

"So, this is it," Nathan said.

"It would appear so," Astrilla replied.

It took Nathan several attempts to push the heavy stone doors open. By the time he'd shoved them wide enough to get through, Nathan was sweating. He tied back his thick dark hair before venturing inside.

The temple was completely empty. It was old, dusty and faded. The walls were the same greyish white as the exterior with no sign of decoration or character. Tough brown blades of grass and weeds sprouted between gaps in the floor.

"I finally see where the 'wealthers get their lack of imagination," Nathan remarked.

Astrilla didn't acknowledge his sarcastic attempt at humour. Instead, she stepped inside and paced around the derelict building.

"It is just like every other Enkaye structure," she remarked.

"So every other Enkaye structure has been in a dream you've shared with a complete stranger?" Nathan said.

The Evoker didn't answer and continued exploring. Nathan did the same and pondered what the purpose of the building had once been. There was nothing; no sign of function or intent. The temple was utterly dormant.

Guess that's what a few thousand years will do, Nathan thought.

The Enkaye had —supposedly— been on Earth. At least that was one of many theories. To Nathan, it was a concept that made complete sense. Languages across the galaxy, including Earth's, were almost identical. Ancient Egyptian hieroglyphs had been found on Enkaye relics. The Greek myths were eerily similar to a long-dead Maruvian religion known as Olympyism.

Regardless of the theories posed by scientists, historians and clerics, none of it mattered. The Enkaye were gone, and all that was left of their dynasty was old buildings riddled with dust and decay.

Astrilla suddenly grabbed Nathan by the arm and halted him.

"Can you hear that?"

Nathan focussed his hearing, and then the whistling became apparent. It was so high pitched that he could barely hear it at first, but once Nathan had concentrated on the noise, it became hard to ignore.

They followed the sound to the south-facing wall, and with every step, it grew louder and louder. Astrilla stopped at the stonework and reached out her hand to touch it. The whistling became so piercing that Nathan thought his eardrums may give way, but once Astrilla's hand made contact with the stone, the noise ceased.

Something shifted inside the temple, and a flare of light peaked through the cracks in the floor. A few seconds later, the ground behind them split in the middle without a sound and opened up into a steep downward staircase.

"Well, you don't see that every day," Nathan remarked.

"The Enkaye technology is reacting to my presence," Astrilla said. "Amazing it still works after all this time".

Nathan peered into the dark chasm at the bottom of the stairs and immediately felt unsettled by the darkness. He grabbed a small flashlight from his bag and drew his gun.

"Let's go find out what your relatives left here," Nathan said.

After taking a few steps, a low hum emanated from the bottom of the stairs. Nathan stopped and pointed his pistol into the dark. To his surprise, Astrilla proceeded past him, unhindered by the droning hum.

Nathan followed, and after two more paces, a sphere of blue light appeared. It danced in front of them for several seconds, almost as though it were watching them. The ball rotated a couple of times and started leading them down.

"And from the darkness, there will come a guiding light," Astrilla said softly. Nathan shot her a questioning stare and she shook her head, "It's a passage from the Evoker Legendarium".

"Is that some kind of Evoker holy-book?"

"Not exactly," she answered. "The only way we learn is from that which happened before".

At the bottom of the stairs was a small chamber, no bigger than Nathan's cabin aboard the Phoenix. At the centre of the room was a hip-height device, designed for a creature far shorter than the modern human. The same faint blue light poured into the room and somehow merged with the console.

From the device, a warm yellow glow emerged, and within it arose a figure. For a moment, Nathan wasn't sure what he was looking at until he realised that two giant black eyes were staring back at him. The projection depicted a creature of alien origin, with a small human-like body and a large hairless head. There was no doubt in Nathan's mind; he was looking at a holographic projection of an Enkaye.

"Greetings," it said in a monotone voice.

"What are you?" Astrilla said.

The holographic creature blinked before answering;

"I am a virtual intelligence, designed by the Masters to impart a message unto their descendants

"What message?" Astrilla said.

The console whirred again, seeming to process the question and form an appropriate answer. The hologram distorted and its voice skipped a few times.

"Before the downfall of the Enkaye Dynasty, my people were at war with an enemy of immeasurable power. To combat the threat, the Enkaye built war machines; weapons of inconceivable destruction".

There were two parts of the hologram's statement which made Nathan nervous when he thought about them. The Enkaye, a species likened by many civilisations as gods, had built war machines. It was a completely and utterly terrifying prospect. However, there was something far more frightening that sent shivers of ice up Nathan's spine: *who was the enemy that they needed to fight?*

He wanted to ask the question as soon as it popped into his head, but he was cut off by the projection before he could open his mouth:

"The Masters defeated the enemy, but it came at a cost. Many were lost in the war, and in the end, only a few remained." The holographic alien paused as though it were stopping for breath. It focussed its gaze on Astrilla. "The Masters left me here to show you the way".

"Show us the way to what?" she asked.

"My people made every attempt to destroy the remaining war machines, but there wasn't enough time. One of those ships is now under the control of a man who would seek to use it for evil".

Nathan turned to Astrilla with a raised brow. This was the weapon she had referred to earlier —the one that the Revenant now had in their possession— the same device for which they required Astrilla.

"The Masters called this particular war machine, the Messorem," the hologram recounted.

"How do we kill it?" Nathan asked.

The hologram stopped and stared at him with a look somewhere between indifference and curiosity.

"This is why we're here, isn't it?" Nathan said.

The Enkaye nodded; "You are correct. The Masters knew all that was to come. You, like me, are here to fulfil a purpose: to stop the Messorem and the man who controls it".

"How?" Astrilla and Nathan said at the same time.

"Before the Great Exodus, my creators scattered three pieces of a device known as the Omega —a failsafe designed to destroy the Messorem". The hologram didn't take its black eyes off of Astrilla as it spoke. "I am programmed to show you the way".

From inside the hologram, two pieces of metal emerged.

"The first of these two devices is a piece of the Omega. The second is a map to the next piece". The hologram gestured to the two cylindrical metal chunks. "You must not fail".

Before Nathan or Astrilla could say anything else, the hologram disappeared. The light in the room failed, and the two pieces of metal dropped to the floor with a dull thud. As Nathan scooped them from the floor, Astrilla called out to him through the darkness;

"Please tell me you still have that flashlight".

CHAPTER TWENTY-SIX

Agent Leviticus Dines would often describe the Commonwealth as the lesser of two evils, though in recent years he'd begun to question whether or not two evils could be measured in the same way. There was no doubt in Dines' mind that the Revenant were the enemy, but he knew in his heart that the men who gave him his orders were corrupt beyond belief. The 'wealth had become something that Dines didn't recognise anymore, but he remained loyal nonetheless. Leviticus Dines didn't serve out of some misguided sense of loyalty to the politicians or even The Grand Master Of The House: he did it because he truly loved his fellow citizens.

Dines was under no illusions. Most of the Commonwealth's people were far from perfect. The Founders had strived to create a fair and equal society, committed to defeating the fascist, Revenant Monarchy. Unfortunately, the foundations that had built the Commonwealth had changed over time. The fat, corrupted politicians used the values of the Founders as a shroud to mask an agenda of control and oppression. The citizens didn't challenge it either out of fear or obedience. In the case of Lieutenant Harrt Oxarri, Dines knew he fit the latter rather than the former, but he sensed that something had changed since they'd last met.

Dines found Harrt in the gardens of the Evoker Enclave. The Lieutenant offered a salute, and Dines reciprocated the gesture. It was all formal, just as he'd expected from *the hero of Maru Seven*. After saluting, they shook hands, and the formality between them dropped.

"How the hell do you keep finding yourself in the middle of bad situations and surviving?" Dines said.

Harrt offered a shrug, "Guess I'm as hard to kill as you are".

They waited until a meeting room became available, exchanging small talk in the process. After a few minutes, a droid escorted them to an empty hall, and the formality returned. For the best part of an hour, Dines reviewed every line of Harrt's report. It was a thorough process that he had to follow. Neither of them liked it, but it had to be done. Dines would often liken the task to a cog that had to turn in the right way to keep the machine moving. After asking all of the mandatory debrief questions, Dines switched off his datapad and set it down.

"I want to ask you an off-the-record question," Dines said.

"Okay," Harrt replied sceptically.

Dines cracked his knuckles and cleared his throat, "How do you think the Revenant knew your FTL coordinates?"

There was a long pause. Harrt sat back with his palms on his temples for a few seconds before answering:

"Isn't it obvious?" he murmured.

"Maybe," Dines shrugged. "But I wanna hear it from you".

It was a gesture of pure passive-aggressiveness on Dines' part, but he didn't care. Harrt Oxarri had denied the existence of a mole before; refusing to believe that Commonwealth citizens would do such a thing. Harrt's rejection of Dines' intel had been the catalyst for Maru Seven, and billions had been lost as a result, including Harrt's wife and child.

C'mon you fool, say it, Dines thought.

Harrt looked uncomfortable, just as Dines intended. It was about time that men like Harrt woke up and realised that perhaps the 'wealth wasn't as perfect as they'd been taught to believe.

Finally, Harrt leaned forward in his seat and replied;
"I think someone betrayed us".

▲

*"To be Revenant is to be reborn in the image of those who
came before. Once the dead are returned to the Void, they
understand our holy mission. They are devout to the cause;
to the crown; to me".*

Seig's earliest memory was witnessing a living heretic
converted by the river Prynn. The sinner had begged, cried
and resisted, but in the end, he'd succumbed to the mighty
waters. For a child of any other race, witnessing the end of
another being would be traumatising, but for Seig it was
enchanting. Just as the scriptures said, the act of mutation
was far from murder. It was an act of righteousness —the
end of a sinner and the rise of a saint.

That was the mission that Seig had to undertake. To
cleanse the universe of chaos.

All life was his by birthright: just like his father and
grandfather before. The problem was that the people had
turned to a life of intolerable sin; resisting the law and order
that came with Revenant rule. Therefore it was Seig's duty
to guide the citizens of the universe toward the river Prynn
—purging them of evil.

Every time a new planet fell, the deceased were
transported to the nearest Revenant flagship and the
conversion ceremony would begin. They were then placed
in giant pools of water, taken directly from the River. What
followed was a twenty-hour cycle where the dead would
rise, die and rise again. With every death and rebirth, a sin
against the Revenant monarchy was washed away. The
process was always accompanied by the guttural screams of
the immoral as they succumbed to the cleansing. After the
twenty hours had elapsed, the converts would willingly step
from the water. Most of the time they'd be simple-minded
footsoldiers, other times they'd be hunters, and on some rare

occasions, a Paladin would step from the waters. For Seig, it didn't matter so long as they were committed to the cause.

Despite the enemy fighting for their own sinful reasons, it was respectful to be present at the conversion ceremony. Regardless of their previous purpose in life, the deceased would become disciples to the crown.

The conversion process for Yenex was no different. A few trillion were placed in the waters, and Seig spoke a passage from the Revenant Creed. What followed was the usual cacophony of screaming that the King had become accustomed to.

After witnessing only the early stages of the ceremony, Seig was interrupted by one of his advisors. Usually, he would have killed for such a disturbance, but this particular priest had come with important news that couldn't be ignored.

When Seig sat upon his throne, the holographic projectors in the room activated. A hologram of Grand Admiral Olbori formed. The Maruviun turncoat was kneeling before his King and didn't rise until Seig ordered him to stand.

It was hard to ignore that Olbori was getting old. Despite the erosion that came with time, Densius Olbori had remained the same brutal tactician that Seig needed in his circle of advisors. He certainly hadn't gone soft in his old age, but Seig knew the old man had twenty years at most.

Olbori was unlike any of the other key advisors that Seig had at his disposal. He was not born a pure Revenant or even a convert. The truth was that Densius Olbori had once served the Commonwealth as a senior officer. He'd led battles against the Revenant and even destroyed one of Seig's flagships many years ago, but as it turned out, such victories were hollow.

Thanks in part to Seig's son, Baylum, Olbori was captured and eventually recruited as a Revenant spy. Initially, it troubled Seig that a man would turn on his own so quickly. He assumed that the Admiral was simply a double agent just biding his time. However, Olbori proved him wrong and earnt Seig's trust.

The Admiral knew that the Commonwealth was far more flawed than its politicians cared to admit. Like all senior officers, he'd seen the corruption and cronyism first hand. When Prince Baylum took Olbori to the Void, it had spoken to him. The river Prynn showed him the criminal nature of the Commonwealth. He'd witnessed every sinful act that his leaders had carried out. Most important of all, the Void had shown him a path to salvation —serving the Revenant.

Ever since that day, Olbori was committed to the cause. After helping Seig lay waste to the Commonwealth world of Maru Seven, he'd been promoted to Grand Admiral. Since then, Olbori was responsible for the invasion and conversion of the Outer Worlds. He'd been very successful in the role too; laying waste to almost two hundred worlds in just under eight years.

"I wish to hear of your exploits," Seig said. "How goes our campaign in the Juno Galaxy?"

"The fleet continues to make excellent progress," Olbori replied. "Seven planets have fallen in the last seven days. We've stripped them all of their resources, including the dead".

Seig didn't immediately reply. Seven planets in seven days was excellent —better than Seig had ever achieved— but he knew that the priorities of the fleet had to change. The Messorem represented the greatest threat to the Commonwealth he'd ever known. Finding Astrilla had to become the main objective for the majority of Seig's forces.

"I would like you to assume command of the first, second and third fleets, Admiral," Seig said.

Olbori looked at him as if to ask a question, but he quickly acquiesced.

"It'd be my honour, your grace," Olbori replied. "What of the fifth and sixth though? There are many planets we can harvest out here".

Seig held up his hand, "Where is my son?"

The wrinkles on Olbori's dark-skin tightened as he frowned.

"The Prince will be joining us shortly, my lord," Olbori

answered. "He just returned from battle and was covered in the blood of our enemies. You would have been very proud".

Seig dismissed the answer with another wave of his hand. He knew that his impulsive son would be revelling in the field of battle.

"See that my son is ready to take over from your command," Seig ordered. "Bring the sixth fleet with you as well".

Olbori looked at him with a questioning expression, and Seig knew why. Bringing a large group of ships together was risky, but Olbori didn't understand the true power of the Messorem.

Not like Seig.

Once he had Astrilla captive, the plan was to push to the Capital Worlds and cut out the heart of the Commonwealth. Seig knew this would be the key moment, and he needed every gun he had to ensure his victory.

Olbori bore the look of a man who wanted to protest.

"Is there a problem, Admiral?" Seig said.

The Admiral's jaw tensed and he shook his head, "No, your grace. We will rendezvous with you at the Messorem".

Seig nodded, and the hologram deactivated. There was an odd feeling that overcame Seig for a moment. It was the realisation that this was the closest he'd been to defeating the Commonwealth. After centuries of fighting and planning, this was his moment to finally put an end to them. With the Commonwealth and Evokers gone, there would be nobody significant standing in his way. Just as it had been prophesied, Seig would cleanse the universe of all its sins, and all he needed was Astrilla.

I am the saviour that will bring order where there is only chaos. I am the moral: the noble: the righteous.

▲

After the Enkaye hologram deactivated, Nathan's first impulse was to check the temple for anything else that could have been left behind. Astrilla, on the other hand, insisted they return to the Enclave to consult with the Elders. Nathan decided that there was little point in arguing with her, so he completed a quick sweep of the temple, and they began hiking back.

As Nathan stepped outside, he noticed that the pulling sensation was gone; replaced by a mix of confusion and disbelief. A far less cynical person would have been overwhelmed by what he'd seen in the temple.

The Enkaye was considered by some to be the former masters of the universe: gods who may have forged entire star systems. If a true believer had experienced what Nathan had, they would fall to their knees.

Even the most sceptical of people would have been in awe of what he'd experienced. Rationally speaking, the Enkaye were a long extinct species. For a modern Earther it would be like talking with a dinosaur —if dinosaurs built spacecraft and understood the finer points of faster-than-light-travel. For what little factual evidence there was, the consensus was clear about one thing: the Enkaye were technologically advanced —far more than the Commonwealth.

After five minutes of hiking in silence, Astrilla turned to Nathan:

"Do you believe in destiny?" she asked.

"Excuse me?"

"It's a simple question," Astrilla shrugged. "Do you believe in destiny?"

Nathan felt his throat tighten. He'd hoped to avoid conversation about superstition with her, but he knew it would only be a matter of time. Nathan peered warily at her, then shifted his gaze to the horizon. It was easier that way — he didn't need to see the judgement on her soft features.

"My uncle Jack used to have this saying," Nathan began, then paused for breath. "It is not in the stars to hold our destiny, but in ourselves."

"And you believe that?"

"The thing you've gotta know is that it's a really fucked up universe out there, and I've seen the best and worst that it has to offer," Nathan continued. "I've seen two stars merge and become a kilonova. I've walked on the surface of a comet. I've even delivered a baby".

Astrilla's lips formed a smirk of mild amusement, "And is there a point to this grand list of achievements?"

"There is," Nathan nodded and stopped to tie his shoe.

"And that is?" Astrilla looked at him expectantly.

"My point is that a lotta shit has happened to me since the Fall, some good, some bad, but not once has it ever made me believe it was a part of some lofty predetermined plan".

He paused for a moment and glanced at her. The Evoker was looking at him with her arms folded. He could tell that she knew he'd not fully answered her question, so he continued;

"Then… we crash-landed on Yenex, and all of these *strange coincidences* started happening. The kind of coincidences that are pretty hard to ignore".

"So, you're saying *you do* believe in destiny?"

Nathan lifted his hands and answered;

"I'm saying it's nice to have the illusion of choice".

CHAPTER TWENTY-SEVEN

The Enclave was home to the ancient archives: a vast library that encompassed the history of the Evokers. Everything from the intimate journals of the first Evokers to the study of Enkaye culture was held there. Astrilla learned many years ago that history had a tendency of second-guessing itself. Accounts varied on the finer details of specific points in time, and a perfect example of this was the Formation of the Commonwealth. Most texts stated that the Founders enlisted the help of the Evokers during the early days of the Revenant war. However, some accounts directly contradicted this. Some scribes stated that the Evokers were coerced into forming an alliance with the Commonwealth. Others had wholly denied the existence of the Founders, instead citing that it had been the Evokers who united the galaxy against the Revenant.

It made Astrilla question how history would look back on her and everything that was going on. Her heritage was of the Enkaye —at least part of it— and they were considered to be a myth by some modern historians. The thought left Astrilla wondering if she would be the subject of debate in centuries to come.

Would they think she was a myth?
Would she be labelled as a fraud?
Would history even remember her?

In the grand scheme of things, it didn't really matter. Astrilla accepted the fact that she was part-Enkaye a long time ago. The difference now, was that she finally understood the purpose of her heritage —to find the Omega. To stop King Seig.

Astrilla wanted nothing more than to jump in a ship and follow the map to the next piece of the Omega, but she knew better than to simply follow her impulse. Seeking council from the Elders was imperative —regardless of Nathan's earlier protests.

The Enclave was the epicentre of Evoker learning. Every day for generations, students would study within its walls; learning to fight; to negotiate; to survive. Training the next generation of Evokers was an essential practice. It was the very reason why four of the most respected Elders lived on Pelos Three.

After leading Nathan through the busy halls of the old stone building, Astrilla stopped at the doors to the great hall. She stared at him for several seconds, noting that his boots were covered in dirt from the hike and his jeans were ripped at the knee. Astrilla wondered if the Elders would cast judgement on the scruffy Earther, but she reminded herself that there were far more important issues at stake.

"What?" Nathan said, noticing she'd been staring for some time.

"Nothing," Astrilla shook her head. "An audience with the Elders is rarely granted at such short notice. Just try to behave yourself in there".

"You're the boss," he shrugged.

Astrilla wasn't quite sure if she could trust his response. She'd already gathered that Nathan's vocabulary was *colourful*, to say the least. The swearing and cursing he used was mostly Earther and meant nothing in the 'wealth, but the sentiment of it wouldn't be appreciated by the Elders. Despite her misgivings, Astrilla proceeded to push the doors to the Great Hall open.

There were four of the fifty Elders based on Pelos Three: Yuta; Marx; Xanthur and Repla. They were a diverse and seasoned group who had dedicated their entire lives to the order, and yet Astrilla only gravitated toward two of them.

It was no secret that she was closest to Yuta. The old human woman had become like a surrogate mother to her over the years. Yuta was warm and only ever showed kindness to others. She was one of the few people that Astrilla had met that didn't cast doubt on others at a whim.

Xanthur was the oldest and the wisest of all. He'd survived more wars than any Evoker in the entire order. Despite his thin and boney appearance, Xanthur was an incredibly powerful warrior and swordsmen. He'd fought off the Revenant in more battles than any other Evoker in the entire order. More importantly, he had lived to tell his tale.

When Astrilla was a child there had rumours around the Enclave that Xanthur had faced and defeated the previous Revenant King at the Battle of Barium Two. When questioned on the matter, Xanthur and the other Elders simply called it a hoax, but Astrilla always suspected that he knew more than he was letting on.

Regardless of his skillset and influence, Xanthur was a kind and wise man, and Astrilla appreciated his company. It wasn't to say that she didn't respect Marx or Repla —quite the opposite.

As a Sillix, Repla found it challenging to form emotional connections with others, so it made her appear cold and uncaring. When she was young, Astrilla found Repla to be intimidating and mean-spirited, but in reality, Repla simply didn't understand what it meant to feel anything. The fact was that Repla was a master of summoning energy.

Marx, on the other hand, was entirely different from all of them. He came from an incredibly rare avian species known as the Florus: tall bird-like creatures with stern eyes and giant feather-covered bodies. Much like the Earthers, the Florus were a victim of the Revenant's campaign, and only a few hundred remained. As a result, Marx often struggled to stay objective about the Revenant. In Astrilla's opinion, that very characteristic made Marx a brilliant and fearless tactician in the field of battle. However, it also made him reactive and unfocused.

The seats of the four Elders formed a semi-circle that faced inward to where Astrilla and Nathan stood. The room was circular and domed, supported by several ornate pillars at intervals. The shape of the chamber was deliberate, intended as a reflection that all life was both connected and cyclical.

Astrilla cleared her throat before addressing the four Elders:

"Thank you for meeting us on such short notice," she said.

She allowed a moment of silence to linger before continuing;

"I would like to introduce you all to Nathan Carter. He was one of the people who helped me to escape Yenex".

She turned her head to look at the Earther, who simply raised his hand in greeting to the Elders.

Marx was the first to speak:

"We extend our thanks to you, for the part you played in saving Astrilla". The Florus stared at Nathan as he spoke from behind his golden beak.

"No problem," Nathan shrugged.

It wasn't the most impassioned or skilful response, but it was simple and effective; that was all Astrilla could hope for. She reminded herself that Nathan wasn't an Evoker. She couldn't expect him to understand the gravity of what it meant to meet with the Elders.

Before Astrilla could say anything else, Repla stood from her chair;

"What is the purpose of this meeting, Astrilla?" Repla asked, her voice monotone.

Astrilla felt Nathan tense at Repla's stern tone of voice. Like always, the Elder appeared aloof, but Astrilla knew it was simply her nature.

Astrilla spoke about everything from the dream she and Nathan had shared right up to the Enkaye Ruins. She practically quoted the holograms exact words as she told them about the Messorem, the Omega and the mission she had to undertake. After she'd finished speaking there was a long silence from the Elders. In the years that Astrilla had been a part of the Evokers, she had never seen the four of them so quiet. It made her realise the gravity of the situation.

As usual, Marx was the first to comment:

"This is most disturbing," he said. "Did the hologram share any detail of the Messorem's structural or engineering flaws?"

"No," Astrilla shook her head in response.

She became aware that Repla's attention had shifted away from her and toward Elder Xanthur instead.

"You've studied the Enkaye ruins on this planet for years. How is it that you never stumbled upon this underground chamber that Astrilla speaks of?"

Xanthur's snow-coloured brows knotted. The frown suggested annoyance, but Astrilla was sure that the old man was crafting a thoughtful response to the challenge.

"Need I remind you that the technology of the Enkaye only responds to those who share their genetic pattern?" Xanthur answered. "The Enkaye didn't want their technology getting into the wrong hands, so they put safeguards in place".

Astrilla felt a sense of relief when Yuta interrupted:

"Show us what the hologram gave you".

As always Yuta played the impartial party. By simply not acknowledging the tension, she was able to move the conversation forward. It was the same method she used to deescalate heated debates during forums.

Astrilla presented the two items to the Elders. The first was the unmarked cylindrical piece of dark metal referred to by the hologram as the Omega. The metal bar was no longer than half a metre in length, yet despite its size, it was surprisingly light, and the metal felt unusually cold to touch. Astrilla could only assume that the second piece would fit it somehow, but there were no discernable markings or joints.

The second item was an old scroll, housed in an Arcane metal casing. The parchment inside appeared to be entirely new. Upon the bright white page was a detailed star map leading to the next piece of the Omega. The route and destination were clearly marked on the map. By Astrilla's best estimate it would lead them to the other side of the galaxy —deep into the Mironium System.

The Elders studied the relics for several minutes. As Astrilla suspected most of their attention was focussed on the map rather than the Omega. Eventually, Xanthur came to the same conclusion as Astrilla.

"It's pointing to the Mironium system," he said with a level of scepticism.

Something tickled at the back of Astrilla's mind. An instinct. An impulse. For the first time in a very long time, she found herself saying something that wouldn't appease her Elders.

"I intend on going there," Astrilla said. "I intend on finding the next piece of the Omega".

"Are you mad?" Repla snapped. "That system is controlled by gangs and outlaws. If they discover who you are…. we might as well hand you to the Revenant ourselves".

The logical part of Astrilla agreed with the Sillix. After all, she'd barely escaped Yenex, but Astrilla knew that it had to be done.

"Normally I would agree with you," Astrilla replied, bowing her head out of respect to Repla. "I cannot escape the feeling that this is something that the Enkaye intended for me to do. This is a path that I must walk".

The room went quiet.

It was the first time in Astrilla's life that she'd directly challenged an Elder. The silence was so eerie that it made Astrilla wonder if it was the first time that anyone had disagreed with an Elder.

After a few seconds, Xanthur climbed from his chair and addressed his peers;

"My friends we must face a harsh reality," Xanthur said. "We are at war, and our enemy grows stronger with every day that passes. Yes, Seig has an Enkaye weapon, but he adds new soldiers to his ranks every day. Commonwealth analysts are estimating that at least fourteen billion soldiers were added to his ranks from Yenex alone."

"I'm inclined to agree," Marx said. He held out the

Omega and added; "Fate has provided us with the means to strike at Seig first. This is all a part of the Enkaye's great plan, and it seems that Astrilla is a part of it".

Repla seemed to chew at the inside of her mouth for several seconds. She focussed her gaze on Nathan.

"What do you think about all of this Captain Carter?" she asked.

Astrilla looked at Nathan. At first, he looked positively stunned that she'd addressed him as Captain, but after his initial shock had faded, he stepped forward.

"I don't believe we are walking a predetermined path. I believe in what I can see, what I can feel," Nathan said. "That being said, I've never shared a dream, never spoken to long-dead Enkaye tech. This means something, and quite honestly, you'd be total fuckin' morons to not see that".

Astrilla scrambled to make sure that Nathan's cursing went mostly unnoticed. She outlined a simple yet effective plan for the Elders, wherein she and the crew of the Phoenix Titan would travel to the Mironium System without a Commonwealth escort. She substantiated this point by arguing that travelling in a single private freighter would make her harder to find.

Of course, each of the Elders had their doubts, but none of them argued with her. When Astrilla was finished outlining the plan, the Elders spent a few minutes to discuss the issue amongst themselves. After some deliberation, they agreed.

"And you're happy to undertake such a risk, Captain Carter?" Yuta asked.

Astrilla could see the mix of bravado and gravitas in the Earther's face as he answered;

"I am," he nodded.

CHAPTER TWENTY-EIGHT

Ever since the Pluvium Civil War, Koble had lived somewhere between vagabond and criminal. Of course, a large proportion of that time had been aboard the Loyalty; working with a crew. Koble had been raised to live a different life entirely; one of honour and value. Instead, fate had forced other plans on him, and Koble had adapted.

When he'd first come aboard the Loyalty, the Captain had been a man called Theo Arturious, and Jack Stephens had effectively been his second in command. When Theo died under *questionable circumstances*, Jack had inherited the title of Captain. On the night of Theo's memorial, Koble and Jack had spoken about the new responsibility of Captain.

"My father used to say that change is the only certainty in the universe," Jack said. "We have to learn to adapt. If we don't, we may as well join Theo in the ground".

Jack's statement had stuck with Koble ever since. He never expected things to go according to plan; there had to always be a backup. That way he'd never be caught off guard. It was a lesson that served him well for the longest time, but ever since arriving at the Evoker Enclave, he'd questioned its validity.

The fact that he had aided in the rescue of an Evoker was mind-blowing by its own merits. Stranger still, he was standing at the foot of the Evoker Enclave; deep in Commonwealth space. The very thing Jack Stephens had discouraged. And yet neither of those facts were what troubled Koble the most.

Astrilla was part-Enkaye: the implications of that alone were enough to send shivers through Koble's spine and all the way to his tail. It was the kind of thing that was ripped straight out of the old myths, and Koble was living it.

For the whole night, Koble laid awake in his bed, debating how he could adapt to everything that was going on around him. Eventually, he got to sleep and dreamt of fishing in the middle of an ocean.

A loud banging at his cabin door woke him from his slumber.

"Koble, you need to get up," Vol said.

Words failed to form in Koble's mouth as he slowly sat up. Part of him wanted to curse her for disturbing his sleep, but there was an urgency to the Uvan's voice that he couldn't ignore.

"What's so important?" he finally replied.

"Nathan has called a crew meeting," Vol replied. "So drag your sorry ass out of bed".

Koble rolled out of bed and adjusted his fur in the mirror, before venturing from his cabin. With a craving for caffeine, Koble headed to the kitchen and found a bag of Xatiun coffee stashed in a cupboard. It wasn't the same as the slurry that the Loyalty's crew had drunk back in the day, but it gave him the fix he'd been craving. With a fresh cup to hand, Koble followed the sound of voices to the living area. When he got there, Koble found the entire crew waiting for him.

"Good to see you've finally joined us," Astrilla said.

Koble took a sip from his mug and sat down in an armchair, shaking off the grogginess he was feeling.

"I didn't sleep well last night," Koble replied. He turned to Nathan; "So what's so important that you felt the need to call a crew meeting —if that's what we're calling ourselves now?"

"We need to talk," Nathan said.

The account that Nathan and Astrilla played back to the crew made Koble's fur stand upright. Shared visions were one thing, but a functioning Enkaye hologram was something else entirely. Once again, Koble found himself wondering;

How can I adapt?

Before his brain could process such a question, Nathan said something that made every hair on his body stand to attention.

"The next location on the map is the Mironium System".

The Earther's eyes settled on Koble. Both of them knew why, but neither of them wanted to say it aloud.

"Which planet in the Mironium System?" Koble asked.

The edgy look in Nathan's eyes told Koble everything he needed to know.

"It's pretty close to Mironium One," Nathan replied. "I'm not one-hundred percent sure, but it's close".

Koble's mouth became dry, and for a moment, it felt as though all the blood in his body had left.

"You're joking, right?" Koble folded his arms. "Of all the planets and systems in the galaxy, and the Enkaye are sending us there?"

Koble and Nathan exchanged looks: both of them terrified to return to the corporation-controlled system.

From the other side of the room, Harrt leaned forward in his chair;

"What's so important about Mironium One?"

Koble frowned at the question. Before he could open his mouth, Astrilla answered for him:

"Mirotose Station is in orbit around Mironium One".

It took Harrt a moment, but when he finally realised the significance of Mirotose Station to Nathan and Koble, he stiffened. Harrt leaned back in his chair and rubbed his eyes either out of frustration or worry.

"So, what does that mean?" Harrt sighed. "If someone spots one of you are we gonna have a problem on our hands?"

Koble couldn't help but roll his eyes at the question. It was another example of just how little the 'wealthers understood the galaxy outside of their own space. The

Mironium System was almost entirely lawless. The corporations would battle amongst themselves for power, but in reality, the gangs and mafias ran the show. Mirotose Station was no different. Like most corporate-controlled systems, the space station was densely populated, and billions would travel through it daily.

"No one is gonna recognise us," Nathan said to reassure the 'wealther. "It's been a decade since I was in the system".

"Me too," Koble nodded.

As he sipped his coffee, Koble watched Harrt's increasingly sceptical frown grow.

"Don't worry 'wealther. It'll be fine," Koble said, tipping his mug to the Lieutenant. "Trust me".

Koble felt a tightness in his chest when his eyes met Nathan's.

"It can't go any worse than the last time we were there," Koble said, under his breath.

▲

After the crew meeting, Harrt told Nathan and Astrilla that they needed to speak in private. There was a nervousness in the wealther's eyes that told Nathan that whatever he had to say was important, so the request could not be ignored.

They met Harrt on the landing pad. As the night set in, automated lights flickered to life on the Phoenix's hull, allowing Nathan to make out the silhouettes of Harrt and another human.

The man accompanying Harrt wore a Commonwealth officers uniform. He had silver hair which transitioned to a darker well-trimmed beard: it was an attempt at gravitas that tried and failed to lend to his boyish features. Despite the colour of his hair, the 'wealther appeared closer to Nathan's age rather than Harrt's.

"Who's this guy?" Nathan said.

Harrt introduced the 'wealther as, Special Agent Leviticus Dines. The fact that Harrt called out his full title in addition to his name suggested that Dines was perhaps his superior.

Agent Dines stared at Nathan for several seconds without saying a word. He was the type of 'wealther that Nathan had always imagined when Jack spoke of the Commonwealth's strict communist regime.

"I tried to do my research on you, Captain Carter," Dines said. "We had a surprising lack of intel on you. Usually, I'd call that questionable, but Lieutenant Oxarri has vouched for you".

It was a strange comment to make, but Nathan wasn't the slightest bit surprised. Jack had intentionally kept the Loyalty away from the Commonwealth to protect the crew from the Commonwealth's violation of citizen records and data.

Nathan cleared his throat and took a step closer to Dines:

"And Harrt's opinion is enough for you?"

Dines nodded with a confident look in his eye.

"Intelligence is my designated specialism. You could say I know the people I can trust," Dines said. "I'd trust Lieutenant Oxarri with my life".

"So, what are we here to discuss?" Astrilla asked.

Dines and Harrt exchanged a glance; a tiny human jolt of communication that said more than words ever could. Nathan was unable to decode any of it, but he assumed the 'wealthers were going to tell him something that he didn't want to hear.

Dines was the one to speak first;

"The Lieutenant and I have a theory about how the Revenant was able to shoot the Vertex out of FTL"

"It's obvious," Astrilla cut-in. "Someone betrayed you and gave the slipstream coordinates to the Revenant".

Nathan nodded in agreement. In his opinion, Astrilla was entirely correct. There was no other way for the Revenant to know the exact slipstream coordinates and timing of the Vertex's crossing.

"That's the theory," Dines nodded.

"Any idea who it could be?" Nathan cut in.

Both of the 'wealthers shook their heads, which made

Nathan nervous.

"So what the hell do we do about this?" Nathan said. "In a few hours, we're heading to the Mironium System to retrieve an Enkaye device. What's the likelihood that when we arrive, I'll be looking at a few dozen Revenant warships?"

Dines let silence hang in the air for a moment, then shook his head;

"It's possible," Dines shrugged. "If there really is a spy, then the key is to keep the number of people who know your whereabouts to a minimum".

Nathan noticed Harrt shooting Dines a look of disapproval. It was common knowledge, that 'wealthers followed the chain of command without question. What Dines was suggesting was entirely contradictory.

"I know, the Elders know, and the crew of this ship knows," Dines counted using his fingers. He turned to Harrt and added; "I know you aren't comfortable with this, but you need to trust me to deal with the Admiralty and politicians".

Nathan noted that Dines was directing his gaze at Harrt the entire time he was speaking. There was a history between the two —Nathan could feel it.

"So, what's your plan?" Harrt said.

"I'll go to Kamen first, then the Grand Master," Dines shrugged. "After that, they'll have to call a meeting with the Admiralty. I figure that buys you a minimum of twenty-four hours".

Harrt didn't talk for several seconds. When he did, his voice was calm but wary.

"You better be right about this, Dines".

▲

The conversation with Leviticus Dines ended the moment that the Enclave's mechanics returned from their break. The Elders had agreed to get the Phoenix fully operational, and it looked as though they were almost finished. Nathan was no mechanic, but it was evident that the ship was in a far better state then when it had left Yenex. Knowing that in a matter of hours, he and his *crew* would fly to the Mironium System with a fully operational ship was a reassurance.

After Dines left the group, Nathan headed back to the Phoenix, but was interrupted along the way by a delivery droid, with a small crate in its hands. It was a postal droid of simple design with the logo of Gerrick Shipping on its skeletal metal frame.

"Excuse me, sir," the droid called out. "I have a package for a Captain Nathan Carter?"

Packages and letters were something Nathan wasn't familiar with. Nobody was supposed to know where he was; Jack had always made that clear, so to be looking at one intended for him was an alien concept.

That's how they get you, Jack's voice rang inside Nathan's skull. *Once they know who you are and where you are, they control you.*

Nathan forced himself to remember that it was just a delivery droid. It was unarmed and probably incapable of combat, so he answered with a nod of the head.

"Yeah, that's me".

The droid handed him the crate and produced a datapad for Nathan to sign. Once their transaction was complete, the droid said in a robotic but joyful tone;

"You have a great day".

The wooden crate was no bigger than a case of Sphinax wine, but it was surprisingly heavy for its size. Nathan checked the outside of the box for any return address details, but he only found his name printed on top.

"I thought you weren't registering the ship's location?" Astrilla said.

"I didn't," Nathan shook his head.

"You're violating about thirty Commonwealth laws by doing that by the way," Harrt chipped in.

Nathan chose to ignore him.

They took the box back into the ship, and Nathan cut it open with a knife. The whole time, Astrilla hovered behind him nervously, watching over his shoulder. As he opened it, Nathan saw the contents and felt his heartbeat quicken. His brain wanted to communicate an expression of shock, but he was overwhelmed. He stepped back, words unable to form in his mouth.

It had been ten long years since he'd laid eyes on it — the gun that had once belonged to Jack Stephens.

The weapon emitted a cold, yet fearsome glow. It was forged from the shell of an old Earth revolver and turned into a hybrid. The barrel was as he remembered it —a mix of carbon-suminite and Earth steel. The grip, though weathered, still looked sleek and battle-worthy. Nathan took ahold of it and placed it on the table.

He noticed a folded piece of card at the bottom of the box. Printed on the ivory-white parchment were the words;

Never let them see you bleed.

It made Nathan's gut cease up. The words of Jack Stephens along with his gun were there, right before him. Nathan couldn't help but wonder; *What if he's still alive?*

"What is it?" Astrilla finally asked.

It took Nathan a moment to form a coherent response;

"It's Jack's gun. I think he sent this to me".

CHAPTER TWENTY-NINE

Eventually, all of us must return to the darkness from whence we came. It is for that reason that every monarch must ensure that the royal bloodline continues. There must always be an heir of pure Revenant blood, and they must be prepared to take up the mantle.

As he meditated, Seig allowed the ice-cold water of the river Prynn to wash over his grey body. He used the time to commune with the Great Void; to ask it how he could fulfil his destiny.

Seig's meditation was cut short by the sound of his communication terminal chiming. He climbed from the water and allowed his body to acclimatise to the slightly warmer environment. He saw the meeting request on his screen and knew it was something he couldn't ignore. He ordered one of his servants to pass him his robes.

After dressing, Seig keyed in his access code to the communications terminal and a holographic projection of his son formed. Prince Baylum stared at his father, his robes covered in blood and entrails.

Every time Seig looked at his son, he thought he was looking into a mirror. Baylum had the same imposing stature; the same grey muscular skin covered in ceremonial tattoos of the Revenant Creed. Unlike his father, Baylum was covered in a plethora of scars and war-wounds: a result of his aggressive and combative nature.

Baylum was trained in every form of combat imaginable, just like Seig and all the other monarchs before, but Baylum was different. The Prince was filled with rage. He didn't care for the holy mission in the same way that his father did.

Seig believed that it was his duty to guide the sinful to salvation by any means possible. He didn't like it, but at the same time, he didn't hate it. It was simply his purpose. There was no joy to be taken in the killing of the heretics.

Baylum, on the other hand, revelled in the slaughter and chaos of battle; almost treating it as though it were a sport. As a result, the Prince had suffered many injuries over the years, but it had made him a wise combatant.

"It is good to see you, my son," Seig said. "I hear your exploits in the field of battle have been most successful".

"They have," Baylum answered, bowing his head in respect to his father. "We've taken an entire system this week. The people believed that if they surrendered, they would be spared. How wrong they were".

It didn't take much effort for Seig to picture his son cutting through waves of yielding infidels. He could only imagine Baylum's pleasure in delivering those souls to the river Prynn after the slaughter. It made Seig both proud and fearful at the same time, so he chose not to acknowledge it.

"I presume Admiral Olbori has told you of my plans?" Seig asked.

Baylum nodded but didn't say anything. Seig knew that his son would feel excluded, but he didn't care. The Prince was dangerous, and having him around at such a critical time would be most unwise.

"It is regretful that you'd prefer me to not be there," Baylum finally said. "To witness the downfall of our greatest enemy would be an honour. I implore you to reconsider and let me help you lay waste to the Commonwealth".

Seig shook his head:

"I need you out there. Should I die, you will be all that remains of our bloodline. The cause cannot afford to lose both of us".

Baylum's jaw tightened, but he didn't argue.

Seig found it interesting to watch his son pretending to be angry. It was almost authentic, but the intelligence in Baylum's eyes told Seig everything he needed to know. The prospect of slaughtering more lives without the hindrance of military strategy had already sent adrenaline coursing through Baylum's veins. Without Olbori in the way, Baylum could do precisely as he wanted, and in turn, would convert billions more.

"As you wish, Father," Baylum bowed his head.

Sensing that his son was going to deactivate the comm-link, Seig interrupted him:

"There is something else that I need from you".

The Prince stopped and awaited his fathers instruction:

"I need your spy to start submitting reports on Astrilla's whereabouts," Seig said. "I suspect that she fled to Commonwealth space".

Baylum narrowed his eyes with a look of reticence on his face. The Prince had many spies; it was how Olbori and many others had been recruited, but this particular mole was different. Even Seig didn't know his or her true identity. All he knew was that the spy had been working for them for over fifteen years and they'd proven themselves particularly useful.

"I'll see what I can do, but it may take some time," Baylum finally answered. "*We* cannot risk losing this particular spy, Father".

"Just make it happen".

The holographic projection of Prince Baylum nodded and disappeared. Seig knew that the mole would deliver the intel; it was only a matter of time. Knowing that he needed to channel some patience, Seig removed his robe and moved back into the river Prynn.

I embrace the plan you have laid out for me. I shall deliver the heretics to salvation. I will fulfil your divine mission and bring about the end of chaos.

▲

During the escape from Yenex, the Phoenix's engines had only been at eighty percent thrust capacity. It was a slightly terrifying fact that the engineers had shared with Harrt after they'd finished the repairs. The ship had still outrun the Revenant fleet, but evidently, it was by a hair. Either it was dumb luck, or the Phoenix Titan really was a one-of-a-kind ship. It was when Harrt flipped the switches to activate the engine that he realised that it was the latter rather than the former.

The Phoenix Titan roared as it lifted off from Pelos Three. The shift of gravity as they entered the zero-g atmosphere was astounding. It felt more like flying a small fighter than a freighter.

Once the Phoenix entered the gentle embrace of open-space, Harrt spun the pilot's chair around and looked at Koble in the co-pilot's seat.

"And I thought this thing was impressive when we were getting away from Yenex," Koble remarked. "Ol' tricky Jack surprises us once again".

"Tell me something," Harrt began as he keyed a series of coordinates into the terminal beside him. "When your old crew got sabotaged at Mirotose Station, what were you doing there?"

Harrt couldn't help but wonder why the Sphinax nervously checked over his shoulder before answering in a lowered voice.

"Technically it was intended as a kinda shore leave for the crew," Koble said. "But, well, there was a small delivery job we needed to do".

"What were you hauling?"

Koble shrugged in response;

"Jack used to have this contact on Paradisium who sold and traded old heirlooms with other Earthers. Guess it was some old Earther crap that this guy was selling to another lost soul".

"So you didn't know what the cargo was?" Harrt raised his brow.

"I know it wasn't dirty if that's what you're implying," Koble said. "The point is that the job was simple; collect a crate of old Earther crap from a delivery hub near Nebar Point then haul it to Mirotose Station".

"Why Nebar Point?" Harrt said as he plotted the route for FTL into the nav terminal. "That's a hell of a journey from Paradisium".

Harrt noted that Koble checked over his shoulder again.

"Jack didn't care for Paradisium or other Earthers for that matter. I guess he had some history back there," Koble said. "Besides, his contact on Paradisium liked to remain anonymous. Nobody on the crew knew who he was".

"Not even Nathan?" Harrt said.

Koble waited for a moment then shook his head:

"None of us knew".

"Your old crew didn't share much," Harrt said, saying it more like a question than a statement.

"We didn't," Koble shook his head. "The Loyalty was a crew of orphans, misfits, and nomads. I'm pretty sure there were a few criminals amongst us. We wanted nothing to do with the 'wealth, the Revenant or the corporations".

"How come?" Harrt questioned. "The Commonwealth offers its citizens everything they'd ever need to live a happy life. They'd have welcomed your people with open arms, just like they did with the Earthers".

Koble shrugged.

"Like I said, Jack had a history with some of the Earthers. Doesn't change the fact he was one of the finest men I've ever known".

Harrt could tell that Koble was holding something back, but he didn't acknowledge it. Koble's history was his to share at his own discretion, just like his own.

"So, what happened at Mirotose Station?" Harrt asked.

Koble unfastened himself from the co-pilot's seat and stretched.

"We got to the trade and found our recipient dead. Then, all of sudden this..." Koble paused as though he were searching for the right words. "This small army sabotaged us. They weren't like anything I'd ever seen before. No gang would be that well organised".

"You think they were Revenant?"

Koble shook his head almost immediately;

"No. These guys were a highly organised unit. They wore masks, combat armour and carried some serious weaponry".

Harrt felt a lump form in the back of his throat as he digested the new information. What Koble described sounded like a Commonwealth Black Ops unit, but he couldn't be entirely sure. Then again, why would the Commonwealth concern themselves with a group of pirates in the Outer Worlds?

"All I know is that I saw all the people I cared about die," Koble said, his voice becoming thoughtful. "And that was for the second time in my life".

"What was the first time?"

"The Pluvium Civil War," Koble said stoically. "But that's a story for another time".

As Koble exited the cockpit, Harrt was left with a strange, empty feeling in the pit of his stomach.

Perhaps we aren't that dissimilar, Harrt thought.

▲

When Nathan finally got to his cabin, he locked the door behind him and slumped on the bed. Despite his overwhelming sense of fatigue, Nathan was unable to sleep. He felt restless, but it wasn't because they were heading to a potentially dangerous world. It was because of Jack.

Are you still out there, old man?

Nathan turned in bed a few times, before finally sitting up. His eyes were drawn to Jack's gun on the mantle. Someone had arranged the delivery to Pelos Three; to the Phoenix Titan: the very ship that Jack had left for him.

That can't be a coincidence, Nathan thought.

He climbed from the bed and took ahold of the firearm. It was the same gun Jack had carried with him on the day of the Fall. Jack had used that very weapon on the Revenant soldiers who'd murdered Nathan's parents and grandmother. To hold it now felt strange —like he wasn't supposed to have it.

Nathan recalled something Jack said in his final message;

The path ahead is gonna be fuckin' hard, but I know you can do this.

Did Jack know this was going to happen? Nathan wondered, but he shut the thought down quickly. *Don't be fuckin' stupid,* he told himself.

Jack was a simple man with a simple desire to survive. He didn't care about the Enkaye or the war. All that mattered to Jack Stephens was the Loyalty and his crew.

What if someone's fucking with me? Nathan wondered.

He placed the gun down in frustration and took a deep breath. Before he could summon another thought, there was a knock at the door. He was more than happy to entertain the distraction.

He opened the door to find Astrilla. The Evoker was wearing a dark robe, with a large hood pulled over the top of her head.

"Why aren't you asleep?" Astrilla said, rubbing her eyes.

Nathan allowed the words to linger until the irony became apparent. It was clear from her dark eyes that Astrilla was utterly exhausted too.

"Maybe you should be more concerned with *your* lack of sleep than mine," Nathan folded his arms.

The Evoker narrowed her brown eyes in frustration:

"I can't sleep because all I can sense is the ambivalence radiating from you and this cabin".

Nathan stared at her for several seconds. He was amazed that even in her sleepy state, she could form such an eloquent sentence. After a moment, her frown softened, and she pulled back her hood.

"It's the gun, isn't it?" she said softly. "That's what's troubling you".

In the back of his mind, Nathan heard the voice of Jack;

Never let them see you bleed.

For the first time in a very long time, Nathan shut Jack

out. He'd followed his uncle's lessons for years, and what did he have to show for it? A sense of trepidation and hostility. Yes, he'd left Nathan the Phoenix Titan, but it didn't replace the pain of being alone for so long. Jack was gone, and it was time to move forward.

Nathan looked to Astrilla. The Evoker nodded at the gun again;

"Would you like to talk about it?"

There was something in her eyes that made Nathan question himself. He wondered if he'd imagined it, or if perhaps there was a flicker of something between them. It wasn't something that he'd ever considered. The truth was that he'd not thought about romantic encounters in a long time. People had a tendency of letting him down, and previous relationships had undoubtedly confirmed that. Besides, Astrilla was an Evoker, and he was a freelancer. They were two very different people.

Nathan didn't realise he'd paused to mentally prepare his response until Astrilla tilted her head to one side, with her brow raised:

"Well?" she said. "Would you like to talk about it?"

The tone in her voice suggested impatience, like she already knew he was going to say yes.

"Sure," Nathan answered. "I could use a drink".

CHAPTER THIRTY

With most of the crew asleep, the only thing that could be heard was the faint hum of the FTL slipstream. There was something oddly relaxing about it that Astrilla could never quite identify. It was like meditating during a rainstorm: soothing, contemplative and yet somehow chaotic and uncontrolled.

Astrilla sipped from her mug of warm floral tea as she listened to everything Nathan had to say. It was evident from the moment they'd met that the Earther had lived through some tough times, and Jack seemed to be at the centre of all of them. Of course, Astrilla couldn't form a clear picture of the man, but she sensed he'd had a flexible moral code. From the outside looking in, Jack was the cause of Nathan's burdens. Rather than getting his son and nephew the counsel they needed after the Fall, Jack had dragged them into a life of crime and chaos. It was that same lifestyle that ultimately resulted in Jack's murder.

Nathan described the ambiguity of his death as *uncertain.* Jack's demise had resulted in the destruction of the Loyalty and the break-up of what remained of his crew. It was clear that Nathan felt responsible, but he said that Jack's final message served as form of closure. Then the gun had shown up and thrown everything up in the air once again.

"And you think Jack is still out there?" Astrilla said.

"What do you think?"

"I think the universe works in mysterious ways".

Her answer seemed to frustrate Nathan, so Astrilla decided the best course of action was to share her experiences.

"I lost my entire family too. After I left to become an Evoker, my homeworld was destroyed by the Revenant."

A sorrowful expression filled Nathan's eyes, but only for a heartbeat. It was evident that the Earther didn't like to show emotion around other people. He'd clearly learnt to shield himself from others a long time ago.

"I'm sorry," he said, clearly unsure of what else to say.

"For months, I struggled with the same kind of guilt that you described," Astrilla said.

"You seem pretty well adjusted," Nathan said stoically. "How'd you get past all those shitty feelings?"

"Elder Yuta told me that the dead are gone. Rather than mourn what could have been, we should celebrate that which was," Astrilla said. "The Revenant may have taken your home, but they could never destroy the love you had for those people. The same applies to your uncle. Don't mourn what could have been: mourn what was".

There was a moment where neither of them said a word. Astrilla wondered if Nathan would take anything from what she'd said, or if he'd simply brush it off. He reminded her that life was bitter and harsh, and Astrilla appreciated that she'd grown up with the appropriate support.

"It's about time someone put an end to the Revenant," Nathan said, staring into his cup. "Those bastards can't keep making orphans like you and I".

Astrilla could only nod in response.

▲

They spoke for another twenty minutes until Nathan finally decided to go to bed. Just as Astrilla hoped, talk had helped to ease the Earther's worries. As Nathan shuffled to his cabin, Astrilla felt something strange.

What is this? she wondered. *Is it perplexity, or*

fascination?

Astrilla smiled regardless. Whatever it was she couldn't quite put her finger on it, but that was ok. The feeling was unintrusive and didn't serve as a distraction. Rather than examine it any further, she wandered back to her cabin and climbed into bed.

▲

Memories of the Fall flooded into Astrilla's sleeping mind, but they weren't hers. Fires roared across the landscape causing the once blue skies to turn red. Dylan Carter rushed toward the enemy but was sliced down by a Revenant hunter. His body slammed into the wall, pinned by a jagged metal spear. His tortured final screams filled the dream. As Liza Carter begged for her son's life, an officer turned his weapon on her and pulled the trigger.

There was darkness, then there were stars.

Despite the cold emptiness of the lifeless vacuum, Astrilla could feel something call out to her across the void.

Mirotose Station was far off in the distance, and yet, Astrilla could tell that she had to go there: that the Omega laid within the station's cold metal walls.

In the blink of an eye, she was transported to the middle of a desert. She stared at her new surroundings, hoping to find something —anything— that would help them to locate the Omega. Instead, Astrilla found a wooden bench, that she knew was out of place.

She took two paces toward it, and voices began to swarm her.

"From the darkness, there will come a guiding light".

"Find the Machine".

"It'll be an easy job, Nate. Sneak aboard, grab the goods then make a break for it."

Astrilla reached for the bench and placed her hand down on its warm surface. The voices didn't subside and instead grew louder.

"I've been waiting for you for what feels like a lifetime".

"LOYALTY!"

"You're an arrogant little bastard, Carter. Just like that uncle of yours".

There came a woman's scream from one of the sandy dunes, but Astrilla tried to shut it out.

"Find the Machine!"

The final voice was that of Jack Stephens. He stared down into a dark void with his hand reaching out for something that was falling. His scream was one of desperation and sadness.

He yelled a name. "Krell".

Astrilla awoke cramped and cold beneath her bedsheets. There was a discomfort in her chest where her heart had been pounding so hard that it ached. The vision was far more visceral than the first. She didn't know why, but Astrilla felt a distinct sense of loss and failure, but she knew it wasn't her own.

"Find the Machine, and you will find the Omega," Astrilla repeated.

Astrilla sat up, took a deep breath and assessed what she had seen. Something instinctive told her that Nathan had shared the same vision. It was clear that whatever purpose these visions had, they meant something important. For one reason or another, the universe was guiding them toward Mirotose Station.

Toward the Machine.

▲

Many years ago, Vol had learnt that the best thing to do during a long haul FTL journey was to sleep through it. Some people experienced gravity sickness if they stayed planetside for too long, others experienced panic attacks. In Vol's case, she suffered headaches. She figured it was far more comfortable to sleep through the pain rather than suffer.

She spent the evening examining the repairs to the Phoenix. Then when the headache had started, she sat with Harrt in the cockpit. They discussed the ship, the mission and her experience fixing an old Pelosian racer. After that, she fell asleep in the co-pilot's chair.

She dreamt about repairing the engine on a modern Belfort Linkrider, before waking.

"We're here," Harrt said as he nudged her awake.

Vol stretched until the joints in her shoulders popped. She looked out of the window to examine Mironium One. The first thing she noticed was a giant swampy ocean dividing seven distinct continents, all of which had been heavily industrialised.

In the distant orbit of the planet was Mirotose Station: the space station that served as the economic trading centre of the system. Even from a distance, a few thousand kilometres away, Vol could make out the cylindrical silhouette against the barren starscape. A vast sprawling city was built across the entirety of the Station's inner and outer shell.

"So, where are we landing?" Vol said. "Planet or station?"

Harrt turned to her and shrugged;

"I don't know. Maybe we should—"

"Mirotose Station," Nathan interrupted as he entered the cockpit. He handed Harrt a datapad and pointed at the screen. "We're heading for the gambling district. Whatever it is we're looking for, it's there".

There was a sense of certainty in Nathan's voice that Vol hadn't felt since they'd first met. It was as though he'd gained perspective.

"You had another dream, didn't you?" Vol asked.

Nathan chewed the inside of his cheek and nodded quietly in response.

▲

It took slightly longer than Nathan expected to gain landing clearance. After several minutes of arguing with a particularly obstinate flight controller, Harrt was able to convince him that they weren't from Jareth Corps or from Roth Industries. It took some time, but eventually, the

Phoenix was cleared to land.

"There it is," Nathan sighed. "One of the more fucked-up, shady places I've ever been".

Mirotose Station was a giant floating hub, with queues of traffic going in and out of the trading district. As the Phoenix Titan approached, it became clear that the expansive city structure had only grown since the last time Nathan had visited.

After docking, the crew gathered in the cockpit to discuss a plan of action. Harrt and Vol brought up a publicly available schematic of the station, while Koble ate a breakfast of pungent-smelling fish.

"So, where are we heading?" Koble drawled.

In Nathan's mind, there was no doubt that the vision — or dream— was trying to tell him something, but it was unclear. Amongst the cacophony of muddled voices, Nathan had been able to identify one of them as his former employer, Don Guttasnype Galassini.

What the hell does that weasel have to do with all this? Nathan wondered.

There was no reason for Guttasnype to have any involvement with Enkaye relics, the Commonwealth or the Revenant. He was a self-serving criminal, whose only interested was making money. Conducting business as far out as the Mironium System would be a breach of a hundred unwritten mafia rules. For Guttasnype to do business on another Don's territory could put the entire criminal syndicate on his back. The Icktus was certainly not that stupid.

"Nathan?"

He snapped out of his train of thought and glanced up from the holotable to Harrt, who was looking at him, expecting an answer.

"Sorry," Nathan shook his head. "Say again?"

The 'wealther sighed through his nostrils and repeated; "I think it'd be wise if a few of us stayed here to guard the ship".

"Agreed," Nathan nodded. "I've not been here for a while, but it doesn't look like it's changed much".

"Looks like its gotten worse if anything!" Koble gestured out of the window. The Sphinax climbed to his feet and stared at the schematic for several seconds. "This is one hell of a big station to be looking for an Enkaye relic," Koble folded his arms. "What exactly did you guys see in this dream of yours?"

"It was a *vision*," Astrilla corrected him. "It was hazy. There was a desert and a park bench and voices".

Koble clicked his teeth sarcastically, then turned to Nathan with a raised brow.

"What kinda voices?"

Nathan reflected on the dream.

"One of them was Jack," Nathan said with certainty. "Guttasnype was another".

When Nathan mentioned Jack, Koble's eyes lifted, but as soon as he spoke of Guttasnype, they lowered into a frown.

"Great," Koble pressed a paw against his forehead in frustration. "Where there's Guttasnype there's trouble".

"Am I missing something here?" Harrt said. "Why is this Guttasnype such an inconvenience for you guys?"

"Well for one, he's the guy who hired me to sneak aboard the Vertex," Nathan answered. "Secondly, he's a part of the Criminal Syndicate and has some interesting associates".

"Plus he's an all-round asshole," Koble added. The Sphinax placed his bowl down and focussed on Nathan and Astrilla. "Did these voices have anything else to say?"

"Two of them kept screaming," Astrilla said, she turned to Nathan for confirmation; "They were saying Loyalty and..."

"Krell," Nathan finished her sentence. "It was Jack screaming the name, Krell".

Koble seemed to stiffen. He lifted his head and peered back at them with a confused look.

"W-what did you say?" Koble said with a dry mouth.

"Jack was looking down at someone called Krell," Astrilla confirmed.

Koble took a step closer to Nathan, his fur standing

upright in displeasure. It was a rare sight to see a Sphinax with hairs standing to attention and made Koble appear bigger than he already was.

"And you're sure he was saying the name, Krell?" Koble said with a low voice.

"Positive," Nathan nodded. "It's a Sphinax name, right?"

"It is," Koble nodded. "It was my mother's name".

There was a tension that lingered in the air for a moment too long. Nobody wanted to discuss the Pluvium civil war; least of all, Koble. Nathan knew that Koble had lost his entire family in the war, but didn't know the exact details. Bringing up the subject with the rest of the crew around would be insensitive, so Nathan didn't press the Sphinax for answers.

Koble stared at the schematic for a few more seconds, twiddling his whisker in deep thought. Finally, he turned to Nathan;

"I think I know where we gotta go"

CHAPTER THIRTY-ONE

Mirotose Station felt like a living creature. Its streets were alive, and Nathan knew that there were eyes on every corner. He forced himself to remember that unlike Yenex, the Revenant wasn't there — for now.

If anything we are safer here than we were on Yenex, Nathan told himself.

He walked beside Astrilla, several paces behind Koble. The Sphinax led them through the busy gambling district toward a club called Cambino's. Nathan was unfamiliar with the area, but it seemed just as unsafe as the rest of the station, so he kept his hand close to his concealed gun.

"Who is he taking us to?" Astrilla said, nodding toward Koble.

Nathan shrugged, "Beats me. The last time I was here, this part of the station was still under construction".

The answer didn't satisfy the Evoker's curiosity. She took a deep breath and looked around their dingy surroundings.

"There's something that's been troubling me about our last vision," she said.

Besides the fact, we're sharing dreams? Nathan thought but didn't speak aloud.

"What is the significance of this mobster, Guttasnype?" Astrilla said.

Knowing that by merely saying the name of a Mafia Don could attract some unwanted attention, Nathan checked over his shoulder to make sure they weren't being followed. He gestured to the Evoker to lower her voice.

"I don't know," Nathan whispered. "Guttasnype doesn't operate out here. The Syndicate would kill him if he was working so far from his territory, so I highly doubt he's got anything to do with this".

"The Syndicate?" Astrilla asked in a hushed tone.

"It's a kind of criminal network," Nathan replied. "All the Don's in the Outer Worlds simply trying to keep the peace".

"Does it work?"

"What d'you think?" Nathan raised his brow.

"I think you know an awful lot about this criminal network…"

There was no hint of judgement in Astrilla's eyes, and Nathan wasn't ashamed of the life he'd led. It was all he'd known.

"I've lived in places like this since I was five," Nathan admitted. "Outside of the Commonwealth, this is how many are forced to live".

The look of pure compassion on the Evokers face was enough to make Nathan pause for thought. He'd never asked for sympathy —or pity— from anyone: he certainly hoped it was the former. This was the way it had been, and there was no one to blame but the Revenant. When Nathan glanced back at Astrilla, her dark eyes had softened considerably. He could only see her pity —as though his mind wouldn't allow him to see anything else.

Never let them see you bleed, Jack's voice echoed around his skull. Nathan listened to his uncle's words and did his best to disregard Astrilla's compassion.

"We should catch-up to Koble," Nathan murmured.

Cambino's was at the top of a neon-soaked promenade; sandwiched between a nightclub and a casino. Koble led Nathan and Astrilla straight past a fast-talking pimp, whose gaze lingered on the Evoker's rear for an uncomfortable amount of time.

If only he knew that she could set him on fire, Nathan thought.

It was the kind of thing that was to expected on Mirotose Station. Social decency didn't exist here. Instead, it was replaced by lust, greed and the type of immorality, that Nathan associated with degenerates.

Koble stopped them at the door, and with a deadpan look on his face.

"Let me do the talking, got it?" The Sphinax looked at both of them, then pointed at Astrilla. "And please try not to offend anyone".

Astrilla straightened up, ready to argue, but by the time she was ready, Koble had pushed open the doors.

The interior of Cambino's was luxurious in an old-fashioned, seedy manner. There was a bar at one end of the club looking onto a large stage with patrons sitting around, either doing business or watching the dancers. Half-a-dozen scantily dressed young women waited tables, while heavy-set armed bouncers watched from every corner. There was a thumping bass line of a track punching through the sound system. An announcer's voice boomed over the top;

"Loosen your collars and get ready for something scorching. Put your hands together for Shaneyqua."

A female human burst through a pair of red velour curtains. She floated into the dazzling glare of a red spotlight, spinning her half-naked body around. As the stripper began to perform, Nathan turned to Astrilla; her face flush with disgust.

"That is... rather vulgar," she said.

"Welcome to Mirotose Station," Nathan replied, while shrugging with his hands. "Whatever your vice, this place can cater for it".

He nodded in the direction of the stripper, who'd already tossed her bra into the audience. When Nathan turned back to Astrilla, the Evoker frowned at him.

"Believe it or not," Nathan shrugged, "this is kinda tame".

Astrilla's look of disapproval deepened.

"Guys," Koble said over the loud music. "Stop

gawking. We have a galaxy to save, remember?"

Koble walked past the stage to a door at the back of the club. A large male Horrus with a coat of greying fur stood guard with his bulky arms folded.

"Staff only," the dog-like creature said as though reading from a script.

Nathan saw it for what it was: a polite yet firm way of telling them in no uncertain terms *to turn around and fuck-off.*

"I'm here to see Flotonius," Koble said.

"Never heard of him".

Koble smirked and rolled his eyes;

"Of course you haven't.."

"Sir—"

Koble grabbed the Horrus by the collar and pulled him in close. "You find Flotonius and tell him that Koble is here. Tell him it's time for him to repay his debt".

Koble released his grip on the Horrus. The bouncer straightened, gritted his giant canine teeth at Koble, then pulled a communicator from his belt.

"Boss," he said into the device. "Got a guy called Koble here to see you. He's saying something about debts".

There was a pause, and then a husky male voice replied;

"Bring him through".

At some point during the flight to Mirotose Station, Dines sent Harrt a message and an update with the latest Commonwealth intel.

OXARRI, I HAVE BRIEFED THE GRAND MASTER ON OUR SITUATION. IF THERE IS A MOLE, YOU CAN EXPECT A REVENANT PRESENCE WITHIN TWELVE HOURS. GOOD HUNTING.

Dines' intel provided a useful download of the latest

Revenant movements. The first page detailing the Revenant's withdrawal from the frontlines was interesting, but the second proved to be far more provoking. An image of the disgraced former Commonwealth Commander, Densius Olbori, popped up as Harrt opened the page. Involuntarily, Harrt's hands formed into fists at the sight of his former CO and mentor.

"I will find you," Harrt said to himself. "Mark my words. Even if I have to hunt you to the ends of the universe, I will find you, and I will kill you".

Beneath the picture of Olbori was a single paragraph:

GRAND ADMIRAL OLBORI HAS ASSUMED COMMAND OF THE REVENANTS, FIRST, SECOND AND THIRD FLEETS. REPORTS SUGGEST THAT KING SEIG HAS JOINED HIM.

Harrt pulled up a galaxy-map on the holotable and clashed the data from Dines' intel against it. Where the Revenant had withdrawn, it looked like a victory for the Commonwealth. At least that was what it was supposed to look like. The withdrawal was nothing more than a calculated move, straight out of Olbori's book of military tactics.

Rally the forces, then make a final push, Harrt thought.

The question was, *why?*

The Messorem may have been in the Revenant's hands, but it was inoperable. The simple fact was that Seig needed Astrilla. Without her, the Enkaye war machine would be nothing more than a floating piece of old space junk.

So why is Olbori pulling them back? Harrt wondered.

He pondered every tactical scenario that sprung to mind, but not one of them felt concrete. In Harrt's mind, the only possibility was that Olbori was focussing his efforts on something else: likely the search and capture of Astrilla.

"We gotta be careful," Harrt concluded.

He deactivated the holotable when Vol came into the cockpit. She carried in her hands two food cartons, which she'd bought from a street vendor outside. Judging by the spicy aroma, it was a Mironium version of a Yexian stew. Vol handed him one of the steaming cartons and settled into the co-pilot's seat.

"Nathan and Koble weren't exaggerating," she said. "I don't know what's filthier; Mirotose Station or the thoughts of some of the people living on it".

"That's precisely why I didn't want to leave the Phoenix unguarded," Harrt replied. "Places like this outside the Commonwealth are a breeding ground for crime and indecency".

A gentle smirk formed on Vol's lips. "You haven't travelled much outside of the 'wealth have you?"

Harrt knew that the Uvan's mockery was camaraderie, but at first, he wasn't sure how to respond. He opened the carton of fragrant stew and stirred it with his fork.

"I'll have you know that I spent six months in the Darrum System," Harrt replied.

"The Darrum System?" Vol scoffed, almost choking on her food. "That's more like a honeymoon destination than an Outer Worlds planet. You may as well have gone to Paradisium and worked on your tan with the Earthers".

In some small way, Harrt knew that she was right. Granted, the Darrum System wasn't technically a part of the Commonwealth; it wasn't like Yenex or any of the worlds in the Mironium System. Far from it. All of the planets, from Darrum One through Six, were a paradise, devoid of the level of crime on Mirotose Station.

"What were you doing in the Darrum system, anyway?" Vol asked as she prodded at her food.

Harrt was reticent to answer her question at first, but the friendly way in which Vol looked at him, made him feel safe.

"You ever heard of the festival of lights?" Harrt asked.

Vol stopped nudging her food and looked up at him.

"Sure," she nodded. "You light a lantern and let it go into the sky as a commemoration for a loved one who's passed. The Sphinax do something similar." Vol paused before asking; "If you don't mind me asking, who was your lantern for?"

Harrt took a mouthful of his stew as Vol spoke but almost spat it out when the spice hit the back of his throat. He forced himself to swallow the red-hot mix of tank-bred peppers, rice and fish, before setting the container down.

He cleared his throat; "The lanterns were for my wife and son". He coughed against the spice of his food and added; "I always promised that I'd take them to Darrum One, but, well—"

Harrt stopped.

There was the sound of a crash from the living area which prompted Harrt to dart from his seat. By time he was up, Vol had done the same. He drew his gun and gestured to the Uvan to do the same.

Someone was aboard the Phoenix. Harrt knew it.

Carefully, they proceeded toward the back of the ship. The sound of rustling and gentle footsteps seemed to grow as they drew closer to the lounge. Harrt moved in with his weapon raised. He spotted two male Sphinax checking the bar. One was several decades older with a coat of blue fur, wearing a fedora on his head. The second, no older than his teens, had a stripy black and brown coat of fur and carried a crossbow.

"Check the cockpit," the older one said. "We need to make sure that Jareth Corps hasn't planted any trackers or bugs on this thing".

Harrt stepped out from cover with his gun pointed at the pair.

"I don't think so," Harrt said. "Get the hell off of this ship before I start shooting".

The youngest recoiled when he saw Harrt's gun. His older counterpart stood his ground.

"You don't look like the usual Jareth Corps mercs". The fedora-clad Sphinax had a voice that was smooth and sophisticated: not what Harrt had expected from Mirotose street thugs at all.

"Get the hell off of this ship," Vol ordered.

"I strongly advise you follow the lady's advice," Harrt added.

The younger Sphinax backed away while the other

didn't budge an inch. It told Harrt that this wasn't the first time he'd stared down the barrel of a gun. To Harrt's surprise, the hatted Sphinax took a pace forward.

"Tell me, where did you get this ship?" he asked.

Harrt's finger poised over the trigger.

"Last chance," Harrt warned. "Turn around and leave".

The blue-furred Sphinax eyeballed him arrogantly.

"Y'know, it just seems strange to me that you two are all the way out here aboard a dead man's ship," he mused. "I heard that the Revenant bombed the living crap outta Venin Towers along with the rest of—".

In a move of sheer aggression, Harrt stepped closed and pressed the barrel of his gun against the intruder's forehead. In reaction, the smooth-talking Sphinax didn't flinch a muscle.

"Vikor Venin is in a Commonwealth cell," Harrt said through gritted teeth. "You won't be so lucky if you keep trying my patience".

The fedora-wearing Sphinax smiled at Harrt, which seemed very out of place.

"And you, my friend, need to check corners before entering a room…"

Harrt turned only to get struck over the head with something heavy. It suddenly became apparent that another Sphinax had tucked himself behind the doorway — allowing him to get the jump. Before Harrt could slump to the ground, the Fedora-wearing Sphinax caught him and gently lowered him safely to the floor. As Harrt fell in unconsciousness, he was only partially aware that they had surrounded Vol and taken her gun. He could hear the smooth talker say to his accomplices;

"Take these two back to the lady. You three, guard this ship with your lives".

CHAPTER THIRTY-TWO

Astrilla didn't know what was worse —the club or the backstage area. The dressing room was filled with a varied cast of strippers of every species and gender known. There was a sad desperation that Astrilla tried to push to the back of her mind as she stared at the semi-naked flesh of the dancers.

It wasn't right that people had to live like this: that people had to parade their bodies before an audience to make a living. The experience was a stark reminder of all the things Astrilla had taken for granted. Had Yuta and the Evokers not found her, she could have ended up no different.

Astrilla felt a tug on her upper arm and noticed that Nathan was pulling her down the hall. She didn't realise she'd been staring at the rabble of half-naked dancers for an awkward amount of time.

"You really shouldn't stare," Nathan said. "If one of them is an addict they'll shiv you for sure".

"I wasn't staring," Astrilla shook her head. "I was just —"

"I know," Nathan interrupted. "It's awful and inhuman, but there's nothing we can do about it".

The bouncer escorted them to a dark corridor at the back of the club. When they reached a chipped and dented metal door, the guard knocked three times, and a voice called from the other side;

"Come in".

The office wasn't much better than the club. There was an aroma of exotic smoked herb that had seeded its way into the walls and furniture. At one end of the office, soft velour chairs lined the wall, beneath a collection of vulgar neon signs. The other side was in total contrast. The utilitarian influence reminded Astrilla of the Commonwealth warships and Capital Worlds.

The black desk held no clutter. There was a holo-monitor, a moveable lamp and a single glass of kor. Behind, was an overweight male Horrus, sitting upon a posture improving chair. He wore a black business suit atop his short-styled fur with a gold chain around his neck.

This was Koble's contact, Flotonius.

The guard ushered them inside and closed the door, while Flotonius glared at Koble.

"You've got a lotta brass coming back here, Sphinax," Flotonius mumbled.

Astrilla noticed that Koble didn't react.

"I'm not here to interfere with this little operation that you've got going," Koble replied. "Just here to call in my debts".

"Your debts?" Flotonius choked and slammed his paw on the table.

"Fine, let's call it a favour," Koble shrugged.

"The last time you called in a favour from me, I ended up losing a paw".

"And because of me that's all you lost," Koble replied. "You owe me. More importantly, you owe Jack".

Astrilla took note that Nathan tensed at the mention of his uncle. It was clear that the Earther was unfamiliar with Flotonius or the involvement Jack had with him.

"Jack Stephens is long dead, my friend," Flotonius replied. "People on this station still talk about that massacre down in the docks like it was yesterday. You're lucky to be alive."

"A life debt is a life debt," Koble said. "We saved your ass back on Pluvium. If it weren't for me, Kornell would have thrown you over the city walls, just like he did to my mother".

Flotonius sighed; placed the cut cigar between his lips and pressed the flame of a match to it. The Horrus took a long drag and blew the smoke through his nostrils.

"Pluvium Forever," Flotonius nodded to Koble.

Astrilla found the gesture to be strange, but to her surprise, Koble nodded and repeated the words back. Even though Flotonius wasn't a Sphinax., the statement meant something to him as well.

"So, what do you need?" Flotonius said, taking another long drag on his cigar.

"You still control the facial-recognition out of here?" Koble asked. "The one we used after the attack at the docks?"

Flotonius climbed from behind his desk and waddled across the room. He stopped a few inches ahead of Koble;

"What do you need it for?" he asked.

Koble licked his lips and replied, "I need to find someone".

▲

Astrilla could only assume that Flotonius had once been far more than a strip club manager. He had a background in technology or cyberwarfare at some point in his life, that much was clear. She watched the Horrus as he hooked his holotable up to an old-style computer. Flotonius worked a keyboard and began to bypass and breach the station's computer network. Within minutes, he'd used his elaborate setup to hack into Mirotose Station's mainframe.

"So, who are you looking for?" Flotonius glanced at Koble.

"I need to see every adult Sphinax who's come through here in the last week," Koble said. "Start with females".

Flotonius worked the keyboard, and within a minute the computer returned over a hundred results.

Koble shook his head in annoyance, "Filter out any under sixty cycles of age".

Flotonious reloaded the information, and only five

results came back. Koble studied each of the pictures intently, but none of them was what he was looking for.

"Shit," Koble cursed to himself.

Nathan moved toward the holotable and Astrilla noticed a quizzical look on the Earther's face.

"Does this thing search by name?" Nathan said.

"I wouldn't be much of a hacker if it didn't," Flotonius remarked.

Astrilla could hear Nathan grinding his teeth.

"What are you thinking?" Astrilla said, placing a hand against his shoulder.

Nathan looked at Astrilla's hand, which she promptly withdrew. The Earther paced awkwardly around the projection. His expression was thoughtful yet filled with dread. Finally, he looked to Astrilla;

"The voices said *Loyalty*, right?"

"I believe so," she nodded.

Nathan closed his eyes and took a deep breath. Astrilla could tell that what Nathan was going to say was far from easy. The Earther turned to Flotonius and said,

"Search for Jack Stephens".

The raised brow that Flotonious shot Nathan was undoubtedly born out of confusion. The Horrus looked to Koble, who simply shrugged in response.

"You heard the kid, search for Jack".

Flotonious carried a cynical expression but continued to work the computer nonetheless. It took far longer to load than the previous searches, and during that time, Astrilla was sure she could feel Nathan's heart pounding. Eventually, the search returned a series of images that dated back over a decade.

Over a few minutes, Nathan studied the two dozen moving images of his uncle carefully. Astrilla did the same but unlike Nathan, she did it out of curiosity. The man who Nathan and Koble had described appeared relaxed in most of the footage. In one video it showed him sitting in a cafe with a young woman, who Koble nostalgically identified as *Merri*. In another piece of footage, Jack conversed with a more youthful and less bearded version of Nathan. They exchanged conversation while loading a large crate onto a trolley. It was strange to see a snapshot of the past, but it helped Astrilla to understand. Jack had been a paternal figure. Not just for Nathan and his own son, but also for Koble, Merri and many others. Maybe there was something redeeming about him after all.

"And, this is all you've got?" Nathan looked at Flotonius. "Anything from the docks?"

The Horrus tapped a button on his control panel. The two dozen videos that had been there before were replaced by footage of violence and chaos. The group that Jack Stephens was fighting off wore black masks and armour. They weren't Revenant, and they weren't a street gang. The organised nature of the hostile force reminded Astrilla of the Commonwealth marines she'd faced during her escape from the Vertex.

In one video, Jack helped an injured Horrus to his feet and began firing at the opposing force. In another, a young woman was cut to shreds by laser fire, while Jack called out to her in horror. Every piece of rolling of the video showed a member of the Loyalty's crew being slaughtered. The enemy —whoever they were— had showed no mercy.

Astrilla knew in her gut that it had been intended as an assassination.

"We were supposed to be delivering some antiques to a guy down on the docks," Nathan said stoically. "Then these guys showed up..."

Astrilla swallowed the lump in her throat. It seemed pointless for Nathan to torture himself over the events of something that had happened ten years prior, so she asked, "What are you hoping to find in this footage?"

Nathan didn't answer her question and instead turned to Flotonius.

"I need you to track that package," Nathan said, pointing to a wooden crate in the videos. "Can you do that for me?"

Flotonious nodded, and the computer returned a diagram that showed the movements of the Loyalty's final delivery. Container LOY8476-J had undisclosed contents.

The sender and recipients names were redacted from the station's records. There was, however, a trail of its movements. The Loyalty's final delivery was now stored in an apartment on Mirotose Station: registered to someone called Kornell.

Nathan and Koble's brows raised at the name.

"Son-of-a-bitch," the Sphinax said through gritted teeth. He turned to Flotonious and ordered him to run a search on the name. What returned was an image of a lean male Sphinax with dark fur and a giant scar across his face. Astrilla noted the time stamp in the bottom right corner was from just a few hours prior.

"Oh fuck," Nathan said wide-eyed. "What the hell is he doing here?"

"I don't understand," Astrilla said, pointing at the hologram. "Who is that?"

Koble turned to her, his face awash with a look of untamed rage. To her surprise, Flotonius stared at the image with a look of dismay in his eyes as well.

"That is Chief Kornell of the Pluvium System," Flotonius answered grimly.

Then Koble added, "He's my brother".

▲

The faint sound of voices caused Harrt to wake from his unconscious state. At the back of his nose was the distinct aroma of Sphinax wine. There was a ringing in his ears, but it subsided after a few seconds. He opened his eyes to a darkened room with a table directly in front of him. As Harrt reached for the dull ache at the side of his head, he felt something grounding him. His hands were tied behind his back, and his feet were shackled to the ground.

"I'm sorry that my man had to inflict such pain upon you, my friend," a voice said. "My people have been seeking revenge against Jareth Corps for the longest time, but they fail to understand the complexities of your corporate lifestyle".

When Harrt's sight settled, he could make out the

fedora-clad Sphinax from earlier sitting across the table.

"My medic checked you for injuries," he added. "You'll have a headache for a few hours, but you'll be fine".

"Wheres Vol?" Harrt said, struggling to form the words.

The Sphinax looked at him with compassion, "She's unharmed and in the next room".

Harrt straightened up in the chair to get a better look at his captor. The blue-haired Sphinax was older than he'd initially thought: somewhere around fifty cycles of age, but it was hard to tell. His coat of fur was a mix of navy blue and sapphire, peppered with the odd grey here and there. It was rare to see a Sphinax with such irregular colouring, especially this far out from the Pluvium System.

"My name is, Rain," he said, placing his fedora on the table. "My people have been tracking the movements of ships in and out of this station for the last month. That is how we found you".

Rain produced a datapad from his jacket and began to read from it;

"Serial number 8527-PAR-68. Modified Titan-class frigate, codename: Phoenix. Registered to the Jareth Corporation over ten years ago". The Sphinax placed the datapad down and stared at Harrt for an awkward amount of time. "Where is David Jareth?"

Harrt shook his head, "I told you, we aren't from Jareth Corps".

Rain climbed from his chair and took a few strides towards Harrt.

"Cast off the corporate shackles my friend," Rain replied. "You don't owe your employers a thing. Your loyalty to them will not be reciprocated. Trust me".

"I told you," Harrt replied. "We aren't from Jareth Corps".

"Then how do you explain the ship?"

"We stole it—"

There was a knock at the door, which caught Rain's attention. The blue-haired Sphinax turned from Harrt and shuffled away. Harrt couldn't see who was at the door, but he could hear Rain speaking to a woman in a lowered voice. The only thing Harrt could definitively make out was Rain saying;

"That's impossible".

Finally, Rain circled around to Harrt with the other Sphinax. The grey-haired female wore a grey hood over her head, and her eyes were stern. She shot Harrt a steely glare, while Rain pulled up a chair. In his paw, Rain carried the old Pluvium flag that Koble had crudely nailed to the wall of his cabin. Harrt noted the look of surprise on Rain's face.

"Where did you get this?" he said, placing the flag down on the table.

"One of my crewmates is a Sphinax," Harrt said nonchalantly. "He fought in the civil war."

Rain exchanged a look with the hodded Sphinax, and they moved to the back of the room to confer. For several seconds, the sound of hushed voices was all that Harrt could hear. Then he heard one of them knock against the door and call out to whoever was on the other side.

"Bring her through," Rain said.

Harrt heard the door behind him swing open, and Vol was led in by two more hooded Sphinax. He was relieved to see that Vol was unharmed. Harrt exchanged a look with Vol, and she nodded to him. Rain directed Vol to take the seat next to Harrt, and she warily followed her captor's order.

"Okay, let's say you aren't from Jareth Corps," Rain mused. "I want to know who you are, and I want to know the name of the Sphinax aboard your ship".

Harrt was reticent to give away their identity, but he didn't have much choice. The group of Sphinax were adamant that he and Vol were from Jareth Corps and it didn't fill him with hope.

"Commonwealth Lieutenant Harrt Oxarri. Serial Number 04673–"

"I told you he's a 'wealther," the hooded Sphinax interrupted and rolled her eyes at Rain. "Get those binds off of them."

As Rain cut the rope from Harrt's wrists, the second

Sphinax pulled her hood, revealing a far older face than Harrt was expecting.

"What is a 'wealther doing with a Jareth Corps ship?" she asked.

"It's not a Jareth Corps ship, anymore," Vol interrupted. "It was left to our Captain by his uncle. Jarrth Corps just stole it".

"Sounds incredibly elaborate if you ask me," Rain interjected.

"It's been a hell of a week," Vol replied.

The female Sphinax grabbed the old Pluvium flag and held it up to them. She stared at Harrt and Vol with the same hard-nosed and authoritative expression she had earlier: "Who's the Sphinax in your crew?" .

CHAPTER THIRTY-THREE

Koble forced himself to unclench his fists. His brother, Kornell, hadn't changed over the last two decades. He still looked as arrogant as the last time they'd seen each other on Pluvium One, and it made Koble's blood boil.

"I don't understand," Astrilla said, pointing at the image of Kornell. "*That* is the Chief of the Pluvium System?"

Koble took a deep breath to push the anger out of his voice.

"Yup,"

"And *he's* your brother?"

"That'd be about right".

"So, what does that make you?" she asked.

Koble stared at his feet and sighed. Everyone who'd known what he'd gone through during the Pluvium civil war was dead. Either they'd perished in the war, or with the Loyalty and her crew during the Mirotose incident.

Koble knew that Nathan's *loose understanding* of the Pluvium Civil War was heavily filtered by Jack. The old man had censored specific parts of the story, while Koble had avoided talking about it all together —at least with the youngsters aboard the Loyalty. Vol knew even less. Koble had told her some parts, but he never wanted to discuss who he really was in any detail.

For the longest time, that was the way Koble wanted it; buried away where he didn't need to think about it. The war had happened, and he'd survived. Everything else was redundant.

Seeing footage of his brother brought everything back. Koble could feel his guts turning in anxiety and all of his fur standing to attention. Knowing that Kornell was standing on the same station as him; breathing the same recycled air as him, made Koble's claws itch. He circled the projection again. Kornell was far more lean and muscular than the last time Koble had seen him.

The enormous diagonal scar that ran from Kornell's face was a result of Jack Stephens: as was the missing thirty centimetres of his tail. It seemed strange that even with all his riches, Kornell had never erased those war wounds. *Maybe he wore them as a badge of honour.*

Jack got you good, Koble thought.

He turned back to Astrilla, who repeated her question; "Who are you?"

Koble sighed through his nostrils and prepared to reply, but Flotonius answered for him;

"He is the true heir to the Pluvium Chiefhood," the Horrus said.

"Heir?" Nathan turned his head to Koble in confusion. "You never said you were the heir. You said you were from a rich family".

Koble sighed again and rubbed a piece of stray fur from his brow.

"Well that's the thing," Koble said. "I *was* the heir".

"Care to elaborate?" Astrilla asked.

"Nope," Koble's response was blunt. He turned to Flotonius; "Can you get me the address of his apartment?"

"You sure that's wise?" Flotonius said. "Kornell ain't gonna—"

"Can you get me that address; yes or no?" Koble raised his voice.

Flotonius reluctantly nodded and brought up a new projection of the station. The apartment was several miles from their current location, but in the same district as the strip-joints and casinos.

"What are we doing here?" Nathan said in a lowered voice. "Remember the mission? We are here to find the next piece of the Omega, not get into a fight with your brother".

There was no denying that Nathan was right, but Koble had the same overwhelming feeling that he'd had back at the Enclave: the idea that something was guiding them toward an end goal.

What if this is it? Koble thought.

He scratched his chin as he moved to a minimised window on the hologram. In the video, he saw Jack Stephens standing by the final delivery that the Loyalty was ever supposed to make. Koble recalled that LOY8476-J was a wooden crate far too heavy for one person to carry. Jack had been acting strangely in the days leading up to Mirotose Station, but at the time, Koble had assumed that it was just Jack being Jack. The Earther could have won an award for his distant, self-loathing nature; but Koble knew it was for a reason.

When he squinted at the video of his old friend, Koble saw something that wasn't right. During the time he'd been looking at the picture of Jack, he'd assumed it was paused footage, but it wasn't. Jack had been staring into space, completely still and mouthing something.

"Can you expand that image?" Koble said to Flotonius.

The Horrus obliged, and the video of Jack filled the space where Kornell had been. It looked as though the paused footage had been taken hours before the crew were sabotaged. Jack stood with his hand on his gun, staring at the wooden crate marked LOY8476-J.

Koble gestured to Flotonious to play the video. Jack didn't move for an odd amount of time. For the better part of twenty seconds, the Loyalty's crew worked around him, offloading the ship and sharing conversation, yet Jack didn't move. Koble beckoned Flotonious to roll back the footage and play it again. He studied the projection of Jack from several angles, and then he saw it again. While his eyes were locked on the crate, Jack's lips moved, but he wasn't talking to anyone. Koble turned back to Flotonious;

"You got audio on that thing?"

The Horrus huffed as he turned the dial on his old computer. When Flotonius hit play, Jack's voice could be heard, and it kept repeating the same three words over and over:

"Find the Machine".

▲

Up until his experiences on Yenex, Nathan never believed in fate. There was no reason to trust anything. In his view, there was no pre-determined path to walk. Everything was in a state of uncontrolled chaos, and Nathan had learnt to live within its boundaries. Back on Yenex, he'd questioned the idea that something more significant was guiding him. On Pelos, he'd started to embrace that idea. Now, he was sure of it.

After leaving Flotonious' club, he'd experienced a wave of emotion that he couldn't quite put into words. Jack had spoken to him through a decade-old piece of footage. The fact that he'd recorded it just hours before his death, on the same station where Nathan was standing felt ominous.

What the hell is going on? Nathan thought, but he didn't have time to ponder the question.

LOY8476-J was in Kornell's possession. It had always been in his possession, and now Nathan was heading to his apartment. He wasn't sure what they would find, but he knew one thing for certain: Kornell had questions to answer.

Flotonius' directions led them out of the gambling district and into a giant marketplace. The smell of unsmoked herb and fish filled the air around them. Traders competed to announce their offers over the sound of the busy market. It reminded Nathan of a simpler time; back when he'd been aboard the Loyalty. Usually, he didn't get nostalgic, but there was something about those times that had been easy. Going from job to job, unburdened by the war or the Revenant now seemed like a distant memory.

"Well," Koble drew the word. "That stuff with Jack was kinda...strange?"

Nathan turned to the Sphinax as they walked, unsure of how to respond. At least Koble appeared as baffled by the situation. That was reassuring in some strange way that

Nathan couldn't quite describe.

"How is something like that possible?" Nathan said. "I mean... that footage was from ten years ago…"

"I think it's a foregone conclusion, Nate," Koble interrupted. The Sphinax lifted his paw and gestured around them; "Destiny; fate; the universe. Whatever you wanna call it...that's what it is".

Nathan didn't dignify it with an answer. It wasn't that he disagreed, it was that he didn't want to appear foolish. Fate and destiny were the kind of bullshit spouted by fortune-tellers and self-appointed psychics. The problem was that Nathan was starting to believe in it, and he didn't know if that scared him more than the mission.

"I'm sorry I never told you," Koble nudged Nathan. "The Chiefhood stuff. When I joined the Loyalty, that shit was kinda raw. Plus Jack didn't want you kids exposed to what had happened down there. Things were kinda rough, and I didn't really wanna talk about it at the time".

"So, what happened?" Nathan asked.

Koble paused for several seconds, and the sounds of passers-by and market traders filled the silence.

"My father was gonna sign our system up to the Commonwealth," Koble said. "My brother, the traditionalist, disagreed with him. Jareth Corps got their claws into Kornell and supplied him with a private army. My brother murdered my father and started a civil war in the hope he could take over".

"I take it that's the simplified version?"

"Not really," Koble shook his head. "That's pretty much how things went. My brother was, or is an idealist. He believed that systems outside the Commonwealth could still function without actually being a part of the 'wealth".

"And you think he was wrong?" Nathan said.

"Most of the citizens thought he was wrong," Koble replied. "No offence, but Earth is living proof that if you don't have a socialist big-brother with a big-ass military to cover your butt, you're kinda screwed".

Nathan didn't reply, and Koble continued.

"Unless we all stand together, the Revenant will get us

all eventually," he said. "You know I don't like the Commonwealth, but I don't see any other way of pushing back Seig. He's got his forces united, that's a hell of a lot more than everyone else".

Sensing that their conversation was heading to a political or philosophical place, Nathan opted to change the subject and address the elephant in the room.

"What was Jareth Corps' interest in Pluvium?"

"No idea," Koble shrugged. "All I know is that we fought a war. Jack and the others got caught up with us, and we ended up allies against Kornell and his followers".

"So," Nathan said, drawing the word out to three syllables. "You lost?"

Koble's jaw tensed, and he nodded.

"Kornell had greater numbers thanks to Jareth. He captured my mother and threw her over the edge of the city walls. After that our resistance was finished. Anyone that didn't lay down their arms was executed."

"How the hell did you get off Pluvium?" Nathan said.

Koble turned back to him with a knowing, yet mournful smile; "Jack".

▲

Even by Mirotose Station's standards, the apartment complex was a slum. A small gang comprised of Humans and Uvans were hanging around the entrance, playing loud music from a datapad. Nathan made sure not to maintain eye contact. Despite his discomfort, Nathan fought the urge to drop his hand to the butt of his gun. It was the right call. Once they entered the building, the gang stopped watching and returned to loitering.

The smell of freshly smoked herb reached Nathan's nostrils as they proceeded toward a staircase. The inside was almost as grim as the exterior. It was the type of ill-designed building that would have been condemned by Commonwealth standards. Nathan could hear the sound of loud music, holopads and the occasional scream of drug-induced hallucinations.

When they reached the apartment numbered 1984, Nathan drew his gun and Koble did the same. Unlike the other apartments, Kornell's front door was made from a reinforced alloy; impenetrable by gunfire or blunt force.

"This is it," Nathan said.

Astrilla placed her palms on the door but didn't push. She studied it for a few seconds before looking over her shoulder.

"I can blow it from the hinges," Astrilla said with a lowered voice.

"Got it," Koble nodded. "You blow the door. I shoot first then we ask questions later".

Astrilla turned to Nathan and frowned.

"He's kidding," Nathan said. "I hope".

Astrilla raised her palms, and a bright light flared from her hands. What followed was a whoosh of air that felt like a ship passing by. The summoned energy burnt through the steel hinges, and within a heartbeat, the door was gone.

Nathan was the first through the doorway. He raised his gun, checking the corners on entry. The apartment was soaked in crimson by an overhead LED, and the smell of sweet perfume permeated the air. The first thing he saw was a startled half-naked woman. She scurried to cover her naked body with a bedsheet and raised her hands in surrender.

Koble pushed toward her with his gun and yelled; "Where is Kornell? Where is he?"

Nathan moved into the kitchen, while Koble continued to shout at the woman, who Nathan now suspected was a hooker. The kitchen was also illuminated by the same red light, but the smell of perfume was replaced by cheap alcohol. From the shadows, a tall figure emerged and darted toward Nathan with a kitchen knife. Fortunately, the attacker wasn't very agile. Nathan was able to dodge the swipe and follow it up with a strike to the head. Nathan felt trimmed, coarse hair as his fist connected. The punch caused the aggressor to fall to the floor. Nathan pointed his gun at the goon and made out a pair of cream coloured paws which were raised in surrender.

"Whoa, c'mon let's talk about this, huh?"

Nathan recognised the voice immediately and by the time Astrilla found the light switch his suspicions were confirmed. Below a pair of dark eyebrows, two yellow eyes stared at Nathan. It was not who he'd expected at all.

"Guttasnype," Nathan said.

"Nathan?" the mobster appeared equally surprised. Then his tone became friendly, "Nathan, my man, I've been lookin' all over for you. After you went missing on that job I thought you were dead and—"

Nathan refused to allow him to finish his sentence. He grabbed Guttasnype by the collar and pulled him to his feet. He slammed his former employer into the fridge.

"You son-of-a-bitch!" Nathan yelled. "You set me up".

"Nathan, I don't know wh—"

Nathan slammed a closed fist into Guttasnype's head, causing the mobster to crumble to the floor.

"You got this all wrong," Guttasnype groaned. "I never set you up,"

Nathan resisted the urge to boot the Icktus in the gut and instead pointed his gun at Guttasnype's head.

"Get-the-fuck-up". Nathan yelled.

Guttasnype reluctantly dragged himself from the ground and limped into the next room. The hooker was at the other end of the apartment, still wrapped in a bedsheet to cover her modesty. Koble was checking the bathroom and when his eyes met Guttasnype his brows dropped.

"Oh perfect," Koble cracked his knuckles. "It's been a very long time Guttasnype".

The Icktus sighed; "I take it you are here for Kornell?"

"Among other things," Koble nodded.

Guttasnype's eyes settled on Astrilla.

"Who's the broad?" he said, pointing with his chin.

Nathan shot a cursory glance at the Evoker, and answered, "She's precious cargo".

CHAPTER THIRTY-FOUR

Many of your enemies must fall in the pursuit of the cause. The act of this chaos and brutality should not be heralded or celebrated. When the fallen are returned to the Great Void, the violence that I, the King, commit will be washed away. It is this divine gift of absolution that makes me more than just a prophet. It makes me Revenant.

From a distance, the Messorem looked like nothing more than a grey speck against the darkness of space. The sheer scale of the Enkaye war machine only became apparent when Seig compared it to his fleet. The black pyramid lurked in the coldness of space like it belonged. There were no discernible markings on the hull. No identifiable sections from the exterior. It was only when Seig's ship neared that he was able to make out a number of protrusions from the hull — towers and spires hidden within the shadows. He also spotted a perfectly circular crater, measuring several miles in diameter on the front face of the ship. Seig felt a strange sense of pride, knowing that he was looking at the Firing Array: the weapon that would lay waste to his enemies.

After his flagship docked with the Messorem, Seig left his throne room and made his way aboard the Enkaye vessel. He was greeted by Admiral Densius Olbori at the airlock, who knelt before him. Seig ordered him to stand, and they proceeded into the bowels of the ship.

Even with the retrofit lighting that the engineers rigged up, Seig found it hard to navigate the Messorem. Every long, winding corridor was precisely the same as the last. The walls, floor and ceiling, were made from the same lifeless black metal.

"You'll be pleased to know that Prince Baylum's spy is ready to communicate details on Astrilla's whereabouts," Olbori said, handing Seig a datapad. "Our forces are on standby. Once we receive word of her location we will find her".

Seig studied the datapad as they walked along the empty corridors on the Messorem. The intel that Baylum's spy had provided was comprehensive. Not only did the data show Astrilla's movements after Yenex, but it also disclosed information on those who'd aided in her escape. Seig studied the list of names and recognised one immediately.

"Lieutenant Harrt Oxarri," Seig said, turning to Olbori. "He was once your second in command?"

Seig already knew the answer. He'd been on the ground at Maru Seven; though far from the frontlines.

Olbori's reply was just as Seig expected;

"Yes, he was, your grace".

Harrt Oxarri was a name that Seig wouldn't forget. The Maruviun was one of the few who'd stood in Seig's way and lived to tell the tale. Motivated by a burning desire for revenge, Harrt Oxarri had rallied what little Commonwealth forces remained and held off the Revenant ground forces as they made a final push. On that day, Lieutenant Oxarri and a few hundred had held the line, while a large proportion of the Maruvian people fled.

Seig continued to scroll through the data. Besides Oxarri, the crew of the Phoenix Titan were nobodies. There was a Uvan Engineer, a Sphinax with more citations than Seig had ever seen and an Earther.

Seig and Olbori continued walking for several minutes until they reached a set of doors that had been prised open by the engineers. Olbori led the King into a vast pyramidic room. At the centre was a large platform, suspended high above a pool of grey liquid: just like the river Prynn.

For the first time in centuries, the tiny hairs on Seig's arms stood.

Olbori pulled him back into the moment, by gesturing toward the platform high above.

"That is where the power source must go, my lord," Olbori said as he led them deeper into the expansive chamber. "The men have fit bindings so that when the Evoker is apprehended, she won't be able to escape".

The engineers and workers, at least the ones who weren't mutations, paused as they laid eyes on their King, but immediately got back to work.

"What is the status of the investigation?" Seig asked, turning his head to Olbori.

It was more than hopeful to presume that the engineers could circumvent the lack of a living Enkaye aboard, but Seig had learnt to never rule anything out. The look on Admiral Olbori's face was enough of an indication to tell there had been little-to-no progress.

"The power chamber remains inoperable, your grace. They cannot bypass the Enkaye's failsafe, but they identified something in the water you may want to see," Olbori said.

As they neared the pool, Seig felt strange. It was like being near the river Prynn. He could hear the Void clawing at the back of his mind; urging him to find the Evoker.

"What is it?" Seig asked as he looked into the water.

"It's a conductor for the device above," Olbori said. "The water shares eighty percent of the same chemical compounds as the river Prynn".

"And what is the other twenty percent?"

"We are currently investigating that," Olbori answered.

There was something about the way the water moved that made Seig feel uncomfortable. The Void seemed to move through its waves like a predator. Once again, it called out to Seig, but he couldn't make out the words.

He knelt before the water and, despite Olbori's protests, carefully placed his hand into it. Seig suddenly felt a burning sensation as the grey liquid seared into his skin. He tried to pull his hand free, but the water clung to him;

"You dare to defile our creation?" it screamed. "We shall resist".

Suddenly it released its grip on Seig, and forced him to fall. Olbori rushed to his king's aide, while engineers called for the medics. Seig stared at his hand for several seconds. Initially, it felt like he'd suffered a severe burn; like his hand had been soaked in acid. To his surprise, the pain only lasted a matter of seconds, and his skin returned to normal.

Embrace the Void where there is no pain or suffering. Channel that which overshadows the light and use it to rise again. There is no fire in the darkness; there is only the Void.

▲

Astrilla watched Guttasnype Galassini squirm as Nathan pressed his gun to his head. She could feel an unbridled rage boiling at the back of the Earther's mind, unlike anything she'd ever felt before.

"You set me up you fucking filthy rat," Nathan said through gritted teeth. "I oughta blow your head off right now".

"No, no, no," Guttasnype squealed. "Nathan, my man, I'd never turn on my best people. You know that better than anyone".

"Shut up," Nathan yelled, pressing the gun harder into the Icktus' skull. "What was your plan, huh? Feed me to the 'wealthers so that I didn't find out what you did?"

"Wait, what?" Guttasnype's eyes widened, and he scrambled to form a coherent sentence. "Nathan, I swear I didn't set you up, I—"

Guttasype didn't finish his sentence as Nathan struck him in the head. It was an act of sheer aggression that Astrilla didn't appreciate.

Koble was at the back of the room, sitting on an armchair, watching the whole thing play out. He'd not said a word the entire time. It was evident that both Nathan and Koble had a history with Guttasnype, but it didn't matter.

The fact that Guttasnype was unarmed was one thing, but it didn't look like the Icktus knew how to handle himself in a fight. Even if he was the one who'd ordered Astrilla's capture, she disagreed with what Nathan was doing.

She watched Nathan grab Guttasnype by the collar and drag him to his feet.

"Did you kill him?" Nathan said. "Did you kill Jack?"

It should have been obvious, but for one reason or another, Astrilla didn't realise it until that moment. All of the violence on display was not because Guttasnype had set up Nathan, as much as the Earther wanted Astrilla and Koble to believe it. The brutality and anger were because of Jack.

"Nathan, I loved your uncle like he were my own brother," Guttasnype said. "I'd never harm him or you. I didn't kill Jack, I swear".

There was nothing genuine in the way Guttasnype spoke. Astrilla suspected that most of what he'd said was a lie, but she couldn't allow the violence to continue. She placed her hand on the barrel of Nathan's gun.

"No," she shook her head. "This isn't the way to deal with him".

The look of anger on the Earther's face remained hardened. Astrilla could tell she'd struck a nerve, but she didn't care. Convictions were the only things separating them from the Revenant. If Astrilla allowed her moral code to be breached, she'd never forgive herself.

"Can't you see he's lying?" Nathan's brow lowered.

"Maybe he is, but executing him is not going to get us any answers".

"He had something to do with my uncle's murder," Nathan hissed. "Why the hell is he in the same apartment where the Loyalty's final shipment was delivered".

"I don't know," Astrilla replied. She glanced at Guttasnype, "Vol will be able to separate the truth from the lies. Maybe you should bring her here and cool off".

She stared into Nathan's dark eyes, hoping that he would lower his gun, which after a few seconds he did. The Earther's face was awash with reticence as he holstered the weapon. He took a step back, and Guttasnype slid down the wall in relief.

"Fine," Nathan muttered. He pointed at Guttasnype; "Don't take your eyes off of him for one fuckin' second".

"Don't worry," Koble said from an armchair at the other side of the room. "If he so much as flinches, I'll kill him myself".

Astrilla frowned at the Sphinax. It irritated her that Koble could have stepped in at any time, but he'd chosen not to do a thing: as though watching Nathan execute an unarmed man didn't trouble him in the slightest. Before leaving the apartment, Nathan and Astrilla exchanged a long stare that said more than words ever could.

▲

In the ten minutes after Nathan left, there was no conversation. Astrilla didn't want to interrogate Guttasnype until Vol arrived, and she didn't want to argue with Koble in the presence of a prisoner. She knew that they needed to appear united to intimidate Guttasnype. That meant that Astrilla had to bite her tongue and fight the impulse to scold the Sphinax for his failure to act.

Guttasnype remained on the floor, with his long and spindly back against the wall. After a while, he lifted his head and stared at Koble for an awkward amount of time. When it seemed as though Koble was about to say something, Guttasnype spoke up:

"So," Guttasnype mused. "You and Nate found each other after all this time. What a strange universe we live in".

Astrilla watched Koble slowly climb to his feet and shuffle across the room. His paws had already formed into fists, but Astrilla was willing to give him the benefit of the doubt. She'd only intervene if things turned ugly.

"Y'know what Jack Stephens used to say about you?" Koble said. Guttasnype shrugged in response and Koble continued, "He used to say that there was a hint of a good man beneath those shitty suits and mobster bullshit"

"So?"

"*So,* how about you tell us why you're *really* here?"

Astrilla glared at Guttasnype across the room. "You are standing in the apartment where the Loyalty's final package was delivered: the same apartment which is owned by Chief Kornell of Pluvium."

The Icktus lifted his thick eyebrows and turned to Koble, who shrugged in response;

"The lady has a point. As far as Nathan's concerned, you are as good as guilty. Even if my Uvan friend confirms what you say about Jack, I can't guarantee that'll be enough for Nate."

Guttasnype was quiet for a long time. His eyes seemed to dart from side to side as he processed his options. Finally, after growing impatient, Astrilla folded her arms and approached him;

"Well? What is it going to be?"

"The truth," Guttasnype nodded. "Kornell keeps the Loyalty's final package in a safe beneath this apartment". The Icktus pointed with his chin to a large bookcase at the side of the room. "There's a door behind that thing".

Within seconds, Koble had pushed the solid piece of furniture to one side, revealing a metal blast door and accompanying keypad that was set into the wall. Smashing it open with blunt force or firepower was pointless as the metal appeared to be several inches thick.

"Stand aside," Astrilla said to Koble.

She readied herself to cast a summon that would break through the vault, but Koble stopped her.

"I wouldn't do that if I was you," the Sphinax said, knocking his paw against the door. "This vault is a VX52".

"Is that supposed to mean something to me?" Astrilla frowned.

Koble chewed the inside of his cheek before answering.

"For one thing, VX52's are made from a highly durable Rubian alloy. Cutting through that would probably take you a day or two," the Sphinax paused and rubbed the back of his neck. "They are also rigged with a nasty little failsafe".

"Let me guess," Astrilla exhaled. "Is it the explosive kind of failsafe?"

"Bingo," Koble replied. "Once the system detects that you're tinkering with the outer layer of the door... kaboom. Explosion would likely take down this entire block if not half the station".

Astrilla could almost feel her frown deepen. If Koble was right, which he likely was, then it meant that they'd need to enter the vault's passcode manually.

Astrilla glanced at Guttasnype.

"What's the code?"

"I don't know..." he answered.

"Then who does?" Koble said.

Guttasnype's eyes narrowed, and his mouth turned upward, forming a thin, devious smile.

"The guy who owns this apartment," Guttasnype said. "Kornell".

CHAPTER THIRTY-FIVE

While Nathan walked back to the Phoenix, he got the strange sense that someone was watching him. The logical part of his brain told him that Mirotose Station never slept: that hundreds of thousands of people were going about their lives throughout the station. It was his instincts that told him that somewhere amongst the moving ocean of people, that someone had their eye on him. Nathan looked over his shoulder, checked every corner, and glanced at every rooftop, but nobody stood out.

Once he reached the Phoenix, his gut-feeling was proven to be correct. From the docks, he could see through his cabin window. His bedside lamp, which he'd intentionally left on, had been switched off.

When anchoring somewhere hostile, leave a light on or draw the shades as a marker so that you know you aren't walking into an obvious trap.

He wasn't sure if it was one of Jack's tricks, but he knew it had come from his formative years on the Loyalty, and it had served him well ever since.

Nathan drew Jack's gun —no, it was no longer Jack's. Nathan drew *his* gun from its holster. He felt the weight of the modified Earth revolver in his hand. Where there had once been a round chamber to carry bullets, there was now a custom cylinder. Despite the many customisations that had been made to the revolver, the most distinctive was also the least functional. From the end of the 'wealther military grade barrel to the grip was a detailed engraving of a wolf baring its teeth. Being armed with the same weapon that Jack carried for years made Nathan feel strong. Even if someone was watching him and intending on doing him harm, he felt protected. Despite every fibre of his being telling him not to do so, Nathan entered the ship with his weapon raised.

The first corridor past the airlock was clear, as was the cargo hold, so Nathan doubled back toward the front of the ship. When he neared the living area, he heard someone behind him.

He glanced over his shoulder, spotting a crossbow in the darkness. He darted to one side, and a bolt flew by him. As the intruder attempted to reload his weapon, Nathan slammed an elbow into the hostile's jaw, forcing them to the ground. Nathan felt the thick, warm fur of a Sphinax as his strike connected. With his attacker down, Nathan kicked the crossbow away and pointed his gun toward the enemy.

"Don't move," Nathan warned.

It was only at that moment that Nathan felt the cold barrel of a gun press against his back. He couldn't help but kick himself for not assuming there had been another onboard.

"I give you my word; your people are unharmed. My men are bringing them back right now," A deep voice said from behind.

Nathan kept his gun trained on the first attacker while replying to the second;

"Sorry, but your word means nothing to me," Nathan replied through gritted teeth. "I suggest you drop the gun before I start shooting".

Nathan could hear the one behind him clicking his tongue, while the second kept his paws raised in surrender. Both were Sphinax —he was sure of it. The second hostile had a distinct accent very similar to Koble's, which left Nathan wondering if the pair were working for Kornell.

"Well? What's it gonna be?" Nathan said, raising his voice. "Do we start shooting each other, or are you putting that gun down?"

He hoped it would be the latter rather than the former. To Nathan's surprise, he heard Koble's voice from the direction of the airlock.

"I suggest you put down the guns," Koble said. "Unless you guys fancy your chances against Kornell's worst enemy and an Evoker".

Nathan could see the green targetting laser from Koble's handgun through the dark. Astrilla stood behind him with a blue flame forming inside her palm.

He was grateful to see them, but he couldn't help wonder why they weren't at the apartment. Guttasnype peered into the ship nervously, and Nathan noticed that his hands were bound together. Something had made them come back, but it was not the right time to ask why. Instead, he had to focus on the gun pressed against his back.

There was a long moment of silence until Koble flicked a light switch. With the overhead L.E.Ds switched on, Nathan could see that his first attacker was a female Sphinax. She was no older than twenty cycles of age, with red fur and a grey hood pulled over her head. He hadn't realised that the hostile was a female, but it was hard to tell a Sphinax from a Horrus under cover of darkness, let alone gender.

He couldn't see the one behind, but Koble did, and the expression on his face was not what Nathan expected.

"Nero..." Koble said, his jaw dropped several centimetres.

There was a pause. Nathan felt Nero pull the gun away and stepped around him toward Koble. The look on Nero's face was both of shock and reverence. He stopped at Koble and dropped to one knee. To see someone kneeling before Koble was a strange sight, and yet there it was.

"My Chief," Nero bowed his head, and his voice wavered slightly. "We thought you were dead".

Koble shook his head in embarrassment and pulled Nero to his feet.

"Cut the kneeling crap," Koble said as he dragged the other Sphinax to his feet. Once Nero was standing, Koble pulled him into a tight embrace and patted him on the back.

"I thought you were a goner. What the hell are you doing here?"

"My friend," Nero swallowed a lump in his throat. "The universe truly smiles upon us".

▲

Nathan secured Guttasnype in the cargo hold, just as he'd done with Venin days earlier. The Icktus tried to plea his way out of the situation, but Nathan didn't listen to a word.

Before sealing the door, Nathan looked at his former employer, slumped at the back of his cell. It was unusual to see the mafioso in a position of weakness, let alone as a prisoner. Guttasnype had always been the one holding all the cards and calling all the shots, and now he wasn't.

"When I come back, you and I are gonna have a chat," Nathan said, his voice calm but authoritative. "You sit here and think about how you want that conversation to go".

He sealed the door before the Icktus could reply and took a deep breath. He could sense that Astrilla was nearby, and more importantly, he knew that she was going to preach to him about right and wrong.

As he turned down the corridor, his senses were proven right. Astrilla sat atop a wooden crate, her legs folded one atop the other and her brown hair tied into a neat bun.

She explained that Guttasnype gave up Kornell's safe, but she had been unable to access it. Nathan's first thought was to ask Vol to take a look at it, but when Astrilla showed him images of the vault, he knew it would take weeks, if not months to break open.

"So, are you glad you didn't beat Guttasnype to death?" She pointed her chin in the direction of the brig.

I knew that was coming, Nathan thought.

He could see through her narrowed eyes, a look of judgment: as though what he'd done was wrong. The harsh truth was that Guttasnype's tongue had been loosened as a result of the beating he'd received. Nathan wasn't sorry for Guttasnype in the slightest. He didn't like that he'd inflicted pain on another, but it had to be done. Sometimes a bit of brute force was required. It was something that Astrilla would never understand. She didn't know what life was *really* like in the outer-worlds, and Nathan did.

He also knew Guttasnype, and understood the way the Icktus saw the world — the way he'd sell his own mother to make a quick credit. But despite everything Nathan's gut told him, he couldn't ignore Astrilla staring back at him hopefully. It made him realise that she thought he was someone he wasn't. Maybe she believed he had the potential to be a virtuous and upstanding member of society, just like she was.

The truth was that Nathan wasn't that person.

"Trust me," Nathan growled. "Guttasnype deserved a hell of a lot more".

Astrilla's frown deepened. "If I hadn't stopped you, we wouldn't have the safe".

"Without the access codes, we *don't have* the safe," Nathan replied. "And now I've got my dirt-bag former employer using up precious oxygen".

Astrilla cast a stricken look at him —somewhere between offended and irritated. Nathan couldn't be sure.

"Do you want to know what I think?" she said, her tone growing argumentative.

"Not really," Nathan answered.

"Well, I'm going to tell you anyway".

Rather than allow the Evoker to talk, Nathan began walking toward the front of the ship, but of course, Astrilla followed. The Evoker grabbed him by the forearm and halted him from going anywhere.

"I think you have been on your own for far too long." she said. "You don't need to pretend that you are something you are not. You are not Jack. You are Nathan Carter; Captain of the Phoenix Titan".

Never let them see you bleed.

Nathan pulled his arm from her grip and scowled. For a moment, he thought of a million ways to respond, but what he ended up doing was walking away.

Her words cut deeper than Nathan cared to admit. He didn't like it, but some part of him knew that she was right.

Nathan had lived behind a hardened facade that Jack had made for him. Maybe it was inadvertent or perhaps Jack had intended it to be that way: to craft Nathan into an uncaring survivor just like him. Regardless, Nathan realised he'd ended up like Jack and he'd never felt more conflicted by it.

When Nathan returned to the living area, he found Koble in discussion with the other Sphinax. Nero was an old resistance fighter who'd fought shoulder-to-shoulder with Koble during the Pluvium Civil War. The younger one, Kesi, was Nero's daughter.

Nero told them that Vol and Harrt were under the care of his men and that they were on their way to the Phoenix. He'd described their capture as a *mix-up*; believing the 'wealther and Uvan to be Jareth Corps spies.

As Nathan poured himself a drink, he listened to the two Sphinax talking.

"Just you wait till they get here," Nero said. "You are not going to believe who's with us".

"It can't be any more surprising than seeing you, pal," Koble replied.

"Wanna bet?" Nero said with a knowing smile.

▲

They didn't have to wait long. The sound of the airlock opening caught Nathan's ears, and he saw Harrt and Vol enter. They appeared mostly unharmed, though Nathan noticed Harrt rubbing the side of his head.

What followed was a group of at least ten armed Sphinax. All except one wore grey hoods over their heads, just like Nero and Kesi. The one who stood out from the pack was an older male Sphinax with a blue coat of fur and an old fedora on his head.

As they came into the living area, Koble climbed to his feet and stared at them nervously. Nathan could tell that Koble and the one wearing the hat recognised each other.

"So, it is true," the hatted Sphinax turned his head to Harrt then back to Koble. "Your crewmates are honest people, my old friend. That is almost as hard to find as the chances of you being alive".

"Rain?" Koble took a step forward, and his jaw twitched nervously. "I….How are you alive?"

"I could ask the same of you". There was a twinge of emotion that made Rain stammer as he stared at Koble. "I think there is someone else that you need to see".

Rain pulled his hat from his head and beckoned to another Sphinax to enter. She, like the others, wore a hood. The greying fur on her body suggested that she was several decades older than the others, but she was strong and carried herself like an old warrior. The way that her bow was slung over her shoulder implied that she wasn't to be messed with. When she pulled back her hood, Koble took a step back, and his fur stood to attention. Tears formed in Koble's eyes, and for several seconds, he was unable to form a word. Finally, after several failed attempts, he managed to talk.

"Mother?"

CHAPTER THIRTY-SIX

The Evoker scriptures taught that the universe was guiding all things at all times: that every event, no matter how insignificant, was part of a predetermined path. Astrilla believed that destiny, fate, and miracles were as real as the air she breathed. Everything happened for a reason, and Astrilla's faith had never wavered. Seeing a mother and son reunite after two decades had only reaffirmed that belief.

For several minutes, she watched from the bar as Koble and his mother spoke for the first time in years. To witness their emotional reunion play out before her eyes was nothing short of breathtaking.

After some time, Koble introduced his mother to the rest of the Phoenix's crew. Astrilla's first impression of Krell was that she was a warm person, despite having the look of a hardened soldier. Koble introduced Nathan as *Jack Stephens' nephew* and Krell hugged the Earther as though he were her own son. It was clear that Nathan wasn't comfortable with it, but he quietly accepted the embrace nonetheless.

Once the introductions were completed, Koble and Krell went to the cockpit to have a conversation in private. The Sphinax soldiers milled around until the blue-furred one, Rain, ordered them to take watch.

The older Sphinax seemed to swagger as he walked toward Astrilla. When he reached her, he pulled his hat from his head and bowed.

"I am Rain," he said, his voice oozing with charm. "Hell of a ship you people have. When I first saw this thing dock I thought David Jareth had treated himself".

"This isn't David Jareth's ship," Astrilla shook her head. "What makes you think it belongs to him?"

"That's what I kept trying to tell them," Harrt said as he joined them at the bar. He looked at Astrilla and added, "This ship is tagged and registered to the Jareth Corporation; not Viktor Venin".

Astrilla recalled something that Venin said about stealing the Phoenix from Jareth Corps, but she'd dismissed it as the ramblings of a fool. Perhaps there was some validity to what he'd said.

"Well, it's a good thing the Chieftess can smell a 'wealther from three miles away," Rain patted Harrt on the shoulder and added; "No offence of course".

"I've been called worse," Harrt shrugged.

For a moment, Harrt and Rain engaged in companionable conversation, like two old soldiers at a veterans party. It seemed friendly, and it probably was, but Astrilla sensed there was another reason for the group of Sphinax to be on Mirotose Station. The troops that Rain and Krell commanded were a highly organised and heavily armed militia. They certainly weren't there for Koble: that much was clear.

She interrupted the friendly banter between Harrt and Rain, and asked the question that needed an answer;

"What brings you and your people here?" Astrilla said.

Rain straightened up as though he were still working out if he could he trust her. His expression grew severe, and he swallowed before replying;

"We're here to carry out an assassination".

▲

Vol stared across the room at Guttasnype Galassini, while Nathan paced back and forth behind her. As soon as she'd stepped inside the makeshift brig, she sensed that there was something unusual about the Icktus. There was no denying that he was afraid, but it seemed as though everything going on around him was an inconvenience.

Nathan, on the other hand, was conflicted. There was a mix of anger and frustration with a strange hint of regret. The animosity was easy to read; Nathan believed that Guttasnype had wronged him; it was as simple as that. The guilt —or shame— that Nathan tried to push aside was harder to distinguish, but Vol was sure it had something to do with Astrilla. It was only after she'd taken a closer look at the bruises forming on Guttasnype's angular face that she put two and two together.

Ah, that'd be it, Vol thought.

Nathan spent several minutes glaring at Guttasnype, with his arms folded. Vol was sure it was intended to come across as threatening, and for the most part, it did. After sitting in silence with the two men for what felt like an uncomfortable amount of time, Vol turned to Nathan;

"Can we get this show on the road?" she said impatiently.

Nathan's display of macho bravado wouldn't get them anywhere, in fact, it was wasting time. If Guttasnype wanted to lie, he would. There was no use in posturing.

Nathan sighed through his nostrils and took several paces toward Guttasnype. Vol noticed the Earther's hand twitching over his holstered revolver.

"I'm gonna ask you some questions, and if you lie to me, I will shoot you," Nathan said, his voice low and serious. "Did you kill Jack?"

Guttasnype stared at the Earther, then at Vol.

"No," he shook his head. "As I told you before, I had nothing to do with it".

Vol concentrated on the thoughts that itched at the back of Guttasnype's brain. None of them indicated that he was lying, but there was something in there: something that he didn't want Nathan to know.

Nathan looked at Vol expectantly, and she answered;

"He's telling the truth".

For a moment, Vol wondered if Nathan was disappointed by the answer, but she didn't have time to explore his thoughts. Nathan turned back to Guttasnype;

"If you didn't kill him, who did?"

"I dunno," Guttasnype shrugged.

Again, Vol sensed nothing, which meant that Guttasnype was telling the truth. She nodded to Nathan, and the Earther pressed his lips together in frustration. He turned back to the Icktus, and his questioning became less personal:

"What are you doing on Mirotose Station?"

There it was. Vol felt it at the back of Guttasnype's mind —the makings of a lie. It was like touching a small tremor with her pinky finger, but Vol was sure it was there, and Guttasnype knew she could feel it. The Icktus stuttered for several seconds and finally conceded.

"The Syndicate Dons called a meeting," Guttasnype said. "All of us, including Chief Kornell, Adrian Walker, you name it. All of us in one place at the same time".

That was true, but Vol sensed he was holding back.

"Why?" Nathan said. "Why now?"

"Rumour has it that Prince Baylum wants to cut us a deal," Guttasnype said leaning against the wall. "The talk of the town is that King Seig is starting to lose his marbles, and the Prince wants his throne".

Vol took a step back. That part was almost certainly real, in the sense that Guttasnype believed it. She wondered why the Revenant Prince would be interested in cutting a deal with the Criminal Syndicate.

"Prince Baylum of the Revenant wants the mob to help him?" Nathan said, his voice lifting in surprise. "That makes no sense at all".

"And yet, here I am," Guttasnype shrugged with his palms. "You don't turn down an opportunity".

"Wait," Vol said, halting the Icktus mid-sentence. "Are you saying the Revenant Prince is coming here to meet your people?"

Guttasnype sneered in amusement before answering, "Seems that way".

Once again, Nathan looked back at Vol to confirm if Guttasnype's answer was true or false. She verified

Guttasnype wasn't lying.

"One last question," Nathan said, taking another step closer to Guttasnype. "When you hired me to sneak aboard that 'wealther ship, did you know I was gonna get captured?"

When she delved inside Guttasnype's brain, Vol felt an odd sensation that she couldn't quite put into words.

"No," Guttasnype shook his head. "How could I know such a thing?"

Somehow he was both telling the truth and lying at the same time, but Vol couldn't distinguish where the fact or fiction began. She wanted to drill into the answer more, but she knew it could take hours, and that was not a luxury they had. Prince Baylum was aboard Mirotose Station. That simple fact alone carried more weight than Guttasnype's true intentions.

▲

While Nathan and Vol questioned Guttasnype, Koble walked his mother to the cockpit where they could have a private conversation. It was strange to see her; to hear her voice; just to know she was alive after so long.

Koble sat her down with a glass of Maruviun kor. He spoke of how Jack Stephens had saved him from Kornell during the final days of the Civil War. Then he attempted to explain a condensed account of the last two decades. Finally, when he was done talking, there was one question on his lips;

"How in the hell did you survive falling from the city walls?" Koble said. "I saw Kornell throw you over the edge. I saw Jack try to save you and I saw you plummet into the badlands. That's over a thousand feet!"

Krell looked at him with a stony expression, then her lips turned into a reluctant smile.

"You wouldn't believe me if I told you," she said. "It's a little crazy".

"Try me".

Krell pulled a communicator from her belt and spoke

into it. Koble didn't recognise the voice at the other end.

"Go for Krish".

"Krishnan, can you get the droid out of storage?" Krell said.

"Of course, ma'am. I'll be over there in fifteen minutes".

Krell turned back to look at Koble, and the reluctant smile returned to her face.

"Something caught me before I hit the ground," she said. "At first, I thought it was a spirit or something supernatural. Then I realised it was a droid".

"A droid?" Koble raised his brow. "A droid caught you?"

Krell nodded.

To Koble, it seemed far-fetched, but he reminded himself of the events of the last few weeks. Things had undoubtedly been unusual, and this was just another item to add to the list.

"The droid caught me, and when I was safe, it deactivated," Krell said. "For months, while I survived in the badlands, I tried to fix him, but nothing seemed to do it. When I escaped Pluvium, I brought it with me".

"You kept it?" Koble raised his brow sceptically. "Why the hell would you do that?"

"That droid saved my life, and I'd like to return the favour," Krell replied. "In between trying to stop your brother, I've gone from place to place trying to repair it, but nobody has managed it yet".

"Well, Vol is a pretty kick-ass engineer. Maybe she could take a look at it for you," Koble said.

His mother smiled in appreciation, and for several minutes they shared more stories of the last twenty years. Koble told her more about his time on the Loyalty and his love for the Earther beverage coffee. Krell shared some details about Pluvium and the ongoing battle against Kornell's regime. Even after two decades, there was a resistance movement against his brother. Kornell had committed atrocities against his own people, forcing them into slavery and almost bankrupting the system.

Kornell had become precisely what Koble and many others had feared during the war. His brother had always been a narcissist, but with the added political power of the Chiefhood, Kornell had developed a full-blown god-complex.

The thing that surprised Koble the most was that not only had his brother cut ties with Jareth Corps, he'd also declared war on the Corporation. One of Kornell's most notable supporters in the war was now his worst enemy. That fact alone meant that Kornell was fighting on at least two fronts.

"What caused this little feud between Kornell and Jareth?" Koble asked.

"We're not entirely sure," Krell shook her head. "All we know is that Kornell visited David Jareth for a meeting on Paradisium. After that they were sworn enemies".

Koble considered what she'd said. The fact that David Jareth no longer supported him meant that Kornell and his regime were in a weakened position. It suddenly made Koble realise that his mother, Rain, Nero and the others were on Mirotose Station for a reason.

"What the hell are you guys doing here?" Koble asked.

There was a long pause, and Krell's smile disappeared.

"We're here for your brother," she said. "We've been trying to take him down since the war, but we've never had a shot like this. He's here, on Mirotose Station with a small group of bodyguards."

"You're here to kill him?" Koble raised a brow.

"If it means freeing our people, then yes".

"Huh…" Koble mused. "Well, ain't that something".

CHAPTER THIRTY-SEVEN

Nathan waited patiently for the Sphinax resistance fighters and his crew to take their seats in the lounge. He'd gathered them all there because it was clear that both factions shared a similar goal —taking down Kornell. The difference was that the Resistance wanted the Pluvium Chief dead, and Nathan needed him alive.

He poured himself a whisky from the bar, and a robust wooden aroma filled the air around him. Every eye in the room was on him, and he felt it as though it were a physical force bearing down on him. They were looking for the direction of a leader, and he wasn't too sure how to begin. For a split-second Nathan froze, realising that this was who he was now. The Captain of the Phoenix Titan couldn't be the uncaring vagabond that he'd been for the last decade. People needed him now; just as he depended on them.

He thought back to the best and only Captain he'd ever known, Jack. Nathan tried to picture how his uncle would address a twenty-to-thirty-man crew back in the day, but he quickly realised that his uncle had improvised every time.

"You are not Jack. You are Nathan Carter".

Astrilla's statement from earlier that day circled in his head. He stared at the Evoker across the room, wondering if she knew just how much those words had hurt him. Not because they were cruel, but because they were right.

Nathan glanced at Astrilla and she looked back. Their eyes met, and for a while, everything seemed to slow down. He wanted to apologise for earlier, but something told him that she already knew. She nodded to him in encouragement, and Nathan began to speak.

"Nero," Nathan called out to the ginger Sphinax who was still standing. The room went quiet, and for several seconds nobody said a word. "You said earlier that the universe smiles upon us today. I can't help but agree. It would appear as though opportunity has presented itself to us".

No one else spoke. Koble was staring at the hologram of Kornell in front of him. Harrt sat on one of the barstools beside the Sphinax, sipping from a glass of kor.

"So," Nathan said, to fill the void. "Here are the facts..."

He spoke for the better part of fifteen minutes, sharing his account of the Mirotose Station incident, Jack's murder and their mission to stop Seig. When he explained why they were on Mirotose Station, what they were looking for and why, Rain raised his paw.

"Go on?" Nathan said.

Before climbing to his feet, Rain removed his fedora and placed it on the coffee table in front of him. There was a particular type of confidence about the way Rain carried himself that Nathan admired. The Sphinax was a strong leader; there was no doubt about it, but what Nathan idolised was the relaxed, charismatic charm that practically oozed from him.

"You expect me to believe that this woman is part-Enkaye?" Rain said, pointing at Astrilla. "Because she certainly doesn't look like one".

Nathan was about ready to fire back, but Koble interrupted.

"She's Enkaye," Koble replied. "She may not have the grey skin and giant head, but somehow she's one of them, and I vouch for her".

"Astrilla is the key to stopping the Revenant," Nathan added.

"From what exactly?" Rain asked.

"Total annihilation," Harrt said, from his barstool. "The

Messorem isn't just an old ship. The Enkaye built it for war. If Commonwealth intel is correct, then this thing is more than capable of destroying a planet in a single blast".

The Sphinax resistance fighters began chattering in hushed tones until Rain signalled for them to stop. He turned back to Nathan and continued:

"I mean you no disrespect when I say this, but you do understand that we are not here to fight Revenant?" Rain said. "We are here to take down the man who destroyed our democracy".

"And that's fine," Nathan nodded. "Once we've got the contents of the safe, Kornell is all yours."

Rain bowed his head in agreement. Nathan did the same and waited for Rain to take a seat.

"So," Nathan said. "How do we go about crashing a syndicate meeting and bagging ourselves a dictator?"

Again, Rain raised his paw;

"I've got a plan". He clicked his tongue against his teeth and smiled. "Your uncle used to have this saying; *no risk, no reward*. I think that it applies to this situation".

▲

Rain's plan was ballsy. That was the only word Nathan could think of as the Sphinax outlined the details of the mission. He used the holotable to draw out an elaborate operational diagram, that reminded Nathan of the way Jack planned heists back in the day.

The Syndicate meeting was due to take place at one of Mirotose Station's high-rise penthouses. Rather than fight through several layers of security by going through the front door, Rain intended on dropping his people from a moving ship straight into the meeting room on the three-hundredth floor.

"The element of surprise can be a fickle bitch," Rain said with a smile. "Trust me, Kornell will never see it coming".

Nathan wasn't opposed to high-risk operations; he'd seen more than his fair share over the years, but Rain's idea was amongst the most insane that he'd ever heard. Going directly into the meeting room wasn't the main problem. The tricky part was extraction from the roof, especially if Kornell or the other attendees had a ship in the immediate airspace.

But we have the Phoenix, Nathan thought. *We could drop people in and guard the airspace while we grab Kornell.*

Nathan suggested a few alterations to the plan, which involved using the Phoenix Titan as the primary dropship. Rain agreed, but when he asked to pilot the ship himself, Harrt stepped in.

"No offence intended, friend, but this is our bird," Harrt said. "We're still working out the kinks".

The older Sphinax shrugged as though it were no big deal, though Nathan could tell he was slightly disappointed.

"Maybe another time, eh?" Rain said with a smile.

For five minutes, Nathan, his crew and Rain studied the operational schematic and the intel. The Sphinax resistance had amassed a wealth of data on the attendees. Kornell's name was highlighted among a list of twelve that would be there in person. Another five were joining via hologram, including Prince Baylum.

There was no denying that the plan was solid if a little dicey, but it wasn't foolproof enough. Nathan had learnt that if there were gaps, it was best to close them, and when he looked at the schematic, he saw a giant gaping hole. He hadn't noticed it at first, but once he spotted it, Nathan couldn't ignore it.

"We need a man inside that meeting room," Nathan pointed at the hologram. "The Syndicate could have escape routes or more guards than Rain's intel suggests".

Nathan could almost feel Astrilla's brows raise.

"What are you proposing?" she said. "One of us just walks through the front door with all the other criminals?"

Nathan didn't realise that his lip had curled into a cocky smirk. Astrilla couldn't read his expression, whereas Koble saw it from a mile away:

"You gotta be kidding me..." Koble shook his head.

"No. No way! Uh-uh! Nope!"

Nathan wanted his shrug to suggest confidence rather than arrogance, but he was pretty sure it came across as brash.

"I don't get it," Harrt said. "What are you thinking?"

"We already have a ticket to that meeting, and he is sitting in my brig," Nathan said.

▲

"Where the hell do you get off?"

Guttasnype glared at Nathan across the room with an expression of pure disdain. Nathan had never seen that side of his former employer before. Generally, Guttasnype maintained a calm yet weaselly demeanour. He didn't get angry or raise his voice, so Nathan could tell he'd struck a nerve.

"You are just like that uncle of yours," Guttasnype continued, shaking his head vigorously. "Do have any idea what the Syndicate would do to me if they found out?"

Nathan wanted to reply, but Koble beat him to the punch:

"They'll probably chop off your head," the Sphinax shrugged. "Personally, I was thinking of doing the same thing, but this soft Earther thought you might listen to reason".

"Reason?" Guttasnype laughed. "You call that reason? These people are no joke. They make me look like the 'wealther's healthcare system".

Nathan took a couple of paces toward Guttasnype and deactivated the bindings around his wrists. The Icktus stared back in surprise while rubbing his forearms. It was a gesture of goodwill that Nathan hoped would add weight to what he said next;

"Surely we can find a way for this to work for both of us…" Nathan said. "Think about it... There's something to gain here, right?"

The mobster's eyes darted from side to side and for a split second Nathan could have sworn he saw the credit symbol in the Icktus' pupil. Nathan knew that Guttasnype Galassini was many things, and greedy was most definitely one of them.

"I'm all ears," Guttasnype lifted his palms. "What have you got for me, Nate?"

"Your life, for starters".

Guttasnype snorted in response:

"Life ain't worth living if there ain't no profit," Guttasnype rubbed his fingers together. "I need me some scratch".

"Fine," Nathan nodded. "The contents in Kornell's safe are yours, except the Loyalty's final shipment".

Guttasnype pressed his lips together until they were thin.

"I can work with that," he said.

▲

Though the mission lacked the type of military finesse that Harrt was accustomed to, he admired the way that the Sphinax resistance collaborated with the crew to bring it all together. Using the Phoenix Titan as both a dropship and as the primary aerial defence was a wise move. It meant that Rain and his squadron of pilots could cover the airspace without having to worry about the ground forces.

The part that involved Nathan accompanying Guttasnype made Harrt nervous, but then he'd realised that there was logic buried within the madness. On the one hand, Nathan could signal if it was a trap, and on the other, he could find out what Baylum was hoping to gain from the meeting. That kind of intel could go a long way, especially if Baylum was as loose-tongued as rumours suggested.

Harrt pulled himself into the pilot's seat, while Vol checked a terminal on the co-pilot's side. Krell and Nero were going to be operating the gunnery chambers, meaning that the Phoenix would be at full combat capability.

"Engines are looking good," Vol said, reading from a display on her left side. "Oh, I also scrubbed Jareth Corps from the ship's registry".

"Nicely done," Harrt nodded.

Once Harrt had the all-clear, he activated the station beside him and watched his heads-up display flicker to life. He double-checked the system's overview and began lift-off procedures. The Phoenix rose from the dock and the landing gear retracting into the belly of the ship. Harrt steered the vessel to a safe distance and looked at Vol;

"You wanna take the helm for this one?" he asked.

"So let me get this straight, you don't trust the experienced Sphinax fighter pilot to drive this thing, but you trust me?"

"Yeah," Harrt nodded, his voice lifted an octave. "I mean, we make a good team, right?"

The Uvan smiled back at him, and for a moment, Harrt wondered if she'd read his mind. If she had, then she'd have known just how much he'd meant it. With that in mind, Harrt stuttered before adding;

"Only makes sense that you get used to flying this tub under stressful situations, right?"

For a long moment, they were silent. The chimes and buzzes of the cockpit's systems filled the room. For one reason or another, Vol leaned across the space between them and jabbed him in the arm.

"Thanks," she said.

Harrt began to wonder if she'd intended the gesture as camaraderie or flirtation, but by the time the thought had popped into his head Rain was speaking through the comm;

"I have eyes on Nathan and Guttasnype. I think it is go time!"

CHAPTER THIRTY-EIGHT

It had been fourteen days since Nathan and Guttasnype met to discuss the job that led him to the Vertex, the Phoenix Titan and his new crew. For one reason or another, Nathan felt as though it were much longer. The man who'd worked for Guttasnype Gallassini didn't care about the war. He'd lived without a cause, going from one job to another without meaning.

Maybe that was the thing I lacked for so long?

Simply surviving was not a purpose, and the crew and their journey had helped him to realise that. When Nathan looked back on who he'd been, he realised that Astrilla was right all along. He was not Jack and didn't need to pretend any more. On the one hand, Nathan was eternally grateful to Jack for teaching him how to survive, but as a result, a part of his humanity had gone. The thing Nathan realised as he walked with Guttasnype into the penthouse reception was that Jack had bestowed hundreds of lessons upon him, but he'd missed out something important;

A man must live with a purpose.

Maybe that explained why it was so strange to be acting as Guttasnype's henchman. He followed his former employer through the reception and to a security checkpoint. The guards didn't check them for weapons, which didn't surprise Nathan in the slightest.

They were now playing by Syndicate rules. Everyone was a potential target. The mobsters had to trust each other or else their kind and their ventures would cease to exist. It was for that reason that Nathan knew he'd be safe, right up until the moment that the drop team crashed the party.

A group of heavily-armed guards escorted Nathan and Guttasnype to a glass elevator. When they got inside, the guards left them to ascend alone. Nathan tapped the control panel, which looked as though it were made from a rare white crystal from the Outer Worlds.

"Care to explain why you are going to all of this effort for an old box that the Loyalty hauled?" Guttasnype mused.

"No".

"All I'm saying is, what if you get this thing and it turns out to be a case of Sphinax wine?" Guttasnype said, lifting his hands. "I mean... that's an awful lot of effort, right?"

Nathan resisted the urge to grab the Icktus by the collar.

"All you need to worry about is getting us inside and staying alive," Nathan said.

The Icktus clenched his jaw and scowled in silence. Nathan was more than comfortable with the absence of Guttasnype's nasally voice, but it didn't last for long. Like always, the pressure became too much for Guttasnype to bear, and he caved.

"Y'know how insane this plan is, right?" Guttasnype said, chewing the inside of his cheek. "It's borderline suicidal".

"And that is exactly why it'll work," Nathan replied.

The meeting room was functional in its décor. A wide black table and eight chairs were the only pieces of furniture. Two flags were suspended either side of a large screen that measured at least seven metres in width. Nathan recognised one of the flags as *the paw of independence*; otherwise known as the symbol for New Pluvium —Kornell's regime.

At the table sat seven members of the Criminal Syndicate; including Guttasnype Gallasini. The rest were a mix of Human, Uvan and Horrus that Nathan recognised from Rain's intel. There was a hostile atmosphere that couldn't be ignored. None of the mafiosos spoke to one another which left a silence so void Nathan could hear his own heartbeat. One of the mobsters that Nathan recognised as Adrian Walker, impatiently checked his watch and huffed. A female Horrus with dark fur rolled her eyes and tapped on the desk.

Kornell was making them wait.

Nathan positioned himself two metres behind Guttasnype and tried his best to look as formidable as the other bodyguards in the room.

After several minutes, Chief Kornell entered with an entourage of five bodyguards. Nathan saw a slight resemblance to Koble in the shape of Kornell's head and ears, but that was where the similarities ended. Kornell was tall and lean, but his physique was not the result of athleticism. The Sphinax's muscular upper body were the consequence of several expensive surgeries and steroid enhancements. Nathan could tell from the tiny patches of missing fur and the way Kornell's lip twitched that the Sphinax had recently undergone a beautification surgery.

Nathan tapped the transmitter inside his jacket pocket. At that very moment, an almost undetectable signal was going straight to Harrt and the others, telling them that Kornell was there and the mission was a go. It was just a case of waiting. According to the plan, the Sphinax Resistance would breach the building in under five minutes, while the Phoenix held the airspace.

This plan is going to work, Nathan told himself.

The silence lingered as Kornell took his seat. The Sphinax gestured to a man in the opposite corner to activate the screen. Three rectangular windows appeared on the vast display, two of which were completely blank. Prince Baylum was in the centre pane, staring through the camera with an expression of sheer indifference.

Adrian Walker was the first to speak up;

"So it's true," Walker spat. The arms dealer turned to Kornell, and his brow lowered several inches in anger. He pointed at the Revenant Prince, and growled; "I will not do business with this man. We may all be criminals, but we have a code. I will not aide the man who destroyed my people".

Kornell didn't move.

"Everyone of us, including you, Adrian, have committed atrocities," Kornell said. "And you know as well as I do that the Prince is not entirely to blame for the Fall of Earth. We are here to discuss the future, not the past. So I suggest that you allow the esteemed Prince to speak before you cast any judgement, just as I did when he first came to me".

Kornell's voice was an octave lower than Koble's. He spoke with an opulence that gave the impression he was far more educated than he looked. The Sphinax watched Walker like a predator. It was intended as threatening, but Walker matched it pretty well right up until the moment he climbed from his chair.

"No," Walker said, throwing a diamante jacket over his torso. "I will not work with the Revenant".

Nathan noticed one of Kornell's men reach for a gun as Walker made for the door. To his surprise, Kornell halted his bodyguard by slitting his throat with a knife. Everyone in the room winced as Kornell's man fell the floor in a pool of his own blood. Even Walker glanced over his shoulder to see what was going on.

"Go if you must, coward," Kornell spat. As Walker and his guard turned to leave, Kornell called out; "Should you see David Jareth, tell him that I'll be seeing him very soon".

Walker didn't reply and left in silence. As the elevator door hissed shut, Kornell clapped his paws together and looked around at the seven mafiosos in the room.

"Well... shall we get down to business?"

In one of the incognito windows on-screen, Nathan saw a pair of human hands emerge from the darkness, with a silver watch on the left wrist. Nothing moved on the second anonymised screen.

Prince Baylum was grey-skinned and bore the look of a man who'd seen war. His dark, soulless eyes peered through the screen and studied the men sat around the table. He looked amused by Adrian Walker's protest — as though he knew something that nobody else did.

"I have only worked with a handful of you in the past, so I do not expect any of you to trust me immediately," Baylum said, picking his words carefully. "My Father is a man of devout faith who will continue to fight until he dies. I, on the other hand, am a man who understands the value of *specialists* like each of you".

"What is it that you are proposing?" a Horrus mobster said to the left of Guttasnype.

Baylum's expression didn't change.

"My father is on the verge of controlling an Enkaye war machine. Once it is fully operational, he will begin laying waste to planets, starting with the Commonwealth Capital Worlds". Baylum paused as though he were waiting for questions, but none came. "The good news for all of you is that there is room in the new world for industrious, loyal people to thrive, unmutated".

With a growing sense of dread, Nathan listened to Baylum talk. The speech was well-rehearsed, maybe even scripted, but it worked.

"If you help me to find that which I seek, you shall be rewarded in the new world," Baylum continued. The Prince allowed a moment of silence and his lips curled upward into a knowing smile. "I presume we have a deal?"

An awkward silence followed, finally broken by a Uvan mobster sitting nearest to Kornell;

"You'll have a deal once we know what it is you want".

The three windows where Baylum and the two anonymised attendees were on-screen became smaller as a fourth window popped up. An image of Astrilla formed, and Nathan felt a cold chill run down his spine.

"This woman is the only target any of you should be concerned with," Baylum said. "If you bring her to me dead, I will burn your entire syndicate to the ground. If you bring her to me alive, you will live among the blessed in the new world. I will reward each of you with kingdoms fit for gods. I—"

The screen deactivated, and everything went dark. An

instinctive feeling at the back of Nathan's mind told him that it hadn't been five minutes. Whatever happened was not the Phoenix and the drop-team.

The doors to the right side of the room burst open, and Nathan heard the unmistakable hiss of a smoke grenade landing on the floor.

▲

Once Nathan's signal was received, Koble felt the Phoenix lurch forward. He placed a comms device over his ear and checked that the audio was coming through correctly. He helped Astrilla to fit the complicated straps of the drop-suit over her small human frame.

"Have you ever done something like this before?" he asked, checking the harness around her shoulders.

"Yes, we covered drop-ship procedures at the Enclave when I was twelve" she nodded.

"Uh-huh," Koble mused. "And have you dropped out of a moving ship since you were twelve?"

"Not exactly," Astrilla said nonchalantly. "Have you?"

Koble wanted to challenge her on it. Most Sphinax weren't great at telling the age of humans out of their teenage years, but Koble had been around enough of them to know that Astrilla was much older than that —he guessed she was somewhere close to Nathan's age.

Over the crackle of the comm, Koble heard chatter from the cockpit. He heard Vol speaking in an alarmed tone of voice.

"What the hell is that thing?"

Koble raised his brow to Astrilla, who'd also heard it.

"That can't be good".

He left Astrilla with the Sphinax warriors and rushed to the cockpit. When he got there, he found they were well within visual range of the skyscraper. What he didn't expect to see was an ivory white gunship deploying armed marines onto the roof.

"Who the hell is this?" Koble said, leaning past Vol and Harrt to get a closer look.

"That is a Jareth Corps gunship," Vol said. "Things just got a whole lotta' complicated".

CHAPTER THIRTY-NINE

Smoke filled the room with a cloudy haze, obscuring Nathan's view. Every door to the meeting room burst open at once, and a dozen marines armed with automatic weapons rushed inside. The new group of hostiles, whoever they were, opened fire on the gangsters and mafiosos without a second thought.

Out of the corner of his eye, Nathan saw Kornell and his men dip into a corner to take up cover. Guttasnype threw himself to the floor as a line of laser fire smashed through the Uvan mobster beside him.

Nathan grabbed his gun and took cover beside Guttasnype.

"Someone across the room was yelling; "Hands up! Show me your fucking hands, right now!"

The accent was American —east coast by Nathan's best estimate, but he couldn't be entirely sure. Somebody from Kornell's last position began shooting from the opposite side of the room. A yelp of agony told Nathan that they'd hit someone. Guttasnype peaked from cover, and a string of gunshots flew past him. Nathan grabbed the Icktus by the collar and pulled him down.

"Keep your head down and don't do anything stupid," Nathan growled.

He darted from cover and leapt behind an overturned table; barely avoiding a hail of slugs that tore up the floor and wall. Nathan peeked at the other side of the room, where Kornell had drawn a dagger and was fighting off an attacker.

It was the first time that Nathan had been able to get a good look at the new group. They were all human, carrying advanced rifles. They moved together in the same highly organised fashion as 'wealther marines, but their weapons and armour suggested they were Corporate Enforcers.

One of them was moving toward Nathan on the right side of the room. Without hesitation, Nathan took a couple of shots but was sure he'd missed when the man ducked into cover.

"Son-of-a-bitch!" Nathan heard another American accent.

The same man popped up and began firing wildly. The gunshots forced Nathan to remain sheltered behind cover. Gunshots erupted from the other side of the room, and the hostile slammed against the wall in a haze of blood and laser fire. Nathan turned to the source of the gunshots and spotted Guttasnype clutching a smoking rifle.

Didn't see that one coming, Nathan thought.

He scrambled across the room to the dead hostile, narrowly avoiding a blast of incendiary rounds from the centre of the room. The man that Guttasnype shot was dead. Nathan grabbed his discarded assault rifle and saw the words *Jareth Corps* across the barrel.

They must be here for Kornell, Nathan thought.

Nathan took up the weapon and began shooting into the smog and chaos around him. He fired, taking down one of Kornell's men and clipping a Jareth marine in the shoulder. Another three or more began firing at Nathan, and he was forced back into cover.

A burst of laser fire hit the wall opposite and blew debris into the air. Nathan forced himself to crawl along the floor, passed the dead marine to attain a new firing position. He returned fire, using his handgun and caught one of the Jareth marines. Again, there was the distinct twang of American accent cursing and swearing.

At that moment, Nathan looked out of the window and spotted the Phoenix Titan on approach. The red frigate was moving toward the building at such an alarming pace that Nathan thought it wasn't going to stop. At the last moment, the ship banked up at a steep angle, and a burst of gunfire followed, smashing the long windows open.

Nathan forced himself to shield his eyes as tiny fragments of glass rained down on him. Koble dropped through the window, followed by the Sphinax Resistance Fighters and Astrilla. Knowing that back-up had arrived, Nathan summoned the courage to dart from cover.

▲

"They made it inside!" Harrt's yell was somehow celebratory and wary at the same time.

It took several seconds for the Jareth Corps gunship to detect them, but once it did, it opened fire. Vol pushed the Phoenix in an upward motion that almost made her stomach turn, but it was necessary. Jareth Corps was well-known for being a highly successful security business. Money was no object, and that meant they had the best weapons and technology on the market.

Vol jammed the thruster forward and sped over the tower, twisting and turning to avoid laser fire.

"I've got your six fast movers," Rain's voice came through the comm. "Where the hell did that gunship come from?"

"I couldn't care less," Harrt answered. "We need to disable that thing before it shoots us out of the sky".

"So, what are you thinking?" Rain yelled.

As Vol sent the Phoenix into a downward spin, control panels and sensors alarmed around her. A flash of pulsing light swept past her and collided with the tower. Huge chunks tore away from the building and plummeted toward the heart of Mirotose Station. Vol concluded that it had been a rogue missile that the Jareth ship had fired speculatively.

"Okay, new plan," Harrt said, working his terminal. He punched a button and shared the flight plan with Vol, the gunners and Rain's people all at once. "We will be the bait! Rain you and your guys need to focus all weapons fire on that gunship, while we pass over them. Take out the weapons system and propulsion, I want these guys alive. We'll double back and give you a hand once we're clear of any fire".

There was a murmur of agreement that came from Rain, which Vol took as *yes*. She tapped her own comms unit called out to Krell and one other, in the Phoenix's gunnery chamber;

"Watch our ass for any projectiles," Vol said.

She turned back to Harrt, who was monitoring the enemy movements;

"I think you may be the craziest 'wealther that ever lived," Vol said.

"You've got this," Harrt nodded.

Vol adjusted a few settings to the engines and shields, then sent the ship into a sharp climb. The Phoenix Titan flashed through the battle, dodging flak and laser bolts from the enemy gunship. They were only a few dozen kilometres from the Jareth Corps warship when a pair of small fighters whipped across their path.

"Shit," Vol cursed and sent the ship spiralling to avoid the enemy craft. "Jareth Corps has back-up".

▲

Once Koble and the Sphinax resistance had made it inside, at least a third of Kornell's men were dead or incapacitated. Astrilla positioned herself in the middle of the room, which Nathan saw as slightly arrogant, but she held the spot well.

After years of pulling heists and jobs with the Loyalty's crew, Nathan couldn't help but feel that having an Evoker on his side felt like cheating. It was too easy to send a *magic-wielding* brunette into a hostile situation, and to an extent, it took the challenge out of the job.

Astrilla made light work of the mafia goons and what remained of the Jareth Corps mercs. She threw what looked like balls of fire at any hostile that looked menacing. The attack she used wasn't the same as the one he'd seen on Yenex. Her strikes didn't cause anyone to disintegrate into a pile of ash and instead incapacitated.

Nathan became aware of someone heading toward his position. They were moving low and fast toward one of the exits, and it seemed fair to assume they didn't know he was there. When they got close enough, Nathan tackled the assailant and slammed him into the wall. It was only when Nathan got the attacker in a headlock that he realised it was Kornell. The Sphinax wrestled with him but stopped when Nathan placed his gun against Kornell's skull.

Nathan saw Koble dash toward him, after shooting dead two of Kornell's bodyguards. By the time he arrived, Kornell was already shouting at Nathan.

"Get your hands off of me," Kornell protested. "You're making a big mistake!"

Nathan looked to Koble, and he saw rage on his friend's face. It was clear that Koble wanted to harm Kornell, but the situation wasn't right. All of a sudden the gunfire in the room ceased and all Nathan could hear over Kornell's complaints was an American accent:

"Cease-fire! Cease-fire!"

It came from the opposite side of the room; directly beneath the giant screen where Baylum was projected earlier. The meeting room fell into complete and utter silence. Nathan glanced out of cover to check on Astrilla. She was still in the centre of the room, and her hands were glowing white.

Beyond Astrilla, the Jareth Corps marines had seemingly stood down. A large man emerged from behind a piece of overturned furniture, with his hands raised in the air. He was in his forties with a shaved head and trimmed beard, which complemented his tanned skin.

"It seems that we are all here for the same reason," he said, looking to Astrilla and then to Nathan. "Let's take a breather, stop shooting at each other and talk about this".

The American stood at around two metres in height and had one of the most muscular physiques Nathan had ever seen. Unlike Kornell, this man's incredible two-hundred-and-fifty-pound frame was not the result of surgery or augmentation —it was natural.

"Tell your ships to stop shooting first, then we'll talk," Nathan yelled from cover.

Kornell began to protest again, but Nathan slammed the Sphinax's head into the floor, knocking him unconscious. He returned his gaze to the Jareth Corps mercenary, who was a matter of metres from Astrilla. To Nathan's surprise, the burly American pulled a comms device and called for a cease-fire.

"Done," he said, looking back to Nathan's position. "So, how about you come out here, and we have ourselves a nice little chit-chat?"

"Think I'll be just fine back here," Nathan replied. "You guys could have a sniper back there".

The mercenary seemed to chuckle, which seemed odd under the circumstances.

"I mean you guys are the ones with the Evoker, right?" The American pointed at Astrilla. "She could turn me into Grandma's ashes in the blink of an eye".

Nathan let the uncomfortable silence linger for a moment longer, then snapped at Koble to keep hold of Kornell, who was unconscious. As he moved to the centre of the room, Nathan noticed just how threatening the mercenary looked. He was at least half a foot taller than Nathan, and his bulging arms looked as though they could bench over two-hundred pounds without breaking a sweat.

"The name's Ralph Hayward: head of security for Jareth Corps," he said as Nathan drew closer. "And you are?"

"Taking a war criminal prisoner," Nathan said. "Kornell is ours".

Hayward placed his meaty hands on his hips and stared at Nathan for several seconds with his eyebrow raised.

"Name your price," he said. "Jareth Corps is more than happy to award freelancers such as yourself with compensation for situations like this".

"He's not going anywhere," Nathan shook his head. "I'm giving you and your men one shot to walk away from this situation. Go back to Paradisium and tell David Jareth that Kornell is dead."

"That ain't gonna happen, son," Hayward shook his head.

Nathan saw the bulky American reach for something in his vest, and Nathan immediately pulled his gun from its holster. The sound of panic followed from both sides, but Hayward halted his men. The mercenary didn't pull a weapon, and instead, his gaze lingered on Nathan's revolver for an awkward amount of time.

"That's one hell of an interesting gun you've got there..." Hayward said thoughtfully. "You're an Earther, right?"

"That doesn't concern you," Nathan shook his head. He wrapped his finger around the trigger, sure that at any moment all hell could break loose.

"Well, it kinda does," Hayward replied. "See, that gun in your hand is a modified revolver".

"So?"

"So, answer my fuckin' question, kid," Hayward replied. "Are you an Earther or not?"

Nathan finally conceded;

"Yes, I'm an Earther".

Hayward's eyes widened, and his jaw lowered. Nathan wasn't quite sure what to make of it. If it was a tactic to distract or draw Nathan's attention away from something, it was undoubtedly a strange one. Hayward took another step closer, and Nathan fought the urge to move back.

"Answer this for me," Hayward said in a lowered voice. "How often do they see you bleed?"

For a second or two, Nathan thought it was a threat, then he realised it wasn't. He didn't allow his expression to flicker, even though his head rang with a silent scream. Every part of Nathan's being wanted to grab Hayward by the collar and demand why, but he couldn't.

It was a passphrase: the kind of old trick Jack would have used to ensure that an ally was really an ally. The phrase was something between Nathan and Jack: nobody else.

"Never," Nathan answered with a dry mouth. "Never let them see you bleed".

Hayward's face softened a degree, and he stepped back. The burly American tightened his jaw and looked at Nathan with a degree of scepticism.

"Kornell is all yours, kid," Hayward said with an imperceptible nod of the head. "We stand down".

For a moment, Nathan thought he'd misheard, but when Ralph Hayward turned to his team and told them to *prep for exfil,* his suspicions were confirmed.

"What the hell do you mean, he's all ours?" Nathan said, following behind Hayward. "We just shot the living shit out of this place, and you're just willing to walk away".

"You knew the override countersign, kid. Plus that gun you're carrying…." Hayward stopped and cleared his throat. "If you still wanna throw down, I'll happily oblige, but its a fuck-ton of paperwork if I end up killing you."

For one reason or another, *Never let them see you bleed* was the countersign. Jack's gun was delivered to Nathan with the same words printed on an accompanying card: the exact phrase that Jack had drilled into him as a child. For Nathan, it all meant one thing. Somebody inside Jareth Corps was looking out for him.

CHAPTER FORTY

During the Pluvium Civil War, Jareth Corps supplied a small army to Kornell. Their numbers were nothing exceptional, but they had the weaponry and technology. During a particularly vicious battle at Triumph Place, Koble wished that Jareth would recall their militia and leave the fighting to the Sphinax people. Of course, that never happened. Kornell's forces propped up by Jareth's people overran Triumph Place, and Koble's people were forced to flee.

The Earther who'd identified himself as *Ralph Hayward* ordered his men to pack up their gear and return to their dropship. To see a group of Jareth mercenaries withdrawing, made Koble feel on edge. Jareth Corps had never strayed away from a fight. Ever.

The Earther-led Corporation was known for its ruthless nature in the field of combat. They'd even given the Revenant a run for their money, which was a feat that few could claim. Yet the Jareth Mercs were pulling back: all because Nathan had said the words;

Never let them see you bleed.

It was the kind of thing that Jack Stephens would have said back in the day; when he was playing the part of *tough-teacher*. It was evident from the way Hayward and his men stood down that the phrase meant something of significance —both to Nathan and Hayward. It raised more questions than Koble cared to count.

After Hayward and his small army left, Koble called one of Rain's men to take Kornell away. His brother was still unconscious on the floor. It should have felt more like a victory, but Koble was too preoccupied with the Jareth mercs to celebrate.

At the centre of the room, Nathan stared quietly into space, his eyes wide. It was evident that the Earther was just as baffled by the whole thing as everyone else.

"What the hell was that?" Koble said. "Never let them see you *bleed*?"

Nathan was quiet, and his face darkened.

"I..." he said, but never finished the sentence.

Koble watched Nathan slouch down against one of the overturned tables. The Earther pressed the back of his palm against his forehead and exhaled.

"It was something that Jack used to say," Nathan peered up at Koble. The Earther lifted his handgun —the same one that Jack had left him. "This gun and a business card were sent to the Phoenix a few days ago. The business card had that fucking phrase printed on the back of it".

Koble scratched his chin and looked at Astrilla, who appeared just as perplexed. The Evoker didn't say a word.

"Are you implying that Jack is...communicating to you?" Koble folded his arms.

"I dunno," Nathan shook his head. "All I know is that Hayward used that phrase as a fucking countersign. That can only mean that someone inside Jareth Corps is trying to help us".

"Do you know how crazy that sounds?" Koble replied. "Why the hell would Jareth Corps help the likes of us?"

Before Nathan could say anything, the sound of shouting came from the other side of the room.

"Unhand me this instant," Kornell screamed at the Sphinax who was pinning him to the ground. "Do you know who I am? I'll have your head for this, you wretch!"

Koble turned back to Nathan and Astrilla, realising that there were more pressing matters to attend to. The Jareth mercs had withdrawn. The reason didn't matter. Getting Kornell away from the area before any reinforcements arrived was now the priority.

"Can we continue this conversation later?" Koble said. "I've got a lil' family reunion to attend to".

Nathan nodded, but after Koble took a few paces forward, the Earther called out to him; "Get us that safe code".

"You got it, boss," Koble nodded.

"Question him on the Phoenix," Nathan added. "We'll head to the apartment. Get us on comms when you've got something".

Koble heard a stark contrast in Nathan's voice from seconds earlier. It was decisive and confident. Like the Captain of a ship. Like Jack.

▲

After the Sphinax resistance fighters bound Kornell's wrists, they dragged him to the Phoenix Titan. The Chief of Pluvium protested, but nobody paid any attention to it. Koble followed several metres behind, refusing to allow his brother to lay eyes on him. After everything that Kornell had done, Koble wanted to savour the moment where Kornell realised that not only had he lost, but he'd lost to him.

While he waited for Rain's men to complete their search, Koble spoke to Harrt and Vol over the comms. He explained that Nathan, Astrilla and Guttasnype were heading back to the apartment and that it would be wise to get the Phoenix out of the area. Harrt agreed, and Koble felt the Phoenix Titan rumble to life.

"So I take it you got him?" Rain's voice came through the comms.

"Your boys are in the process of settling my brother into his temporary pad," Koble replied with a smile. "I'm going to enjoy a lil' family reunion once I've been given the all-clear".

"Planning on having all the fun without me, boss?" Rain laughed. Koble could hear a sense of achievement in his old friend's voice.

It felt good.

It didn't take long for Rain's men to give Koble the go-ahead. They presented Koble with everything they'd found on Kornell. It didn't surprise him that his brother had several knives and a tracking device concealed within his fur and clothing.

"Destroy the tracker then let Vol and Harrt know that Kornell may not be alone on this station," Koble ordered.

He waited until the soldiers had disappeared toward the front of the ship before taking a deep breath. He'd spent twenty years wondering if this moment would ever happen, and now that it had arrived Koble found himself afraid.

"You can do this," Koble said, and he forced himself to enter the cargo hold.

Kornell sat in the middle of the room, his cuffed paws resting in front of him. Two of Rain's men stood in the corner of the room to oversee him and yet somehow Kornell managed to look in control of the situation. The indignant look in Kornell's eyes only grew the moment he saw Koble. There was a tension that felt so raw, Koble was sure he could cut it with a knife. He'd never experienced anything quite like it.

"Well, after all these years, I was starting to wonder when you'd resurface," Kornell said, his voice calm and calculating. "I see the years haven't been as kind to you as they have me, dear brother".

Koble resisted the urge to lean across the table and break his brother's jaw for the petty insult. Instead, he sunk into his chair and placed his feet on the table to match the same arrogant confidence as his brother.

"You realise you're finished, right?" Koble said. "The only reason you are still alive is because of me. All these pissed off Sphinax resistance fighters would prefer to see your head on a spike".

Kornell stared back and didn't say a word. Koble wondered if it was an act of arrogance or if the shame of defeat weighed down on his brother. He allowed the silence to linger before continuing:

"Why do you have the Loyalty's final shipment in your vault?"

Kornell's lips curled up at the question, forming a smile. The expression was unsettling and sent a shiver up Koble's spine.

"It won't take my people long to find out what happened here and when they do, you and your friends will die," Kornell hissed.

"I disagree," Koble stretched his arms, while giving his brother a smug look. "When your loyalists find out that you've been conspiring with the Revenant, I'm pretty sure they'll be pretty pissed off. You see I may not have been to Pluvium since the war, but I'm pretty sure that kinda thing isn't acceptable by our people's standards —even the traitors and cowards".

Kornell wasn't expecting it. His smirk disappeared as quickly as it had formed. Koble took his feet off the table and leaned forward in his chair to look his brother in the eye.

"As we speak, footage of that meeting we just crashed is being sent to Pluvium for broadcast," Koble said. "Now, here's how this is going to work; I ask you some questions, and you will answer. In return, I'll see to it that you receive a fair trial. If you don't answer, I walk out that door, and leave you in the hands of the Sphinax resistance, and they'll probably execute you without a second thought".

Kornell chewed the inside of his cheek as he weighed up the options. The response Koble received was just as he expected;

"Quite frankly, dear brother, you can go to hell".

Koble's fake smile only grew more. There was a part of him —a large part— that wanted Kornell to push his buttons. He wanted to react. He'd tried the calm and collected approach, but now he just wanted a reason to take off the gloves, and Kornell had obliged.

"I don't think so," Koble said, mock hurt in his voice. "You see, you and I had unfinished business after the Civil War. You took people from me; people I loved".

"You —" Kornell started, but Koble kept speaking.

"Then I find out that the Loyalty's final shipment is in your apartment. That suggests that you had a hand in the deaths of a few more people that I loved". Koble cracked his knuckles, "So how about you drop the act and smell the roses, dear brother. You have lost, and we have won. Answer the questions I have, and I won't kill you. Question one: did you kill Jack Stephens?"

Kornell rolled his eyes. "I didn't even know that fleshy meat-bag made it off Pluvium after the war".

"Then how the hell do you explain the Loyalty's shipment being in your apartment?"

"Must have just landed there…"

Koble could smell the bullshit from a mile away. The animosity between them stretched and Koble could tell that his brother wasn't willing to give anything away. What Koble did next felt wrong, but he didn't care. In the blink of an eye, he drew his gun and fired a single round into Kornell's knee.

A mix of blood, ligament and bone flew into the air, and Kornell let out an agonising guttural scream. The howls of torture that came from Kornell's mouth were so striking that the burly guards at the back of the room flinched.

"You shot me!" Kornell cried as he nursed the grizzly looking wound on his leg. "You—"

Koble grabbed his brother by the windpipe, halting him mid-sentence. As Koble stood there with his paw clamped around the throat of the man who'd killed his father, he felt tempted to snap Kornell's neck. As he watched his brother gag for air, the thought seemed so right. He knew that anyone in his shoes would do the same, and yet Koble couldn't do it.

Killing him may have been easy, but it wasn't the right thing to do. Plus Kornell's followers would turn him into a martyr, and that was precisely the opposite of what the Sphinax resistance wanted. Reluctantly, Koble released his grip on Kornell's throat and watched his brother cry in agony.

"I wasn't aiming for your leg…" Koble growled. "Now, do I have to go back to my original target to get some damn answers?"

Kornell's response was a hasty nod.

"Did you kill Jack Stephens?" Koble repeated.

Kornell winced and shook his head.

"No,," Kornell said. "I—"

Koble took up his gun again, aiming for Kornell's other leg, but to his surprise, his brother yelped,

"Wait! Wait! Wait!"

Koble withdrew his gun and looked at his brother impatiently.

"Answers," Koble demanded. "Now!"

Kornell gulped and took a deep breath.

"I didn't kill Stephens, I swear," Kornell said. "The package from the Loyalty is not mine. I was storing it for an old contact. I meant to destroy it months ago".

Koble placed his pistol back in its holster and peered at his brother.

"Who is your contact?"

Kornell gulped nervously, "David Jareth…"

CHAPTER FORTY-ONE

After leaving the tower, Nathan led Astrilla and Guttasnype to an inner station transport. The single pod that they travelled aboard was full of civilians, so there was little room for conversation. Usually, an enclosed space full of people would have irritated Nathan, but on this occasion, it didn't. He needed the time to think.

His first concern was that Prince Baylum had reached out to the Criminal Syndicate. The Revenant wasn't known for working with others. They'd never kept allies or associates in the past, but evidently, something had changed. Perhaps their goal of tracking down Astrilla had taken priority, or maybe Prince Baylum was far more dynamic than his father. Either way, it wasn't good news.

Ralph Hayward and the Jareth Corps mercenaries were another problem. For one reason or another, Hayward knew to use the catchphrase on Nathan: the very same words that Jack had instilled in him as a child. Nathan knew it wasn't a coincidence, but when he tried to make sense of it, he kept coming to the same conclusion: that someone inside Jareth Corps was looking out for him.

Eventually, the inner-station transport stopped a few blocks away from Kornell's apartment. Guttasnype took the lead for most of the journey, while Nathan walked side by side with Astrilla in silence. The station was quieter than it had been earlier. White LED's in the ceiling simulated a nighttime sky, while motion-activated street lights illuminated the sidewalk.

After walking past a particularly seedy bar, Astrilla cleared her throat and looked at him. Nathan didn't immediately look back. He wasn't sure what kind of reaction he would garner from her after their tense conversation earlier that day.

"What does never let them see you bleed mean?" she asked.

He should have predicted that question would come up. It wasn't something he'd ever discussed with anyone. The lesson was between him and Jack and nobody else. Koble may have recognised the phrase as one of Jack's, but it wasn't something the Sphinax could truly understand.

"It means that you don't show weakness," Nathan replied.

Astrilla seemed to frown as though he'd stated something obvious.

"Those words are of significance to you, aren't they?"

"It doesn't matter," Nathan shook his head. "We got lucky. You should be thankful for that".

"I disagree," she shook her head. "That man from Jareth Corps knew to say that exact phrase to you because he was testing you. Given the fact that they withdrew means that you answered correctly. Therefore those words are clearly of significance".

Nathan turned his eyes forward to Guttasnype. The Icktus was several metres ahead, so he wasn't within earshot of their conversation.

For one reason or another, Nathan grabbed Astrilla and forced her into a closed doorway. Initially, she fought back but quickly stopped when she realised he wasn't going to harm her. There was an intensity to the moment that, for Nathan, was loaded with several emotions. He was aggravated by her questioning, but he was more irritated with himself for letting his guard down. He could've avoided the whole topic if he'd stuck to what Jack said.

"You're right," Nathan said, his voice low. "Those words mean something of significance to me, but I don't need to explain it to you".

"Why?" Astrilla raised her voice. Nathan saw the stubbornness in her eyes.

"The fact that some asshole inside Jareth Corps knows those words and what they mean to me implies that there is far more at play," Nathan argued. "What that phrase means to me, is my business. If you think—"

"What are you so afraid of, Nathan?" Astrilla cut him off mid-sentence. "Do you think if I see your weakness or fears, I'll think less of you?"

Nathan's jaw tightened, and he could feel his stomach seize up. For the second time that day, Astrilla was completely and utterly right about him.

"I've seen your memories. We have shared the same visions," she said.

"You don't know a fucking thing about me!" Nathan snapped. "I lost my entire family to the Revenant. I watched the soldiers and hunters murder my family, right in front of me, and for years I relived those moments every time I closed my fucking eyes."

There was a moment where Nathan wondered if the expression on the Evoker's face was of realisation or anger. It didn't stop him from continuing his rant. They were too far down the rabbit hole.

"Do you want to know what stopped me from being scared of those fucking dreams?" Nathan yelled. "It was Jack. He taught me to *never let them see me bleed.* I have lived by those fucking words all my life because I needed to be tough enough to survive".

Silence lingered between them.

Nathan couldn't tell if the look she gave him was of pity or remorse. He wanted to continue shouting: to tell her that, *not everyone had grown up at some safe Evoker compound, protected from the harshness of the galaxy,* but he forced himself to stop.

Astrilla placed a trembling hand against his face. She looked back at him and didn't say a word. Her eyes conveyed a kindness that Nathan had seldom seen in the last decade. He wanted to push her hand away, but for one reason or another, he couldn't do it.

He stepped away, allowing her to move from the doorway.

"C'mon," he said. "We've got a safe to open".

▲

When they arrived at Kornell's apartment building, the smell of smoked herb and piss had grown more potent than it was earlier. Nathan could have sworn he was getting a contact high, just by walking through the grim corridors of the complex. As it had been earlier, the sounds of loud music, arguing, and general debauchery filled the lobby. It wasn't pleasant, but Nathan resisted the urge to comment as he knew they'd be getting out of there soon enough.

They entered Kornell's apartment, which was the same as when he'd left. Regardless of that fact, Nathan rechecked all the rooms just in case Kornell or Jareth Corps were going to try anything. Fortunately, he didn't find anyone lurking in the apartment, and when he returned to the main living area, Guttasnype had thrown himself into an armchair, whilst Astrilla checked her datapad.

"Any news from the others?" Nathan asked.

The Evoker shook her head, "No. I think I'll try to get a signal from the balcony".

Astrilla hadn't said much since they'd argued a few minutes earlier, but Nathan was sure that she wasn't pissed off with him. If anything she understood him more, but whether that was a good thing or not remained to be seen.

With Astrilla checking for a signal outside, Nathan became aware that he and Guttasnype were alone together for the first time since the Syndicate meeting. Nathan cleared his throat as he sat directly opposite the Icktus.

"I guess I should thank you," Nathan said.

"For what?"

"You saved me back there, so thanks for that..." Nathan eyeballed Guttasnype tentatively. "But I gotta ask, why'd you do it?"

Guttasnype folded one long leg over the other.

"I told you, I always look after my people. I looked after you just as I looked after Jack." Guttasnype shrugged. "I'm a man of my word, and I keep my promises".

Nathan couldn't deny that there was a hint of something genuine in the Icktus' voice, but it wasn't enough to convince Nathan his intentions were anything but self-serving. He knew Guttasnype all too well: the Icktus would do anything if it meant making money.

"You do understand that I still don't trust a single fucking word that comes out of your mouth, right?" Nathan said.

"Guess so," Guttasnype shrugged. "Maybe I can take the first step to build back some trust?"

"I'm all ears," Nathan said.

Guttasnype exhaled, and his pointy face settled into a look of resignation.

"Back in the day, Jack had a contact back on Paradisium that gave you guys on the Loyalty a whole bunch of work, right?" The Icktus paused for Nathan to respond. When Nathan nodded, Guttasnype continued, "It may interest you to know that Jack's contact was David Jareth".

Nathan straightened as he absorbed Guttasnype's statement.

"Bullshit," Nathan said, flatly. "Jack hated the corporations. He always told me never to trust them, especially Earther ones".

"And yet he worked for David Jareth," Guttasnype spread his hands wide. "Certainly explains why those Jareth Corps mercenaries left the moment you said that passphrase".

Nathan wanted to argue, but everything seemed to fall into place. Perhaps Guttasnype was telling the truth, and if he was that was worrying in and of itself.

"So, that means the Loyalty's last shipment was for Jareth?" Nathan said.

"I guess so," Guttasnype shrugged. "But I don't see wh
—"

"So, let me get this straight," Nathan interrupted. "The Loyalty hauls something on behalf of David Jareth, and the moment we arrive for drop-off, we get sabotaged. No —not sabotaged— murdered. Murdered by a highly organised militia…"

Nathan's mouth became dry, and he forced himself to stop speaking. It felt like a shockwave passing over him when he realised what Guttasnype was implying— that Jareth Corps were the ones who'd slaughtered the Loyalty's crew.

He thought about it for a second, then realised that what he was thinking was entirely possible. The Jareth Corps mercenaries that he'd run into earlier that day were highly trained and heavily armed. Given that Jack had worked with, or for, David Jareth in the past, made the theory seem that little bit more plausible.

▲

Nathan paced around the apartment as he waited for Astrilla. Every few seconds, he'd stop to look at the balcony door in the hopes that she'd got some news from the Phoenix. When he realised that nothing had changed, he'd do another lap of his dingy surroundings.

Eventually, she emerged from the exterior with a hopeful look on her face. She passed her datapad to Nathan. A nine-digit code was on the screen, which he quickly entered into the safe's control panel. After hitting the unlock button, the safe whirred to life. The metal door opened with a loud hiss and a cloud of dust followed.

"Looks like Koble nailed it," Nathan concluded.

To say the safe was larger than expected was an understatement. Nathan thought it would be a standard ten-foot-by-six-foot vault, but what he found was more like a bomb shelter. A narrow staircase led into what Nathan could only assume was the apartment below. Metal walls were built over the building's existing foundations and fabrications. They looked thick enough to survive an outer planet bombardment, which meant that Kornell was storing something precious inside.

The vault itself looked more like a warehouse, with floor-to-ceiling racks outlining the room. The contents inside Kornell's vault varied greatly. There were priceless jewels, exquisite piece's of art and enough weapons to supply a small army.

"Well, hot-damn," Guttasnype said excitedly. The Icktus reached for one of the guns but stopped when he realised that Nathan had drawn his pistol.

"Don't even fuckin' think about it," Nathan warned.

Guttasnype shrugged, "But, we had a deal?"

"Our deal didn't include firearms," Nathan replied. "You can have everything else, but the guns are going to the Sphinax resistance".

Guttasnype shook his head and grabbed a long rifle with a rounded ammunition magazine from the rack. The Icktus examined the weapon and slung it against his shoulder, looking just like the Earther mafioso's that Nathan had seen in old books and movies.

"One for the road," Guttasnype said with a thin smirk. "Besides, it matches my eyes".

Nathan resisted the urge to punch the lanky Icktus in the head by reminding himself of why he was there. At the back of the room, Nathan saw the crate marked LOY8476-J, and he felt a lump form in his throat.

"So, this is it," Astrilla pointed at the container. "What do you think is inside?"

For one reason or another, when Nathan tried to answer, his voice trailed off. He stopped to clear his throat and ran a hand through his wavey hair. He stared at the Loyalty's final delivery, wondering if he was looking at the very thing that had catalysed the murder of his previous crew and uncle.

"Let's find out," he said.

Nathan looked for something to force the crate open and found a metal pole on one of the racks. Guttasnype warned him that the silver item was a priceless piece of Augustian Art that predated the Commonwealth, but it didn't stop Nathan using it as a crowbar.

Several layers of a thick foam-like material were stuffed inside to protect the contents from damage. Nathan removed what he could and found two boxes at the bottom of the container. The first, and far larger of the two, was empty and had already been opened. Nathan noticed the name *David Jareth* printed on one side.

Shit, Nathan thought.

The second was no bigger than a standard hand-held datapad, but when he opened it, he found a few layers of protective material around a sealed envelope which had his name written on it.

"What in the hell?" Nathan said, recognising the distinct handwriting.

He carefully opened the envelope using a thumb, and inside he found a carefully folded piece of paper. Nathan could feel Astrilla lurking behind him, almost certainly glancing at the letter, so he took a deep breath and began to read aloud:

Nathan,

If you are reading this, then you are on the right path. That's the good news. The bad news is that things are not going to get any easier. You must find Doctor Gordon Taggart. He will be essential in what is to come. I know this is vague, and I can only imagine how difficult this has been for you, but you need to do this.

Stay Strong. Stay Vigilant.
Jack

When Nathan turned his eyes to Astrilla, he noticed her expression was a strange mix of confusion and sympathy. He didn't say anything and instead reread the letter: this time in his head. When he'd finished processing the message that Jack had left him there was one question in Nathan's mind;

Who the hell is Gordon Taggart?

CHAPTER FORTY-TWO

"Doctor... Gordon... Taggart..."

Koble's voice boomed through the speakers on Nathan's datapad. Astrilla could imagine him stroking his chin as he repeated the name. The Sphinax sounded far more thoughtful than usual, which made Astrilla nervous, though she wasn't sure why.

"Well, you can shave my fur and call me a Uvan's brother," Koble remarked. "Yeah, I've come across Gordon Taggart in the past".

"I presume you mean in the past with Jack?" Nathan replied into the datapad. "Right?"

There was a pause from Koble's side, which seemed to last longer than necessary.

"That'd be about the half of it," Koble answered. Then after a moment of consideration, "Trust me, Nate, this is something we shouldn't discuss over comms".

"Fine," Nathan nodded. "We'll be back in the hour".

"So, did you find the you-know-what?" Koble asked.

Nathan looked at Astrilla with a justified frown on his face. Despite the vision they'd shared, the second piece of the Omega was nowhere to be found. Even amongst the priceless works of art and treasure that Kornell had hoarded inside his safe, there was no sign of the Enkaye device.

The defeated look on Nathan's face almost prompted Astrilla to say, *this isn't a loss*, but it wouldn't have been right in the moment. Instead, she watched Nathan pace to another side of the room and answer Koble's question:

"No, we didn't, but let's discuss when we get back to the ship".

"You got it," Koble drawled.

Astrilla wanted to keep her eyes on Nathan, but the sound of Guttasnype excitedly whistling at his newly acquired plunder served as a distraction. She turned to the Icktus who was busy examining what looked like a jewel-encrusted lampshade with an optical magnifier.

"I presume you're quite happy with the way this worked out?" she said, trying to mask her annoyance.

"Do you know how much a piece of old shit like this could fetch?" Guttasnype said, placing the lampshade back on the rack. When Astrilla didn't comment, he answered for her; "About three-hundred-thousand. That kind of money could go a very long way".

"To what? Building your little empire?"

"You're damn right," Guttasnype nodded. "Building an empire that wouldn't dream of collaborating with the Revenant".

Astrilla sensed that Guttasnype was implying that somehow he was the lesser of two evils. She didn't see it that way, but she didn't see any reason to argue with him either. Guttasnype Galassini was the type of person who would find ways to justify the worst acts imaginable. Astrilla knew there was no point in trying to debate morality with him: it was likely that the Icktus had no concept of a moral code.

▲

After Nathan packed all of the guns from the vault into a floating storage container, he signalled to Astrilla that it was time to leave. She waited at the top of the stairs while Nathan bid farewell to Guttasnype. Astrilla tried her best not to eavesdrop, but now and then she overheard the odd sentence between the pair. Finally, she gave into temptation and listened to what they were saying:

"For the record, I hope you find whatever it is that you

are looking for," Guttasnype said.

"Thanks," Nathan replied. "And for what its worth, I'm sorry I beat the shit out of you earlier".

There was a break in the conversation that prompted Astrilla to listen closer. At that moment, she imagined all the history between Nathan and his former employer: all the history with Jack. There was bad blood there, but Astrilla sensed that something had changed in Nathan. It was hard to tell if the Earther was extending an olive branch to the Icktus or if the pleasantries were a way to say goodbye.

"Best of luck to you, Carter," Guttasnype said with a strange softness to his voice. "When you decide you're done with this saving-the-universe-bullshit, look me up. I might be able to find you some paid work again".

"I don't think so," Nathan said. "I'm done with that life".

Seconds later Nathan emerged from inside the vault with the sealed container of guns floating behind him. Together, he and Astrilla retraced their steps toward the docks. Mirotose Station at night was considerably quieter than in the day. Like most stations, the lights on Mirotose would dim and brighten to simulate the traditional day-to-night cycle. It still felt dangerous and overpopulated, but it didn't stop Astrilla enjoying the peace.

▲

After docking the Phoenix inside Mirotose Station, Vol rechecked the ship's onboard systems for any gaps in engine or weapons performance. She suspected there were no problems, but Vol had always preferred to err on the side of caution.

An hour later, her suspicions were proven correct: the Phoenix Titan was running like a dream. She wiped the sweat from her brow and crawled out from under the cockpit's main control panel. There was a slight pain in her right shoulder which served as more of an annoyance than a distraction. Still, it had been a long day, and the need for a drink and some bunk-time was needed.

She made her way to the bar for a drink. Along the way, she passed a group of Sphinax fighters who invited her to play a game of cards, but she declined. For a few seconds, she debated which alcoholic drink she'd treat herself to, and eventually settled on a glass of Maruviun kor.

If Harrt swears by this stuff its gotta be okay.

She poured herself a glass and took a tiny sip of the smoky alcohol. The taste was a mix of fragrant notes accompanied by a distinct zesty spice that contrasted nicely. It wasn't the best drink she'd ever had, but given the sense of victory she felt, the Maruviun kor tasted like triumph.

Vol was about ready to take the drink back to her cabin when Krell joined her at the bar. There was no denying that she shared a slight resemblance to Koble. They had the same thick fur and bright eyes, but her ears were lower than Koble's, and her frame was significantly smaller: though Vol suspected that Koble's stature was due to his diet rather than something he'd inherited from the family gene-pool.

"I'm told you're a marvellous engineer," Krell said as she reached for a bottle. "Would you mind taking a look at something for me?"

The tired part of Vol's brain wanted to decline or at least delay Krell's request, instead, she found herself nodding out of politeness.

"Sure," she said. "Do you need me to take a look at one of your ships?"

"No," Krell shook her head. "What I need you to look at is something very precious to me: a droid that saved my life many years ago".

Vol couldn't help but raise her brow out of sheer curiosity.

"A droid saved your life?" Vol said. "That sounds like something I really need to take a look at."

Krell smiled in appreciation before sipping from her glass. The older Sphinax pulled her communicator and spoke to someone at the other end;

"Krishnan, can you bring the droid up to the Phoenix's living area?"

After thirty-or-so seconds another Sphinax entered,

carrying a big crate using a cargo barrow. He placed it down in the middle of the room, and Vol moved in to take a closer look.

The droid was of a very odd design. Its head and body were spherical, made from a taupe-coloured metal. There was a single ocular sensor on its head, which suggested the droid once had communicative functionality. From both sides of its body, were two thin arms, which were hooked at the ends. Vol noticed that instead of legs, the droid had some kind of propulsion system on the base of its body.

Perhaps it was a mining droid or some sort of hauler? Vol thought as she stared at the mechanical carcass.

"How did this thing save your life?" Vol turned to Krell.

"Long story short, he caught me; lowered me to safety and deactivated," Krell replied. "I've been trying to get him working for years, but no engineer has been able to make repairs".

"Well," Vol said, pushing a stray piece of hair from her face. "I'll certainly give it a shot!"

▲

The electronic nerves and ganglia within the droid, were mostly intact. A few bolts here and there were loose or rusty, but for the most part, it was fine. Vol searched within its dome-like head for something that resembled a power source, but she was unsuccessful.

The other thing Vol struggled to identify was the material that the droid was made from. A scan from her datapad wasn't able to recognise the dark metal at all, but when she scanned at the molecular level, Vol's eyes widened. The readings suggested that the droid not only predated the Commonwealth, but it predated modern history.

That is entirely impossible, Vol thought. *Unless...*

Vol tampered with her datapad to scan for black market materials, removing any Commonwealth restrictions from the device. When she rescanned the droid's carcass, the reading on-screen was enough to send shivers through her body.

"What is it?" Krell asked.

Vol turned back to the Sphinax and showed her the datapad.

"This little guy is made from Arcane!" Vol said. "Where the hell did it come from?"

▲

When Nathan and Astrilla reached the docks, they found the Phoenix Titan amongst the sea of ships that the Sphinax Resistance had at their disposal. There were a few dozen fighters and a large freighter that was probably five or six times the size of the Phoenix: positively making the Titan-class frigate look like a much smaller ship by comparison.

"Just how many people do Krell and Rain have…" Nathan remarked.

"She told me earlier that this is only a small group sent here to carry out the mission," the Evoker replied. "From what I gather there's a flotilla out there dying to take back Pluvium."

"With Kornell out of the picture that might just become a reality," Nathan replied.

Upon entering the Phoenix, Nathan heard the sound of Kornell's raised voice coming from the cargo hold. Fortunately, it sounded like the entitled yelling he'd been making earlier rather than the sounds of torture which Nathan had expected.

Koble was standing in the entrance to the ship with Rain. The pair were sharing a smoking pipe which reeked of Sphinax Vine. Blue trails of smoke floated up to the ceiling, filling the air around the Phoenix with a sour, fishy smell, that was not pleasant to the human sense of smell.

"Could you two smoke that outside the ship?" Astrilla said, shielding her nose from the scent. "That is rather pungent".

Koble handed the pipe to Rain and breathed a giant plume of vapour through his nostrils.

"Don't come bitchin' to me because your weak human scent glands can't handle the sophisticated aroma of blended Pluvium vine and atomised mackerel," Koble replied, his voice surprisingly jovial. "This stuff is sacred; kinda like champagne to an Earther".

"Back home this stuff is considered quite the delicacy." Rain added. He held out the pipe to Astrilla; "You should try some my dear. They say it's good for human hair and cell regeneration".

Astrilla declined as politely as she possibly could and gestured to the floating crate of guns.

"These are the weapons from Kornell's apartment. Nathan thought that your resistance would find them useful".

Rain took another drag on the pipe before handing it back to Koble. The blue-furred Sphinax staggered down the landing pad to examine the guns and after a few seconds whistled.

"This is a very kind gesture, my friends," Rain said, picking up one of the military-grade rifles. "I sincerely hope that with Kornell in custody that his regime will crumble. It'd be a shame to use these weapons."

"A good man once told me to always have a back-up plan," Nathan said, glancing to Koble then at Rain. "I hope this is the start of an alliance between us".

Rain patted Nathan on the shoulder and smiled.

"You may not have the fur of a Sphinax, but you certainly have the soul," Rain replied.

"Thanks," Nathan replied awkwardly.

While Rain and his men loaded the guns into the Resistance freighter, Nathan headed back up the boarding ramp to Koble and Astrilla. He stopped Koble from taking another drag on the pipe and asked:

"Who is Gordon Taggart?"

The Sphinax chewed the inside of his cheek and nodded. The grave look in Koble's eyes said more than words could, which made Nathan nervous.

"Well?" Astrilla said. "Who is this person?"

Koble sighed, "Let's get a drink".

Nathan nodded, and they followed Koble to the living area. When they entered the room, they found Vol and Krell examining what Nathan assumed was an old engine. He grabbed a bottle of Xaxian rum and poured himself and Koble a shot. Nathan offered the bottle to Astrilla, but she politely declined.

"So," Nathan leaned on the bar. "Gordon Taggart?"

Koble was about to answer his question when the sound of something mechanical hissed behind them. Vol and Krell moved back in alarm. When Nathan turned, he saw the cause of their distress.

In the middle of the living area was a floating spherical droid. The way its metal arms and appendages spiralled and extended from its torso was almost spider-like. Nathan drew his gun and was about ready to open fire, but when the droid stopped, it focussed its red ocular sensor on him. Its arms stopped moving, and there was a strange hum that came from within its body.

"What the fuck is that thing?" he said, trying to mask the panic in his voice.

Before anyone could reply, something audible came from a speaker on the body of the droid. It was complete gibberish, but the frequency and pitch seemed to adjust with every noise and beep it made. The droid looked beyond Nathan to Astrilla. A cacophony of noises and high pitched sounds poured out of the droid's body until finally, it said something coherent.

"Enkaye genealogy detected. Commencing start-up procedures". The red-eye on its carcass turned blue. "Greetings".

CHAPTER FORTY-THREE

The droid's arms twitched as it stared at Astrilla. Despite looking like something from a bad nightmare, it seemed harmless. It's arms reached out toward her, but as soon as it spotted Nathan's raised gun, it stopped. That meant that the droid could understand human behaviour.

"You are Enkaye?" it asked.

Astrilla exercised a level of caution as she took a step closer to the hovering machine. It whirred and buzzed before gently floating over to Astrilla. It studied her, and its eye became turquoise. Another series of unrecognisable words and dialects came from the droid's spherical skull.

"I think it's trying to talk," Nathan said.

The droid stopped and focussed on Nathan. All the beeps, boops and attempts to communicate halted and for a moment, Astrilla thought the droid had burnt out a component.

"Detecting language parameters…" it said.

"What the hell is it doing?" Koble said from the bar.

Astrilla looked back, noticing that the Sphinax had a gun in one hand and a bottle of wine in the other. Before she could answer, the droid caught her attention:

"Apologies, this unit has been inactive for forty-three-thousand hours. Language functions were disabled to preserve energy". The voice had softened, though it was still robotic. "I detect that you share the genealogy of the Enkaye…"

"I do," Astrilla nodded. "May I ask, what are you?"

The droid continued to buzz and whir as it processed the question.

"This unit is of Enkaye construction: designed as a storage guardian," it said. "My purpose was to wait for the Masters to return".

"How long have you been waiting?"

"Approximately seventy-three-million solar cycles," it replied.

Astrilla turned to Nathan, and they exchanged a look. She could see that Vol was already trying to quantify the number.

"You were built by the Enkaye?" Astrilla asked.

"Correct," it answered. "Now that you are here, I can impart to you the item I have been holding".

"What item?" Astrilla said.

"The Omega," the droid replied, stating it as though it were obvious.

There was a sudden flash of blue light, which seemed to alarm everyone except Astrilla. Something formed in the droid's hands that looked like a thin bar constructed entirely of light. Astrilla looked on as the droid seemed to assemble the item from nothing. When it was finished, the droid held out a metal rod that measured around fifty centimetres in length.

"This is the second piece," it said, handing the item to Astrilla.

She felt the smooth piece of metal against her delicate skin. It was like holding an icicle that was both cold and boiling at the same time. Much like the first piece, the second didn't seem like much of a weapon. It was a blank piece of metal, with no discernable markings or purpose. It looked more like a tool that would be used for opening crates rather than saving the universe from evil. Astrilla realised as she pressed her thumb into the metal that the visions that she and Nathan shared had steered them toward Mirotose Station: toward Guttasnype and eventually Krell.

There is a path for all of us, Astrilla thought.

Before she could say anything else, Nathan spoke up,

"Are there more parts to the Omega?"

"The Masters would never keep such an item in one place," the droid said. "After the great war, what was left of the Enkaye dynasty scattered the pieces across several planets".

The droid moved around the living room with a surprising amount of delicacy. The way it hovered in the air so silently was a magnificent feat of engineering that even Astrilla could admire.

"I detect that you have the map?" the droid said. "I must show you the way".

Nathan grabbed his backpack from behind the bar and opened it with his free hand, producing the scroll they'd acquired back on Pelos Three. The droid spun around, watching the Earther's every move.

"You mean this?" Nathan said, holding the scroll up. The droid moved to him and snatched it from his hands. "Hey!"

The droid ignored him and unravelled the scroll, placing it on the bar. The diagram on the parchment began to change. The dark lines that indicated star systems and planets twisted and reformed, creating an entirely new map, with a new location.

The droid handed the scroll back to Nathan, then shifted its focus to Astrilla. There was a strangeness to the droid that Astrilla hadn't noticed up until that point. It was the machine: the same *machine* mentioned in her visions. Whatever destiny had in store for her and the crew of the Phoenix, this was undoubtedly it. Fate had brought them all to that very moment, and the realisation of that was terrifying.

As the droid closed the gap between itself and Astrilla, Nathan stepped in the way. He took up an interrogative stance rather than one of aggression and pointed at Krell.

"A few years ago, you saved our friend here," Nathan said. "Right?"

The droid glanced at Krell and buzzed a few times before giving a reply;

"Yes, seven-thousand-one-hundred-and-twenty-seven

days ago, this unit saved this Sphinax female from a life-threatening fall." It turned to Nathan, "From my scans, she appears to be intact; therefore, this unit was successful".

"Just incredible…" Krell marvelled. "You are working again! I want to thank you for saving me".

The droid didn't acknowledge her at all. It turned away and moved to Astrilla's side. The droid whirred, and its voice faded;

"Mission complete. Commence final shut-down. Terminate all files. Deactivate drive core. Purge memory banks. Delete all subroutines…"

There was a dreadful, lifeless thump as the droid crashed to the ground. The whirring and beeping from inside its torso ceased. Its limbs and appendages sagged to the floor as its ocular sensor faded to black. Nathan took several paces toward the metal corpse and gently tapped it with his boot.

The droid didn't react.

"Did this thing just self destruct?" Nathan asked.

Vol paced over to the droid and knelt beside it.

"I think that was more of a failsafe," she said, nudging the droid with a wrench.

"Can you fix it?" Astrilla asked.

"I'm not a historian," Vol shook her head. "I don't know the first thing about Enkaye technology."

"Maybe not," Koble said from the bar. The Sphinax clicked his fingers together and looked at Nathan, "But I know someone who might…Doctor Gordon Taggart".

▲

After all the excitement with the droid, Koble felt the need to get some fresh air. The Phoenix was getting slightly crowded, and he needed some time to think about Gordon Taggart: or at least how to explain who he was.

The hangar where the Phoenix and Sphinax resistance had docked was quiet, and the temperature was comfortable, which Koble appreciated. He stretched his thick legs as he sipped from a bottle of Fish Wine and hummed a tune which had been stuck in his head for several hours.

"Okay," Koble said to himself and took a deep breath. "This is gonna be a tough one".

In a strange way, Koble wanted to curse the universe for throwing a curveball like Gordon Taggart at him, but at the same time, he couldn't. The universe or fate had reunited him with his mother; with Rain and with Nero: people who'd he'd thought were long dead. He knew that he needed to be grateful, but Gordon Taggart was a complication that couldn't be explained away.

After less than five minutes, Nathan joined Koble in the hangar with a glass of dark liquor in his hand. Koble could tell the Earther was exhausted just by looking at him.

"So," Nathan said, taking a seat on one of the crates. "You gonna tell me what's so special about Gordon Taggart?"

"Well, he's an Earther, like you," Koble replied carefully. "Jack had a little bit of history with him."

"So what's the story?" Nathan replied.

That was a moment that Koble dreaded. It was the making of the lie —a deception that would protect the legacy of a friend while sparing another.

"Back in the old days, Jack took this job protecting a science crew on Diem Nine, during the labour strikes. One of them turns out to be this guy, Gordon Taggart."

Nathan stared at him with a blank expression and took a sip from his drink.

"So, Jack knew him before the Fall?" Nathan raised his brow.

"I think so," Koble nodded. "But that's not the interesting part. During our time protecting Taggart and his group, he took a swing at Jack."

"So?" Nathan shrugged. "A whole bunch of people tried to attack Jack. What's so special about this guy?"

Again, Koble felt the dread creep up his spine.

"Jack didn't hit him back," he said. "I knew your uncle for a long time, and I've never known anyone to strike him and get away unscathed."

"So, why'd Taggart hit him?" Nathan asked.

Koble felt his gut sink.

"I don't know," he lied. "Jack didn't want to speak about it".

Lying to Nathan didn't feel right. It was shameful, but Koble knew he had to keep his word to Jack. Honouring the memory of his long-dead mentor and friend meant more than the disgrace he felt. He wondered for a split second if Nathan could see through it, but the Earther shrugged and drank from his glass. Thankfully, they returned to casual conversation, discussing Kornell and the droid, but all the while Koble couldn't push aside his guilt for lying.

The conversation ceased when Rain's men led Kornell out of the Phoenix in shackles. Seeing his brother defeated should have felt like a grand victory, but to Koble, it was underwhelming. The truth was this was the early stages of freeing Pluvium from the tyranny of Kornell's regime. Kornell would have supporters who would fight to the bitter end to defend the man who'd kept their people from becoming 'wealthers: or at least that was the story Kornell wanted them to believe.

Koble halted the guards and stood directly in front of his brother. For several seconds, there was a silence between them, which Koble allowed to drag as long as he possibly could.

"I need to know," Koble began. "Did you kill Jack Stephens?"

Kornell's smirk was eerie, and Koble forced himself not to take a swing at his brother.

"Sadly not," Kornell hissed. "As much as I wish I had, none of it was my doing".

"So who did it?" Nathan said, moving to stand beside Koble. "Who killed Jack?"

Kornell licked his lips, and the same sinister smile returned;

"That, my boy, is a question for David Jareth," Kornell said. "If anybody knows what happened to Jack Stephens, it is undoubtedly him".

Nathan's eye contact with Kornell didn't waver: not even for a split second. For a moment, Koble wondered if the Earther would react violently, but he didn't. The Loyalty's final shipment was addressed to Jareth. That meant something. Perhaps Jareth had murdered Jack all those years ago, or maybe he knew who had. *Perhaps someone inside his corporation*? Either way, it was another step closer to unravelling the truth.

"I'll see you back on the ship," Nathan said, turning to Koble.

Koble watched as Nathan walked around Kornell and the guards and returned to the Phoenix. He wanted to follow his friend, but he had more to say to his brother.

A severe expression replaced the devious smirk on Kornell's face as they looked at one another.

"You know this will never be over, dear brother," Kornell hissed. "Pluvium will never bow to the will of your soft 'wealther friends. The Sphinax are an industrious people that understand the meaning of sacrifice. They will suffer through the darkest of times to build something grand".

"I do not doubt the capabilities of our people," Koble shook his head. "But you cost billions of people their lives, including our Father: all to protect your outdated views of the universe."

"I suppose time will tell," Kornell smirked arrogantly. "History will look at me as the man who stood against the decay of our traditions and culture. I will be remembered for the heroic sacrifices that I had to make. I did what I had to in order to preserve our people from the curse of communism". Kornell stopped and the hubris in his eyes seemed to grow. "You, on the other hand, will be remembered as the man who fed our cultural identity to 'wealthers. You will be known as the one who allowed them to wash away everything that makes us exceptional".

Koble didn't say anything, because it was a hard point to argue. To an extent, Kornell was right about the Commonwealth, but he'd failed to understand that the 'wealthers were the lesser of two evils. The Revenant were the real enemy. They posed a greater threat to all life in the galaxy than communism. Regardless of Kornell's arguments, he had condemned countless Sphinax lives in the name of his crusade. That was something Koble could never forgive.

"You're right, time will tell," Koble nodded to the guards, and they led Kornell away.

CHAPTER FORTY-FOUR

Before bidding farewell to the Sphinax Resistance, Rain offered Harrt and the crew some additional supplies. Initially, Harrt declined, but the blue-furred Sphinax was surprisingly insistent. They spent the better part of an hour, loading crates of food and ammo onto the ship. During that time, Harrt and Rain swapped stories of their past. Harrt spoke about the Vertex, the Commonwealth and eventually Maru Seven, while Rain told him about the Pluvium Civil War. He found himself telling Rain more than he would anyone else, and it reminded him of the long conversations he would share with Rooke about the trials and tribulations of war. He told Rain of Densius Olbori and the cost of his betrayal at Maru Seven. Even though Harrt had undergone years of grief counselling and emotional rehab, there was something therapeutic about discussing the subject with a fellow veteran.

"What will you do if you ever find the man who betrayed you?" Rain asked as he set down a crate.

Harrt didn't have to think about his answer.

"I will kill him".

"May I ask you another question?" Rain said as he helped Harrt to pickup another crate. Harrt nodded, and the Sphinax continued; "Why do you think that man turned on your people?"

"Well," Harrt strained as they moved the heavy box across the hangar. "High Command always maintains that he was greedy and mad for power."

"That's not what I asked," Rain said. "Why do *you* think he betrayed your people?"

Harrt stopped and looked back at the Sphinax. Rain raised a brow and stared at him expectantly.

"You and I both know that wars do not start on a battlefield, they begin in a fancy building full of well-educated people with agendas," Rain said. "You can't make a traitor overnight. It takes something to make them do what they do".

"Are you saying Olbori is justified in what he did?" Harrt said, his voice growing defensive.

"Not for a second," Rain shook his head. "What I'm saying is that the establishment may tell you he was motivated by a lust for power, but that's oversimplifying it. You 'wealthers are incredibly committed to your cause. If this Olbori was once one of you, then it stands to reason that at one time or another, he held the same values as you. Imagine what it would take for you to jump to the other side as he did."

"There is nothing that would make me turn my back on the Commonwealth".

"Maybe not, but if you are committed to killing this man, make sure you do it for the right reasons," Rain said. "Regret is a fickle bitch that you don't want on your mind. Trust me".

They lowered the crate to the floor, and Harrt wiped the sweat from his brow. In his mind, he disregarded everything that Rain said. Olbori was a traitor, and his actions had cost Harrt his family and homeworld. There was no rational explanation for that.

▲

While Nathan sat at the bar, he pondered why someone like David Jareth would have any interest in Jack or the Loyalty, but finding an answer was impossible. Out of pure curiosity, Nathan pulled all public information on the Jareth Corporation and spent some time reading from his datapad.

According to various marketing materials, Jareth Corps had started as a private security firm but had quickly moved into other fields such as medical research and engineering.

The CEO and founder of Jareth Corps, David Thomas Jareth was a British businessman who'd survived the Fall of Earth. He'd graduated from one of Earth's finest universities and had gone on to work for his father's banking firm. Jareth had undoubtedly survived the Fall, but there was no information on how he'd managed to escape. Instead, buzz-words and catchy slogans filled the paragraphs that described the corporation's CEO.

Words like *innovation, resilience* and *synergy* were thrown onto the page like it was going out of fashion.

Nathan's gut told him to ignore the corporate bullshit as it was a fabrication made to create business for business' sake. Instead of researching the company, Nathan figured it would be wise to look at the man behind it. Commonwealth public records on David Jareth were relatively bland, so Nathan focussed on the multimedia coming out of Paradisium. What he found wasn't exactly mindblowing, but it did paint a picture of the kind of man David Jareth was.

Across various articles, Jareth was referred to as either a brilliant visionary or as an arrogant and ungrateful bigot. Although Jareth had never publically stated his views of the Commonwealth, the speculation in the media was that he opposed them in almost every way. The most recent article Nathan found, spoke of a Commonwealth investigation into Jareth's tax returns, but it wasn't the headline that grabbed Nathan's attention it was the photograph.

David Jareth was now in his sixties and had a thin-face with a head of silvery blonde hair. He didn't look like a murderer, but Nathan knew that looks could be deceiving.

Why would you kill Jack? Nathan wondered as he stared at the picture.

When Nathan lifted his head from the datapad, he noticed Krell placing something down on the bar beside him. It was an unlabelled bottle of clear alcohol.

"It's for you," she said, pointing at the bottle.

Nathan picked it up and unscrewed the cap. He took a sniff, but couldn't identify the distinct scent.

"What is it?" he asked.

"You don't know?" The Sphinax raised her brow. Nathan shrugged in response, and Krell looked at him sympathetically; "It's called vodka. It's one of yours".

"One of mine?"

"An Earther drink," Krell replied. "It was your uncle who introduced me to it. Obviously it's not an original, but we have some excellent people that can reverse engineer most things".

"I appreciate that," Nathan said, nodding to Krell.

He was about ready to deactivate his datapad when Krell glanced the picture of David Jareth on the screen. Nathan knew that the rest of the crew had been talking. By now, Jack's message and all the things Kornell had disclosed would be common knowledge. Krell stepped around the bar and examined the datapad with a frown.

"David Jareth is a fascinating man," she said. "In a way, he should be applauded for his ambition. He should also be shot for what he did to Pluvium".

"I don't disagree," Nathan replied. "It doesn't make any sense. Why the hell would he involve himself with your people's war? What the fuck did he have to gain?"

Krell shrugged as she took a seat beside him.

"I've learnt that not all questions can be answered," she said. "But, if it turns out that Jareth murdered Jack, please put a gunshot in him for me".

Nathan looked back at her in surprise, and she smiled in response.

"Your uncle was one of the finest men I've ever known," Krell said. "He tried to save my life when Kornell threw me over the edge of Triumph Place. All I remember was holding onto his hand for dear life. When he lost his grip, I fell. I thought I was going to die, and yet, all I kept thinking was that Jack looked so scared; so terrified".

It was at that moment that Nathan realised that he'd seen Krell's fall in his dreams. He recalled seeing Jack reaching out to someone as they plummeted from a great height. It was fair to assume with everything Krell had described that he was right. Still, Nathan couldn't help but wonder *why he was seeing such things? What purpose did it serve?*

Krell went quiet for a moment, and her eyes bore a look of sadness. She placed a paw on Nathan's shoulder;

"Thank you for helping us," she said, her voice returning to its stoic tone. "Thanks to our joint efforts, we are one step closer to freeing Pluvium. Captain Carter if you ever need anything — safe harbour, food, medical— you have a friend and ally in the Sphinax Resistance."

Krell reached out her paw and Nathan took it. They shook hands and Nathan wished her safe travels.

"Are you taking Koble with you?" he said. "I guess now that Kornell is captured, that makes Koble the new Chief?"

"Technically, yes," Krell nodded. "I asked Koble to come along, but he insisted that he must stay with you to see out this mission. He said something about destiny being on your side and I couldn't help but agree".

▲

When it came time to bid farewell to the Sphinax Resistance, hugs and handshakes were exchanged. It reminded Nathan of the celebrations that often followed a job-well-done back on the Loyalty. It felt strange: not like a victory, but the start of something new. When Nathan shook Rain's hand, the Sphinax pulled him into a hug, which he wasn't expecting.

"If you ever need a decent pilot, give me a call," Rain said. "I'd be happy to help, especially if it means I get the pleasure of flying that ship of yours".

"I might take you up on that one day," Nathan replied.

▲

Nathan understood it would take Koble longer to say his goodbyes than the rest of the crew, so he waited patiently in the cockpit. He checked the Phoenix's communications terminal to see a message request from Agent Dines.

Probably wants an update, Nathan thought as he shut down the terminal. *I'll let Harrt deal with that one.*

Slowly the rest of the crew filtered into the cockpit. When Koble arrived, Nathan noticed a skip in the Sphinax's walk. Koble was always the happy one, but Nathan had never seen him so chipper. Despite everything the universe had thrown at him, the Sphinax had always maintained a mostly upbeat nature. It was one of the things Nathan envied.

"Well," Koble drawled, slapping Nathan on the shoulder. "Where's our next stop?"

Nathan furrowed his brow and looked to Astrilla for direction. He noticed that she was still clasping the scroll that the droid had updated hours earlier.

Astrilla paced to the holotable at the centre of the room. She placed the scroll down along with the two non-descript pieces of the Omega. She unravelled the scroll and the rest of the crew crammed around the table to get a better a look.

"At least this one is inside Commonwealth space," Harrt said, keying the location into the star-map. "Looks like a straight FTL jump to the Calidi System".

"Wait," Nathan replied his voice heavy with dread. "Whereabouts in the Calidi System?"

Harrt rechecked his datapad, and answered;

"Paradisium…"

Koble's ears pricked upward at the mention of the Earther refugee planet:

"Oh shit," Koble said in mock celebration. "Cocktails all around. Maybe I'll get a nice tan!"

"How the hell does a Sphinax get a tan?" Vol remarked. "I mean, all that fur?"

Koble lifted a single finger and smirked, but before he could say his witty reply, Nathan cut him off:

"How long will it take to get us there?" Nathan looked at Vol.

He became aware that there was an abruption to his

question that could seem rude. Nathan considered apologising but quickly realised that Vol had already picked up on the thought before he'd even realised.

"Less than a day," she answered with a knowing look. "Maybe eighteen hours".

"Sounds good," Nathan said with a long breath. "I think a bit of rest would do us all some good".

CHAPTER FORTY-FIVE

Less than thirty minutes into the journey, Harrt found himself sending an encoded reply to Leviticus Dines. He updated the Agent with the details of their mission and their new destination. He hit the send button and reclined in his seat, watching the blue flashes of the slipstream pass over the Phoenix.

There was always a delay in sending and receiving messages during the slipstream leg of any journey, so Harrt didn't expect a quick response. Rather than wait for Dines to message him back, he engaged Koble and Vol in friendly conversation.

For over an hour they shared a bottle of Xax and spoke about their lives before the Phoenix Titan. To Harrt, it seemed like a lifetime ago, but it had only been a few weeks. He found himself realising that the crew he'd surrounded himself with felt like a family: it wasn't something he was used to. Back when he served aboard warships like the Vertex, he was friendly with the crew, but it was formal and rehearsed. Of course, he had a friendship with Commander Rooke, but that was different: they'd fought at Maru Seven in the trenches of battle.

Fraternisation and friendships were something High Command disapproved of. The logic was that if a senior officer was too close to those they commanded, he or she would lose perspective, and to an extent, Harrt couldn't disagree. Perspective was important as a senior officer.

Aboard the Phoenix it was different. He was the only military officer on board, and more importantly, he wasn't technically in command. It meant that Harrt could be himself, and it felt damn good.

When his datapad chimed with a response from Dines, Harrt excused himself from the conversation to read the update.

Oxarri,

Glad to hear you are in one piece. Revenant activity in Commonwealth Space has been spiking in the last two days. Intel suggests that Seig has got several military units searching for Astrilla and the Phoenix Titan. I suspect it's only a matter of time before one of them finds you. It is for that reason that the Grand Master, along with the council, have instructed me to meet you at Paradisum. I'm sorry, I tried to keep the circle as small as possible, but what can I say, politicians have to have their way.

I still suspect there is a mole within our ranks. As the councillors, Evoker Elders and anyone in a Commonwealth uniform knows, its fair to assume our mole does too. If I'm right, which I hope I'm not, they know where you guys are heading. That means the Revenant won't be far behind.

I'll be at least eight hours behind you, so whatever you need to do, do it quickly and quietly. Do not draw attention to yourselves.

Dines
P.S. Public information on Doctor Gordon Taggart attached.

Harrt read the message two more times, before switching off his datapad. He audibly sighed as he placed the tablet down on one of the cockpit terminals.

"What did your guy say?" Koble asked.

"Nothing good," Harrt shook his head. "Dines suspects we may have some company at Paradisium, so the Commonwealth has elected to send a few ships as a back-up".

"Firepower is firepower," Koble replied, taking a sip from his drink. "When it comes to the Revenant, we gotta play this smart. The way I see it, more guns means less Revenant".

At the back of the room, Vol tinkered with the Enkaye droid which was laid out atop the holo-table. She lifted her head, to look at Harrt and said;

"Plus, there is Jareth Corps to think about".

She was right.

The Earther corporation presented a different challenge to the Revenant as they were neither friend nor foe. David Jareth had personally dedicated hundreds of military assets simply to be a thorn in King Seig's operation. There was some nobility to that, but Harrt couldn't ignore the fact that Jareth was a greedy capitalist. That meant he stood for everything the Commonwealth didn't.

"So, have either of you ever made it to Paradisium?" Harrt asked. He wasn't sure why he suddenly craved light and companionable conversation, but it felt right.

Koble sipped his drink and shook his head quietly in response, while Vol said;

"Nope, never. Far too rich for my blood".

Koble scoffed in response to the Uvan's reply, almost choking on his drink. He nudged Harrt with his elbow and asked;

"You ever been there, Oxarri?" The Sphinax stifled a cough and returned to his drink.

"No. I've heard it's gorgeous though; golden beaches and beautiful oceans," Harrt said. "The survivors of Earth did quite well out of being refugees, I guess."

"From what I've heard, most of the survivors were the very rich and the well connected," Koble remarked. "Jack always told me that these elite types had the means to save billions of people but instead saved their own asses".

"The Fall of Earth has always been a tricky one," Harrt replied. "The people that survived were effectively given a paradise by the Commonwealth: that's not something we usually do for refugees."

"There's gotta be a reason for that, right?" Koble lifted his paws.

"The Commonwealth failed all those people," Harrt said regretfully. "Normally we would rush to the defence of a small, undeveloped world if the Revenant were attacking it, but we arrived over thirteen hours into the attack".

"So, you think Paradisium is like an apology?" Koble asked.

"The Commonwealth recognised that they'd made a mistake," Harrt nodded. "So, yes, I guess Paradisium is some sort of restitution".

There was a loud crash as Vol bashed the droid with a metal tool. It drew Harrt and Koble's attention to the back of the room, and when the Uvan lifted her head she smiled:

"I've found something that looks like a CPU," Vol exclaimed. "We might be able to repair this little guy after all".

▲

After spending the better part of an hour trying to sleep, Nathan decided to clear his mind by strolling through the Phoenix's corridors. He found himself climbing into the ship's topside gunnery chamber, which boasted an impressive three-sixty view of the FTL slipstream.

He reclined in the leather chair with his hands behind his head, reflecting quietly on everything that kept him awake. Like always, thoughts of the mission and Jack circled Nathan's mind, but they weren't the main thing that was bothering him.

The idea of going to Paradisium made Nathan's gut tighten. He cursed under his breath, thinking of the tropical world, its inhabitants and everything they represented. Though Nathan had started to question many of Jack's lessons, all his claims about Paradisium and its occupants were hard to ignore. Most survivors from Earth were the well-connected types, and Jack wasn't the only one to make those claims. Over the years, there was a handful of Earthers aboard the Loyalty, and every one of them shared the same view.

Paradisium was not Earth, and it's people were not Earthers. The people of Earth may not have been perfect, but it had been a damn sight better than what had grown on Paradisium.

It's a planet filled with former politicians, celebrities and captains-of-fuckin-industry, Jack had once said over a drink. *Stay the fuck away from there unless you wanna leave in a body bag.*

Nathan heard someone climbing up the ladder toward the gunnery chamber, and after a few seconds, Astrilla emerged from the opening in the floor.

"I hate to tell you this, but sitting up here and brooding will not help," she said, sliding herself into the seat opposite.

"I'm thinking," Nathan replied.

Nathan sensed that Astrilla's smirk was sarcastic, but he couldn't be sure. The Evoker leaned back in her chair and stared at streams of light sailing over the ship. Nathan could just about make out his reflection in the glass amidst the slipstream.

"Would you care to share what's on your mind?" Astrilla said, keeping her gaze locked on the window.

Nathan felt a tension begin at his shoulders and creep up his neck. He didn't want to admit it, but there had been an uncomfortable tension between them at Mirotose Station. Despite only knowing her for weeks, Nathan felt as though he finally understood her. Astrilla was persistent, tenacious and incredibly perceptive. Most importantly of all, she cared. That was a rarity in Nathan's experience.

"You were right," Nathan admitted.

Astrilla peeled her gaze away from the window and faced him; "About what?"

"I'm not Jack," he said, referring to their argument

earlier that day. "I've been on the defensive for so fucking long that I lost sight of that. When I was a kid, I struggled with what had happened during the Fall."

"That is—"

"Never let them see you bleed was a saying that Jack told me. He wanted to toughen me up to survive. I guess in some fucked-up way, Jack believed it was the right thing to do," Nathan said. "Whether it was right or wrong doesn't matter. I'm still here because of him, but I'm afraid that it cost me a piece of myself that I'll never get back".

Astrilla leaned across the space between them and carefully placed her hand atop of his.

"There's a passage in the Evoker Legandariums," Astrilla said. "I can't remember it exactly, but the core of the message is that losing a part of yourself leaves room to gain something new. Maybe this ship and the crew is the next step of your journey".

Nathan nodded, and she withdrew her hand.

He got the sense that nothing else needed to be said. He'd opened up, and Astrilla had accepted what he'd had to say. Nathan didn't feel any weaker for sharing his innermost thoughts, but it still felt odd.

Astrilla rose from the chair, but rather than climb out of the gunnery chamber she stopped and their eyes locked. For a long time, Nathan didn't know what to say, and he was sure that the same applied to her.

She held his gaze a moment longer, then they drew into one another. Their lips met under the sapphire lights of the FTL slipstream. Seconds later, they removed each other's clothes, and their bodies met.

▲

Memories from the Fall forced their way into Nathan's sleeping mind like a tsunami. The once blue sky had turned to the colour of blood. The brutal murder of his grandmother, father and mother, followed. Usually, the dream would end at the point where Nathan realised he couldn't fight back, but this time something changed.

He was no longer the cowering unarmed child. He was an adult, and he was armed. Nathan took up his gun and fired. The Revenant officer who'd murdered his mother, fell to the ground in an explosion of blood.

It took what felt like an hour for Nathan to become aware of his new surroundings. Water surrounded him for miles and miles, as far as the eye could see. The bright yellow sun beat down on him and reflected off of the waves.

"I'm not that kind of doctor…" A male voice called out in panic.

There was a violent flash of red light, and Nathan found himself in a dark metal chamber. He looked to his left for Astrilla but found that he was alone. The room was of Enkaye design, similar to the temple on Pelos, but far more expansive. Out of the darkness, a figure emerged. Nathan attempted to get a better look, but with every step, the presence moved away.

"Life such as this reminds us that there can still be harmony," a soft male voice spoke from the darkness.

"I'm not that kind of doctor…"

The spectre lingering at the back of Nathan's mind pushed its way through the Enkaye-built room. A pair of dark eyes stared into Nathan's very soul, but they weren't hostile.

"And at what cost does your harmony come, my old friend?"

There was another flash of red light, and the pair of dark eyes were replaced by the ocean.

"You will need allies in the days to come".

"I'm not that kind of doctor…"

There was a loud squeal that overpowered Nathan's senses. The sound was too intense to bear, and it snapped him out of the dream.

As he shot up in his bed, Nathan noticed a lingering voice in his ears, which left him wondering if it were real or not;

"This is simply the first step".

He exhaled and ran his fingers through his dark hair in an attempt to calm himself. After a few seconds, he turned to Astrilla, sitting up in the bed beside him.

CHAPTER FORTY-SIX

May the river Prynn wash the heretics of that which makes them violent. May it soak away the primitive sense of evil that lies within every living being.

In the days since docking the Messorem, There had been no word of Astrilla's whereabouts. Baylum's complex network of spies was usually prompt, but there was a hold-up, and it made Seig feel impatient. Rather than focus his attention on something he couldn't influence, Seig spent his days meditating in the presence of the river Prynn. He hoped that the great waters would guide him to the Evoker, but instead he became aware of another presence lurking within the Void. Whoever, or whatever the spectre was, it didn't show itself: it merely observed from a distance. Seig had never felt another being within the waters. Ever.

For hours, he searched and searched, but the phantom was elusive. Something had changed, and it didn't take long for Seig to realise what it was. He had touched the liquid in the Messorem's power chamber, and it had reached out to him and burnt him.

What if it did more than burn my skin? Seig wondered. *What if it severed my connection to the river Prynn?*

In that moment of realisation, the apparition passed by him. He couldn't see it, but he knew it was there; stalking him.

"What are you?" Seig said, but he was met with no reply.

His connection to the Void was severed the moment his communication panel chimed. Seig awoke in his chamber, kneeling at the edge of the pool. He felt cold and uncomfortable, which was something he wasn't accustomed to. The communications panel chimed once more, and Seig resisted the urge to put his fist through the screen. Instead, he answered the message with a raised voice;

"Did I not give you explicit instructions not to disturb me?"

Prince Baylum's visage appeared on the screen, and Seig swallowed his anger.

"What news do you bring, my son?" Seig said, his voice carrying less rage than before.

Baylum's lips curled into an arrogant smirk, which only made Seig want to reach through the screen and slap the pride off of his face. Instead, he reminded himself of the work that Baylum and his spies had undertaken. *Perhaps they had found something of interest.* Baylum's smile seemed to be victorious which filled Seig with a sense of hope: so much so that he could feel himself leaning toward the screen in anticipation.

"I bring good news father; my informant has made contact," Baylum said. "The Evoker and her crew, are heading to Paradisium. It appears that the Commonwealth is sending warships to defend them."

"You're sure?" Seig asked, placing his hands on the control panel.

"I'm certain," Baylum nodded. "Father, I believe we should rally our forces at Paradisium. The Jareth Corporation will undoubtedly attack once—"

"No," Seig cut him off with a wave of the hand. "The line must continue. Do not come to Paradisium".

"But—"

"I have spoken," Seig growled. "Do not force me to repeat myself".

Seig forced himself to bite down his disappointment. The thing Baylum failed to understand was that he was the last of their sacred line. Heritage meant everything to the Revenant monarchy. To remember where you came from was more holy than the river Prynn.

Baylum tightened his jaw in an attempt to mask his wounded ego. It was another sign of how immature the Prince was. He couldn't inherit the crown: not yet.

"I will be in touch over the next few days," Seig said, keeping his voice low. "Update the fleet if you receive any further intel".

Baylum was silent for a long time, and the scowl on his face seemed to deepen. Finally, he answered;

"As you wish".

After Baylum's face vanished from the screen, Seig sent strict orders to Grand Admiral Olbori. There was no doubt in his mind that there would be a fight at Paradisium, and it wasn't limited to the Phoenix Titan and her crew.

The darkness guides all. The darkness will spread, anything else until then is of little meaning.

▲

Astrilla didn't know how to feel about spending the night with Nathan. It had been months —years in fact— since she'd even thought of such things. It was not for lack of desire, but rather an unwillingness to let her guard down with another. Connection on a spiritual or an emotional level was essential: otherwise, it'd be a casual encounter, and the idea of that made Astrilla feel sick to her stomach.

There was no denying that in the weeks since Yenex, that something had developed between her and Nathan, but it was hard to ignore the fact that they were very different people. She was a well-spoken, scholarly Evoker, while he was a foul-mouthed scoundrel; albeit an educated one. Still, she couldn't deny that they shared a connection, and it had only grown over time. Whatever it was between them, Astrilla knew it was more than she'd first thought. It may have been awkward; tense and at times, heated, but it made her feel alive. That was something she hadn't felt in a very long time.

After sharing another vision, they stayed awake for several hours. Initially, they discussed what they'd seen in the dream and tried to make sense of it. Of course, the vague nature of it meant that it was hard to piece together.

Instead, they laid under the sheets and spoke for hours. They talked about hopes and dreams; of their childhoods and of their families. Astrilla gathered from that conversation that the one thing Nathan missed most was a family unit.

From the way, Nathan described the relationship he'd shared with Jack, Astrilla could tell that he'd meant the world to him. As questionable as Jack Stephens' parenting methods sounded, Astrilla couldn't deny there was something admirable about him. To raise a child that was not his own was commendable by its own merits, but to raise a child in an environment so hostile and uncertain was something else entirely.

The idea of Jack finally made sense to Astrilla. She understood why the subject was so sensitive to Nathan. Simply put, he missed the man who'd been like a father to him. The only closure he'd ever had regarding Jack's fate had come in the form of a hologram; almost a decade after his disappearance. With so many unanswered questions concerning his uncle, it had left Nathan, confused and angry.

"Your cousin is still out there," Astrilla said. "If family means that much to you, why don't you go find him?"

Nathan frowned at her question and shook his head.

"James is —or was— someone you don't want to be around," he answered.

"You think he's dead?"

Nathan sighed. "James was an addict, and the drugs made him into the worst possible version of himself. He became violent, aggressive and reckless. Ultimately, I had to cut ties".

"That must have been difficult".

Nathan sat up in bed and leaned against the headboard.

"You know what scared me the most about that whole situation wasn't leaving my cousin with all his demons and addictions. It was the fact that I didn't feel an ounce of guilt when I walked away. I still don't". He paused for several seconds, and Astrilla noticed that his jaw had tensed.

"So you feel guilty for not feeling guilty?" Astrilla surmised.

"In a way," Nathan nodded. "James killed a lot of people —*innocent people*. When I confronted him about what he'd done, he said that *those people's lives meant nothing*. To this day I don't regret the decision to leave him".

There wasn't an ounce of anger or remorse in his voice.

"For the record, I think you did what you needed to do," Astrilla said. "Yuta always used to have this saying; *It isn't blood that binds us, it's love*. I'd say the short time I've known you that you embody that saying".

"What do you mean?"

"I mean this crew," she answered. "We've all been brought together by mere circumstance, and yet it feels as though we're a strong unit. Now, I believe in happenstance and destiny, but I don't think the bond between this crew is because of that. It's because you are at the heart of it".

Nathan appeared taken aback by what she'd said, but seconds later he allowed himself to smile. Astrilla rested her head on his chest, and she felt his heartbeat. She wrapped an arm around him, and they sat in companionable silence until she fell asleep.

▲

After six hours, a gentle alarm woke Harrt Oxarri from his slumber. He blinked, opened his eyes, then shut them again as the overhead LEDs activated. Most people would remain between the covers for another couple of hours, but Harrt wasn't like most people.

Once he'd climbed from his bed, Harrt shaved, showered and changed. It still felt strange to wear informal clothing, rather than a uniform, but he accepted it as a necessity for the mission.

After making his bed and ensuring that his hair was combed, Harrt left his cabin and made his way to the cockpit. He found Vol in the pilot's seat, tinkering with a metal item as she watched the slipstream. Koble was at the back of the room, drinking something that had a bitter aroma while watching something on his datapad. The strange scent was coming from a half-empty pot of dark liquid that the Sphinax had placed on the holotable.

"Want some?" Koble gestured to the container.

"What is it?"

"It's called coffee," Koble answered. "Earther drink — well a replication of an Earther drink anyway. It's good, gives you a nice buzz in the morning hours".

"I'm good," Harrt replied, wondering how the Sphinax could derive pleasure from the taste of a human beverage.

Harrt passed by Koble and took the co-pilot's seat beside Vol. The Uvan was busy trying to repair a component she'd found inside the droid.

"It's like trying to thread a needle using a wrench," she said, holding up the coin-sized piece of metal. "Let's hope this Doctor Taggart knows what he's doing".

"Let's hope so," Harrt replied.

He spent a half-hour carrying out the same routine checks he would have done back in the days when he'd been a helmsman. Harrt ticked off the mental checklist, stored in the deepest recesses of his mind. Engines; Navigation; Environmental controls: everything was operating at optimum capacity. Before Harrt could double-check his findings, the terminal beside him buzzed, indicating that their destination was approaching.

The drop out of FTL felt smooth: like the Phoenix was a leaf gently floating across a puddle. It reminded Harrt just how remarkable the ship was.

The pale sapphire world of Paradisium looked like a gem amongst the darkness of space. If terraforming was considered to be a form of art, then Paradisium would be a masterpiece. It looked every part as beautiful as Harrt had heard. A magnificent blue ocean divided the continents and tiny scattered islands. The perfect proximity to the local star ensured that Paradisium had the ideal climate to sustain a healthy ecosystem.

There wasn't the usual traffic of supply vessels and civilian transports coming off of the planet. Instead, there was a small Commonwealth fighter squadron patrolling the area: as was protocol since the Earther refugees were rehomed there.

As Harrt expected, the fighters hailed and demanded the immediate transmission of clearance codes. He did, and after several seconds of silent static, the squad leader said;

"And what is it that brings you here, Lieutenant Oxarri?"

"We are here on behalf of High Command and the Evokers," Harrt replied. "Our mission is classified so I can't really say much. I can give you a heads-up though; a few of our big-birds will be dropping into the system in the next couple of hours as part of our mission".

"You expecting some trouble, Lieutenant?" the Squadron Leader said. "We aren't used to combat situations around these parts".

"Hopefully not," Harrt answered. "Just a formality. You know how it is, right?".

More silent static followed.

"You are cleared for landing. Two of my guys will guide you to a suitable landing pad".

"Thanks," Harrt said.

The Fighters escorted the Phoenix through the planet's defensive shield network and into the atmosphere. The ocean stretched for miles, meeting the horizon and reflecting rays of light from the sun. Luxurious boats and yachts could be seen floating in the sea as they passed over.

After several seconds a mass of land became visible. The first thing Harrt spotted was a harbour, where more yachts and cruisers were anchored. To the east, there was a long golden beach with parasols and sun loungers amongst the pristine sand. Tropical trees were planted around the paths, which led to countless rows of extravagant gated mansions.

"You 'wealthers really went all out for these people,"

Vol said. "Don't think I've seen anything quite like this".

The ship passed over hundreds of ostentatious houses, each boasting well-maintained gardens and swimming pools. Vol almost gawped at the sight of the tropical paradise. Harrt said nothing and instead kept his eyes fixed on the escorting fighters ahead of them.

In many ways, Vol was right. The Commonwealth had gone out of its way to see the Earthers were kept in the lap of luxury. No other refugees had received treatment quite like it, and it was a point that had come under scrutiny inside the Commonwealth Council chambers many times.

Of course, it didn't matter if the Earthers lived better than some 'wealthers. The Commonwealth knew it had to take responsibility for its failure to protect the Earth. Billions had died, and Seig had added most of them to his ranks. It was the kind of failing that the older generations felt ashamed by. Worlds had been lost to Seig in the past, but never one so primitive. The only way to recover from such shame was to make amends to the people who'd been wronged.

The simple truth was that Paradisium was restitution for a colossal failure, but at least the Commonwealth could recognise where it had failed.

CHAPTER FORTY-SEVEN

Koble knew that people saw him as *a comedian.* As a loveable clown. For the most part, he found that there was nothing wrong with it. He rather enjoyed bringing a smile to those he cared about. The problem was that with the reputation came the assumption that he wasn't astute; that he couldn't detect subtly. Of course, it was a misconception, and over the years, those who'd grown to know him well, knew just how perceptive he really was.

Nathan was one of those people.

When Koble noticed the Earther entering the living area with Astrilla oddly close behind, he took note. When he saw the pair exchange a discreet glance, it confirmed Koble's suspicion.

Well, at least they got that over and done with, Koble thought.

He poured two cups of coffee and returned to the seating area, where the others were reviewing a map of the local area. Koble handed Nathan one of the steaming cups and took a seat. The rest of them were already in deep conversation. Harrt was pointing at a part of the holo-map that looked distinctly residential.

"There it is: 1955 Hemlock Street," Harrt said pointing out Gordon Taggart's address on the map. "Looks like it's less than a thirty-minute walk".

"Then we should leave immediately," Astrilla replied.

"Hold up," Koble interrupted her mid-sentence and

held up a paw. "Trust me when I say this: Taggart is the jumpy type. If we all turn up on his doorstep, we will spook him."

"Any chance he's mellowed since you last saw him?" Nathan said.

"People like Gordon... don't mellow," Koble said, picking every word delicately. "Trust me; it's better if he sees a familiar face".

Nathan raised his brow, and for a heartbeat Koble was sure he'd said too much. Koble knew that the Earther was shrewd and could usually spot dishonesty, but Nathan also placed a great deal of faith in those he trusted. Fortunately for Koble, Nathan's trust for him outweighed his wisdom.

"Fine, but at least take Harrt with you," Nathan said. "Just in case we need to drag Taggart back here".

It wasn't the answer Koble had hoped for, but it was good enough. He nodded and sank back in his seat and masked his relief by drinking from his mug. As he gulped back a mouthful of bitter coffee, Koble peeked out of the corner of his eye at Vol. Koble could see the expression of scrutiny on her face from a mile away. It was likely that she couldn't get a precise reading on what he was thinking: that was a rare skill that only a handful of Uvan's had. Instead, Vol would probably detect a spike in emotion, and he hoped it would be of relief, not evasion.

Getting Gordon alone was the key. Koble had to get to the doctor before Nathan: to make sure that he wouldn't say the wrong thing. Jack's secret had to remain buried: just as Koble promised.

Jack was dead, but his memory was not. The one thing that Koble cared about most was that Nathan remembered his uncle for the honourable man he was.

▲

With Koble and Harrt on the way to track down Gordon Taggart, Nathan decided to venture out of the ship to find the Portmaster. The Phoenix needed her fuel topping up, and he figured that he could gather some local intel at the same time. When he walked out of the ship, Nathan found a thin man standing at the bottom of the landing-pad, wearing pressed a linen suit.

"Captain Carter?" he said, stepping a few inches closer to Nathan.

"Who's asking?"

The thin man fished a piece of folded paper from his breast pocket and handed it to Nathan.

"Declan Montague; Assistant Chief of staff to Mr Jareth".

Nathan resisted the urge to reach for his gun: "Is that right?"

"Yes, sir," Montague replied, his voice oozing with regality. "Mr Jareth would kindly like to invite you to his private estate for tea. He wishes to discuss some business with you".

Nathan became aware that his brow had raised involuntarily.

"Tea?" he said.

Montague looked at him with a hint of disdain: as though Nathan was saying something profoundly stupid.

"Yes, sir," Montague repeated and pulled a datapad from his pocket. He checked a diary on the screen then looked back to Nathan; "I can pencil you in for noon?"

It became painfully evident that Jareth's employee was nothing more than an administrator. He wasn't one of Jareth's security henchmen like Ralph Hayward. Perhaps it was a trap or something else, but Nathan had to go. He had to find out what Jareth knew about Jack.

He looked back at Montague, whose thin fingers hovered above his datapad in anticipation.

"Sure," Nathan nodded. "Noon".

Montague nodded and a polite smile formed on his face.

"Excellent," he said. "The address is on the back of my business card. It's a short walk east along the beachfront. When you get to the front gates, tell security that you have an appointment with Mr Jareth and they'll see you to him".

With his business attended to, Montague bid Nathan a

pleasant but rehearsed farewell. As Nathan watched the thin man disappear into the crowded spaceport, he heard the sound of Astrilla and Vol walking down the landing pad.

"Who was that?" Astrilla asked.

"You are not going to believe me," Nathan said, handing her the business card.

▲

Paradisium was nothing like Yenex: it was like no world that Vol had visited in her life. The temperature was pleasant, and the ocean was almost as blue as the clear skies above. It was a kind of perfection that poets would spend years trying to describe, and yet it made Vol feel sick to her stomach. Knowing that the Commonwealth had bank-rolled Paradisium for the Earthers, despite many of the 'wealth's citizens struggling to make ends meet, wasn't right. The harsh reality was that some Commonwealth systems struggled with poverty, and yet Paradisium thrived. Yes, the Earthers had lost their planet, and yes, the 'wealth had failed them, but they were one of a billion other races effected by the war. No other refugees had received anything quite like Paradisium.

So, what made the Earthers so special? Vol wondered.

For a while, she walked side by side with Nathan and Astrilla. She sensed that something had changed between them since Mirotose Station. Vol didn't need her sixth sense to tell what had happened. The telltale signs were already there, but the pair of humans did a good job of keeping it under wraps, so she elected to do the same out of respect.

Vol couldn't deny that the beach attire for Paradisium's residents lacked modesty. The only other time she'd seen so much exposed flesh was in the dance clubs back on Yenex. Vol could sense Astrilla's discomfort to the sight as well, so she nudged the Evoker:

"If this is their usual attire, where the hell do they keep their gun?" she jested.

Astrilla smiled in amusement.

"It's a good thing that these people don't have winter

here," she remarked. "Or farming for that matter. Clothing like that would be most unsuitable".

The Evoker made a good point. the Earthers had nothing better to do than work on their tan. Paradisium wasn't a resort; it was their home. They'd spent the better part of two decades living a life of pampered luxury.

There was one woman in particular who caught Vol's eye: a beautiful, elegant young lady with sunkissed skin and blonde hair. She stared at Vol and the others for a moment, before turning away and reaching for a glass of champagne. She was perhaps a half-decade younger than Astrilla and Nathan, which meant she likely didn't recall the Fall; or she wasn't Earth-born at all.

It was strange to think that an entire generation had grown up only knowing the luxury of Paradisium. They wouldn't understand what it was like outside the comforts of their new home. They couldn't understand the meaning of real sacrifice, like Vol or the rest of the crew: *how could they?* Paradisum was all they knew.

After a mile, the group reached a harbour, where a dozen yachts were anchored. It seemed like the appropriate place to stop, so Vol pointed out a beachside bar serving breakfast.

"Seems like a good spot," she said.

"Sure," Nathan shrugged. "Hopefully the locals might have some info on Enkaye ruins".

▲

The beach bar was a large open hut, made from a wooden base with matching supports. A leaf thatched roof was suspended above the establishment, providing shade from the warm morning sun. Nathan found himself becoming increasingly aware of the stray glances from the locals. Evidently, Paradisium didn't get many visitors.

Astrilla picked a booth at the back: away from the other customers. Nathan took their drinks order: tea for Astrilla and something fruit-based for Vol.

A jukebox at one end of the room played rock music at

a low volume. The wailing vocals and guitar-driven melody reminded Nathan of sitting in the back of his parents' car. He took a seat on one of the barstools. While he waited for service, Nathan glanced at the three-dozen bottles of alcohol that were available: he'd only heard of half of them.

"Sorry for making you wait, dude," a voice said from the end of the bar.

Nathan drew his eyes over to the barman who moved in front of him. The young man was African American; tall and slender; likely no older than his early twenties. Unlike the other Earthers —or Paradisians— with their bare chests or floral shirts, he wore a dark t-shirt and jeans.

The barkeep stuffed a dishcloth in his back pocket then clapped his hands together;

"What'll it be?"

His American accent was strange: west coast with hints of something else that Nathan couldn't identify.

"Well, for my friends, tea and a glass of whatever your best fruit juice is," Nathan said. He glanced again at the jumble of alcohol and soft drinks and shrugged; "And as for me... Surprise me!"

"Ah, an off-worlder," the barman said as he began preparing his order. "We don't get many of you guys around here".

The young man's comment felt like a punch to the gut. It wasn't because Nathan felt insulted, but because he realised that his kind didn't recognise him as one of their own. He was a bonafide survivor of the Fall. More importantly, he was an Earther —born on Earth.

"What makes you think I'm not from Earther?" Nathan said, watching the bartender slice something that resembled a lemon.

The young man looked at him and smiled;

"I said *off-worlder,* not *Earther:* there's a distinct difference," he said. "Besides, nobody around here says *Earther* anymore, 'cept the older folks".

"So, what do they say?"

"Well, the people that were born here call themselves Paradisians".

"But not you?"

The barman scooped up a handful of fruit and tossed it into a juicer. As the machine gurgled and buzzed, he turned to Nathan;

"Do you see me working on my tan or drinking champagne at 10 am?"

Nathan shook his head.

"Exactly," the barman said, grabbing a teapot from a shelf. "I don't have to work, but I choose to do it. I hope to own my ship and fly as far away from this rock as possible".

Nathan leaned forward on the bar; "This place is a tropical paradise. Why would you want to leave?"

The barkeep spread his hands wide.

"My Pops once told me that a man has gotta have a purpose in life," he said. "The way I see it, this place is where purpose comes to die".

Nathan agreed. The survivors of Earth and their offspring had become lethargic. He also couldn't help but notice how similar the barkeep was to him at that age. It made Nathan wonder if he'd have ended up the same had he lived on Paradisium. He waited for the young man to finish preparing the drinks and paid him a handsome tip.

"What's your name, kid?" Nathan said, handing the young man a credit chit.

"It's Russell".

"Thanks for the drinks and conversation," Nathan said, picking up the tray of drinks. "For the record, I think your father was right: a man needs purpose".

CHAPTER FORTY-EIGHT

The thirty-minute walk to Gordon Taggart's house was surprisingly pleasant; though Harrt didn't care for the tropical weather. Along the way, he and Koble passed an elderly couple walking a four-legged creature on a leash. The strange animal was unlike anything Harrt had ever seen: like a primitive, devolved version of a Horrus, but far smaller, and walking on all fours.

"The Earthers call those things, *Dogs*," Koble said, using his fingers to make air-quotes. "If you think that's weird, you should see the weird Sphinax cousins that evolved on Earth".

As the pair passed the luxurious gated homes, they discussed the events of the last few days; particularly about Koble's new position of *Chief*. The chunky Sphinax didn't acknowledge the title at all, and throughout their conversation, tried to change the subject: that told Harrt that Koble didn't want to lead.

"Let me ask you a question," Koble said, in an attempt to divert their conversation. "Was it just me or did I notice some glances exchanged between Nate and the Evoker?"

"I'm not doing this," Harrt shook his head.

"Doing what?"

"Gossiping," Harrt answered. "It's their business: not mine or yours".

"Yeah, but come on!" Koble's voice shifted an octave. "The peace and quiet is great, but how long till they are back at one another's throats?"

Recognising that their conversation had drifted, Harrt changed the subject. "What can you tell me about Gordon Taggart?"

Harrt could've sworn he saw the slightest flicker of resentment in the Sphinax's eyes, but when Koble turned to look at him, there was clarity.

"Well, I met the guy years ago," Koble said. "Gordon is kinda like Nathan. He's one of those Earthers who doesn't like other Earthers".

It was something that, up until now, Harrt hadn't fully understood. He'd always believed in his fellow citizen: just as the Founders had commanded. Since arriving on Paradisium and seeing the inhabitants, he was slowly starting to realise why Nathan abhorred his people so much. The planet oozed of excess and luxury; something that wasn't common on refugee worlds.

After several minutes, they arrived at the home of Doctor Gordon Taggart. Unlike the other houses, Gordon's was far more understated. Harrt thought it was smaller than his standard-issue bungalow back on Maru-Seven. Koble and Harrt proceeded along a path of cobbled stones to the front door. Along the way, Harrt noticed that patches of the garden were neatly divided into floral, herbal and vegetation.

How odd, he thought, as a muddled mix of aromas met his nostrils.

"Let me do the talking..." Koble said.

Harrt nodded, and Koble proceeded to knock on the door. There was a short silence before it opened. The first thing Harrt noticed about Gordon Taggart, aside from his surly expression, was his dark hornrimmed glasses. The spectacles seemed to lend to the Earther's teacherly appearance. Gordon's exact age was hard to pin down. His slim build, dark greying hair and trimmed beard suggested he was in his late fifties. However, the careworn expression on his face made him look a decade older.

He studied the pair through the glasses on the bridge of his nose for several awkward seconds.

"Koble?" Gordon's sigh made him sound annoyed, rather than surprised.

"Gordon," Koble nodded.

"What are you doing here?" The doctor's face seemed to turn sour as he peered at the Sphinax.

"I'm here on business," Koble replied.

Gordon's disenchanted expression deepened.

"I'm not interested in any business that involves Jack," The doctor shook his head and began closing the door.

"Wait!" Harrt grasped at the door to hold it open. "We are here on Evoker business,"

Gordon Taggart stopped and reluctantly stepped outside. He pushed his glasses up to his face and stared at Koble.

"You're working for the Evokers now?"

There was an awkward hint of surprise in Gordon's question: as though the notion of Koble doing legitimate work was ridiculous.

"You could kinda say that," Koble replied, rubbing the back of his neck.

Sensing that Gordon's hostility was growing by the second, Harrt decided to cut in:

"Doctor Taggart, we are on a mission concerning Enkaye technology: a subject I believe you are highly specialised in. I hate to sound dramatic, but a lot is riding on this and—"

"You're a 'wealther?" Gordon interrupted, his eyes growing wide. He turned to look at Koble. "Let me guess, Jack didn't want to see me, so he sent you and this 'wealther in his place?"

Koble shook his head. "Jack's dead; he's been gone for years".

Gordon took a step back in surprise, "Jack is dead?"

Harrt noticed a sad and mournful look in the doctor's eyes, but the sour expression quickly returned.

"So what the bloody hell do you want with me?" Gordon looked at Harrt.

"Doctor Taggart, we are on a mission of grave importance," Harrt said. "If you'll allow me five minutes to explain…"

"You've got three," Gordon said, looking at his watch. "Then I'm closing the door and returning to the wonderful book I was reading".

For the first thirty seconds, Gordon listened to every word that Harrt said with a look of scepticism that bordered on cynical. It was only when Harrt mentioned Astrilla's heritage that the doctor's eyebrows lifted and his expression softened. When Harrt was done, Gordon removed his glasses and rubbed his eyes.

"Has your friend made any progress repairing the droid?" Gordon asked.

"Not much," Harrt shook his head. "She's done what she could".

Gordon hummed, and Harrt struggled to tell if it was voluntary. As the doctor processed whatever it was in his head, he stroked his beard. Finally, he turned to Koble.

"What is it that you aren't telling me?" Gordon shot the Sphinax a glare.

Koble cleared his throat.

"Our captain is a guy called Nathan Carter," Koble stammered. "He's Jack's nephew".

Gordon's eyes narrowed a degree, but then he seemed to laugh to himself. It was not the reaction Harrt had expected at all. The doctor paced back and forth, muttering to himself as he looked off into the distance.

"All this time and the old man still surprises me," Gordon said to himself.

Koble and Harrt exchanged a confused look, while the doctor looked at them expectantly.

"This captain of yours, he's here now? On Paradisium?" Gordon asked, looking at both men.

Harrt nodded, and Gordon rushed into his house, eagerly inviting the pair to wait inside. Harrt found the sudden change in Gordon's mood quite disconcerting, so he entered the house with a degree of caution. Much like the exterior, the interior was understated. The walls were decorated with a few paintings, which sat perfectly flush against exposed brickwork walls.

"That went better than I thought," Koble whispered.

Harrt didn't reply. Instead, he examined a framed photograph on Gordon's cabinet. It showed a much younger version of Gordon, stood in a white lab coat aside a much older man. Somehow they seemed like father and son, despite the fact they looked nothing alike.

Several minutes later, the doctor emerged from the next room with a suitcase in each hand and a satchel over each shoulder.

"I thought you said a *few* things?" Koble remarked.

Gordon pushed past him to the cabinet, snatching the framed photograph from Harrt. He stuffed it into one the satchels and shrugged at the Sphinax:

"Equipment, books, tools, clothing," Gordon said, ticking off each item from the list in his head. "Oh, and my gun!"

"And you need all that?" Harrt furrowed his brow.

"Of course," Gordon answered. He looked at them expectantly and added, "Surely you don't expect me to carry all of this on my own..."

Harrt and Koble grimaced in unison.

▲

For the better part of fifteen minutes, Nathan discussed what to do about David Jareth's invitation with Astrilla and Vol. Both women agreed that the idea of going was foolish, and they were probably right. But despite their advice, and agreeing with it, Nathan knew he had to go.

David Jareth had something to do with Jack, and Nathan needed to know what that was. There was a good chance that Jareth Corps were the ones who'd murdered his uncle, and if that was the case, Nathan owed David Jareth a bullet to the head.

For a while, he phased out and simply stared at his surroundings. The beach-side bar was filled with strange pieces of memorabilia that were no doubt from Earth. In another life, items like a framed sports jersey could have meant something to him, but all Nathan saw were the relics of a dead race.

Something caught Nathan's attention. He turned to the bar, where two men were arguing in hushed tones with the bartender. The first man was thin and handsome, with cropped blondish hair and a pair of expensive sunglasses resting on his head. The second was the muscle of their operation. He was in his twenties, bald and wearing a white vest and shorts. The thing that Nathan noted was the gun tucked into the bald thug's waistband. The barman seemed to argue back with the pair; even going so far as to raise his voice and threaten them.

"You got a problem with it, you take it up with management, asshole," he warned.

Nathan didn't realise he'd been staring until it was too late. The bald one spotted him and swaggered toward the table. In an attempt to appear menacing, the henchmen leaned over and snarled at Nathan;

"You got a problem, pretty-boy?"

Nathan looked to Astrilla first. The expression in her eyes practically said; *Please don't start a fight.*

"Yo!" The bald beefcake banged his fist on the table, drawing the attention of the patrons outside. "I'm talking to you! You got a fucking problem?"

Nathan took his eyes off of Astrilla and cleared his throat. He could almost hear the Evoker's eyes roll as he climbed from his seat.

"Take it from me," Nathan said, stepping an inch closer to the vest-wearing thug. "This ain't a fight you wanna pick".

The bald man jerked his head in the direction of his companion, seeking some sort of approval. When he turned back to face Nathan, he was caught off guard. The hard right that Nathan threw was enough to take the man off his feet. Before the punk could reach for a gun, Nathan booted him in the head; knocking him unconscious.

Nathan wasn't surprised by the lack of combat experience in the slightest. This was Paradisium, land of the lethargic. The closest thing to combat that most pampered Paradisians had experienced was either on the tennis court or against one another in drunken bar fights. They'd never needed to know how to fight because they didn't need to.

The blonde associate was caught by surprise. Seeing his backup fall so easily startled him and he reached for something in his pocket. Nathan's first impulse was to grab his gun and shoot, but when the blonde man produced a pathetic excuse for a switchblade, he stopped.

"Really?" Nathan shrugged at the knife.

"Step back," the thug threatened. "Don't you know who I am?"

"Don't know and don't care," Nathan shook his head. "Now how about you put that... *knife* down and we all walk away from this unharmed".

The blonde attempted to rush at Nathan, swiping the switchblade wildly. Nathan caught his attacker's arm and followed it up with a left hook that sent his attacker stumbling toward the bar. Nathan didn't want to shoot the man: he was another entitled asshole who'd grown up in the lap of luxury on Paradisium and simply didn't know any better.

"That's enough," Nathan said, lowering his voice. "Drop the knife and walk away: last chance".

The blonde refused and lashed out with the blade, but Nathan could see the attack from a mile away. He grabbed the attacker's arm, twisting it behind his back until he dropped the weapon. Without mercy, Nathan planted the man's head into the bar, using enough force to leave a mark, but not to kill.

Another pair of armed goons rushed into the bar to aide their fallen comrades. Nathan was ready to take them on, but they stopped in their tracks, the moment he unholstered his pistol. It suddenly became apparent that they'd halted for a different reason.

The barkeep, Russell, pointed a shotgun at them while standing on the bar. It was the kind of weapon that would certainly kill one of them before he'd need to reload. In addition, Vol had her handgun trained on both of them. The two goons looked sheepishly at one another: no doubt realising they were outgunned and outmatched.

"Take your friends and walk away," Nathan warned.

Thankfully, the backup team had more brain cells than the bald muscle and the blonde switchblade enthusiast. The burly bald man climbed to his feet slowly and could not walk in a straight line, while the knife-wielding blonde was carried out of the bar by the backup team.

"He broke my fucking nose!" the blonde one said to his men. "Just wait until Father hears about your incompetence".

Nathan holstered his gun and looked at the barkeep. The young man placed his shotgun down and took a deep breath.

"Are you okay?" Nathan asked.

"You got any idea whose nose you just broke?" Russell said. "You shoulda' just let them get their pound of flesh outta me".

"Why?" Astrilla asked as she reached the bar. She gestured in the direction of the retreating thugs. "Who was that?"

Russell raised his brow at the Evoker.

"Lady, that guy was Thomas Jareth," he answered, as though she should've known. "He's David Jareth's son".

CHAPTER FORTY-NINE

"Did you really need to escalate that situation?" Astrilla said.

"Yes. If I hadn't stepped in, they would have shot the kid," Nathan nodded in Russell's direction. "Besides, the bald one started it".

Nathan folded his arms and shot her a cocky smirk. She couldn't help but admit that it made him look handsome, but it was still infuriating. It was likely that the violence could have escalated if Nathan hadn't stepped in when he did, but Astrilla knew there was no use in debating it after the fact.

They watched from the beach as the young barkeep received a dressing down from the establishment's owner. For several minutes all that could be heard was shouting. Russell eventually emerged with a backpack in one hand and his shotgun in the other.

"Well?" Vol asked as he stopped in front of them.

Russell let out a long sigh. He rubbed a hand through his dense hair and shook his head.

"I got fired. Turns out that pointing a gun at one of the elite is considered an *insurance risk*".

Astrilla turned to glare at Nathan: his boyish smirk was gone. He straightened up and climbed to his feet.

"I'm sorry, kid," Nathan placed a hand on Russell's shoulder. "Can't help feel like I'm to blame for this..."

To Astrilla's surprise, Russell laughed at what Nathan said.

"I mean you kinda escalated things, but you saved my ass from a beatdown," Russell replied. "Thomas Jareth's been on the warpath with all the local businesses around here for a while. If you hadn't stepped in, it probably would've been me with the broken nose".

"How come?" Nathan asked.

"Let's just say the gentleman clubs around here have some weird initiations," Russell replied. "The last place my father worked got burned down to the ground by one of the Roth kids. Rumour has it that it was all part of an elaborate initiation to join Alpha-Sigma-Epsilon. I tell you those guys are fu—"

"Do you want a job?" Nathan interrupted the young man mid-sentence.

There was a moment of awkward silence between the four of them. Astrilla couldn't help but crane her neck to glance at Nathan. She could feel her brows raise involuntarily. It was good to see him emote to Russell's situation, but Astrilla couldn't escape the feeling that he was rushing into hiring the young man. It was evident from the way Russell stepped back that he was just as surprised as she was.

The barkeep stuttered then stifled a chuckle, "Thanks, but I don't have a clue what you guys do".

Nathan seemed to wait a moment to consider his answer. It was a look that suited him well. Gone was the brash arrogance Astrilla had seen in the past, and its place was something reflective yet decisive. It was the look of a Captain.

"Earlier you said something about a man having a purpose," Nathan looked at Russell. "What if I told you that our purpose for being here is the most important thing in the universe?"

"I'd say y'all have a superiority complex!" Russell

laughed, but his smirk quickly vanished. "You're kidding, right?"

▲

After a thirty minute hike back to the Phoenix Titan, Harrt felt like he'd got a good measure on Gordon Taggart. The Earther seemed smart and capable, but Harrt questioned if he could handle the dangers that the mission could present.

Yes, he brought a gun, but that doesn't mean he knows how to use it, Harrt thought.

Along the way, Gordon seemed to direct his questions to Harrt rather than Koble, which seemed strange, considering that the pair shared a history. He asked Harrt about the mission; the droid and whether they'd run into any trouble. Harrt had kept his answers brief and factual, which the doctor seemed to appreciate.

"So, this captain of yours, will he be at the ship when we arrive?" Gordon asked.

There was a hint of excitement there that seemed entirely out of place. Harrt wasn't sure what to make of it, so he chose to downplay his response.

"I don't know," Harrt shook his head. "He was planning on heading into town to get the lay of the land".

"Well, when he gets back I'd very much like to speak with him," Gordon insisted. "It's of the utmost importance".

When they got back to the Phoenix, Harrt gave Gordon a quick tour of the ship and allocated him a cabin close to the galley. He then escorted the doctor to the cockpit, where Vol was storing the Enkaye droid. Gordon's expression became almost reverential when he laid eyes on the lifeless machine. He carefully placed a hand on the droid's metal shell and took a deep breath.

"What do you think?" Koble said. "The Enkaye made it, right?"

Gordon didn't answer immediately. He pulled off his glasses and knelt to look at the exposed circuitry and inner workings that spilt out of the metal carcass.

"It's one of theirs," Gordon confirmed. "The fact that this thing shows no signs of rust or decay is testament to its builders.... Incredible".

"Can you fix it?" Harrt asked.

Gordon pulled a small flashlight from his pocket and shone it inside an opening on the droid's body. He gestured to Koble and Harrt to get a better look.

"I can rebuild most of the internal components," Gordon said. He directed Harrt's eyes to a cube-shaped mass between the plethora of circuitry and wiring. "The intelligence processor is fried. *If* I'm able to make repairs, it may not remember a thing".

"So, there's a chance this thing could be a glorified toaster?" Koble shrugged.

"Perhaps," Gordon replied. "But think about it: what if the droid remembers? What if it has an understanding of the Enkaye culture or their history? Think about the impact that will have..."

Harrt couldn't help but agree. If the droid had a shred of information on its builders, the discovery would be monumental — possibly the biggest discovery since FTL.

"What do you need?" Harrt said to Gordon.

The doctor looked back at him, his expression empty: "Time".

▲

After hiring Russell Johnson, Nathan asked Vol to escort the former barman back to the ship. He also asked her to tell Harrt and Koble that he was going to see David Jareth.

"Are you sure that's wise?" she said. "Jareth Corps is dangerous. It could be a trap..."

"Maybe," Nathan nodded. "But David Jareth has

answers, and I intend on getting them".

Vol could tell from the tone of Nathan's voice that there was no dissuading him. She turned to look at Astrilla, knowing that the Evoker was just as concerned.

"Surely, you can't think this is a good idea?" Vol said.

Astrilla hesitated, then folded her arms. For a tiny, insignificant flicker of time, Vol was able to read the Evoker. It was something she'd been unable to do since they'd met.

Vol was surprised to find a strange mix of fear, anxiety and uncertainty that festered inside Astrilla's head. It wasn't what she expected as the Evoker always seemed so confident.

"If David Jareth knew we'd docked at the spaceport then he's likely been watching us since we entered the system," Astrilla answered. "I think we should go, but err on the side of caution".

"So, what are you thinking?" Vol asked.

"I'll accompany Nathan to the meeting," Astrilla replied. "Evokers tend to send a message in hostile situations. If he wants to attack us, then he won't get far".

As they parted ways, Vol couldn't help but wonder if Astrilla was over-estimating her abilities. Evokers were deadly, and Astrilla had proven that point several times over, but Jareth Corps were an unknown entity: a private corporate army with a history of questionable actions.

▲

The shack that Russell Johnson called, *home,* was a stark contrast to the other buildings on Paradisium. Unlike the other Earthers, Russell didn't live in an ostentatious mansion. There was no private swimming pool; no carefully crafted garden with accompanying water sculptures. Instead, the former barkeep lived in a wooden shack about half the size of Vol's cabin aboard the Phoenix.

"You wanna come in while I get my stuff together?" he asked.

Sensing Russell's apprehension —*or dread*— that she might say *yes,* Vol declined and opted to wait outside. The wave of relief that flooded Russell's mind told her that it was the answer he'd been hoping for.

Less than five minutes later, Russell came out with a duffle bag over one shoulder and an old backpack on the other. Vol thought it was odd that he was able to pack an entire life into two bags. It was when they started talking on the way back to the Phoenix that she understood why. Russell grew up in what he'd described as a moderately sized house on the other side of Paradisium. His parents were administrative workers on Earth, but when they arrived at Paradisium, they started a new life and eventually opened a restaurant. Russell said that his parents always encouraged him to seek out a *life of purpose* and to him that meant exploring the galaxy. Then a few years prior, Russell's parents died in a freak boating accident, and he'd lost everything.

"Didn't your parents have a will or something?" Vol asked.

Russell snorted at her question.

"Hell no," he answered. "The house went back to the 'wealth, and the restaurant owed a significant amount of cash to Equinox banking".

"Okay, I get the part about the restaurant, but I thought this planet belonged to the Earthers. Why'd you have to give the house back to the Commonwealth?"

"That's the law around here," Russell said, stating it as a fact. "They probably had a big family to move in there or something. The 'wealthers tend to shuffle people about on the northern hemisphere, but they won't touch this side of the planet".

"How come?"

The young man looked back at her with a raised brow and frowned.

"Southern hemisphere is where the big dogs live — people like David Jareth, Markus Holland, Fawas Hussein. They are the kinda people the Commonwealth doesn't wanna upset". Russell looked at Vol and noticed her blank expression. "Y'know, the hardcore separatist types, who make a whole lotta' noise?"

"There are separatists?" Vol raised her brows, and she felt her voice lift an octave. "You mean there are people who don't want to be part of the Commonwealth? After everything they've given your people for the last twenty years?"

Russell shrugged. Vol sensed that it wasn't the first time he'd refused to share his opinion on the matter, so she didn't push for an answer.

Ten minutes later, Vol and Russell reached the Phoenix Titan. As they climbed the boarding ramp, the former barkeep whistled from behind his teeth:

"This is one helluva' ship," he marvelled. "So, you guys stole this thing?"

"Technically, no," Vol replied. "Nathan inherited it from his uncle. We just stole it from the guy who stole it from Jareth Corps".

Russell chewed the inside of his cheek as he made sense of her statement.

"Sounds...complicated," he remarked.

You don't know the half of it, Vol thought.

She took Russell to the living area where they found Koble sitting at the bar. The Sphinax watched an older human working on the droid at the coffee table.

"Is that him?" Vol gestured in Gordon's direction.

Koble nodded, then turned his attention to Russell: "Who's the kid?"

"Long story," Vol replied.

Before she could properly introduce Russell, the young

man eagerly offered his hand to shake with Koble.

"Name's Russell: Russell Johnson," he said in a friendly tone. "I've never seen a Sphinax in the flesh before! Is it true that your people drink wine that's made from fish?"

"Huh, a Paradisian with a knowledge of different cultures," Koble remarked as they shook hands. "What's your line of work, kid? You a smuggler?"

Russell looked at Vol with a hesitant smirk, then back to Koble:

"I'm a former mixologist," he said with pride.

"A what?"

"Well as of an hour ago I was a bartender," Russell said. "I specialise in cocktails".

To Vol's surprise, the cynical expression on Koble's face faded and was replaced by a look of delight. The Sphinax placed a meaty paw on Russell's shoulder.

"You and I are gonna get on just fine," Koble said. "This could be the start of a beautiful friendship."

Vol left the pair as they began to discuss exotic liquor. She walked to Gordon, who seemed to be too engrossed by his work to notice anything else around him.

"Doctor Taggart?"

It took a moment for Gordon to notice, but when he finally did, he diverted his attention away from the droid and over to Vol.

"Ah," he said, climbing to his feet. "You must be the engineer I keep hearing so much about. I'll have you know that Lieutenant Oxarri speaks very highly of your work".

She wasn't sure why, but for one reason or another, Vol felt herself blush, and she did her best to resist. There was an odd flutter of excitement, knowing that Harrt had complimented her work to a total stranger.

"Harrt likes to exaggerate," she replied as they shook hands. "I see you've already got to work on the droid?"

"Yes, I hope you don't mind. I couldn't resist taking a look at it".

"Not at all," Vol said. "From what I gather, you are quite the expert on Enkaye tech?"

Something at the back of Gordon's mind called out to Vol. It was a sadness that she couldn't quite explain. She allowed herself to explore it. There was a shadow of overwhelming horror that Gordon Taggart had locked away for many years. Vol couldn't see the details, but what she could read was almost overwhelming: a single voice behind all the misery that the doctor had clung onto:

Promise me, Gordon: promise me you'll find him.

The only thing Vol could ascertain was that the voice belonged to a much older man who had meant something to Gordon. She wanted to explore the thoughts behind it, but before she could do so, Harrt called out to her:

"Hey?"

Vol snapped out of the moment and looked at Harrt. The 'wealther handed a set of tools to Gordon and placed a hand on her shoulder:

"Are you okay?"

"Yeah," Vol said, shrugging his hand away.

She knew that Nathan's plan to meet with Jareth would serve as a point of contention for Koble, so she subtly directed Harrt to the cockpit. When they stepped into the room, Vol sensed the words on Harrt's lips, but she permitted him to say them aloud.

"Who's the kid?" Harrt nodded toward the living area. "And where are Nathan and Astrilla?"

"Nathan sent me back: he's going to meet with David Jareth," Vol replied. "And the kid is called, Russell: Nathan hired him".

"Why?"

"Because Nathan got him fired from his job," Vol said.

"No," Harrt shook his head. "The other thing: he's meeting with Jareth?"

CHAPTER FIFTY

After passing through a security check-point and entering the grounds, Nathan got a good look at David Jareth's home. The gargantuan property must have spanned over forty acres in size, looking more like corporate headquarters than a living space. There was a certain modernist aesthetic that made it stand out from the other homes on Paradisium. The three-storey building took up at least a third of the grounds: its dramatic V-shaped frame leaving ample space for the gardens to flourish.

A trio of armed guards escorted them up a cobble-stone path to the house. Initially, Nathan was surprised that they hadn't ordered him to relinquish his handgun, but when he studied the Jareth Corps armour and rifles that the guards were carrying, he knew why. They were armed with the finest firepower that money could buy. Nathan knew that if things turned south, he'd need to empty an entire magazine just to break through the protective gear.

Fortunately, things hadn't turned south —yet.

They entered a reception hall, where another pair of armed guards and an administrator were already waiting for them. The administrator politely offered them a seat, and after a couple of minutes, she stood from behind her desk:

"Mr Jareth will see you now".

Nathan tensed his jaw as he and Astrilla climbed from their chairs.

"I apologise," the administrator interrupted them. "Mr

Jareth is only expecting Captain Carter. Ma'am, I must ask you to wait here".

"No," Nathan protested. "She comes with me".

He could almost feel the guards tension as his voice reverberated around the room. There was a long pause, and the administrator didn't say a word.

"It's fine," Astrilla said in a lowered voice. "You go. If things turn ugly, I'll handle it".

Reluctantly, Nathan nodded.

He was escorted to a marble staircase at the back of the building, which seemed to go on forever. When he reached the top, one of the guards pointed him to a pair of black wooden doors.

"Mr Jareth will be in shortly," the guard said. "Please feel free to make yourself at home".

Nathan entered and closed the doors behind him. The expansive room that he found himself in was immaculate. The white marble floor had been polished so rigorously, that it reflected the sunlight peeking through long windows on the other side of the room. To the right, there was a giant bookcase that scaled the length of the wall. Nathan's eyes were drawn to a large piece of furniture beside the window. The name was on the tip of his tongue, but he only remembered when he placed his palm on the hood.

"Piano," Nathan whispered to himself.

He circled the instrument; noticing the sun reflecting from its varnished surface. He ran his hand across the smooth lid, recalling that his grandfather had one very similar back on Earth. When Nathan reached the black and white keys, he couldn't resist pushing down on one. The piano emitted a smooth note, and for some reason, it served as a reminder of Earth. Of what was once home.

"Beautiful, isn't it?" A voice came from the door.

Nathan's gaze was drawn upward to David Jareth. Just as he'd appeared in the press, Jareth looked calm and collected and sinister, all at the same time. Jareth closed the door behind him and straightened his grey linen jacket.

"I had that piano recreated a few years ago; based on Bechstein's late-nineteenth-century designs. If you have space on the Phoenix Titan for a similar piece, I'd be more than happy to give you his business card".

Jareth was in his early sixties by Nathan's best estimate, though his whitish, blonde hair suggested otherwise. He spoke with an upper class English accent; each word enunciated perfectly.

"Let me guess," Jareth said. "You've not seen a piano since Earth?"

Nathan moved his hand away from the keys and circled toward Jareth. "I didn't come here to discuss musical instruments with you".

David Jareth looked him up and down, and his thin lips curled upward into an arrogant smirk.

"No, you didn't. I suspect you didn't come to Paradisum to get into a bar brawl with my son and his idiotic friends either".

"You got a problem with the outcome of that fight?"

Jareth chuckled to himself. "For someone in his late twenties, my son has not had the necessary experiences to mould him into a man of action. You could say that he deserved a life lesson. I see that Jack did a good job raising you. He would be proud".

Nathan took a step closer to Jareth, resisting the urge to reach for his gun.

"Did you kill him?"

To his surprise, Jareth laughed at his question and strode over to a nearby cabinet. He picked up a glass decanter along with two glasses.

"Let me guess, that's what Kornell told you?" Jareth set the glasses and decanter down and smirked. "Or perhaps it was that upstanding member of society, Viktor Venin…"

"You still haven't answered my question," Nathan growled.

Jareth paused as he poured them each a drink.

"For the record: I did not murder Jack," he said.

"How do I know you're not lying?"

Before Nathan could reach for his pistol, Jareth replied;

"Need I remind you that you are armed, and I am not" Jareth's hands lingered in the air for a split second, then he pointed to the gun at Nathan's hip. "How do you like the family heirloom that I returned to you?"

Nathan did his utmost to hide his reaction. His jaw dropped a degree, and he shuffled across the room to Jareth.

"You were the one who sent me Jack's gun?"

Jareth stroked his chin and nodded. It was evident that the years of corporate negotiations had made his expression almost unreadable. Nathan could imagine the old man being an excellent poker player.

"How did you find Jack's gun?" Nathan asked.

Jareth took a sip from his whisky and looked at him thoughtfully.

"How much did you know about your uncle?" Jareth tilted his head to one side and studied Nathan's reaction. "It's evident that you didn't know he was working for me".

Nathan scowled, but resisted the urge to react. Jareth grabbed the second glass of whisky from the table and took a step closer to Nathan. There was no doubt that David Jareth had the gift of the gab when it came to verbal sparring. His words may have been true, but Nathan couldn't trust them.

"By now it is probably of little surprise that your previous crew were hauling goods on my behalf?" Jareth said. "Including the Loyalty's final shipment; which I believe you discovered in Kornell's apartment".

"Where did you get the gun?" Nathan asked for the second time.

Jareth's expression hardened, and his eyes became flat. He handed Nathan the drink and proceeded to circle around him.

"Three days before the Loyalty was sabotaged, I received three explicit instructions from Jack. The first was to ensure that the Phoenix Titan was held in a storage facility out of Peresopolis Station. The second was to send you his gun on a precise date to a series of precise coordinates on Pelos —it's clear that it reached you".

"And the third?"

Jareth turned and one of his eyebrows arched;

"The third, and most important of all was to find you,

and when we did, to utter the phrase, *never let them see you bleed,"* Jareth paused. "He said it would let you know that I am not your enemy".

The old man's snake-like eyes made it impossible to tell if there was a shred of truth to any of it. A small part of Nathan wanted to believe him: he wanted to believe that Jack always had a plan, but it seemed too convenient.

"How do you explain the Phoenix?" Nathan said. "Jack never said a word about it. If the Phoenix was once his ship, why the hell did you have it?

Jareth's jaw twitched; "Let me be clear with you. Jack kept our partnership a secret for the same reason he didn't allow you to live on Paradisium. People from the old days wanted him dead".

"But not you?"

Jareth's knowing smirk returned, and he raised his glass in mock-toast;

"Not me," Jareth replied. "I kept the Phoenix Titan because your uncle said that one day you would need it for something important. How right he was. You are here, which means you and Astrilla are looking for the Enkaye Relic: just as he said you would".

Nathan felt a cold chill run down his spine: *how did Jareth know about their mission?*

"What are you talking about?" Nathan's scowl darkened.

"You're trying to stop Seig from using the Messorem," Jareth said, taking a final sip of his whisky. He placed the glass down on the coffee table in front of him. "Avenging our people is rather commendable".

"So, Jack told you about this?"

"He did".

Nathan narrowed his eyes, "How could he possibly—"

"I do not know," Jareth cut him off. "And that fact alone is more terrifying than anything the Revenant could ever throw at us".

Jareth's expression grew thoughtful and anxious at the same time. He tried to mask it by casually shuffling to the window and staring at the ocean outside.

"Tell me something, Captain Carter. Do you hate the Revenant? Do you believe they should be destroyed for what they did to our people?"

"I do".

Jareth looked at him for a moment, then shifted his gaze to the ocean once more.

"As do I," Jareth said, his voice growing distant. "When the Commonwealth brought us here, to this paradise, I vowed that Jareth Corps would continue. But, instead of banking and investments, we would find a way to avenge those who died in the Fall". Jareth turned to Nathan, his eyes wide and his jaw clenched. "Over the years, I have invested countless resources into researching the Enkaye. For that reason, I know that the device in Seig's possession is called the Messorem. I also know it can only be brought to power when someone with Enkaye DNA is placed within its power chamber".

Nathan stepped closer to Jareth with only a few inches separating them.

"The Loyalty's final shipment was an Enkaye device: a key," Jareth said. "Jack knew what it was, and I think the people who killed him and your previous crew did too. Personally, I think Jack died hiding it from the hostiles because he knew it couldn't fall into their hands".

When Nathan whittled through the list of questions in his head, he pushed aside the ones relating to Jack. He sensed that Jareth wasn't telling the whole truth, but logic told him that the old man had brought him there for a reason.

"If it was a key, then what does it open?" Nathan asked.

David Jareth's lips turned upward, forming a thin smile.

"An Enkaye temple, seven miles beneath the ocean," Jareth said. "I believe that what you seek is down there. All it needs is an Enkaye-half-breed to switch it on".

There was a long, uncomfortable silence until Jareth added;

"But, there is a slight problem. The surrounding facility

was recently compromised by a... hostile force".

"Define *hostile* force?"

"Let's just say that Enkaye technology doesn't respond well to interference," Jareth replied.

"What the fuck does that mean?"

"It means that *I* made a mistake," Jareth said. "For that reason, I'll be sending an armed unit with you. They will escort you through the facility and get you out of there".

"And I'm supposed to simply trust you?" Nathan folded his arms. "I go to a place miles beneath the ocean with a group of your armed goons? Sounds like suicide if you ask me".

Jareth nodded, and his ambiguous smile returned; "If I wanted to kill you, you'd be a corpse."

"That's a pretty shit guarantee..."

"Life has no guarantees," Jareth mused. "The choice is yours: walk away, Seig wins. Trust me, and we may stand a chance of stopping him once and for all".

CHAPTER FIFTY-ONE

When Nathan returned to the reception hall, he found Astrilla standing at the opposite side of the room with a wary look in her eyes. Nathan sensed that she was on edge, and when he reached the bottom of the stairs, he saw why.

Ralph Hayward leaned against the administrator's desk with a bowl of cereal in his hand, while a group of six men casually unloaded weaponry from crates. There was something in Hayward's eyes that made Nathan feel unsafe —like a predator stalking its prey. He tried his best to ignore it.

"Didn't think I'd be seeing y'all again," Hayward mused, before scooping a spoon of cereal into his mouth.

"Looks like you've got enough firepower to take on the Revenant". Nathan said, gesturing to the modified assault rifle, that Hayward had slung on the desk behind him. "What the hell are we dealing with in this facility?"

Hayward stared at Nathan with a blank expression, then nodded in the direction of Astrilla;

"I suggest you calm her down before she starts setting fire to things".

Reluctantly, Nathan broke away from Hayward and headed over to the Evoker. Astrilla shot him a nervous glance as he neared, and for a moment, he felt her anxiety.

"What happened?" she said. "The mercenaries are saying that they are taking us to an Enkaye temple—"

"Jareth is sending these guys as back-up," Nathan

interrupted. "There's something hostile in the temple".

Astrilla frowned and stepped past him. She marched toward Hayward and his men:

"I am not going anywhere until you tell us what we're walking into," she demanded.

For several seconds the only sound in the room was of Ralph Hayward chewing. The broad-shouldered American continued shovelling the contents of his bowl into his mouth and didn't respond to Astrilla's demand. Finally, after tipping the leftover milk into his mouth and placing down his bowl, Hayward answered.

"Twenty-eight days ago there was an incursion on our research station. We don't know what the attackers are: all we know is that they are very, very dangerous". Hayward cleared his throat and gestured to them both, "My mission is to escort you into the Enkaye temple so that you can commune with whatever technology is left. So, how about you quit worrying about my job and worry about yours".

▲

Hayward escorted them to a launchpad built into the east wing of Jareth's mansion. With every step, Astrilla sensed a growing darkness draw closer. She couldn't be sure if it was pursuing her or if she was going toward it, but it was near, and that was all that mattered. The sensation was the same cold anxiety that she'd felt aboard the Vertex. It sent shivers up her spine.

At the launchpad, an ivory white Jareth Corps dropship was waiting for them. Once they'd boarded the small craft the engines kicked to life with a roar. It was a matter of seconds before the dropship was over the open sea. Astrilla looked out at the vast ocean as they soared through the sky. It was hard to escape the realisation that everything she saw was just like the previous night's vision.

Strange music blared from the pilot's radio: a cacophony of percussion, distorted stringed instruments, and howling vocals. The music mutated in Astrilla's head into violence, and at that moment, she could feel the Revenant king's presence.

I see you, half-breed, Seig said. *The river Prynn sees you.*

Astrilla grabbed Nathan's bicep and nodded toward the back of the ship.

"Something isn't right," she said, giving an uneasy look to the Earther.

"I know; these guys are packing some serious heat," Nathan replied. He gestured to Hayward, and the other mercenaries; "Whatever is below the surface has these guys spooked".

"Not that," Astrilla shook her head. She took a step closer to Nathan and whispered into his ear; "I cannot explain it, but I think the Revenant are coming here".

Nathan's expression grew hard, and he bore the look of someone that wanted to take action.

"We need to find the Omega and get you away from here as soon as possible," Nathan replied. "When we land I'll comms the Phoenix and get Harrt to prep the ship".

The tone in his voice was nervy, and Astrilla could tell he was trying to mask his fear. Astrilla wrapped her hand inside his, and took a deep breath;

"I've already asked a lot of you... But I must ask you to make me a promise."

"What is it?" Nathan said.

Astrilla swallowed a lump in her throat, and she could feel the colour drain from her face. What she said next, wasn't easy, but in her head, it seemed right:

"If it looks like they are going to take me..." She stammered and took a breath. "I need you to make sure they don't take me alive".

Time stood still, and all either of them could do was look back at the other.

"I won't let that happen," Nathan finally said. "None of us will".

"You can't guarantee that," she interrupted. "If they take me and plug me into that Enkaye death-machine, all hope is lost. I cannot allow that to happen: *you* cannot allow that to happen. Do you understand?"

Astrilla fought back the emotion she felt. It was an

awful thing to put on someone, but she knew it had to be said. Nathan's jaw clenched, tight enough to break a tooth and finally, he conceded with a nod.

▲

"You are where? With who?" Koble raised his voice, unable to quench his distress at what Nathan had told him. "Are you insane? Do you know what David Jareth is capable of doing? Get the hell off that ship: jump in the ocean if you have to!"

Koble could feel the hairs on his neck spike down to his tail as he awaited Nathan's reply. Harrt shot him an equally concerned expression as the pair stared at each other across the cockpit.

"Calm down," Nathan replied in a no-nonsense fashion. "Now listen, I'll send you the coordinates as soon as we land. Once you've got them you need to hightail it over here and be ready to pick us up".

Koble cursed under his breath as his tail swung anxiously. Rather than slapping the table in frustration, Koble looked at Harrt, hoping the 'wealther's calm demeanour would help sway Nathan's choice. Harrt's expression hardened, and he casually circled the holo-table to Koble's side.

"Why the sudden rush?" Harrt said into the communicator.

There was a pause from Nathan. The sound of static filled the Phoenix's cockpit, and before Nathan spoke, Koble could tell that his old friend was worried.

"Astrilla says she can feel the Revenant getting closer," Nathan answered.

It took Koble a moment to realise that his tail had stopped swaying. He glanced at Harrt, and the dark-haired human moved toward the pilot's station to check for proximity alerts. Before Koble could utter a response, Nathan continued to speak.

"I'll get you the coordinates ASAP. Just be ready. Harrt, if you can get a message to your 'wealther pal, tell him to hurry".

"Already on it," Harrt said, spinning in the pilot's seat. "Just get me those coordinates".

"Will do," Nathan replied, before killing the commlink.

For a moment, silence filled the cockpit. Koble placed his head in his paws and leaned against the holotable. Harrt continued tapping at his datapad and finally stood from the pilot's seat.

"Well, there's no sign of Revenant activity in the system, but that could change at any moment," Harrt said, pinching the bridge of his nose. "As for Dines, we may be waiting a few hours".

Koble lifted his head and frowned at the 'wealther:

"What in the hell is Nate thinking?" Koble shook his head. "Meeting David Jareth unaccompanied is one thing, but flying out to one of their facilities with a bunch of their armed thugs..."

Koble stopped, noticing Gordon Taggart in the doorway. The Earther's eyes had widened, and his greying eyebrows lifted.

"Jareth facility?" Gordon stepped toward Koble.

"Nothing to worry about, Doc," Koble waved his paw dismissively. "Just a communication from the Captain: nothing to—"

"Did he say which facility they're taking him to?" Gordon interrupted.

"Some kinda underwater station," Koble said.

Gordon's jaw dropped a degree, and he shakily pulled off his glasses. The Earther turned away from Koble and anxiously paced back and forth for several seconds.

"The hell's got you all worked up?" Koble remarked.

Gordon stopped in his tracks and shot him a frown; "Your friends are in danger".

▲

The Jareth Corps dropship stopped several miles from the coast. As Nathan looked at the emptiness surrounding them, he couldn't help but wonder how anyone could find a temple so far from civilisation.

Ralph Hayward leaned out of the dropship, then returned to the interior with a serious expression on his face. He tapped a series of commands into a datapad, and a klaxon began to sound from under the sea.

Tiny bubbles began to form on the surface of the ocean in the shape of a square. A low hum followed, then a giant mass arose from the depths of the blue sea. The water crashed and folded as a landing pad emerged from under the waves.

Hayward ordered the dropship to land and once they touched down the burly American slid the doors open. The six marines that had accompanied them filed out of the ships in a military-like fashion. Nathan and Astrilla were the last to step out. As Nathan's feet touched the ground, he felt a strange sinking sensation. He realised seconds later that the platform he was stood on was an elevator slowly descending into the ocean.

"No need to be alarmed, Carter," Hayward yelled with a smug grin on his face. "This tunnel will take us down to the facility.

Nathan looked up and saw that the sky was beginning to shrink: it was like seeing the light at the end of a dark tunnel. A strange sense of dread came over him as he watched the sunlight disappear into a speck. Nathan felt something cold and heavy shove into his chest. When he peeled his eyes away from the diminishing sky, he found that Hayward was handing him an assault rifle.

All the suspicions that Nathan had about Jareth, leading them into a trap seemed to fade. He took up the weapon and checked the magazine to make sure it was fully stocked.

It was.

Nathan glanced back at Hayward, and the muscular man nodded:

"I assume you know how to use one of these?" Hayward said. "It's got a modified barrel: kicks a bit, but it'll shred anything that gets in the way,"

Nathan examined the weapon a little closer. He recognised the shape and design. It was the type of gun that Jack would have carried back in the old days: an Earth weapon, enhanced to fight a far more deadly enemy than man.

"So, what the hell are you expecting to run into down there?" Nathan asked.

Hayward's expression was severe. The American strapped an armoured plate to his chest and huffed:

"As I said, we don't know," Hayward answered. "But, I'll offer you a word of advice: if it moves, shoot it, and don't stop shooting until it is dead."

CHAPTER FIFTY-TWO

The platform screeched to a halt. It was so loud that it made Astrilla's ears pop.

"Game on boys: standard formation," Hayward bellowed.

The men met his orders with a unified chant; "Oorah!"

It was a strange custom that Astrilla didn't understand, and judging from the raised brows on Nathan's face, he didn't get it either. Hayward cocked his rifle and swaggered to a hatch on the other side of the platform, and his mercenaries followed.

"You two in the middle," Hayward said, pointing Nathan and Astrilla to a space in the pack. Once they were in position, Hayward looked at the group and said in a low voice; "Down to the temple, in and out. If you see anything you blow it straight to hell".

Once Hayward was satisfied that his men understood the order, he moved to the hatch and spun the locking mechanism around. After a few rotations of the wheel, a sharp thud followed, and the hatch opened.

The door led onto a dark and damp hallway. A broken light flickered in the darkness, making the sterile metal corridors seem hostile. As they stepped inside, Astrilla noticed that the ground was wet and that the air felt thick and muggy.

At the front of the pack, the mercenaries moved with their guns raised, shining flashlights into the dark corridor.

As a single unit, the group moved silently through the passageway, weapons ready to cut down anything that dared to get in their way. They checked every corner —every shadow. They reminded Astrilla of Commonwealth marines, but somehow this group seemed far more efficient —or maybe that was what she hoped.

The smell of stagnant water seemed to become more potent with every step Astrilla took. She tried to ignore it and focus on the task at hand, but when she did, Astrilla felt her stomach tighten in dread.

I see you halfbreed, Seig said.

Eventually, they turned a corner and found a staircase leading downward. Hayward signalled to proceed, and when the group reached the bottom, they stopped suddenly.

On the floor was the top half of a human carcass, its skin replaced by a shiny grey substance. Two metres up the hall, behind a trail of blood and entrails, was the bottom half —discarded by whatever had killed it.

"Fuck," Hayward whispered, kneeling down to examine the body. "Looks like Doctor Taggart was right all along."

Astrilla took a closer look at the warped remains. The human features were gone; replaced by something far more vicious. She didn't bother guessing if it had once been male or female, but she did focus on the grey slime covering its skin.

It looked like the sacred waters of the Revenant: or at least the descriptions Astrilla had read. Such a thing was impossible. The Revenant were bound by their creed to keep the river Prynn —as they called it— in the darkness of space.

Hayward knelt beside her and prodded the corpse with his knife. The grey goo fizzed as the small blade made contact with it. To Hayward's surprise, his knife disintegrated almost instantaneously, and he tossed the remains aside.

Is Jareth Corps experimenting with Revenant technology? Astrilla wondered.

"Did you say, Taggart?" Nathan said to Hayward. "As

in Doctor Gordon Taggart?"

Ralph Hayward rose to his feet and signalled for silence.

Astrilla frowned and took a step closer to the giant Earther. She pointed at the corpse; "Is that what I think it is?"

Ralph Hayward didn't answer the question and instead pulled a silenced pistol from his belt. He pushed past her and fired a bullet into the skull of the corpse.

"What the hell are you doing?" Nathan whispered.

"Making sure it's dead," Hayward answered. The bulky man shifted his gaze to Astrilla, "I sure as shit hope that it isn't what you think it is, because if it is... we've got a big fuckin' problem".

Hayward gave the signal to continue, and the group moved out. They passed through an area which Astrilla could only assume had once served as a laboratory. There was smashed glass everywhere, and splattered blood covered the walls and ceiling. It was as though a predator had feasted on its prey at the end of a long hunt.

Upon spotting more bodies covered in the grey goo, Hayward signalled his men, and they fired silenced gunshots into the skulls of the dead. It wasn't dignified, and it didn't show respect for the deceased, but if her suspicions were correct, then Astrilla knew it was justified. If the grey liquid was Revenant holy water, things could take a turn south very quickly. Astrilla had fought mutated Revenant soldiers and hunters many times, but the difference was that she'd not faced them seven miles beneath the ocean, in a confined space.

The group continued through the labs and down another flight of stairs. At the bottom, they entered a large circular chamber. There was a two-metre stone monolith at the centre of the room, set into a pool of the same grey liquid.

Astrilla looked to Nathan, and for a moment, she could feel his terror as though it were her own. The sense of trepidation they both felt came from the monolith, but neither of them could explain why.

"You feel it too?" Astrilla asked.

Nathan didn't say a word but managed to nod in response. Astrilla was sure that he was overwhelmed by the intense agitation that emanated from the monolith.

"I think we all feel it," Hayward said.

Something primal in the back of Astrilla's head told her that the monolith was Enkaye technology, but it wasn't working as intended. Someone had tampered with the device, and it had broken.

Despite her sense of dread, Astrilla took a few steps toward it, and when she got within five metres of the pool, she was overcome with a sense of danger. It was as if the device was warning them to stay away.

"What the fuck is this thing?" Nathan glared at Hayward.

"Enkaye tech," Hayward replied, nonchalantly.

Astrilla spun on her heels to look at him;

"That thing was working long before I arrived," Astrilla said. "How did you get it working?"

"Jareth Corps employs some very talented scientists," Hayward replied. The bulky man then took a step closer to the monolith and glanced at the grey whirlpool below; "Looks like someone fucked up. That liquid was crystal clear last time I was down here".

"But you understand what that water is, don't you?" Astrilla said. "That is the Revenant holy water!"

Hayward nodded and produced an explosive device from his vest; "That's why I'm blowing this place straight to hell when we're done here".

Astrilla couldn't argue with his logic. They waited for Ralph Hayward to set four charges around the pool and monolith, before pushing through to the next room. It took Hayward several attempts to open the next door, and when it finally gave way, an armoured corpse fell through the doorway. There was a loud thud as the body slammed into the metal floor.

At first, Hayward raised his weapon, but relaxed when he realised that the body served no threat. Astrilla glanced down at the distinctive cladding on the metal armour. She was surprised to see that it didn't bear the logo of Jareth Corps. Instead, there was a gold and black text which read; *Roth Industries.*

"Ah fuck," Hayward muttered.

A sudden inhumane scream came from the labs and was followed by the sound of frantic running footsteps. Astrilla knew the sound all too well, but she didn't want to believe it was possible. Suddenly, Hayward was barking orders to them and shoving Astrilla and Nathan into the next room with his men.

"Move!"

▲

Vol attached a series of wires to a new component that Gordon had provided. From her best estimate, the green circuit board was some kind of regulator, but she couldn't be too sure. The plugs snapped into place perfectly, just as Gordon predicted.

When the doctor returned to the living area, he was followed by Harrt and Koble. Vol didn't need a sixth sense to tell that the three men were rattled.

"What do you mean they're in trouble?" Harrt said as he pursued Gordon into the room.

The doctor stopped and looked at the 'wealther with a frown. He then began to pace back and forth while nervously scratching at his greying hair. Vol could hear something at the forefront of Gordon's thoughts. It was a realisation of some sort that he'd tied back to someone of great significance.

A teacher? Vol thought. *No, that's not right, a father? No, that's not it either.*

Before she could mine into his thoughts, Gordon stopped pacing and took the seat opposite. He took off his thick-framed glasses and placed them down on the table beside the broken droid.

Gordon sighed; "Years ago, David Jareth and his cronies uncovered an Enkaye temple, miles below the ocean. For years his people kept trying to hire me, and I refused. It was only until one of them came to me with a drawing of a specific artefact that I decided to accept the job".

"Why?" Harrt asked.

"Because I saw something just like it on Earth, and it cost my friend his life," Gordon replied. "I had to take the job to make sure it wasn't the same as the one we found on Earth".

"And was it?" Vol asked.

She narrowed her eyes and studied Gordon's facial movements as he formulated an answer. She was certain that he wasn't lying, but at the same time, the doctor wasn't intending on telling them the whole truth either. Behind his tired eyes, Gordon Taggart hid a sense of loss and betrayal, which couldn't be quantified.

"No," Gordon shook his head. "It was nothing like the item my team encountered on Earth. However, what Jareth had found was still dangerous".

"So what the hell is it?" Koble said.

Before Gordon could answer, his dark memories bubbled to the surface and for a split second Vol felt consumed by them. She saw a massacre: men and women cut down by primitive Earther weapons. In Gordon's mind, he associated those events with a great sense of betrayal. Vol realised that the hazy, distant memory was a tragedy that Gordon had never been able to move beyond.

Promise me, Gordon, a weak male voice said. *Promise me...*

Vol was able to pull herself out of the darkness of Gordon's thoughts, right as the Earther answered;

"Simply put; it is switched on, but it is broken," Gordon said.

"But it's Enkaye tech?" Vol interrupted. "How the hell did you get it working without a living specimen?"

The doctor stared back at her with a pleased look on his face: evidently, her intrigue had impressed him.

"It never switched off," he answered. "Just think, for thousands of years it was running and nobody—"

"Can we cut to the chase?" Koble said, waving

Gordon's words away impatiently. "Why are Nate and Astrilla in danger?"

Gordon frowned as he leaned forward in his chair;

"The monolith has... mutagenic capabilities".

Koble looked at Vol, then back to Gordon, "Meaning?"

"*Meaning*, that it mutates the makeup of anything it comes into contact with," Gordon answered. "Jareth wanted me to conduct experiments on it, but I refused. Naturally, I stormed out, and he brought in some young whippersnapper to run tests on the device".

"Let me guess," Vol raised a brow; "It went horribly wrong".

"The mutations overran the facility," Gordon nodded. "Then, with every task force that Jareth sent down there, the body count just kept piling up. I'd say your friends are safe from the monolith, provided they don't touch it or the waters that surround it, but I can't say the same for the mutants".

Harrt's hand terminal chimed with an alert, and the 'wealther glanced at the screen. A wide-eyed expression formed on the 'wealther's face and Vol noticed the corners of his mouth dropping into a frown.

"Is that Nathan's coordinates?" she asked.

Harrt looked at her with a blank expression, then shook his head.

"No..." he stammered. "That was a sensor alert. Three Revenant warships just entered the system".

CHAPTER FIFTY-THREE

Nathan followed the mercenaries through another corridor that was indistinguishable from the last. Despite moving at a hurried pace, Hayward kept his rifle raised while checking every dark corner, while the rest of his men stuck to a tight military formation. Nathan tried his best to focus on the path ahead, rather than the deathly screams that followed, but it was impossible. There was something familiar about the animalistic howls that Nathan couldn't quite identify. They sounded primitive, hungry, and most importantly of all, tortured.

The group halted when Ralph Hayward held up a closed fist. Nathan kept his rifle raised as he examined the blocked path ahead. Directly in front of them was a giant stone door, engraved with symbols and hieroglyphs, just like the ones Nathan had seen on Pelos. It must have measured at least ten metres in height and width. Where the Enkaye temple began, the Jareth Corps facility ended. It created a strange contrast that Nathan found hard to ignore, and he imagined that Jareth had built the facility around the opening.

"Shit," Hayward said, shining the flashlight on his gun over the sealed door. "We've got a big problem: this thing wasn't shut last time we were down here".

There was another scream, and Nathan was sure that it came from the next room. He looked at the heavy stone door, knowing that it couldn't be forced open. He turned to

Astrilla but didn't have to say a word;

"I think I can get it!" She placed a glowing hand on the door and looked back at him; "It's going to take me a minute".

"We ain't got a minute," Hayward barked, as the device on his wrist began to alarm. "We've got fast-movers heading our way".

Astrilla's hand glowed red the moment she began to pull at the door. Dust and debris rained from the ceiling but nothing else moved.

"You'd better keep me covered," Astrilla said.

Hayward frowned, then turned to his men and began barking orders;

"Form up, take up defensive positions!" Hayward took up his gun, and looked at Nathan; "You too man-bun. We're gonna need all the firepower we can get".

Nathan watched as the group of six men formed a semi-circle around the Evoker; each of them aiming their weapons into the darkness ahead. He pushed the stock of his assault rifle into his shoulder and joined Hayward.

The screams from the next room grew louder and louder, and then there was nothing. For a split second, the only thing that could be heard was the sound of sparks emanating from Astrilla's hands. Suddenly a scraping noise began. It sounded like it was metres away. The pulsing alarms from Hayward's wrist device grew louder and closer, indicating that whatever was stalking them was near.

The sound flatlined.

It was right on top of them.

Nathan looked up at the ceiling panel, but there was nothing there. Metres away, he heard Ralph Hayward muttering;

"What the fu—"

Before he could finish, the mesh metal floor beneath Hayward was forced into the air. Nathan watched Hayward crash into a laboratory window, and disappear into the darkness. He snapped his gun back to the hole in the ground, and something grey leapt out. Chaos erupted as the fast-moving creature leapt onto one of the mercenaries. It pierced the man's armour and body with something sharp. Before it could do any more damage, Nathan and the rest opened fire.

The monster howled in agony, and when it turned to face Nathan, he shot it in the head. The human-like skull exploded in a shower of grey and black blood. The carcass fell to one side with a hollow thud.

For a second, Nathan got a good look at the monster. It had once been human, but something had changed it into a warped abomination. The skin was torn in several places, and the jaw had expanded into a jagged mess. From Nathan's best guess, it was where the stress of extreme muscle growth had caused the human body to rip open and form something new. Its hands were no longer human. Not only had they grown, but where there were once fingernails, there were long dagger-like claws.

It's just like a Revenant hunter, Nathan thought. *But easier to kill.*

He turned to the mercenary who'd been attacked by the creature but found that he was dead. The not-hunter had cut through the man's metal armour and sliced into his chest.

Before Nathan could react, there was another shriek from the darkness, but this time it sounded more like a war-cry. The noise was so piercing that Astrilla took her eyes off the door for a moment. The sound of footsteps grew louder and closer, and Nathan knew what was coming.

"Here they come," one of the mercs yelled. "Light these fuckers up!"

Ahead, another mutated creature emerged from the darkness. Then three others. Then five more. Then there were too many to count. Nathan and the mercenaries opened fire as the monsters pounced into action. The creatures moved in swarms, which wasn't a problem for the Jareth Corps mercs. They were able to concentrate their weapons-fire down the corridor and dispatch groups of the creatures.

After firing at least fifty-rounds, Nathan had to reload his gun. He released the magazine and allowed it to drop to the ground. As he placed the second one into the gun, he suddenly became aware of something approaching from his right.

When he turned, he felt a crushing sense of dread as he laid eyes on a second group of the freaks, climbing through a broken grate in the ground. Without a second thought, Nathan slammed the mag into his gun and opened fire.

The spray of laser fire dispatched the first, then the second, but before he could take aim at the third, it leapt into the air. The monstrosity soared passed Nathan and landed on one of Hayward's men, plunging its spiked claws into the unsuspecting man's throat.

The other mercenaries reacted and took the creature down in a hail of gunfire. Nathan rapidly turned back but was sideswiped by one of the animals. He slammed into the mesh floor, dropping his rifle in the process.

The creature darted toward him, and for a moment, Nathan thought that was it: that was where he was going to die. He looked at the bastardised version of a human being, and it gazed at him with a soulless empty look in its black eyes.

The creature pounced at Nathan, but before, it could reach him, it was cut down by a single, precise gunshot. Nathan looked up, to see Ralph Hayward, holding a smoking revolver.

"Get-the-fuck-up!" Hayward yelled, dragging Nathan from the floor.

Nathan rushed back to his feet, just in time to see another mercenary cut in half by one of the hunters. Despite crimson blood splattering in every direction, Ralph Hayward snapped up his rifle and shot down the mutated abomination before it could move any closer. Nathan scooped his rifle off the ground and began to fire round after round at the oncoming attackers.

"If there was ever a time to get that door open, it's now," Hayward yelled at Astrilla.

Nathan took his eye off the incoming horde and peered at the Evoker. She wrestled to get the door open as multi-coloured sparks of electricity flew from her hands.

C'mon! Nathan thought. *Don't let us die down here.*

Suddenly, the door shifted, and the glow from Astrilla's hands turned blue. There was a sense of relief that washed over Nathan, and when his eyes met the Evoker's, he knew she felt it as well.

The moment didn't last.

The last of Hayward's men were overwhelmed by a swarm of the hunters. The sound of screams lasted all but a moment.

"Move!" Hayward yelled, firing the last few bullets from his rifle. "Get inside!"

Nathan pushed Astrilla into the next room and felt a cold chill as he entered. The new chamber was shrouded in darkness, and the only source of light came from the previous room. Nathan went to grab his flashlight, but his attention was quickly diverted back to Hayward. The American backed into the new space, firing his sidearm at a group of attackers.

"Could use a hand here," Hayward called out.

Nathan became aware that Astrilla had climbed to her feet and that her hands were glowing. As she raised her palms ready to strike, a turquoise ball of light formed in the centre of the room.

As before on Pelos, the light scanned them. Nathan ignored it and continued firing at the hunters. He tossed his sidearm to Hayward: aware that the burly man had run out of ammo.

He became aware of a new voice in the room;

"Deploying countermeasures".

The light suddenly changed into a flat vertical sheet that spanned from floor to ceiling. White lights lifted from the walls, allowing Nathan to see the energy barrier move through him like a gust of wind.

After passing, the sheet of red light seared into the flock of incoming mutants. It sliced through the creatures with machine-like precision, causing them to dissolve on impact. Nathan was certain that the temple's technology could tell the difference between the living and the mutated. There was a perfection to the way the machine had executed its task. It was too perfect —too precise.

"Now that was a close call," Hayward laughed then dropped to the floor to catch his breath. "I got nine of those ugly fuckers. How many did you score, Carter?"

Nathan ignored the question. As he walked deeper into the room, Nathan noticed the ivory stone walls were covered in hieroglyphs. Unlike the temple on Pelos, this one was preserved perfectly.

He felt a shudder at his back when he neared Astrilla. It was as though they were supposed to find this place —like it was meant to be. He couldn't explain the sensation, but he knew it was real.

When the blue turquoise ball returned, it shifted and formed the shape of an Enkaye.

▲

Harrt did his best to shut out the sound of blaring proximity alerts as he piloted the Phoenix over the ocean. Beside him, Vol took up the co-pilot's seat and tried her best to direct him to the coordinates that Gordon had provided.

"How much farther?" Harrt yelled over the alarms.

As he glanced over his shoulder at the Uvan, he caught a glimpse of the nav terminal. Multiple Revenant warships were in the solar system, and they were drawing closer to Paradisium.

"Three... maybe four minutes," Vol replied frantically.

Harrt took a breath, then eyed the nav terminal. They were cutting it close. By his best estimate, the first Revenant warship would break the atmosphere in just over twelve minutes.

Harrt turned to Koble; "We're gonna go into that facility and get them out ourselves!" He then nodded towards Russell; "Koble, I need you to give the kid a crash course in the gunnery chambers. Things are gonna get real dicey!"

Koble nodded, and proceeded to lead Russell to the back of the ship. After a minute, Harrt relinquished control of the Phoenix to Vol. She picked up the helm from the co-pilot's station and adjusted a setting on her side.

"Dicey, huh?" She raised a brow. "Dressing up the situation a little, aren't you?"

"Doesn't matter," Harrt said, unbuckling himself from his seat. "Get us in low and hold the airspace".

At first, she looked apprehensive, then her expression hardened.

"Be careful," she said.

"You too!"

Harrt slid out from his seat and grabbed his pistol and holster from the holotable. He made for the rear of the ship, passing Gordon Taggart in the living area. The bespectacled Earther was still attempting to fix the dead droid, despite the ship's buckling.

"This is bad; this is very bad," Gordon muttered to himself. "If the old man was right, then this is how—"

"Maybe this isn't the best time!" Harrt yelled as he walked past. "We've got Revenant warships incoming. Make yourself useful!"

Gordon shook his head and muttered something inaudible. Rather than acknowledge Harrt's order, the doctor continued his repairs. Harrt resisted the urge to raise his voice and instead continued toward the airlock.

Koble was already waiting for him at the back of the ship, beside the closed hatchway. He handed Harrt a pulse rifle, then gestured to the airlock. When Harrt looked out, he saw a giant gaping hole in the ocean, leading to a dark abyss.

"All set," Koble yelled, over the sound of the Phoenix's engine.

The Sphinax handed him a descent cord, and Harrt buckled it around his waist. He checked Koble's rope, and the Sphinax returned the favour.

"So, I kinda noticed you didn't volunteer for the dropship team when we went after Kornell," Koble mused. "Something you wanna tell me? You afraid of heights?"

Harrt couldn't help but let out a small laugh. Even at the very moment, where they were facing insurmountable odds, Koble cracked a joke. It lightened the mood, if only for a split second.

"C'mon," Harrt said, nodding at the airlock. "Let's do this".

Koble slapped the airlock control, and there came a giant whoosh as the hatch opened. The sudden rush of moving air caused both of them to shield their eyes. Once the Phoenix's environmental controls had compensated for the gusts, they secured their lines to a clamp. As the pair moved to the edge of the Phoenix's airlock, Koble looked into the hole;

"Well," Koble drawled. "At least I won't get wet".

He then leapt from the Phoenix, sailing down into the darkness. Harrt looked up at the blue skies; took a deep breath then jumped.

CHAPTER FIFTY-FOUR

The Enkaye projection studied Astrilla with an insatiable curiosity, that seemed different from the one they'd encountered on Pelos. It appeared older and more experienced. The alien's skin was a lighter shade of grey, and there were deeply rooted wrinkles around its eyes and mouth.

It circled the room, pressing its tiny hands together while blinking nervously.

"We're here for the Omega," Nathan said.

"I know," it replied in a solemn tone of voice.

The hologram turned to face him. The blank stare that it gave Nathan seemed full of regret, but that was impossible. It was a hologram: a piece of data, stored in the facility for thousands of years to fulfil a purpose.

The Enkaye glanced at Astrilla, took a deep breath and continued;

"We don't have much time," it said, passing through Nathan as it moved to the centre of the room.

"Why?" Astrilla asked.

The hologram didn't immediately reply. Instead, it summoned a pillar of white light at the centre of the room, no taller than a metre in height.

"The ones you call, *Revenant*, are in orbit. They are the ones in possession of the Messorem". Again, the hologram's expression formed into a frown: at least that's what Nathan thought it was.

"What are you?" Nathan asked.

The Enkaye didn't answer. It placed its holographic hands against the pillar of white light, and something began to materialise from within. A metal bar, just like the other pieces of the Omega emerged, and the hologram held it out to Nathan.

"Do you have the map?" it said.

"Yes," Astrilla said. The Evoker pulled her backpack to one side and held out the scroll.

"You still require the final piece," the projection said, as it took the map from her. It studied the scroll for a second, then circled a particular star system. "You will find it here".

"But, there's nothing there?" Astrilla said, glancing momentarily at Nathan.

"I assure you, it is there, for I am talking to you from there".

A shudder ran down Nathan's spine. The hologram was not a piece of data: it was a communication. They were talking to a living Enkaye.

Suddenly, the whole facility started to shake. Dust and grit fell from the ceiling. Rumblings came from all directions, causing the hologram to flicker.

"I must initiate this facility's self-destruct sequence; you must leave now," the Enkaye said. "I detect that a large number of hostiles are heading toward you. Come to the next location; I will explain what I can when you arrive!"

"Wait," Astrilla shouted, but the hologram dissolved into the air.

Seconds later, all the lights fell, plunging the room into darkness. Nathan didn't dare close his eyes. Every time he did, his mind filled with a cascade of questions and thoughts

That was a living Enkaye, he thought. *A living-fucking Enkaye.*

He wasn't sure why, but it felt both overwhelming and disappointing at the same time. Somehow they had communed with an extinct creature, whose race had died out thousands of years ago. It should have been impossible, but there it was—a monumental moment, not just for Nathan or

Astrilla, or Hayward, but for all living beings. They'd spoken to a creature, that many cultures believed were the creators of all life. It should have felt tremendous, but it didn't. Nathan didn't feel as though he'd spoken to a living god. Quite the opposite. It felt like talking to just another ordinary alien. Maybe that was monumental: that the creators of everything were just like everyone else.

Ralph Hayward cracked open a flare, and the controlled red flame illuminated the room.

"We've gotta move," Hayward said, "That grey guy said that this place had a self-destruct function. We shouldn't hang around".

"He also mentioned Revenant," Nathan said. "We've got Commonwealth warships coming to rendezvous with us here, but I think we've still got an hour before they arrive. I take it Jareth Corps can put up a fight?"

Hayward nodded; "Once we get top-side, I'll call it in, but right now, we gotta move".

Together, they raced through the facility. Another series of rumblings caused the ground to shake. When Astrilla stumbled forward, Nathan steadied her. They stopped at another indistinct intersection. The semidarkness made it difficult for Nathan to tell if they'd passed through earlier, or if Hayward was leading them a different way. The air seemed fresher, so he could only assume that was the case. Hayward checked the device strapped to his wrist, which was beeping frantically.

"I've got two bogeys, standing right in our path," he said, nodding to one of the corridors.

Nathan unholstered his handgun and proceeded to follow the burly American. With every step they took, the alarm on Hayward's wrist grew more frantic, until they reached a hatch.

"Get ready," Hayward whispered, his hand poised over the door controls.

Nathan nodded, then he heard something muffled through the door:

"I mean, we can see in the dark; at least way better than you hairless meat-bags," Koble's voice echoed. "Besides, hot-wiring doors isn't exactly my speciality. You want an engineer; she's back on the ship..."

Nathan looked at Astrilla, and the Evoker frowned.

"It's our people," she sighed.

Hayward raised his brow as if to ask a question, but he didn't say anything. He punched the door control, and they found Koble on the other side, kneeling at an exposed panel. Harrt quickly raised his gun, then lowered it once he realised they weren't in danger.

"Oh," Koble drawled. The Sphinax looked over his shoulder at Harrt and added; "Told you we'd bump into them".

Harrt ignored the poor attempt at humour, and as always got straight down to business.

"Revenant warships are inbound," he said. "We've gotta get you—"

"We know," Astrilla interrupted.

Nathan could almost see the word, *how,* linger on Harrt's lips —albeit for a second. Then the military-man nodded.

"Let's go".

A scream emanated from the passageways behind them. Nathan swung his head around to see the source of the feral cry. He didn't need to look to know what it was, but he did it anyway.

He glanced another horde of the mutated creatures heading straight toward them. The monsters dashed from the other end of the corridor, screeching and howling as they spilt toward them.

"What the hell are those," Koble said, his voice raising an octave or two.

Nathan didn't answer and instead shoved Koble and Harrt in the opposite direction.

"Run!" Nathan yelled. "Get us back to the ship!"

As they sprinted back the way Koble and Harrt had come in, Hayward fired his gun over his shoulder. It was a poor attempt at keeping the enemy away.

"Looks like the grey guy didn't get 'em all!" He yelled.

Finally, they reached a hatch door that led to the

elevator. Harrt and Koble were the first ones through, closely followed by Astrilla and Nathan. When Nathan looked back, he saw Ralph Hayward facing the enemy horde with two pistols drawn. He fired wildly into the pack, but it was futile; The mutants had the numbers.

"Hayward!" Nathan yelled.

The American ignored him and continued to fight off the monsters. Nathan went to grab him, but Astrilla pushed past. She raised her glowing palms, and the air around her whipped up.

"Hayward!" Nathan repeated. "Get the fuck outta there!"

This time, Hayward listened, and he leapt through the hatch. As the swarm crashed through the doorway, Astrilla unleashed a pillar of blinding light, pushing the monsters back into the facility. As Astrilla lowered her palms, Koble tossed a grenade at the crowd of not-hunters, then slammed the hatch shut, sealing the monsters inside.

Nathan grabbed the hatch wheel and with Koble's help sealed the door. An explosion followed from behind the hatch, causing water to spill out from tiny gaps in the seal.

"That was a close one," Koble exhaled.

The Sphinax moved toward him with a worried look on his face, but Nathan waved him off. As the elevator began its long ascent, Nathan slumped on the floor and regained his breath.

For a matter of seconds, Nathan could hear his heartbeat, and it felt like everything had the volume turned down. His mind lingered between conscious and unconscious, then as he looked up in the sky, the roar of the Phoenix Titan shook him into the moment. As Nathan sat up, he spotted a Revenant fighter plunge from the skies toward them, only to be cut-down by the Phoenix's top-side cannon.

"Great shooting kid," Koble yelled into a communicator. "Vol, get the ship down here now, we've gotta—"

A deafening hum stopped the Sphinax mid-sentence. The noise bellowed from above for several seconds, then a gust of hot air followed. Nathan turned his eyes skyward to see what had caused the sound.

A Revenant warship emerged through the clouds. The steely grey and black mass loomed over Paradisium like a shadow; eclipsing the sky in every direction.

I see you, Earther. I finally see you.

The deep voice that filled Nathan's ears filled him with the same dread he'd felt at the monolith. He didn't know who or what it was, but it was there; Nathan knew it.

Above him, Nathan could hear the sounds of Revenant fighters launching from the warship. He imagined the Revenant bridge crew, yelling orders to obliterate the Phoenix Titan.

No, Nathan thought. *Not today.*

"Get to the fucking ship," Nathan screamed at the others.

The Phoenix was landing, and whoever was in the top-side gunnery chamber was doing a good enough job of holding off the Revenant fighters. A boarding ramp emerged from the Phoenix's underbelly, hovering metres from the landing pad.

Harrt was the first to make it to the ship, leaping across the gap with ease, then Hayward. As Nathan and Astrilla sprinted to the Phoenix, a stutter of gunfire erupted, landing a metre across their path, cutting through the Jareth Corps dropship they'd travelled aboard earlier. The gunfire sliced through the ivory vessel, and it exploded. The blast sent Nathan hurtling to the floor, and for a split-second, he lost sight of everything.

Thick plumes of black smoke filled the air, accompanied by the smell of burning fuel. The pain on his side suggested he'd cracked a rib, but Nathan couldn't be sure. He couldn't see much farther than a few metres ahead. His sight clouded by the smoke around him. Amid the confusion, Nathan became aware of Koble on the other side of the elevator platform. The Sphinax was calling out to him while firing at the fighters passing overhead:

"Nate? Astrilla?"

After a second, Nathan struggled to his feet and

scrambled across the platform to Astrilla. The Evoker was sprawled out on the floor. For a heartbeat, Nathan thought she was dead, but when he turned her over, she coughed. There was a bloody wound on the side of her head, and she strained to speak.

"I've got you!" Nathan yelled. He screamed in Koble's direction, feeling the pain in his ribs as he strained to lift Astrilla; "Koble! Need a hand here!"

He scooped the Evoker up into his arms, and when Koble reached them a second later, Nathan nodded at Astrilla's satchel. Fortunately, he didn't need to tell the Sphinax that the Omega was inside, the look on his face conveyed all it needed to. Koble nodded and grabbed the bag; securing it over his broad shoulders.

Nathan became aware that the squadron of Revenant fighters was doubling back and that it would be a matter of seconds before they were in firing range.

"Go!" Nathan yelled.

As they sprinted, the sound of the fighter's engines grew louder. Nathan could see the Phoenix's top-side cannon firing wildly into the air to provide cover. Koble leapt onto the Phoenix's boarding ramp and hurried on all-fours into the ship. Nathan was a metre behind, and as he moved up, he saw Harrt at the airlock door with his hand reaching for Nathan;

"C'mon; Hurry!"

Within inches of his reach, Nathan extended his hand, while clinging to Astrilla with his other. For a fleeting moment, Nathan believed they'd done it: that they'd escaped the Revenant once again. His fingertips touched Harrt's, and then he was clinging to the 'wealther.

We made it, Nathan thought. *We-*

I see you, Earther. I finally see you. The river Prynn sees you.

Suddenly, a gunshot from one of the Revenant fighters, collided with the Phoenix, causing the ship to buckle violently under the impact. The Phoenix tipped forty-five degrees, and Nathan felt himself falling. Astrilla was beside him, as was Harrt.

As he fell, Nathan looked at the Phoenix Titan. He spotted Koble gripping to the airlock for dear life. The Sphinax was screaming something at Nathan, but his mind could not process it. The adrenaline running through Nathan's veins muted everything around him, and he realised that he was still clutching Astrilla.

Before Nathan's mind slipped into unconsciousness, he heard a male voice clawing at the back of his mind. It was just like the visions, but far clearer;

"This is simply the first step".

CHAPTER FIFTY-FIVE

Koble looked at Vol, and he noticed that her eyes carried the weight of defeat. The Phoenix had been forced to flee: outnumbered and outgunned by the Revenant warships and fighters. Despite the Phoenix Titan being a one-of-a-kind frigate, it wouldn't have stood a chance against such insurmountable odds. Vol landed the ship to the far side of Paradisium, hiding the vessel on a small island, so she could try and contact the Commonwealth. Koble paced back and forth in the cockpit, clutching the third piece of the Omega in his paw.

He felt angry. Not just with the Revenant, but with himself. He should have got Nathan and Astrilla onboard first, but he'd rushed ahead. Every time he replayed the moment, Koble felt himself sinking deeper into despair.

You are an idiot, he told himself. *You idi—*

Vol punched the holo-table and shot him an angry look:

"Thoughts like that aren't going to help," she said. "Start thinking proactively: what do we do now?"

"We've gotta get them out!" Koble answered as though stating the obvious.

From the corner, Ralph Hayward folded his arms and offered up a sigh that Koble assumed was irritation.

"Afraid that's easier said than done," Hayward shrugged.

"Nobody asked you, gym-rat," Koble raised his voice. "If we don't save our people that's bad news for everyone".

Hayward frowned, forcing Koble to wonder if the lumbering human was planning to retaliate. Koble sighed through his nostrils and shook his head at the Earther.

Not today, he thought.

He realised that the man before him was not David Jareth: he wasn't the man that had aided in Kornell's rise to power. The only way they would stand a chance of saving Nathan and the others was to ask for Jareth Corp's help. It made Koble feel sick to his stomach.

▲

"Wake up".

Harrt's mind lingered between consciousness and a dream-like state that made him feel as light as a feather. Somewhere buried deep in the recesses of his psyche, Harrt was aware that he'd landed in seawater. He could taste the salt on his lips, and his body ached all over from the impact.

"Wake up!"

The back of a palm slapped against his face, hard enough for Harrt to know that his captor was wearing a ring. He became aware of a heaviness constricting his arms and legs, then he felt an overwhelming sense of nausea. Harrt turned his head and vomited a mix of saltwater and blood onto the floor. When he turned his head back to face his attacker, Harrt opened his eyes.

He was in a dimly lit room, his arms and legs secured in place by metal restraints on an upturned platform. He realised that Nathan and Astrilla were not with him, even though he was sure that they had fallen from the Phoenix as well. It took Harrt longer then it should have to recognise the uniformed Maruvian standing before him. Maybe the muddled mess inside his mind wasn't working as it should, or perhaps his former mentor had aged more than Harrt had ever anticipated.

Densius Olbori: former hero of the Commonwealth, stood before Harrt; his expression unapologetic.

"You bastard," Harrt spat. He pushed against his

restraints, hoping to lunge at Grand Admiral Olbori, but he was held in place. As Harrt struggled, he screamed at his former friend; "I'll kill you!"

Olbori circled him with an expression as cold as ice. There was no sorrow in his eyes —no semblance of regret for what he'd done: for the billions who'd lost their lives at Maru Seven.

"It's been a long time, old friend," Olbori said. "I barely recognised you when they dragged you out of the water. I suppose that you are no longer the bright-eyed young officer that you were all those years ago".

"And you are an old man and a traitor," Harrt spat. He pushed himself up against his restraints and screamed; "You helped them to destroy our home!"

Olbori's stare didn't waver.

"You may have aged, old friend, but I see you are still the boy I knew back then. You still believe that the Commonwealth are righteous".

Harrt was unable to contain his rage. He willed with every fibre of his being that the restraints would buckle and that he could kill the man who'd taken everything from him.

"They call you the hero of Maru Seven, don't they?" Olbori said. "The man who was willing to sacrifice everything to save the civilians from the Revenant".

"Mark my words: I will kill you for what you did; to my family, to our people," Harrt said behind gritted teeth.

Olbori's face shifted: his eyes grew wide, and his jaw tensed uncomfortably:

"I'm sorry for what happened to your family; to Jophy and Hailam; their deaths were unfortunate," Olbori said.

"Don't even say their names," Harrt yelled, but Olbori continued to talk over him;

"I did what had to be done".

"You betrayed all of us," Harrt yelled. "You betrayed us for the rank of Admiral in Seig's mad conquest!"

"No!" Olbori bellowed.

Harrt noticed the old man's hand tremble as he regained his composure.

"I betrayed the Commonwealth because it betrayed all

of us," Olbori said. "For centuries, the politicians have hidden behind sentiments of acceptance and tolerance, but in reality, all they care about is asserting control. How are they any different from the Revenant? The 'wealth consumes every culture it inducts. They destroy religions, creeds and ideologies because they don't want people to know the truth".

"What truth?" Harrt spat.

"The truth that the Enkaye had a plan for all living things," Olbori said. The Admiral took a step closer, and for a split second, Harrt eyed the handgun on the old man's hip. "Harrt, I have looked at the Great Void, just like the Revenant king. It showed me all the atrocities committed by the Commonwealth; things that would make any man question his loyalty".

"You're insane," Harrt shook his head. "You are the madman who murdered my family, and I swear I will kill you if it's the last thing I ever do".

Olbori's smirk was like a predator, who'd already claimed its kill:

"Your threats of revenge will do you no good now," Olbori replied with a stoic expression on his face. "We have Astrilla: *we* have the means to power the Messorem and bring about the end".

Olbori snapped his fingers to a pair of soldiers who had remained hidden in the darkness during their entire conversation.

"Bring in his friends," Olbori ordered.

When the soldiers disappeared into the next room, there was a lingering silence. Harrt wanted to kill Densuis Olbori. For almost a decade, it had been the thing that had fueled the fire of pure hatred in his soul. Grand Admiral Densius Olbori was once a proud and decorated Commonwealth officer. Many had believed him to be a hero. Now, he was a weathered, old man, wearing the uniform of the enemy: the enemy that mutated its victims into brainless husks. Killing him would be easy. Getting to him was the tricky part.

Minutes later, Astrilla and Nathan were brought in.

Both of them were restrained in the same way as Harrt. Nathan appeared unconscious, while Astrilla was groggy at first, but when she laid eyes on Admiral Olbori, she lurched forward against her Evoker-resistant bindings.

"You!" The Evoker hissed. "You murderous warmonger!"

It was the first time that Harrt had seen the Evoker genuinely enraged. Her nostrils flared, and her eyes were so wide that she could've burst a blood vessel.

"Please, spare me your name-calling, and outrage," Olbori said, his voice oozing with callousness. "The King shall be joining us very soon, and I assure you, he will not appreciate such behaviour from you, dear girl".

Harrt took his eyes off Astrilla, as he heard Nathan cough. The Earther shook off his daze and confusion, then took in the surroundings and their situation. His gaze met Harrt's, but only for a second, as Olbori continued to taunt Astrilla:

"The King is looking forward to finally meeting you," Olbori gently ran the back of his hand against Astrilla's cheekbone. It was a classic power-move that Harrt recognised immediately: a poor attempt to intimidate and assert control over one's captives. Olbori closed his hand around the Evoker's face and squeezed on her jaw.

"Take your fuckin' hands off of her," Nathan yelled from the corner.

Olbori looked back at Nathan, with a wide grin spread across his face, but it lasted a second. To Olbori's horror, Astrilla was able to twist her head and sink her teeth into several of his fingers. The Admiral's yelp of agony felt like music to Harrt's ears. Unfortunately, the agonised screams didn't last long.

Several of the Olbori's men rushed to aide him. One of them struck Astrilla over the head with the end of a rifle, causing her to release the animal-like grip she had on the Admiral's hand. Olbori dropped to the ground with a look of sheer horror on his face. His hand was covered in blood, and when Harrt got a good look, he realised that the Admiral had lost a finger.

Despite being bloody and barely conscious, Astrilla spat the severed finger onto the floor, inches from Olbori's reach. She shot him a hostile scowl that was made more threatening when Harrt realised she was covered in Olbori's blood.

"You bitch!" Olbori yelled.

The Admiral gestured to one of the soldiers, and the guard passed him a sidearm. After examining the gun, Olbori moved closer to Astrilla and placed the barrel against her head.

Harrt could see Nathan push against his restraints, as Olbori hissed in Astrilla's ear;

"Go on you Evoker bitch, beg for your life."

Astrilla icy glare didn't change. She tilted her head toward Olbori's gun, and pulled herself forward against the restraints, bringing herself inches from the Admiral's face.

"Go ahead: kill me," Astrilla said.

Olbori plastered a casual smile on his face and laughed to himself. The old man pulled the gun away and stepped back.

"Mark my words, if his royal highness didn't want each of you alive, I'd have sacrificed you all to the Void," Olbori said. The Admiral bent down and scooped his severed finger from the ground. He straightened up and held it out, causing blood to drip onto the floor. "You will witness his highness ascend to greatness. He will use the Messorem to cleanse the universe of its sin and deliver every lost soul to salvation".

Olbori turned on his heel and looked at Harrt. His smile was thin and calculating. There were no words exchanged. Olbori's stare lingered for several seconds until finally, he left with his men.

When they were alone, Nathan was the first to speak; "Did you seriously bite that guy's finger off?"

Before Astrilla could respond, there was a rumble, followed by a loud crash. It didn't feel like an FTL jump, and it certainly didn't feel like an engine spinning up.

No, Harrt thought. *Someone just took a shot at the Revenant.*

CHAPTER FIFTY-SIX

As a Commonwealth Special Agent, Leviticus Dines learned long ago that fear was the enemy's greatest weapon. Managing such impulses was at first difficult. It was during one of his first assignments that Dines realised the depravity of the Revenant Purebloods. The mission was among the worst of his career. It was an undercover assignment wherein he spied on Grand Priest Arlagog: King Seig's half brother.

Dines posed as a Revenant officer and bore witness to the Revenant's way of life. He'd seen the Revenant sacrifice settlers from a small mining planet to the river Prynn. Seeing the dead return, suffer and die all over again had changed him forever.

Dines accepted that like all other Special Agents, he would meet his end, and it would likely be unpleasant. He understood that he wouldn't be afforded a peaceful death surrounded by his loved ones. Instead, he lived knowing that he'd probably die at the hands of the enemy, but it would be in service of everything the Commonwealth stood for.

On the final night of his mission, Dines disregarded his orders and planted a bomb in Arlagog's chambers. It detonated an hour later, killing Arlagog and over half a million Revenant soldiers.

The fact was that the very moment Leviticus Dines took up the mantle of Special Agent, he ceased to be a citizen. Instead, he became what his people needed him to be: a blunt instrument designated to protect the values that the Commonwealth was built upon.

For the first time in as long as Dines could remember, he felt nervous. Ever since he took command of the warship Signet, Dines felt a tightness in his chest. Often, he'd undertake many different roles in the service of the 'wealth. He'd been called a spy; a torturer; a hitman, but he'd never been a leader. It was a terrifying prospect, but he'd asked to command the mission himself. Someone was pulling strings, and the only person he could trust was himself.

The Signet was a Colossus-class warship, manned by a crew of over seven-hundred. The ship was among the 'wealth's finest vessels —a two mile-long war machine that could obliterate a moon in a matter of seconds.

Usually, such ships were reserved for the frontlines of battle, but Dines made a case to he Commonwealth Council. The fact was that he needed more than just a fleet of standard warships, and fortunately, the politicians agreed.

In addition to the Signet, the Council sent the Adonis and the Zenith as escort. They weren't the newest or the most advanced ships, but they were commanded by two excellent officers who Dines trusted —for the most part.

A ship-wide alert told him that it was ten minutes before the drop from the slipstream. As he made his way to the command centre, Dines checked his messages to see if Harrt Oxarri had made contact, but the interference from FTL was causing a thirty-minute delay.

The command centre was a vast room, based at the top of the Signet, filled with consoles and overhead monitors. A mezzanine floor looked over the twenty-plus bridge crew, where usually the CO would be based. Dines had no intention of looking over his people. He wanted to be in the action, as though he were in the field.

He was greeted by the X.O, Lieutenant Verk, who handed him a datapad.

"Sir, we are picking up all kinds of proximity alerts in the system," Verk said, tipping his pig-like head to one side and stretching his short neck.

"Revenant?"

"There's no telling," Verk replied. "Could be Jareth Corps doing military exercises, or—"

Dines cut him off, "Put us on alert, and instruct the Zenith and Adonis to do the same. I don't wanna get caught with our trousers down when we leave the slipstream".

There was a hint of protest in Verk's eye, but he didn't say anything. He simply nodded and executed the order. A klaxon sounded throughout the ship, and the overhead lighting shifted to orange. Dines moved to the middle of the bridge and took a good look at the officers around him. Knowing that he was responsible for all of them and the many others onboard made Dines feel queasy.

"Agent Dines, Sir, we're coming upon Paradisium".

Dines looked across the bridge and nodded to his helmsmen. He walked to the comms station and issued a command to the officer manning the terminal;

"As soon as we drop out, make contact with the Phoenix Titan".

"Aye, Sir".

When Dines turned back to the viewing port, the flashing blue lights of the FTL slipstream dissolved into the darkness of space. The Signet and Adonis reported in, and for a second, Dines allowed himself to think that everything was alright.

Too easy, he thought.

Proximity alerts and target-lock warnings began to fill the combat centre. When Dines looked over to the tactical terminal at the centre of the room, he felt his heart sink. He counted four —no five— Revenant warships in orbit over Paradisium and a sixth was heading straight toward them.

"Battlestations! Launch all fighters!" Dines yelled. Before he could draw breath, he issued his next command to the helmsmen; "Evasive manoeuvres".

The ship jolted as it began to take fire from the approaching Revenant warship. Dines knew the damage would be minimal from such a distance, but it was a fact that was about to change quickly. He looked at the tac-terminal and saw the Zenith and Adonis following the same path, while also launching fighters.

The comms officer called out; "Sir, we're receiving an incoming transmission". There was a pause, then, "Confirmed; it's the Phoenix Titan!"

"Put it on my terminal," Dines replied.

The holographic projector at his station lit up, and the images of a Uvan woman and a heavy-set Sphinax appeared in front of him. Dines recognised the pair from the Phoenix's manifest: Vol Volloh and the mercenary known as Koble. As a loud crash caused the ship to rumble violently, Dines skipped the pleasantries;

"Where the hell is Oxarri?"

"Aboard that Revenant flagship," Vol answered. "They captured him, Astrilla, and Nathan".

Dines felt his gut tighten. If Astrilla was a captive of the Revenant, then all hope was lost. There was another impact to the Signet's hull, and Dines was forced to steady his footing.

"We have a plan," Koble said. "But you ain't gonna like it: I know I certainly didn't at first, but hear us out..."

There came a momentary hiss of static which cleared after a second. On the Phoenix's side of the communication, someone new moved into view. Dines recognised Ralph Hayward immediately, from his short beard, bald head and muscular build. The square-jawed Earther regarded him with a no-nonsense nod of the head.

"I think we can extract the Evoker. Good news is that Jareth Corps has back-up inbound" Hayward said.

"And the bad news?"

Ralph Hayward folded his arms; "We're gonna need you guys to create a distraction so that we can drift the Phoenix through their shields. Once we are through, we'll latch onto the side of that thing. I don't need to tell you that time is of the essence".

Dines felt his gut sink.

"How long till Jareth Corps' back-up arrives?" He asked.

"At least ten minutes, but you and I know the Revenant could jump at any moment".

Hayward was right. Now that the Revenant had Astrilla, all they needed was an open patch of space to make the FTL jump. Dines needed to position his small fleet directly in the Revenant's path. It was the only way to buy the Phoenix Titan, and its crew some time.

"So, Agent Dines," Hayward said. "What'll it be?"

Dines swallowed a lump in his throat and answered; "Do it. We'll keep them busy!"

▲

As soon as Dines killed the comm link, Vol threw herself into the pilot's chair. A drifting manoeuvre was not easy, especially in a frigate the size of the Phoenix. Hayward assured her that the interference from Paradisium's extensive satellite network could cause the best proximity sensors to go haywire —particularly around the southern hemisphere.

"Trust me," Hayward said. "The 'wealthers mistake small ships for asteroids or space-junk all the time. How'd you think Jareth Corps smuggles things past the Commonwealth patrols?"

Vol knew that the drift would be easier to execute in a link-rider or a racing skiff, but they were out of time. The manoeuvre was simple, blast the engines until reaching high velocity, then switch off every non-essential system on-board. The idea was to create the illusion that the ship was nothing more than debris drifting through space.

The only thing Vol could hope was that the Commonwealth warships would keep the Revenant busy long enough for her to get the Phoenix Titan through the shield array. As she prepped the ship for drifting manoeuvres, Koble sat down beside her, clutching a heavy rifle in his paws.

"Tell me something…" he began. "When you and I first met at that casino back on Yenex, did you ever think we'd be doing something like this?"

Vol shot him a smirk; "Attempting to execute a high-risk drift to board a Revenant warship?"

Koble's smile was anxious, reflective and nostalgic all at the same time. It was a look Vol had never seen on him.

"Remember when it was all just about stealing a ship and getting even with a total asshole?" he said.

"Yeah, I do".

Koble gazed at the tactical screen, filled with blips to indicate the Revenant warships and fighters.

"They were simpler times," he sighed.

"Yep, they were".

▲

For several minutes, Astrilla strained to destroy the metal bindings that held her in place, but it was useless. The restraints were designed to resist elemental summons. No matter what Astrilla threw at them, they would not break.

Everything seemed to shake and rumble. With every impact, the red overhead lights flickered. Astrilla was sure that the Commonwealth hadn't broken through the Revenant's shield array, but they were getting close.

"C'mon Dines, kill those Revenant bastards," Harrt whispered to himself.

Astrilla peered across the room at Nathan. He looked tired and frazzled —as though the fall from the Phoenix had knocked the life out of him.

We have to get out of here, Astrilla thought.

She cast her mind back to her formative years at the Enclave, trying to recall the wise words of Elder Xanthur. The old man once shared an account of how he had escaped Revenant capture. Astrilla's mind suddenly became foggy. She could picture the Enclave and Xanthur's wrinkled old face at the front of a classroom, but she couldn't recall any specifics from his lessons. Astrilla searched the winding corridors of her mind. She tried to find anything that could be of use, but she kept going around in circles until finally, she stumbled on something else.

It wasn't something from her memory, and it certainly wasn't a dream or a vision. The grey rocky dune Astrilla found herself standing on felt like something invading her mind. She was sure that she was standing on a lunar-body, orbiting a blue planet in the distance. It was cold —freezing in fact— but Astrilla knew that what she experienced was real.

"You are hurt," a male voice said across the barren landscape.

Astrilla wanted to answer, but something told her that the question wasn't intended for her.

"We don't have time for that," a second voice answered. "They are right on my tail".

In her mind's eye, Astrilla saw two spirits talking to one another. The first was old —very old. The second seemed oddly familiar, and when Astrilla drew closer, she saw the face of Jack Stephens. He was injured, and his clothes were covered in blood.

Astrilla hovered above the scene for several seconds, watching Jack. He staggered forward and almost fell to the ground, but somehow he managed to stabilise himself.

Astrilla watched as the spectre rushed to Jack's side.

"Did you secure it?"

Jack nodded while clutching his stomach; "Yeah, it's on my shuttle. I gotta get outta here before they track me to you."

"I don't think that's wise!"

"Doesn't matter what you think!" Jack raised his voice. "I'll lead them away and mask my trail. Just make sure everything goes according to plan!"

Astrilla watched the ghostly spirit nod at Jack; "I will".

The apparition around Astrilla collapsed in on itself. The walls dissolved, and Jack faded away. The image of a barren moon lingered in Astrilla's head for a few more seconds, then she was back in the room with Nathan and Harrt.

She felt her breath quicken as her heart began to race. What she'd seen was a memory that was not her own. Every fibre of Astrilla's being wanted to question its purpose. She wanted to ask why the universe would show her such a thing. When Astrilla leaned forward, she noticed that the bindings around her had loosened. As soon as she cast an elemental summon, the metal restraints broke apart in a blaze of white light.

Take care of my boys, Jack's voice reverberated inside her head. *Make sure everything goes according to plan.*

CHAPTER FIFTY-SEVEN

Nathan shielded his eyes. The blaze of light that Astrilla cast was almost blinding. He wasn't sure how the Evoker had broken through the restraints, and before he could ask a loud alarm began to screech.

As Astrilla broke Harrt free, Nathan yelled over the alarm; "We gotta get outta here".

Almost as soon as Nathan said the words, a single Revenant soldier rushed inside the chamber. Before he could open fire, Astrilla cast a summon and sent the mindless Revenant troop crashing into the wall. Nathan took up the dead soldier's rifle then searched the body for a sidearm, which he promptly threw to Harrt.

"We've gotta get the hell outta here," Nathan said for the second time in less than thirty seconds.

Harrt stepped across the room toward him, and Nathan noticed a sombre look in the 'wealthers eyes.

"You two should head to the hangar bay and commandeer one of their fighters," Harrt said.

Nathan noted that the 'wealther didn't include himself in his suggestion.

"What about you?" Nathan asked, already anticipating Harrt's answer.

"Densuis Olbori betrayed me at Maru Seven," Harrt's expression hardened. Then, "He's the man responsible for the murder of my wife and son. I can't let that go unpunished. Not now, not while he and I are standing on the same ship."

There was a finality to the 'wealther's voice that Nathan couldn't ignore: as though Harrt had already made up his mind. The 'wealther was willing to sacrifice himself to avenge those he'd lost. On the one hand, Nathan found it to be commendable, but on the other, he realised just how foolish an act it was.

Astrilla stepped in and began to protest, telling Harrt, *he shouldn't throw his life away*, but it was no use. Harrt's mind was made up. The 'wealther, looked at her, then at Nathan with a concluding expression on his face. At that moment, Nathan spotted something that he'd failed to see up until that point.

He realised that since meeting aboard the Vertex, he'd seen Lieutenant Harrt Oxarri as the logical type: as the kind of man who didn't let his impulses rule his decision making. Seeing him now, consumed by his demons and hatred was a stark realisation that Nathan and Harrt were never that different after all.

Nathan felt his heart sink when he reflected on that thought. He couldn't deny that he would do the same if faced by Jack's killer or the Revenant soldiers that murdered his parents and grandmother. Instead of protesting or trying to change the 'wealthers mind, Nathan nodded and swapped Harrt's pistol for his rifle. Harrt's face seemed to soften as he recognised the gesture.

In his heart, Nathan wanted to stop him from going, but he knew that there was no changing Harrt's mind, and they didn't have the time to debate. Giving Harrt the rifle gave him a fighting chance; at least that's how Nathan decided to look at it. Astrilla was silent, as she watched Nathan hand him the gun.

"Thanks" Harrt swallowed a lump in his throat.

They shared a moment that felt almost brotherly. Neither needed to say a thing to the other. There was a part of Nathan that wanted to tell Harrt, just how much of an impact he'd made on him, but he didn't. Such a gesture wasn't required.

As Harrt turned to leave, he looked back at Nathan and

Astrilla; "Finish the mission. Find the crew: find the Omega and end this".

Nathan nodded, and Astrilla did the same. He knew that the Evoker disapproved, but they couldn't waste time arguing the point. Too much was at stake.

▲

After parting ways with Harrt, Nathan and Astrilla carefully sleuthed into the next room, where they found a non-mutated human officer. He appeared to be shouting into a communicator about the alarms, unaware of Nathan's presence. The officer was too late to realise that they'd snuck up behind him. Once Nathan got the weaselly man in a chokehold, he demanded to know where the Revenant had taken their weapons and supplies. Nathan hoped that if he could be reunited with his communicator, he could radio the Phoenix or even the Commonwealth.

At first, the officer resisted, but after Nathan applied more pressure he caved;

"Storage locker.... 42a," the man choked and tried to point at the other end of the room.

Nathan ordered Astrilla to check, and she pulled his backpack and guns from the locker. The officer began to plead, but before he could make his case, Nathan snapped his neck. It was a cold, ruthless act of murder, and for a split second, Nathan embraced the guilt he felt. Then he reminded himself, that the officer was a non-mutant and didn't deserve pity. In Nathan's head, those who willingly served the Revenant were worse than the mutants —at least they'd not been given the choice.

Astrilla didn't protest and instead handed him his backpack in silence. Nathan checked his bag's soggy contents and instantly recalled that he'd given Astrilla's satchel to Koble right before their capture.

"The Omega and map are aboard the Phoenix," Nathan said in relief.

He gestured to her to cover the door and pulled his datapad from his backpack. The screen flickered a few times and was slower to respond than usual, but it was still working. Nathan tapped the device, opening a scrambled channel to the Phoenix Titan.

The sound of static filled the room, and Nathan nervously bit his lower lip. He took a deep breath; waited and finally spoke into the device;

"Come in," he said. "Phoenix Titan, come in?"

The crackle of empty static followed.

"Koble... Vol... if you can hear this, please respond..." Nathan said. "It's Nate... I'm aboard the Revenant warship... please respond!"

There was no reply, which meant the Phoenix had fled, or the Revenant had destroyed it. Nathan looked up, and his gaze met Astrilla's. He felt his heart sink into his chest, realising that they were alone.

"Try an open frequency," Astrilla said. "Maybe the Commonwealth will pick up the transmission—"

There was a whistle from the open comms channel. Then interference, before finally a voice;

"Nate?" Koble said. "Your signal is weak, but I think I can hear you.."

▲

From what Astrilla could gather from Koble's garbled message, it sounded like Vol was in the process of attempting a drifting manoeuvre: a high-risk move to sneak aboard the warship while the Revenant and Commonwealth battled. After that, Vol would latch the Phoenix to the warship's underside and cut through the hull, creating a sealed vacuum between the Phoenix and the enemy vessel.

It was dangerous, but the one thing Astrilla had learnt was not to underestimate Vol or the Phoenix Titan. Despite the poor connection, Koble transmitted a crude diagram of a rendezvous location. The Sphinax had picked a spot, not too far from their current position, but there was a big problem. It meant travelling through one of the ship's unsanitised areas: where the mutated soldiers, hunters and abominations lived.

The moment Astrilla moved toward the datapad, the comms-connection to the Phoenix Titan died.

"Signal's dead," Nathan sighed. He turned to Astrilla; "Did you see those rendezvous coordinates?"

Astrilla nodded.

"This day can't get any better," Nathan added.

▲

Dines surveyed the carnage of battle from the semi-comfort of the Signet. In the space of five minutes, Dines lost over three dozen fighters and many more crewman. The good 'wealther in him said that *they were necessary sacrifices in the field of battle,* but the honourable man in him disagreed.

He watched the Revenant warship where Harrt Oxarri and his companions were captive —the same ship that the Phoenix was attempting to board. It had been a matter of minutes since the Titan-class frigate went dark, but with all the madness around him, it felt like hours. To keep the Revenant busy, Dines ordered the Adonis to focus on blocking the enemy's path: preventing their jump to FTL

Like always, the Revenant put up a good fight and had bombarded the Adonis, but 'wealther resolve was firm, and the Adonis held its space. The Zenith focussed on keeping one group of the Revenant crafts separated from the main flagship. This move enabled the Signet to get in the middle of the Revenant's formation and keep the enemy busy.

After two minutes, Dines and his small fleet laid waste to one of the Revenant warships, but that still left five. The Revenant had the numbers, and Dines knew that the three ships under his command could only last so long. The Adonis was starting to suffer, as it was directly in the line of fire.

"Get the fighter squads to cover the Adonis," Dines said to the Tactical officer. "Tell them to take out that Flagship's weapons systems and—"

He didn't finish the sentence. One of the Revenant warships crashed through the Adonis. The Commonwealth warship, with a crew of several hundred, exploded in unison with the giant enemy ship. The kamikaze move told Dines just how desperate the Revenant were to clear the path to FTL He wanted to mourn the brave men and women aboard the Adonis, but he knew he couldn't: not yet.

Instead, he called out to his helmsman, "Put us in the path of the flagship".

For a moment, Dines considered setting a collision course. Of course, it would mean killing everyone aboard the Signet, including himself, but it would guarantee that Seig wouldn't get his hands on Astrilla.

The needs of the many, Dines thought.

As they moved into the enemy ship's field of fire, Dines was ready to issue the order, but something stopped him. An alarm came from the tactical station and Dines rushed to get a look.

"We've got an unidentified ship inbound," Verk said, peering across the workstation. "It's a Jareth Corps ship!"

When Dines turned to the windows, he saw a giant white ship drop out of FTL The massive vessel was slightly larger than the Signet, with an ivory white body and an impressive weaponry arsenal across the hull. The Jareth ship soared over the Signet as it joined the battle, unleashing incessant weapons fire at the Revenant warships.

Dines wanted to breathe a sigh of relief, but he couldn't. It was only one ship, but it was a start. He pushed the thought of setting a collision course aside.

"You better hurry Oxarri," Dines said under his breath.

▲

At some point in the early years of Harrt's military service, a senior officer bestowed an important lesson;

When the enemy shows you their hand, bite it off before it becomes a fist.

Densuis Olbori had said those words to Harrt, along with fifty other fresh-faced recruits. Harrt remembered it so clearly because Olbori was a Maruvian like him. At the time, it was rare to see a high-ranking Maruvian officer with so many honours.

Upon reflection, Harrt noticed the irony of the situation. He was pursuing the very man, who'd taught him to strike the moment opportunity presented itself.

As Harrt snuck through the warship's upper levels, he noticed a strange feeling in the pit of his gut. He'd sacrificed the mission, leaving Astrilla and Nathan to escape without him. He had abandoned his people —his friends— in the name of vengeance. All because of Admiral Densuis Olbori: the traitor. The strangest part was that Harrt was ready to die. He was willing to sacrifice it all if it meant killing the man who'd taken everything from him.

Harrt navigated the complex network of nondescript corridors with great care. Despite arming himself with one of the enemy's assault rifles, there was no need to draw unwanted attention. He wasn't a one-man army: he wasn't an Evoker.

Harrt heard the unmistakable sound of hurried footsteps from up the hall, so he darted into the shadows of a narrow passageway. A cluster of Revenant troops and hunters hurried past him; unaware of his presence. He was sure that they were headed toward the cells, probably to recapture Astrilla and Nathan.

He paused to make sure the troops passed, before starting down the corridor. Harrt felt his gut tighten, knowing that his friends were in danger, but tried to ignore it. All that mattered now was killing Olbori.

When Harrt got to the end of the corridor, he found himself staring at a door that led to the command centre, guarded by two non-mutated soldiers. Without flinching, Harrt moved from cover and shot both men, before either knew what was happening.

All paths led to the death of Densuis Olbori, and Harrt was to be the executioner. It was the way it had to be. Harrt took a deep breath, then pushed through the doors to find his prey.

CHAPTER FIFTY-EIGHT

Ten minutes.

Vol placed her dimly lit datapad down and sighed. Ten minutes until they'd glide through the flagship's shield array. It seemed too long —as though the seconds were taking minutes to pass by. Once they were latched to the warship's hull, it'd be at least another minute before they could get into the enemy ship.

Nine minutes.

The plan was loose, but then again, how could it be anything else. Vol would stay aboard the Phoenix, keeping the engines hot while guarding the airlock. Koble would go aboard the Revenant ship and find the others.

One Sphinax versus a warship's worth of Revenant soldiers. I don't like those odds. Vol thought.

To Vol's surprise, Russell volunteered to accompany Koble. It was something she didn't expect in the slightest. She didn't dismiss it, but it was astounding in a way. Less than six hours prior, he'd been serving cocktails at a bar, and now he was volunteering for a suicide mission.

Eight minutes.

When Nathan's transmission came through Koble's datapad, the signal was weak —terrible in fact— but it didn't matter. They were alive and more importantly, they'd gotten loose.

There was a moment of elation, between Koble and Vol, then panic. The Sphinax hastily drew a crude rendezvous location over a schematic and hit send. The signal became weak, and for a moment, Vol worried that the transmission had failed. Seconds passed, and finally Koble's datapad let off a cheerful chime, indicating that Nathan had received the diagram.

Seven minutes.

The Phoenix Titan floated through open space, like a feather caught in a breeze. Vol found something oddly peaceful about the slow drift. Where before the cockpit was awash with beeping terminals and flashing monitors, there was nothing: replaced by blank screens and deactivated systems.

Six minutes.

She and Koble sat in the pilot and co-pilot's seats watching the battle unfold against the barren darkness of space. It was a scene of complete contrast when compared to the silence of the Phoenix's cockpit. It made the whole thing seem unreal: like they were watching something on the newscast.

Five minutes.

Three Commonwealth warships fought against what Vol could only assume was an entire armada of Revenant ships. To their credit, the 'wealthers fought bravely, but Vol knew the Revenant had the numbers. One of the 'wealther ships put itself directly in the enemy fire line and was caught in an array of missiles.

Four minutes.

It was only when a Jareth Corps warship dropped from FTL that things seemed less desperate. The mile-long white vessel pushed into the field of battle like an untamed animal fighting to keep its territory. The Jareth ship immediately went on the offensive, moving at the Revenant like it had a death wish. Tiny drones launched out into space and began picking off the Revenant fighters. Ralph Hayward lingered behind Vol's seat, watching the battle play out like a sports game.

"That's my boys!" Hayward boasted. "Jareth Corps' finest right there."

Vol ignored the comment, wishing that the peace and

quiet she'd experienced minutes earlier would return.

Three minutes.

As the Phoenix closed in on the Revenant flagship, Vol noticed signs of damage on the hostile ship. The hull had suffered several breaches, and at least two cannons were gone. She chose to focus on those facts alone, rather than the size of the looming enemy vessel. With everything going on around the Phoenix, Vol knew that they'd appear as a floating piece of debris to the Revenant. The enemy's onboard systems weren't the problem, it was the naked eye that worried her. If a shrewd fighter pilot spotted them, it would be over. If the Revenant had someone using the manual scopes, they would be screwed.

Two minutes.

"Once we're on board, we gotta be in and out," Koble said, as he unbuckled himself from the co-pilot's seat.

Over Vol's shoulder, Russell was checking a gun for ammo, while Ralph Hayward hadn't moved from behind her chair. It felt like having a supervisor —as though Hayward was watching her every move. Vol wanted to read his thoughts, but she couldn't —not during a stressful situation.

Focus, she told herself.

She became aware of Koble stopping in his tracks, as though Hayward said something offensive.

"What the hell do you mean, *you ain't going?*" Koble raised his voice.

Vol spun in her chair, to see Koble clutching a gun in one paw while pointing at Hayward with the other.

"Your friends are not my problem, muchacho," Hayward shrugged. "My concern is with the good people of Paradisium."

"What?" Koble inched toward Hayward, and Vol felt the immediate twang of outrage that ran through his brain.

"I'm not gonna sit by and let the Commonwealth ignore the people of Earth all over again," Hayward protested. "Jareth Corps' main directive is to put the people of Earth back on the map, where we belong. We can't do that if the Revenant have their way".

Vol didn't need to read Koble to know what he was

thinking. The Sphinax would have taken a swing at Hayward under any other circumstance, but he didn't. He couldn't. Time was of the essence. The only thing that mattered was saving the others, and Koble knew that.

One minute.

After arming himself and Russell with enough firepower to take on a small army, Koble looked at Vol. She sensed fear, anxiety and all the other things that seemed appropriate.

Russell was the same, but far more than Koble. He grasped a heavy assault rifle in his hands, looking like someone who didn't belong in the situation. Still, Russell was willing to go, which was more than could be said for Hayward.

"Well," Koble drawled as he stared at Vol. "I guess this is—"

Vol sensed the word *goodbye* on his lips, so she cut him off.

"Get in; find the guys; get outta there," she said, swallowing the lump that was forming in her throat.

Neither Vol nor Koble needed to say goodbye: the look they shared said enough. Koble nodded, and when Vol looked at Russell, the former barkeep smiled at her assuringly.

"Come back in one piece," Vol added.

As she watched the pair, disappear from the cockpit, Vol sat in silence with Ralph Hayward. The countdown on the datapad hit zero, and she activated the Phoenix's onboard systems.

Never a dull moment, Vol thought.

▲

As Koble passed through the Phoenix's living area, he rechecked the list of weapons he was carrying in his head. Everything was locked and loaded from the shotgun over his shoulder to the assault rifle in his paw.

Going aboard a Revenant warship is fuckin'

lunacy, Jack Stephen's voice seemed to play inside his brain, but Koble realised it wasn't Jack at all: it was his own intuition.

Koble huffed when he laid eyes on Gordon Taggart. The Earther was kneeling at the coffee table with a soldering iron, still attempting to repair the droid. Despite all of the carnage going on around them, Gordon hadn't offered to lift a finger. The doctor appeared to ignore Koble and Russell as they passed through the room. It was selfish and disrespectful and cowardly all at the same time.

How the hell did Jack resist beating you to a pulp? Koble wondered.

As he and Russell walked passed Gordon, Koble heard the bespectacled Earther mutter something to himself;

"If you were right all along... Dammit!" Gordon shook his head. "Shit: not enough bloody time!"

Koble chose to ignore the insane ramblings and led Russell to the airlock instead. There was a time and a place to deal with Gordon Taggart, and this was not it.

▲

When Harrt Oxarri made it inside the command centre, he saw several non-mutated Revenant officers staring back at him. There was a certain camaraderie about it that didn't sit right with Harrt. As he looked at the bridge, the officers and the way they worked, he felt uncomfortable. It all seemed eerily similar to Commonwealth ships he'd served aboard in the past. The Revenant crew seemed just like ordinary military officers, but Harrt knew they weren't. These were people who willingly served King Seig.

They were monsters.

Before any of them could raise a weapon, Harrt opened fire. He mowed through a group of them with his rifle, sending crimson blood flying in all directions. One man wearing a Commander's uniform darted toward cover, but Harrt's aim didn't waver. Another reached for his sidearm, but the gunfire cut through her brittle human body as though it were made from paper.

This was a slaughter, and Harrt was aware of it. He didn't like it, but it was justified. The enemy had taken so much away from him —from the Commonwealth. They deserved death, for servicing such a cruel monarch.

When it was done, Harrt tossed his empty rifle aside and looked at what remained of the command centre. Blood stained every surface. Bodies of his enemies lay around their stations, unable to attend to the blaring alarms around the room.

Not one of them was Densius Olbori.

Harrt moved to the commander's console at the end of the room. As he laid eyes on the monitor, Harrt saw the reason for all of the proximity alarms. The navigation readouts indicated that something big was about to drop from FTL and it had a Revenant signature.

Before Harrt could draw a conclusion, he heard the sound of someone coughing a few metres away. He turned on his heels and drew his sidearm from its holster. A human male leaned against the wall in a pool of blood. His uniform was peppered with gunshot wounds, while his skin had grown pale from severe blood loss.

Harrt moved toward him, keeping his weapon trained on the dying man's head.

"Where's Olbori?" Harrt growled.

To his surprise, the Revenant officer's blue lips formed a calculating smirk. He didn't say anything, and when Harrt pressed the barrel of his gun against the man's head, his expression only grew:

"Tell me, and I will grant you a quick death," Harrt said.

The officer laughed, then coughed a mouthful of blood onto the floor.

"The King is coming," he spluttered.

The officer's laugh became maniacal, leaving Harrt with a sense of dread. Olbori wasn't there, which meant he had somewhere more important to be.

"His royal highness is coming for the Evoker," The officer smiled, showing the blood that stained his teeth. He nodded at Harrt's gun with his chin; "Take my advice, use that weapon on yourself. Die in service of the Revenant rather than resisting. There is no stopping what is to come".

"We'll see about that," Harrt said.

The Revenant officer leaned back against the wall, and his laughter grew louder and more disturbing until Harrt finally shot him in the head. It was an act of mercy that wasn't deserved, but Harrt knew it was the right thing to do.

He holstered the smoking gun and moved to the comms station. Harrt pushed a dead officer from atop the terminal and wiped away just enough blood so that the screen would respond to his touch. He scrolled through page after page of logs, messages and tactical alerts. After a few seconds, Harrt found a recent report from a ship marked RV3. When he looked closer, Harrt discovered that it was a Revenant behemoth-class warship. It was on an intercept course to their current location, and someone using Olbori's credentials had supplied docking procedures.

Harrt imagined Densuius Olbori tucked away in a safe room somewhere aboard the ship, just waiting for evac. It stood to reason that the old man would hide away and leave his crew to handle the dirty-work: all the while surrounded by bodyguards and soldiers.

I'm playing straight into his hand, Harrt thought. *This is what he wanted me to do.*

Harrt memorised the exact location of where the behemoth was due to dock, then he smashed the control screen with his fist. Slowing down the Revenant was now his main objective. He took up his gun and fired into the tactical station, then the navigation terminal.

On the way out, Harrt grabbed a communicator from one of the many dead bodies. He adjusted the frequency, hoping to make contact with Nathan and Astrilla. He barked into the handheld device, calling out to the pair in the hope he could warn them about Seig.

The voice that answered was not what Harrt expected;

"Harrt?" Vol said, her voice nervous. "Where the hell are you? Why aren't you with Nate and Astrilla?"

"No time to explain," Harrt said hurriedly. He looked at the screen, noting that Vol's transmission was nearby. "We've got a big problem".

CHAPTER FIFTY-NINE

The unsanitised areas of the Revenant warship were like something carved from a nightmare. Slime-caked bodies were fused to the walls and ceiling, leaving a rotten smell that Astrilla tried to ignore. She wasn't sure which side of the resurrection cycle the bodies were on, but it didn't make it any less horrifying. The eyes of the dead were bloodshot and hollow, and their skin had become pale and miscoloured.

They may just be dead bodies, Astrilla thought in a poor attempt to reassure herself. When she considered her thinking, it made her feel ill.

Just dead bodies.

Astrilla wanted to kick herself for thinking such a thing, but upon reflection, she embraced it. Regardless of her Evoker training, she was human: or at least, mostly human, besides the minor peppering of Enkaye somewhere in her genealogical cocktail. Astrilla realised that a primitive survival instinct had booted up inside her brain —likely the human part. Her heart pounded, and her palms became sweaty. Astrilla could feel the adrenaline coursing through her veins like fuel to a ship's engine.

Once she recognised that everything she felt was a physical and mental response to her surroundings, Astrilla felt the fear dilute. There was a strange meditative acceptance about everything. It was an understanding that at any moment a swarm of footsoldiers or hunters could spring from anywhere and strike.

Nathan pointed his handgun into the darkness as they moved together through their nightmare-ish surroundings. Neither of them said a word to the other; both out of horror and fear that they could draw unwanted attention. They heard a cacophony of screaming from deep within the ship. The noise echoed toward them like a gust of wind and sent a cold chill up Astrilla's spine. Despite being unlike anything she'd ever heard, Astrilla knew exactly what it was:

"This must be where they mutate the bodies," Astrilla whispered.

He didn't look at her, and instead kept his gun trained on the darkness ahead.

"There's nothing we can do about that now," Nathan insisted. "All that matters is that we keep moving, and we get the hell out of here".

It was a cold, harsh truth, and she couldn't help but agree. Under any other circumstance, Astrilla would have searched for a way to destroy the mutation chamber, but Nathan was right—escaping was their only option.

They continued to creep through the unsanitised areas, avoiding a group of soldiers that staggered around their bleak surroundings, unaware of Nathan and Astrilla's presence. After the husks had passed, the pair continued to navigate the grim corridors and junctions, until they reached a doorway.

Braced with both hands, Nathan pushed, and the door shifted slightly. Something screamed from up the hall, and Astrilla felt her heart sink. She was certain it was a hunter. The word *hurry* formed on Astrilla's lips, but before she could say it, Nathan booted the door open.

For a moment, Astrilla was certain that Nathan's blunt force would draw attention, but strangely, it didn't. Instead, the hostile howl seemed to grow distant and less aggressive. It was moving away.

▲

Dines squeezed the bridge of his nose as he looked over the tact terminal. Despite the aggressive flight-path that the

Jareth Corps' warship had taken, the Revenant's forces refused to back down. Rather than stare at a screen, Dines moved to a giant window at the end of the command centre. Surveying the field of battle with his own eyes, added some clarity to the situation. Anti-fighter cannons on both sides of the skirmish flashed against the dark backdrop of space. It was evident that the Revenant flagship was desperate to escape. Every time the behemoth-sized vessel tried to plot a new jump the Signet would block its path. The Revenant needed Astrilla alive, therefore, they wouldn't risk jumping through another ship.

"They need a clean jump," Dines said to himself.

Suddenly a new alarm began to sound from the tact terminal, and when Dines made it back to the workstation, his eyes grew wide. A new object appeared on the screen. There was no callsign or recognisable drive signature: no early indication of what was about to emerge from the slipstream.

At the edge of the battle, a gigantic ring of energy flared into existence. A blue wormhole that to the naked eye looked like a thunderstorm. Someone—or something's—idea of a ship emerged from the event horizon. It was a dark, jagged thing that completely dwarfed every vessel in the area.

It took Dines a moment longer than it should have to realise that the crew around him had gone silent. Consoles alarmed and the Signet rocked from gunfire but his officers didn't make a sound.

An officer turned to him; "What the hell is that thing?"

"I think that is a Revenant behemoth," Dines stuttered, then realised the weight of what he'd just said.

Dines was staring at Seig's royal destroyer, and it was terrifying.

The behemoth bared down on the battlefield, pushing toward the other Revenant ships. The Jareth vessel appeared to move into the behemoth's path, concentrating its weapons fire on the hulking mass. The behemoth remained on its trajectory.

Dines swallowed a lump in his throat, then called out to

the comms officer;

"Tell Jareth Corps to get outta there!" He yelled.

The behemoth sped up, and in the space of a single breath cut straight through the Jareth warship. To Dines, the sight evoked images of swords slicing through skin. The behemoth was like a bullet from a gun, and the Jareth vessel was mere flesh. Dines and his crew watched as the Jareth ship exploded in a ball of red and green fire. The behemoth emerged unharmed and unhindered by the collision. Seconds later, it began to dock with the Revenant flagship.

▲

After safely navigating the unsanitised areas of the ship, Nathan exhaled heavily. It was a poor attempt to rid the stench of hunters from the back of his throat that failed to work. He didn't care to admit that the scent evoked powerful memories of the Fall.

For several decks, the pair snuck by Revenant patrols with ease: darting into empty rooms and using the cover of darkness to avoid detection. When they got to the bottom of the eighteenth deck, they were forced to fight.

Astrilla made light work of three hunters: tearing them limb from limb using a powerful summon that Nathan hadn't seen before. It was only when she faced down a fourth hunter that her attacks seemed less powerful, and it wasn't intentional. Rather than incinerating the mutated beast, Astrilla held it in place while Nathan fired a round through its skull at close range.

Astrilla released her summon, and she staggered forward drunkenly. Nathan was barely able to steady her;

"What's wrong?"

Astrilla blinked, and her breathing seemed to quicken:

"I-I don't know," she stuttered. "I think... I think they may have drugged me with some kind of inhibitor".

Nathan hoisted her arm over his shoulder and gestured to the path ahead of them.

"We're not far now," he said, checking the crude schematic Koble had sent earlier. "Just a couple more decks and we're outta here".

While he had the communicator to hand, Nathan checked for a comms signal, hoping to radio Koble or Vol. To his dismay, the screen was empty, and the device established no connections. Nathan cursed then swapped the communicator for his handgun.

He dragged Astrilla through the bowels of the warship, and with every step, he could feel her weaken. When a pair of unsuspecting Revenant officers turned a corner, Nathan had no choice but to gun them down. The first didn't see it coming. By the time the second realised what was happening, it was too late. His head snapped back in a haze of red, and his carcass slumped to the ground.

"Almost there," Nathan said, but Astrilla was unconscious. Regardless, he repeated it, unsure whether it was reassuring himself or the Evoker.

▲

When Nathan reached the rendezvous location, he found Koble and Russell at the end of a long hall. The pair had set up a defensive position next to an elevator which Russell jammed open using an overturned storage locker. Over two dozen dead Revenant soldiers were strewn up and down the long room, where the pair had successfully held the spot.

"I see you guys had some fun," Nathan remarked. "Where's the ship?"

"Next floor down," Koble nodded at the elevator. The Sphinax looked as though he were going to continue, but he stopped and looked around. "Where the hell is Harrt?"

Nathan's brow lowered, "He had a score to settle".

Koble straightened up, and his long whiskers drooped slightly.

"Are we sticking around for him?" Koble said.

Nathan hoped his expression said all it needed to. As he was about to explain the sound of yelling came from up the hall. Out of the corner of his eye, Nathan saw a full squad of Revenant soldiers heading straight toward them.

"Let's go," Koble said, raising his gun and firing down

the hall.

After Russell helped Nathan carry Astrilla into the elevator, he pushed the upturned storage locker clear of the doors. Nathan returned fire, cutting down one of the pursuing soldiers. As soon as Koble was in the elevator, Nathan slammed the control panel, and the doors sealed shut. For a few seconds, there was the dull thud of laser fire ricocheting against steel, but the shots failed to break through the metal.

As the elevator descended, Nathan looked at Astrilla. Her eyes were wide but dreary, and all the colour in her face had drained. Nathan could only assume that she'd taken a hit of some kind of powerful tranquilliser —likely something designed for use on Evokers. Despite looking like she could pass out at any moment, Astrilla remained aware of what was going on around her.

"Once we're onboard the Phoenix we'll get something into your blood to get rid of whatever they've given you," Nathan said, trying his best to reassure her. "We're almost out of the woods".

To his surprise, Astrilla laughed gently. It was a gesture that made Nathan wonder if the sedatives in her blood were finally reaching her brain, but he was proven wrong:

"I rather enjoy a stroll in the woods," Astrilla said wistfully. "I assume that's another one of your Earther sayings?"

"Yeah, I think it is," Nathan said.

Astrilla took a deep breath; nodded sagely. "What a terrible saying".

▲

It is only through your enemy's despair that a king finds victory. Once the spirit is broken, so too is the soul. The heretics shall perish in defeat. Many will suffer, but always remember that they will be reborn. The river Prynn will wash them of the sin and hubris and create loyal subjects for our righteous cause.

As soon as Seig stepped aboard the flagship, he could feel Astrilla's presence. It was a strange, magnetic sensation that he'd felt before at Yenex, but this time it multiplied. For one reason or another, the Great Void was guiding him toward the Enkaye half-breed: toward his ultimate victory.

Rather than allow his Kingsguard to escort him, Seig instructed them to find and evacuate Admiral Olbori. It would seem like a foolish move to an outsider, but Seig knew the situation was unique. It was the only opportunity to ensure Astrilla's capture, and Seig had grown tired of the failure of others.

He ventured alone into the dying warship, and the Great Void acted as his shepherd through the chaos. All around him, the once-proud Revenant war machine withered under the immense pressure of battle. Usually, Seig would have mourned such destruction, but given the circumstances, he told himself that the flagship and all those on board were a necessary sacrifice.

We will rebuild, Seig affirmed.

He embraced the Void, allowing it to guide him toward her. With every step, the sensation grew stronger, until finally, the river Prynn spoke to him:

This is simply the first step.

Seig stopped at a dark junction, illuminated by the red emergency lighting. He studied the four-way intersection, taking note of the elevator directly ahead of him. Despite the descending staircase on his right, and another long corridor to his left, Seig knew she was on the elevator: the Great Void showed him. He waited patiently in the darkness, and when the elevator door opened, Seig laid eyes on his target:

And so my ascent to greatness begins.

CHAPTER SIXTY

The imposing figure standing before Nathan was almost as broad as he was tall. The robed creature lingered in the shadows like an immovable, motionless object. His long black robes accentuated his already menacing appearance. Whoever —or whatever— the hooded man was, Nathan knew he was dangerous. More importantly, he stood directly in their path. A miasma of fear shrouded the area, leaving Nathan with a sense of terror he'd never experienced before.

Nathan raised his gun, and Koble and Russell followed his lead. They moved out from the elevator as a pack, keeping their weapons trained on the stationary hostile.

Over his shoulder, Nathan noticed Astrilla slowly climb to her feet and follow. Nathan could feel all her fear and anxiety as if it were his own —as though the creature standing before them was radiating horror.

The robed figure pulled back his hood, revealing a thin crown made of dark metal atop a scarred bald head. His face was mostly human, but his grey tattooed skin and black eyes had evolved from something else entirely. His eyes were empty and soulless: devoid of emotion or humanity.

"Seig," Astrilla trembled.

"Our paths cross at long last, Evoker," the Revenant king said in a low voice. "Although you have proven to be a highly elusive prey, the time for running is over."

Nathan pulled the trigger on his gun. The single bolt of energy should have torn through the Revenant king's body, but instead, it seemed to fade into nothingness. King Seig twitched slightly from the attack, but it seemed nothing more than a mild inconvenience.

"Violence will do you no good, my friend," Seig shook his head. "I urge you to lay down your weapons and surrender yourself to the Great Void. Spare yourselves the pain and suffering of combat and instead become servants to our cause".

Nathan chanced a look at Koble, and the Sphinax glanced back with a look of defiance.

Seig raised his palms; "What will it be; pointless acts of violence or obedience to a higher being?"

Nathan swallowed his shuddersome sense of trepidation. He twisted his head slightly until the wrinkle in his neck popped, then pursed his lips together.

"You aren't taking her," Nathan growled.

Seig's brow lowered —as though what Nathan had said was offensive. A grey hand emerged from under his dark robes, and a black flame formed in Seig's palm. It looked just like an Evoker summon to the naked eye, but everything in Nathan's mind told him otherwise. As Seig hurled the fire toward them, the group dispersed. Nathan darted to one side, just in time to spot Koble firing. As before, all weapons fire was ineffective against the Revenant king.

In the time it would take to draw breath, Seig pounced forward and landed a kick on Koble. The impact was so powerful that it sent the heavy-set Sphinax hurtling to the ground with a thud. Russell opened fire, but the King cast a summon that forced the former barkeep into the wall. In all the chaos, Nathan continued to fire at Seig, hoping that one of the shots would eventually cause some damage.

At the same time, Astrilla summoned a beam of white energy that seemed to burn the King, albeit partially. In response, Seig cast an attack of his own. A purple and black pulse erupted from his hand, knocking Nathan off of his feet.

For a heartbeat, Nathan's mind drifted between conscious and unconscious. He felt Seig's attack surge through every nerve in his body. After a few seconds, Nathan regained some semblance of what was going on. He lifted his head, spotting Astrilla at the other end of the corridor, fighting a losing battle with Seig. Koble was, at best unconscious. Russell was the same.

As he climbed to his feet, Nathan saw Astrilla stumble. Seig sent another pulse of dark energy into her, and the impact launched the Evoker down the hall. In that moment, Nathan realised that he had to do something. The drugs had weakened Astrilla, and the others were out of action. He couldn't stand by and let Seig win.

Nathan rose to his feet, placing himself directly in the King's path.

Seig bore an almost predatory look in his soulless dark eyes. It was the kind of expression intended to incite fear, but all Nathan could see was a man possessed by purpose. Shadows clung to the Revenant king as he stepped toward Nathan.

"You cannot win, Earther," Seig said without emotion. "Stand aside, or you will perish in the most painful way imaginable".

Nathan said nothing, refusing to show any sign of weakness. He waited split-second, then swept up his pistol. Nathan pulled the trigger over and over again. Every shot connected with Seig's torso, and his robes began to burn.

The Revenant king was unaffected.

Once Nathan's pistol ran out of ammo, he took a step back, and the King stopped.

"How very disappointing," Seig said before tossing his charred robe to one side.

Dark tribal tattoos that looked more like scars covered Seig's muscular body. The markings seemed to depict a complex pattern that was both violent and illustrious. The same design was stitched to his black trousers, belt and sheath. To Nathan's surprise, Seig didn't immediately attack. Instead, the King stared at him with an unreadable expression:

"Tell me something, Earther..." Seig hissed. "Why did you ally yourself with the Commonwealth?"

Nathan didn't answer the question. He waited, knowing it would be a matter of seconds before his ammo would recharge.

The King's lips twitched, almost forming a smirk, "They never told you the truth about the Earth, did they?"

Nathan knew it was an attempt to incite an emotional response. Seig was trying to distract him: trying to get inside his head.

"I may have harvested your world, but the Commonwealth had plans to lay waste to Earth long before I'd heard of it". Seig took a step forward, and Nathan held his ground. "Your people represented a far greater threat to the Commonwealth than I ever could."

It was almost the same thing that David Jareth had said earlier that day. Nathan tried to process the implications of what the Revenant king was saying, and it filled his head with questions:

What if it's true, Nathan thought. *What if—*

In a swift motion, Seig unsheathed the sword at his left side and lunged toward Nathan. Adrenaline kicked in, and all of Jack's life lessons and combat training kicked into overdrive. He saw Seig's attack coming and darted downward, narrowly avoiding the blade. Nathan rolled to the right and grabbed the second of Seig's swords. In a single motion that vaguely resembled that of a pickpocket, Nathan hijacked the weapon and used it to parry another of the King's swipes.

Based on Seig's widened eyes and marginally dropped jaw, Nathan assumed that it was the first time that anyone had offered him a challenge.

"Impressive, but foolish," Seig remarked.

The Revenant king began to edge his way back into the fight, becoming the aggressor once more. The swords collided over and over; electrical sparks flying as metal clashed with metal. Nathan was able to land a strike that cut into the King's upper arm. Arrogantly, he moved in for the killing blow, certain that the battle was over.

Nathan realised his mistake too late.

Seig cut into his midsection without mercy. A heartbeat

later, the Revenant king plunged the jagged blade viciously through his flesh. Nathan made no sound as he felt the cold steel penetrate his torso. The impact caused him to stiffen. All the blood in his body felt as though it had turned to ice, but when Seig wrenched the blade from his torso, everything burned.

For several seconds, Nathan stood motionless, fighting against the shock of what he knew was a lethal blow. He staggered, and a haziness formed in his eyes. The sword in his hand fell to the floor, and Nathan Carter crumbled to his knees.

His first thought was to force himself to stand and face his foe, but his body wouldn't allow it. At first, there was fear. Then there was defiance: a willingness to go on. Nathan stared at his killer, refusing to embrace death.

"I thank you for your sacrifice, my friend," Seig said, his voice callous and remorseful at the same time. "Do not fear death, for you shall be reborn Revenant".

As Seig swung back, a strange primitive sensation permeated Nathan's mind. It was acceptance. He was going to his death, and it was a fucking terrible way to go. He wanted to live longer. He didn't want to become a Revenant drone. He wanted to be with his crew —his family. If he were given a second chance, he'd tell them all how much they meant to him; how much they'd affected him. He'd tell Astrilla how he felt about her. Most importantly of all, he'd live a better life.

▲

Astrilla's mind jumped between two distinct states. The first was slow to comprehend what was going on around her. She was aware that Nathan was facing Seig alone and that he was in danger. Astrilla needed to step in, but every time she willed her body to move, the second state would take over, and her consciousness would wander.

She found herself standing in the same desert she'd seen in her dreams. As before, a spectre lingered in the background, but this time when Astrilla called out, he answered, and what he said mattered.

"This is the way it is has to be".

Once Astrilla's mind returned to the moment, she saw Seig thrust his sword into Nathan's torso. The cocktail of dread and horror that swept over Astrilla was overwhelming. She knew that Nathan had sustained the kind of wound you could not recover from. As Nathan fell to the ground, Astrilla tried everything in her power to claw to her feet. She wanted to help Nathan —to spare him from Seig— but the drugs hindered her ability to move. The Revenant king pulled back his sword, and Astrilla despaired.

Something changed, and the King's sword didn't touch Nathan.

Astrilla became aware that someone else had intervened. When her eyesight finally settled, she saw Harrt Oxarri firing a heavy rifle at Seig. The gunshots made little impact, but it was precisely the distraction Astrilla needed to act. Suddenly, everything the spectre said finally made sense, and as Astrilla climbed to her feet, she knew what she had to do. It didn't make any sense, but everything the universe had shown her up until that point meant something.

Astrilla chose faith over logic.

She raised both palms, willing the universe and all the energy around her to manifest. She drew power from where there was none. Despite the drugs and the exhaustion, her passion fuelled the summon that formed in her palm. The air whipped up around her like a violent storm. A boiling heat circulated her. When Astrilla finally unleashed the summon, it sent pillars of light careening through the corridor.

The attack struck Seig. It wasn't enough to kill him: it was barely enough to hold him in place, but its grip was firm. The summon would restrain Seig long enough for the others to escape.

"Get out of here!" she yelled to Harrt. "Go!"

At the back of the room, Astrilla could hear Koble and Russell. The Sphinax was complaining about an ache in his neck. Harrt scrambled across the floor to Nathan's side.

"Go!" Astrilla screamed. "I can't hold him for long. Get out of here!"

Amongst the pillar of Evoker magic, Seig managed to break his hand free from the storm of energy. He cast his own summon to meet Astrilla's. Seig's attack was far more substantial, and Astrilla knew she didn't have much time.

She watched Harrt, Russell, and Koble wrestle Nathan to his feet. Blood was everywhere, and Astrilla was sure that the Earther was unconscious. She made eye contact with Koble, and the Sphinax looked at her as if asking, *what the hell are you doing?*

Astrilla shook her head, and Koble raised his brow in confusion. Astrilla knew that this was the way it had to be.

"You must get Nathan out!" Astrilla shouted. "Go!"

Koble nodded reluctantly, and when he looked over to Harrt, the 'wealther did the same. Astrilla doubted they could ever understand her reasoning, but they trusted her decision: that was what mattered.

As Harrt, Koble, and Russell carried Nathan out of the area, Astrilla fought to hold off Seig. For minutes, she endeavoured, struggled and eventually succumbed.

When she was struck by King Seig's summon, Astrilla crashed into the cold metal floor. Her eyesight became foggy, and her head felt as though it had been cracked open like an egg. Astrilla felt as though she were floating at sea, but the ocean was searing hot at the surface.

When she finally made out the visage of King Seig, he looked victorious.

"There is no shame in defeat, my child," Seig said, shaking his head. "You fought valiantly, but now that fight is over".

The last thing Astrilla felt before falling unconscious, was the impact of a powerful summon.

CHAPTER SIXTY-ONE

There was a very good reason why Revenant behemoth's were seldom seen: they were reserved for members of the Revenant monarchy. Dines had only ever seen the viciously designed craft in intel reports, so to see one in the flesh was a new experience entirely.

It had been a very long time since Leviticus Dines had felt such fear. He looked on as the behemoth spun up its engines. In a way, there was something marvellous about the speed with which the giant vessel rotated and adjusted its heading. The way it slithered through space reminded him of the Warialle Sharks that dominated the southern seas on his homeworld.

They've got what they came here for, Dines thought.

He wasted no time in issuing his next command;

"Order every ship to take that thing down," Dines said. "We cannot let it escape".

Dozens —if not hundreds— of fighters crossed space toward the behemoth. All Dines could see was a flurry of laser fire, but it was all to little avail. The behemoth adjusted its course, returned fire and allowed its shields to do their work. Dines ordered his helmsman to block the hostile craft from getting the FTL jump its pilot so desperately craved. Unfortunately, the behemoth had both the scale and the speed to outmanoeuvre the Signet.

In a sudden flash of blue, that vaguely resembled an electrical storm, the behemoth vanished. When Dines realised that the enemy ships was gone, he felt his mouth become dry. Slowly the other Revenant warships vanished into FTL leaving only the battered remains of Densius Olbori's flagship and a sea of debris.

▲

A trail of blood followed behind Harrt as he and Russell carried Nathan to the Phoenix Titan. Koble led from the front, gunning down any Revenant soldiers that stood in their path. For the longest time, Harrt didn't concern himself with the unmistakable rumble he felt in his gut. In his mind, there were two objectives: escape to safety and save Nathan. Nothing else mattered.

Harrt had seen enough injuries on and off the battlefield to know when the outlook wasn't good. The stab wound on Nathan's torso was well over two inches wide and he was bleeding profusely. Like all Commonwealth officers, Harrt had trained as a field medic, but it wouldn't be enough to save Nathan's life. Gauze, bandages and alcohol could only do so much. Nathan needed a surgeon in a sterile environment with the right equipment.

Ralph Hayward was waiting for them at the Phoenix's airlock. The giant Earther provided them with cover fire, cutting down any persistent pursuers.

Once they were on board, Koble rushed ahead and yelled to Vol in the cockpit;

"Get us the hell out of here! Comms the 'wealthers, tell them we need an emergency medical team over here!"

As he and Russell carried Nathan to the living area, Harrt felt the unmistakable whir of the Phoenix's engines. When Harrt's eyes settled on Gordon Taggart, he felt a rush of anger. Despite everything going on around them, Gordon was still working to fix the droid. He'd placed the dead machine over the coffee table and was sealing something on the outer shell with a welding pen.

Harrt pushed back his sense of outrage —which wasn't easy— then called out:

"Get that thing off the table. We've got an emergency".

When Gordon turned around and saw Nathan, all the colour faded from his complexion. To Harrt, Gordon bore the look of a man who'd never witnessed violence before.

Typical Paradisian, he thought.

Despite Harrt's order, Gordon froze. Rather than waste any time, Koble shoved the droid off the table, ignoring any cries of protest from Gordon. They placed Nathan down in the droid's place, and for the first time, Harrt got a good look at the damage that Nathan had sustained.

The Earther was unconscious, and his blood was everywhere. What Harrt saw sent a chill down his spine. By his best estimate, it would be at least five to seven minutes before they'd dock with the Commonwealth ships, and Nathan didn't have that long. Harrt knew he had to do whatever it took to save his friend. He took a deep breath, willing his pounding heart to slow and for his mind to clear. After that, Lieutenant Harrt Oxarri shot into action.

He placed a hand on Russell's shoulder, then gestured to the bar; "There's a red medic pack in the third cabinet on the right. Bring it to me and bring me a bottle of strong alcohol".

Russell didn't even nod; he rushed to grab the supplies as ordered. Harrt then turned to Koble; "I'm going to need sheets: lots of them".

"You got it," Koble nodded.

When Harrt turned to Gordon Taggart, the older man seemed overwhelmed.

"I'm gonna need your help," Harrt rushed.

"Mine?" Gordon said in a shrill tone of voice.

"Yes, yours!" Harrt said, raising his voice. "You are a doctor, right?"

"I'm not that kind of doctor!" Taggart's eyes grew wide as he looked down at Nathan. "But I—"

Russell handed Harrt the medical pack, and before Gordon could formulate a full response, Harrt shoved the red bag into his chest. Harrt tore Nathan's shirt apart to gain access to the injury. The stab wound went straight through the Earther's chest to the other side. In addition, Nathan's breathing was weak and shallow, leaving Harrt to wonder if

Seig's sword had penetrated a lung.

To Harrt's surprise, Gordon seemed to jump into action. The older man yanked a heart monitor from the medical pack and attached its receivers to Nathan's neck, chest and wrists.

"He doesn't look too hot," Russell said as he peered at Nathan.

"He's lost a lot of blood," Gordon replied.

It felt like the doctor was stating the obvious, but Harrt didn't acknowledge it. When the heart monitor booted up seconds later, it beeped in line with Nathan's weak pulse. Harrt checked the medical bag for a bio-repair tool, but the one he found was for use on mild burns and cuts. There was nothing he could do to fix the gaping hole on Nathan's chest: *not yet anyway.* His only option was to slow the bleeding long enough for the Commonwealth medical team to arrive.

Harrt sensed his mouth becoming dry with panic as he yelled to Vol in the cockpit;

"What's our ETA with medical?"

"At least twelve minutes," she answered.

It was much longer than Harrt expected. He wanted to curse and swear, but he didn't have the luxury of time. Koble rushed into the room carrying a stack of a half-dozen towels. Once Harrt had one to hand, he placed it over Nathan's bloody wound and applied pressure.

"He's going to need a blood transfusion," Gordon said.

As the doctor rolled up the sleeves on his shirt, Koble's stare bounced between Nathan's injury and Harrt. It was the first time that the Sphinax had looked visibly terrified in the time Harrt had known him.

"I'm no medical expert, but don't you Earthers have weird blood?" Koble said. "This one time Jack—"

"I don't wanna hear about Jack-bloody-Stephens," Gordon interrupted. He snatched the medical pack from Harrt and, after some rummaging, removed a needle and tube from the bag. "Back on Earth, they would've called me a universal donor".

The term meant very little to Harrt, but he understood

the gist. Whatever it was that Gordon wanted to do, it was better than nothing. The doctor began to pierce the skin at his forearm, hoping to place the needle inside his vein and syphon off his blood. Just watching the act made Harrt feel queazy.

All of a sudden, the heart monitor produced a long continuous note. The regular pulsing noise that had been there before was now a single, droning note.

Nathan's heart had stopped beating.

"No!" Koble shook his head as he looked at the flatlining monitor.

As much as he wanted to, Harrt didn't say a word. Koble looked emotional, and Gordon was bewildered. Experience told Harrt that someone had to stay in control of the situation, and as always, it had to be him.

Gordon handed the needle and tube to Harrt and moved to Nathan's side. Initially, Gordon wore a bewildered expression, which Harrt could only liken to that of an inexperienced greenhorn on their first mission, but then Gordon's face shifted. His brow lowered, and his jaw tensed, and after a deep breath, he got to work.

Harrt, Russell and Koble watched in silence as Gordon attempted to save Nathan. He applied firm compressions to Nathan's chest.

"Cmon, Cmon!" Gordon yelled. "I made a promise to the old man, don't you dare die on me now."

None of it worked. Nathan Carter's skin was pale, and his lips were starting to go blue.

Death had taken him.

Harrt looked to Koble, but the Sphinax didn't make eye contact. Gordon continued to apply cardiopulmonary resuscitation until Harrt placed a hand on his shoulder.

"It's over," Harrt swallowed a lump in his throat. He didn't want to believe the next thing that came out of his mouth, but he knew it needed to be spoken aloud. "He's gone."

The doctor reluctantly halted his efforts, and a look of disappointment came over him. For several uncomfortable seconds, Gordon stared at his blood-soaked hands. With a disheartening sigh of defeat, he stepped away from the table.

Harrt turned to look at Koble, and he found the Sphinax slumped against the wall, with his giant paws resting on his head. Russell remained stoic, but it was obvious that it was the first time he'd seen someone that wasn't a Revenant die.

For a while, there was a mournful silence that seemed immeasurable. Time seemed to slow down, and Harrt wasn't sure if it was a sign of his brain trying to process what had happened or if he was simply overcome with mourning. Everything other than the moment at hand seemed so trivial.

When Vol entered, her eyes widened at the sight of Nathan's bloody remains. At first, the Uvan didn't move, but she stumbled when she finally took a step forward. Harrt placed an arm around her shoulder for comfort.

"Damn it!" Gordon growled as he wiped Nathan's blood from his hands. "I'm sorry, Bill, I'm so sorry".

Harrt didn't notice what the doctor said. He didn't care. It took Harrt several minutes before noticing the blood staining his hands and shirt. After a minute or two, he let go of Vol and proceeded toward the bar to wash his hands. Clumsily, Harrt stubbed his toe on the lifeless Enkaye droid, still strewn across the floor. Harrt cursed, but the pain was only momentary and didn't compare to the overwhelming sense of loss that he felt.

As warm water met his skin, Harrt looked over his shoulder and allowed himself to wipe away a tear. While he splashed his face with water, Harrt became aware that Vol was questioning Koble.

"What the hell happened?" she said, stifling a sob. "Where's Astrilla?"

At first, Koble answered with silence. Harrt imagined the Sphinax slumping against the wall and shrugging with his meaty paws. When Koble replied, his voice sounded broken:

"Seig took her. Nate faced him and—"

Koble didn't finish what he was saying. Harrt heard a noise from The Sphinax that seemed somewhere between a gasp and sheer panic. Harrt assumed it was nothing more than Koble getting choked up by what had happened, so he continued washing his hands. It was only when a shrill and panicked yell came from Russell that Harrt turned around.

His eyes widened at what he saw next.

The Enkaye droid drifted slowly across the room. The previously dead ocular sensor on its spherical torso was emitting a pulsing white light. The droid floated over to Nathan's body and lingered above him.

Harrt's first instinct was to pull his gun, but something deep in his gut told him to wait. When he looked at everyone else, they seemed equally shocked.

Spider-like arms spilt from inside the machine's body, and the flashing light from its eye blinked at quicker intervals. Everyone watched in stunned silence as blue sparks filled the Phoenix's living area. A low hum came from the droid's torso, and the pulsing light in its eye intensified. Large bolts of something that looked like electricity whipped through the air.

Harrt resisted the urge to cover his eyes from the glare, but eventually, he gave in. The humming sound went from being uncomfortable on the ear to downright deafening. It felt as though the droning bass riddled tone was invading Harrt's ears and left him with a sense of being underwater.

A handful of seconds passed, and all of the chaos ceased. The blinding light faded, and the noise dulled, leaving a stark absence of sound which seemed alien in comparison. When Harrt opened his eyes, he saw the Enkaye droid emitting a gentle green pulse over Nathan's body. Unhindered by fear, Harrt stepped forward with his gun trained on the droid. The machine showed no sign of hostility. Once he was within a metre of Nathan's body, Harrt's eyes widened at what he saw.

Where seconds earlier, there had been a bloody stab wound, there was smooth, fresh skin. A healthy complexion returned to the Earther's face.

Nervously, Gordon reached out to check for a pulse, but the moment his hand got within a few inches, Nathan grabbed the doctor by the wrist. A look of animalistic hysteria set in on Nathan's face. Gordon yelped in panic, and Harrt jumped back in horror, but after a few seconds of heavy breathing, Nathan Carter calmed himself and released Gordon's sleeve from his vice-like grip.

"Harrt…" Nathan coughed, reaching out for him. "What happened? Where is she? Where is Astrilla?"

CHAPTER SIXTY-TWO

There was a sharp, icy sting to Nathan's veins that felt utterly alien, as though all the blood in his body had become citric. The sensation was mostly limited to his arms and legs, but every time Nathan moved his neck, he felt himself grow lightheaded. Rather than climb to his feet, he opted to remain seated in an armchair. Everything around him seemed to move faster than it was supposed to. Conversation between the others was muted, and the air felt somehow refreshing and heavy at the same time.

For an extended period, Nathan was sure that he was recovering from a loss of consciousness, but somehow he knew it was more than that. As his brain pieced together everything that happened aboard the Revenant warship, the realisation struck him like a moving ship.

He'd died due to his injuries.

He was dead.

For minutes he had no pulse, no brain activity, yet somehow, he was alive. His heart was beating again, pumping new blood around his body as though he'd never lost any in the first place. Nathan recalled being stabbed in the chest by Seig, so much so that when he focussed his mind, he could still felt the cold steel cutting into his body. Despite the false sense of lingering pain in his chest, there was no injury. Where there had been a gaping hole, there was healthy skin.

When the 'wealther medical team came aboard, they

checked his vitals and ran several scans. Everyone aboard the Phoenix seemed to gasp in unison when the chief medic said;

"There's no sign of any blood loss."

Vol and Russell exchanged a look of confusion while Harrt and Koble questioned the medic. Nathan heard the pair say things like *that's impossible,* and, *are you sure?*

It took Nathan a while to comprehend what exactly had happened after he'd lost consciousness, but eventually, he made sense of it. Doctor Taggart had fixed the Enkaye droid, and for one reason or another, the machine had revived him: *how that was even possible was up for debate.*

Doctor Gordon Taggart wasn't what Nathan expected at all. He didn't look like the kind of guy that would take a swing at anyone, let alone Jack. Gordon was a tidy man with a well-trimmed beard and thick-framed glasses that lent well to his age. He was an inch or two taller than Nathan, but there was no sign of muscle or athleticism at all. He looked like the kind of seasoned Earther who —in another life— could've been a university professor. For a long time, Gordon didn't say anything to Nathan. Instead, the older man sat at the bar, switching his attention between the droid and Nathan.

When the medics packed away their gear, Nathan heard Koble raise his voice. When Nathan turned, he saw the Sphinax pointing angrily at Ralph Hayward, leaning against the bulkhead.

"Why the hell didn't you help us?" Koble growled. "If you'd have helped us aboard that ship, we could have stopped Seig. Now he's got the girl."

Hayward moved from against the wall, unfolding his massive arms:

"I just brought a gun to a fuckin' knife fight," Hayward declared. "That was a fifty billion credit warship that Jareth Corps sacrificed back there. So don't for one minute—"

"What about all the people that died?" Vol cut him off.

Nathan noticed that Koble's tail was swinging in a side-to-side motion that indicated agitation. It was obvious that Koble was a breath away from striking Hayward.

Emotions were at an all-time high, and Nathan knew the Sphinax well enough to know that he'd act on impulse. Nathan was about to dissolve the situation, but as he moved to stand, Agent Leviticus Dines entered the room.

It was clear from the careworn expression on his face that Dines was not having a good day. His once well-groomed silver hair was messy, and dark bags filled his otherwise youthful eyelids.

Suddenly, the tension in the room tripled, and Nathan wasn't sure why. Harrt stood ready to offer a salute to the Agent, but Dines didn't seem bothered by protocol and instead waved a hand in decline.

"Hope I'm not interrupting something here?" Dines said, peering at Koble and Hayward. "I'd hate to call the marines down here to break up a fight".

Koble eventually stood down, but only after he spent a few seconds glaring at Hayward. After a moment of silence, Dines looked at Nathan then at Harrt;

"Seig's got her, hasn't he?"

"Yeah," Harrt nodded before Nathan could respond. "They got her".

Leviticus Dines swallowed a lump in his throat; "I need to inform High Command. Once the Revenant power-up the Messorem, they'll likely attack the Capital Worlds".

"So, that's it?" Nathan said, his voice hoarse. "Final stand at the Capital Worlds?"

Dines brow lowered, and he lifted both hands as if to question him. "You got any better ideas, Captain Carter?"

"We've got three pieces of the Omega and an updated map to the next piece," Nathan replied, pointing at Astrilla's satchel. Just seeing the Evoker's bag made Nathan's stomach knot.

"How the hell do you hope to get anything Enkaye to respond without Astrilla?" Dines said with a degree of futility. "She's the key to operating their tech after all".

The silver haired 'wealther was right. The symbiotic relationship between Enkaye tech and Enkaye operator was essential. Without Astrilla's presence they'd be unable to activate the technology.

Gordon Taggart stood from his seat, and raised his palm, "That's not necessarily the case.."

Nathan turned his head to look at the doctor, noticing the unusual accent that sounded like a blend of American, English and something else.

"I think our droid has proven he is more than he appears," Gordon pointed at the floating robot that casually lingered around the room. "It is undoubtedly of Enkaye origin, and I'm confident that it could interact with their technology".

For a moment, Nathan was sure he saw the droid stop and turn to face Gordon — aware that someone was talking about it.

"That droid looks pretty unremarkable to me," Dines shrugged. "You honestly expect me to believe that thing is capable of complex tasks?"

"Believe me, pal, if you saw what we just saw, you'd be quaking in your standard-issue 'wealther boots," Vol cut in. "We just witnessed that little guy perform a miracle".

Dines appeared to disregard the Uvan's statement and turned to Harrt:

"We're going to need every ship we can get to defend the Capital Worlds," Dines said, before turning to Harrt. "Lieutenant Oxarri, I want you to take command of this ship and join us at the Capital Worlds".

Who the fuck do you think you are? Nathan thought before he could say it aloud. *I'm not letting some communist stake a claim on my ship or my crew.*

Before Nathan could offer his protest, Harrt beat him to the punch:

"Leviticus, you and I have known each other for a very long time, so I need you to trust what I'm about to say," Harrt stopped and waited for Dines to nod. After the Commonwealth Agent reluctantly agreed to hear him out, Harrt pointed at the droid: "Today that thing performed a real-life miracle, and you know I don't normally say things like that."

"What's your point?" Dines replied cynically.

"I can't explain it, but I know that something is guiding

us toward the Omega," Harrt answered. "We need to see this through, with or without Astrilla".

Nathan climbed to his feet and focussed his gaze on Dines.

"You ain't staking a claim my ship," Nathan said, looking at Dines. "So whether you agree with Harrt or not, we're going to the next location and finding the Omega".

A tension fell over the Phoenix's living area. Nathan didn't care if he'd insulted the 'wealther: nobody was taking his ship or his crew. There was an absolute clarity that came with death and resurrection that told Nathan he had to keep those he cared about safe, and that included the Phoenix Titan herself.

To Nathan's surprise, Agent Dines seemed to brush away his outrage and turned his gaze to Harrt:

"You really believe this, don't you?" Dines waved his index finger in a circular motion. "All of this is happening for a reason?"

"I do," Harrt nodded. "I swear on the Founders of our great Commonwealth that this is something we have to do. The Omega is the key. It's like all of this is happening for a reason. I don't think any of us can explain it, but we know it's there…"

Harrt trailed off when he realised that the Agent wasn't listening. Dines pulled his datapad to check a message. At first, Nathan assumed that the Agent was dismissing everything that Harrt said, but he was proven wrong. Leviticus Dines looked nauseous as he read from his datapad.

Nathan recognised the expression of horror on the 'wealther's face.

"What is it?" Nathan asked.

When Dines was finally able to fathom a cohesive sentence, he could not hide his state of alarm:

"Revenant forces are dropping out of FTL near the Capital Worlds," Dines stammered as he scrolled back through the report. Warily he lifted his head and stared at Harrt; "If you swear on the Founders that the Omega is the key to stopping that mad Revenant bastard, then I believe you".

As soon as Dines finished speaking, he started heading out of the room, only to be halted by Harrt;

"What about you?"

Dines looked over his shoulder, and with a steely look in his eyes, answered; "I'm taking my ship to the frontlines".

Nathan watched the 'wealthers exchange a military salute. Before Dines left, Nathan climbed to his feet and nodded in Hayward's direction:

"Dines, can you take this guy with you? Maybe he can convince his boss to take some action".

Hayward chuckled and stepped away from the bulkhead. He squared up to Nathan, puffing out his chest in an attempt to look intimidating. It failed to elicit a single ounce of fear in Nathan: after all, he'd faced down the self-proclaimed King of Darkness. He'd seen death first-hand and lived to tell the tale. In comparison, Ralph Hayward was nothing more than a loyal gun-for-hire.

"What makes you think Mr Jareth has any concern with the Commonwealth's survival?" Hayward said.

Nathan squared up to the broad-shouldered American, refusing to break eye contact.

"Tell David Jareth that Seig has the means to power the Messorem. Tell Jareth that the enemy of my enemy is my friend".

Hayward considered it, then reluctantly broke away. As he grabbed his black jacket from the floor, Ralph Hayward said his farewell;

"I'll be seeing you around, Carter".

▲

With a refilled fuel tank and one less Jareth Corps employee aboard, the Phoenix Titan pushed away. Nathan stared out of the cockpit window at the Signet. The mile-long ship under Agent Dines' command peacefully floated amongst the stars for all but a minute. Once the Phoenix was clear of the hot-zone, the 'wealther warship spun up her FTL drive and disappeared into the slipstream.

It seemed strange to think that thousands of ships, just like the Signet, would be returning to the Capital Worlds at that very moment. Harrt explained that nobody had ever attempted an attack on the Capital Worlds. Ever. To strike at the single most defended system in the known universe was suicide, and yet Seig was doing just that.

He's confident, Nathan thought. *That means he knows how to use the Messorem.*

Once the Signet left the area, Nathan gathered the others around the holotable. He was about ready to address his crew, but the moment his mouth opened, his voice cracked. Rather than acknowledge it, Koble handed him a mug of black coffee. After sipping the warm, muddy contents of his cup, Nathan cleared his throat.

As if sensing that Nathan was about to say something important, the Enkaye droid drifted into the cockpit. It floated silently in the corner of the room like a peculiar mechanical voyeur. At first, he tried to ignore the strange machine's presence, but when he got around to contemplating what to say, he chose to embrace it:

"I guess I should start by extending my thanks to all of you. So, from the bottom of my heart, thank you". Nathan said, looking at each of the crew. He turned to face the droid and added, "That includes you too".

While the droid didn't acknowledge the sentiment, it didn't ignore it either. It simply floated in the corner of the room, watching everything that was going on.

Nathan turned back to the others and clapped his hands together; "So, let's take a look at the map and the Omega: let's find out where we are heading next".

Koble handed over Astrilla's satchel. Just holding the leather bag sent chills down Nathan's spine. Despite everything he'd done to protect her, Astrilla had fallen into Revenant hands. At first, Nathan felt guilty, but when he thought about the fact that he'd died trying to save the Evoker, a strange sense of absolution washed over him.

After rooting through the bag, Nathan pulled out the map and the third piece of the Omega. He unravelled the scroll, allowing the others to take a look at the updated star chart.

The next destination was an odd-looking star-system far beyond Commonwealth space. It sat in the desolate regions, where worlds were either ravaged by the war or completely uninhabitable. Nathan counted a single glowing star, along with a lunar body and nine planets, though one of them could have been a large moon by 'wealther standards.

At first, Nathan didn't recognise the location at all. The system was so far from civilisation that nobody would think to venture that far out. It was only when Doctor Gordon Taggart cast his eyes on the map that Nathan realised where they were heading;

"That's the Sol System," Gordon said, raising a brow. "I think your map is leading us to Earth".

CHAPTER SIXTY-THREE

Every Revenant pureblood is born in the Great Void. We understand what it is to feel fear. The cold, dark embrace of the river Prynn teaches us the value of true suffering, thus moulding us into instruments of its divine will.

As Seig stepped aboard the Messorem, he felt a great sense of triumph. Of course, he anticipated his own unevolved desire to validate his accomplishment, so he shut it down as quickly as it arose. Yes, victory was closer than it had ever been in history, but there was still much to do. Hubris and arrogance were a path to failure, and Seig wouldn't allow himself to fall into that trap like the many others who'd come before. Even when Astrilla was dragged aboard the Messorem and all the previously dead systems activated, Seig stifled any sense of achievement he may have felt.

Heavy restraints around the Evoker's ankles, wrists and neck kept her from lashing out. Two dozen soldiers armed with a mix of riot shields, electrified staffs, and non-lethal firearms forced her to walk through the vessel. The small army surrounded her in a military formation designed to escort a prisoner while keeping them at a safe distance.

With every step that Astrilla took, the Messorem's onboard systems activated. The overhead lighting began to switch on; control panels flickered to life, and oxygen regulators began to pump cool air. As the pack moved through the slowly awakening Enkaye ship, Admiral

Densius Olbori turned to Seig. The Maruvian turncoat bore a victorious expression, which to Seig felt grossly misplaced. There was no denying that Olbori had initially captured the Evoker, but it had been temporary. More to the point, most of the ships that Olbori took to Paradisium were either destroyed or severely damaged. Seig didn't appreciate the dramatic loss of resources in the slightest.

"I cannot express what an honour it will be to witness the downfall of the Commonwealth by your hand". The Grand Admiral smiled at Seig as he spoke: it left the King feeling angry at the arrogance emanating from the man.

"See that the rest of our forces are mobilised for the attack," Seig said, ignoring Olbori's boot-licking comment. "The first wave will only last a few hours; we need to be ready to strike".

The Maruvian hid his frown far better than he did his pride. Olbori respectfully bowed his head to Seig; "As you command your grace".

▲

Seig stepped into the Messorem's power chamber and immediately felt as though the conducting liquid watched him. Days earlier, the grey water latched onto him, and ever since, Seig hadn't felt the same. Despite sharing over eighty percent of the same chemical properties as the river Prynn, the conductor was something completely different.

In the briefest of moments, it told the Revenant king; *We shall resist.* It was a statement delivered free of fear and intended solely as a threat. Of course, Seig saw no reason to burden himself with worry. Yes, Enkaye technology was far more advanced than its modern-day counterpart, but it was nothing more than machinery. It still needed an operator: someone to tell it where to aim and when to fire, and that job now belonged to Seig.

As Astrilla walked into the power chamber, the lights flickered, and the air became thick and humid. Astrilla was led to a large metal platform, suspended high above the grey pool. Seig noticed the water begin to swirl as though it had a gentle current. For a heartbeat, there was the faintest hint of a shimmering light beneath the surface of the twisting water.

The Messorem was slowly waking up.

A chest-high podium at the centre of the platform served as the main power terminal. The moment Seig's guards forced Astrilla's hands onto the slab, everything switched on at once.

As one of the soldiers moved to restrain her, Astrilla resisted. Defiantly, she struck one of the guards with such force that he fell from the platform. When the Evoker turned her attention to Seig, the Revenant king saw the look of hate on her otherwise delicate human features. It was obvious from her gritted teeth, flared nostrils and rage-filled eyes that she wanted to kill him. Even with all the odds so heavily stacked against her, Astrilla resisted. In a way, Seig found it admirable, but the reality was that her defiance was futile.

Before Astrilla could summon an attack, a kingsguard struck her in the neck with an electrical staff. The Evoker fell to her knees and writhed on the floor, and her screams filled the room.

"There's no point in resisting, my child," Seig said as he knelt beside her. "This is the way it is meant to be".

"You cannot win, Seig," Astrilla shook her head. "My friends will stop you".

The guards dragged the Evoker to her feet and once again restrained her hands against the stone podium. A noise followed that sounded like a wild animal howling in the night. At first, Seig assumed it was Astrilla, but he quickly realised it was the Messorem.

Thick steam began to rise from the water below, and the walls glowed red. The howling seemed to shift, and when Seig turned his attention to Astrilla, he realised that she was now the one screaming. Blue sparks of electricity wrapped around her weak, human frame as the Messorem awoke. For the first time in thousands of years, the Enkaye's greatest weapon was alive.

Finally, everything is in motion, Seig thought.

He waited for the Evoker to cease her feeble cries, but

they only seemed to dull to a whimper.

"Your friends are inconsequential now," Seig hissed.

Even with all the agony that she was suffering, Astrilla looked at him with the same hateful expression. It was still admirable. Seig stared directly into her angry human eyes;

"Once I have completed my holy mission, I will release you from this life as painlessly as possible. I swear it".

Astrilla was not grateful for his promise. Instead, she seethed with the kind of fury and hatred that Seig associated with the reprehensible.

△

It was hard to ignore the difference that power made to the Messorem. Every system was fully operational, just as it had been during the days of the Enkaye dynasty: back when the little grey creatures would masquerade as gods. To think that entire religious orders had once been built around such charlatans made Seig feel disgusted.

Thanks to the river Prynn and the knowledge it shared, Seig knew the truth. He knew that the Enkaye were not the deities that so many believed them to be. Yes, they had once been the utmost dominant force in the galaxy, but superiority wasn't the same as divinity.

Like all creatures, the Enkaye's single greatest motivation was the continuation of their seed. In that manner, they were no different from any other primitive being and in Seig's eyes, there was nothing godly about it. Unlike the Revenant, the Enkaye did not serve a holy purpose: they didn't seek to rid the universe of all its chaos, even though they had the means to do so. The Messorem and the river Prynn were a testament to that fact.

Seig peered around the command centre as the bridge officers reported operational systems. When the final one called out, Seig allowed himself to smile, albeit for a heartbeat. The Messorem was fully functional and ready for its first firing test. The FTL drive spun to life, and the ship lurched into the slipstream.

My forerunners built devices of great power, but they did not possess the courage to use them. I possess that which they lacked, and I will bring order.

△

Despite her many years as an engineer and pilot, Vol had never grown entirely accustomed to FTL travel. It seemed strange to think that the Phoenix could fly past entire systems in the time it took to draw breath. Vol always assumed it was because the mind hadn't evolved to a point where it would unconsciously comprehend the high-speed and sudden shift in gravity, but after reflecting on Nathan's death and subsequent resurrection, she realised that it was something far more simple. There was no forward motion to speak of whatsoever: no sense that the Phoenix was moving at all.

For a long time, Vol pondered how she could've missed something so glaringly obvious. At first, she wanted to believe that she'd been naive, but the more Vol wondered, the more she realised the truth. Seeing a close friend die had changed the way she perceived the everyday. Death had that effect on people. They would evaluate the norm and perhaps see things from a new perspective: Vol knew that fact from first-hand experience.

Although Nathan had lived —thanks to the droid— he'd still died, and Astrilla was now in the hands of the Revenant. The whole thing served as a stark reminder of just how dangerous the mission was. People could die —people had already died— and many more would follow if they failed. For a time, Vol sat in quiet contemplation, debating the complex subject of mortality. She became so wrapped up in her thoughts that she barely registered the distinct fish-like aroma emanating from Koble's bowl. Vol wasn't sure how long the Sphinax had been sitting there, but she guessed it wasn't much, based on the steam still rising from his dish.

"Crazy couple of hours," Koble remarked before shovelling a spoonful of fish into his mouth.

"You can say that again".

"I've seen some crazy shit in my time, but everything that just happened is... kinda freaky," Koble continued, his voice nostalgic and reflective. "I mean... Nate was dead — like *really* dead. People don't just come back to life after being stabbed through the chest".

Vol shrugged with her hands and continued looking out at the slipstream; "Maybe we underestimated the droid's capabilities".

Koble raised a finger, readying himself for a reply, but someone else beat him to the punch;

"Or perhaps the droid wanted you to underestimate it".

Vol turned to the back of the cockpit, where Gordon Taggart lingered. He stared at them through his dark-framed glasses without a readable expression: though Vol could still hear a flicker of his thoughts.

"Why would it do such a thing?" Vol asked.

Gordon opened his mouth, ready to answer her question but stopped himself as if to consider his words carefully.

"In my years of study, I've learnt that Enkaye technology is not as it appears," Gordon said. "Perhaps the droid needed to be sure it could trust us?"

"You think it's capable of that?" Koble mused.

Vol could feel Gordon brush aside a superstitious thought: as though his inner-critic was filtering the absurd from the plausible. The word, *yes,* ambled on Gordon's tongue, but to Vol's surprise, he didn't say it. Instead, the doctor rubbed his hands together and awkwardly changed the subject:

"Which cabin belongs to the captain?" Gordon asked.

Vol suddenly sensed Koble's thoughts halt, and there was a moment of panic, which he quickly concealed the moment his eyes met hers.

"W-why? Koble stuttered but covered it with a cough. He repeated the question, "Why?"

"I was thinking it's about time I had a chat with him," Gordon replied, folding his arms. "Is that okay with you?"

An awkward silence lingered between the two men,

which only raised Vol's suspicions. Koble's jaw tightened, and his tail flicked from side to side.

"No problem at all," the Sphinax said. "Nate's room is second on the right; next to the bar".

"Thank you," Gordon replied as he slowly backed away.

As Gordon left, Vol turned to Koble with her brow raised. She was about ready to question him, but she sensed a wariness from the Sphinax that told her not to ask. It was as though he were warning her not to get involved; that it was something deeply personal —something the Sphinax had never spoken aloud. When Vol delved deeper into his thoughts, she felt the promise Koble had made to himself, but it was indecipherable: like reading a book of blank pages.

CHAPTER SIXTY-FOUR

Nathan's body wanted him to sleep, but his mind refused. For what felt like hours, he laid in bed, staring at the ceiling, willing his mind to not imagine the horrors Astrilla was facing. Of course, it was inevitable that his thoughts would conjure up the darkest of images, so Nathan eventually gave up his attempt to sleep. As he climbed from the bed, Nathan embraced the horrible realisation that Astrilla was now in the hands of the enemy.

He took up the armchair in the corner of his cabin, with a shallow glass of liquor to hand. As he stared around his empty room, Nathan felt as though he was aboard an entirely different ship. Somehow the Phoenix didn't feel the same as it had the morning prior. Maybe it was the intensity of the last few hours that made his room seem so unfamiliar, but in his heart, Nathan knew it was much more.

Astrilla wasn't there. She'd sacrificed herself to keep him alive, even though he'd suffered a fatal injury. It was an act of bravery that was so unquantifiable that Nathan knew she'd done it out of love rather than logic.

Love; just thinking about it made Nathan's chest ache. There had never been room in his life for such luxury, and yet there it was. Nathan recalled a thought that ran through his mind before death;

If I was given a second chance, I'd tell her how much she meant to me.

He felt a sense of shame and anger and something

more complicated that wasn't ready to be put to words. King Seig had taken her, and there was nothing that could be done about that now. There was no point wallowing in failure or assigning blame. All that remained was to take action and get her back. The only option left was to go to Earth, find the Omega's final piece, and hope that it would somehow stop Seig.

For five minutes, he sat in quiet contemplation, wondering what awaited at Earth. A gentle knock came at the door. Before climbing to his feet, Nathan kicked back what was left in his glass and set it down. He didn't want the others thinking that he was drinking away his worries, like some pathetic old drunk.

When Nathan opened the door, he found Gordon Taggart on the other side, clutching a old duffle-bag. The old man studied him from the doorway for all but a heartbeat, then after clearing his throat, he spoke;

"May I have a moment of your time?"

For the first time, Nathan took note of Gordon's appearance. The doctor seemed somehow familiar, but Nathan could be sure why. Somehow Gordon reminded Nathan of a simpler time: before the Fall.

Nathan invited him into the cabin and the first thing Gordon did was shake his hand.

"I thought I should introduce myself properly," the doctor smiled nervously. "I must say, you certainly don't look anything like Jack".

Gordon's observation came as no shock to Nathan. He and Jack and James shared zero resemblance at all. Back in the day, many would assume that there was no relation between them at all. Jack often compared Nathan's looks to his father and his personality to his mother. The truth was that Nathan could barely remember either of his parents. Regardless of Gordon's comment, Nathan still felt compelled to understand the doctor's history with Jack. After all, anyone who could throw a punch at Jack Stephens and get away scot-free must've had a story to tell.

"When your name came up at Mirotose Station, Koble mentioned that you knew Jack," Nathan said.

"Did he now?" Gordon murmured thoughtfully.

"He said you two shared a history; said you knew Jack before the Fall," Nathan shrugged with his hands. "He also mentioned that you are one of the few people to punch my uncle and live to tell the tale".

Nathan took up the armchair opposite Gordon and watched the doctor's reaction. Gordon's dour expression didn't change, which under normal circumstances would put Nathan on edge, but something told him he could trust the man.

"That was a very long time ago," Gordon replied as he set his duffle bag on the ground. "The truth is I met Jack a few times on Earth, but I didn't know him particularly well".

"So you two didn't share a history?"

"Not quite," Gordon said, with a knowing smile. The doctor reached into his bag. He produced a wooden picture frame and passed it to Nathan. "I didn't know Jack well, but your grandfather Bill Stephens, I knew very well".

Nathan wasn't quite sure how to respond. He took the frame from Gordon and examined the photograph inside. The image showed a much younger version of Gordon Taggart —thick framed glasses included— standing beside his grandfather. Both men were grinning at the camera while dressed in white lab coats.

Nathan reclined in his chair and brushed away a stray piece of dark hair from his face. After such a long time, seeing a new picture of his grandfather filled him with an uncomfortable emotion that he couldn't quite place: it was a misplaced nostalgia that was neither happy nor sad. The strangest thing of all was that Bill Stephens looked exactly as Nathan remembered: a tall man with a full head of thick grey hair, Hornrimmed glasses at the bottom of his nose, and a charming smile that couldn't be forgotten.

"Your grandfather was the best of men. He was both a mentor and friend to me," Gordon said wistfully. "We worked together for many, many years, right up until the Fall".

Something Gordon said triggered a memory in

Nathan's mind. It was the last time he'd seen Bill Stephens at the family home —the same day that Nathan snuck into his grandfather's shed and unearthed the only known photograph of his great-grandfather. That was the same day that his Grandpa Bill had offered Nathan some words of wisdom;

No matter how bad it gets, there is always a way to keep moving forward.

After everything Nathan had been through, those words meant so much more than anything Jack had ever passed on. *Keep moving forward* was far better life advice than *never let them see you bleed*. It also dawned on Nathan that his last memory of Bill Stephens was watching him get in a car with a young man in dark-framed glasses.

Nathan studied Gordon's face again, then referred back to the framed photograph as a benchmark for what a young Gordon looked like. Nathan wondered if perhaps Gordon was the same man from his memory, but it was impossible to be sure. Twenty-five years had passed, and the picture in his mind was the recollection of a child.

I can still wonder, Nathan thought.

Gordon produced a whisky bottle from his duffle bag and proceeded to unscrew the cap;

"You look a bit like Bill, you know," Gordon remarked as he poured himself a glass. He gestured at Nathan before adding, "Not so much the hair and beard. I imagine he'd tell you to have a haircut and shave".

Gordon offered Nathan a glass of the Paradisian whisky, and of course, he obliged. After gently sipping the copper-coloured drink, Nathan leaned forward;

"You could say that haircuts haven't been top of my agenda the last few years".

"I can certainly believe that," Gordon quietly nodded in response and matched Nathan's stance. "I heard that you were in the care of Jack many years ago. I can't say that Bill would have approved of the lifestyle, but life throws us these challenges, and we all must learn to adapt".

Nathan exchanged a questioning glance with the doctor.

"Jack did his best," Nathan replied, staring down into the shallow glass. "He was far from perfect, but he did what he thought was right".

"I'm sure he did," Gordon said, giving a half-smile that seemed forced.

Nathan wondered if the doctor felt as though he'd overstepped his mark. As it happened, he had, but Nathan wasn't offended at all. Still, he couldn't escape the feeling that Gordon knew more about Jack than he was letting on.

"Tell me something," Nathan said, placing his glass down on the arm of his chair; "What exactly was it that you and my grandfather did back on Earth?"

Gordon's eyes widened, and his expression conveyed a mix of confusion and excitement.

"You mean, Jack never told you?"

"Well, he always said that my grandfather was a scientist, but as you know, Jack wasn't exactly the chatty type".

Gordon removed the glasses from his face and proceeded to wipe the lens with the tail of his shirt. He took a deep, sobering breath;

"We were a part of a *unique* research group," Gordon answered. "Almost every government on Earth would call on our team to study unusual phenomena".

"You mean, paranormal shit?" Nathan leaned forward in his chair, almost knocking over his drink. "You realise just how fucking crazy that sounds, right?"

The doctor hid his amusement behind his glass as he nodded in response.

"I was more of a spectator to it all, to be honest," Gordon admitted. "Bill was the main draw. The rest of the team were talented, of course, but your grandfather had an exceptional mind that even to this day boggles me".

Nathan couldn't help his smile. Though Gordon's words were entirely different from Jack's, they both described Bill Stephens in the same way.

He was a fuckin' genius, Jack had said. *Smarter than any of us.*

Nathan listened to Gordon for the better part of thirty

minutes. He savoured the conversation as he did the Paradisian whisky. There was a strange familiarity to Gordon that Nathan wasn't expecting at all. For one reason or another, it felt as though he were speaking to a long-lost relative.

Gordon answered every question that Nathan asked: questions about his grandfather, Gordon's past and what life on Earth was like before the Fall. Unfortunately, there was one question about Bill Stephens that Nathan felt compelled to ask, and it filled him with dread;

"My grandfather was on a trip to Russia at the time of the Fall," Nathan said. "I was only a kid at the time, but I remember him getting in a car with a young guy wearing dark glasses. I assume that was you?"

Gordon stared at him thoughtfully, and said in a flat tone, "Yes".

Nathan continued, "A few days later, the Fall happened, and we never found out what happened to him…"

Gordon sighed, rubbing the corner of his eye with a thumb. He clearly knew what Nathan's question was before he even asked it.

"I guess what I'm trying to say is, do you know if he made it off of Earth?" Nathan said.

There was a long pause. Gordon necked what was left in his glass, then proceeded to pour himself another. He set his glass down, then with a sobering expression, answered;

"I'm sorry," Gordon shook his head. "Bill didn't make it off of Earth".

"Were you with him at the end?"

Gordon swallowed a lump in his throat and reluctantly nodded. The doctor's answer should have filled Nathan with sadness, but it felt somewhat like a relief. If Bill was anything like the man Jack and Gordon had described, he wouldn't have appreciated the retired life on Paradisium.

Sensing that their conversation had taken a downward turn, Nathan leaned back in his chair and changed the subject; "So, why do you think the droid saved me? Better still, how the hell did it bring me back to life?"

"I wish I knew," Gordon shrugged. "I've been researching the Enkaye since before you were born. I've never seen it do anything quite like that before".

Nathan leaned forward; "But you fixed that droid, and it resurrected me."

"I only did what I could," Gordon said, his voice growing defensive. "I removed all the broken components and replaced them with old computer parts and what little I had in my tool kit. That droid did the rest".

"Maybe we can question it," Nathan said, snapping his fingers. "When it activated back on Mirotose Station, it spoke to Astrilla, maybe—"

"It won't work," Gordon shut him down mid sentence. "Besides the fact, your Evoker friend served as some kind of battery for the droid, I was unable to salvage its processor and memory core. It won't remember a thing. Most of the components in that droid's head are from scrap parts I found on Paradisium".

"Are you telling me that thing has the brain of a calculator?" Nathan raised his brow.

"More like the brain of a U.S. submarine," Gordon tilted his head in mild amusement. "I had a friend at the Museum of Earth who wanted to trade some old clutter for a few books I had".

Nathan tried to switch off the part of his mind that compared Gordon to a modern-day doctor Frankenstein and took a large mouthful from his glass.

After Gordon finished his drink, he climbed from his seat and gestured at the frame in Nathan's hand; "Keep the picture; I've got another copy back on Paradisium".

"I appreciate that," Nathan said, placing it on his chest of drawers. "It's been good to talk with someone who knew my family before the Fall. I hope we can do it again if we make it out of this alive".

Gordon seemed to consider the invite, then nodded when he realised he'd taken too long to reply. As Gordon walked toward the cabin door, Nathan knew there was one more question he had to ask;

"Why did you punch Jack?"

Gordon stopped in his tracks, and his head lowered. Nathan couldn't see Gordon's face, but he could see the older man's shoulders drop an inch. Gordon didn't turn to face Nathan when he replied;

"That is a story for another day and another bottle".

CHAPTER SIXTY-FIVE

As Koble waited patiently in the living area for Gordon, he couldn't help but imagine Jack lingering at the bar. The look of judgement on his old friend's face was terrifying, and Koble forced himself to break eye contact with the hypothetical spectre. The truth was that Jack wasn't aboard the Phoenix Titan at all. At best, what Koble saw was a figment of his imagination and, at worst, a manifestation of his guilt. It wasn't a secret Koble wanted to keep, but preserving Jack's legacy and sparing Nathan the awful truth, meant more to him than he cared to admit.

Koble owed Jack his life, and for that, he'd protect Nathan from the truth. Jack was gone, and there was no reason to soil his good name. The problem was that Gordon knew, and he'd been alone with Nathan for over forty-five minutes.

Koble imagined Nathan's reaction to the truth. At first, the Earther would be angry enough to punch a hole through the bulkhead. Then he'd fall into a pit of despair, just like Jack would do. That was the best-case scenario. If Nathan were to find out that Koble had known the truth for as long as he had, bullets would likely fly.

When Gordon emerged from Nathan's cabin, his eyes met Koble's. Neither of them said a word until the door behind Gordon sealed shut.

"So, what did you tell him?" Koble asked.

Gordon's glare was cold and judgemental, with just a

hint of hatred. Koble knew that most of that was directed at Jack rather than himself.

"So that's what this is all about..." Gordon shook his head in disappointment, "You're still protecting Jack?"

"Just answer the question!"

To Koble's surprise, Gordon took a step closer to him and puffed out his chest aggressively.

"I told Nathan precisely what he needed to know," Gordon growled. "Fortunately for Jack, that didn't include any detail about what he did".

Koble's feline ears involuntarily pricked up at Gordon's response. It wasn't what he'd expected at all.

"You didn't?"

"Nathan doesn't deserve the weight of Jack's actions on his shoulders". Gordon started to walk around Koble, but he stopped, and with a low voice added, "Nobody deserves that kind of burden, including you, Koble".

Gordon's words clung to the air like a frosty chill. The weight of Jack's crime was more than Koble cared to admit. He'd shouldered the load for too long, but Gordon was right: Nathan didn't need to know the awful truth. Nobody did.

$$\triangle$$

It took Harrt just under an hour to do a full inventory of all the weapons and ammo aboard the Phoenix Titan. It should have taken thirty minutes, but he found himself distracted by the events of the last few hours. Knowing that his fellow citizens were laying down their lives to protect the Capital Worlds left his gut in a knot. In part, Harrt felt a measure of guilt for not following Dines to the field of battle. Every 'wealther would be doing their part to protect the freedom and liberty of the Commonwealth while he was counting missiles and pulse magazines.

Deep down, Harrt knew that his absence from the battlefield wasn't the only thing twisting his stomach. Coming face-to-face with the murderer of his family would distract the best of soldiers, but witnessing the death and sudden resurrection of a friend was completely and utterly alien.

Still, the Phoenix wasn't shy of ammo, and that was all that mattered —at least that was what Harrt told himself. The Sol System may have been devoid of life, but experience taught Harrt that trouble was around every corner. Knowing the ship was stocked and ready to fight alleviated some of the stress he felt.

After reloading the top and bottom gunnery chambers, Harrt stowed the excess ammo in the cargo hold. As he placed the final magazine down, Harrt heard the doors behind him hiss open. He glanced over his shoulder to see Nathan in the doorway clutching a cup of coffee, with his long dark hair pulled into a bun.

"Shouldn't you be resting?" Harrt said.

"I could say the same about you," Nathan replied, pointing his mug at Harrt. "You okay if we talk for a minute?"

Harrt hadn't known Nathan a long time, but he knew the Earther didn't ask permission to speak often. Whatever he wanted to discuss was serious: Harrt could feel it in his bones.

"What's on your mind?" Harrt said.

Nathan took a deep breath as he stepped into the cargo hold;

"Jack raised me to believe that all you 'wealthers were the same. He said that you want to control everyone and make them think what you think".

Perhaps it was a response to his years and years of patriotism classes at school, but Harrt anticipated that the following words out of Nathan's mouth would be a verbal attack on the Commonwealth. He involuntarily straightened up and lowered his brow and waited for Nathan's statement. By the time Harrt realised that he'd taken an aggressive stance, Nathan was already talking;

"My point is that while you and I disagree on a lot of things, we still found common-ground back on Yenex. I never thought I'd see the day where I'd break bread with a 'wealther, but here we are," Nathan said. "You stopped Seig from cutting my fucking head off, even though I was a deadman. I can never properly thank you for that".

Nathan's enigmatic expression hinted at regret, but it was impossible to tell.

Harrt hesitated. Then said, "You don't need to thank me".

"Yes, I do," Nathan's brow lowered, and the tone of his voice grew severe. "I need to thank you because I need you to know that I am not your enemy; I am your friend. I need you to know that because what I'm about to say could be controversial, and we don't need any drama".

Harrt shot him a puzzled glance, "What is it?"

Nathan slowly exhaled, and looked him hard in the eye. "Back at the Revenant ship, Seig told me that the Commonwealth planned to destroy Earth before the Fall. He said that Earthers represented a greater threat to the Commonwealth than the Revenant ever could".

Nathan's tone wasn't accusatory, so Harrt assumed it was a joke. He allowed the tension in his shoulders to soften, but when he realised that Nathan was entirely serious, he straightened up again.

"And you believed him?" Harrt narrowed his eyes and took a step back. "You believed Seig?"

"Normally, I wouldn't," Nathan said. "But David Jareth happened to say the same thing to me a few hours earlier".

"Seig is a monster: the same monster that destroyed your home, as well as mine," Harrt said, trying to mask his outrage. "As for David Jareth, he's not exactly the most credible source of information".

"Do you think there's any truth to it?"

For a moment, the tension in the air became so apparent it was practically palpable.

"No," Harrt replied with absolute certainty. "The Commonwealth protects other cultures. We do not destroy them, we defend them".

Harrt realised just how defensive he sounded and took a breath. Nathan stepped closer, and for a split-second, Harrt wondered if the Earther was going to react violently.

"Good," Nathan nodded, his voice milder than it was before. Then as if their previous conversation never happened, Nathan gestured at the ammo supply; "So, we all good if shit turns sideways?".

It was an unsettling contrast from their previous subject, but Harrt could tell that Nathan was equally as uncomfortable as him. As they discussed the weapons inventory, Harrt wondered if there was any shred of truth to what Seig and Jareth had told Nathan.

Of course, twenty-five years had passed since the Fall. Harrt would have been a cadet at the time, and he didn't run in the right circles to be privy to such information.

Then again, would I be entitled to such information today? he wondered. *After all, I'm just a Lieutenant.*

△

By the time the Phoenix was due to drop from FTL, the entire crew gathered in the cockpit. Vol and Harrt were at the helm while Gordon, Russell, and Koble stood around the holotable examining the Omega. As Nathan looked around the group, he realised that this was what a functioning crew was supposed to look like. Everyone, regardless of their differences was united.

An entirely new sensation of peace and security washed over Nathan: albeit for a heartbeat. Of course, it was exhilarating to feel like part of a team, but he couldn't fully embrace it: not while Astrilla was a prisoner to the Revenant king.

Minutes later, the Phoenix Titan erupted from the FTL slipstream. When Nathan glanced out of the window, the first thing he saw was the unmistakable glow of the sun.

As far as solar-bodies went, Sol was mostly unremarkable. Nathan had seen hundreds of stars since the Fall —everything from red giants to white dwarfs— but for one reason or another, he found himself entranced by the burning sun. It was strange to think that he was the first in his family to have not lived beneath its glow. Everyone from his parents to his distant, primal ancestors had thrived under its warm embrace.

The sight left Nathan with a thought that was unsettling yet undeniably beautiful: his existence was fleeting and insignificant when compared to the generations that came before him. Nathan had known his parents and grandparents, but he couldn't say the same for his great-grandparents. He didn't even know their names. It was with that thought that Nathan realised that one day nobody would know his name or who he'd been, but that was okay.

The moment passed, as did Nathan's sense of acceptance and was replaced by dread, as what remained of Earth came into view. The planet that Nathan once called home was a scorched husk with no oceans or identifiable continents. Most of Earth was shrouded in a blanket of black cloud. A deep crack spanned most of the southern hemisphere where the Revenant had siphoned the planet's core a quarter-century prior.

It took Nathan longer than he expected to digest the sight. He'd not seen his homeworld since the Fall, but then again, he had no reason to do so —nobody did.

"Well?" Vol said, looking at him over her shoulder. "Where are we heading?"

"I don't know," Nathan shook his head. "I've not had any dreams or seen anything since Seig took Astrilla".

As Nathan turned to check the scroll, he unexpectedly bumped into the Enkaye droid. He'd not been aware of the droid's presence at all, so when he nudged into the floating machine, it came as a surprise. The droid jerked to one side to avoid the impact, then prodded Nathan with one of its tiny mechanical hands. The droid extended its arm and murmured something indecipherable.

"Gordon? What is it doing?" Nathan said.

The doctor pulled off his glasses and approached the droid as it continued to wave its arm.

"I think it's trying to tell us something," Gordon answered.

The droid prodded Nathan again, then gestured to the window. He decided to humour its request and walked to the pilot's station. The droid attempted to vocalise something as it followed, then as if it were growing frustrated, shoved passed Nathan to the window. It knocked it's tiny metal hands on the glass, then buzzed again. Nathan was sure that Harrt would grab the droid out of sheer frustration, but the 'wealther must have seen something that Nathan couldn't. Harrt shifted the Phoenix's pitch, and a white lunar body came into view.

"Moon," the droid said, its voice calm and absolute. "Moon…"

CHAPTER SIXTY-SIX

It is the duty of every Revenant monarch to become the monster that the uncleansed fear above all else. The heretics will resist and will fight, but once the work is complete and order is forged from chaos, you will be their saviour.

The Ravow system was a small farming colony on the outskirts of Commonwealth space, comprising of two stars and six planets. Seig chose it because he knew that there would be little military presence in the area.

He was mostly correct. As predicted, the Commonwealth placed the survival of the Capital Worlds above all else. The politicians selfishly recalled their defences to protect the central nervous system —thus protecting themselves. This left a single Commonwealth cruiser to defend the Ravow system. Olbori estimated that it was likely staffed by a crew of eighty. The small vessel opened fire to no avail and was obliterated in seconds by the Revenant armada, leaving the Ravow System entirely undefended.

The Commonwealth's loss was Seig's gain.

The Messorem was operational, but the ship hadn't undergone a full field test. Seig decided it would be ill-advised to rush to the Capital Worlds without understanding the Messorem's offensive capabilities first. He set his sights on Ravow Three —the most populated of the system— and issued a command to fire the Messorem's orbital cannon.

Seig waited patiently beside Adrmial Olbori as the crew

carried out the order. Neither man said a word to the other, and Seig presumed that Olbori was overwhelmed by everything going on. The silence was broken when a tremendous noise erupted around them. It was a low roar like the sound of a million war-drums all being played at once.

Seig looked through the windows to see a prism of red light forming in the cannon. The mass of energy sparked violently in a way that reminded him of an untamed electrical storm. The mountain of savage fire and frantic lightning bolts grew to the size of a small planet. Then the wait was over. The streak of light that dashed toward Ravow Three was beautiful, haunting and vile all at the same time. Seig watched in awe as the spear of light poured onto the planet with unbelievable force. The fiery storm dispersed amongst the forests, oceans and cities like an unstoppable flood. Seig counted the time it took for the inferno to spread from one side of the hemisphere to the other.

Five heartbeats was all it took to snuff out six billion lives.

Seig was wordless. All he could do was marvel at the sheer magnitude of the Messorem. He knew that this unstoppable device would be the downfall of all those that would dare stand in his way.

"Before, I was divine. Now, I am a god," Seig whispered to himself. There was a stunned silence from the command crew, which Seig interrupted. He pointed toward Ravow Two and barked his new command; "Destroy it".

The corporal operating the weapons station nodded in confirmation, and Seig turned back to the view. The Messorem adjusted it's heading, and Seig watched patiently.

After thirty seconds, the King realised he'd been waiting for too long. He glanced at the corporal, who nervously hammered at his alarming console.

"Is there a problem?" Olbori barked as he moved to the workstation.

The corporal tapped at the screen frantically; "The weapon isn't responding, sir".

"Try again," Olbori snapped.

"It's not working, sir," the nervous man replied. "I've

tried everything, but it's impossible. It's as though the Evoker is resisting".

Seig loomed over the corporal, noticing the man's lower lip twitch nervously. The King didn't offer him a chance to speak his plea. In a single motion, Seig drew his sword and cut the corporal's head from his shoulders. The headless torso crumbled to the floor and a streak of blood splattered across the workstation.

Everyone, including Olbori, stopped in shock. Seig took a sobering breath, and handed his blood-soaked sword to a servant. He looked around at the concerned faces of the crew and shook his head in disappointment.

"I will not allow words such as *impossible* aboard this holiest of vessels," Seig bellowed. "I have already achieved the impossible. This ship is a testament to that fact. If anyone tells me otherwise, their neck shall meet my blade. Do I make myself clear?"

Silence followed. Nobody offered a protest. Seig turned to Olbori, who was checking the dead officer's workstation.

"Well?" Seig said impatiently.

"It appears that either the ship or the Evoker requires some cool-down time between shots," Olbori answered. "I can have the engineers take a closer look, but from what I can tell, we're looking at ten, maybe fifteen minutes between firing".

"That's not good enough," Seig clenched his fist.

"I agree your grace, but we must be mindful. We could risk killing the Evoker if we overuse certain functions," Olbori replied nervously.

"Then I shall go and loosen her sense of resistance," Seig said, gritting his teeth.

I am an instrument of the Great Void, destined to bring an end to the chaos and sin that plagues our existence. Nothing will stand in my way.

△

A full scan of the lunar body revealed nothing of interest, but Nathan's gut told him that this was where he was supposed to go. Harrt suggested taking the Phoenix in for a closer look, to which Nathan agreed. For five minutes, Nathan watched mile after mile of the barren moonscape pass him by. The Moon was a cold and eery wasteland; as devoid of life as it had been before the Fall.

A proximity alert buzzed at the pilot's station, and Harrt pointed at something on the horizon;

"What the hell is that?" he said, slowing the ship to one-quarter speed.

Nathan's eyes settled on a small metal structure nestled amongst the dust and craters. He initially assumed it was a piece of debris, but he recognised it as some kind of primitive spacecraft, held in place by four metal legs.

"Well, how about that..." Gordon marvelled. "Magnificent!"

Nathan narrowed his eyes at the strange metal husk, wondering how something so flimsy could operate in the empty vacuum.

"What is it?" Nathan asked.

Gordon's puzzled frown quickly evolved into a wry smile; "That is the lunar lander; this is where our people first walked on the moon."

As they neared the landing site, Nathan spotted footprints etched in the grey soil, each one as freshly cut as the day the astronauts made them. It was hard to ignore how enamoured Gordon was by the lunar module, and Nathan wondered if he should have felt the same way. Of course, where Gordon saw a monument to one of Earth's most significant achievements, all Nathan saw was an archaic space capsule and an old flag waving in a nonexistent breeze.

After passing the lander, the Enkaye droid began to gesture downward:

"We go here," it said. "We land. We dock".

Harrt and Vol exchanged a look, then Harrt shrugged; "What the hell, let's humour the little guy".

It was only when the Phoenix touched down that

Nathan realised the droid had halted them over a sizeable patch of smooth ground, unencumbered with craters or ditches. It was the perfect landing spot.

After flipping a switch on the command console, Vol spun her chair to look at Nathan;

"Well?" she said. "What now?"

All of a sudden, there came a rumble —too mechanical to be an earthquake. When the Phoenix began to descend, Nathan's suspicions were confirmed. The Phoenix had landed on a primitive docking platform. There was a tired creak to the machinery, which told Nathan that it hadn't been used for quite some time.

"I thought your people didn't have this kind of technology?" Koble said, peering at Nathan, Gordon and Russell.

"We didn't," Gordon said with a stark expression on his face. "This is quite unusual".

The docking pad came to a grinding halt with a loud screech. Lighting flickered to life, allowing them to see that they'd docked inside an underground facility.

△

Astrilla knew precisely when King Seig fired the Messorem's orbital cannon. There was a moment where the only thing she felt was torment. The agony was immeasurable. It felt as though a magnetic force was shredding the very essence of Astrilla's being from its rightful place. Her body wilted under the immense pressure of the Messorem's pull. Time ceased to pass and Astrilla hoped for nothing more than death: to submit to the nothingness toward which she was drifting. Then there was nothing.

When she regained consciousness, Astrilla found herself slumped across the stone plinth. Her hands were still tethered to the top of the podium, creating the circuit the Messorem so desperately needed to operate.

"Rise," someone said.

Astrilla lifted her head to see Seig staring up at her from beneath the platform. There was a certain savagery to the his expression, which left Astrilla feeling more terrified than she'd been previously. Before he'd looked reserved — in control of the situation. Now he looked like a man possessed by his own madness.

"The first firing test of the Messorem was a complete success," Seig said as he circled toward the platform walkway. "Six-point-five-billion lives snuffed out in the blink of an eye. Some would say that kind of power would only be matched to that of a god, wouldn't you agree?"

Astrilla refused to answer, knowing that the Revenant king was either trying to incite a reaction or feeding his ego. Seig had been a psychotic murderer with a lust power long before he'd obtained the Messorem. Now with an Enkaye warmachine at his disposal, the King had ascended beyond madness —beyond control.

As Seig walked up the ramp toward her, he spoke, and his deep voice reverberated around the room;

"Much like the Evoker Legendarium, our sacred texts refer to the Enkaye several times," Seig said, stopping within a metre of Astrilla. "Do you have any idea what killed the last Enkaye?"

Astrilla didn't dignify him with a response, but it didn't stop the King from continuing;

"It is said that after their dynasty fell, the last Enkaye settled on a primitive world. They were arrogant enough to believe they could create a new generation that would be devoid of that which caused the collapse."

"Is there a point to this?" Astrilla gritted her teeth.

Seig's expression hardened, and his jaw tensed. It was a very human reaction that Astrilla hadn't entirely anticipated.

"They tried and failed to procreate naturally. So, the Enkaye muddied their blood with the primitive creatures with whom they shared a planet." Seig took a step closer. "Thus creating new life, free of the sinful impulses that caused their downfall. My point is that you and I are not that different; in fact, I'd say we are the same".

"We are nothing alike," Astrilla spat, willing her body to break the shackles that bound her.

The Revenant king shot her a vindictive yet knowing smirk. Though it was only a twitch of the lip, the expression sent shivers down Astrilla's spine.

"You and I were assigned our roles long before we were brought into existence," Seig said as he circled her. "You, the conduit to this magnificent device and I, the rightful heir of the Enkaye's legacy".

Something that he said didn't sound right, and Astrilla replayed it in her mind. *How could Seig be the rightful heir to the Enkaye's legacy?*

Astrilla was the only one that possessed their DNA: she was the only one who could power their technology.

"I see it, you know," Seig hissed. "The chemical reaction inside your mind that is prompting the very emotion that blinds you from the truth".

Astrilla maintained eye-contact with the Revenant king as he passed in front of her, "What truth?"

The look on Seig's face didn't change.

"The truth that I and every Revenant pureblood are the true descendants of the Enkaye; the next generation, free of our ancestor's inclination for chaos," Seig said. "I am their heir, selected by the Great Void to purge the sin from this universe".

What he said was impossible. The Enkaye wouldn't do such a thing.

"You're lying," Astrilla shook her head. "They would never craft a monster like you".

Seig shot her a pompous smirk.

"How wrong you are," Seig said, his voice oozing with hubris. The King gestured to the swelling pool of liquid below; "The waters that flow beneath us are just like the river Prynn: just like the waters that gave life to my people. The same sacred river washes the heretics of their sin and creates my loyal warriors".

Astrilla pushed against the bindings that held her in place, willing them to break.

"I've seen that water on Paradisium," she seethed.

"Your sacred water is nothing more than broken technology. You are a fool to believe it's anything more than—"

Seig struck her with a backhanded slap that jolted her head to one side. Astrilla wanted to turn back to face him, but something inside her wouldn't allow it. She became aware of an unpleasant ringing in her ears, which served as a momentary distraction. The King grabbed Astrilla by the hair and yanked her back.

"If you dare speak ill of the Great Void, I will make your stay aboard this vessel far more unpleasant," Seig growled furiously then released his grip.

He stepped back, and Astrilla spat a mouthful of blood on the ground. She took a moment to consider what he'd said and realised that there was a gaping hole in the Revenant king's explanation. It was made more apparent the moment Astrilla said the words aloud;

"If you are a descendant of the Enkaye, why do you need me? Why is it that their machinery doesn't respond to you, Seig?"

His expression hardened as though she'd said something deeply offensive. For a second, Astrilla thought he would strike her again, but he did no such thing. Instead, Seig straightened up with a frown.

"Kings rise, and kings fall: it is that passage of time that has diluted that which makes me Enkaye". Seig turned and climbed down from the platform. He slowly walked to the floor below and looked up at Astrilla; "Simply put, you are more Enkaye than I am".

CHAPTER SIXTY-SEVEN

As Nathan stepped off the landing ramp, he found it hard to ignore the ghostly feel that shrouded the lunar facility. Most of the overhead lights had blown, allowing the darkness to cling to the walls. There was a certain stagnation to the air that suggested they were the first people to dock in a very long time.

Russell was the first to join him in the hangar. The young Paradisian handed him a torch that barely cast a metre of light ahead. The rest of the crew joined them seconds later, including the droid.

"What is this place?" Russell asked as they moved toward the entrance.

"I wish I could say," Gordon answered. "Our people had barely scratched the surface of space when the Fall happened; something like this cannot be ours".

Nathan tried his best to shut out the conversation and focussed instead on how they'd get through the giant metal doors ahead. Fortunately, he didn't need to think about it for long, as once they were within a few metres, the doors opened automatically.

What lay ahead wasn't what Nathan expected at all.

His eyes settled on a sterile, corporate-looking atrium. The vast room opened out onto a curved glass facade that went up for six storeys. A frosted glass staircase was suspended against the wall by several thick steel beams. A welcome desk at the left side indicated that the room had once served as a reception hall.

"Welcome to the United Nations Lunar Facility," Gordon read from a sign hanging above the desk.

"We had a Lunar Facility?" Nathan raised his brow in question.

"I guess so," Gordon shrugged.

"Why the hell would they hide something like this?" Russell said as he began rooting through the desk. "Do you think they were up to no good?"

"If you want to keep a secret, you hide it from everyone," Gordon said. "People always said the governments were hiding secrets from the public".

Nathan hoped that Gordon would expand on that point, but before he could say another word, Koble interrupted;

"Can we continue this trip down memory lane when we're off of the haunted station?" the Sphinax said. "This place gives me the creeps!"

After a sweep of the Atrium, the group proceeded to explore the abandoned facility. The first three floors were near-identical office spaces, each as prescribed as the last. When they reached the fourth floor, the droid beckoned them to follow. It pointed toward the east and said in a garbled, messy voice;

"We are close".

It led them through another office that was precisely the same as the others. The droid didn't stop and continued to lead them to a drab dead-end meeting room, complete with an empty water cooler and a dead plant. Once the entire crew stepped inside, the droid spoke again;

"Stand clear of the walls".

Suddenly the door behind them snapped shut, and the whole room began to sink downward with a hydraulic hum. It was so unexpected that everyone except Gordon drew their weapons in shock.

"It's okay," Gordon beckoned them to lower their guns.

The elevator descended past a long window that looked out onto the empty moonscape, then into a dark shaft. When it finally halted, the doors parted to reveal a decidedly different part of the Lunar Facility. The signage in the Atrium said that this was a research facility, yet it was all wrong. What looked like a waiting area furnished with chairs and leather couches faced a glass-enclosed military command centre raised several metres above the main floor.

As the others explored, Nathan's attention was drawn to the wall opposite him, where two seals were mounted high. The first bore the flags of Earth's mightiest nations arranged in a circle. At the centre were the words: *Earth Defence Alliance*. On the second, a complex carving made up the image of an eye looking over the Earth along with the phrase; *Novus Ordo Seclorum.*

"Earth Defense Alliance?" Nathan peered at Gordon.

The old man eyeballed the seal and shrugged.

"The EDA were a top-secret government agency; about as corrupt as they come," Gordon said bitterly. The doctor shifted his gaze back to Nathan; "Did Jack mention the EDA to you?"

"No," Nathan shook his head. "Should he?"

"Well, yes," Gordon replied. "He worked for them".

"When?"

"Back on Earth," Gordon said, as though stating the obvious.

Gordon's statement brought up a question that Nathan wanted to ask, but he wasn't sure if he'd like the answer. Jack had always been cagey and secretive about life before the Fall, and it left Nathan to assume that it was because his uncle didn't like talking about it. Knowing that Jack had worked for a *corrupt government agency* made Nathan wonder what kind of man Jack was before. Perhaps against his better judgment, Nathan pushed his questions to the back of his mind and focused on the task at hand.

He circled the room to what appeared to be a small television studio in the corner. A lighting rig was suspended from the ceiling, illuminating a podium and two flags. A blue curtain served as a backdrop, while a pair of old-cameras were trained on what Nathan assumed was a stage. Someone important was supposed to be there: to broadcast a message that had never been made.

What the fuck is this place? Nathan wondered.

Before he could speak his question aloud, Russell called out from the other side of the room in alarm;

"Guys!"

The sheer terror in the young man's voice was enough for Nathan to tell that something wasn't right. He drew his pistol and darted across an empty desk toward the sound of commotion.

Russell and Harrt had been exploring a room that looked like a computer centre, filled with rows of decommissioned monitoring stations from a by gone era. As Nathan neared, he saw the pair pointing their guns at something standing in the shadows. It was only when Nathan got to within a few metres that he saw the cause of their distress.

The creature was no taller than a child. It had a head that seemed out of proportion with the rest of its tiny frame, and its dark eyes were almost indistinguishable from the shadows.

It was a living, breathing Enkaye. More importantly, Nathan recognised the creature from the hologram on Paradisium.

"Put down your guns," Nathan said to the others. "He ain't gonna hurt us".

Nathan didn't wait for them to follow his order and instead approached the Enkaye with caution. The little creature didn't show any sign of emotion; it simply stood in waiting, as though it had been expecting them all along.

"Nathan Carter, I've been waiting for this moment for a very long time". The creature beckoned him to follow, "Come; we don't have much time".

△

The Enkaye walked with a limp that suggested age over injury: at least that's what Nathan could only assume. It slowly led the crew to a waiting room situated behind the television studio. There was a row of seats that had been fashioned into a bed. Every wall was covered from floor to ceiling in tally marks.

The Enkaye gazed at Nathan as it sat down; "You recognise me, don't you?"

There was a strange hint of surprise to the creature's otherwise monotone voice that Nathan found hard to ignore.

Nathan nodded, "You were the one on Paradisium that gave us the second part of the Omega".

There were no changes to the Enkaye's blank expression:

"My name is Moshia".

"How did you get here?" Vol said from the back of the room. "I didn't see any other ships on the way in".

The Enkaye blinked once. It was as though the tiny creature didn't —or couldn't— convey emotion: *perhaps the Enkaye had evolved to the point where the very notion of expression was redundant?*

"I have been waiting for you for a very long time," Moshia finally answered. "It is my purpose to provide you with the means of stopping the Messorem".

"You are talking about the Omega?" Gordon said.

The Enkaye blinked again before answering, "Yes, among other things".

Moshia tapped a control panel, and a pillar of green light formed at the centre of the room. Something emerged from the energy, but this time, it differed from the other parts of the Omega. A sharp blade engraved with a complex pattern appeared in the blinding light. It floated freely until Nathan took hold, then all the light surrounding it dissolved into the air.

He carefully examined the sharp foot-long piece of cold metal, realising that it wasn't a traditional blade at all. It was, in actuality, a spearhead, sharp enough to cut through stone.

"Let me get this straight, Nathan said, looking at Moshia. "You are telling me that we've done all of this for a spear?"

Moshia shook his head, "The Omega is a failsafe. It

will enable you to pass through the Messorem's defences unharmed".

"Are you saying this thing is a shield disruptor?" Gordon said, as he took a closer look.

"I shouldn't need to tell you of all people, Doctor Taggart, that our technology isn't all it appears on the surface," Moshia replied.

There was a moment of strange tension between Gordon and the tiny creature that Nathan noticed immediately. It was awkward, as though Moshia knew something that Gordon preferred to keep buried. The moment ended almost as quickly as it began, and Moshia turned back to face Nathan;

"Once you're onboard the Messorem, there is a room where they will be keeping Astrilla; this is where the ship draws the energy from her." Moshia interlinked his long grey fingers and sat back in his seat. "Inside the chamber, you will find a mechanism that works with the Omega. When the time comes, you will know what to do".

For a time Nathan wasn't sure what to make of Moshia's explanation. The whole thing sounded too simple.

"So, that's it?" Koble said boisterously, his loud voice reverberating around the room. "Break onto the Messorem and use the Omega to blow the thing to hell?"

"The Omega is the catalyst," Moshia answered. He pointed toward the next room; "In there, you will find the necessary data and weaponry to ensure the Messorem's destruction".

Nathan gestured to Russell and Vol to check it out, then turned back to Moshia. The Enkaye extended a hand, beckoning Nathan to come closer. He knelt down and Moshia reached out to him. It seemed like a strange, almost human gesture that was out of character for the stoic, unemotional creature. Then again, Nathan knew very little about the Enkaye: nobody did. Nathan took Moshia's hand, and the first thing he noticed was the warmth of his leathery skin.

"For me to fulfil my purpose, I must die here," Moshia said.

There was no fear in his voice at all, which only made what he was saying seem more sombre. Nathan wasn't sure if his frown was voluntary or not, and all he could say was;

"Why?"

"Whenever an Enkaye dies, there is a displacement of potent elemental energy. The Omega is designed to absorb that power. Mark my words; you will need it in the battle to come," Moshia answered. "Use what I have given you here to get Astrilla to safety and destroy the Messorem".

"I will," Nathan nodded.

Moshia turned to Gordon; "I sense you have questions?"

"More than I care to count," the doctor replied. "But there's two that seem most pertinent; I assume you already know what I'm going to ask before I say it?"

Moshia nodded; "My people built the Messorem as a response to the war we were fighting. We were on the verge of extinction, desperate to survive while fighting an enemy more powerful than you could possibly imagine."

There was a long pause before Gordon replied: "What about my second question?"

Moshia's answer came in the form of a nod and nothing else. Whatever it meant satisfied the doctor's curiosity. Nathan pretended not to notice Gordon pulling the glasses from his face to rub a tear from his eye. Whatever his second question had been, it was personal, and that was the sort of thing Nathan actively avoided.

"We don't have much time left," Moshia said, turning his attention back to Nathan. "You must assemble the Omega and place it in my hands".

Nathan looked to Koble, and the Sphinax hurriedly handed him his satchel. The four pieces of the Omega came together with an almost magnetic force. When combined, all four parts formed a spear, measuring around two metres in height. As Nathan held the surprisingly light weapon, he felt the metal warm to his touch.

He placed the staff in Moshia's hand, and the Enkaye looked at him with an expression that Nathan saw as acceptance.

"For a long time, I've known that yours would be the last eyes I would ever see," Moshia said. "It's strange now, knowing that my part of this grand plan is drawing to an end, but it brings me peace knowing that I've done my part".

Nathan saw something in the darkness of Moshia's eyes. It looked like a glittering white sand cast into a whirlwind.

"Use everything I have given you here to destroy the Messorem," Moshia said behind a shallow breath.

Gentle plumes of sparkling green mist rose from the Enkaye's glowing skin as his voice grew weak. The Omega's glow matched Moshia's illuminated skin. Tiny, ineligible symbols appeared on the surface of the blade and spread all the way down to Moshia's long fingers.

"He... He would be so proud of you," Moshia stammered.

Nathan's eyes widened at the statement, but before he could say a word, Moshia and the Omega were enveloped by a cloud of blinding white light. A terrible distorted scream followed for several seconds —loud enough to shake the dust from the walls.

Then there was silence.

The light cleared, and Nathan opened his eyes. Where Moshia had been, there was only the Omega.

Where there was chaos, there was peace.

It was the death of an Enkaye.

"Well, I didn't see that one coming," Koble drawled.

CHAPTER SIXTY-EIGHT

History said that the Founders never opposed religion, but they disapproved of the cultural divisions it created. In the dark ages, entire wars were waged over which Enkaye god to pray to. Logically, the Founders saw that as a waste of life and the first citizens were encouraged to open their minds to tolerance and open-mindedness.

Like all Commonwealth citizens, Harrt never believed in the supernatural. He was taught that there was no such thing as gods or destiny: that such notions were the by-product of old religious hokum. Despite his upbringing and education, Harrt couldn't ignore the feeling that something greater than he or the 'wealth was working. Everything up until that moment led the Phoenix and her crew to Moshia, and now it was pointing them toward the Messorem. Of course, all of it could be a coincidence, but that meant ignoring the impossible things Harrt had borne witness to.

Even if he wasn't a man of faith, he was certainly a man who believed in that which he could see or touch. To dismiss everything that had happened —and was happening — went against everything he stood for.

Nathan took up the Omega from where Moshia had been. The spear was still glowing but in a more restrained fashion than it had previously. Small symbols and markings appeared in the metal, and it looked warm to touch.

"What d'ya think we just saw?" Koble asked, his voice low and thoughtful.

Gordon shook his head with a bewildered look on his face. It said a lot that the foremost expert in the Enkaye didn't have a clue what they'd just witnessed . Harrt's next impulse was to look at Nathan for the answer, but he didn't know why. To his surprise, Nathan's expression was solemn but confident.

"Moshia sacrificed himself so that we stand a fighting chance," the Earther said. Then with a hint of determination to his voice, Nathan added, "C'mon, let's go see what data and weaponry he left us".

△

The next room was an empty armoury. Two of the four walls were covered in open gun racks, which lacked the weaponry Harrt was hoping for. There was a messy workbench covered in scraps of metal and rusty components that made the tidy 'wealther in Harrt cringe. There was a slightly outdated but working computer that Vol had hooked up to her datapad.

When Harrt looked closer, he saw three crates of Commonwealth military ammunition where Vol was resting her boot.

"Guess we can check ammo off our list," Harrt said, kneeling down beside her to examine the box. The consignment date on the crates went back over ten years, which caused Harrt to pause and wonder where they'd come from.

"That's not all," Vol nodded and she pointed at the computer screen. "That Enkaye has given us a full-blown schematic of the Messorem; check it out".

The Uvan wasn't exaggerating.

The diagram on the old dusty screen showed a detailed map of the Messorem, but it also highlighted two key locations. The first was situated deep inside the Messorem's lower levels, while the second was at the very top. Each of the two points was labelled: *power chamber* for the first and *detonation site* for the second.

Harrt stopped to consider, then he said something that seemed stupid but needed to be said.

"What the hell does he mean detonation site?" Harrt leaned on the workbench as he looked at Vol. "Did he expect us to——"

"Stop!" Gordon interrupted with a loud, terrified yelp. The doctor's complexion lost all its colour, and his mouth twitched in what Harrt could only assume was fear. The Earther stammered before gently insisting, "Harrt, Vol, you need to step away from the desk very, very slowly".

"Why?" Vol asked.

"That," Gordon pointed to the pile of shrapnel and wiring that littered the workbench.

Harrt noticed the doctor's hand trembling. When Harrt looked closer, he saw the cause of the doctor's alarm. The rounded piece of metal looked like a retired torpedo shell. It was painted a dark green and bore a series of symbols that Harrt couldn't understand.

Once Harrt stepped aside, Gordon moved in and began examining the metal device. There was a tension to the doctor that nobody else seemed to understand, which put Harrt on edge.

"What the hell is it?" Nathan asked.

Gordon didn't answer immediately, and when he turned around, he had to force himself to take a breath.

"Well?" Russell said, trying to hurry an answer out of the doctor.

"It's a bomb," Gordon said, nodding his head nervously. Gordon twitched a couple of times, then after composing himself, "It's a nuke".

Nathan visibly stepped back, as did Russell. Harrt noticed that Koble and Vol didn't react in the same way, which suggested the term *nuke* was some kind of Earther slang.

"Whats a nuke?" Koble asked, raising his paw in question.

"You serious?" Russell barked in panic. "Nuke, as in nuclear bomb; as in we gotta get the fuck outta here before that thing blows up".

The Sphinax visibly tensed, and Vol backed away from the workbench. Every fibre of Harrt's being wanted nothing more than to run, but something in his gut told him that this device was just another part of the journey.

"Detonation site," Harrt pointed at the onscreen schematic. "I think Moshia wanted us to plant this bomb on the Messorem".

"An Earther-made weapon versus an Enkaye war machine?" Koble said sceptically. "That's like going after a Revenant hunter armed with a pen; it'll barely make a dent".

"Maybe," Nathan said, pursing his lips in contemplation. The Earther silently turned to Gordon and gestured at the bomb, "Can you check out the components inside that thing?"

"Are you seriously asking me to open the shell of a nuclear bomb?" Gordon replied as though what Nathan was proposing was insane. "Do you know how utterly ridiculous that is?"

"That's precisely what I'm asking," Nathan nodded. "Astrilla was right all along; all of this is happening for a reason. I dunno why, but I get the feeling that bomb is something we are gonna need".

Gordon turned to the bomb and muttered something incoherent, likely an Earther curse word. He carefully placed a hand against the metal shell of the nuke and sighed. Then as though he'd squashed all his fear to the back of his mind Gordon grabbed a tool from the workbench and got to work.

$$\triangle$$

It took Gordon less than ten minutes to dismantle and remove the front nose of the nuke. After which, he scanned the contents of the weapon using his datapad. At first, Vol wondered why he hadn't simply run scans before removing the heavy metal faceplates, but when she took a look at the innards of the bomb, it all made sense. Amidst the primitive Earther components, there were pieces of Enkaye technology.

"Is that what I think it is?" Vol peered at Gordon, and the old man took a step away.

"It most certainly is," Gordon mused. "Moshia must have retrofitted this thing with his own parts".

"Why would he do that?" Nathan said from the back of the room.

"I'll need to examine it closer, but I think he made it more powerful," Gordon replied with certainty.

"Powerful enough to take out an Enkaye warmachine?" Vol asked.

Gordon looked at the bomb, then back at her;

"I think so".

△

Once the nuke was stowed aboard the Phoenix, they gathered in the cockpit and congregated around the holotable. There was a nervous stir amongst the crew, which Vol tried to ignore.

She loaded the Messorem's schematic to the holotable, the detailed plan was projected in holographic form, including Moshia's annotations. The Messorem was — according to Moshia's data— almost the same size as the very moon where the Phoenix was docked. The engineer in Vol wanted to quantify the energy required to power such a thing, but just imagining those numbers gave her a headache.

The crew stared at the hologram, and for a long time, nobody said a word. Despite the lull, Vol could still hear the others anxious thoughts and worries. The silence was broken by the chime of Harrt's datapad. The 'wealther checked the screen, then sighed through his nostrils.

"Three more Revenant armadas just entered Capital World space. According to Dines, that brings the total number of hostile ships to over a thousand," Harrt placed his datapad down and sighed.

"Well, if that's where he's taking the Messorem, then that's where we're heading," Nathan said.

The Earther placed his hands against the edge of the holotable and keenly examined the projection. Nathan bore the look of a man who was no stranger to plotting and planning; it seemed natural. He adjusted the hologram, rotating and zooming in on the key locations. Then after a few seconds, he circled an area that looked like a hangar. Finally, after a few seconds of mulling over his scheme, Nathan looked back at the crew;

"I don't think any of you are gonna like it, but I think I've got a plan".

△

Not that long ago, Nathan would've said that the plan was stupid, but of course, the *old* him hadn't seen or experienced the things the *new* him had. In his mind, Nathan saw the logic and reasoning behind what he was proposing. The fact was that everything since the Vertex had happened for a reason.

Maybe David Jareth was right; perhaps Nathan was supposed to *avenge the people of Earth,* but he knew it meant more than that.

His plan was simple. It was also bat-shit-crazy, but Nathan tried his best to shut out the part of him that clung to his old self. He was no longer that man. While Gordon ran checks on the fully assembled Omega, Nathan outlined the first phase of his scheme: getting aboard the Messorem. Effectively, Harrt or Vol would pilot the ship and allow the Omega to disrupt the shields, just as Moshia said it would. Nathan saw the look of doubt on Vol's face from a mile away, but when Gordon confirmed that the device was as Moshia told them, she relaxed, albeit slightly.

The second phase was arguably more dangerous than flying head-first into a shield network.

"Two teams," Nathan said after clearing his throat. "Team one takes the bomb and plants it at the detonation site".

"Whoa, whoa, whoa," Koble waved a paw in

disagreement. "Why can't we just get Astrilla out, then throw the bomb in the torpedo tubes? Y'know fire that bad boy from the safety of space?"

Nathan readied himself to answer, but Gordon beat him to the punch;

"I can say with absolute certainty that we Earthers didn't design our warheads for outer space". The doctor pointed at one of Moshia's annotations; "And of course, our Enkaye friend marked this spot for a reason, right?"

"So you're saying this thing needs to be detonated from the inside?" Koble said. Gordon nodded in response. "Peachy, just freakin' peachy!" Koble muttered. After twiddling one of his whiskers in quiet contemplation, Koble lowered his paw and nodded to Nathan to continue.

"While Team One takes the bomb to the top, Team Two goes to the power chamber and grabs Astrilla," Nathan folded his arms. "I'd like to be the one to get her if there are no objections?"

"I'll come with you," Vol said. "It may take two of us to get her out".

Nathan wanted to say no, but he couldn't argue with her logic. If Astrilla was injured, it could take one to carry her while the other led the way.

"Fine," Nathan nodded. He turned to the others, "I guess that makes the rest of you Team One".

"Why so many of us?" Russell questioned. "Surely you need some backup".

"Two of you to carry the bomb, two of you to cover," Nathan answered. "That bomb has to be the priority. If we fail to get Astrilla out, then at least we can blow the place sky-high."

There it was: the moment they'd all tried to ignore up until that point. This was likely going to be a suicide mission.

"Victory or death," Koble snorted sarcastically. "You are starting to sound a lot like Jack".

"That may be, but he's not wrong," Gordon replied. "So long as the Messorem has a power supply, it's a threat. I hate to say this, but the bomb has to be the main objective of this operation; the Evoker is secondary".

"Okay," Koble said, climbing to his feet and casually strolling toward Nathan. "And what about Seig?"

Slowly, the crew turned back to Nathan, watching him as though he could anticipate their chances of failure. There was a good chance they'd all die: he had been killed at the hands of the Revenant king. The odds were stacked against them in a way that they'd never been before.

Nathan's response wasn't the one he wanted to give, but he knew it was the right one to protect his crew.

"Don't do what I did," Nathan said coldly as the risk of the mission finally hit him. "If you see Seig, you run as fast as you can".

Nathan allowed the answer to sink in. It suddenly became clear that he'd been through a journey since the Vertex, and it had changed him. He was no longer the lonely, criminal vagabond; he was a leader: he was the captain of the Phoenix Titan.

Nathan cleared his throat, refusing to allow the weight of it all to show.

"Look, I ain't gonna lie, this mission is gonna be dangerous," he said. "If any of you wanna get off the ship before we jump, say so now or forever hold your peace".

There was a silence, but none of them took the offer.

"I think I speak for all of us when I say, we're with you, dude," Russell said with a nod. "I saw you resurrected by a floating basketball; that's gotta mean something".

CHAPTER SIXTY-NINE

Koble had learnt that the worst part of any mission or job was the wait that came beforehand. Somehow time acted as a multiplier for his fears, and with every passing second, he found a new thing to worry about. Of course, he'd never let it show and would instead appear cool and calm. It was far easier that way: nobody needed to acknowledge how slim their chances of survival were.

He typed out a long message addressed to his mother, expressing his wishes to free Pluvium from Kornell's loyalists and that if he made it out alive, he'd be on the frontlines. After hitting the send button, Koble typed another message, this time intended for Rain. Rather than get bogged down in any emotional mumbo-jumbo, he simply wrote;

If I don't make it out, take care of my mother. See that our people are freed, and treat yourself to a new hat.

As Koble hit send, Nathan joined him at the bar. The Earther grabbed a bottle of something suited for a human palette and poured them each a shallow glass. Nathan sat down beside him, and the pair shared a companionable silence that lasted several minutes.

"Funny, ain't it," Nathan mused. "To think where you and I started all those years ago".

Koble breathed laughter and turned to face him; "You think we're gonna make it?"

"I dunno, but what I do know is that this is something

we have to do".

Koble tipped his glass to Nathan, "To Jack and all the other guys we lost on the Loyalty."

"For all of them," Nathan replied.

△

On the Nav terminal, there was a red countdown timer, which would tell the pilot when the drop from FTL would happen. Harrt had never taken much notice of the instrument, but for some reason, he'd found himself staring at it for an inordinate amount of time. There was a harsh but absolute truth that he acknowledged as the timer hit the one hour mark: in sixty minutes, the Phoenix would drop out of the slipstream and into the middle of the largest skirmish in known history.

As Harrt mulled over the plan outlined by Nathan, he watched the slipstream pass by. There they were in a floating tin-can, hurtling across the endless void. Sure, they could die fighting Seig, but then again, they could all die due to a failed FTL drop at any moment. Death could be random; Harrt had to remind himself of that.

He was thankful when Vol interrupted his thoughts. She passed him a steaming mug of something that looked like tea but smelt like fuel.

"The kid made it," Vol said, referring to Russell. "He called it liquid courage".

Harrt took the mug, and despite the pungent aroma, took a large sip. It didn't taste as bad as it smelt, but it certainly wasn't a glass of Maruvian kor.

"I guess we could all use a little courage," Harrt replied, stowing the cup in his holder.

He glanced at the timer, which had now whittled down to fifty-five minutes. Something instinctive told him that he needed to settle all the conflicts raging inside him. Densius Olbori was still there, lingering in his brain with a traitorly smirk on his ragged old face, but the vengeance wasn't the main thing on Harrt's list.

He wanted to not just live but to feel as alive as he had for the last few weeks. He realised that for too long, he'd been a shell of the man he'd been before Maru Seven. Part of him died with his wife and son, but somehow the Phoenix and her crew had restored something once lost.

When Harrt turned to Vol, she was already looking at him. He could tell that she already knew what he was going to say, but that was fine.

"What say, when this is all over, you and I get a few drinks and get blind-stinking-drunk?" she said, her voice surprisingly playful and upbeat. "You look like you need a night on the town".

For the first time in a very long time, Harrt reached out. He pulled Vol close and hugged her. It wasn't intended as a romantic gesture, even though they both wanted it to be that way.

"Thank you," he whispered.

"Same to you," Vol said softly. "Guess we've got a war to win".

$$\triangle$$

After sharing a drink with Koble, Nathan moved to one of the armchairs in the living area. He checked both of his pistols, then one of the assault rifles from the lock-up. As Nathan finished adjusting the sight on the heavy weapon, Russell took the seat opposite. The former barkeep nervously clutched the shotgun he'd brought with him from Paradisium.

"Take this," Nathan said, handing his assault rifle over. "You are gonna need something with a bit more bite than an old shotgun".

Russell took the weapon and nodded; "Guess I ain't dealing with drunks and rich-kids anymore".

No, you certainly aren't, Nathan thought.

It was clear that Russell was out of his depth and knew it. Yet he'd remained aboard the Phoenix. It made Nathan wonder if the kid had a death wish or if he was the type of brave that some would call stupid.

"You don't need to do this," Nathan said, keeping his voice low. "You don't owe me a fuckin' thing".

"You're right; I don't owe you shit, but I wanna do this because it's the right thing to do," Russell said as he checked the ammo on his new weapon. "I might only be a barman, and I'm not the best shot, but I can damn sure carry that bomb to where it needs to go".

For the first time since they'd met, Nathan found himself in awe of Russell Johnson. The former barkeep was willing to lay down his life based on a moral choice. That act alone told Nathan the kind of man that Russell Johnson was: the kind of man he wanted on his crew.

"You are a good man, Russell," Nathan said as he shook hands with the young man. "If we make it through this, I'm buying the first round".

△

"Get me an update," Dines yelled over the wail of klaxons and emergency sirens.

He stumbled as another missile struck the Signet but was able to steady himself. When Dines reached the tact terminal, he found the operating officer either dead or unconscious at his station. Dines didn't bother to check for a pulse as another projectile struck, this time knocking him off of his feet.

"We're gonna need medical up here!" Dines yelled to anyone who was listening. Then to his comms officer, "If Admiral Quoga's ship is gone, find out who the hell is in charge!"

"Aye, sir!"

Dines shuffled to the nearest window, not noticing the blood dripping from his eyebrow. Tens of thousands of ships were in Capital World space; all of them engaged in the most significant conflict in history. Despite the scenes of war unfolding before his eyes, Leviticus Dines couldn't quite believe it. Nobody had ever been brave enough to attempt an attack on the Capital Worlds. He'd been taught as a boy that such things were impossible: that the Capital Worlds were a powerful symbol of liberty that would stand until the end of time.

Maybe this really is the end of days, Dines thought as he watched another Commonwealth warship explode in the distance.

With every passing moment, more Revenant ships of varying sizes blinked into existence from their slipstreams. It seemed as though Seig was bringing everything he had to the battle, which implied the King was confident, foolish or insane.

"Sir," the comms officer yelled. "We're getting a signal."

As Dines waited, he hoped that Quoga, Sovoc or any of the Admiralty were still out there. He didn't want to be the one in charge: not under the circumstances.

"Who is it?" Dines demanded.

"The Phoenix Titan!"

Dines felt a momentary jolt of something that felt like hope; though he didn't trust it.

"Patch them through to my station," Dines said frantically.

A sudden crash caused the Signet to shake violently again, forcing Dines to brace. Once it subsided, Dines straightened up and watched the image of Harrt Oxarri appear before him.

"Your sense of timing isn't great," Dines commented as he looked at the Lieutenant. "Please tell me you've found the Omega?"

"We've got it," Harrt nodded. "But we're gonna need some help here!"

Dines didn't allow himself to breathe a sigh of relief. "What do you need?"

"We need an escort to get us in close to the Messorem," Harrt replied. "The Omega is some kind of shield disruptor; it'll allow the Phoenix to break through. Then we're gonna blow the thing up from the inside".

"You want to go inside that thing?" Dines yelled. "Are

you crazy?"

Dines was forced to duck as a series of electrical sparks flew from a panel on the level above. The plan that Harrt Oxarri offered was far from ideal, but then again, he wasn't entirely sure what ideal could even look like anymore.

"Can you do it?" Harrt barked impatiently.

"I don't see what other choice we've got," Dines surmised. "We'll get you an escort and buy you as much time as we can".

"Copy that," Harrt nodded. "Good luck".

"You too," Dines nodded as he deactivated the comm-link.

It was the final thing Dines could offer the hero of Maru Seven. They'd never been friends, but they'd never been enemies either. Sure, Harrt was a thorn in the side, but so were all the other bureaucrats, politicians and soldiers. The difference was that Harrt Oxarri believed in what the Commonwealth stood for, not what the aristocracy had made it.

After taking a deep breath, Dines turned to the communications officer;

"Put the word out to our fighters; provide an escort for the Phoenix Titan," Dines said. He waited for the officer to respond, but the young man simply looked at him with a bewildered expression. "What is it?" Dines demanded.

"The Admiralty aren't on available comms, sir," he said anxiously. "They aren't even on the battlefield."

"What?" Dines snapped. "Are you sure?"

"Yes, sir," the officer nodded. "Admiral Embala is with the twelfth fleet, but the ETA for arrival is unconfirmed".

In other words, I'm in command, Dines realised.

He rolled his eyes, trying not to grimace in front of his crew. They needed leadership, now more than ever.

"Your orders, sir?" Another officer looked at him expectantly.

Leviticus Dines didn't hesitate; "My orders still stand; get the Phoenix Titan a fighter escort, then patch me through to the entire fleet".

He stepped to the tactical terminal, where a half-dozen

officers worked rapidly to provide real-time updates to the fighters. The Phoenix Titan was now on the holographic map amidst the thousands of ships. Dines could already see his support fighters rallying around the Phoenix as it veered toward the Revenant fleet —toward the Messorem. He ordered the senior tactical officer to get the Phoenix as much support as possible. As soon as Dines finished at Tactical, the comms officer told him that an open channel to the fleet was waiting for him.

That was when it hit him.

Leviticus Dines, Special Agent, lone wolf and hitman, was now in command of the Commonwealth's entire military arsenal. He was the one responsible for defending the Capital Worlds. He was the one that history would remember as either the victor or as the man who allowed liberty to die.

Dines stepped over to the comms station and stood before the holographic recorder. For several moments, he stood quietly at the station, staring awkwardly into the faces of his expectant crew: imagining the thousands more aboard the other ships.

Then, without knowing where to begin, he began.

CHAPTER SEVENTY

Despite Vol's advice to remain seated, Nathan stood, gripping the back of Harrt's chair. He needed to get a better look at what they were up against. What he saw was beyond comprehension.

Mile-long warships crowded the space around the Capital Worlds, and laser fire flashed on all sides. Smaller gunships and fighters fought at closer range while avoiding the shrapnel and anti-aircraft flak that filled the space between. Nathan wasn't quite sure of the right words to use as he gazed at the scale of the Revenant forces. He'd never seen so many ships in one place: he doubted that anyone ever had.

Every terminal and console aboard the Phoenix was chiming with alerts, and yet somehow, Vol and Harrt remained calm. Vol's hands flew over the control panels, weaving the ship between the crossfire and wreckage, while Harrt dealt with Dines over comms.

The 'wealther's conversation didn't last long, and by the time it was over, at least thirty Commonwealth fighters formed a defensive formation around the Phoenix.

"When this is all over Nathan, I'm teaching you how to fly this damn ship," Vol said as she plotted a new course. "A captain needs to know the basics".

Before Nathan could respond, the Phoenix whipped sideways, narrowly avoiding a burning chunk of something that had once been a fighter.

"Fine by me," Nathan said as he clung to her chair.

Hartt continued to push the Phoenix to its maximum velocity, all while dodging the chaos around them. The 'wealther fighters did what they could, but the battlefield was too frantic, making it almost impossible to keep a tight defensive formation.

The Phoenix whipped across the bow of a Revenant warship and spewed laser fire into the hostile ship's hull. The attack barely left a mark, but it was at least something. When Vol fired the port jets, the Phoenix kicked to the right, spinning them away from the larger ship. A group of enemy fighters attempted to follow but were cut down by either Koble or Russell in one of the gunnery chambers.

"Yeah, get some of that, you Revenant bastards!" Koble's voice was so loud he didn't need comms.

Once they were past the bulk of the Revenant's armada, Nathan's eyes settled on the Messorem. He felt a sudden primordial fear that he'd never experienced in his life. Instinct told him to turn the ship around and run as far away as possible, but as soon as Nathan thought of Astrilla, it was gone.

"Guess this is the home stretch," Russell's voice came through the speakers. "Let's hope that Enkaye knew what he was talking about".

The former barkeep was right: this was the moment that mattered. If the Omega worked as Moshia said, it would allow the Phoenix to pass through the Messorem's vast shield network. Nathan didn't want to think about what would happen if the Enkaye was wrong.

He peeled away from the pilot's station and turned to the rear of the cockpit, where Gordon was holding the Omega. The spear-shaped device had taken on a deep green glow since the Phoenix had entered the battle. Nathan wondered if the device was readying itself for what lay ahead.

"Is this gonna work?" Nathan asked.

Gordon's expression was a mix of nerves and uncertainty, which didn't fill Nathan with confidence.

"I certainly hope so," the doctor answered.

Koble heard the answer through the comm-link and replied, "What kinda chances of survival are we looking at here, Doc?"

"About eighty percent," Gordon said, bobbing his head as though he were calculating something. "Maybe eighty-five".

"Uh-huh," Koble drawled sarcastically. "So what happens if that magic stick doesn't work?"

"Well," Gordon drew the word out into three syllables. "In the event that we don't break through the shields, we'll all die in a horrible fiery explosion…"

The comm-link from Koble went quiet, and Nathan imagined the Sphinax grimacing at the odds.

"Of course, if that happens, we'll all be dead in a matter of seconds," Gordon said, stating it as though it were the bright side of his hopeless scenario.

Nathan turned back to the pilot's station. On the tact-screen, he saw that three large 'wealther gunships had joined in the charge, along with the fighter escort.

"Here we go," Vol said. "Everyone hold onto something".

The ship's engines rumbled, causing the ground to quake beneath Nathan's boot. When the Phoenix began its hard burn toward the Messorem, Nathan felt the shift in momentum in his veins. The support ships cut through any head-on attackers with ease; then, after clearing a path to the Messorem, the 'wealthers proceeded to launch an array of missiles at the Enkaye warmachine.

The Messorem's shields did what Nathan thought they would. A quarter-mile from the surface of the looming vessel, the missiles detonated in midair. A green ripple cascaded across the vast shield network that surrounded the Messorem.

As the Phoenix neared, Nathan heard the panic in Koble's voice through the comms. He could sense the apprehension that radiated from Gordon. Harrt and Vol were yelling *pilot-talk* at one another as the escort ships broke away from the charge. Despite all the chaos around him, Nathan knew it would work. It had to work.

Nathan closed his eyes and held his breath. He recalled the night he'd spent with Astrilla. He thought about the deep conversations they'd shared: the things he'd told her —that he could never tell anyone else.

When the Phoenix Titan met the Messorem's shields, Nathan opened his eyes to look at the Omega. The device shifted its glow to a warm orange that seemed to pass over the ship and crew. The moment ended, and the Phoenix broke through as though the shields were never there.

Russell's voice erupted triumphantly through the comms; "We did it,"

The cockpit speakers became alive with excitement as Koble and Russell shrieked in celebration. Harrt and Vol excitedly cheered and exchanged a high-five.

Nathan didn't join in, and he noticed that Gordon didn't either. It was as if both of them knew that something far more challenging lay ahead.

"You're gonna need this," Gordon said, handing him the Omega. Something had changed in the older man's voice, but Nathan couldn't be entirely sure what it was.

As the Phoenix drew closer, the Messorem eclipsed the view, and eventually, all Nathan could see was the dark stone-like surface of the Enkaye ship. Like the Omega, the Messorem's hull was detailed with tiny symbols illuminated by a light source inside the thick metal surface.

"Incredible," Gordon said as he examined the view. He pointed at a cluster of hieroglyphs, "I could swear that one is Egyptian".

Nathan looked back at the doctor with a blank expression. He didn't want to dismiss Gordon's inquisitive nature, but under the circumstances, entertaining it didn't seem right either. Fortunately, Nathan didn't have to say a thing, as Harrt interrupted;

"There!" Harrt pointed to a triangular opening in the Messorem's hull. "That's our way inside".

Harrt slowed the Phoenix and took them into the opening. What lay ahead was a long, darkened tunnel that seemed to go on forever. Of course, Nathan had seen the schematics and knew that the Messorem's central hub was buried miles inside the structure. At every hundred metre interval, shafts of green electricity poured from the walls and into the passage. A series of massive superstructures crossed the giant V-shaped tunnel, carrying what looked like water from one side to the other. Even though the Phoenix was moving at pace, the sheer scale of the Messorem made it feel like they were casually drifting.

Nathan glanced at Moshia's schematic, overlayed with the Phoenix's location in real-time. Their destination was a hangar roughly halfway between the two main objectives. Nathan's gut told him they would meet resistance there.

$$\triangle$$

Three minutes later, the Phoenix Titan entered the hangar, taking a platoon of unsuspecting Revenant troops by surprise. The enemy force scattered in every direction, attempting to avoid the unforgiving onslaught of the Phoenix's cannons. By the time the last soldier fell, the ship had touched down, and the crew were ready to disembark.

Despite carrying a heavy assault rifle, a shotgun, two hand cannons and a grenade launcher pre-loaded with a dozen grenades, Koble felt decidedly unarmed for the situation. It was hard to tell what they were about to walk into, but nothing he'd seen suggested it would be a cakewalk —far from it. Even with all the firearms, and ammo that his stocky frame could carry, Koble knew he didn't stand a chance if he came face to face with the Revenant king. He tucked a concealed combat knife beneath a thick tuft of hair on the back of his neck, knowing that if were captured, it would come in useful.

At least I can shiv the Revenant king if he gets close, Koble thought. *Take that big bald bastard by surprise.*

Beside him, Gordon and Russell were preparing to lift the bomb onto a metre-wide trolley. The plan was that two of them would push —or carry— the bomb while the other two covered: Koble knew that was easier said than done. Still, at least they had the trolley to take away some of the effort.

While Harrt handed out spare ammo clips, Vol checked the trolley. Koble could tell that something had evolved between the pair. It seemed unlikely, but then again, so was everything else going on around him.

Nathan stood at the airlock, with the Omega in one hand and his pistol in the other. Though Koble suspected otherwise, he couldn't help but admit that Nathan looked calm and ready to face whatever lay ahead. He bore the look of a leader and captain. Nathan looked like Jack: minus the blonde hair, ocular implant and the self-loathing nature.

"Time to go," Nathan said. Before pushing the door control, Nathan looked back at the crew. "If we don't make it out..." The Earther paused and swallowed a lump in his throat.

Sensing that his friend was uncomfortable, Koble spoke for him, "I think what Nate's trying to say is; whatever happens, don't get shot".

It was a light moment: something to break the tension they all felt. It felt good, but it ended the moment the airlock door opened.

$$\triangle$$

On this day, I, Seig, son of Mezug, begin my ascension to greatness. The Great Void lives in me, as I in it. Today the agents of chaos shall cower before me like the omnipotent god I was destined to become.

Seig watched as another armada of Revenant ships joined the battle in a flanking position. The flagship led the charge into the enemy formation like a wild animal. The two dozen warships cut through an ocean of Commonwealth ships, leaving behind a trail of debris, fire and burning gases.

It was violent and marvellous at the same time.

Seig chose to look at life as a flawed masterpiece painted upon a canvas of unimaginable scale. Regardless of the artist, it was a miracle, but that fact alone didn't mean that existence could be acquitted of its sin. Life was violent

and bloodthirsty, and it was his mission —no, his destiny—
to wipe the metaphorical canvas clean so that something
new could begin. *To reset existence* was the Revenant cause
at its simplest. That was the holy mission, set by the river
Prynn.

Seig found himself pulled away from the scenes ahead
of him by Olbori. The aged Maruviun-human bowed, then,
with an uncertain grimace, addressed Seig.

"Your highness, we are receiving a priority transmission
from your son".

Seig fought to hide his outrage. The fact that the Prince
was willing to interrupt such a historical moment was a
testament to his hubris. It proved that Baylum's sense of self-
entitlement knew no bounds.

"I will deal with my son; put him on my terminal," Seig
snapped. Then after composing himself, "Charge the weapon,
and take aim at the nearest of the Capital Worlds. When I am
finished with the Prince, I would like to see one of their planets
reduced to ash".

"Of course, your grace," Olbori nodded.

When Baylum's visage formed in the holographic
projector, Seig didn't offer his son a fatherly greeting.

"What is it?" Seig barked.

Baylum made little attempt to hide how offended he was
with his father's tone. There was a petulance to it that Seig had
expected, but there was also a look of agency to the Prince that
seemed entirely out of place.

"I have received some disturbing reports," Baylum said,
his voice hard. "Allies of the Commonwealth possess a device
capable of not only breaking through the Messorem's shields
but also destroying it".

"Impossible," Seig said, shaking his head.

"It's true, Father; they are heading your way. I implore
you to abandon the battle," Baylum said. "We must be smart;
we need to rally all of our forces and ensure that nothing can
destroy the Messorem".

"I will do no such thing," Seig said, trying to mask his
rage with false politeness.

"But, Father—"

Seig slammed his fist into the control panel before him.

"I will not run away from this fight like a gutless coward!" Seig's angry outburst caught the attention of the entire bridge crew. A part of him wanted to regain some semblance of composure, but Baylum's interference had awoken the rage that often lay dormant. Seig refused to appear weak before his subjects, so he continued to bellow at the top of his voice. "There is no room in my sacred domain for cowardice. This is the time and place where I will fulfil the destiny bestowed upon our entire race by the mighty river. Chaos has reigned for too long, and this is where we will draw the line. If one of those anarchists has secured a weapon, let them come for me; I will slaughter them as I will the rest".

The rant was a warning both for his son and his subjects. Usually, Seig would regret such an outburst, but this time he didn't regret a thing. *How could he turn back now?* Such an act was impossible. Seconds passed, and the expression on Baylum's face devolved from petulance to outrage.

"You fool," Baylum snarled. "This will be the death of you and our kind".

Seig slammed his fist into a control panel, unable to quell his rage any longer; "You dare question my authority?"

Baylum's glare didn't waver.

"Fine. Go to your death, old man," Baylum snarled. "For when you die, I shall be crowned king. Mark my words, my reign will not be plagued by the same superstition and idiocy as yours. I will be the one to fulfil our purpose".

Seig gritted his teeth, readying himself to scream at his traitorous son, but before he could say a word, the comm-link died. He couldn't tell if Baylum killed the line or if a disturbance from the battle caused it. Either way, Baylum had made his position clear.

It would seem I have a new enemy, Seig thought.

When Admiral Olbori stepped forward, awaiting his orders, Seig pointed at one of the Capital Worlds;

"Fire the weapon".

I shall watch my betrayers burn as I do my opponents in battle. Nobody, including that of my creation, will be spared..

CHAPTER SEVENTY-ONE

There were a few storage crates scattered between a half dozen docked Revenant shuttles. At each side of the vast room were two large metal doors, one to the upper decks and demolition site, the other to the power chamber, where Astrilla was held.

As Nathan and the crew disembarked, Revenant reinforcements rushed into the hangar. Vol was the first to open fire, followed by Harrt. Nathan moved to cover behind a shipping container and fired his pistol at the hostile force. His gunshot met its target, and in a haze of grey blood, the soldier fell to the ground.

Harrt joined him behind cover, and together they provided surpressing fire, allowing the others to offload the bomb safely. The next few seconds of the gunbattle were utter chaos. As Gordon and Russell carefully pushed the bomb down the Phoenix's boarding ramp, Koble went ahead of them and raised his assault rifle. The Sphinax fired a wide arc of laser fire that cut through several enemy targets.

Nathan moved from cover, and with Harrt and Vol at his side, they pushed toward the soldiers. Nathan fired at the hostile force, counting three more kills as he darted behind another container. He reloaded his gun, barely taking notice of the sharp staccato of laser fire that filled the hangar.

As if acting out of pure instinct, Nathan rolled right, narrowly avoiding the deadly swipe of a Revenant hunter. The creature's claws lodged into the metal container wall, and for several seconds the enraged beast fought to free itself. Nathan wasn't sure why, but he found himself taking up the Omega rather than his pistol. A ripping sound followed as the hunter jerked its hand free of the metal, then dashed at Nathan like a ferocious animal.

Nathan stood his ground right up until the moment the hunter was within a metre. After dodging a rapid swipe, Nathan stabbed the Omega into the hunter's chest, slicing through the brute's metal armour as though it were made from paper. The savage monster shrieked in a mix of agony and confusion before disintegrating into a cloud of ash.

Nathan stared at the Omega in disbelief as his vanquished foe disappeared into nothingness. The device had behaved like an elemental summon. It was an impossible feat, and yet it had happened. It became clear to Nathan that the Omega was more than it seemed.

$$\triangle$$

It didn't take long to clear the hostile threat from the hangar, but when the last soldier fell, Nathan noticed that the Messorem was starting to shake. It wasn't like the slipstream, and it certainly wasn't laser fire from the battle outside: it was coming from inside the ship. Something that looked like liquid flooded through a piping system overhead. When Nathan looked closer, he saw sparks of green electricity inside the water. For a moment, it felt as though all the oxygen in the room tightened until finally, the quaking pulse and deafening howl ceased.

"What the hell was that?" Koble yelled.

To Nathan, the answer seemed obvious, but he didn't want to say it aloud: none of them did. He felt the rush of the Messorem's power in the very fibre of his being. The weapon had been fired: he was sure of that much. The real question that Koble should have asked was, *where did Seig aim the gun?*

"Unity," Harrt stammered, almost dropping his datapad. "That mad bastard took out Unity".

Nathan circled over to the 'wealther and looked at the datapad for himself. He stared blankly at the screen for several seconds, unsure of how to process what he saw.

"How many people lived on Unity?" Vol said slowly.

"At least a trillion," Harrt answered, his voice growing low and vengeful.

The number was unquantifiable in Nathan's mind. He'd never cared for the Commonwealth or their political agenda, but they were still people nonetheless. People whose lives had been snuffed out by the Revenant king. The realisation hit Nathan like a moving ship: many more lives would be lost if they failed.

He knew that the plan had to change. After seeing the speed at which the Messorem could destroy an entire world, Nathan knew in his heart that they couldn't allow Seig to fire again. He turned and called Vol and Russell over;

"You know where the firing array is on this thing, right?" Nathan said.

"Yeah," Vol nodded. "But why—"

"We are the only ship inside their shields," Nathan said quickly. "We need to take advantage of that".

"What are you thinking?" Russell raised a brow.

"Get the Phoenix out there and do everything you can to stop Seig firing again," Nathan replied. "Throw everything we've got at it".

"What about getting Astrilla out?" Vol said. "You can't do that alone".

Taking out the Messorem was the primary objective. Astrilla was secondary. All of them knew that before embarking. The most important thing for Nathan was to prevent as many innocent deaths as possible.

"I'll be fine," Nathan answered, then turning to Russell, "Vol's gonna need a decent gunner out there. Can you do that?"

Russell bore the look of someone who was about to offer a protest, but before he could open his mouth, he saw something and gestured toward the bomb. The Enkaye droid had emerged from inside the Phoenix and casually floated over to Gordon and the warhead. The droid extended its metal arms and took ahold of one side of the heavy bomb.

"We lift and push together," it said to Gordon.

In stunned silence, the doctor nodded; "Sure".

When Russell turned back to Nathan, his answer was simple.

"I'm the man for the job".

$$\triangle$$

Harrt Oxarri had faced down death more times than he cared to count. He'd seen and done things in war that would make any normal man question their sanity. The difference for Harrt was that he stood by every decision he'd ever made — at least up until now.

As Harrt watched Vol climb aboard the Phoenix, he debated what to say. There was a good chance that neither of them would make it back in one piece.

This has to count, Harrt thought.

A million thoughts raced through Harrt's mind like autumn leaves caught in a current. Everything from a simple farewell to a full-blown declaration of fondness or more swept through.

Before getting close to selecting one of the many things he wanted to say, Vol interrupted him.

"Remember that whole thing I said about getting blind-stinking-drunk?" she said across the hangar.

"Of course".

"Well, I just wanted to let you know that you're buying the first round," Vol nodded.

It was as close to goodbye as either of them could get, at least within their unspoken boundaries of comfort. Harrt realised that, in a way, it was perfect.

"Be careful," he said as Vol began to close the airlock.

Her reply came with a simple nod.

Then Vol disappeared into the Phoenix and the airlock sealed shut.

$$\triangle$$

As I watch the heretic symbol of Unity burn, I feel nothing. I am the boot that destroys the insect nest: I am the wildfire that burns fields of crops. I am the tsunami that wipes continents off the map.

Unity was gone, engulfed by a green fire that spread for miles. No one could survive such superior firepower. Of course, it meant that the dead couldn't be sacrificed to the Void, but Seig knew that the river Prynn would forgive him.

For the first time in a very long time, Seig allowed his lips to form a satisfied smile. Watching Unity burn was beyond words. Nobody, not even his great-grandfather, had even breached Capital Space.

Nobody until Seig —*the destroyer of worlds.*

"Congratulations, your highness," Olbori said, looking out at the devastation. "We are charging the weapon; reports suggest we will be at firing capacity in twenty minutes".

Seig did not answer. Instead, he savoured the beauty of Unity's death. As he watched the planet crumble in on itself, Seig realised that he had ascended far beyond his creators' design. Yes, the Enkaye had built the Messorem, but they failed to vanquish their enemy. Seig would not make the same mistake.

He suddenly became aware of a man's worrisome voice over his shoulder. When he turned, Seig saw a senior officer presenting Olbori with a datapad. There was a nervousness to the man that Seig couldn't ignore.

"When was this recorded?" Olbori snapped at the officer. "When?"

"Less than a minute ago, sir," the officer answered nervously.

"How did they make it through the shields?"

Before the officer could answer the question, Seig stepped forward and snatched the datapad. What he saw on the screen filled him with a mix of rage and confusion.

The prospect of failure crept over his scalp, causing goosebumps to form on his skin. Not only did he see Lieutenant Harrt Oxarri, but he also saw the Earther: the same man who he'd critically injured on the Flagship.

How is he alive? Seig wondered.

It didn't matter. The crew of the Phoenix Titan were there to save Astrilla, and Seig couldn't allow that to happen. Olbori was throwing out orders to the security personnel, but Seig halted him mid-sentence.

"Where are they now?" Seig growled at the officer.

"It looks like they are moving to the top of the ship. We can have soldiers cut them off in seconds".

The power chamber wasn't their destination, or that is what they wanted it to look like. Seig knew in his gut that they were there for Astrilla: *they had to be.*

Knowing that Harrt Oxarri and his crew were there to take everything that mattered from him, Seig clenched his fists. The time for action was now. Nobody would take anything from him: not after everything that Seig had sacrificed to get to this point.

The choice was simple, and Seig chose chaos. He took up his sword from the wall, and Densius Olbori shot him a confused look.

"What are you doing, sir?" Olbori said.

"Admiral Densius Olbori, I want you to personally lead the defence of this ship. See that Harrt Oxarri and any of his companions are killed without mercy".

Fear circled in the Admiral's withered expression.

"Of course," Olbori bowed his head. "But what about you, your grace?"

Seig brandished his sword.

"Not all of them are heading for the top; I sense that some will try and free the Evoker. I shall deal with any of them personally".

Olbori tensed his jaw but didn't offer a protest. "As you wish".

Seig drew back silently and began to walk the halls of the Messorem. No one would stand in the way of his ascension to godliness: that included the Earther. It didn't matter how he'd survived a sword through the chest; all that mattered was stopping him from freeing the Evoker.

From this moment, I cease to be a king; I cease to be the

creation of my flawed architects, for I am the one who controls the power of gods.

△

The sound of control panels alarming and officers yelling in panicked tones was all that Dines could hear. He didn't know what to say or think as he watched Unity collapse in a ball of fire. There were no words to describe the horror he felt, but Leviticus Dines was not a poet; he was a Commonwealth Agent. Experience taught him to fight harder when his back was against the wall, and in Dines' mind, this situation was no different. He couldn't allow the Messorem to fire again, even if that meant sacrificing every warship he had at his command.

"Sir?"

It took Dines a few seconds to snap himself back to reality. He peeled his eyes away from the scenes of destruction outside and set his sights on the comms officer.

"What is it?" he said.

"We've got more incoming," the officer replied.

Dines glanced at the tact terminal and spotted twenty-to-thirty fighters coming up on the battlefield. The ships didn't have a Commonwealth or Revenant drive signature, which left Dines to ask;

"Who the hell are they?"

The comms officer took longer to answer than Dines expected.

"They appear to be Sphinax fighters," the officer said. "They are very old models but quite nimble with the right pilot".

The intelligence officer in Dines wanted to question it, but the man in charge of the fleet didn't have the time. The situation was too desperate to be picky.

"We'll take whatever help we can get," Dines said, patting the officer on the shoulder.

△

Inside the cockpit of his ship, Rain grinned. He began a steep climb over the surface of a 'wealther warship, arching his fighter around the giant steely mass. It was the perfect manoeuvre to distract his pursuer. The Revenant fighter never saw Nero coming and exploded in a ball of fire seconds later.

"Guess you never forgot how to fly, old man," Nero's elated voice came through the comm-link.

"I suppose not," Rain said, trying his best to stifle any hint of humour from his voice. Then to the rest of the squadron, he said, "Eyes open people, let's locate the Phoenix Titan and our Chief".

CHAPTER SEVENTY-TWO

The Messorem was a complex maze of greenish-grey corridors, occasionally interrupted by strange hexagonal intersections. Koble doubted that he'd be able to navigate such a complicated layout without Moshia's schematic, which Harrt was checking every hundred metres.

Resistance up until that point had been light, suggesting the Revenant were either operating with a skeleton crew or rallying ahead. It didn't stop Koble from keeping his gun raised and checking every corner and doorway they passed. He half expected a hunter or Paladin to spring out of nowhere, and Harrt's movements suggested the same.

Gordon and the droid remained a few metres behind, pushing the bomb and trying their best to keep up. Koble didn't question how the droid was able to lift such a heavy load. Instead, he accepted it as part of *the-grand-master-plan.*

Suddenly, two soldiers appeared at the end of the corridor, paused, and aimed at Koble and Harrt. As Koble opened fire, a larger squad rounded the corner, and all hell broke loose.

Koble darted into cover while Harrt shoved Gordon to one side. The booming clatter of laser fire filled the long corridor. Instinctively, Koble waited for an opening, then when an opportunity presented itself, he dropped to one knee and peaked from cover. The Sphinax acquired his target and squeezed the trigger. Once he'd confirmed the kill, Koble shifted his aim to the next hostile. He continued until the moment his assault rifle overheated. As Koble reloaded, he became aware that Harrt was fighting off a second group from the rear.

"Shit," Koble exclaimed, slinging his rifle over his shoulder and taking up his grenade launcher. "Time to break out the serious firepower".

△

Harrt leapt over the warhead, firing his gun erratically in the hopes that he could take out one, if not more, of the hostiles. Once his feet hit the ground, he darted behind a column for cover and spotted Gordon firing his Earther shotgun into the new pack.

The sudden roar of a grenade explosion came from Koble's position up the hall. When Harrt turned to look, he confirmed that the Sphinax had switched weapons.

To Harrt's surprise, Gordon was holding his own, occasionally moving from cover and picking off easy targets with remarkable accuracy. There was something about how Gordon handled his weapons that suggested he'd received more than basic firearms training.

Harrt bolted from cover and opened fire. Between him and Gordon, they began to make light work of the small platoon, leaving Koble to worry about the enemies blocking the path ahead.

It was all going too well, and Harrt knew it. His suspicions were confirmed the moment he laid eyes on a hunter sprinting toward them. Harrt shifted his aim toward the fast-moving behemoth without hesitation, but suddenly the hunter leapt into the air, ready to strike.

For a heartbeat, Harrt was sure that this was to be his final moment. Everything seemed to slow down. He noticed the light reflect against the hunter's jagged claws as the creature bore down on him. He felt the recoil of his rifle as round after round of laser fire penetrated the enraged animal's torso to little effect.

If this were to be his death, then at least he'd die for something.

Then as though someone hit the fast forward button, the hunter veered to one side as a tightly formed pack of Earther-bullets ripped through its body. The beast crashed into a wall just metres from where Harrt was standing. He'd never seen a hunter take damage quite like it. He gazed over his shoulder to see Gordon clutching a primitive Earther shotgun. The hunter growled as it clumsily tried to climb to its feet, but Harrt emptied the rest of his ammo into its skull.

When he looked at Gordon, the doctor shrugged.

"Experimental rounds," Gordon said, reloading his gun. "Looks like they worked. It was just a theory of mine but—"

Harrt tackled the doctor into cover as a stray round whizzed by. Harrt turned his weapon on the perpetrator, but Koble beat him to the punch, cutting down the revenant officer with a precise gunshot.

"Are we clear?" Koble said, checking in every direction.

The Enkaye droid popped out of cover and let off a series of cheerful sounding beeps.

"I think that means, not for long," Gordon replied. "C'mon, we've gotta move".

△

With every step that Nathan took, he could feel a strange cocktail of emotions seep into his thoughts. There was an innate sense of dread that didn't belong. It was as though something inside the Messorem was whispering to him.

In the same way someone would turn on a light switch, Nathan suddenly felt Astrilla again. It was the same magnetic feeling that had guided them to the temple on Pelos, the same sensation that was ever-present in their shared visions. Nathan embraced the connection and allowed it to guide him. As he sleuthed through the convoluted network of corridors, halls and intersections, the sensation grew. It told him that Astrilla was exhausted and in a great deal of pain, but she was alive.

That was all that mattered.

He took cover to avoid a fast-moving group of soldiers, who sprinted to an ascending elevator. The hopeful fool in Nathan proposed to him that perhaps the power chamber was not the Revenant's focus, but the sceptic knew better. It was more than likely that the Revenant were on their way to intercept Harrt, Koble and Gordon.

Rather than remain hidden until they'd vanished, Nathan decided to help his friends by thinning the enemy forces. As the last of the soldiers filed inside the cramped elevator, Nathan made his presence known by tossing a cooked grenade into the pack. Before any of the hostiles knew what was happening, they were engulfed by a fiery explosion.

It was a dirty tactic that Jack would have called *brilliant,* and it worked.

He continued to follow the connection to Astrilla until he reached a large metal doorway, guarded by two Revenant Paladins. Each of the hooded men was unarmed, but that didn't mean they weren't deadly. Nathan had gone toe-to-toe with one back on Yenex and almost lost in the process. He knew that a head-on attack would likely fail, but there was no time and no other options.

When Nathan stepped out in front of them, the two men straightened up in surprise. Rather than draw his pistol, Nathan kept hold of the Omega. He couldn't explain why, but he knew he had to use it.

"You dare stand aboard this hallowed weapon?" one of the Paladins said, raising his palms.

"I do," Nathan gritted his teeth.

Silence lingered between the three men.

"Then you shall die," the other Paladin declared.

At that instant, both Paladins moved in tandem, hurling pillars of energy at Nathan that would kill on impact. When Nathan raised the Omega, he found that the spear was guiding his body and mind through the fight: as though it could anticipate his attackers' every move.

A searing hot bolt of energy ricocheted from the Omega and collided with one of the Paladins, causing the man to crumple to ash. The second came at Nathan with a raised palm of fire. As before, the Omega told Nathan exactly where to go and what to do. He parried the attack, then swept the Omega from left to right. The Paladin's head flew from his body with a sickening crack. Before the skull could hit the ground, it was no more than dust. The corpse keeled over to one side, then like the head faded into nothingness.

Nathan took a sigh of relief.

He'd been barely able to stand his ground against the Paladin on Yenex, and yet he'd just killed two of them armed only with a spear. Of course, Nathan knew in his heart that the Omega was far more than it appeared.

With a loud, metallic groan, the massive doors slowly began to open. A thick cloud of acrid white smoke emerged from the clearing. It spilt out from the power chamber and into the corridor where Nathan stood. For a long time, all he could see was the thick smog, but eventually, the clouds cleared, and he saw the power chamber.

The room was entirely pyramidic in shape, with a single point in the ceiling. The transparent walls and floor looked out onto a bubbling greyish liquid that went up and down for more miles than Nathan cared to guess. The mechanical whir of machinery filled the room while thick plumes of steam spewed from piping overhead.

At the centre was a large opening in the ground, leading to the water surrounding the room. The pool of whatever the steaming grey substance was, looked violent to the naked eye. It was just like the liquid that Nathan had encountered at the Jareth Corps facility.

Nathan lifted his eyes to a platform suspended high above the pool. That was when he saw Astrilla. The Evoker was hunched over what looked like a stone plinth. Of course, like everything else of Enkaye design, it wasn't as it appeared. Nathan's gut told him that the device was somehow syphoning power from Astrilla and into the Messorem.

Without wasting any time, Nathan moved deeper into the room. When he was within a few hundred yards of Astrilla, he saw a staircase leading up to the platform. In his head, Nathan made a checklist of new objectives. The first was to remove Astrilla from the device, thus powering down the Messorem and giving the Commonwealth a fighting chance. The second was to find the mechanism that would work with the Omega, just as Moshia said before death.

An escaping cloud of steam blocked Nathan's view, forcing him to stop. It was at that moment that Nathan realised he was not alone. He waited for the loud hiss of machinery to cease, then he heard the footsteps approaching from behind.

King Seig strode through the white vapour with a sword to hand. Unlike the last time he had battled with the Revenant king, Nathan noticed the rage on Seig's face. He didn't seem like the same calm and collected warrior that Nathan had fought before. Something had changed, and it left Nathan to realise that the one thing Seig feared wasn't the Commonwealth or the Evokers. What the Revenant king feared was failure to fulfil his destiny: a destiny handed down over generations.

Despite the realisation that his foe had a weakness, Nathan acknowledged that Seig was the stronger combatant. It was likely that Nathan would die in the fight to come, but he couldn't walk away.

There was only one choice. It was a choice Nathan had made before he'd even stepped foot aboard the Messorem. He would fight to save Astrilla and the crew he'd grown to love. Not because he wanted to save the Commonwealth, but because it was the right thing to do.

In the end, he was a true son of Earth, raised by a man who only tried to do the best he could. He was Nathan Carter, Captain of the Phoenix Titan, led to his crew and ship by destiny.

"In my centuries of conquest, nobody has survived direct combat against me," Seig said in a low voice.

"Guess I broke your streak," Nathan said, reaching for his holstered pistol. "I wonder what else I can break".

Seig raised his sword; "You may be the first, but I promise you will also be the last".

CHAPTER SEVENTY-THREE

The Phoenix raced through the labyrinth of tunnels to return to the Messorem's exterior. Once the ship was soaring across the giant hull that made up the Enkaye war machine, Vol gazed upward. There was less than a mile between the Messorem and the complex shield network overhead, meaning that there was little room for aerial manoeuvres requiring verticality.

That wasn't a good thing.

Violent crackles surged across the shields as the 'wealther ships tried and failed to breakthrough. It was a stark reminder to Vol that the Phoenix was entirely cut off from reinforcements; not to mention out of its depth. Before she could even quantify the odds of survival, alarms began to shriek.

The proximity sensors picked up multiple Revenant fighters heading straight toward the Phoenix. Vol glanced at the screen, noting that they were launching from the Messorem's underside.

"How long till they're on our ass?" Russell's voice came through the comm.

"Ninety seconds," Vol answered. Then after checking that the gunnery chambers were ready to go active, she asked, "You good up there?"

"Sure," Russell's reply was loaded with sarcasm. "So, when we make it to the big guns, what are we going to do?"

"Exactly what Nathan said; we throw absolutely

everything we've got at it."

The words, including the ship itself, lingered on Vol's lips, but she didn't say it aloud. That was the doomsday scenario, where if all hope was lost and the others didn't make it out alive, she would plunge the Phoenix Titan into the firing array. It was a simple plan, cobbled together in seconds, yet Vol wouldn't have had it any other way.

Seconds later, gunfire whipped across the Phoenix's bow as the pursuing enemy squadron gave chase. Vol counted eleven —no twelve— ships in the immediate area, but the Revenant was launching more by the second.

She tried not to focus on the weapons terminal beside her, which flashed every time Russell fired a shot. Instead, she kept both eyes on the path ahead, trying to shut out the unforgiving bark of the proximity sensors.

Vol punched the thruster control, sending the Phoenix hurtling forward. She used the Messorem's tangle of protrusions and channels to out-manoeuvre the pursuing enemy craft, which must have worked because seconds later, Vol spotted a stream of laser fire pass by.

The Messorem's firing array was a mile-wide crater in the hull, surrounded by four giant spires that met at a central tip. A preliminary scan of the fifteen-mile superstructure concluded that the bowl-shaped mouth was an advanced reactor designed to handle energy far beyond that of the modern era.

More importantly, the Phoenix wouldn't leave a dent in the paintwork.

The spires were a different story altogether. They could most certainly be destroyed. From Vol's best guess, the four structures were power regulators, designed to focus all of the Messorem's collective energy into a single world-ending bolt of death.

"We've gotta take out those towers," Vol said over the ship's communicator. "Be ready to shoot".

Russell's reply came seconds later, "You've got it".

Vol sent the Phoenix hurtling across the metal crater. Then to throw off the pursuing fighters, she jerked the ship right and made a beeline for the closest spire. Once they were within weapons range, Vol saw the weapons terminal flash, and Russell opened fire.

Suddenly, a loud crash rocked the Phoenix, sending the ship into a violent downward spin. Every instrument around Vol began to shriek as the artificial gravity system strained to reorientate.

"What the damn hell was that?" Russell shrieked.

Vol didn't want to imagine what it was like for Russell in the gunnery chambers without gravity, but she knew it wouldn't do his stomach any favours. Once she regained control of the ship, the cause of the sudden attack became crushingly apparent.

"Shit," Vol cursed, spotting a second and third fighter squadron heading their way.

Without thinking, Vol yanked on the throttle, throwing the Phoenix in the opposite direction. She quickly eyeballed the proximity monitor and grimaced as she counted the number of new ships.

"You okay up there?" she yelled.

"I think so," he groaned. "But my breakfast... not so much".

Vol tried to shut out the mental image and instead turned her attention to the next monitor. Thanks to the last impact, the Phoenix had sustained some mild damage to the starboard side, but it was repairable. The greater concern was that the shields had taken the brunt of the attack, and Vol wasn't sure how many hits they could handle after that.

"We need to get another run at those towers," Russell's voice boomed through the comm. "We can do this".

"Not yet," Vol replied. "There's way too many of them. You need to get them off our ass, and then we'll make another approach".

Vol's attention was then directed to an alarming sensor. When she glanced at the tactical terminal, she saw a fourth group of Revenant fighters approaching from the front. She sent the Phoenix into a sharp left turn, narrowly avoiding a wall of gunfire from the new ships.

Eventually, the tact terminal proved to be more distracting than helpful, so she yanked a cable from the underside, killing the alarm.

△

By the time they reached the detonation site, Harrt had lost
count of his confirmed kills. Maybe it was the stress of the
situation, or perhaps something had changed. Commonwealth
military training was clear; *you always kept count;* that way,
you knew your contribution to maintaining liberty.

The final Revenant in their way was an unmutated
human officer, but Harrt couldn't care less. Mutated or
unmutated, the man was serving the Revenant king. The
same king who'd murdered trillions in the blink of an eye.
Harrt took aim and fired three times. Each shot met its mark
and sprayed three clouds of crimson blood against the wall.

He made sure to count that kill.

The detonation site was an enormous room that Harrt
could only assume was an engineering deck. Throughout the
chamber were several rows of giant liquid-filled vats, linked
together by metal piping. Retrofitted walkways loomed
overhead, while massive support beams from the original
structure held everything together. It all led to a much larger
container at the back of the room, which strangely
resembled a giant FTL drive.

"Gordon, is that what I think it is?" Harrt pointed.

The doctor's eyes widened behind his spectacles. "If
that is an engine..."

"This bomb will make one hell of an explosion," Koble
interrupted, then unapologetically turned to Gordon;
"Right?"

"That's one way of putting it," the doctor nodded.

Harrt rechecked Moshia's schematic, confirming that
this was the right spot. He studied the room, noting that
there were only two ways in and out: in the event of
Revenant reinforcements arriving, that wasn't a good thing.
Strategically speaking, it wasn't the most defendable area
Harrt had seen, but there was room to play with. The giant
pillars would make for decent cover, as would the complex

network of vats and pipes. The overhead walkways could double as an excellent vantage point, provided the shooter had a worthy aim, but that could also play into the enemy's hand.

The challenge was to get in and out as quick as possible; at least, that's how Harrt saw it.

"Okay," Harrt said, looking to Gordon and the droid. "You guys get that bomb set up next to that drive core".

As Gordon and the droid rushed ahead, Harrt grabbed Koble by the arm.

"You go with them," he said. Then while gesturing to the door behind them, "I'll hold up here and buy you as much time as possible, but they'll try and use the other entrance".

The look of someone who wanted to disagree was all over Koble's face, but the Sphinax didn't offer up a challenge. Instead, he quietly handed Harrt the last of his grenades. The pair shared a moment of companionable silence that spoke for them.

"Don't get yourself killed," Koble said. "You owe Vol a drink; I'm holding you to that".

"Thanks," Harrt nodded.

With everything said and done, Harrt got behind cover. He aimed his rifle at the door, ready for whatever was about to walk through.

Within seconds the doors hissed open, and another group of soldiers began to rush inside. Harrt threw a grenade into the pack, and moments later, it detonated, sending bodies flying across the room. With only one way in —at least on this side of the room— there was a bottleneck, and Harrt took advantage of it. He moved out of cover and mercilessly fired into the open doorway.

Eventually, his assault rifle overheated, and Harrt was forced to take up his sidearm. He retreated back into cover, firing off a few shots as Revenant forces began to spill into the room.

He took a deep breath. Knowing that the enemy numbers were increasing meant that his chances of survival were getting slim. There was a certain deja-vu to the situation that Harrt recognised immediately. It was just like Maru Seven, but with one key difference;

Harrt Oxarri had something to fight for, other than the Commonwealth.

He darted from cover, took aim and fired, killing a soldier in a single glancing shot to the head. He then turned his aim on the next soldier and fired, then the next, until finally he was struck in the shoulder by a laser bolt.

The blast penetrated his clothing and his skin in the blink of an eye, but it didn't stop Harrt from fighting. He raised his gun again, but another gunshot caught him in the leg, causing him to fall.

Unmutated soldiers surrounded him, pointing their guns in his face, and ordering him to relinquish his weapon. Harrt did his best to resist, but they wrestled the gun away from him.

Why haven't they killed me? Harrt wondered.

The answer to his question came seconds later, as Admiral Densius Olbori strode through the doorway with a smug look on his aged face.

"We need to stop meeting like this," Olbori said. Then to his troopers; "Find his Sphinax friend and bring him to me".

$\triangle$

The sound of gunfire ceased from the other side of the detonation site, making Koble's heart sink. It meant one of two things; either Harrt had fought off the entirety of the Revenant forces, or he was dead. Koble hoped for the former, but he knew the latter was more likely.

For several seconds Koble impatiently watched Gordon set up the bomb. The Earther took his sweet time, but eventually, he finished.

"We've got fifteen minutes," Gordon said.

"You are sure they won't be able to deactivate it?"

The doctor nodded before grabbing his shotgun; "So, what now?"

"Now, we've got a fight on our hands," Koble replied.

Together Koble, Gordon and the droid retraced their path through the intricate network of vats and piping. There was an acidity to the air that left Koble craving the comforts of the Phoenix Titan. The truth was that he didn't want to be there, and he certainly didn't want anyone to die, but in some strange way, Koble knew he had to be there.

This was his purpose.

Around the halfway point, Koble halted the group, making sure they were well hidden before peeking from cover. He needed to confirm what he thought he'd seen. Then when he laid eyes on what was ahead, Koble groaned.

The good news was that Harrt was alive; the bad news was that it may not be for long.

Harrt was on his knees at the centre of the room, surrounded by a mix of two dozen Revenant marines, hunters and soldiers. Behind Harrt was a uniformed old man who had his pistol pressed against the 'wealther's skull.

They must have realised that Koble was there. A sudden warning shot passed by and bounced off of the vats before dissipating into thin air. Koble was ready to open fire, but before he could, the officer at the centre of the room called out;

"Hold your fire," he yelled at his people. Then to Koble, "Chief Koble of Pluvium, I strongly urge you to drop your weapons and come out with your hands raised".

CHAPTER SEVENTY-FOUR

Nathan leapt to one side, barely avoiding the angered swipe that Seig sent his way. There was undoubtedly something different about the way the Revenant king fought this time. Gone was the shroud of confidence and decorum, replaced by blind fury and rage.

If Jack had taught Nathan one thing about combat, it was to identify the opponents' weakness and exploit it. Seig's fighting was dictated by fear. It made him heavy-handed and unwieldy. Nathan's gut told him he could take advantage of the situation.

He landed, using his forward momentum to roll across the floor. It put some distance between him and Seig, allowing Nathan to draw his pistol and empty several rounds into the King's torso. The laser bolts connected but made little impact.

Seig closed in, swinging his giant broadsword at Nathan without restraint. When Nathan used the Omega to block the attack, electrical sparks flew out in every direction. The pair went back and forth across the power chamber, exchanging hits and parries for over a minute.

Suddenly, Nathan saw an opening in Seig's offence as clear as day. The Omega whispered something to him, and Nathan shifted one way to avoid a heavy-handed swipe, then, in the same breath, he plunged the Omega into the King.

The blade cut into Seig's bicep, and the Revenant king

grimaced in pain. Seig retreated several paces and stared at the burning wound left by the Omega.

"No man has ever drawn my blood," Seig said in disbelief. "You shall—"

Nathan rushed forward, refusing to let him finish his sentence. He blocked one of Seig's attacks. Then another. The Omega whispered to Nathan, and he embraced it.

He became the aggressor. He deflected, dodged and anticipated Seig's movements, forcing the King closer to the pool of steaming liquid at the centre of the room.

He saw another opening, but the Omega urged him to exercise patience. Nathan chose to ignore it and instead swung, only for the Revenant king to ungracefully block the attack. Both men lost grip on their weapons, and as Nathan attempted to regain the Omega, Seig punched him in the head with a closed fist.

The strike was harder than Nathan expected. He stepped back, attempting to regain his footing, but Seig was too quick. The King booted him in the midsection, sending Nathan crashing into the wall. He clawed at the ground, pushed himself onto his knees and spat a mouthful of blood onto the floor. As he rose to his feet, Nathan lowered his brow and stared across the void between them.

"Your allies do not deserve your bravery," Seig said thoughtfully. "They will never truly accept you for what you are".

"It doesn't matter what I am or what the 'wealthers are," Nathan replied. "What matters is doing the right thing".

Seig's soulless eyes grew wide. His almost human mouth formed a smirk of amusement. The Revenant king raised his right palm, summoning a ball of white and black elemental energy between his spider-like fingers.

"You, son of Earth, shall die," Seig replied before hurling the summon.

Something inside Nathan changed. It wasn't the same feeling he'd had before death, but it felt eerily similar: almost dream-like. His eyes processed the image of Seig's attack, but what his mind saw was completely different.

There were hills of sand, rounded by mountains and a clear blue sky that went on for miles. A pleasant northerly wind whipped by, creating goosebumps on Nathan's pale skin. It wasn't a pre-death hallucination, and he was pretty sure it wasn't the afterlife. A strange sensation told Nathan that something was reaching out for him, and he embraced it.

As Seig's summon neared, Nathan raised his hand. What followed felt as natural as gravity, but he couldn't explain it. From his palm emerged a white bolt of elemental energy, meeting Seig's attack.

It was an Evoker attack: strong, precise and most importantly of all, deadly.

When the two summons collided, there was a loud crash. Blue flames and sparks erupted at the centre and cascaded outward. Long threads of light and energy crackled in the air. The heat of an open flame emerged from the epicentre.

Nathan didn't know how he could summon such power, but he told himself it didn't matter at that moment. He focussed everything —his mind, energy and spirit— on pushing through Seig's attack. Nathan twisted and contorted his ribbon of light until finally, it broke through Seig's summon and struck the King in the torso. The impact of the attack sent the Revenant king smashing into the wall with a bone-churning snap.

Seig's smoking body went limp, and his dark eyes were devoid of life. Nathan wasn't sure how, but he'd defeated the Revenant king, using an elemental summon.

It was impossible.

Before he could question how he'd been able to pull it off, the liquid surrounding the room began to bubble behind a red light. Crimson fell over the power chamber, and steam violently rose from the centre pool.

On the platform, Astrilla seized up, and she began to cry out in agony. Her body twisted and writhed violently as she was enveloped by thick bolts of lightning and electricity.

Without thinking, Nathan grabbed the Omega from the floor and rushed up the stairs to Astrilla. It was when he reached the platform that Nathan noticed the strange crackle of electricity surrounding him. There was a deep, thumping noise that hammered on the inside of his skull: an all-consuming, all-powerful moan that overpowered the senses.

It was at the moment that Nathan saw the Omega's true purpose.

The platform was covered in subtle carvings that made up a pattern on the ground. Despite the perfect symmetry in the design, Nathan's eyes were drawn to something at the edge.

In his mind's eye, Nathan saw a hole in the stonework, big enough for the Omega. He wasn't sure how he knew such information, but he knew it had to be done. As Nathan plunged the Omega into the mechanism, he felt the spear pull away from him. It rotated into the platform like an old key twisting to open a lock.

All of a sudden, everything stopped. The waters stopped bubbling, and the lights behind shifted from crimson to neutral. The ringing in Nathan's ears ceased, and Astrilla was no longer screaming.

When Nathan rushed to her side, he used his gun to break apart one of the bindings holding her. A wretched squeal escaped her throat as she regained consciousness. Nathan could swear that there was a fading web of electricity between her hand and the panel.

"Am I glad to see you," he said, yanking a piece of the broken metal from her wrist. "I'm gonna get you outta here, just hold on".

It took Astrilla longer to respond than Nathan anticipated.

"Kill me..." Astrilla muttered. "Please, kill me".

Nathan glanced back at her, noticing that her dark eyes were rolling back drunkenly. He chose to put her request down to injury and proceeded to smash apart the second restraint around her wrist.

"Please, don't let them use this weapon again," Astrilla yelled.

After a few seconds, the bindings around her wrists were gone, and Astrilla crumpled onto the ground in exhaustion. A surge of energy came from the monolith as the connection was severed. The circuit powering the Messorem was finally broken.

"It's done," Nathan said, kneeling down to help Astrilla up. "C'mon, we've gotta—"

Something elemental struck Nathan in the back.

He staggered and stumbled before falling to the ground. For a long moment, Nathan felt like the flesh on his bones would explode if he moved. The impact seared deep into his skin like a wildfire spreading through a forest. The agony and torment expanded over his every nerve and muscle until all Nathan could feel was burning.

It felt like dying all over again.

"You feel it don't you?" Seig mocked as he stepped onto the platform. "You feel the embrace of the Void".

Panic gripped Nathan, but to his surprise, the words of Jack scratched into his mind; *Never let them see you bleed.*

Nathan looked up in defiance as the Revenant king snatched the Omega from the mechanism. Helplessly, Nathan tried his best to move, but his limbs felt heavy and sluggish. Seig met his gaze with a hateful and vicious glare. Then as though the Omega were nothing more than a piece of junk, Seig tossed it into the waters below.

"Do not look at death as though it is a failure, my friend," Seig said, his voice sounding almost remorseful. "You have been a most worthy adversary, and I thank you for the challenge."

Nathan willed himself to move, but despite all his efforts, his body simply wouldn't respond. He peeled his gaze away from Seig, choosing instead to gaze upon Astrilla one last time.

Even behind her tears, Nathan still saw her beauty. She was as perfect as the first time he'd laid eyes on her. Granted, she'd thrown him through a wall seconds after their first encounter, but that wasn't the point. She was something to him that no one else had ever been —that nobody else could ever be.

Neither he nor Astrilla needed to say a thing. The connection was still there. He felt what she felt and vice versa.

"May the Great Void bring you peace," Seig declared. Then like a woodchuck kicking down a partially hacked tree, the Revenant king booted Nathan in the chest, sending him from the platform and into the pool below.

As Nathan hit the water, the only thought he had was of his crew and of Astrilla. He didn't want to embrace what was next.

$$\triangle$$

As soon as the early casualty reports began to hit Dines' datapad, he turned the device off. It was a breach of command protocols that would ordinarily be met by court martial, but Leviticus Dines did not care about consequences anymore. He was done with all the bureaucracy and politics.

Trillions died the second Unity was struck by the Messorem's weapons array. More were dying by the second as the battle raged on. Dines ignored the part of himself that said that all of those deaths were on him. He knew that the moment he started questioning his own command was a moment he couldn't afford.

Behind the sound of shrieking terminals and the rumble of battle, someone was calling him across the bridge. It took Dines' brain longer than it should to cut through all the background noise and realise that an officer was calling out to him.

"Agent Dines, Sir!" The tactical officer yelled. "Looks like something has happened to their shield array. We're detecting unusual spikes in energy".

Dines pushed past the officer to gaze out of the window. Before, the Messorem's shields looked like a solid green outline against the blackness of space. Now they looked more like a blinking light, switching on and off every few seconds.

Dines turned to the officer;

"Can our fighters get through?"

The officer seemed to consider his words carefully.

"They would have to be suicidal," he answered with a cautious nod. "But if they are quick...maybe".

As Dines was about to give the order to proceed, a ship-wide proximity alert began to howl. He glanced out of the window again, noticing several ivory coloured ships entering the battlefield.

There was only one corporation in the galaxy with spacecraft like it: Jareth Corps. For a split second, Dines was elated. He wanted to believe that finally, David Jareth had put aside his separatist values and seen he shared a common enemy with the 'wealth. Of course, reality dragged Dines back to the moment when the Jareth ships didn't advance toward the battlefield.

"Sir, the Jareth flagship is requesting communication with you," the comms officer said.

Dines took a deep breath. "Patch 'em through to my station".

Seconds later, the holographic image of Ralph Hayward formed in front of Dines. The Earther folded his big arms and regarded Dines with a sharp, professional look.

"Mr Hayward," Dines nodded in greeting. "I see you convinced your boss to join the fight. Did Carter's little speech help?"

The bald, muscular Earther glanced back at Dines sternly and didn't say anything for an awkward amount of time. His expression was almost unreadable.

"Mr Jareth wants to offer the Commonwealth some assistance during your hour of need," Hayward said. "Of course, we wouldn't be much of a business if we didn't ask for something in return".

There it was: the deal. Dines had seen it coming seconds before, but he was still surprised. It made him sick that David Jareth was still plotting and scheming away even in the most desperate of situations.

Regardless of Jareth and his capitalist dream, Dines forced himself to put aside his pride and values. Trillions of lives were at stake.

"What do you want?" Dines narrowed his eyes at Hayward.

The big Earther's expression turned a mix of sinister and arrogant. It left Dines feeling as though the muscle-bound Earther was reading his mind. It was a most unsettling feeling.

Finally, Hayward cleared his throat and gave his answer.

"Jareth Corps kindly requests a data transfer; right now," Hayward shrugged in an almost apologetic fashion. "Specifically, we want all Commonwealth data regarding Earth, the Fall, and everything that ever concerned our homeworld".

Intel such as that was regarded as classified, and there was a good reason for it. The sharing of secretive documentation was a punishable offence, especially if it cast shade on the Commonwealth. Dines knew he'd be breaking dozens, if not hundreds, of patriotic commandments if he went through with it. He also knew that there wouldn't be much of a Commonwealth left if he didn't act swiftly. More Jareth Corps warships and drones began to enter Capital Space, but none of them engaged in the battle.

It wasn't ideal, but it was the best bet Dines had to even the odds. He knew there would surely be consequences for what he was about to do. The thing was, Leviticus Dines didn't care about consequences anymore. All he cared about was saving lives. He hit the transfer button, sending thousands of classified files to Jareth Corps.

CHAPTER SEVENTY-FIVE

Laser fire chased the Phoenix from every direction. Vol could've sworn that her number of pursuers was increasing by the second. She spotted another group of enemy fighters heading straight toward her. Without thinking, she slammed the Phoenix hard to port, allowing Russell to snap off several precise shots. In the corner of her eye, Vol saw a small batch of the fighters explode. Then, before she could even think about smiling, the Phoenix jolted violently. A single bolt struck the ship's starboard quarter, and a warning warble followed.

"It's getting rough back here!" Russell's panicked voice cried out through the communicator.

Vol ignored him, twisting the Phoenix in a corkscrew between two protruding structures on the Messorem's hull. She noticed something flicker overhead and assumed it was enemy gunfire. Then she looked again. The Messorem's shields were blinking, almost as though someone was flicking them on and off.

"Are you seeing this?" she said into her comm.

Russell's reply came a few seconds after;

"Yeah," he said. "You think the guys did it?"

Vol didn't want to speculate, especially not while fleeing a few dozen Revenant fighters in a closed space. She twisted the Phoenix around a skeletal tower. Behind, two of the fighters broke out from the pack in an attempt to ram the Phoenix. Unfortunately for them, Vol anticipated the overly aggressive move and jolted the ship to one side. Both Revenant fighters met a grizzly end as they smashed into the tower.

When Vol circled the Phoenix around to get another run at the firing array, she saw what they were up against. To say that the enemy had the numbers was an understatement. The Phoenix's instruments detected three dozen fighters, but it looked like a lot more to the naked eye.

"Still think we're gonna make it?" Russell asked grimly. "That's a whole bunch of Revenant, and we're all alone in here".

A sudden crackle broke the comm, and for a moment, Vol was positive that the ship had been struck again. A familiar, boisterous voice emerged through the static interference.

"You need to lighten up, my friend; you'll live longer!"

The accent was Sphinax, heavier than Koble's and oozing a hell of a lot more charm. Vol recognised Rain's voice immediately.

"The Phoenix Titan will never be alone," Rain said.

Sphinax fighters rushed across the Messorem, meeting the Revenant in battle. The numbers were starting to look good, not great, but far better than they'd been twenty seconds earlier.

"Rain?" Vol said in surprise. She rechecked the proximity monitor, almost unable to believe what she was seeing. "You got through their shields!"

"We detected that you were in a little trouble, my dear." Rain answered. Vol could almost imagine the blue-furred Sphinax beaming ear to ear as he attempted to charm her over comms. "We saw the shields on this thing were partially working, so thought we'd take the risk and show the 'wealthers who has the best pilots in the galaxy."

"Not complaining or anything, but you are one crazy bastard," Russell interjected.

The Revenant fighters broke formation, splitting out in every direction as the Sphinax pilots began to demonstrate the sheer strength of their flying abilities. There was something to be said for the proficiency and skillset of a pilot over sheer numbers. An average aviator could just about pull a corkscrew, but it took a genuinely savvy aerialist to do it while taking on four other ships at the same time.

"So," Rain drawled. "Gimme a rundown of the objectives here, and while we're at it, where the hell is Koble?"

Vol outlined the plan in a single breath.

"Destroy the firing array at these coordinates." She tapped the nav terminal and sent the details out to Rain and his people. "Then I gotta return to the interior and exfil the others".

"Sounds like a challenge," Rain mused. "Okay, we'll keep your Revenant friends busy while you do what you need to do."

"Sounds good to me!" Vol said. "First round of drinks on me when this is all done, pal".

There came a short chuckle from Rain; "I hope you both like Sphinax wine."

"Never tried it," Russell said. "I hear it tastes kinda fishy?"

Vol pictured the devilish smirk on Rain's face as he answered, "Only slightly".

△

Astrilla looked down as Nathan disappeared beneath the surface of the thick grey sludge. The water twisted like a whirlpool as it swallowed him into the abyss. Seig had condemned him to the same fate as the mutated. It was a fate worse than death.

Astrilla wanted to cry. She wanted to mourn the man who'd made her feel alive again.

The Revenant king laughed maniacally. Astrilla bit back her sense of sadness. She wiped a tear from her eye and unsteadily climbed to her feet, focusing her steely gaze on the Revenant king. Seig had spent months searching for her. He'd uprooted her entire life to power an Enkaye warmachine. He was the one who'd used her to fire the Messorem, not once but twice. He'd used her to slaughter trillions.

Subjecting Nathan to such a death made things personal: not only would Astrilla fight him and kill him, but she'd allow hate to dictate her actions. If the Revenant king were to die, he'd die in a lot of pain.

"I am the bringer of death," Seig declared. He glared at her with wild eyes and began to recite a passage from his holy texts. "I am law, I am order, I am pain, I am fate, I am Revenant, I am Seig, and I shall—"

Astrilla didn't allow him to continue. She cast a summon of fire and threw it directly into his face. It wasn't intended to kill, only to torture: Astrilla wasn't going to let Seig die that easily. The attack connected, mercilessly burning into Seig's flesh like acid. Before he could react, Astrilla followed up with a dropkick, sending the King crashing to the ground below.

She leapt from the platform to face her enemy. As the Revenant king climbed to his feet, he wiped his hand across the bloody, burning wound on his face.

"We are not done," he hissed. "You will finish the work we started. For only then will I grant you death".

Despite the anaesthetics and overall sense of exhaustion, Astrilla didn't want an easy fight: she wanted to inflict pain on the Revenant king. Astrilla wanted him to suffer as she had.

△

"You have one minute to come out with your hands up," Olbori yelled. Koble peered from cover to assess the situation. The Admiral had his gun pointed directly at Harrt's skull, and around two dozen Revenant personnel had rallied around him.

"If you do not emerge after that time has elapsed, I will shoot Lieutenant Oxarri in the head," Olbori continued.

"Don't do it, Koble," Harrt yelled. "Blow the bomb,

don't let these bastards—"

One of the Revenant marines slammed the butt of a rifle into Harrt's head, knocking the 'wealther onto the floor. Koble couldn't help but wince at the strike. Two of Olbori's men dragged Harrt back to his knees, and the Revenant Grand Admiral resumed his tirade:

"I will kill him," Olbori threatened. "Mark my words, you Sphinax scum, this is not a fight you can win".

Koble didn't like being insulted, and he felt the need to respond in kind. The phrase, *wrinkled-old-prunus-fruit,* formed on Koble's lips. Then some other profanities inspired by Jack and Nathan came to mind.

He was about ready to reply with his own witty insult, but then he realised something. Olbori was only referring to him, not the droid or Gordon.

He debated the question for a moment, wondering if perhaps he'd found an opportunity. If he was wrong, they'd all die in a horrible gunfight, either that or the bomb would explode, and they'd all die anyway. On the other hand, there was a slim chance that Olbori hadn't accounted for Gordon and the droid. If that were the case, Koble knew he could exploit it.

Just as Jack used to say, find a weakness, Koble thought.

He turned to Gordon, who was wiping sweat from his brow. The droid was hovering low to the ground with its ocular sensor fixed on Koble.

"What are we gonna do?" Gordon said.

The Earther's voice didn't sound as anxious as Koble expected. Over the years, he'd come to understand the human response to high-pressure situations. Most humans would perspire, breathe rapidly and, in many cases, get highly emotional. Gordon was only one of those things, and it left Koble feeling as though he'd misjudged the older man. Rather than being the *lab-geek* that Jack had described him to be, Gordon Taggart looked decidedly calm.

"How good is that aim of yours, Doc?" Koble said in a low voice. Then after checking over his shoulder, "You got any issues shooting a non-mutated type?"

Gordon's gaze turned steely, and he tensed his jaw before answering.

"I've killed before," the doctor nodded, with a low factual voice.

Gordon's answer, despite not being what Koble expected, was good enough. He handed the Earther his heavy assault rifle.

"Okay, here's the score," Koble began. "That gun will charge up to three hundred rounds: point and shoot, simple as that".

Seeing Gordon holding the gun made Koble realise just how bulky he was compared to a human. It positively made Gordon look like half a man in height.

"I'm gonna go out there and stall them," Koble continued. "When I give you the signal, you come out of cover and rain down all kinds of hell on these bastards. I'll deal with the old guy; you just worry about the soldiers. Start on the left and work your way right. Don't stop firing until they are all dead. Got it?"

Gordon nodded.

Koble took a deep sobering breath. Then, as he was about to move out and initiate the plan, Gordon halted him.

"For the record," Gordon said. "Jack was a bastard for what he did; I could never forgive that, but you are a far better man than he ever was".

Koble nodded, then as he began to turn, Gordon stopped him again.

"One more thing, what's the signal?"

"Hmm, let's see..." Koble mused. After a few seconds, he snapped his fingers in a eureka moment and said the words aloud; "My left ear".

Gordon nodded, and with that said and done, Koble moved from cover with his paws raised in surrender.

The back of the room was lined with more soldiers than Koble expected. Each of them trained their weapons on him as he stepped out into the open. It felt like suicide to see so many weapons pointed at him at once. Several metres ahead of the pack was Admiral Olbori, with his gun pressed against Harrt's head. As Koble got within five metres, the

Revenant Admiral ordered him to stop.

"Not another step," Olbori hissed.

The senior Revenant officer looked unwell. There was a certain thinness to his face that suggested a life of hardship. His mahogany skin looked almost ashen under the harsh overhead lighting.

Koble was more than confident he could kill the man without breaking a sweat, but that wasn't the problem: getting the gun clear of Harrt's head was. Fortunately, Koble had a plan to deal with that particular issue, but first, he had to distract his enemy and make them think he was a fool.

"Whoa," Koble smiled arrogantly. "Fellas, can't we just talk about this for a minute?"

"Silence!" Olbori bellowed, and his voice reverberated off the walls. Just as Koble hoped, the Admiral pulled his gun from Harrt's head and gestured with it. "Get on the floor, with your filthy Sphinax paws behind your head".

"Whoa, whoa," Koble said, raising his voice as a distraction. "Cool it with the insults. We're all friends here, right? We can talk to one another with a bit of respect".

Koble knew that one would cause a bit of controversy. He could almost see the vein in Olbori's forehead that was about ready to burst, which meant his plan was working. Before the Admiral could say another word, Koble began to speak in the most obnoxious, over-the-top manner he possibly could.

"Listen here, guys," Koble said with a cocky smirk. "We're at an impasse here. Let's sit down and discuss this like civilised people".

Olbori's jaw tightened to the point where it looked like he'd break a tooth if he applied any more pressure. The soldiers and troops around Olbori began to glance at one another in confusion. Harrt stared at Koble with an expression that practically said, *what the hell do you think you are doing?*

"Now, what say we all just lay down our weapons and talk this out?" Koble finally stopped for breath, allowing a look of sheer arrogance to mask his true intentions.

Olbori pointed his gun directly at Koble. The anger and

rage were painted across his wrinkled visage so blatantly that Koble could've seen it from space.

"Get on your knees," Olbori seethed. "Hands behind your head".

Koble winked at the old man, but it wasn't intended for him at all. It was for Harrt. Koble raised both paws and placed them on his head. As he continued to talk belligerently at Olbori, Koble reached into the thick tuft of fur on his neck and grabbed the concealed combat knife he'd hidden earlier.

It was a dirty move straight out of Kornell's playbook, but Koble couldn't help but admit it was genius. He ranted a little more until finally, he was ready to give the signal to Gordon and the droid.

"I knew you guys wouldn't be willing to talk," Koble said dramatically. "I bet my left ear with the other guy but —"

Olbori's gaze shifted, and Koble heard the unmistakable chatter of his assault rifle. As Olbori turned his gun on Harrt, Koble took up his knife and launched it toward the Revenant Admiral.

CHAPTER SEVENTY-SIX

Nathan opened his eyes.

Amid great darkness was a single point of radiance from a great distance. Before Nathan knew what was happening, the light surrounded him. The gravity accelerated exponentially, dragging him down as if caught in a drain. The momentum got stronger and stronger until finally, everything stopped.

Everything became serene. There was no sense of falling, no motion at all. Nathan had time to wonder if he was dying, dreaming or hallucinating. All he knew was that he should have been dead, and there was a good chance that maybe he was. Somehow Nathan sensed that wasn't the case. He couldn't begin to explain how or why; he just knew.

He was sat at a park bench in the middle of a desert, the same one from the visions he'd shared with Astrilla. The sand beneath his feet was coarse and warm. The breeze stirred gently and carried with it a pleasant Earthy aroma. If this was death, then at least it was peaceful.

"I've been waiting for you for what feels like a lifetime, my dear boy". The voice was familiar.

Nathan turned.

Sitting beside him was a familiar gentleman in his early seventies. He wore a brown tweed blazer atop a button-down shirt. His glasses were dark, with thick frames that somehow reminded Nathan of Gordon. The way his dark grey hair curled at the ends and the striking blue of his eyes were just as

Nathan remembered: just as they looked in his memories.

The man beside him was his grandfather, Bill Stephens.

Everything Nathan knew told him that it was impossible, that Bill Stephens had died over a quarter of a century ago: *after all, that was what Gordon had said.*

Yet there he was, alive and in the flesh, and more importantly, unaffected by the ravages of time. Given that it had been twenty-five years since Nathan last saw him, Bill Stephens should've looked like a man in his nineties. But, instead, he looked just as Nathan recalled. Nathan wanted to probe for questions, but he had to stop and marvel at the significance of it.

They were both present in a single moment: grandfather and grandson, reunited outside the boundaries of life and death. Nathan wanted to say all the things he'd stored up over the years, but instead, he found himself asking the most obvious of questions.

"Am I dead?"

Bill Stephens offered a dry smile in response. "No, my dear boy: quite the contrary in fact".

Nathan raised a brow to his long-dead grandfather, unable to quite grasp what his cryptic response was meant to imply. He gestured to the peaceful landscape surrounding them and asked;

"Are you sure about that?"

"Pretty sure," Bill nodded assuringly.

"So, how come the last thing I remember is being aboard the Messorem and falling to my death?" Nathan asked. "How come I'm looking at you? How come I'm looking at a man who's been dead for years?"

As Nathan stood, he noticed that his clothes were not the same as those he'd been wearing aboard the Messorem. Gone was his dark shirt and jeans, replaced by linen trousers and a light shirt that somehow seemed climate appropriate for whatever this place was.

"Well, the answer to all of those questions is very simple," Bill said, folding one leg over the other. "You and the Omega are still aboard the Messorem, inside the very life force that powers the machine".

"You mean the grey liquid?" Nathan raised a brow. "The stuff that turns dead people into Revenant soldiers?"

"Correct, but that is not its true purpose," Bill answered. "You see, the Revenant king made a fatal error in judgement. He cast you and the Omega into the waters, which was a rather stupid move on his part, but it's an excellent thing for you".

Nathan couldn't help but frown at his grandfather's statement. Nothing he said made any sense, and it caused Nathan to ask, "Why?"

Bill smiled at him without humour. He used the same look back in the day when asked something that had an obvious answer, at least to him. The funny thing was that Nathan recognised the same expression not only in himself but also in Jack.

"After thousands of years, the Enkaye's plan is finally coming to fruition," Bill answered. "You see, for any normal being, contact with the great waters would be fatal".

The old man peered through his glasses at Nathan expectantly. It was almost as though he were prompting Nathan to understand something obvious.

"What do you mean, *normal being*?"

It was at that moment that Bill Stephens climbed to his feet. He shuffled across the sand to Nathan's side and placed a hand on his shoulder. It felt real —it was real.

"Isn't it obvious?"

"No," Nathan shook his head. "It isn't".

"By chance, you happen upon a woman, with whom eventually you share a strong connection: a woman who is of Enkaye descent: a woman with whom you share visions," Bill stopped and gazed at Nathan wistfully. "Then, on Pelos Three, you and her were drawn to an ancient place that had laid dormant for thousands of years: that is until you arrived".

Something in the old man's words prodded in Nathan's mind. Every logical part of him said that he was okay, that Bill Stephens was simply trying to make a point; however, instinct urged him to resist. Nathan tried to take a step back, but his grandfather clasped his shoulder and continued to speak.

"When you first came aboard the Phoenix Titan, you found messages left to you by Jack. On Pelos Three, you were given a map that led you to Mirotose Station, to Krell and more importantly, to the droid," Bill barely stopped for breath as he recounted everything that Nathan had been through. "Jack sent you looking for my old protege, Doctor Gordon Taggart, in the hope of repairing that droid. After facing Seig the first time, you died a horrible death".

Nathan could still feel the broadsword cutting into his flesh. The memory sent chills down his spine, forcing him to break eye contact with his grandfather. Bill placed his hand on Nathan's face, drawing his gaze upward. The very human gesture was intended to comfort him, as though Nathan were a small child with a grazed knee. It told him that the man he was speaking to was the real deal and not some hallucination.

"I am so sorry that you had to go through that, my dear boy," Bill's voice softened. "Unfortunately for the Revenant king, you were miraculously revived by that droid".

Bill's voice trailed off, and he glanced out at a distance. While he'd been speaking, the sun had set against the horizon. As a northerly breeze passed them by, Bill looked at him with an apologetic expression. He sighed;

"That droid can only activate in the presence of a living Enkaye, or at least someone with their DNA".

"Astrilla was nowhere near the droid when it resurrected me," Nathan argued. "Gordon fixed it..."

Nathan's voice trailed off as the realisation set in. Then, finally, he saw the answer laid out before him as clear as day, but he didn't want to believe it.

"You mean that the droid would only activate in the presence of someone who possessed the Enkaye DNA.." Nathan stopped and allowed the thought to wash over him. Then as though he were a curious child once again, Nathan looked at his grandfather, "Are you saying that I'm like Astrilla? Are you saying that I somehow possess Enkaye DNA?"

Bill nodded once.

"The heritage you possess is both of Earth and of the Enkaye," he answered. "You, like me, and Jack and your mother, possess the blood of the Enkaye. We have and will always be a part of their grand plan. You are a child of two species, destined for greatness".

In a state of disbelief, Nathan stared at Bill. His mind whirled with those words. For a moment, Nathan didn't know how to process it. He was unable to breathe, unable to fathom words with the realisation that he'd always been more than just human. His mind filled with a hundred questions at once, *How is something like that possible? Who is my Enkaye ancestor? How did I never know about this?*

Then one thought overrode all others.

"Jack knew, didn't he?" Nathan looked at his grandfather. "Jack knew that we are descendants of the Enkaye..."

Bill's shoulders slumped ever so slightly. It was a subtle emotional cue that conveyed a sense of something that looked like defeat.

"Not the whole time," Bill said remorsefully. "It was only toward the end that he found out the truth".

Nathan saw the sadness creep into his grandfather's eyes. The old man gazed across the enormous dunes without saying a word. It left Nathan wondering *how long Jack had known before Mirotose Station.*

"You see, Jack came to understand that much like you, he had a part to play in the Enkaye's plan. He knew that you and Astrilla were going to find one another, and more importantly, he knew what that meant for the future".

Nathan felt a sudden tightness in his throat. "What do you mean, *future*?" he asked.

"That is all to come," Bill answered with a knowing twinkle in his eye. "All you need to know is that Jack did everything he could to make sure you had the best chance of success. He loved you so much that he sacrificed himself to ensure you arrived here; at this moment; in this place".

Nathan tried his best to push back the overwhelming urge to tear up at the statement. The words *never let them see you bleed* seemed inappropriate given his present company, but he still embraced the notion. With a stiff upper lip, Nathan nodded, and Bill continued:

"Now, to the task at hand. We need to get you out of here and back into the fight; otherwise, that mad Revenant bastard is going to take more lives. Personally, I'd say he needs to be stopped, wouldn't you agree?"

Nathan wanted to press him for more answers, but the old man was right. While Astrilla was aboard the Messorem, Seig had the capability of killing countless more. Reluctantly, Nathan chose to nod, and his grandfather continued;

"Now, I just want to let you know that the river that runs through the Messorem has some..." Bill paused for thought. "Let's just say, supernatural properties".

"Meaning?"

"Meaning, that for you, it feels like we've been having this conversation for several minutes," Bill said, glancing at his watch. "In reality, you've been in the liquid for maybe fifteen seconds".

"What?" Nathan said flatly. "You mean all this—"

Bill continued to speak over him as though he were in a rush.

"When you wake up, you must reacquire the Omega and use it to put an end to Seig," Bill said. "Once it is done, you will face a choice that will dictate everything that is to come. It is your decision to make, and yours alone".

"And how do I know that I picked correctly?"

"You'll know," Bill answered.

Suddenly, the breeze grew strong, whipping the sand into the air. The sky above seemed to rip away as everything began to vibrate violently. To Nathan, it was like the universe falling in on itself. Through the riptide of space falling around him, Nathan looked at his grandfather. The old man was calm, as though everything going on was completely normal.

"Will I ever see you again?" Nathan called out over the noise.

Bill's nod was accompanied by a faint smile.

The sandy dunes began to wash away as though caught in a rough current. Within the crumbling sky, Nathan saw stars and planets rush by and decay into nothingness.

"Oh, can you do me a favour?" Bill yelled. "Next time you see Gordon, tell him that I said thank you; he'll know what for".

"I will," Nathan nodded. Then out of sheer curiosity, he asked, "What about Jack? Why wasn't he here to meet me?"

The spectre of Bill Stephens looked at him with a blank expression that didn't give anything away. Nathan stared at his grandfather's face eagerly, hoping that the old man would say something about Jack, but there was nothing. Before Nathan could ask again, Bill Stephens was swept away with the sand. Everything around Nathan collapsed, like a dream coming to an abrupt end.

When Nathan opened his eyes, he saw darkness. He was floating aimlessly in the rivers of the Messorem. It was just as his grandfather said. As Nathan looked around, the grey liquid began to change, transforming from a muddy sludge to crystal-clear water.

Metres ahead, Nathan saw the glow of the Omega, and he reached out for it. The moment his hand made contact, he felt something powerful course through his very being. The sensation that flooded his spirit was like a crashing wave in the ocean. Thousands upon thousands of voices were calling out to him: not in terror, but in salutation. The Messorem had recognised who, or rather, what he was, and now Captain Nathan Carter was in control of the system. He could feel all the long-dead Enkaye ripple against the tide: as though they were watching everything unfold.

A white light emerged from the Omega, illuminating everything in all directions. The liquid around Nathan began to bubble like a pan of boiled water, but it was neither warm nor cold. It was a guiding current, sending Nathan back to the power chamber: back to Seig and, more importantly, back to Astrilla.

As he neared the surface, an unfamiliar voice spoke inside his head.

"You have the power of a million generations within you," it said. "Make them proud, s*on of Earth*".

CHAPTER SEVENTY-SEVEN

Two elemental summons met at the centre of the power chamber, casting sparks and fire across the vast room. Astrilla reached into her very being, willing herself to push through Seig's attack. Despite being in the fight for a short while, she knew that her strength was starting to waver. The giant incandescent flares bursting from her palms would not hold out for long, and she knew that another course of action had to be taken. Astrilla spotted Nathan's rifle on the floor. Despite knowing that the weapon would inflict minor damage on the Revenant king, it was a chance for her to recover.

She veered off, breaking her summon away while dodging Seig's. She retreated toward the gun, casting two quick summons that were intended as a distraction. The first missed, but the second connected with Seig, searing into his hip.

The tactic bought her less than a heartbeat.

Astrilla lunged for the gun, grabbing it by the barrel and swinging it in a wide arc. The modified metal stock slammed into the King's jaw with a crunch, knocking his head sideways. Seig straightened his head and spat out the shattered remains of a tooth. Astrilla rotated the rifle into a firing position and squeezed on the trigger, but no laser fire followed.

Seig shot forward, grabbing Astrilla by the throat and slamming her into the ground. The impact sent pain surging up her spine and neck. Her head banged against the hard metal floor, causing her ears to ring and her vision to shake.

The Revenant king eyed her thoughtfully as his spider-like hand tightened around her windpipe. Then, he lifted her by the throat, holding her in the air like she were nothing more than a ragdoll. He could've killed her with the slightest twist, but he did no such thing.

"When you and I have finished the work, I shall truly enjoy watching you die," Seig hissed. "Until then, you will power this magnificent machine".

A blinding white light emerged from the walls. Giant forks of lightning materialised from the liquid pit, washing away any hint of shadow from the room. The air whooshed through Astrilla's hair as though she were standing on the peak of a tall mountain. The webs of electricity grew in both scale and brightness until finally, they reached out, striking the Revenant king across the room and forcing him to release his grip.

When Astrilla sat up, she blinked furiously, clearing the colourless glare from her eyes. She turned her gaze back to the liquid pit, where the water swelled into a violent vortex. Everything about the whirlwind of liquid and lightning should have been terrifying, but somehow Astrilla knew it was the opposite. It was Enkaye technology working as intended. Not the bastardisation that the Revenant had twisted it into.

Gone was the poison sludge that subjected the dead to conversion, replaced by something pure.

At first, Astrilla thought it was her presence that had caused the change, but when Nathan emerged from the vortex, she realised that there was more going on than she'd first thought.

▲

As Nathan emerged from the waters, armed with the Omega, his gaze met Astrilla's. There was so much he needed to say, but there wasn't the time. Bill Stephens had sent him back with both a purpose and a vital objective that needed to be completed.

He set his eyes on Seig. The Revenant king was stood with his broadsword drawn, ready for battle. The expression of raw anger and madness was presenting in the monarch's dark eyes.

"Why won't you die!" Seig screamed with burning rage.

Nathan didn't respond. He felt the power of both the Messorem and the Omega flowing through his veins, along with the blood of his ancestors. Astrilla stepped to Nathan's side, raising her palms and forming perfect spheres of elemental fire.

They were ready to face Seig. Together.

In a frenzy of madness, Seig lifted his sword and dashed toward them. The look on his warped features implied that he was sure of his victory. As Seig brought his broadsword around in a sweeping motion to strike them both, Astrilla leapt over the blade, while Nathan brought the Omega up to block the attack.

When the two weapons met, there was a crash. Seig's expression changed the moment his sword shattered into a million pieces.

As Nathan looked into the eyes of his enemy, he heard one of Jack's lessons play out in his mind;

Never let them see you bleed: never, ever let them win. You keep fighting until the day is done or die trying.

Nathan plunged the Omega into Seig's heart.

The stricken Revenant king gasped in disbelief as the cold metal weapon sliced through him. A mix of curiosity and defeat filled Seig's face as he stared down at the blade still lodged in his heart.

When Nathan yanked the Omega from Seig's body, there was an almighty crack. The Revenant king fell to his knees in a pool of his own blood, inches away from the liquid pit.

"You!" Seig spat a mouthful of blood onto the floor. Then, he nodded in Astrilla's direction, "You are an Enkaye half-breed like her, aren't you?"

Nathan didn't dignify him with an answer.

"You destroyed Earth," Nathan said behind gritted

teeth. "You destroyed so many worlds, and for what?"

"Everything I have done is in the pursuit of order," Seig answered with a hiss. "That is something your kind could never truly understand".

Nathan could still picture the slaughter of his family at the hands of the Revenant. He felt the weight of the Omega as the pain and agony washed over him.

The dying Revenant king lifted his head to look Nathan in the eye. It was hard to ignore the thick dark blood that trickled from the corners of his eyes and mouth.

"This war will not end with me," Seig coughed. "You cannot stop the darkness that is to come—"

Astrilla threw an elemental summon straight through Seig's chest, obliterating flesh and organs in a merciless burning strike. An explosion of blood burst from Seig's torso, spraying against the floor and walls. The King's dark eyes went wide with shock, then he fell backwards into the River.

The waters dragged Seig under the surface, and he didn't come back up.

For a moment, Nathan couldn't believe it. He stood in silence with Astrilla as he watched the Revenant king disappear beneath the bubbling surface of the water.

"Are you okay?" he finally said, turning to look at the Evoker.

Silence lingered between them.

"Better now," she gestured to the blood riddled pool that had absorbed her former captor.

Astrilla turned and set her gaze on Nathan. The look in her eyes suggested that she had a few million questions. Then as she took his hand, she asked with a soft voice;

"You're like me, aren't you?"

Darkness whirled there. And truth. Nathan didn't want to admit it, but the prospect of what he really was frightened him.

"Yeah," he whispered. "I am".

He felt the ten thousand emotions, thoughts and sentiments that washed over her mind. But, in the end, all that remained was a realisation that he wasn't alone anymore. At that moment, Nathan wanted nothing more than to leave with her and get as far away as possible.

All of a sudden, Nathan's datapad alarmed with an incoming communication. He assumed it was one of the others, calling to tell him that the bomb was set and that it was time to hightail it outta there. Without hesitation, Nathan drew his soaking wet datapad from his pocket, which had somehow survived the submergence, and accepted the communication. The hologram that started to form was slow and pixelated, as though the transmission signal was suffering interference.

"Harrt?" Nathan said, hoping for a reply.

The projection twisted and contorted until finally, the snake-like face of David Jareth appeared on the other side of their communication.

"Hello, Mr Carter," Jareth said.

▲

The very second that Gordon opened fire, Koble took action. Olbori turned his gun on Harrt, and without hesitation, Koble flung his combat knife across the space between them. The moment his concealed blade left his paw, Koble leapt toward Harrt, hoping he could save the 'wealther before it was too late.

A barrage of laser fire cut through the unsuspecting Revenant marines as Gordon rained hell from left to right. The familiar clatter of Koble's modified heavy rifle filled the room as its new operator used it with surprising accuracy.

As Koble pounced across the five-metre gap toward Harrt and Admiral Olbori, he watched his knife soar toward its target. There was a certain sparkle to the glistening blade that he'd never noticed. It was beautiful in a weird way.

Then as quickly as the moment started, so too it ended.

The combat knife sliced deep into Densuis Olbori's arm, sending a cloud of crimson blood into the sky. The old man fell to the floor, relinquishing his weapon in the process. Koble landed just shy of Harrt's position, but fortunately, the 'wealther had darted to the floor out of instinct.

The roar of gunfire was so overpowering that for a while, it was all Koble could hear. With every round that Gordon fired, a high pitched chatter followed. It was then accompanied by either the blare of ricocheting gunfire or the sound of laser meeting flesh.

All at once, the whir of Gordon's gun ceased, and Koble lifted his head. The first thing he saw was Harrt, just inches away, looking back at him with an equally stunned expression.

"You good?" Koble said in disbelief.

Harrt nodded, "Yeah. You?"

"I guess," Koble's reply was musical, yet sardonic. "I mean, that was my good knife, but hey, you can owe me, right?"

There was only a second of levity between the pair. As Koble lifted his head, he saw the devastation around him. The bodies of over two dozen Revenant soldiers littered the floor. Blood was everywhere. Gordon was still holding the smoking rifle with a bewildered expression on his face.

Behind, Koble heard a cough. Admiral Densius Olbori clawed at the floor in a feeble attempt to escape. The knife was still lodged deep in his arm, and a trail of blood followed the old man as he slithered across the floor.

"It's over, Densius," Harrt said as he climbed to his feet.

Olbori tried to crawl but quickly realised it was to no avail. The Revenant Admiral rolled onto his back and chuckled to himself.

"Do it," Olbori said with a defeat in his voice. "Get it over and done with".

Koble watched Harrt grab a discarded pistol from the ground. He could already see the years of anger and rage bubbling to the surface of Harrt's hardened expression. Koble knew what Harrt had lost, and he could relate.

A mix of instinct and experience told him to not get involved, so he watched from the sidelines.

"There's one thing I need to know before we get this

over and done with," Harrt spoke slowly and in a low, intimidating voice that hinted at a darkness that Koble had never seen in the man. "Why did you do it? Why did you turn your back on everything you ever believed in? Why did you give up the dream of liberty? Why did you burn our homeworld in service of the Revenant?"

Olbori's expression grew thoughtful.

"Because *liberty* is a lie, told to us by a government so corrupt that they no longer represent the people," Olbori said. "The Commonwealth Council believe that they are so pure and virtuous that they are entitled to tell people how to live their lives; how to think, speak and act".

"Stop it," Harrt said, but Olbori continued to speak over him.

"Ask yourself, why do they tell the citizens how to feel? Why do they try to control our thoughts? Why do they tell us who we can and can't love?" Olbori raised his voice. "I did what I did because the dream of liberty —*true liberty* is dead. It has been replaced by a shroud of lies and deceit, intended only to control".

"What about my wife and child?" Harrt yelled. "They were innocent!"

"What's the first thing you learn at the Academy about war?" Olbori said. "Loss of life, civilian, military or otherwise, is to be expected".

Harrt's brow furrowed, and for a second, Koble wondered what was going through the 'wealthers head. It was a strange moment of conflict that Koble had never experienced before.

Olbori struggled to his knees, and as he straightened up, he looked Harrt in the eye.

"I will not beg for my life," Olbori said to Harrt. "But I will offer my apologies for that which I took from you, my old friend".

Even as Harrt raised his pistol, Admiral Olbori's gaze didn't wander. There was a metallic click, followed by the sound of a laser bolt meeting flesh. In a single brutal moment, Olbori's head snapped back in a haze of crimson and his corpse keeled over.

Silence filled the room.

With his vengeance completed, Harrt Oxarri tossed the gun aside and looked at Koble;

"Let's get outta here".

▲

Alas, this is how I die: meeting my end in the same waters where I was born. I return to you now, great river, for I have failed.

As his blood failed to circulate, Seig felt the cold chill of death before noticing that he was drowning. The river Prynn was not the same: changed by the Enkaye half-breeds into something new. The water consumed him from the inside out, tearing through flesh and bone without forgiveness.

Seig tried and failed to scream as he dissolved into the river Prynn.

He realised that his visions of a universe free from sin and chaos would not come to pass as death met him.

Not under his rule, at least.

But Baylum was still out there.

Maybe he could finish the work...

Maybe he could fulfil the Revenant purpose...

Maybe that was the reason for Seig's entire existence: to bear a son who would finally bring order to the chaos.

Seig, the destroyer of worlds, did not feel the moment he ceased to exist.

CHAPTER SEVENTY-EIGHT

The Phoenix Titan began its pass of the firing array, flanked on both sides by two Sphinax fighters. The Revenant kept sending reinforcements, but Rain and his squadron were able to keep them busy.

"The way I see it, we've got one shot at nailing this," Vol said to Russell over the comm. She eyeballed the nav terminal, which displayed a sea of red blips on the screen: each of them a Revenant fighter. "I'm gonna bring us around the crater; you need to take down those towers".

She couldn't deny that it was a lot of pressure to put on the kid, but Vol couldn't fly and shoot at the same time, at least not without a co-pilot. When Russell replied, his voice was free of anxiety.

"Just point me in the direction of those towers".

"Good," Vol nodded. She swiped on the weaponry terminal, sending control of the missiles to Russell. "Use these," she added. "They'll drag a little, so try to fire in advance. Use the guns—"

"I got this," Russell interrupted. "Just get me the shot. I'll take care of it".

Vol banked the ship into the giant crater that served as the firing array. She took the Phoenix on a route around the outskirts of the bowl, allowing Russell to line up his shot. Vol imagined the former barkeep, rolling the gunnery chamber around with gritted teeth. She pictured him dragging the crosshairs of the HUD to meet with the looming metal protrusion. It would take one, maybe two seconds, for the targeting sensor to confirm target-lock. By that stage, the Phoenix would be less than a kilometre from the tower. Finally, Russell would pull the trigger, sending both torpedos and laser fire toward the target.

Before Vol knew what was happening, an explosion erupted from the first tower. A glorious flash of fiery light painted the shadows on the Messorem's rocky hull. The Phoenix buckled with the shockwave, but Vol's steady hand kept the ship stable, avoiding the falling spire as it collapsed. The second and third towers fell as quickly as the first, caving in under their weight as Russell fired.

Up until that point, Russell had been silent, hopefully concentrating on the task at hand. Then, after the third, he spoke up.

"Looks like we can actually kill this thing!" His voice sounded almost giddy.

Vol disregarded the comment and instead jammed the throttle forward. There was no point in getting excited: not yet anyway. There was still one more tower to go, and then there was the challenge of exfilling the rest of the team afterwards.

As Russell fired, Vol spotted the laser fire arc toward the giant superstructure. Two missiles followed, leaving purple trails between the Phoenix and the firing array.

The final tower contorted, and a series of small explosions erupted from the inside out. A shockwave followed, sending debris in every direction. Vol punched the Phoenix's throttle as the last spire fell, throwing the ship in a wide arc to avoid the fallout.

"That's what I'm talking about!" Russell's elated cheer boomed through the comm.

Vol could almost imagine him punching the air in victory. She couldn't deny that his whooping was almost infectious, but Vol knew she couldn't celebrate yet: not until the others were safe.

"Settle down," she said, trying to mask her sense of accomplishment. "We're not done yet".

▲

There came an unusual moment, which caused Leviticus Dines and his entire crew to stop everything they were doing. The Revenant fleet became disorganised, losing the sense of direction and purpose. A handful jumped to FTL, leaving the majority behind. Some floated aimlessly in the endless vacuum, while others collided.

In all his years, Dines had never seen anything quite like it. The sight of a few thousand warships lifelessly drifting across the open void was almost haunting.

Where there had been war, there was nothing.

Dines didn't care what had happened. All he saw was the opportunity to strike.

"Open fire," he ordered. "Destroy every last one of them".

▲

The last person that Nathan expected to hear from during the most suicidal mission in history was David Jareth. Given everything that had transpired in the previous fifteen minutes, Jareth was alien to the situation. And yet, there he was, looking at Nathan as though he belonged to the moment.

"What the hell do you want?" Nathan said, half-tempted to cut off the connection there and then.

Jareth held his gaze but didn't respond. Nathan could see from his datapad that there was no signal delay in their communication. Wherever Jareth was, he was nearby.

"It's just as Jack said," Jareth marvelled. "That you and I would arrive at this historic moment".

"What the fuck is that supposed to mean?"

Yes, it was a blunt response, and no, Nathan didn't regret it. His gut told him that the businessman was up to no good.

"*It means* that I need you to stop what you are doing and listen to what I have to say," Jareth leaned forward in anticipation.

"And why the hell would I do that?"

"The Commonwealth lied to you, Nathan; they lied to our entire race," Jareth said.

"What the fuck are you talkin' about?"

"I have irrefutable proof that the Commonwealth Council failed our people on the day of the Fall," Jareth said, his voice low and considered.

Nathan waved off the comments dismissively, "We all know they arrived on the scene too late".

Jareth's frown deepened.

"I have acquired a series of classified Commonwealth documents that prove the Council had prior knowledge of the attack on Earth".

"What?" Nathan said, exchanging a glance with Astrilla. "What do you mean?"

"They knew," Jareth said apologetically. "They knew, and they were willing to let us die".

The statement caused Nathan to stop everything he was doing. He looked at Jareth's deadpan expression with scrutiny, trying to assess if the old man was being deceptive.

It was impossible to tell.

"They knew twenty-four hours before the attack commenced. The politicians debated whether or not to save us for over thirty hours," Jareth said. "By the time they'd agreed to take action, the Revenant had been laying waste to our world for over ten hours. Add on two hours for FTL travel, and low and behold, they arrive at Earth thirteen hours after the Revenant arrived".

A sudden crash caused the Messorem to rumble, sending a wave of water crashing against the edges of the room. It served as a stark reminder to Nathan that he and Astrilla were —in essence— stood on a powder keg.

"Why the hell are you telling me this?" Nathan demanded as he glared up at Jareth. "What do you want from me?"

Behind the lens of his holographic recorder, David Jareth took a long, slow breath.

"I need you to stop what you are doing," Jareth answered. "The Messorem represents an opportunity for our people to reclaim our rightful place in the universe. Give the people of Earth —your people— a weapon that will cement our dominance: just as the Enkaye intended".

"You're insane," Astrilla shook her head at Jareth.

"Am I?" Jareth tilted his head. "Why do you think the Commonwealth waited so long?"

It was a question that neither Nathan nor Astrilla could answer.

"They waited because they feared Earth," Jareth continued. "They put the survivors of the Fall on a quiet, secluded world, where they could keep us tucked away: never to grow or change or innovate. The Commonwealth did this because they knew that our people would evolve into something far more than they ever could be".

Nathan couldn't deny that maybe Jareth was right: perhaps Paradisium was as much a prison as it was a paradise. There was something valid to that argument, Nathan could see it from miles away, but he couldn't deny the ache in his mind that told him that David Jareth wasn't trustworthy. There was a certain unconscious grace gained from years of experience that gave people like Jareth the edge in talking-the-talk: whereas people like Nathan, and Jack, and Koble could walk-the-walk. That was how you survived in the harsh realities of the universe: at least if you didn't have the luxuries of Paradisium. More importantly, that was how you knew if the crew you shipped with were credible.

"Jack kept you away from Paradisium because he knew that the 'wealthers were trying to hinder our kind," Jareth said almost apologetically. "He knew, Nathan. He knew all along that they would never truly accept our people. And now here we are at a crossroads".

Nathan realised that this was the choice Bill had warned him about.

"How the fuck do you expect me to trust someone like you with a machine like this?" Nathan said, gesturing to the walls of the mighty Enkaye warship.

"Not me," Jareth shook his head. "Give it to *our people* just as the Enkaye planned all those years ago. We do not need to use it as a weapon; we keep it as a deterrent for those who would seek to halt our progress".

Nathan found it terrifying that Jareth was starting to make sense. There was a hint of truth in Jareth's eyes, as though he genuinely believed in everything he was saying.

"Nathan, we cannot allow our people to be hindered any longer," Jareth continued. "Don't do it for me. Do it for those we lost on that terrible day: people like your mother and father. People who died fighting an enemy that could've been stopped. Don't let their deaths be in vain."

It was a cheap and desperate plea that Nathan didn't appreciate. But, while it raised questions about how Jareth knew about his mother and father, none of it mattered. Yes, there was a possibility that the Enkaye had intended for Earth and its people to inherit the mantle. Nathan was living proof of that now.

"Let our people thrive again," Jareth begged. "Please..."

In Nathan's mind, the problem was that the Messorem was dangerous: too dangerous for any one man or government to control. It was the kind of weapon that should never exist in the first place. It fell into corrupt hands with Seig, and he'd killed trillions with it. It would be no different in the hands of Earthers or 'wealthers.

"We can do this together, son," David Jareth said.

Nathan saw the comment for what it was: a cheap attempt to appeal to the part of him that had once craved a tender and loving father figure. It was fruitless.

Nathan chose: the Messorem had to die. With his decision final, the Omega spoke to him and told him exactly what to do.

Nathan looked up at Jareth and said, "No".

He moved to the liquid pool and the centre of the room, ignoring Jareth's futile arguments and pleas.

Jareth called out. "Don't do this..."

Nathan dropped the Omega into the waters and it disappeared beneath the surface. A short hum followed, and the glowing water turned to a deep red.

The room began to shake uncontrollably, and Nathan steadied himself and Astrilla. Large cracks formed in the glowing walls, and the liquid housed behind began to boil violently. When Nathan looked back at David Jareth, the old man was practically seething with anger. His striking eyes had narrowed into a hateful frown, and his jaw twitched with displeasure.

"You've made an enemy today, Captain Carter," Jareth growled. "The people of Earth will not forget this".

Jareth's image dissolved into obscurity, leaving Nathan and Astrilla alone inside the shaking red chamber. Suddenly the liquid pool began to boil over, throwing huge scarlet clouds into the air. The cracks in the walls began to spread, and water spat through the gaps.

"Nathan, we have to go," Astrilla tugged at his hand.

As they sprinted out of the power chamber, the walls caved in, flooding the room.

This was how an Enkaye warship died.

This was how it was meant to be.

CHAPTER SEVENTY-NINE

Harrt dashed toward the hangar, closely followed by Koble, Gordon and the droid. All around him, the Messorem vibrated with the seismic force of an earthquake, making it tough for Harrt to stay balanced. Behind the retrofitted emergency alarm system, a new booming noise rushed from deep within the Messorem. It sounded like a wild animal howling endlessly into the night, either in pain or in fear; Harrt couldn't be sure.

Despite the searing pain in his shoulder and leg where he'd sustained wounds earlier, Harrt endeavoured to escape. He was finally free of the revenge he'd so desperately craved, and now he had no intention of dying.

When Harrt and the others reached the hangar, they found the Phoenix Titan, exactly where it had been for the drop-off. Russell was clutching a heavy rifle while stood on the docking ramp. Harrt had never been happier to see the former barkeep. At first, Russell looked ready to gun down anything that moved, but when his eyes settled on Harrt, he urged them to hurry.

"C'mon, we don't have much time!"

"Did Nathan make it back?" Harrt said, grabbing Russell's forearm.

For a split second, Harrt felt his gut tighten. He didn't want to hear that he'd lost another friend in combat. Not again. Fortunately, Russell's lips turned upward, forming a gentle smile.

"See for yourself," he answered, gesturing to the lounge.

Harrt walked to the end of the corridor, turned the corner then looked out onto the living space at the centre of the Phoenix. There on the couch was Captain Nathan Carter, pressing a damp cloth against Astrilla's forehead.

Before Harrt could say a word, the Phoenix's engines whipped up, and he felt the ship accelerate at an alarming pace. Despite the disbelief that they'd all made it —Astrilla included— Harrt knew the Phoenix needed a co-pilot.

When he got to the cockpit, Harrt strapped himself into the chair beside Vol. He took one look out of the window, then immediately wished he hadn't. The Messorem was caving in on itself. The vast network that had served as the guts of the warship twisted and warped into a collapsing tunnel. A series of explosions chased the Phoenix out of the Messorem.

"What took you so long?" Vol asked, not taking her eyes off the path ahead.

"We encountered a little bit of resistance," Harrt answered.

They shot through a narrow triangular aperture with only centimetres to spare, plunging into the open void of space. The pursuing explosions engulfed the Messorem as though it were being eaten from the inside out.

Harrt didn't hear the explosion or see it, but he felt it in his bones. At first he could've sworn that there was the slightest hint of a tremor. Then something cascaded through space that vaguely resembled a shockwave, but felt different somehow.

Once they were clear of the blast, Vol slowed the Phoenix and turned the ship to look at what had once been the Messorem. All that remained of the Enkaye war machine was a dying ball of burning gases, that was slowly fading into nothingness.

"Still buying me that drink?" Vol asked with a raised eyebrow.

"Absolutely".

▲

The moment that the Messorem exploded in a ball of white fire, Leviticus Dines had to look twice. The flare of light appeared more like a star burning brightly in the endless vacuum than a dying warship.

In a way, it was beautiful, *if you didn't know otherwise.*

Around him, the bridge crew began a gleeful cheer of victory, which Dines did not immediately share. Yes, it was a win, *but at what cost?* David Jareth now possessed proof of one of the Commonwealth's most significant failures. Dines could only wonder *what Jareth would do with that information.*

As he thoughtfully stared out at the fiery blaze that had once been the Messorem, the crew began to sing the Commonwealth anthem of victory.

RISE MIGHTY CITIZENS, UNITED BY OUR CAUSE,
PROTECT OUR LIBERTY FROM THE DARKNESS,
I WILL FIGHT FOR MY COMRADES,
I WILL PROTECT THEM FROM INJUSTICE,

As the first verse ended, Leviticus Dines reluctantly joined his crew in song. With every line he sang, Dines felt his anger toward the admiralty and the politicians grow. They should have led the battle. Not him.

▲

A Commonwealth medical team boarded the Phoenix less than fifteen minutes later. While Harrt received treatment for his unpleasant-looking gunshot wound, Nathan poured a stiff drink at the bar and took a moment to reflect.

He was part Enkaye, but he was still part-Earther. He wasn't sure what that meant, but he was damn sure going to find out.

Once the medics were gone, Nathan gathered the others in the living area. After pouring them each a drink, Nathan proposed a toast to their victory. Then he proceeded to tell his crew —his new family— everything that had transpired aboard the Messorem. They listened, and Nathan spared no detail. When he finished talking, there was a long silence that seemed to drag. The truth of his heritage was now among those he trusted most. It didn't help answer the thousands of questions that Nathan had, but it made him feel like he could face down anything with the crew around him.

"So," Koble said, drawing the word out thoughtfully. "That means Jack was part Enkaye too..."

Nathan nodded.

"I always thought there was something special about that guy," Koble said as he twiddled a whisker. The chunky Sphinax leant forward in his seat, looking at the others. "We can't let anyone else know about this. That kinda information will put a target on all of us".

To Nathan's surprise, all of them nodded in agreement, including Harrt. When Nathan looked at the 'wealther, he could see that something had changed. He seemed somehow more aware: as though his eyes had opened to something greater.

"I'll just leave that little detail out of my reports," Harrt said, tipping his glass to Nathan. "Besides, I don't think high command would believe me if I told them".

Suddenly the awkwardness of the moment dropped — if there had been any in the first place. All the tension that Nathan had melted away.

Gordon passed an old bottle of whisky around while Russell played old Earth music from his datapad. It was a crew celebration that was well worth the wait.

▲

Twenty four hours after the Messorem's destruction, Harrt was summoned to Commonwealth High Command. Before the Phoenix landed on the Capital World of Valour, Harrt slipped into his military dress uniform. After everything he'd been through since the Vertex, wearing the uniform felt wrong.

Feels like it belongs to another man, Harrt thought.

It was that very notion that prompted Harrt to decide that he was done with military life. He'd more than completed his civil service, and the 'wealth had taken more than its pound of flesh. He arrived at High Command with an hour to spare, so he waited patiently outside the campus. The weather was pleasant, and it seemed like an excellent opportunity to finish up his *mostly* accurate report. As Harrt had promised, there was no mention of Nathan's Enkaye heritage. He had no intention of putting his friends in danger: not after everything they'd been through. The events of the last few weeks had proven that the up-tops in the Commonwealth couldn't be trusted.

As he closed his datapad, Harrt saw Leviticus Dines coming out of the building, dressed in uniform. Harrt waved him over, and Dines took the seat beside him. The look of a man with a chip on his shoulder was ever-present on Dines' chiselled, youthful features. Harrt knew the Agent had led the Commonwealth during the battle: something Dines was not equipped to do. Leviticus Dines had done what the Admiralty were too cowardly to do. He'd faced the enemy head-on and refused to back down. He'd made a deal with Jareth Corps, which likely saved trillions. Of course, the Admiralty wouldn't see it that way. Neither would the Master of the House or the other politicians. They would instead dress it all up as a reckless betrayal of the Commonwealth.

When Dines sat down next to him, Harrt pondered a few dozen questions. He wanted to ask about the battle and the data he'd given Jareth Corps, but before Harrt could speak, Dines beat him to the punch.

"So, I think they are going to offer you a promotion," Dines said, nodding at the tall building ahead. "Try to look surprised when they tell you".

"I don't think I want it," Harrt shook his head. "Not anymore".

"Really?" Dines said, keeping his tone neutral. Then with a hint of sarcasm, "Don't tell me the hero of Maru Seven has given up on the dream of liberty?"

"No," Harrt shook his head. "I still believe in freedom and bravery and everything the Founders set out to do. It's just—"

"It's just you realise how broken the system has become". Dines finished the sentence. He stared at Harrt until he nodded, then with a polite smile, the Agent added, "So, what changed your mind?"

Harrt had to think long and hard about why his faith in the Commonwealth had faltered. Rather than a single moment in time, he noted a list of occasions and failings that he simply couldn't ignore. The thing that cemented it all together was what Densius Olbori had said before death:

True liberty is dead: replaced by a shroud of lies and deceit, intended only to control.

Those words cut Harrt deeper than anything else ever could. Some of what Densius Olbori said made sense in its own screwed up way. That alone terrified Harrt more than all the foes he'd faced. The idea that he, Harrt Oxarri, the hero of Maru Seven, could agree with a traitor like Densius Olbori would be seen as unlawful by many.

And yet, Harrt couldn't ignore the fact that Densius Olbori was right: at least from a certain point of view.

"Let me ask you something," Harrt said, looking at the silver-haired Agent with a degree of caution. "*If* the Commonwealth is broken, how do we go about fixing it?"

Dines looked at him with raised eyebrows. Then in a low voice, he answered, "Corruption is like a weed; it grows and spreads under the surface until finally, it emerges in plain sight, by which point its roots are both strong and hidden".

"So, how do we root out that weed and kill it once and for all?"

"You're serious about this?" Dines said, trying to mask his disbelief.

"Someone high up the chain sold us out to the Revenant," Harrt said with a nod. "They sentenced my entire crew to death aboard the Vertex. They told Seig that the Phoenix was on Paradisium and almost got my friends killed. Whoever this traitor is, they've made it personal".

"You do realise that our traitor is only one of many," Dines nodded. "They may not be selling secrets to the Revenant, but they are just as corrupt".

"Then we'll deal with them one at a time".

A satisfied expression filled the face of Leviticus Dines. It was a look Harrt had never seen on the man. It was strange to see the usually dour Agent so pleased.

"If we are gonna do this, Oxarri, I need you one hundred percent behind me; no more pretending that we work for some righteous, all-knowing government".

Harrt nodded in agreement.

"The only way we bring them down is from the inside," Dines said. Then, he gestured to the High Command building, "What I need you to do, is take the promotion. Get assigned to a ship, then get close to the Admiralty".

Harrt felt his gut sink. It was the direct opposite of why he'd come here in the first place. He wanted a life aboard the Phoenix Titan with his friends, and of course, with Vol. The problem was that Harrt believed in liberty —true liberty. Maybe being a selfless idealist was a dumb thing to do, but someone had to do it; otherwise, nobody would. Generations of good 'wealthers would continue to fall into the same trap and allow the aristocracy to corrupt what the Founders set out to do. Harrt wasn't willing to let them use freedom, liberty and unity as a mask to control the masses. The people of the Commonwealth deserved better: they deserved choice.

Harrt turned to Dines, and with a nod, he answered, "So be it".

CHAPTER EIGHTY

King Seig, the foolish, had failed every monarch that had come before him. Such failure was unacceptable in the eyes of the Revenant. Baylum could never forgive his father for squandering everything that hundreds of generations had fought to build. All that remained of his birthright was a mere slither of what Seig had taken into battle.

Hours before his coronation, Baylum meditated before the river Prynn, hoping that the waters would show him the way. He begged and screamed, but the Void did not answer him.

The coronation of King Baylum took place aboard his flagship, the Invincible. He drew his blood and allowed it to drip into the River: signalling that a new monarch had taken the crown. The ceremony was meant to feel monumental, but instead, it felt like rubbing salt into the wounds of failure: a failure that was not his own.

Despite the heavy losses, Baylum found a silver lining to the whole thing. He was now the King. He answered to no one. His father, the fool, was dead, as was his stubborn obedience to the cause. Baylum could finally fight the war the way it was supposed to be fought. The old rules no longer bound him. Baylum could wage wars the way he wanted to.

A council of Baylum's most trusted advisors gathered in the hours that followed the coronation. They wanted revenge as much as he did, but Baylum knew that patience would ultimately win the war.

"Retreat and rebuild," Baylum said to the group. "We will face them when we are ready".

Baylum hated the idea of running away from a fight, but he knew it was the wise thing to do. Even despite the bitter taste of defeat, the new King knew that he still had power lurking in the shadows.

"I will bring greatness to our people," Baylum affirmed.

▲

Koble noticed something strange about Harrt when he returned from his debriefing. The 'wealther seemed distracted and focussed all at the same time, leaving Koble to wonder what had happened. Around an hour later, Koble noticed that Vol seemed pissed off with a control panel. She slammed a wrench into the underside of the console, cursing at it in the old-Uvan tongue.

"You okay?" Koble asked.

"Yeah," she said, trying her best to mask whatever was eating away at her. "I'll be fine. Just a shitty console".

Koble knew Vol well enough to know when she needed her own space, so he left her to continue her work. *It's better to have her hit the console with a wrench than me.*

Later that evening, Harrt announced to the crew that he'd received a promotion from High Command. He'd been allocated a Commonwealth warship and a crew of his own. Of course, that meant he wouldn't be staying aboard the Phoenix.

"I'll be taking the job, *for now*," Harrt said.

Harrt explained that he —along with Leviticus Dines— would investigate a conspiracy inside the Commonwealth. Accepting the role of Commander was the best way for Harrt to get close to the senior military officials. He could find out who had betrayed them.

"We all know that there are traitors," Harrt said. "I'm doing this because I want to keep you guys safe. I'm not letting them screw us over again".

Suddenly Vol's outburst made perfect sense to Koble. She wanted Harrt to stay, but she'd never tell him to do so because he was entirely correct. The best-case scenario was that there was a single mole inside the Commonwealth working for the Revenant. Koble didn't want to think of what the worst case could look like. That was why Vol was so upset: she had a thing for Harrt, and he had placed his mission —his calling— above their potential relationship. On the surface, Koble couldn't deny his actions seemed uncaring, but he knew that Harrt Oxarri was doing it because he wanted to protect Vol. The mole was still out there and still posed a significant threat.

The news came three days later that Kornell's loyalists had surrendered. The Pluvium System was free after twenty years. That meant the rightful Chief had to return home and set right all the wrongs Kornell had made. It was a tall order, but Koble knew with his mother, Rain and Nero at his side, he could do anything. The problem was that he didn't want to leave the Phoenix. Sharing a ship with Nathan felt like being aboard the Loyalty all over again. And now, as it turned out, Nathan was part-Enkaye. Koble knew that it meant something: that his destiny was entwined with Nathan's. Koble wasn't sure how or why, but he knew it.

The Phoenix set a course for Pelos Three a day later, where Harrt would charter a shuttle to his new warship a week later.

At least he's got some time to smooth things over with Vol, Koble thought.

Initially, Koble planned to stay aboard the Phoenix for another month. He wanted to make sure everything was ship-shape before departing. But, unfortunately, duty called. During the final stretch of the FTL journey, Rain arranged to pick him up at Pelos Three.

A few hours before the Phoenix was due to drop out of the slipstream, Koble decided to grab a quiet drink. Most of the crew were sleeping in their cabins, with the exception of Vol and Harrt, who were up in the cockpit. Koble knew better than to disturb them, so he proceeded straight to the bar and lounge.

Gordon was sitting in one of the armchairs, reading an old book while sipping a glass of brown liquor. The pair had barely spoken since the Messorem, and Koble had a few dozen things to say to the doctor. He suspected that Gordon hadn't been entirely honest with the crew. If Koble was going to leave Gordon Taggart aboard the Phoenix, he needed to square a few things off first.

Koble grabbed a steaming cup of coffee from the vending unit and took the seat opposite the doctor. He took a long sip from his mug, buying himself time to think.

"So," Koble said as he put his feet on the table. "I heard you were staying aboard..."

"Correct," Gordon didn't take his eyes away from his book. "Nathan wants me to help him investigate the Enkaye ruins at Pelos Three".

Koble could tell the doctor was trying to avoid the conversation. Maybe Gordon knew that Koble suspected something, or perhaps he was being his usual evasive self. Regardless, Koble wasn't going to leave any leaf unturned, especially as Gordon knew the truth about Jack.

"There's something I've been meaning to ask you..." Koble leaned forward in his chair.

Gordon's eyes finally peeled away from the pages and darted to Koble.

"Let's hear it," he said, tossing his book onto the table.

"When Nathan told us that he was part-Enkaye, you didn't seem surprised.." Koble chose his words carefully, and Gordon's brow lowered a degree.

"Is that a question?"

There was a hint of tension in Gordon's voice that Koble refused to ignore.

"Did you know?" Koble said, keeping his voice flat and non-accusatory.

Gordon held his gaze for several seconds without saying a word. It was an eerie, considered expression that Koble had only ever seen once before: painted on the face of Jack Stephens before a mission. But Gordon Taggart was not Jack Stephens and this was not a mission.

Finally, Gordon shook his head. "No," he said. "I didn't know Nathan was an Enkaye".

Koble sensed there was more to his answer than was

spoken aloud. He took a sip from his mug and stared at Gordon.

"But you knew something was up, right?" Koble leaned forward and placed his drink down. "I mean, you ain't no dumbass, right?"

Silence lingered for a moment, and Gordon swallowed a lump in his throat.

"Okay," Gordon said as he pulled off his glasses. "I worked with Jack's father, Bill, for almost a decade. I came to know that man as both a friend and as a mentor. Did I ever think that Bill was part alien god? No, I most certainly did not. Did I think he was something special? You're damn right I did".

Gordon placed his glasses down on the arm of his chair and leaned forward to look Koble in the eye.

"The truth is that good ol' Bill Stephens said some crazy shit to me before he died," Gordon continued, his voice growing both nostalgic and mournful at the same time. "He said that *one day I'd be essential in saving the universe:* that *I would save Nathan's life.* That all of this was going to happen. The funny thing is that he told me all of that over twenty-five years ago, and everything he said was right".

Koble gawped in shock. For a split second, he wondered if Gordon was lying but quickly laid the thought to rest.

"You mean Jack's father told you that all of this was going to happen before the Fall?" Koble raised a brow in surprise, and Gordon nodded. "Does that mean to say that Bill knew all along?"

"Perhaps," Gordon shrugged. "I've not given it much thought up until now. You see, the thing is, I thought it was complete and utter-bullshit for the longest time. That is until the moment you and Harrt knocked on my front door".

"Then the droid; then Nathan's resurrection," Koble said, filling in the blanks of Gordon's story.

"Don't forget the nuclear bomb," Gordon murmured. "That was the most critical piece of the puzzle".

"Why?" Koble asked.

Gordon nervously tapped his fingers on the arm of his chair. He swallowed anxiously, then climbed to his feet. "Before he died, Bill told me that Nathan would face an impossible choice aboard the Messorem..."

"You mean, Jareth's proposal?" Koble said, raising his brow. "But Nathan didn't give the Messorem to Jareth: he destroyed it. The Omega did what it was supposed to do..."

Koble's voice trailed off, and he stared at Gordon in shock.

"The nuclear bomb was a failsafe..." Koble said with a dry mouth. "In case Nathan handed over the Messorem".

Gordon nodded solemnly. "I guess I have to bite my pride and admit that Jack raised him well. Nathan made the right call and no doubt saved many more lives by not giving Jareth the weapon".

There was silence for well over a minute. Gordon poured himself another drink, and Koble sat thoughtfully mulling over everything they'd discussed. As conflicted as Koble felt about the doctor's actions, it was hard to find fault with the reasoning behind them. Everything Gordon had done was for the greater good.

"Nathan can never know the truth about Jack..." Koble said, breaking the silence. He lowered his brow as he stared across the room at Gordon. "If he found out the truth, it would destroy him. I can't let that happen".

Gordon nodded reluctantly, "It wouldn't be right to shoulder such a burden on him: not after everything he's been through".

"Then we have a deal?"

"We do," Gordon answered. "I'll take Jack's secret to my grave. I swear".

Koble necked the rest of his drink and nodded. He leaned forward in his chair, wondering if it was worth sealing the deal with a threat of violence, but quickly decided against it. Regardless of their differing opinions on Jack, they could both agree that Nathan was a good man: too good to be dragged into Jack's past.

▲

"Rise and shine, folks," Vol's voice boomed through the ship-wide announcement system. "Two hours till our slipstream drop".

Astrilla tentatively opened her eyes, feeling as though she'd woken up too soon. Her first thought was of the mild muscular discomfort in her ribs and back; inflicted upon her by the Messorem. It had taken days, but the pain was finally starting to subside, and she was starting to feel normal again.

Beside her, Nathan mumbled something incoherent and sat up in the bed. Astrilla had noticed that her —for lack of a better word— emotional tie to Nathan had only grown in the days since the Messorem. She found it strange to think that they'd shipped together for weeks, not knowing that they were both part-Enkaye. Astrilla found it even more bizarre to believe that she'd mistaken Nathan for an assassin the first time they'd met. Looking back, Astrilla couldn't deny that she'd been in a bad place before meeting Nathan and the crew, but all of that had changed.

The universe had a plan: there was no denying it. The question remained, *how would that plan unfold?*

There were still things that plagued Astrilla's mind, but she'd tried not to acknowledge them. A few days to recover from the horrors of the Messorem was what she needed, for now at least. A time would come when Astrilla would turn her mind to that of King Baylum and the traitor still operating inside the Commonwealth.

She had every intention of stopping them, but not today. Instead, Astrilla shifted to Nathan's side of the bed and wrapped an arm around him. Astrilla felt good to be in his embrace: as though it was precisely where she was supposed to be.

▲

Hours after docking at the Evoker Enclave, Nathan found himself sitting in the Phoenix's living area. He was alone for the first time ever aboard his ship. He'd never noticed how peaceful the Phoenix Titan was when it wasn't full of people. And yet, it felt strange to be alone, and it left Nathan feeling uncomfortable.

All those years I spent alone, and now I can barely stomach an hour of quiet time, Nathan thought. *Things have changed.*

He distracted himself from the silence by reviewing the ship's repair plans on his datapad. There was no denying that the Phoenix had taken a hammering in the battle, and the repairs were pricey. Usually, Nathan would've found an alternative or attempted to repair the ship himself, but not this time. Thanks to Leviticus Dines, all major repairs were being paid for by the Commonwealth.

A sudden beeping noise emanated from down the hall. At first, it served as a mild inconvenience but quickly grew into an annoyance. Nathan placed his datapad down and followed the sound into the cockpit. The beeping was coming from the holotable at the centre of the room. As Nathan moved toward it, a holographic file loaded up. The projection contorted and twisted, trying to form into something human. There was audio, but it wasn't playing correctly. Nathan wondered if the file had corrupted, but as he went to reboot the projection, an image formed in front of him.

The face of Jack Stephens stared back at him knowingly, looking just as he had the day of the Mirotose Station incident. Nathan felt a chill run up his spine as he stared at his uncle.

"Nathan," Jack said, across the void of time. "You know me well enough to know that I ain't apologising for shit. This was the way it had to be; I hope you understand that".

Nathan couldn't help but smile at his uncle's blunt justification.

"There's a lot more heading your way, kid. It's far from over, so don't get all cocky," Jack nodded. "I'm hoping that by now you are starting to see that the Enkaye's plan is the real deal. I guess it's now your job to understand what it all means and put the pieces together".

Jack Stephens looked at Nathan with an expression of

pride and gratitude. Nathan waited a moment to see if his uncle would impart any helpful information —anything to help him with the path that lay ahead. Instead, Jack drank from a bottle and sighed. He regarded the camera stoically as though the weight of the world were sitting on his shoulders. It was a look that suited him.

"It's all on you now, kid," Jack said. "Godspeed".

EPILOGUE: ROTH

Brothers and sisters of Paradisium, we stand at a critical juncture in our people's history.

Alastair Albon de Freiherr Roth was many things to many people. On paper, he was a Featon Academy graduate and alumni, CEO of Roth Industries, father to two children and, of course, an outspoken critic of the Commonwealth. Off the record —the 'wealther ones at least— he was the reigning chairman of the Society, handpicked by the wise and wonderful Theodore Jareth to continue the work that generations of great men had undertaken before.

After the Fall, Roth initially envied his predecessors for not having to contend with the likes of the Commonwealth. Throughout Earth's history, the Society lived in the shadows by design, but they'd hidden out of necessity since the Fall. If anyone else were left in charge of the Society, it would've crumbled within five years of Earth's downfall. But not under the rule of Alastair Albon de Freiherr Roth. No, under his wise and cunning leadership, the Society continued to thrive —simply waiting for the opportune moment.

For over twenty-five years, we, the people of Earth, have lived under the rule of a government that we did not elect: a government that could have prevented the slaughter of our loved ones.

On his first day at Featon Academy, Roth was instructed by his teacher to give an introductory speech to his classmates. At the tender age of thirteen, such a prospect was terrifying to him. He wasn't much like the other kids. Despite his family's riches and legacy, Alastair Roth wasn't a confident child. He tried his best to deliver a speech but to no avail. Ultimately he failed when a classmate rudely interrupted him: likely a dig at his weight or lack of athleticism.

Of course, things changed as time rolled on. Fifty-seven years after that first day at Featon Academy, Alastair Roth thrived at public speaking.

I can see the sunlit meadows beyond. I can see a world where we are not refugees to take pity on. I can see a world where we, the people of Earth, aren't just on the political stage of the galaxy but are centre stage: the main act.

Roth sat in quiet contemplation with a glass of port, watching the graphics and talking heads of a Paradisian newscast. Over the last day, every news outlet, regardless of affiliation, reported the same story non-stop: King Seig, along with most of his military forces, had been destroyed. To finally see reports of Seig's death made Alastair Roth raise his glass in the name of progress.

"Novus Ordo Seclorum," Roth said to himself before taking a large gulp of his drink.

I believe we would be mad not to take back control from those who once debated our destruction. This movement is a once in a generation chance to say no more.

Late in the night, a knock came at his study door. Roth's assistant, Claire, poked her head through the opening and looked at him with a cautious expression. She was a pretty young thing that likely didn't remember the Earth or life before Paradisium, but she was good at her job and understood the art of subtlety, which was more than could be said for most of the airheads that made up the younger generation. Most importantly of all, she didn't ask questions, and that suited Roth just fine.

"David Jareth is here to see you; he says it's urgent," she said. "Should I send him in?"

As much as Roth despised Jareth, there was a self-imposed etiquette that he had to follow. Yes, David Jareth was the son of Alastair's mentor, but Jareth wasn't a member of the Society. He certainly had a vague awareness of the group, but he decided not to join as a teenager for one reason or another. That meant that Jareth didn't know who the members were. He didn't know the traditions and closely kept secrets of the Society. Despite all of those things, David Jareth certainly had his uses. The saying *keep your friends close and your enemies closer* never felt more apt to Alastair Roth.

"Send him in," Roth said.

This erosion of democracy cannot continue. That is what brings me into this fight.

David Jareth sleuthed into the study with the confidence of a city rat. As always, he looked cool and calm and smug all at the same time. Usually, such a late visit from someone he didn't like would boil Roth's blood, but something was different on this occasion, and he wasn't sure why.

The pair shared a formal handshake and small talk, as was the appropriate custom between business acquaintances. Once Claire had brought them each a shallow glass of whiskey and then excused herself from the room, it was straight down to business. The two men settled in a pair of armchairs beside the fireplace: each waiting for the other to make the first move.

David Jareth, the younger of the pair by eight years, was the first to speak:

"I suppose you are wondering why I have called at such a late hour," Jareth paused and his lip curled in what Roth could only assume was amusement.

"I certainly hope it wasn't just to drink my good whiskey," Roth replied, and the pair shared a chuckle that was far from genuine.

Jareth pulled a datachit from his breast pocket and handed it to Roth.

"And what might be on this?" Roth asked.

Jareth's eyes flicked to the datachit then back again. His expression was thoughtful. It wasn't a look Roth had ever seen on the man in the forty-plus years they'd known one another.

"That datachit contains documents which will aid in our separatist movement," Jareth answered.

The proof of the documents presented on this day shows the corruption of those who govern us.

Jareth's data confirmed what Roth and many others had suspected for years. Until that point, nobody had ever been able to prove the Commonwealth's intention to destroy Earth, but now that had changed.

It took several seconds for Roth to realise the implications of the data Jareth had given him. He felt a sense of euphoria that was almost electrifying.

"So," Jareth said, leaning forward in his chair. "What do you think we should do with this?"

For the first time in twenty-five years, Alastair Roth saw the path forward.

"We use it," Roth answered.

And so, I hereby declare that we, the people of Earth and of Paradisium, will no longer stand for Commonwealth rule. At this moment, I, Alastair Albon de Freiherr Roth, call for a nonpartisan ballot wherein we shall decide our future, either as a Commonwealth member or a sovereign world.

After Jareth left, Roth allowed himself to smile. Of course, the data Jareth provided would serve as the catalyst for a withdrawal movement of some sort. That much was obvious. It was probably why Jareth had shared it in the first place: he and Roth shared a mutual interest in that regard.

The concept of a separatist movement wasn't the reason for Alastair Roth's smile. Instead, he smiled because of what it would allow him to do. Withdrawal would serve as the perfect distraction, thus allowing Roth to execute his ultimate plan: his pièce de résistance.

When you reach the ballot box on that most sacred of days, just remember a vote for independence is a vote for freedom —the freedom we have been denied for a quarter of a century!

After pouring himself his third glass of port for that evening, Alastair Roth ventured to his private room: a reinforced bunker that could withstand the brunt of a planetary bombardment. He made sure to secure the buttons on his collar before stepping onto the holoprojector and making the call.

The communication took slightly longer to establish than Roth expected but eventually, the signal connected. The person at the other end of the communication materialised in the form of a hazy black and white hologram.

He must be far away, Roth thought. *Far beyond corporate space.*

The imposing three-dimensional figure was clad in dark robes and wore a newly-forged crown atop his bald head. His dark eyes held the look of authority, but Roth knew what was hiding behind them. It was the soul of a hateful, vindictive and violent man. They were the eyes of the newly crowned King Baylum.

"Your majesty..." Roth bowed his head, not as a symbol of subservience but as a gesture of respect.

Baylum did the same. "Alastair".

"On behalf of my colleagues in the Society, I would like to extend our congratulations on your coronation". Roth waited for Baylum to reply, but the King's expression didn't change. "On a personal note, I'd like to say that a change of leadership was long overdue. Under your wise and level-headed leadership, I know we will continue to achieve great things together".

Despite recently losing his father and most of the Revenant fleet, Baylum showed no sign of emotion whatsoever. The fact that neither Baylum nor Roth acknowledged Seig's death said everything that needed to be said. Seig was a superstitious fool so bound to his creed that it had cost him his life and legacy: Roth knew that wasn't a mistake that Baylum would make.

To all the naysayers and fearful folk out there today, I say dare to dream of the sun rising over a free and independent Paradisium. Dream of a victory for decent, ordinary people like you and you and you.

"Why do I sense that you have more to discuss than my coronation, Alastair?" Baylum asked with a low voice.

Roth tapped on his datapad, sending all of the stolen Commonwealth data to the Revenant king. None of it came as a surprise to Baylum, and rightly so. He'd known about Earth long before his father, and most importantly of all, Baylum had made the Fall possible. He'd worked with the Society to destroy Earth for a reason, and now Baylum was staring at a collection of documents that would enable them to see their plan through to fruition.

"We've waited for a very long time for the right moment, my old friend," Roth said as he looked up at Baylum's projection. "These documents will serve as fuel for the fire. With your father gone, we can finally move forward with our plan".

Baylum looked thoughtful as he considered the documents. "You are confident that you can use this to our advantage?"

The classified 'wealther documents that we have uncovered clearly show a conspiracy to bury the potential of our people. The Commonwealth seek only to crush our spirits and guide us toward a meaningless future, all while they push their communist ideals on all of us. I, for one, say that enough is enough. Today we say that enough is enough.

Roth nodded confidently. "First, I shall share this with my brothers and sisters in the Society; then, we will push a political movement that will do what it needs to while you and I work in the shadows".

We shall honour those we lost in the Fall by continuing to grow and evolve. Not by caving in or bowing down to Commonwealth rule. We, my brothers and sisters, shall forge our own destiny. Paradisium forever!

"So be it," Baylum said.

"Paradisium forever," the crowd chanted before breaking out into thunderous applause.

TALES OF THE PHOENIX TITAN
VOLUME ONE

HERITAGE

S.M. WARLOW

SMWARLOW_AUTHOR

Made in United States
North Haven, CT
08 September 2022